SORCERER OF ALMORA

SORCERER SEED

By
Curt Sylvester

Acknowledgement

I am deeply grateful to the many fantasy and science fiction authors whose stories have enriched my life and fueled my imagination over the years. Their boundless creativity, rich worlds, and unforgettable characters have transported me to places beyond our own and inspired me in ways I never thought possible. Through their work, they have sparked in me a desire to craft stories that might, in some small way, carry forward the magic they have so generously shared. I owe a great debt to these visionaries for showing me the path and giving me the courage to follow it, aspiring to capture even a fragment of the wonder they have brought to countless readers like myself.

To those creators, both known and unknown, who labor to bring their dreams to life on the page, I extend my heartfelt thanks. May this book honor, in some way, the profound joy and inspiration they have given to me.

Table of Contents

CHAPTER 1 - ARRIVAL

Maylore awoke to a spinning head as dust-ridden wind blew into his eyes and nose. He lay crumpled on the ground, unable to move his arms or legs. He blinked away some of the dust when he saw two bodies lying nearby.

"Oh my, what is this?" he monologued as he tried to move his head. His mind spun wildly, forcing him to lie still. He tried to remember what had happened but could feel his memories burning away as he tried to recall them. "Who am I?" he said aloud as his swirling mind slowly cleared. "Maylore," he said as the name came to him. "That's who I am. At least, I think so. Why are my arms and legs not working? Was I drugged?" he said as feeling began to return to his hands. His body pinned his left arm above his head, but he could move his fingers. Strength began to return to his arms slowly. He could move his left hand enough to feel it touching something. "All right, up I go," he said, pushing his way up to his elbows. His mind was still swirling, but he could see he was in a dry clearing surrousnded by boulders.

There were two motionless people to his right. Above him, a small man slumped against a rock with blood covering his head and body. A small, bloodied club lay near Maylore's hand.

"Did I beat someone?" he exclaimed as he looked between his hand and the club. His mind abruptly cleared at the sight of the carnage above him. "There is blood on the club, blood on the ground, and blood on him. No blood on my hands or clothes, though," he said, looking at himself. He forced himself to rise to his knees, stand, and wobble over to the man. He saw a small man dressed in leather and a once-white headband drenched in blood. He roused as Maylore approached.

"Go to the cave," the little man said, pointing weakly to the left. "Blood Wolves will come soon. Blood draws them. Take the other two, hurry." The little man's head lolled as he fell silent.

Maylore looked at the other two and started walking toward them. They were all dressed like him in rough, one-piece brown fabric robes. Their feet had the same leather sandals.

The first body he came to was a man lying on his side. Maylore bent down to see if he was alive. He appeared to be in his mid-twenties with dark hair and eyes. He rolled the man onto his back and noticed him staring at Maylore.

"Dizzy?" Maylore asked. "Lie still a while, and it will clear. I am Maylore. You will be able to speak soon," he said, patting the man's shoulder as he stood. Maylore moved to the second body, which appeared to be a woman. She was on her stomach with arms on either side of her head. Her robe was splattered with blood and bunched up to her hips. Maylore knelt beside her to check for a pulse. She had a strong pulse, so he rolled her onto her back. Maylore studied her before his mind told him she was a stranger. She is a pretty lady in her mid-twenties with long hair. "No blood on this side of your robe," Maylore noted as he readjusted her robe to the correct length. Her eyes were closed as he said, "Awake if you hear me. We need to move soon." She remained silent as Maylore started scanning the area for the cave the little man told him to find.

The second man's eyes slowly focused on the sky above him. The man calling himself Maylore was talking with someone, trying to reassure them. Blinking dust from his eyes, he found he could clench one fist but not move his legs.

'Where am I?' he thought as he continued trying to move his limbs. 'Why is my mind melting?' Questions started replacing confusion as he tried to remember his name. 'I am Jordin, Jaren. No, Jendrin,' he decided as the mind cleared. He could feel muscle control quickly returning as he lifted his head. A bloody club was on the ground, with a petite figure slumped in blood beside a rock. A voice behind him spoke again.

"We need to move soon. Awaken if you hear me," the voice said. Jendrin raised himself to his elbows to look behind him. The one

2

calling himself Maylore was kneeling beside another body. He was looking into the distance. To Jendrin, Maylore looked to be a man in his early fifties, his dark hair framing a face marked by years unknown. He tried to see if he might have any weapons but did not see any.

"Are you going to beat us, too?" Jendrin asked, pushing himself to his knees.

"Good! You are awake," Maylore said, looking at him. "No, I didn't beat anyone. I am also a stranger here. I assume you are a stranger since we are dressed the same way. Are you injured?"

"My head is hurting, but I don't feel injured," Jendrin said.

"Good. May I ask your name?" Maylore asked.

"Jendrin," he replied. "I have no idea where I am. Is that person alive?" he asked, pointing to the woman.

"She is," Maylore replied, "She is not recovering as quickly as we did. I don't believe anyone beat her, but she does have blood on the back of her robe. You do not have blood on your hands or clothes, nor do I. If one of us attacked the little guy, we would be blood-stained, too. I don't believe she attacked him, either. She does not have blood on her hands or the front of her robe."

Jendrin listened carefully, trying to determine Maylore's truthfulness. He didn't detect any deception, and the evidence rang true. "Do we have any idea of where we are?" Jendrin asked, looking around at the desert scene. "Rocks, some brush, and we are in some kind of crater. It looks like late afternoon."

Maylore looked up to see the familiar twin suns overhead. "Doyen and Trailer will be setting soon. They are higher in the sky than I think they should be." Looking toward the mountain, he noted, "I don't recognize those tall inland mountains."

3

"Dumped in the desert with two strangers," Jendrin said, standing straighter by the minute. "All of us dressed in sackcloth. I don't think I am a criminal, are you?"

"I am sure I am not," Maylore replied, looking back at him. "I don't know where we are or how we got here. I believe the best we can do is help each other and perhaps the little guy. He has lost a lot of blood."

The wind shifted at that moment, blowing off the ocean to a steady breeze toward the hills.

"The little guy told me we must move to a cave before the wolves arrive. He pointed toward the other side of the crater," Maylore said.

"Wolves?" Jendrin asked, looking around.

"He told me they are called Blood Wolves," Maylore said. "He said they are attracted to the smell of blood."

A distant howl caused both men to look into the distance as their bodies snapped to full wakefulness.

"They are distant," Maylore said. "Let me see if I can find the cave he mentioned," as Maylore ran to where the little man lay. Looking to where he had been pointing, he said, "There is a cave opening. Are you recovered enough to pick her up?"

"Yes," Jendrin replied, "You get the little guy, and I will bring her."

Running to where she lay, he picked up the unconscious woman and hurried in the direction Maylore had indicated.

Maylore didn't stop to verify if the little guy was alive. A small pouch lay beside him as he picked them up and started toward the cave. Another howl ripped the air as he looked toward the howls. Two giant wolves were nearly upon them. The little man was light but awkward to carry. Maylore started running toward the cave, but the first wolf knocked him over within a step. The little guy flew away as the impact threw both aside. Maylore scrambled to his knees as the wolf came toward him. The wolf stopped before him as Maylore sat back on his heels. The wolf was taller at the shoulder than his head. The wolf bared its dagger teeth before spinning and joining its teammate in dinner. Maylore couldn't believe the wolf spared him but jumped to his feet before the wolf decided he would be a good snack, too.

Jendrin reached the nearby cave when he heard the wolf attack. He turned to see Maylore on the ground, and the little guy tossed to the side. He started to put the woman down, thinking how he could help Maylore. He realized the size of each wolf would destroy both of them in seconds. He watched long enough to see Maylore get off the ground and run in his direction. Jendrin turned and slipped through the small cave entrance. He had to turn sideways in the narrow opening to allow him to enter with the woman. He paused inside the entrance, trying to locate any dangers.

"What creatures could be hiding here?" Jendrin said, peering into the darkness. He could hear Maylore approaching and decided to move. "Into the darkness," he said as he moved to the edge of the light. Maylore ducked in as he continued to survey the area. The sound of snapping and tearing jaws continued outside. "You have blood all over the front of your robe. I hope the little guy was dead before the wolves got him," Jendrin said, looking at Maylore.

"I am sure he was," Maylore replied, looking at the blood on his robe and hands. "How do we keep them outside?" Maylore said, peeking through the cave entrance. He noticed a small fire pit outside the entrance. "It appears others have used this cave. There is a fire pit outside filled with wood. Perhaps the little guy knew wolves were a problem," Maylore said.

"I will find a spot for her to rest, then see if we can devise a defense," Jendrin said. His eyes were already adjusting to the low light in the cave. It was relatively large inside with a high ceiling. Light from the entrance showed boulders and rocks filling most of the cave. Parts of the cave floor near them were clear of stones. There were several large rocks a few steps in front of him. Jendrin laid the woman against one of the large rocks. He looked around and noticed several holes in the ceiling, allowing light to enter. A stack of wood lay inside the entrance. Wooden poles leaned against the other side. "Somebody was expecting us," Jendrin said as he picked up two poles. "They left us weapons," he said, passing one of the poles to Maylore. They pushed the pointed end outside the opening and watched the wolves. "You are lucky you weren't wolf food," Jendrin quipped.

"I did wonder why they didn't eat me, too," Maylore said, watching the wolves. "I guess they thought I would be too tough to enjoy."

"Perhaps," Jendrin replied as he turned to examine the cave interior. "I don't see sunlight entering from any source except the ceiling. That will help keep the wolves out," he observed. "The woman appears to be still unconscious," Jendrin said, turning his head toward her. Looking back, he noticed Maylore was examining a bag he had picked up. "Did you steal the little guy's lunch?" Jendrin asked.

"I think I did," Maylore replied. "It has some fruit, bread, flint, and rock iron."

"He carried rocks?" Jendrin asked.

"A fire starter kit is my guess," Maylore said, "Let's try starting a fire outside." Digging the rocks out of the bag, he stuck the two together, producing many sparks. Looking again to verify the wolves were still busy, he said, "I will crawl outside and test my fire-starting skills. Warn me if the wolves approach." Jendrin nodded as Maylore crawled out of the cave.

'He is a likable, smart man,' Jendrin thought. 'Perhaps he is trustworthy,' Jendrin thought. 'He does not appear to be dangerous. I wonder if he was a leader of some kind. The woman does not appear to be dangerous either. Although, pretty women can be just as dangerous as anyone else.'

6

Her back ached with a rock pressed into it. She succeeded in opening her eyes but regretted it. Her eyes saw a world spinning around and refusing to stop. She tried moving to ease the back pain, but no muscle would work. Her blazing mind prevented her from forming any coherent thoughts as she slipped back into unconsciousness.

Maylore rested on his knees as he struck sparks onto dry twigs and large feathery husks. It took just a few strokes to start the fire. Maylore could see the fire would need no further tending to continue burning. He crawled back into the cave. The wolves turned in his direction, growled, and then returned to finish dinner. Sliding back into the cave opening, Maylore resumed his spot next to Jendrin.

"Nice fire, Maylore," Jendrin said. "I could have started it in one strike of the stones," Jendrin grinned at Maylore.

"You didn't even know it was flint and iron rock," Maylore smirked at him.

"True, I always used a match," Jendrin smiled.

"You have matches?" Maylore asked.

"No, that is just what I used to start a fire, I think," Jendrin replied, suddenly wondering what a match was. "I don't remember when or where I used them. I barely remember who I am. Thoughts seem to burn away whenever I try to remember something from the past. I do remember my name and how to talk. Maybe I know other things, but I don't have any personal history. How about you?"

"I have tried, but I don't remember my history or people before today," Maylore replied. Looking outside, he saw the two wolves sitting close by, watching him. They seemed to be watching the fire more than him. "We need to keep the fire going to keep them away." Maylore took one of the small chunks of wood and pushed it into the fire using his pole.

An unbidden memory forced its way into her mind. She was watching a faceless man above her. She was lying down and wore

7

lacy garments—an amulet with a brilliant blue stone resting on her chest. The man approached her and started pulling at her clothes. He stepped back before lunging at her. 'Escape! Must get away!' she thought as the memory vanished and her eyes opened. There was no one before her. She looked at her chest, a plain robe with no amulet on her chest. She found she could not move, but her eyesight was clear. Her whole mind felt ablaze like paper burning from its edges. She could see two strange men sitting at a cave entrance.

'Two men? Dark cave? What have I fallen into?' she thought, trying not to panic. 'Where am I? Who am I?' She lay quietly, allowing her mind to begin to clear. 'Airalee, my name is Airalee,' she thought, feeling a small victory in getting her mind to respond. She tried to move her head, but her mind spun so much that she settled back onto the rock. Her arms and legs refused to move. She could see she was not bound. 'Did they drug me, kidnap me to their hideaway? Did they assault me?' Trying to calm herself, she looked herself over. She appeared whole and unmolested.

'That is welcome news,' she thought. 'What am I wearing?' she thought, looking at her robe. Looking at the two men, she thought, 'We are all dressed the same. Am I part of their gang? A group of runaways?' She tried again to move, but her arms and legs refused. Looking again at the two men, she asked, 'Who was attacking me? Was it one of them? How can I defend myself?' She began looking around for a weapon. A fist-size lava rock was within easy reach as she tried to force her hand to move. Her fingers would clench, but her arm complained about her movement. A wave of pain escaped her lips as she closed her eyes.

The loud moan behind them brought the men's attention to the woman. "It appears our associate is coming around," Maylore said, standing up.

"I'll keep track of the wildlife outside while you try to help her," Jendrin said, looking out at the wolves.

Airalee's head was still spinning as she opened her eyes again. A man with a bloody robe had risen and was walking toward her. She stared at the blood on his robe as he approached. "Stay back, whoever you are!" she yelled. Maylore knelt beside her as she whispered some babbling noises.

"Sorry, I don't know what you said," Maylore said softly. "I will try to help you rest if I can." He removed several rocks beside her to create a nearly flat area. "Let me help you lie down," Maylore said, putting a hand behind her head and shifting her to lie flat.

'Don't touch me, murderer!" Airalee yelled, but she didn't have the strength to keep him from touching her.

Maylore saw she looked frightened and heard her mumble something.

"You have nothing to fear from me," Maylore said. "My name is Maylore, and he is Jendrin. I don't expect you to know us since we don't know who you are," Maylore said, looking back at her. "Your head may feel on fire, and you're probably confused. We were both that way when we awoke. We don't know where we are, how we got here, or why. Your muscles may not work yet, but they will recover." She looked at Maylore, attempting to figure out who he was.

"Stay away from me! Who did you kill?" Airalee thought she yelled at him. Maylore heard her mumble something like, "The nekcihc ate all the rocks."

"That would be odd," Maylore replied. "At least you are saying words I understand now."

"Did she say nekcihc?" Jendrin quizzed.

Airalee looked askance at the two men as she tried to shift up to her elbows to yell at both of them. She managed to rise slightly, but the world started spinning faster. Nausea formed in her stomach as she moaned and laid back down.

"Don't touch me while I sleep," she said as her eyes closed.

Maylore heard garbled words from her, including the word sleep.

"I think she said sleep. Probably the best idea," Maylore said, rising to his feet and returning to the entrance.

"I will check the cave for anything else useful," Jendrin stood up.

"Good," Maylore said, sitting in front of the entrance. "I will tend the fire and track our assassins." 'He appears to be a good man,' Maylore thought, watching him leave. 'I am fortunate to have two companions. I hope I am not the reason they are here.'

Jendrin started around the perimeter of the cave. Picking his way through the dark boulder-strewn cave was slow going. 'The center part of the cave is clear of rocks. The rest is rock filled.' He thought as he walked. He listened for any sound that would announce the presence of danger. The ceiling cracks allowed light to stream to the middle and back parts of the cave. He found another wood stack against the outer wall a short distance from the entrance. "Little guy was also a lumberjack," he said as he continued weaving between boulders. He found a small sleeping mat, backpack, and two water buckets.

"The little guy's hideaway," he said, picking up the backpack. "I am sorry for you, but know you have helped us," he said, opening the pack. It was full of dried food and a few clothes. He slung the little pack over one shoulder and continued his search. He crept to the back, following the curve of the cave. He suddenly stopped. Two red eyes stared at him from behind the next rock. The eyes were just above his knees in height. He considered turning back as the eyes disappeared behind the rock. A soft rustling noise followed before stopping a short time later.

"What the Basrah was that?" Jendrin said aloud. "I will leave you alone if you do the same for me," he said in its direction as he started creeping forward. He stayed close to the cave wall, avoiding that rock. He didn't see anything in the darkness behind the rock, regretting he had no weapon to defend himself. He turned to follow the wall, watching the rock for signs of movement. He came to a narrow opening leading into the darkness behind the cave. Jendrin could see the light from the entrance opposite where he stood. Standing in the opening, he could hear the tinkling of running water. A slight breeze blew behind him into the tunnel as he tried to peer into the darkness. He heard low growls from deep within the tunnel. He decided to forego exploring the new tunnel until he could find a source of light. He continued to follow the curve of the cave back toward the entrance. He was approaching the entrance when he nearly stumbled over a group of buckets.

"Buckets?" he said, bending over to examine them. One was empty. The other was small and had a cover with water under it. The last two were large and had a black oily mass in them and a few short clubs sticking out of them.

"Torches?" Jendrin remarked, pulling on one. The oily mass resisted his pulling but finally gave way. Jendrin picked up the water bucket and one pitch bucket as he returned to the entrance. "There was a bucket of water and one of tar over there," Jendrin said, setting the buckets down. "The little guy has a camp on the other side. He had a pack of food we could use and clothing we could not. Perhaps more interesting, a tunnel on the other side of the cave leads deeper into the mountain." Jendrin decided not to mention the growls he heard.

"That is interesting," Maylore said as he examined both buckets. He lifted the bucket's cover to see the water was half gone but looked drinkable. The other bucket had tar in it that was cracked but usable. "Excellent finds, Jendrin. It is concerning, however, that someone went into trouble with preparing this. These buckets are not the little guy's size. Someone else is expecting us. Perhaps the little guy was tasked with making us comfortable until he could contact someone."

"Contact who?" Jendrin asked. "Are we captives?"

"Perhaps, but why would they kill him?" Maylore asked.

Noise from where the woman lay brought their attention to her.

11

"I will check on her," Maylore said. "We may need her ready to move if our captors are returning." Jendrin nodded as he started examining the torch.

Airalee's mind had stopped spinning as she opened her eyes. She propped herself on her elbows as feeling returned to her arms. The same two men were near the cave entrance. The older man was moving toward her again. Airalee studied the two men, trying to determine how dangerous they were. 'I may be able to stop the older man, but not the younger man. They appear to be working together, which would doom me to a life of slavery.' She quickly decided to feign acceptance until she could determine when to flee. A minor ache gnawed at her head as he arrived. "Maylore," she said, surprised she remembered the name.

"Yes," Maylore replied, kneeling near her. "I understand you this time. You were incoherent before your little nap."

"Do you know where we are and how we got here?" she asked, looking around her. She could feel herself shaking with mistrust as her hand closed around the palm-sized lava rock beneath her. Maylore told her what had transpired since they woke up in a desert crater outside this cave.

"Jendrin carried you into the cave while I tried to pull the little guy to the cave," Maylore said. "Picking him up is how I got blood on my robe," he said, looking at his robe. "The wolves knocked me aside and devoured the little guy while I ran to the cave. Why they didn't eat me is a mystery." Maylore looked to the front of the cave again. "We may still be in danger if the little guy's task was to watch us while waiting for his master to arrive. If they mean harm to us, we need to leave here soon. Can you stand?"

Airalee analyzed his comments as she listened to him. 'He speaks with compassion. His body language says he is not dangerous. They both had the opportunity to despoil me but didn't.' Airalee felt some of her fear drain away.

"I believe so," Airalee said as she stood. Maylore was not much taller than she as she followed him to the entrance. Mistrust nibbled at her as she considered her limited options.

"Airalee, this is Jendrin. Jendrin, this is Airalee," Maylore said, pointing from one to the other. "It appears we are now three companions," Maylore said, looking at each. Airalee stood slightly behind Maylore as he spoke, still holding her rock.

"Nice to finally meet you, Airalee." Jendrin said, "I was fortunate you are light to carry away from wolves," smiling at her. Airalee smiled weakly, trying to decide if she should run out of the cave. Jendrin tossed another piece of wood onto the fire. "The fire seems to keep the wolves at bay. I think we are safe in here for now."

"Wolves are outside?" she said, squatting down. "Those two are huge!" Airalee exclaimed, abandoning any thought of running out of the cave.

"Yes. Thoughts of us going that way are gone." Maylore said as he sat down.

"We could wait for them to leave," Airalee said as she stepped farther away.

"The little guy called them Blood Wolves." Maylore said, "He told me blood attracts them."

"Like the blood on your robe?" Airalee asked.

"Perhaps," Maylore replied, "Or the blood on the back of your robe." Airalee looked at the back of her robe, surprised to see blood spatters.

"Sorry, not taking it off," she said.

Both men laughed as Maylore said, "We were not suggesting it. I could be completely wrong about what is holding them here. Nor can we afford to waste the little water we have to wash the blood off." pointing at the water bucket.

"They could be waiting for a master to return to capture us," Jendrin said.

"Do we have any options?" Airalee asked as a different kind of concern replaced her fear.

"I don't believe we can leave the prison cave," Maylore said, looking from the wolves to the desert scene. "Even if the wolves let us pass, there may not be water for a long distance."

"Nice," Airalee said. "We could be eaten by wolves, captured by an unknown party, or slowly perish in a cave."

"There is a tunnel at the back of this cave we might be able to use," Jendrin said.

"A tunnel?" Airalee asked.

"Yes," Jendrin said. "We should explore the passage to see if it leads somewhere. It could be an escape route or perhaps a trap."

"It is dark back there," Airalee said, looking toward the end of the cave. "Do we have a torch?"

"If we can get this tar to light, we will have a torch," Jendrin said. "I will investigate if it lights." Looking toward Maylore, he said, "Let's see if you can light this torch with your rocks."

Maylore retrieved the flint and iron stone from the bag. One strike of the flint lit the pitchy corner of the torch.

"Impressive, you are becoming skillful," Jendrin remarked as he got up. "Suggest bringing more wood and building up the fire. That should keep the wolves from following us if we decide to leave." Jendrin grabbed the torch and headed toward the back of the cave. Maylore nodded and started for the wood pile. Airalee stared, appraising Jendrin. 'He moves like a dangerous man. He appears to be confident and used to being in command. I may need to be wary around him,' she thought before moving to help Maylore.

"Does Jendrin appear dangerous to you?" she asked Maylore as they gathered wood.

"All humans are dangerous," Maylore replied. "Even those who appear mild-mannered can be roused to dangerous levels. I try hard to avoid rousing anyone," he finished with a smile. "We are three companions now," picking up wood sticks. "We will have to trust each other if we are to survive," he said, looking at her. His comments didn't alleviate her fears, but she knew he spoke the truth.

Jendrin used the torch to search for whatever he missed on his way to the back of the cave. The fire slowly climbed the tar as he pushed the torch into the passage. The passage was level and continued to his left. It was at least twice his height and may allow two people to walk side by side occasionally. He entered the tunnel wary of possible traps or animals. He cautiously explored the rock-strewn lava tube, finding no sign of trouble. There were no side tunnels as he approached a narrow spot in the tunnel. A human-sized club lay against the wall. A rock above it had a single line drawn horizontally on it. "Someone has been here. Did they need waypoints in a straight tunnel?" he said aloud. He looked beyond the narrow opening to see the tunnel continuing and a large blackness. "This is probably our escape route," he muttered as he turned and returned to his companions.

Airalee and Maylore sat far apart, watching the wolves as Jendrin returned.

"The little guy had food in his backpack," Jendrin said, retrieving the backpack and the small bucket of water. He sat between them as Airalee moved farther away. Jendrin saw the two wolves had moved farther back from the fires.

"What did you see, Jendrin?" Maylore asked, "Does it look like a possible escape route?"

"I found an inhabitant of this cave on my first trip. It was knee height with red eyes. It didn't seem dangerous and left me as I followed the cave wall. I didn't see it this time. I did find a possible exit from the cave with a tunnel that extends toward the mountains," Jendrin said, pointing to the mountains outside the cave. "My short tunnel exploration showed no traps, animals, or side tunnels. I didn't hear any sounds. There was a waymark at a narrow point in the tunnel. That suggests others have gone that way. It may be an escape route."

"At least we have one possible option. Do we take a vote or what?" Airalee asked.

"I vote we drink this water, eat the little guy's food, and venture into the unknown," Maylore said.

"I agree," Airalee said.

"We all concur," Jendrin noted, moving the little water bucket to the middle of the group. Maylore started unpacking the backpack.

"I hate to do it to the little guy, but I need to wipe some of his blood off my hands," he said, using one piece of clothing to wipe his hands. He next unpacked the food bundle and divided it three ways. The little guy's bucket had a small ladle, allowing them to scoop up some water.

"I hope it is safe," Airalee said, looking at the water. She realized she was still clutching the rock in her other hand and discreetly put it down as she drank.

"The little guy drank it," Jendrin replied, "I would assume it would be safe."

"It has a woody flavor," she said, drinking her first ladle full. "It may be from the bucket itself."

The other two agreed but continued sharing the water until the bucket was empty. The group shared some food, returning most of it to the backpack to carry.

"Do you remember anything before today, Airalee?" Maylore asked when they finished.

16

"I tried to remember as I was eating, but the few things that come to mind burned to ashes," Airalee said.

"Same with me," Jendrin said, nodding. "I remember how to do some things, but no personal information."

"I find only ashes," Maylore said, bowing his head. "I don't even remember what I used to do or enjoy."

Jendrin agreed and reached for more firewood.

"I will put a little more wood on the fire before we go," Jendrin said. Looking at Maylore, he thought he looked asleep. "Maylore?" he asked. Getting no reply, he touched him but had to grab him when he nearly toppled over. "No time for sleeping, Maylore!" he shouted as he tried to wake him up. Jendrin finally laid him down as he continued to sleep.

"Looks like we rest here, Airalee," he said, looking toward her. She was already asleep, lying down on the rock she sat by. "I had better stoke the fire," Jendrin said as he failed to rise from his rock and fell asleep.

Chapter 2 - Escape

A howling wolf startled them awake. The first rays of sunlight entered the cave as the three companions stared wide-eyed at the single howling wolf.

"Basrah! Did I fall asleep?" Maylore exclaimed.

"It appears we all did," Jendrin said, staring out of the cave. "Where did the other wolf go?" Looking back at the first wolf, he noticed the fire had burned down to coals. "I am surprised they didn't attack us," he said as Airalee awoke and leaned away. Jendrin took up his weapon as Maylore readied his. A distant howl filled the air, causing the wolf to look in that direction.

"Reinforcements?" Airalee asked, standing straight.

"Perhaps a dinner bell," Jendrin said as two more wolves arrived and stopped beside the first wolf. The second wolf looked like the first wolf's twin, while the third was older, grey, and even larger. The grey wolf looked at the fire and then the people holding spears. He turned to the first wolf, huffed at him, and trotted away.

"Looks like he was not impressed," Maylore said as the other two wolves lay down. "It appears the dinner party is waiting on us."

"Why didn't they come after us after the fire died?" Jendrin said cocking his head at the wolves.

"Are they still waiting for our human captors?" Airalee asked.

"Perhaps he was waiting for other wolves to help him with the kill," Maylore said.

"One wolf would have easily torn the three of us to shreds," Jendrin said. "We may have been able to defend against one wolf if we worked as a team, but not two."

"We must move out of here before they decide to do just that," Airalee said.

"We decided last night to try the tunnel. Let's go," Maylore said, wedging his pole into the rock. Jendrin did the same and picked up the bucket with torches in it. He grabbed the torch he used the night before. Maylore grabbed the pitch bucket and the water bucket.

"Leave that bucket. I believe the little guy had a sleeping herb in it. The herb he added created the woody flavor we tasted," Airalee said, pointing at the little guy's bucket.

"I will bring the other full-sized bucket instead," Maylore said.

"I can carry the backpack," Airalee said as she picked it up.

"Perhaps one of us should carry it," Jendrin said, reaching for it.

Airalee stepped away from him and pulled the pack to herself.

"I am not a dainty flower," Airalee said. "I can carry it."

Jendrin nodded and used the fire to light his torch.

"We could have done that last night instead of using the flint," Maylore said.

"True. I wanted to see if you could do it." Jendrin said with a smile.

"Before we leave, did you two pick a potty spot?" Airalee asked.

"We used the large boulder to the left," Maylore said, pointing left. Airalee walked in that direction, glancing over her shoulder to verify they did not follow her. She added her fist-sized rock into the pack before returning.

"Did you remember or dream of any other detail of life before we arrived here?" Jendrin asked Maylore as they waited for Airalee.

"I did dream about being a teacher, instructor, tutor, or some kind of educator," Maylore replied. "Do you remember anything else?"

"I saw myself doing physical things such as fixing machines, building, military stuff." Jendrin said, "I seem to recall I have survival skills. I don't remember any people, places, or things."

Airalee returned to the group as Jendrin looked at her.

"Did you remember or dream anything about your past last night?"

"I dreamed I worked in medicine," Airalee replied, "I don't remember any family, friends, places I lived, or what I did for fun."

"Do you feel well this morning?" Maylore asked.

"My head feels clear, and my arms and legs are working," Airalee said, rotating her arms.

"Good," Maylore said, "It seems we have all recovered. Someone or something stole a lot from each of us. It would be nice to know who and why, but we must focus on what we will do now that we are here."

"I agree," Airalee said, feeling more confident about the situation.

"To the back of the cave," Jendrin said, walking between the boulders. Midway through the cave, the group rounded a corner to hear a loud screech and flapping wings. Jendrin saw the red-eyed nekcihc standing atop a rock, berating them. "A nekcihc isn't dangerous unless you are a bug," Jendrin said. "It looks like it will stand its ground. We will go around it on the other side of the boulder." The bird's glowing red eyes watched them as they walked. Maylore watched it for several steps before deciding the bird would not attack them.

Jendrin stopped at the entrance of the tunnel and pushed the torch inside. The torchlight showed an empty tunnel leading away. "I will lead since I have the torch," Jendrin said. "Maylore, would you carry the unlit spare torches and watch behind us for danger? Airalee carries our food and supplies. Ready?" he asked. Both of them nodded, so Jendrin entered the tunnel. The slight breeze pushed them down the tunnel. They arrived at the narrow spot where Jendrin had stopped the night before. Jendrin poked the torch through the opening as Airalee picked up the small club leaning against the wall.

"This may be useful," Airalee said, examining the club.

"Be careful where you swing it," Jendrin said, staring again into the dark tunnel.

"I will not hesitate to use it if something intending evil comes my way," Airalee said, scowling at Jendrin's back.

Maylore continued to watch behind them but saw no movement.

"The tunnel opens into another cave," Jendrin said. "Light is coming in from above, and I don't see any creatures in the tunnel." Jendrin led the group into the tunnel, stopping inside the middle of the cave. Bright sunlight entered the cave from a large ceiling hole.

"The hole is far too high for us to climb out of this tunnel," Maylore said, looking up. The group split up to explore the cave. Airalee found a firepit on one side.

"There have been others before us," she said as she bent down to stir the firepit. She found some very brittle animal bones, some wood, but nothing else. "Whoever was here tossed animal bones into the fire." The two men approached her when a sudden buzzing noise filled the air. They all crouched down, looking in different directions for the source, when shadows moved through the light. "Something went over the top of the cave opening," Airalee said.

"Did you see what it was?" Maylore asked as the buzzing faded away.

"I couldn't tell what it was," Airalee said.

"It seemed to fly over us," Maylore said, standing.

"I have never heard of a buzzing creature save insects," Jendrin said.

"At least not that large," Maylore said. "Let's hope this is not its nest."

"Let's find the continuation of the tunnel before it decides to drop in on us," Jendrin said.

They each walked to a different side of the cave. The torchlight showed an opening in front of Airalee.

"The tunnel continues up from here," she said as she walked toward it. A calm, musky draft blew into her face as she stood before the entrance. A large tuft of fur clung to one side, drawing her attention. "It appears there are large animals," she said, pulling the tuff off the rock. The fur was delicate, and it felt warm in her hand. The two men joined her and examined the fur.

"Time to move on?" Airalee asked, standing near the tunnel.

"Let's light another torch before this one burns out," Jendrin said, holding his torch for Maylore to light. Maylore lit his torch and smoothed Jendrin's torch. Airalee turned to enter the tunnel. "I should lead if we have to fight. I will take the club while you carry our torch," he said, passing her the torch and reaching for the club.

'A little bit arrogant, aren't you.' Airalee thought, but she passed him the club. She grimaced, saying sarcastically, "My hero," as she took the torch. Jendrin ignored her tone and turned to start up the tunnel. Small tufts of hair clung to the lava rock sides of the tunnel as they walked. The tufts would flash to flame as the torch got near them. Jendrin proceeded cautiously, anticipating a creature would rush at them. The tunnel had numerous twists and turns but no side tunnels. Several crater-like depressions in the tunnel forced them to skirt the outside or traverse the crater. Climbing to the top of the latest crater, Jendrin stopped.

"Do you hear that?" Jendrin said.

"It sounds like running water," Maylore said. "It is a trickle somewhere ahead."

"Water would be most welcome," Airalee said as she listened.

The group moved ahead as the tunnel continued to shrink and then grow in height and width. Rounding another turn, they entered another cavern with three tunnels away from it. Water was running from the left tunnel into the cavern's center pool. Another tunnel continued upward, and the third appeared to go down to the right. There did not appear to be any creatures in any of the tunnels. All three walked to the pool and drank deeply of the cool water. They all sat resting on the side of the pool as Airalee sat away from the men.

"I have to get some of this caked blood out of my robe and off of me," Maylore said as he set his load aside and entered the cold pool. Maylore grimaced as the cool water hit his skin. "Cold, very cold!" he said, scrubbing at the blood stains.

"I would like to get the blood off this robe, but I don't want to wear a cold robe," Airalee said. "The air in this tunnel may be warm, but I would be too cold if the robe were wet."

"You could carry it, and I would lend you my robe until yours dried," Jendrin said.

"No, thank you," Airalee said. "After all, what good is a hero without his armor," Airalee said.

"Good," Jendrin said, "I didn't want to do that anyway.

Maylore washed as much of the blood off the robe and himself before the cold water forced him out of the pool. The robe was still stained, but most of the caked blood was gone.

"Don't recommend doing that," Maylore said as he stood by the pool. "Turn, please, Airalee," he said, stepping toward her. She turned, gripping the torch a little tighter. Maylore reached into her pack and pulled out the little guy's shirt. He walked back around a rock and removed his robe. He wrung water from the robe before wrapping the little guy's shirt around his hips. He returned to the group carrying the robe under his arm.

"I was wondering what you were going to do," Jendrin said with a smile. "I wondered how red Airalee would get if you returned in just your birthday suit."

"I would be embarrassed for him, that is all." Airalee said, looking at Jendrin.

"Let's be on our way," Maylore said, draping his robe over the bucket.

"Which path to choose?" Jendrin asked, not wanting an answer. "Let's explore the one on the left." as he walked to the left tunnel.

"Be ready, hero," Airalee said as she thrust the torch into the first tunnel. The tunnel had a pool of water at the entrance and a collapsed ceiling a few paces in.

They moved to the second tunnel as Jendrin stood ready. The torch showed it led upwards into the distance with the same features as the current tunnel.

"This one appears to go somewhere," Jendrin said.

Moving to the third tunnel, Airalee noted more fur at the entrance.

"Fur lines the entrance of this tunnel," she said, examining the entrance.

Jendrin moved before the third tunnel as Airalee pushed the torch into the tunnel entrance. The fur lining the wall flashed into flame, allowing them to see that the tunnel continued downward, but no creatures stood at the ingress.

"We don't need to go that way," Maylore said as Jendrin visually relaxed. The club he carried lowered toward the ground.

"You are off the hook this time, hero," Airalee said.

A loud rumble echoed from deep within the third tunnel. A scare ran through them as they turned to face an unseen enemy. Maylore dropped his load and pulled out one of the torches as a club. Airalee held the torch like a club as Jendrin moved to the group's point. They tensely stood waiting as the sound grew fainter.

"They were afraid of us." she chuckled with relief.

"They probably fear fire since their fur burns so quickly," Maylore said as the sounds diminished.

"I hope you are right," Jendrin said, turning toward Maylore. "Let's light a second torch for you to carry, Maylore. It should keep them from attacking us from the rear." Airalee lit Maylore's torch before turning to the second tunnel. Without waiting for the others, she led the way into the tunnel. Jendrin looked at Maylore, shrugged, and followed. Maylore retook the rear guard using the torch to verify that nothing followed them. They walked steadily with an occasional stop to listen for pursuit. The only sound came from their burning torches. They examined several collapsed branches left, right, upward, and straight down. The companions searched the top of many tunnels to find the blaze showing them the way. Airalee continued to lead as they entered another cavern with several paths leading in different directions.

"Where to start," she said, looking at the options.

The group split up to examine each of the tunnels.

"The first one goes up," Jendrin said, pointing ahead. "There is a club there, and I suspect a wavey line on the wall above it," he said, walking toward the club. "Yes, a mark on the wall."

"It would have been nice if they had marked all the tunnels," Airalee said.

"There is water in this tunnel," Maylore said, bending down to scoop up some water. "I believe my robe is dry enough," he said, putting his damp robe back on. He pulled off the shirt and added it back into the pack. "We should change torches while we can." Maylore lit new torches, doused the old ones, and pushed them into the tar to reload.

"Let's follow the middle tunnel," Jendrin said. He pointed to the marked tunnel as Maylore led the group. Airalee carried her club as Jendrin watched the rear. The trio continued on the marked tunnel, weaving between the rocks and scattered boulders. Maylore suddenly stopped looking up the path.

"Do you feel that?" he asked, gesturing up ahead. "There is a breath of air coming from somewhere ahead."

Airalee stopped beside him and felt fresh air blowing on her. "Yes, I feel it." Jendrin was still checking behind them but said he could feel the air on his body.

"I hope this means we are nearing an exit to this maze." Maylore said. Pushing ahead to another sharp twist in the tunnel, they entered a wide area similar to the cave they started in. Several wide cracks in the ceiling allowed air and some light to enter.

"We can't be too far underground since we can see the light coming in from the cracks," Airalee said. "It is still a long way up. Too far for even a hero to jump," she said, looking at Jendrin.

Jendrin smiled, pretending to jump upward, saying, "You're right, too far."

"These rocks formed a ring around a long deserted fire," Maylore said, examining the area.

"I think it is a hideaway camp," Jendrin noted. "There are a few broken buckets over here," Jendrin said, looking around. "I didn't see any water or food sources."

"This area has not been used in a long time," Maylore said, coming to the center.

"There are bones in the fire pit," Airalee said, examining the area. "A large amount of dust and cracked buckets covered the area. I believe Maylore is right."

"There are clear spots behind the fire pit," Jendrin said, pointing behind them. "It could have been a sleeping area," Jendrin said.

"There is a large amount of fur on these rocks," Airalee said, indicating various large rocks. "It looks like the kind we saw before," she said, pointing to small tufts around the area. Looking to the side, she added, "There are more bones over here." She moved toward the bones, saying, "I believe these are human bones. There are large teeth marks from something gnawing on them."

"Basrah, that means the creatures do come up here," Maylore said, looking back in the direction they had come.

"It could be a group camped here and were attacked when the fire went out." Jendrin conjectured. "We should move out of here and hope our torches hold up.

Jendrin's torch burned low, so he put it out, redipped it in the tar bucket, and relit it from Maylore's torch. Maylore followed his example even though it had not been burning long.

"Let's find the exit," Jendrin said as all three followed the cave wall. The opposite side revealed a smaller tunnel with wavey lines above it.

The group entered the narrow tunnel. The tunnel varied from a single file to requiring the group to duck down or turn sideways to continue. The path ahead was filled with ceiling cave-ins but had an outside path around them. The winding passage came to another fork.

"The fork going up has a mark above it," Jendrin said.

"The fork going down has no markings," Airalee said.

"I don't think we want to go downward." Maylore said, "I hope we can soon leave this cursed tunnel!" as he raised the torch in emphasis.

"It sounds reasonable to me." Jendrin said, "The tunnel guidepost has not let us down yet. Let's go up." Maylore and Airalee nodded as the group started up the tunnel. The tunnel continued twisting as the type of rock lining the tunnel changed.

"It looks like we have gone from lava rock to solid granite," Maylore said, examining the tunnel walls. The tunnel continued slightly down. "Are we sure we want to continue this way?" Maylore said.

"No, I don't." Jendrin said, "But do we have many choices?"

"No, not really," Maylore replied,

"We are not going back, let's see it to its end, or it ends us." Airalee said, "Onward we go." They started down the slight slope of the tunnel.

"Is that rushing water?" Airalee asked as she stopped.

"I don't see any water," Jendrin said, looking around.

"The tunnel is dry." Maylore said, "It sounds like the water is below us." he added, looking down. "Look, the tunnel rock above us has changed to lava rock again. It could be a water-filled tube."

"We could be over an underground river," Jendrin said. "The tunnel we passed going down could end at this river."

"It seems the air is not as dry. Does it smell fresher to anyone?" Airalee asked.

"It smells like an accursed tunnel." Maylore grumped.

"It does seem lighter," Jendrin said, looking up the tunnel.

"Looks like we climb again," Airalee said as she pointed to the rising tunnel. The tunnel climbed at a steeper angle as the three climbed.

"I think I see a light ahead," Airalee said, looking up. The three stopped and looked ahead.

"There is light," Maylore said. "I hope it isn't another cave."

"Listen, do you hear a bird?" Airalee said as all three stood quiet. "That is a bird. I hear a bird chirping!"

"Bird or something," Jendrin said with suspicion in his voice. "Let's walk cautiously to see what it is." The tunnel turned slightly each way before it leveled into a small opening filled with sunshine.

"What a relief," Maylore said, moving toward the entrance.

Jendrin caught his arm, saying quietly, "Let's scan the area first. We don't want to walk into someone's trap."

"Even if there is a trap, where else would we go?" Airalee asked quietly.

"This cave is defensible," Jendrin said. "Let me investigate to see if there is an obvious danger we can avoid," Jendrin said.

"All right, hero," Airalee said, leaning against a bolder.

Jendrin walked to the edge of the cave, which was clogged with brush. He parted the brush to access the entrance and outside the cave. He returned to the group, saying, "I don't see an obvious trap. Let's see what is outside this cave.

"It will be a pleasure to see sunlight," Maylore said as the group made their way through the brush and into the sunlight.

"Greetings, Travelers!" came a voice from above.

"Basrah, now what," Jendrin said.

CHAPTER 3 - FRIEND OR FOE

"Look up," the voice came again. The companions followed the voice into the tree beside the cave entrance. A small man with a bow was looking down at them. "Welcome, refugees. I notified the Beacon even though you made enough noise to alert the village."

"Looks like we made ourselves easy targets," Jendrin said, sliding back into the cave.

"I wonder if all of the people here are small," Maylore said, sliding backward.

"I wonder who he notified?" Airalee commented.

"You have nothing to fear, refugees," the small man said. "I watch the road and cave. Come out and greet us." The three companions looked at each other before speaking.

"Do we take our chances?" Maylore asked.

"We could create a defensive position inside this entrance," Jendrin said, pointing at the brush.

"I am not going back in there," Airalee said. "He could have already shot us with his bow if he wanted to." Looking up at the little man, she asked, "Who are you, and where are we?"

"I am Olach. A sentinel to the village of Olona," the little man said. "I understand some of your language but do not speak it very well. The Beacon will be here soon to answer questions. Wait here." The sentinel climbed higher and disappeared into the tree.

"Is a Beacon a lawman, strong man, slaver, or what?" Airalee asked. "If they are all the sentinel's size, I am sure I can get away into the forest."

"We need to stay together," Maylore insisted.

"We can easily fend off a large group from here," Jendrin said.

"I have no intention of fighting or becoming a slave," Airalee said.

"Nor do we. Let us first hear what the next little guy has to say," Maylore said.

Airalee grumbled and started looking around the area while they waited. "It is getting dark, but at least it is warm out here. There are big trees surrounding this clearing. Over there, a road and two rock huts." Airalee turned toward the mountains, saying, "The mountains beyond are huge!"

"We saw those mountains from where we started," Maylore said. "It looks like we walked under the lava mountain. That granite hill behind it must be the one we recently skirted underground." The three turned to see the mountains fill their view to the left.

"This road goes up this forested lava hill to the left and up the large hill to the right," Jendrin said.

"Look at all the plant life," Airalee said, pointing at the plants and flowers. "We can find food here."

"Indeed, you can," came a voice from behind them. They all turned to see a tall man with a neatly trimmed beard standing by the tree carrying a bucket of water. "Welcome, I am Beacon Rendal." He was a man their size and about forty seasons old, wearing leather with an orange belt. "I serve as the greeter and official leader of the village Olona," he said, pointing behind him. He walked the short distance to where the companions stood and offered a full water dipper. The three hesitated even though they were thirsty. "I assure you, this is just water," Rendal said as he drank the dipper dry. Refilling the dipper, he offered it to the group.

"I will take it," Jendrin said, taking the dipper from him. He offered it to Airalee first.

"A hero with manners, how refreshing," she said, taking the dipper and drinking all of it.

"I try at times," Jendrin said, scooping more water and passing it to Maylore. He drank it and then filled it for Jendrin to drink. The three repeated the process several times before they had enough.

"You are not small like the sentinel," Jendrin said.

"True," Rendal said. "The sentinel you saw is a Tocor. They have a village about a half-day walk sunrise from here," he said, pointing left. "The planet Almora has Tocor, Lemidge, and human villages. There could be others we are unaware of. The valley we are in is called Molia. The name's origins are lost, but we believe it originated with the Tocor. The animal life here ranges from dangerous to benign.

"Dangerous is right," Maylore said.

"How do you stop those huge wolves?" Jendrin asked.

"What are those hairy beasts in the cave?" Airalee asked.

The group started asking multiple questions before Rendal raised his hand, saying, "I will try to answer your questions. Let us move to the visitor's hut," he said, pointing to the hut near the road. "We will bring food and water, and then we can talk," Rendal said, turning toward the hut and waving for them to follow.

Rendal took several steps before Jendrin quietly said to his companions, "Is this a trap? Are we to become prisoners, enslaved, or worse?"

"He did not arrive with guards," Maylore said. "Let's not be so suspicious and go find out." The group followed as Maylore led the way to the hut. Jendrin looked for possible hiding spots that may hold attackers as he walked.

Rendal paused at an opening near a brush. "Let me start by describing directions," Rendal said. "When they say go sunrise, they mean the direction the twin suns rise, which is that way," Rendal said, pointing toward the cave. "Sunset means the other way," Rendal said, pointing to the other side parallel to the mountains. Go mountain is toward the mountains," he said, pointing toward the mountains. "Olona is a coastal city, and the sea is the other way," Rendal said, pointing away from the mountains.

"Seems simple enough," Maylore said.

"Good," Rendal said. "Olona is just beyond these trees toward the sea. The Tocor, Lemidge, and humans all navigate using the same directions. They each have different names, but they mean the same direction."

Jendrin noticed a stick hanging on a rope near the entrance. "Is this a punishment stick?" he asked.

"No," Rendal replied with a chuckle. "It is the stick of measuring. Each village has a stick of a similar length with markings on it to measure objects," Rendal said. Pointing to a rock near the stick, he said, "Besides it, there are two weight-measuring rocks, one large, one small. Each village has similar rocks to measure weights. We measure heat using ice for coldness, the skin for warmth, and boiling water for high temperatures. How do you measure such things?"

The three stared at him. "I should know but don't remember," Jendrin said. Maylore and Airalee gave him the same blank look.

"I suspect you find you don't remember many things," Rendal said.

"I fear much has been stolen from each of us," Maylore replied.

"I understand," Rendal said. "Let us move to where you may rest," Rendal smiled as he walked toward the long hut. Rendal opened the door, saying. "Please enter so we may talk and wait for some food." The three companions entered the dark hut as Rendal followed them in.

Two windows allow light to enter the dark hut. Rendal moved to the far end and added wood to a fire in a small fireplace. The fire added light to the room. Benches lined the walls with a long table in the middle. Four sturdy chairs ringed the fireplace. "Please sit in a chair," Rendal said as he sat in the last chair. They each sat as Rendal started speaking before they sat down. "I realize you have many questions. I will tell you about our valley and village as a way to answer what I can. We do not know all the answers, but I will tell you what we know. Please tell me your names before I begin."

"I am Maylore," Maylore said with a slight wave.

"Do you have other names or titles?" Rendal asked.

Maylore looked at him blankly, saying, "No. I don't think so."

"Maylore, nice to meet you," Rendal said before looking at Airalee.

"I am Airalee. I don't know of any other name or title," Airalee said as Rendal nodded, looking toward Jendrin.

"I heard you named Hero," Rendal said. "Any titles to go with your name?"

"My companion thinks she is funny," Jendrin said, looking at Airalee, who flashed a fake smile. "My name is Jendrin. I have no titles."

"My apologies, Jendrin," Rendal said. "Jendrin, Airalee, and Maylore, I am pleased to meet all of you. Let me explain that refugees who arrive here have a similar situation. They are all dressed in robes and sandals. Men generally have no beards. No one remembers anything before they arrived. The memories and background have been erased from their minds. Most remember their names, speaking skills, and bits of past training. A few don't remember their names, forcing them to choose a new one. Most have headaches for a short time and feel like a fire is burning in their heads. If they remember a fragment of their past, it immediately burns out. None of us understands who, what, when, or why they are here. Refugees puzzle on their predicament for a time before accepting and moving on." Rendal paused to look at their stunned

34

faces. "I understand you are feeling bewildered. All of those who turned up here felt the same."

"That is certainly accurate," Airalee said. "Are you a past refugee?"

"No," Rendal replied. "I was born here like my mother. My mother was not sure where her ancestors lived. Likely, they came here many seasons ago." Rendal could see they were tired and confused but pushed ahead with his talk. "I will try not to push too much information on you. Let me tell you a little about where you are now, and then you can eat, rest, and sleep," he said, pointing to the curtain at the far end.

"To the sunrise, the valley becomes a desert before turning to forest lands beyond," Rendal said, indicating the sunrise direction and then switching to point the other way. "In the sunset direction are small mountains, valleys, rivers, and large lakes. To the sea, there is a vast ocean we have not traveled. A few have tried, but none returned. There are many villages at sunrise and sunset. Some are large, many smaller. There are other human villages in the sunset direction. Olona is the last human village on the sunrise side. There are several Tocor villages on the sunrise side and a few on the sunset side. A few groups just travel the valley, trading and living off the land. The travelers are how we get information about what is happening in this valley. I meet with those groups here and provide them with food, water, and a bed in exchange for what they have seen or wish to trade. Their information is how I can tell you and others what is beyond our village. Our village has 140 people living in it. The land, sea, and trading provide our needs. We trade seafood and what we make to travelers and other villages for other things. Villagers provide for themselves but cooperate with other villagers when needed."

A rattling noise outside the hut drew their attention. It grew louder until the door to the hut opened. Two women entered, one carrying a large pot and the other a small pot and eating supplies.

"Dinner has arrived," Rendal said, pointing to the table. "Mirtha carries the big pot of soup and is our teaching cook. Kai brings water and is our master teaching healer." Mirtha smiled at them as she set the pot on the table. Kai placed the water and eating tools on the table and quickly left.

"This is yfislas root soup," Mirtha announced as she scooped a bowl for each one. "There is more if you wish," she said, moving the pot to the center. Looking toward Rendal, she said, "I have more food to prepare if you do not need me, Rendal."

"No, my thanks, Mirtha," Rendal replied as she smiled and left the hut. "Please enjoy the soup."

The three companions looked at him warily.

"We would not be good hosts if we poison our guests' foods," Rendal said as he scooped a bowl for himself and began eating. After he had eaten several spoonful, the companions moved to the table and started eating.

"This is excellent soup," Airalee said. "It's spicy, smooth, and filling." The other two agreed. No one spoke as they ate. Rendal sat facing the group and filled the water cups from the second pot.

"The water in your cups contains a sleeping draft," Rendal said.

"Spiked water?" Jendrin said.

"We have found it best for refugees to sleep when they arrive," Rendal said.

"The water has a slight mint flavor," Airalee said, looking at her cup. "It doesn't taste like the water the little guy had in the cave."

"It is relaxing, and you have nothing to fear from us as you sleep," Rendal said. "There are six beds in the area behind the curtain. You may choose the one you wish. Tomorrow, you will feel refreshed, and we can continue our talks. Please be comfortable here tonight, and I will greet you all in the morning. A sentinel is living in the tree near this hut. He watches out for you just like he does for

36

the other villagers. I recommend you eat more and drink all the water for a sound sleep." Rendal smiled as he arose.

"We thank you for your hospitality, Rendal," Maylore said.

Rendal smiled, nodded, and left the hut. His footsteps faded before Jendrin spoke.

"I'm not sure we are guests or prisoners," Jendrin said, finishing his soup. "I am going to check outside for guards watching this hut," Jendrin said, peeking out the door before leaving. The other two drank some more water while they awaited his return. Jendrin was not gone long before he reentered. His companions were gone. "Where did everyone go?" he said aloud.

"Back here, Jendrin," he heard Maylore say. Jendrin moved to the rear of the hut and pushed aside the curtain. Airalee and Maylore stood near a bed on opposite sides. "I did not see guards watching the hut," Jendrin said. "The sentinels are small and would easily hide in the darkness."

"I think we should give Rendal the benefit of the doubt," Maylore said as he sat on a bed. "We spent an entire day wandering those cursed lava tubes. No wonder I feel tired." Maylore said, looking at the other two. "I, for one, will take them up on the offer of sleep," as he removed his sandals.

"I am unsure we can trust him or anyone else," Airalee said, moving to the farthest bed.

"I agree," Jendrin said, standing in the doorway. "Rendal appeared to be a friend, but he could just as easily be a foe." Jendrin claimed a bed nearest the curtain where he could see the door. "I will keep a watch on the door," he said, setting his club beside the bed. He closed the shutters on the window above his bed before sitting on it. Airalee set the backpack and small club she carried on a bed beside hers and retrieved her rock. She lay on her bed and watched the two men as she pulled a blanket tightly around her with the rock in hand.

"I don't even need their sleeping draft," Maylore said, laying back on the bed. "I think it is working already."

"We should consider asking Rendal a few questions in the morning," Jendrin remarked. "I wonder how far it is from where we started to here. What kind of beast leaves that fur in the caves?"

"What about those wolves?" Maylore asked.

"Who killed the little man?" Airalee said, propping herself up against the wall to watch the room. Maylore nodded as they spoke. "All good questions. Sleep has come for me. Good night," he said, turning toward the wall. Airalee continued to watch the room but quickly fell asleep, gripping her rock. Jendrin lay on his bed, watching the door, but sleep captured him, too.

Council Meeting

Beacon Rendal asked the council members to meet with him after he left the newcomers. Six elected council members sat at the table in the council hut as Rendal arrived with three others.

"Thank you all for coming to council," Rendal said, moving to the head of the table. "I have asked Marisa, Kai, and Mirtha to join us for this meeting. As most of you know, we received three refugees."

"It has been many seasons since the last refugees arrived," Mirtha said.

"Yes," Rendal said. "This group has two men and one woman. They arrived from the cave in the early evening. The older man's name is Maylore. He appears in his middle fifties, less than two sticks tall, and about four stones. He speaks well and seems to have a calm demeanor. The other man's name is Jendrin. He is in his mid-twenties, a little less than two sticks in height, has a muscular build, and less than five stones. He seems to have an aggressive demeanor to him. The female is in her twenties, one and ¾ sticks, about three stone, and very pretty. I suspect she may be a leader currently deferring to the two men. The two men are probably unfamiliar to

38

her, and her leadership will emerge in time. The story they told me sounds similar to what other refugees have told me. They don't know if they voluntarily left someplace or if someone forced them out. They have no memory of their past lives. They told me they had the same mind-burning sensation that other refugees told us about. I told them it would take time for them to adjust to Almora and the valley's inhabitants. As with past refugees, this council will decide if they remain in Olona or are asked to leave. They may decide to live in our village if we allow them to stay. If they do, we must train them to fit into our society. I would like you to meet with them to decide if we should allow them refugee status first."

"Remember the sadness that befell us many seasons ago," Councilwoman Nenaias interjected. "They turned out to be spies working for the master and the bandits."

"Yes," Rendal said, "We were quick to determine they were not refugees, but they did find out about our village before we pushed them out. We did lose one of our key community leaders to a mysterious disappearance. I still suspect the master was behind it, but I never found proof. This time, we must watch for signs that the refugees are spies. Look for reasons to distrust them or reasons to trust them. Do not reveal who you are or village secrets until this council approves trust is warranted. It should be evident to us quickly if we watch them early. I have asked the sentinels to watch for suspicious activity. Olach said he would ask other Tocor to be sentinels to help him. Their watch from above would allow the refugees to be unaware of being watched."

"We did not have the sentinels watch the last group," Argila said. "This should make it easier to detect any deception."

"I hope it is true," Rendal said. "I have asked Marisa to lead our contact group with them. She will be studying them to determine their integrity. I asked her to bring them breakfast tomorrow and then summon me to discuss our village. She will be showing them the village, and she will be introducing them to you. Throc and Latel will

39

join her to help her guide them until this council says if they may stay or must go."

"I will spy on the spies," Marisa said in jest.

"Mirtha and Kai briefly saw the group," Rendal said. "Do you have any comments?"

"They seemed like fatigued and hungry people to me," Kai said.

"The older man had a blood stain on his robe," Mirtha said. "Airalee has blood splatters on the back of her robe. I considered asking where they came from but decided the time was inappropriate."

"I agree, Mirtha," Rendal said, nodding. "The stains are why I decided they would spend the night in the guest hut instead of inside the village. They did mention they had trouble with wolves, but I decided it was not the time to pursue it. Tomorrow, I will get to the bottom of that story. The sentinels will warn us if they misbehave, but Kai's sleeping draft will prevent misadventure. I do not believe they will be a problem."

"Tension is rising in the valley, and if they bring trouble, it will hurt our village a lot more this time," Councilwoman Caudra said.

"Agreed, Caudra," Rendal said. "Does anyone have a question about them?"

"If they stay, which hut are they going to live in?" councilman Baruo asked.

"I plan to let them use the larger hut the family left a few sunrises ago," Rendal replied. "We have several small huts available they could use separately, but no large huts.

"As long as we can verify they are good people, I would welcome new additions to Olona," Councilwoman Caudra said. The rest of the council verbally agreed and nodded their heads.

"Excellent," Rendal said. "We will hope for the best. We will meet again tomorrow. Thank you, everyone," Rendal said, standing.

CHAPTER 4 - DECISIONS DECISIONS

Maylore's eyes popped open. Daylight streamed into his eyes from the window above Jendrin's bed. The shutters had been closed the night before and were now open. Swinging his feet to the floor, he stood up. Peeking through the curtain, he saw a new fire in the fireplace and food on the table.

"Airalee, Jendrin, wake up, please," he said as he looked toward their beds. Two heads appeared as each started to rise. "The village appears to have a good Samaritan to help its guests," Maylore said, looking at the new food. "We have bread, some kind of juice, and beans for breakfast."

Jendrin looked up at the light in the window above his bed.

"I may have to resign my job as a watcher," Jendrin said. "Someone built a fire and opened the shutters above my head without me noticing," he said as he stood. "I didn't hear a thing last night."

"Even heroes fail," Airalee said, unwrapping the blanket around her.

"Don't be too hard on yourself, Jendrin," Maylore said. "The sleeping potion did its work to perfection. I feel refreshed, hungry, and ready for whatever happens."

Opening the door to check outside, Jendrin noticed the twin suns were high in the morning sky. He spotted an attractive, red-haired young woman sitting on a rock several sticks away.

"Good morning to you," Jendrin said.

"Good morning," she replied, "Please enjoy your breakfast, and then the Beacon will speak with you."

"Oh, thank you." Jendrin replied, "Did you make a fire and bring us breakfast this morning?" Jendrin asked.

"Mirtha made the breakfast," she said. "I delivered it and prepared your hut. I will also be your guide after the Beacon speaks."

"Good," Jendrin said. "What is your name?"

"Marisa," she replied, standing up.

"Would you like to join us, Marisa?" Jendrin asked.

"No, thank you," Marisa replied, "I will bring back the Beacon as you eat," she replied. Jendrin nodded as he closed the door. His companions were sitting at the table as he approached.

"We seem to have a very quiet helper outside our door," Jendrin said, sitting down. "Her name is Marisa. She built a fire, brought our breakfast, and opened the shutters above my bed without waking anyone. I am pleased she did not have a knife or ill intent. She also said the Beacon will come and speak to us."

"We are fortunate you did not scare her off," Airalee said.

"Yes, I am one scary man," Jendrin replied, examining the food on the table.

"You are a big man, hero. She could have been frightened," Airalee replied.

"She didn't look the least bit frightened," Jendrin said, adding food to his plate.

"I suggest we discuss a few things before the Beacon arrives," Maylore said. "Are you two inclined to stay in this village or explore the valley?" Maylore asked.

"Are we going to stay together?" Jendrin asked without looking up.

"I strongly suggest we stay together." Maylore replied, "We do not know what we are facing, and we have met several tests together."

"I have no objection to remaining a companionship," Jendrin said, looking to Airalee.

Airalee could feel anxiety racing about remaining with two men she did not know and barely trusted. 'They treat me like a companion. I could face much worse on my own.' she thought. "I would remain with the companionship," she said.

"That is a relief to me," Maylore said, looking at both of them. "I feel we will accomplish more together than apart."

"Should we remain in a village or travel to see what the valley offers?" Maylore asked.

"If the Beacon decides we are his prisoners, we may not have a choice," Jendrin replied.

"They probably mistrust us too," Maylore said. "We must prove we are trustworthy to alleviate their concerns."

"We will need to live within Olona's expectations to accomplish that," Airalee said.

"Whatever those are," Jendrin said. "Perhaps we should explore the valley before deciding where to settle."

"We should evaluate this village before deciding what to do," Airalee said.

"We could ask the Beacon to show us his village to help make our decision," Maylore said.

"A tour would be welcome before we move on," Jendrin said.

"We may decide to stay," Airalee said a little forcefully.

"If you look too long, you will grow roots and can't move," Jendrin said, looking at her.

"If you move too much, you won't build relationships with other people. They will look at you with suspicion." Airalee said.

Jendrin and Airalee spared back and forth for a short time.

"Please hold your fire," Maylore said, raising his hands. "We need this little group to work together, at least for now," looking at both of them.

"Fair enough," Jendrin replied.

"Ok, Dad," Airalee deadpanned.

Maylore smiled at Airalee, saying, "I guess I am old enough to be your dad. I did sound like one, didn't I? However, you two have too many prickly points to be related to this smooth, even-keeled person," as he smiled at them. They both smiled and ate their breakfast.

"Are we ready to meet the Beacon?" Maylore asked as they finished.

"I would like answers to our questions from last night," Jendrin said.

"I would like to know why the wolves attacked the Tocor, not me?" Maylore said.

"What is leaving all that fur in the cave? Listening to the growls we heard, I assume it is not friendly," Airalee said.

"Why was the camp nearest this end littered with bones? Did they intend to mark the tunnels but failed to mark them all? We spent much time searching along dead ends," Jendrin said.

"I wonder how large this village is? Do they have a social structure we can fit into?" Airalee asked, looking in the direction of the village.

"I wonder if most of them are slaves or prisoners?" Jendrin said.

"Oh my, let's give them a chance to explain," Maylore said as a knock came on the door.

"Right on time," Jendrin said as he stood and opened the door.

"Good afternoon," Rendal said as he entered the hut. "I hope you all had a restful night." He led Marisa inside and sat on the other side of the table.

"Indeed, a restful sleep," Maylore said with a slight wave of his hand.

"I assume you have met your village guide, Marisa?" Rendal said, indicating Marisa.

"We have," Jendrin said. "I am sorry you had to sit so long for us to rise."

"I did not mind," Marisa replied. "It is my task to help you when you need me."

"Thank you all the same, Marisa," Airalee said.

"May we start by asking a few questions?" Jendrin asked.

"Please do. It would be a good way to open our new friendship," Rendal said.

"Why was the little man you call a Tocor waiting for us to arrive?" Jendrin asked.

"The Tocor you met was a greeter. He did not know you would arrive. He was stationed there to meet anyone who did arrive there. Allow me to explain some of the history of the Tocor. The Tocor are native to this region of Almora. They are smaller in stature, measuring one stick in height and one stone in weight. They have sharp eyes and ears. They have feet with a hook or spur on their heel, allowing them to climb any tree easily. Most of them live in groves of Surn trees, which grow higher up in the mountains. They are rarely violent and prefer to stay away from humans. Tocor villages used to assign one of their members to watch for refugees, or perhaps they referred to them as intruders. I am not sure of their meaning from their telling. They tell us unconscious humans started appearing hundreds of summers ago at certain spots in the valley.

The Tocor feared them, and many humans died before the Tocor decided to try to help them. The Tocor sent one villager, whom they referred to as a greeter, to help the humans. The greeter gave the humans food, water, and shelter when they awoke. The Tocor would then lead them away from their village to a location where the humans could provide for themselves. They tell us the Tocor used to monitor many drop points in the valley. They say the number of humans arriving now is few. You three are the first to come here in many summers." Rendal assumed a questioning look as he said, "The greeter accompanies the humans to their new destination. Did something happen to your greeter?"

Maylore looked at his companions to see who would reply. The other two looked at him.

"He was beaten to death by someone before we awoke," Maylore said. "When I awoke, I found a small bloody club nearby and the little guy covered in blood. He lived long enough to point me to a nearby cave. He informed me Blood Wolves would be coming, and we should move into the cave."

Rendal and Marisa intently listened as he continued.

"Jendrin awoke next as I tried to help Airalee," Maylore said. "We were deciding what to do when the wind shifted from a mountain breeze to a sea breeze. We soon heard a wolf start howling. Jendrin carried Airalee to the cave as I tried to pull the little guy's dead body to the cave. The wolves were huge and arrived far quicker than I anticipated. The lead wolf swatted me away as the other wolf claimed the body." Maylore said, looking down.

"That is very sad," Rendal said. "I did not think a greeter would be there. Did you notice his clothes?"

"A worn leather tunic, no decorations, dark hair, and a white headband," Maylore replied.

"A greeter from the Nillon village judging by the white headband," Rendal said. "Their village uses white as their identification color. We will send a message to Nillon to tell them about his fate."

"Why would anyone want to kill him?" Airalee asked.

"A few Tocor now consider it their duty to protect the refugees they encounter. Most will hide until the trouble has passed before trying to help. Perhaps the Tocor saw one of you under attack and tried to intervene."

"It appears," Maylore said, "someone beat the little guy for his efforts."

"Were any of you injured?" Rendal asked. The three companions looked at each other and shook their heads.

"You have blood on your robe. Were you injured, Maylore?" Rendal asked.

"No, I was not injured," Maylore replied. "I got blood on my robe by picking up the little guy to carry to the cave. The wolves got him first."

"The blood splatters on the back of my robe may have come from the attack on the little guy," Airalee said, looking at her robe.

"The Tocor may have saved you and lost his battle," Rendal said, looking down.

Looking at Airalee, Rendal asked, "Pretty women draw birdmen's attention. No one attacked you?"

Airalee did not hesitate before replying, "No one. I am sure of it."

"Good," Rendal replied. "The birdmen have been known to use unconscious refugees."

"Birdmen?" Jendrin asked.

"It is a name the Tocor gave them," Rendal said, looking up. "They tell us a rock splits open, and a large shiny bird flies inside the nest. The bird opens its beak, and a man pulls out one to four sleeping humans dressed like you. The man sometimes uses a sleeping woman before going back inside the bird. The bird then jumps back into the air, and the rock closes. The Tocor claims the rock looks and sounds like a rock with no cracks. The cave you talk about is about a day's walk from here. I have been there a few times and examined the rock myself. It looks like any other boulder in the desert. The Tocor suggested refugees use the cave since it provides shelter from the sun and has water inside its tunnels. The greeter possibly left food for you. Did you find the food he may have provided?"

Airalee retrieved the backpack she had carried. "This is the backpack we found in the cave," she said, giving it to Rendal.

"I suggest we return this to his family in Nillon," Rendal looks toward Airalee for approval.

"Of course," Airalee said.

"Thank you," Rendal replied, passing it to Marisa.

"May I ask about the large wolves?" Maylore asked.

"Yes, Blood Wolves are what you saw," Rendal said, looking up.

"The wolf could have easily killed me outside the cave," Maylore started. "Instead, it only went after the dead Tocor."

"The Blood Wolf is a scavenger," Rendal said. "It is big and could easily kill anything it chooses, but they are aggressive carrion eaters. They sense blood in the air and will wait patiently for a creature to die. Do not try to stop them once they claim a creature, or the wolf will knock you aside."

"Indeed, they do," Maylore remarked.

"There is also a much smaller fierce wolf," Rendal said. "The fierce wolves hunt in packs and are very dangerous despite being small. They are less than one stick in height and attack from hiding. Most packs are in the woods in the mountains," Rendal said, pointing toward the mountains.

"Our advice is to leave the blood wolves alone and climb a tree if you see a fierce wolf," Rendal said. "We are fortunate neither can climb trees."

"The blood on my robe," Maylore said, "do you suppose that is why the blood wolves waited outside the cave?" Maylore asked, looking at the faded blood stain. "Perhaps the wolf was waiting for me to die."

"That would be a good guess," Rendal replied.

"There is a large amount of fine fur lining various places in the cave. Do you know what animal that is?" Airalee asked.

"Eurg, they are called," Rendal said. "They are a large furry beast no one has lived to describe. Several people have seen a glimpse of one moving away, but no clear view. They are afraid of fire since their fur burns so quickly. With so many humans living here using fire, most of the eurg have moved out of the local caves and into the mountain tunnels."

"There is a cavern not far from the tunnel exit with bones and fur scattered throughout it," Airalee said. "Is this where an eurg attack occurred?"

"Yes," Rendal replied. "We sent villagers into the tunnel to restock food and torches. They found the bones many summers ago on one such restocking trip. We believe a refugee group used the light entering the cave during the daytime but failed to light torches at night. The eurg are quiet and would have taken them while sleeping."

The hut was quiet again as Rendal waited for more questions.

"Do you have any other questions before I describe our village?" Rendal asked.

"Are there others besides the Tocor living in this valley?" Jendrin asked.

"Yes. The Lemidge are a traveling group with permanent camps sunset in the mountains. Most are slender, 1½ sticks in height, and

50

1½ stone in weight. They trade services and goods in the human and Tocor villages throughout Molia. They are due to arrive here mid-season. They generally do not stay in villages, preferring to camp between settlements. Does anyone have another question before I begin?"

"No, I am satisfied with your explanations," Airalee said. "I am anxious to hear about your village."

Maylore nodded while Jendrin looked non-committal.

"Excellent," Rendal said. "Let me tell you a little about Olona. We are a human village of about 200 villagers. Some were refugees like you, many were born here, and some migrated from other locations. We have abundant food sources, and each villager gathers their own. Villagers do contribute excess food to the central kitchen. Mirtha will see to the cooking or drying of extra food. Many build non-food items to trade with each other or other villages. We have people skilled in leather, weaving, cooking, healing, history, gathering, pottery, and forest gifts. We are blessed here with a path to descend to the sea from the cliff. Many help with the fishing effort. Seafood is available to those who help with the rest stored or added to the community pots. We trade excess fish and crafts to other villages for needed items. Other villages produce rope, spices, meats, and crafting materials we need. Our villagers don't kill animals, but we will take what we can if we get from a dead animal before the blood wolves arrive. We have a village council of six members. I am the Beacon, lead the council, and have a tie-breaking vote. I speak for the village diplomatically, meet with visitors and refugees, and do the historical records. The council is responsible for deciding and enforcing the edicts of the village and is generally a passive group."

"Who enforces these laws?" Jendrin asked. "Do you have a group to ensure all villagers follow the laws?"

"We do not have a group for that purpose," Rendal replied. "Villagers follow the laws, but if they do not, the offender is forced to live in exile."

51

"If they kill or injure someone?" Jendrin inquired.

"We have other ways to deal with them without violence," Rendal replied.

"How do you accomplish that?" Jendrin asked.

"We will keep that thought for another time," Rendal said. "We have not faced that problem in many summers." Jendrin accepted his comments as Rendal continued. "We believe another group of travelers will arrive today. We meet with them in this hut, so I would like to move you to a hut in the village." All three of the companions nodded and stood up. "I am afraid we only have one empty hut for now. I hope you three can be comfortable staying in one hut."

"Does it have separate areas we each can use?" Airalee asked.

"It has three rooms," Rendal replied. "I hope it will work for you."

"I can accept it if I get a separate room," Airalee said, looking at her companions. The two men nodded to her as Rendal turned toward the door.

"Marisa will be your guide," Rendal said, "I will check with the sentinel to ask if they have seen the next group. Marisa knows where to find me if you need me."

"This way," Marisa said, leading the way out the door.

"A moment, please," Jendrin said. Turning to his companions, he quietly asked, "Do we want to see their village or move up the valley?"

"We agreed we would give them a chance," Airalee quietly said. "They do not act like we are prisoners here," Airalee said.

"We should see their village," Maylore said.

"All right," Jendrin said, turning to the door.

"Lead the way, Marisa," he announced.

Marisa walked the short distance to the opening between the trees leading into the village.

"Your hut will be straight ahead at the end of this path," Marisa said. The companions could see stone huts with large wood and thatch roofs leading away. The path looked wide and branched away at different points.

"Marisa, could we visit the potty first?" Airalee asked.

"Of course. It is straight ahead past your new hut," Marisa said, smiling at them. "Ready?"

CHAPTER 5 - INTO OLONA

Marisa led the way through the wide opening in the trees into Olona. The warm, sunny weather buoyed the companions' spirits as they entered a sparsely treed village. Wide paths branched off, and large and small huts were on both sides of the paths leading into the village. The huts were constructed from lava rocks sealed with mudbrick and topped with tree limbs holding large leaves. A few villagers walked the path, watching the companions with suspicion as they entered. Many villagers wore fabric tunics, robes, or leather tunics. All had various orange touches to their dress.

"This is the council and meeting hut," Marisa said, pointing to the sunrise. "We hold village meetings here, and the councilors meet here." The hut looked the same as the others, only much longer and broader. "We will come back here to meet with the Beacon later."

The companions continued a slow walk, looking down the various paths. Huts lined both sides of the way, all with the same stone construction. People were walking the routes in and out of the multiple houses. Marisa continued to stroll, allowing the companions to take in the sights.

"This is the children's hut, then the birthing hut," she said, pointing to sunrise as she continued to walk. "This will be your hut," she finally said, nearing the end of this path. "We will return here after I show you where to relieve yourselves."

"Is that running water, I hear?" Jendrin asked.

"Yes. A creek runs alongside the village just over this rise," Marisa said as she walked past their hut and started up the slight rise. "The creek flows past the village from sunset, then turns here toward the sea," she said. Continuing down the slope, they came to a large pool of water. "This is our communal bathing area. Everyone bathes here when they wish. A firepit is built below the pool to heat the water from the creek. Several of the older children tend the fire."

"It is cool water," Airalee said, touching the water.

"It is warm compared to many days," Marisa said, touching the water. The group continued to follow the outflow of the pool, which was a short distance to another small pool. "This is our clothes-washing pool," she said, "Beyond it is our dishwashing area. She pointed to each pool before continuing to walk between the brush, stopping on a flat area in the path. "To the sunset, we have the potty," Marisa said. "The elder's huts are at the top of the rise to sunrise. Straight ahead is the drop-off to the sea."

"The sea," Jendrin said, passing beside Marisa. He observed a flat sea that followed a jagged coast from the sunset side to a point just sunrise side of the village. The coastline flared outward into the sea before curving toward the sunrise at the edge of their vision.

"This is the only place we know where people can get down to the shore," Marisa said. "The rest of the coastline is the sheer cliffs to the sea."

Looking over the edge, Maylore said, "It seems like a climbable slope here to those with younger legs."

"This way to the potty," Marisa said, starting toward the sunset. The sound of the creek grew louder as they walked along the lava rock path.

They came to two small huts straddling a narrow crack in the rock. "These huts are where the solids are left," Marisa said. Airalee opened one of the huts and looked in. A rough board straddled a crack in the rock that led to the depths below. Beside the board were soft, feathery husks.

"This looks like a good solution to a human sanitation problem," Maylore remarked. Airalee entered and closed the door. Jendrin used the other hut, followed by Maylore.

When they all finished, Marisa said, "Let's return to your new hut." The group walked back along the same path. Jendrin noticed another path branch along the creek.

"Where does that path lead?" he asked.

"It is a path for another day," Marisa replied mysteriously. "We will explore your hut first then meet with the Beacon." The group returned to the companions' new hut on a more straightforward path than the first one. A loud bird chirped as they walked.

"That is a loud bird," Airalee said, stopping.

"It is a sentinel signaling a visitor is approaching," Marisa said as she continued to walk.

"What is the signal for an enemy?" Jendrin asked.

"We have no enemies," Marisa replied, "But when a dangerous creature approaches, they use a different bird sound. I have heard it a few times when fierce wolves would pass by." Realizing she may have said more than she was supposed to, she shut her mouth and started walking toward their hut. The group remained quiet as they arrived at the companions' hut. Marisa felt her anxiety fade when they didn't ask questions about the sentinel signals or the new path.

"Please enter," Marisa said, opening the door to the hut. The companions entered as Marisa remained outside and held the door. The hut appeared to be about five sticks wide and six sticks to the back wall. A wall of woven wooden sticks created a separate room on the left and the back wall. Two fabric curtains served as doors on the seaside room and the room on the back wall. A bed was set along the wall just inside the door. A fireplace was built on the mountainside rock wall. A small fire was burning with various pots along its edge. A small table with four chairs opposite the fireplace held three piles of clothing.

"I get the first room choice," Airalee said matter-of-factly. She peeked into the room on the seaside. It had a bed big enough for two and a window on the seaside wall. A small cabinet at the foot of the bed left little room for anything else. Stepping to the back of the hut, she opened the curtain at the back of the room. The small window above the bed lets enough light in to gauge the room. A single bed fits along the mountainside wall, with two cabinets at the back. Returning to the center room, she said, "I claim the room on the seaside." Both men nodded in agreement and looked at each other.

"I will take the bed by the door," Jendrin said, "I will assume the task of watching for intruders."

"Our hero is hard at work," Airalee said as Marisa smiled.

"You have little to be concerned about," Marisa said.

"I would be pleased to use the back room. You have as much right to claim it as I do, Jendrin," Maylore said.

"I would prefer to be where I can see comings and goings," Jendrin said. "It is possible we won't be here long anyway."

"Thank you, Jendrin," Maylore said. "I will be pleased for the privacy,"

Marisa pointed to the clothes on the table.

"Our village tailor, Latel, left you some visitors' clothes to wear while yours are cleaned."

"We can wash our clothes," Maylore said.

"Yes, after this courtesy, you will," Marisa said. "One of the tailoring groups heard you and Airalee have blood on your robes and wishes the challenge to clean them. She has helped other villagers with difficult stains in the past and works diligently to clean them."

"I gratefully accept the offer," Maylore said, bowing his head.

"My thanks to her, too," Airalee said. "Won't you come in, Marisa?"

"Greeters are forbidden to enter guest huts unless directed by the Beacon or council," Marisa said. "If you will change your clothes, I will take them to be washed."

"All right," Airalee said, gathering robes from the table and passing one to Maylore. "Did you want to change hero?"

57

"Yes, thank you," he said, catching a robe thrown to him. Airalee and Maylore disappeared into their new rooms as Jendrin prepared to change his robe. Marisa quickly closed the door when she realized he was changing. Jendrin changed and carried his old one while he examined the pots near the fire. Cooked beans filled the first pot. The second pot contained water, and the last was empty. He tasted the pot of beans, noting they had a pleasant flavor. Maylore and Airalee reappeared carrying their stained robes.

"The least we can do is carry these robes to the cleaning person," Maylore said. The other two agreed as they started out the door. Marisa was standing nearby with another man.

"This is Latel," Marisa said. "He is our teaching tailor and will take your robes to be cleaned. Latel, this is Airalee, Maylore, and Jendrin."

"It is a pleasure meeting you all," Latel said, giving them a slight bow. "I will return them late tomorrow, or you may continue to wear the guest clothes if you wish," he said as he accepted their robes.

"Our thanks to you, Latel," Jendrin said with a smile. Latel nodded and walked away with the robes.

"We will await the Beacon in the council hut," Marisa said, pointing back up the path. The group walked past the birthing and children's hut before arriving outside the council hut. "The Beacon is dealing with travelers from another village," she said, indicating the men outside the village entrance. One was a huge man with a small amount of wavy blond hair and appeared to be their leader. The second and third were smaller than him but large compared to many. The leader seemed to be near Maylore's age. The others were close to Airalee and Jendrin's age. The travelers glanced at the newly arrived companions when the mouth of one of the younger travelers dropped open. He stumbled back a step, catching himself before he fell. He pointed at the companions as the other two visitors continued to look in their direction. Rendal turned and made a dismissive wave as he replied to the visitors. The leader turned to his subordinate and also made a dismissive wave, talking to the subordinate.

"You can wait inside," Marisa said, opening the door. "I will see if the Beacon is ready to break away from those men."

The three sat in chairs around the large table as Marisa closed the door and left.

"What was wrong with that guy?" Airalee asked.

"My muscular frame overwhelmed him," Jendrin joked.

"He seemed to know us," Maylore replied.

"Did he recognize us as fugitives?" Jendrin said, suddenly serious. They continued speculating about the visitor's intentions before discussing what might happen next.

"If they think we are fugitives, should we stay here, move to another area, or perhaps go our separate ways?" Jendrin asked.

"Their leader did not seem concerned about us. If we were recognized, he would have come for us," Maylore reasoned.

"We should stay alert to what is happening around us in case we need to leave quickly," Jendrin said. "I don't see windows or a back door to escape through if we need to run," he added, looking around the room.

"We can be prepared, but let's not worry until we need to," Maylore said.

Noticing a back room, Jendrin formulated a plan to defend themselves if necessary. He thought an unlit torch would serve as a weapon and the table for a shield would work. He felt calm with the development of the simple plan.

"If we do stay," Jendrin said, "I wonder if we have a choice of what happens to us? I did not see anyone who looked like a slave."

"Relax, hero," Airalee said. "I believe we can choose what we want. Rendal and Marisa appear to be helping us adjust to the area."

"I agree so far. It does not appear we are prisoners here," Jendrin said.

"Prisoners?" a voice came from the doorway. "No, you are all guests here," Rendal said. "We have no prisoners or enslaved people here. Airalee is correct. I will try to show you what we know about the area. You can then decide your course of action. You are all welcome to leave or stay if you wish."

"That seems reasonable," Maylore said.

"Who were those men you were talking to?" Airalee asked. "One seemed to know us."

"They are from a nearby village," Rendal replied, choosing his words carefully.

"A village of untrustworthy men," Marisa interjected.

Rendal gave her a look of warning as she relented.

"Marisa is correct," Rendal said. "I would rather not discuss them, but if you decide to leave, you must be aware of them. Their leader, Birsha, views all villagers in this valley as his workers who make what his village needs.

"He expects all of us to make what they need with no return," Marisa said.

"They claim they protect us from the dangers in the valley," Rendal said.

"They are the only real dangers," Marisa huffed. "The fierce wolf and the boars we can avoid."

"Villages in this valley are respectful to each other and cause little trouble," Rendal said. "Birsha's villagers practice with their weapons against a foe that does not exist." Rendal sighed.

"Did one of them recognize us?" Maylore asked.

"No," Rendal replied, looking toward Airalee. "Oleg was admiring Airalee. He is Birsha's first lieutenant, and I feared he may well cause trouble. Fortunately, Birsha told him you were too old to serve."

"Serve?" Airalee said, almost spitting it at him.

"Oleg is looking for a mate," Rendal said as his face grew pained. "Birsha will have the final say in the matter. He said you are unsuitable for Oleg."

"Lucky me," Airalee, deadpanning, stared at Rendal.

"Yes," Rendal replied. "Oleg disagreed with Birsha. I fear Oleg will bear close watching."

Airalee stared at Rendal as her companions turned to see her reaction.

"I would like to move on to other subjects," Rendal said.

"Please do," Maylore said, looking toward Rendal.

"Let me start with the weather," Rendal said. "There are two distinct seasons here, both arriving suddenly. Summer melts the ice, grows new plants, and opens the road for trade. We gather food from the forests, grow our garden, and collect fish from the sea. We are near the midpoint of summer now, and the warm weather lets us leave most of our clothing in our huts. Most men wear tunics with no pants like I am wearing. Women wear similar clothes, although Marisa wears much shorter-length tunics than most."

"I am wearing clothing as you requested, Beacon," Marisa said.

"Yes, thank you," Rendal said. "It is tradition for young men and women to do without during the summer. It is their choice."

"I believe I will continue in the old way," Airalee said, looking uncomfortable.

"Let me continue with our weather," Rendal said. "The winter will bring heavy snow and ice to the mountains from sunrise to sunset," he said, pointing in each direction. "Our village gets snow, but we are near the sea, so the ice and snow are lighter here. Do you have any questions about the weather before I move on to the next topic?"

The companions looked at each other and shook their heads.

"We have several different groups living in the valley," Rendal continued. "I have visited a few villages toward the sunset. The human villages are similar to Olona but have different customs. Each has a form of a council to guide their social structure, work, children, and general village life. Buildings are made with materials around them. Some use wood, brush, grasses, rock, or nearby caves. Our village has lava rock behind it, so our huts are constructed from lava rock, limbs, and Surn leaves."

"You said the little guy has a village near here," Jendrin said. "Do they have villages elsewhere?"

"The Tocor live along the entire length of Molia," Rendal said. "They prefer we do not disturb them and hide in their trees if we approach. Their larger villages are toward sunrise. I have not been invited to visit their villages. They do monitor the roads near human villages. I believe they watch what we do more than the dangers on the road. We have two acting as sentinels watching this area and will get two more. Most do not speak the common human tongue, but a few have learned enough to converse with me. Traders visit us a few times each summer, bringing ropes, leaves, and trinkets. We trade our gathering of fish, finished leather, and fabric goods."

"Are the Lemidge the last group?" Airalee asked.

"Yes," Rendal said. "They will remind you of a short human with larger eyes, dark hair, and thinner bodies. They live primarily in the mountains to the sunset but venture to trade along the road each summer. They have a traveling group with a camp about a day from here. We expect them to visit later this summer and trade for dried fish, jewelry, and clothing. Does anyone have a question before I move on?"

"Do these groups expect a tribute like Birsha?" Airalee asked.

"They do not. They trade with us fairly and don't expect anything beyond that," Rendal replied. Not hearing any other questions, he continued.

"We have found sources for food are plentiful in our part of the valley. Our local forest has mushrooms, herbs, vegetables, and some fruits. We are fortunate to have access to the ocean to gather fish, crab, salt, and seaweed. Other villages grow bread trees and different vegetables or fruits from trees we don't have here. We trade the fish we gather for fruits, ropes, raw leather, meat, and decorations we don't have here. Other villages are welcome to join our fishing expeditions, but most choose to trade for ocean foods. We share what we have regardless of if they have anything to trade. We generally have a surplus and can easily gather more when needed. That is why we are not too concerned with Birsha's taking 'his share,' as he calls it." Rendal added with a slight grin.

"What kind of herbs?" Airalee asked.

"Medical, food flavoring, and others I do not know about," Rendal replied. "You may ask Kai when we see her today." Airalee nodded as he continued. "Does anyone have another question before we briefly tour the village?"

"I would indeed like to see the village," Airalee said. Both men nodded in agreement.

"I will leave it to Marisa to answer questions while I prepare for the tour," Rendal said. "Marisa? Will you answer questions when I depart?"

"Yes, Beacon, I will be glad to," she replied.

"I will soon return and introduce you to some villagers," Rendal said, leaving the hut.

Marisa fielded an extensive range of questions dealing with daily life. She discussed bathing, clothes washing, food gathering, firewood collection, and social questions. Rendal returned to a noisy room of conversation. Stepping to the table, he interrupted.

"We are ready for our short tour before you retire to your new hut," Rendal said. "Do not be surprised if some villagers look at you with suspicion. They are all good people, but some are wary of strangers. Marisa will prepare your hut for your arrival," he said, looking at Marisa. Marisa nodded as Rendal said, "This way," as he opened the door.

The twin suns were past their midday point as the group left the hut. Rendal led them down the first row of huts lining both sides of the way. Some were larger than others, and some had attached work areas. He explained who lived in each one and the work huts they used.

The villagers they passed nodded to them as they passed while others turned the other way. A few would greet the group, but most remained silent as they passed. Rendal stopped near a group of six people.

"Greetings, everyone," Rendal said. "I would like you to meet our refugees. Airalee, Maylore, and Jendrin," he said, indicating each one. "This is Nenaias, Caudra, Katiana, Argila, Avahairiel, and Baruo," he said, pointing to each one. "They are fine members of our community, and I am sure you will see them if you stay," he added, looking at the villagers. The groups exchanged greetings and small talk before Rendal said, "We are on a short tour of the village and will not detain you any longer. This way, please," he said as he waved to them and turned up the path. The two groups said their 'glad to meet you' comments as the companions followed Rendal. The route followed the treeline on the mountainside with paths branching toward the sea at different intervals. They could see several other paths going in the same direction between rows of huts.

"Are people living in all of the huts?" Airalee asked.

"Most of them," Rendal replied. "The small huts are homes for one or two people. Larger huts are for those raising families. The connected huts are crafting and storage," he indicated as he walked. Many homes appeared to have small fires, and cooking smells filled the air. A few villagers walked the path, with some seeing the group approach and turning down another path.

"It appears we are scary," Jendrin said as another person detoured ahead of them.

"Some are suspicious of strangers," Rendal said. "Do not take offense from it," as they continued to walk. "We approach the center of our village," he said as they entered a clear area between rows of huts. "Mirtha's kitchen occupies this area." Large pots sat waiting as banked fires glowed. The tables were deserted and clean. Flowering plants and what appeared to be vegetables grew outside the area.

"The kitchen is closing?" Maylore asked, watching the activity.

"Yes," Rendal replied, "Mirtha cooks a community lunch from donations from villagers foraging and fishing. We expect villagers to provide food for themselves except for lunch. Councilors decided long ago to get them to stop working at midday and eat. It allows those who do the physical labor to recharge and rest. Our older villagers prepare and clean up as a contribution. It also provided time for villagers to talk with one another. Community gatherings are held here for entertainment, dancing, and communicating council decisions," he said, pointing in different directions. "Ah, Mirtha," he said as a woman in her forties approached. "Mirtha, you saw our newest refugees yesterday, but I want to introduce them as Airalee, Maylore, and Jendrin. Group, this is Mirtha again. She is our lead cook." The group exchanged greetings and small talk about cooking and feeding large groups. The sky was darkening when Rendal said, "We will let Mirtha complete her day, and I will see you all to your hut. Good night, Mirtha," he said, smiling at her. He indicated the group's direction. The group followed him along a different path until he stopped before another hut.

Knocking on the door, a woman in her late sixties opened it. A flood of scents flowed from the home. "Beacon," she said. "You are here again. What is it?"

"I want you to meet our newest refugees," Rendal said.

"I saw them yesterday," Kai said, looking at them.

"Yes," Rendal said. "Their names are Airalee, Jendrin, and Maylore. Group, this is our village healer, Kai." the group greeted her as Kai turned her head slightly.

"Yes, I will see you all again," Kai said. Rendal turned toward the companions as Kai cracked a smile at the companions and closed the door.

"Kai is a good woman. She can be difficult at times." Rendal said. "You will not find a more dedicated healer when she is needed. Let us return along the outside edge of Olona," he said, walking toward the sea. They came to a ridge of rock before sunrise.

"Is that the creek we heard earlier today?" Jendrin asked.

"It could be. One creek runs alongside the village on the other side of this ridge. It provides fresh water for drinking, cooking, bathing, and washing clothes. Let's continue this way." he said as he walked. A few villagers sat outside their homes and watched the group as they passed. Some greeted the Beacon, but none came to interact with the group. The group arrived at their new hut to find Marisa sitting outside. She arose as the group approached the door. "Is the hut prepared, Marisa?" Rendal asked when they arrived.

"Yes, Beacon," she replied.

"Excellent, thank you, Marisa," he said. "Let's go in," he said, opening the door. The group entered the door and stood in the open area. A small fire was burning in the firepit. Two pots sat on the table. A large pitcher stood on the table with water mugs beside it. Someone had set the table for three to eat. A few small flowers decorated the table inside a small pot.

"We do not have many huts available," Rendal said. "I understand we have one small hut that one person could use. I would guess Airalee could take that one if she wishes."

Airalee considered the offer for a few moments. 'Am I better off living alone in a strange village with men nearby who have intentions I do not know or staying with these two men who have not hurt me yet?' Looking toward Maylore and Jendrin, she thought, 'They are a less dangerous option,' she decided.

"I have already claimed the first room," she said, pointing to the curtain. "I intend to remain here," she said.

"All right," Rendal said. "Do either of you want to use the other hut?"

"I have the back room," Maylore said.

"The bed here meets my needs," Jendrin said, pointing to the bed under the window. "I need to make sure these two don't run away without me in the middle of the night," he added, grinning at his companions.

"Only if I could be so lucky, hero," Airalee said, grimacing at him.

"I fear my bones creak too much to be sneaky," Maylore said.

"Excellent," Rendal said. "Do you need anything else before Marisa and I leave?"

"No, we can get along for now," Airalee replied. "Thank you for setting our dinner for us, Marisa."

"You are welcome," Marisa said, smiling. "Place the pots and dishes outside the door after you eat."

"All right," Rendal said. "Marisa will join you tomorrow. Remember, you are welcome to leave anytime, but I hope you will consider remaining in Olona." He waved and opened the door for Marisa.

Marisa left the hut as Rendal closed the door.

"Shall we discuss our options while we eat?" Airalee asked as she moved to a chair on the opposite side. Maylore and Jendrin sat on opposite ends of the table.

"Options?" Maylore asked as he sat.

"We could move on, stay here, split up, or consider another combination I have not thought of," She said as she sat down. The group was quiet for a few moments.

"I thought we agreed to stay together," Maylore said. "The life of a nomad has no appeal to me. I prefer more certainty and remain here for now," Maylore replied.

"I would like to stay here for the time being," Airalee said. "I don't feel like a prisoner, and there are different things to explore. Did you smell the herbs from Kai's hut? That was intriguing to me. I would be interested if she offered me the chance to learn local herbs and healing techniques."

"I believe I would also like to remain," Jendrin said. "I see many opportunities to improve the function of Olona. It sounds like they should start a village defense force. I believe I can help with that, too."

"A chance to learn the lore and customs of the valley interests me," Maylore said. "Dealing with travelers and documenting their adventures would be interesting. I believe I could help Rendal."

"I believe this is a good place to start," Airalee said. Maylore and Jendrin voiced their agreement.

"We have a consensus?" Jendrin said.

"We all stay," Maylore concluded.

Maylore collected the pots and dishes and moved them outside the door. Darkness had settled over the village, and he saw no movement around the area. Closing the door, he noticed it had a simple latch. Locking the latch, he turned toward the table.

"I think we made the right choice," Airalee said as she moved to her room's door.

"I believe there is something we can contribute to Olona as we work on the puzzle of who, what, and why we are here," Jendrin said.

"Agreed," Airalee said. "I will claim my bed. Good night," She said as she entered her room. She left her clothes on and moved to the far side of the bed. She considered whether she needed to hold her fist rock but decided she could reach it sitting on the bed rail. The small club she carried lay on the wall side of the bed. "A few more days, and I can easily judge their motives," she softly said, setting the rock beside the club.

Council meeting

Rendal and Marisa walked to the meeting hut after leaving the refugees in their hut. Council members Caudra, Nenaias, Katiana, Arguil, Avahairiel, and Baruo were already seated, sharing a snack as they entered.

"I realize that you had a concise talk with the refugees," Rendal said, standing at the head of the table. "What impressions did each of you have?"

"They seemed like good folk to me," Baruo said in his deep male voice.

"I assume you did not tell them who we were, Rendal," Caudra said.

"I did not," Rendal replied. "I wished them to think you were just average citizens."

"Well, that is true no matter what," Katiana said. "They seemed to me to be the refugees they claim to be."

"They did not ask intrusive questions about Olona's inner workings," Caudra said. "The spy that came many seasons ago asked many suspicious questions the day he arrived."

"Based on my impressions, the refugees seemed slightly confused, wondering where they should go and whether they should leave or stay," Nenaias said.

"Rendal, you have become a good judge of people. What do you think?" Katiana asked.

"I believe they would be good citizens for Olona," Rendal said.

"I agree," Dirdin and Katiana said.

"What do you think, Marisa?" Caudra asked, looking toward Marisa.

"I watched them last night and throughout the day. They seemed like honest refugees who could use our help," Marisa said.

"Good," Caudra said. "I believe we should only offer them sanctuary status," Caudra said cautiously. "One day does not prove much to me. We should assign someone to monitor each refugee. They should report to us each day with their impressions."

"It is probably unnecessary, but I have no objections to a short-term watch of each one," Baruo said. The other members agreed.

"I already have Marisa watching them," Rendal said. The sentinels are adding two more Tocor to watch each refugee. I will ask Throc and Latel to help us. Marisa, I want you to pay close attention to Airalee. I will ask Throc to monitor Maylore and Latel to track Jendrin. Is that acceptable to all?" Rendal asked.

The group agreed and passed the motion to offer sanctuary status to the refugees. Rendal was assigned to check with the sentinels each night before a council meeting. Marisa, Throc, and Latel will attend the meeting or pass their comments to Marisa. The council agreed the process would last ten sunrises.

CHAPTER 6 - VILLAGE VISIT

The following day, Jendrin awoke as the sun peeked through the window above his head. The unfamiliar room forced him to consider where he was. 'Olona,' he thought as he swung his legs to the floor. The dark rock walls absorbed much of the light, making it challenging to navigate the room. No one else was in the common area as he moved to the firepit to restart the fire. A few coals still burned as he added more wood to the fire. Light spread into the room as the fire consumed the wood.

"Good morning," a voice behind him said as he tended the fire. Turning, he saw both Maylore and Airalee standing behind him.

"Good morning," he said, standing up. "This hut is as dark as the cave," he added, brushing the dirt from his hands.

"Indeed," Maylore said, "only the light from the window says it is daytime."

"I will check outside then head to the privy," Airalee said, walking toward the door.

"We all need that journey," Maylore said, following her. Airalee opened the door to find three people sitting near the hut.

"Marisa," Airalee said, "You do not need to wait for us to appear. We can find you."

Marisa and the two men beside her stood. "It is part of my task as a guide to be ready," she said as she pointed to the two men. "This is Latel. He is our teaching tailor. He will be Jendrin's guide," she said, pointing to Jendrin. "Our other guide is Throc. He is learning the ways of a diplomat with Rendal. He will guide Maylore," she said, indicating Maylore, who nodded.

"I did not believe we were so difficult that you need more help," Jendrin said, standing beside Airalee.

"No, not difficult," Marisa replied, "I will help Airalee with female interests while they help you with male interests."

"I see," Airalee said. "Right now, this female needs a potty," she said as she stepped out the door.

"We will start there," Marisa said. "We will visit the bathing pool and return here for your breakfast," as she started down the path. The group chatted about the weather, sea conditions, and various foods. The three companions completed their morning tasks as they returned to the bathing pool.

"I will hold your robe while you bathe," Marisa said, reaching out to Airalee.

Airalee looked at the men standing there and then at Marisa.

"I do not need a bath quite yet," she said.

Marisa looked to Jendrin and Maylore, who shook their heads no.

"As you wish," Marisa said. "We will return to your hut for breakfast before we start a new tour," she said, walking away. The group walked silently back to the hut. Marisa held the hut door open as the companions approached. "We will wait outside while you eat," she said as they entered.

The table had food and clean plates as they moved to the table. Their original robes were clean and stacked on the end of the table.

"Being a guest here is wonderful," Maylore said as he sat.

"We should tell them we are staying," Airalee said with a grin.

"What! We would give up this service?" Maylore said in a teasing voice.

"I believe we will contribute more to Olona than they will give us," Jendrin said.

"After sleeping on it last night," Airalee said, "I believe staying here really is the best idea."

Maylore smiled, and Jendrin kept quiet. The companions ate a simple breakfast of beans and soft bread.

"I will tell Marisa we are staying unless you all disagree," Airalee said, looking at her companions.

"I would be pleased to stay," Maylore replied.

"I will go along with the group," Jendrin said.

"Good," Airalee said as she stood. Gathering the dishes, she started toward the door. Maylore pushed the door open as Airalee stepped out.

"We have decided we would like to stay in Olona," Airalee said, "Where do I wash our dishes?"

"I am pleased to hear that," Marisa said, a smile on her face. "The council must yet approve your stay, but they have granted you temporary sanctuary."

"When do we meet the council?" Maylore asked.

"You unknowingly met them yesterday. They were a small group of villagers we spoke to near the kitchen," Marisa replied.

"I see," Maylore said. "They could judge us that quickly?"

"If they had not approved," Marisa said, "It would have been my task to ask you to leave."

"They instead triple our guards?" Jendrin said dryly.

"We are not guards," Marisa said, cocking her head to the side. "You will have more guides to help you adjust to Olona until the council believes you will do well on your own."

Jendrin's crooked smile indicated he was not convinced.

"Don't be so pessimistic, hero," Airalee said. "We need all the friends we can gather." Looking at Marisa, she said, "Since we plan to stay, you will not be cooking and washing dishes for us. Where do we clean our dishes?"

"I will show you all later," Marisa said. "While we expect you to be self-sufficient, you must also participate in village tasks. Different groups will work together to gather food, fish the sea, gather pottery material, grasses for weaving, wood for fires, and hut repairs. You may choose any group on any day. Most tasks finish in less than half a sun cycle. It leaves lots of free time for all villagers to craft, visit friends, or do whatever they choose. Before you decide, we will visit more of the village to see what tasks we do."

"I would welcome that opportunity," Airalee said as both men nodded in agreement.

"We can split into three groups if you choose different areas or a larger group if you choose the same area," Marisa said.

"I wonder what you would have said if we had not said we were staying?" Jendrin asked.

"I would have said the same," Marisa said. "You should be aware of what we expect of you."

"Good," Jendrin said.

"Shall we start?" Marisa said.

"Please do," Airalee said.

Marisa started walking toward the center of the village as she talked. "We will spend time visiting with the crafting teachers as we see all of the village. We will start with Mirtha since we will enter her area first."

Mirtha was instructing two other women when they arrived.

"Add a few more vegetables and some of the usual herbs," Mirtha said. "The stew looks right," she said as she tasted the large pot of stew. "Good morning, everyone," she said, smiling as the group arrived.

"Good morning, Mirtha," Marisa said, as the group replied similarly. We brought Airalee, Maylore, and Jendrin to visit your work area. Would you tell them what your work crew does?"

"I will," Mirtha said, resting against a table. "Our group gathers edible plants, beans, fruit, breadnuts, and vegetables for themselves and our village. They usually start after the sun is entirely over the town and finish quickly. Today, they collected enough for two sunrises and two village lunches. They also finished tending the garden. Most are doing their own activities. I usually have two to six youngsters help with preparing and cooking. This process allows young girls and boys to learn cooking skills and lessen tension with their parents about one subject. Most help prepare vegetables, gather firewood, and maintain the fire plus other odds and ends."

"How many are in the gathering group?" Airalee asked.

"We usually have 20 to 30 different people when we gather," Mirtha said.

"Where do you go to collect?" Jendrin asked.

"We cover from the edge of the mountains to the river and then the sea," Mirtha said, pointing in each direction. "The valley is generous, and everything multiplies quickly. We practice not taking all of any one thing to allow the plants to regrow. We also gather from our garden."

"How do the people know when to come to gather?" Airalee asked.

"I will put a yellow ribbon on the gathering post the day before we gather," Mirtha replied. "Without a ribbon, we do not plan to gather as a group. People are welcome to add food to the village lunch anytime."

"How do you decide what to cook?" Jendrin asked.

"We cook what is available," Mirtha replied. "After a fishing day, we will cook the fish for lunch and allow villagers to use the fire to cook fish to keep the smell out of their homes."

"Do you mind cooking for everyone?" Airalee asked.

"I do not mind," Mirtha replied with a smile. "I see it as my task, and our routine makes it easy. Occasionally, I venture into the forest and meadow to gather herbs with Kai, Marisa, and others. Any other questions?"

"No, thank you, Mirtha," Airalee said.

"Mirtha mentioned the garden," Marisa said. "Let's visit the garden before visiting Latel's group," Marisa said before turning to Mirtha. "Thank you, Mirtha," she said as she waved to the group to follow her. The group continued between the homes to a large open area.

"The garden runs from one side of the village to the creek on the seaside," Marisa said. Row upon row of plants waved in the sun as the group approached. A small group of people carried water to a few dry areas the gathering group missed. A bamboo forest stood behind the garden, running from one side to the other. A hut stood on the mountainside of the garden.

"Who lives in this home?" Jendrin asked.

"My mother, Levyna, lives there," Latel said with a smile. "I grew up helping her prepare the garden, plant, water, and harvest. That is why I became a tailor!" His comments drew chuckles from everyone. "Mom has plenty of outside help, and her life-mate keeps her company. He plays the strings for us at home and parties. You can see her standing near her hut, directing the helpers with water." He waved to her. She waved back to him as the rest of the group waved to her.

"It looks like a lot of vegetables," Jendrin said.

"There are quite a few," Latel said. "We plant at different times so we do not run out of anything. Some are allowed to go to seed for the next crop."

"These look like mostly root vegetables. Where do they gather greens?" Airalee asked.

"Most of the greens grow in the meadow beyond the bamboo forest," Latel said, pointing to the sunset. "It is a large meadow with various greens and fruit."

"What is beyond the meadow?" Maylore asked.

"There is a swamp area on the mountain edge," Latel said, pointing to the sunset. Beyond that, there is a dangerously fast-flowing river that borders the meadow. Its fast current prevents us from gathering farther to the sunset. Our creek originates from that river and flows along the seacoast to its end by Olona."

"Good explanations, Latel." Marisa said, "Shall we move back to your workshop?"

"Ready," Latel said.

"Let's move on," Marisa said. The companions nodded as Marisa led them back into the village. She followed a different path past more homes lining the route. Hammering and scraping greeted their ears as they approached a larger hut closer to the kitchen.

"This is Latel's work hut," Marisa announced, stopping at the door.

"Latel, I leave it to you," she said, opening the door. There were several low benches with two people busy working as they entered. Two others were working at a table behind them.

"Thank you," he said, moving into the room. "We create many leather and fiber clothes for the village. We have two people working in another hut who create sandals and belts." The work stopped as they all looked at the group. "This is Airalee, Maylore, and Jendrin. They recently arrived and are touring our village." Latel said.

"Welcome," they all said.

"This group is creating new clothes for themselves," Latel explained. "We will work as a group to make a few other things as a team. You can create clothes, join our group, or gather supplies."

"Where do you get your supplies?" Jendrin asked.

"We gather grasses from different meadows. We do not kill animals, but an occasional animal falls our way, or we trade for hides. We try to collect the hide before the blood wolves arrive and tear them up. We also trade other villages for leather, fur, and winter boots. We spend part of each winter crushing and stitching various grasses into cloth. We also use fiber from the bread nut and leaves to create clothing pieces. Winters here keep many of our population busy preparing material for clothing.

"I saw several of these short one-piece robes worn by villagers, like Marisa," Airalee said. "I assume you make those too?"

"Indeed, we do," Latel replied. "She made her own a little shorter than the rest. We also make long skirts and pants to wear with them in the winter."

"What are you making?" Jendrin asked one of the villagers who was working nearby.

"I am adding a wolf's fur collar to this tunic Latel made," he replied. "My current mate wanted a new tunic to replace her worn fiber tunic. It will surprise her and should last her many winters," he said. Jendrin noted that the vest bore the orange of the village colors, woven into the stitches.

"How did you convince the wolf to give up his fur?" Maylore asked with a smile.

"Blood wolves die eventually," Latel said. "Blood wolves don't eat their own. This one died outside the mountain pit, so we skinned it."

"How do you make the colors for your clothes?" Airalee asked.

"Kai forms a group to gather flowers when they bloom. They crush the flowers and filter the liquid for various colors. She has one person who is an expert at creating different shades. The village's orange color comes from orange flowers growing in the meadow."

"I would like to learn how you created these pieces," Jendrin said, looking at the vest.

"I would be glad to show you," Latel replied. The companions watched the tailors as they worked on their clothes until Latel said, "Let's move on to the next stop."

"Follow me," Marisa said, holding the door. "We will visit with Kai before returning to the hut to clean dishes and rest before lunch with Mirtha." Marisa led them to a hut a short distance from the kitchen. "This is Kai's hut," she said as she knocked on the door.

"Come in, Marisa," Kai called from inside. Kai sat on the floor behind a low table facing the door.

"Kai. I am showing our new arrivals our village. Kai, this is Airalee, Jendrin, and Maylore. Everyone, this is Kai. She is our healing teacher using various herbs."

"We meet again," Kai said, nodding to the group. "Sit if you wish." indicating the pillows behind small worktables.

"Thank you, I will," Maylore said, selecting a pillow and sitting.

"I hope you all slept well," Kai said, continuing her work.

"Yes." I didn't hear a thing," Maylore replied with a smile.

"What root do you use to help with sleep?" Airalee asked.

"I'll keep that to myself until you join our village," Kai said, looking at her. "If you are allowed to join, I will describe some of our herbs and roots," Kai said, putting down her work.

"Where did you learn your craft?" Maylore asked.

"My grandmother taught my mother, and my mother taught others," Kai said. "I started learning when I was young. She would teach her students, and I would listen. The others decided to learn other skills, leaving me to continue her work. She taught us which botanicals did what, how to use them, and which to avoid. She was very good at closing wounds with her needle and thread. She left it to me to collect and grind healing herbs for the dressings. I always considered it a privilege to follow in her footsteps."

The mention of herbs drew Airalee's attention. "The healing herbs you mentioned, do you collect them nearby?" she asked.

"Many are close by," Kai responded. "Some I have to travel a reasonable distance to find. The special mushrooms grow in the forest sunset of us.

"Do you have a collecting crew like the other groups?" Airalee asked.

"I generally have two others that accompany me," Kai said. "It is specialized knowledge many don't care to learn."

"Could you use another?" Airalee asked.

Kai looked surprised before answering, "Yes, more help is always welcome."

"I want to help you when you gather," Airalee said.

"I will call on you at some point," Kai said.

"Thank you, Kai. I look forward to it," Airalee said.

"If there are no more questions, we will continue our tour," Marisa said, opening the door. "Thank you, Kai," she said, leading the way. Kai resumed her work without speaking.

"We will visit the Beacon's hut next," she said as she walked.

They continued until they reached a hut sitting at an odd angle compared to the other huts. The entrance was on the opposite side. This hut was more extended and broader than the others.

"This is Beacon Rendal's home," Marisa said as she pulled Throc to the front of the group. "Throc works with the Beacon and will take over the explanation."

"I would be glad to," Throc said, moving to the door. "This hut was one of the first huts built in the village. The man who originally lived here was a sorcerer of sorts. Village records do not say why he wanted it made in this manner."

"Does he still live here?" Maylore asked.

"No," Throc replied, "he died many seasons ago. There have been several others who have lived here but no sorcerers." The group could tell he was withholding something back but kept silent. "Let me explain a little of what the Beacon does. The Beacon is the council's leader and, by default, the authority in this village. Most human villages have a council and a beacon to lead them. Beacon Rendal is the keeper of the village charter and official records. My job is to help him enter changes into the records and note the council's decisions. He may still be in council, but we can peek inside," Throc said.

"No need to peek. Please go in," Rendal said, coming from behind them. The companions followed Throc inside to find a table set to the side with four chairs around it. Two small tables lined the opposite wall with a firepit in the middle. A rock sat near the center of the room, and a bookshelf lined the back wall, framing a door.

"I trust you have enjoyed your tour," he said as he and Throc moved to the back of the room. "Please sit," he said as he sat at the end of the table. The three sat at the table while Marisa and Latel sat at a small table near the door. "What have you learned about our village?" Rendal asked.

"It seems relaxed but well organized," Jendrin said.

"The splitting of duties looks to keep the village running and does not overburden the villagers," Airalee said.

"Yes, the villagers all seem content in their chosen tasks," Maylore replied.

"Many seem suspicious, but you warned us of that," Airalee said.

"Indeed," Rendal answered. "They are all warm people and will be to you, too, if you are accepted into the village."

Maylore sat examining the stack of books on the back wall.

"Throc tells us you also handle the writing of the village history?"

"Yes, it is one of the Beacon's jobs in each village," Rendal said. "Throc and I greet travelers, arrange trade, share general information with others, and try to learn what is happening in our valley. If someone has a grievance, I gather our council, and we deal with it. I try to make them comfortable in our guest huts with food and water while they wait. Lore is my real interest. I generally have someone write notes of any lore that may come up. Many of the papers behind me are notes taken by previous Beacons. I also help teach reading and writing to the village children. Several village elders teach the young while their mothers are working."

The group nodded their understanding.

"Does anyone have a question I could answer?" Rendal asked.

"It appears you make and enforce village law?" Airalee asked.

"No," Rendal said. "Not in this village. The Beacon conducts the council, which makes the village's bigger decisions. A few other villages do not have a council, and the Beacon is the village leader. Each village chooses how it wants to run its village."

"The village seems to be very quiet. How do you handle justice if things flare up?" Jendrin asked.

"We are fortunate to have very little trouble," Rendal replied. "The council listens to the complaints and gives their suggestions. Villagers usually accept the council's suggestions, or they leave the village. We have very few who leave for that reason. We have several who arrive from other villages because of a dispute."

"What do you do with someone who kills another?" Jendrin asked.

Rendal and Throc looked at each other for a few moments.

"That has not happened in all my seasons here," Rendal replied. "I do not know what the council would do. Villagers live a simple life. Anyone who needs help for any reason will get it from the village. Does anyone else have a question?"

Airalee looked around the room and asked, "Why is there a black rock in the middle of the hut?"

"Black? It looks like a blue rock to me," Maylore said, looking at the rock.

"Blue?" Jendrin questioned. "Looks pitch black to me too."

"You see a blue coloring in the rock?" Rendal asked Maylore, giving him a sharp look.

"Yes. A kind of shimmering blue," Maylore said, looking at the rock again. The group all stared at the black rock before looking askance at Maylore.

"Interesting, Maylore," Rendal commented, looking toward Throc. "Anyone have any other general questions?" Rendal asked, looking toward the group.

While the others stared at Maylore, he turned his attention to Rendal.

"Yes, I find history and lore interesting," Maylore said. I would welcome interacting with other people and races. Do you need another in your group?"

"It is possible," Rendal said. "We will review this at a future date."

"Thank you, Beacon," Maylore said.

"Good," Marisa said. "Unless you have something else, we will return to your hut."

"Why does Maylore see a blue rock?" Airalee asked, staying in her seat.

"I suspect it is a trick of light from the fire or window," Rendal said.

"Time to wash out your eyes, Maylore," Airalee said, standing up.

"Thank you all for visiting," Rendal said. "Marisa, I have a task for Throc. Can he leave your group?"

"Of course, Beacon," Marisa said as Throc sat down again. The group thanked the Beacon as they left the hut.

The group's footsteps faded as Rendal looked at Throc.

"Maylore could see Almora's energy?" Rendal said. "That ability has not existed in our village for many seasons."

"Kelkalyn is the last to claim he could see part of the energy," Throc said. "It sounded like Maylore could see the energy coating the entire rock."

"Yes," Rendal replied. "Do not tell anyone else about this possible ability. We do not want the master to hear anything about it."

"Yes, Beacon," Throc replied.

"You are assigned to him?" Rendal asked.

"Yes," Throc replied, "I watch him for betrayal and now for ability use."

"Excellent," Rendal said. "I will not tell the council of this yet. I still believe we have a traitor in the village. I don't think it is a council member, but I don't know who it might be."

"You still believe we have a traitor in the village?" Throc asked. "We have not had villagers disappearing in many seasons."

"I suspect everyone," Rendal replied. "New arrivals are particularly problematic. We have yet to determine a trap to find this traitor. If Maylore is not a spy, we need to determine if he has an ability. If he does, we must protect him so he doesn't disappear like others did."

"I agree, Beacon," Throc said.

"Thank you, Throc," Rendal said. "You can rejoin them now if you wish."

The group returned to the companions' hut to find the dishes still waiting for them.

"I will show you all how we wash dishes and clothes," Marisa said, "It is very close to this hut." Jendrin picked up the dishes as they followed Marisa toward the sea. They walked past the bathing pool, which had several people in it. Marisa waved as she chatted with the bathers for a short time. They followed a trail beside a creek that left the bathing pool to another pool hidden behind the clothes-washing pool. The water gathered in the pool before spilling over the rocks. "Here are our clothes-washing and dishwashing pools," Marisa said. "There are pebbles and breadnut husks for scrubbing, soapweed, and washing tools. You may see small crabs at the bottom. They eat scraps of food but do not bother trying to catch one. They have little meat and taste terrible." Marisa grimaced.

Jendrin kneeled to wash the dishes as several small eyes watched him from the bottom. Jendrin quickly finished cleaning the dishes.

"Nice job, hero," Airalee said. "You could be useful yet."

"I can be amazing," Jendrin said as he stood.

"We will return to your hut to rest before lunch," Marisa said, leading the way. Opening the hut's door, Marisa said, "I will bring food to you. You can rest before you eat, and then we will consider what is next." She closed the door after the last companion entered before speaking to the other guides. "I plan to help them find their food and firewood. I can do it alone if you wish to return to your tasks."

"I believe I will continue," Latel said.

"I will also," Throc said.

"One or both of you could remain here while I get their lunch," Marisa said. "I will bring enough for all of us," she said.

"I will help you with the food," Throc said. Marisa nodded as she headed toward the kitchen with Throc. Latel stayed behind near the door.

CHAPTER 7 - WHAT TO DO

Marisa and Throc returned to the companions' hut, each carrying one pot.

"The council believes we should closely watch them," Throc said. "When the Beacon informs them, Maylore may have a small skill, and I fear we may be watching them even closer."

"They seem like trustworthy people to me," Marisa said.

"Rendal thinks we can determine if he is any threat," Throc said as they approached the hut.

"The stew smells as good as ever," Latel said as Throc sat near him.

"I will deliver their stew and then return," Marisa said, collecting Throc's pot. Marisa tapped on the door as Jendrin opened it. All three companions smiled at her as she entered. Stopping, she realized she had entered a guest hut. "Forgive me for entering. I brought some lunch for you all," she said, setting the pots on the table and turning to leave.

"No, we are pleased to see you, Marisa," Airalee said. "Please sit and talk with us," Airalee said, indicating the last chair. Marisa felt relieved but unsure if she should stay.

"Since you asked to be part of the Olona, I believe I can join you," she said, sitting in a chair. Maylore gave her a spare bowl as he filled each bowl.

Discussion during the meal turned to where to gather wood, vegetables, and her life in the village.

"Let us show you where to gather your wood and food for your meals," Marisa said as the chatter quieted. "Bring the largemouth pot to put your food into. The other guides await outside for us to continue."

"Let's go," Jendrin said as they all stood and left the hut. The twin suns were at their late afternoon stage when they started their hunt. Latel and Throc joined them in their gathering.

"Beans are the easiest food to gather," Marisa said, pointing to large bushes lining the paths. "Pick the large pods and remove the beans inside. I usually pick a large batch that will last several meals." The group worked together to fill the pot.

"The branches on the same bush break off easily, even the largest ones," Marisa instructed. "Break them off about one stick in length and gather them together." The group collected a large pile before Marisa called a halt. "Gather half of these and store them behind your hut. These branches dry quickly. You can burn them in your firepit in a few sunrises. Bring the rest of the wood to the kitchen for firewood. Latel, you and Jendrin take the firewood while the rest of us do a cooking lesson."

The group returned to the hut together while Latel and Jendrin continued to the kitchen.

"Does a group gather wood each day for the kitchen?" Jendrin asked as they walked.

"Someone gathers wood for their fire every day," Latel said. "They bring a portion of it to the kitchen. Once this wood dries, it burns slowly, allowing the kitchen fire to burn continuously. Drop your bundle at the end of the stack," Latel said, arriving at the kitchen wood pile.

"I was curious about what lies beyond the village river border," Jendrin said, pointing to the sunset.

"Beyond the river is Birsha's camp, which we suggest you avoid," Latel said.

"Why should we avoid it?" Jendrin asked. "Rendal told us they were traders."

"I see," Latel said. "I will leave it to him to tell that story. It appears he wants to introduce some subjects at a slower pace. Beyond their village, the meadow rises to hills and valleys. The farther you go, the hills turn into mountains. We have heard that you will find dangerous monsters if you scout to the sea from there. It may also be a rumor, but I will not venture there to find out. The Tocor says there is a large lake and many rivers and streams. The valley ends at the sea, with mountains lining the valley." He pointed toward the sea, saying, "You have seen the sea. A few have attempted to cross it, but none have returned," Latel said with a shrug. "We can climb partway into the mountains on the other side of Olona," Latel said, pointing toward the mountains. "Beyond these mountains is a valley before the mountains around it become too steep to climb." Pointing to the sunrise, he said, "Up the lava hill is a desert valley. No one lives in the desert. There are Tocor villages in the hills above the desert. The Surn trees growing there are their homes."

"Have you visited their homes?" Jendrin asked.

"The Tocor disdain visitors," Latel said. "We do not visit them. The Tocor have traders who visit all villages and provide sentinels for those who want them. We have always had sentinels. They will warn us if travelers approach Olona."

"Perhaps we can attempt a visit with them someday," Jendrin said.

"I do not believe they are dangerous, but they are unlikely to meet with you," Throc said. "I admit, the Beacon and I have not tried in many summers to convince our sentinels to introduce us to their village. They politely ignore us."

"What is beyond the desert?" Jendrin asked.

"The Tocor says it becomes grassland then forest again. They claim a large dome of light rises above you as you enter the forest. They say a man who lives there is dangerous. They did not know anything about him and refused to return there."

"I wonder why? It makes an intriguing story," Jendrin said.

"I suspect it may just be a story to keep others away," Latel said. "The Tocor use that land and do not want intruders." Latel pointed higher, saying, "Beyond his dome, the green hills rise with rivers and small valleys in between. The valley ends at the sea, with these same mountains following the valley into the sea.

"You have not ventured to any of these places?" Jendrin asked.

"No," Latel replied. "I am happy to stay near our village. I like my work, the security of easy food, and good people."

"I see," Jendrin said. "I would someday like to see more of this world. I must abide by my choice to stay with my companions, at least for now."

"You are free to leave anytime, Jendrin," Latel said.

"I understand," Jendrin said. "I did promise to remain with them."

"Your friends have a loyal companion," Latel said.

"I like the idea of learning a trade," Jendrin said. "What should I do to prepare to work with you?"

"You must make your tools for yourself," Latel said. "A couple of knives, a punch, needle, hammer or hatchet, and work stone. I will be glad to help you get started to build them."

"I would appreciate your help," Jendrin replied.

"Shall we return to your hut?" Latel asked.

Jendrin nodded and followed Latel back to his hut.

Airalee, Maylore, Marisa, and Throc entered the hut as Latel and Jendrin departed.

"Let me show you how to prepare beans," Marisa said, setting the pot on the table. "They are very nutritious and filling. Many villagers eat them for breakfast since they cook quickly. You can have them with every meal if you wish. Mirtha mixes them with herbs and meat for variety. I suggest you place two handfuls of beans per person into a cooking pot," as she measured six handfuls into a pot from the firepit. "Add water to the beans and herbs if you have any." Marisa poured water into the pot and added an herb from her pocket. "This herb collected a few days ago adds a nice spice flavor. Set the pot next to the fire pit and let it warm."

"I assume you don't just eat beans," Maylore said.

"No," Marisa replied. "Some days, you fix vegetables, meat when we get some or fish. The choice is up to each home. No one specifies what you eat. There are days we collect greens, which you can collect on your own anytime. You do not have to gather when the rest of us do. We collect as a group for safety."

"Safety?" Airalee asked, "From what?"

"Bears, boars, bandits, and fierce wolves," Marisa said. "They leave us alone if we work in a group."

"I thought blood wolves would not harm us," Airalee said.

"Blood wolves will not," Marisa replied. "Fierce wolves are much smaller but dangerous in a pack. They have sharp teeth and move quickly. The blood wolves scare them away since they have thick hides and know their tactics. If you see the grass moving but stop when you look in that direction, it may be a fierce wolf. Climb a tree quickly, or a wolf pack will make you their dinner."

"Guess I will be working in a group," Airalee said.

"We are safe in our valley," Marisa said. "The mountains are where the fierce wolf lives. The wolf prefers the small deer living in the hills. The Tocor and the bandits hunt the deer, too, but we do not. The Tocor trade deer meat and hides for fish several times each summer. I suggest you stay out of the mountains for your safety until you learn where to go."

"Sensible," Maylore said as he added wood to the firepit.

"Do you have what you need?" Marisa asked, looking around the hut.

"Yes," Airalee replied.

"There is one blanket per bed," Marisa said. "Do you not sleep together in one bed?" Marisa noticed Airalee's face turning red.

"We do not!" Airalee said. "These men are strangers!"

"Strangers for now," Marisa smiled.

"Do you sleep with strangers?" Airalee asked.

"I have in the past," Marisa said. "I have a small hut with my mate and no room for others."

Maylore chuckled as Airalee looked aghast.

"Throc, do you have a mate?" Airalee asked.

"I do not," Throc answered. "I have not been asked to share my hut with a stranger either."

Marisa smiled at both of them before saying, "Let's go outside while the beans are warming," as she turned toward the door.

The twin suns were sliding toward sunset when they gathered outside the hut.

"Do you two wish to take a bath before dinner?" Marisa asked.

Seeing the frown on Airalee's face, Maylore replied first.

"I will forgo the bath until the morning," Maylore said.

"Airalee?" Marisa queried.

"I will if others are not there to watch," Airalee said.

"All villagers use the same pool," Marisa said. "Few use it now."

"I will walk to the pool soon," Airalee said as Jendrin and Latel returned. "Before you ask, I will not bathe with him either."

Jendrin stopped trying to determine what Airalee had said.

"I don't recall asking you or you asking me," Jendrin said. "It could be enjoyable," Jendrin smiled.

"Watch it, hero," Airalee said, pointing at him. A low buzz filled the air as the group stood outside the hut.

"There it is again," Maylore said, "the buzzing noise we heard in the cave."

"The firebird may be carrying a dead woca to the sea," Marisa said, looking toward sunrise.

"Firebird?" Jendrin said, looking where Marisa was looking.

"It is what the Tocor call it," Latel said. "There is a green grass valley over this first set of mountains. The Tocor say silver birds bring woca to the valley at the beginning of each summer."

All three looked at him as Airalee asked, "Silver birds?"

"Yes," Latel said, looking for the firebird. "The Tocor say big silver birds fly down from the sky and discharge thousands of woca each time. They leave two firebirds behind to protect the woca and keep them from wandering. They say the firebird shoots fiery warnings if any creature gets too close to the woca. If the creature persists, the firebird's fire cuts off the invaders' heads. We suspect that is why the blood wolves are patient and do not attack living creatures since a young headless wolf is carried out to sea each season. The elder wolves teach young wolves to keep away, but a few will attack and are beheaded each season."

"One way to control wolf population," Jendrin said. "Why do they carry woca?"

"A woca will occasionally die in the meadow," Latel said. "The firebird will pick up the woca and sometimes drop it outside its border. There are always blood and fierce wolves waiting. Sometimes, the firebird carries the woca and drops it into the sea. The firebirds sometimes lose their grip on a sea-bound creature and drop it where we can get it. The firebird doesn't seem to notice the creature fell and continues over the sea. We collect parts of a woca before the blood wolves reach it. We can get part of the hide or a haunch of meat before the wolves arrive. Sometimes, we get the whole animal which provides meat for the village for weeks."

"There it is," Marisa said, pointing between the trees. "Follow me, and we will follow it to the cliff." Marisa led the way to the cliff beyond the bathing pools. When the group arrived at the cliff, the silver and red firebird was over the sea. The firebird was egg-shaped, with a claw protruding from the front and rear. It moved quickly, carrying a headless creature.

"Who controls those things?" Maylore asked.

"We do not know," Throc said. "The Beacon asked the master once and was told he did not need to know."

"That would mean someone else is controlling them but not him," Maylore said. Throc shrugged, offering no further explanation.

"The firebird may drop its load near our shore," Latel said as the group turned to listen to him. Airalee turned back in time to see a blue flash drop from the firebird just as the claw opened and dropped the woca. "It seems to drop them in the same area each time. Anut swims in that area, making short work of the body."

"The anut is a fish, I assume?" Jendrin asked.

"Yes," Latel replied, "A two to four large stone meat-eating fish. We catch a few each season, which can feed several villages."

"Did anyone else see the blue flash fall from the firebird before the woca dropped?" Airalee asked.

"I did not see anything," Marisa said.

The rest of the group shook their heads, making Airalee wonder if she did see it.

"The firebird is going back," Maylore said, pointing skyward. "Do they cause problems for villagers?"

"No," Latel replied. "They only pass over this valley flying near the Tocor village," Latel said.

"I would like to see it someday," Jendrin said.

"You may be able to convince the Beacon to arrange a trip with the Tocor later," Throc said.

"It may be some time before that happens," Jendrin said.

"Let's return to your hut," Marisa said as she led the way back.

The companions asked questions about the duties they could perform for the village. Darkness descended on the village as Marisa turned to the group.

"It is time for us to leave, but we will return tomorrow," Marisa said. "Are you ready to start working with us, Airalee?"

"I look forward to it," Airalee replied.

Marisa nodded to her.

"Tomorrow, Latel will work with Jendrin, and Throc will work with Maylore," Marisa said. "Are you ready for your bath now, Airalee?"

"If no one else is there and these two stay in our hut, I am ready," Airalee said.

"Maylore and I respect your privacy, Airalee," Jendrin sincerely said, opening the hut's door.

"Keep it that way, hero," she said as she started toward the bath.

"I will add wood to the fire and warn others away, Airalee," Marisa said, following her.

Council Meeting

"We can start our meeting," Rendal said as the last council member sat down. "Throc, where is Marisa?"

"She is assisting Airalee," Throc said. "She should be arriving soon."

"Excellent," Rendal said. "We have several things to discuss tonight about the newcomers. Throc, Latel, and I are here to report on observations. I will start with observations from the discussion Throc and I had in my hut. We observed that Maylore was the only one in the group to see the blue Almora energy around the rock in my hut."

The entire council looked up at him and murmured to each other.

"As you all know, Kelkalyn was the last person to be able to see this energy, and he only saw it partway along the rock," Rendal said.

"Did he try to affect anyone using the energy?" Caudra asked.

"No," Rendal answered. "He did not know what it meant and was confused when others could not see it. His companions stared at him, not believing what he said."

"Was it real disbelief or an attempt to make you believe they were surprised?" Nenaias asked.

"It seemed to me they were all surprised," Rendal replied.

"I was alert for any sign of deception," Throc said. "I did not detect any attempt at deception."

"I know Rendal has trained you well in detecting lies," Avahairiel replied. "Rendal's seasons of negotiations with visitors and villagers have given him a strong base to detect deception. I accept your impression that the newcomers are sincere."

"You and I agree on very little, Avahairiel," Caudra said. "This time, I agree with your logic."

"That is something different," Rendal said with a smile. "Let's hear from Throc and Latel so they may leave, Throc?"

"Maylore is my charge, but I have watched the group closely. I came to the short-term opinion that they are likely just new arrivals. Maylore is a quiet, unassuming man. He would be happy to settle here and fit into the village. He seems to watch over his companions as if they were his relations instead of strangers. I suspect he will treat every person he meets the same way. He has asked to learn diplomacy skills from the Beacon and me."

"You have proven to us before that you can characterize people accurately," Nenaias said. "I hope you are correct again."

"I have agreed to allow Maylore to join in diplomatic affairs with Throc and me," Rendal said. "We will not tell him any village secrets until all the newcomers prove trustworthy Olona members." Looking at Latel, he said, "Latel? Your observations?"

"I was assigned to guide Jendrin," Latel said. "Jendrin is an adventurous man who perhaps is happier exploring the valley than living in a village. He expressed interest in the areas around the village and exploring them all. We saw the firebird fly overhead while we were all together. He was very interested in exploring what the firebird was doing. He could be willing to assume the hunter since Werloth retired."

"We do not allow killing animals any more than killing people," Caudra emphasized. "We already sacrifice sea creatures for food."

"Yes, councilwoman," Latel said. "I suggest he help Dirdin process the animals we find for their hides and meat. I did not introduce him to Dirdin since we consider his techniques a village secret. I propose introducing him to Dirdin if Jendrin is accepted into the village."

"I believe he can visit with Dirdin," Rendal said, looking at the rest of the council. "Dirdin does not need to show his processes."

The rest of the council nodded in agreement.

"I will consult with Dirdin about introducing him to Jendrin," Latel said.

"Is he interested in a useful skill?" Nenaias asked.

"He asked to join our tailoring group," Latel said. "I accepted him, believing he would work well with us once he learned the trade. It also allows me to monitor him and finish my work. I judge he will transition to doing physical tasks others avoid. As for his companions, Throc gained more insight than I did during our time with them. They seemed like good people looking for a place to live quietly."

The council room was quiet until Rendal spoke.

"If no one has questions, we will let Throc and Latel go to their beds." No one asked a question, allowing Rendal to dismiss the two men.

"We will continue until Marisa arrives with her report," Rendal said as the two men closed the hut's door. "I asked our sentinels if they detected anything of concern about the newcomers. They indicated they saw nothing that worried them."

"You met with Birsha today?" Katiana asked.

"Throc and I met with Birsha and Oleg," Rendal said. "They informed me it was time to collect their due. We have surpluses of fish, vegetables, and crafted goods. They indicated they would collect from the Tocor village and then from us on their way back to their village. They seemed to have acquired a pole carrier from someone to carry their goods.

"You mean the goods they steal," Avahairiel said.

"I prefer to say we donate to their village," Rendal said as Avahairiel snorted.

"I did not agree to 'donate' my daughter to their village," Avahairiel said.

"No one likes the bandit agreement, but it prevents them from killing our people," Caudra said. "She is, however, back with you now."

"My daughter still fears gathering on her own," Avahairiel said. "We have discussed that old agreement enough to start discussions anew."

"Perhaps it is time to consider changing the agreement and stand up for our girls," Katiana said.

"You are too young to remember the slaughter our village endured before the agreement," Caudra almost shouted.

"Please, everyone, we will not discuss that old treaty and its consequences now," Rendal said. Murmurs continued in the room as a knock came at the door. Marisa entered and moved to the table near Rendal.

"Marisa, please tell us your observations about the newcomers," Rendal said, happy to change the subject in the room.

"I was primarily concerned with Airalee but watched all of them throughout the day," Marisa said. "Airalee is looking for a stable home. I suspect she is a strong woman who is unsure of her surroundings. She does not yet have complete faith in her companions since they are still strangers. I see she puts up a front to keep them at a distance. When we met with Kai today, she expressed interest in joining Kai's collecting group. I believe Kai will allow her to gather mundane items with her group. Kai will not expose her secret herbs until after Airalee proves herself. Jendrin appears to be a self-reliant man who has complete faith in himself. He seemed committed to staying with the group, although he would like to wander. He seems to have an easy relationship with Maylore.

Maylore is a quiet man who seems to glue the other two together. He is committed to his group and seems interested in staying in this village. I did not detect any kind of deception in them. I don't believe they would betray us."

The council listened intently to her assessment and nodded when she finished.

"Thank you, Marisa," Rendal said. "Continue to monitor them and report to us what you find."

Marisa smiled and left the hut.

"I suggest we accept them as guided members," Avahairiel said. The rest of the group agreed, except one.

"We can accept them as guided," Caudra said, "but we should not hurry to accord them full membership until after our agreed-upon ten sunrises. Hut ownership should be even later if they prove them worthy."

"That seems reasonable to me," Rendal said. "Ten sunrises should tell us of any traitorous activity before we allow them to go further." The rest of the council agreed. "I will make a village announcement that we are going to accept the newcomers as guided refugees." Caudra and the rest of the council nodded.

CHAPTER 8 - SCHOOL DAYS

A knock on the door awoke Airalee. Rising from her bed, she entered the main room to find Jendrin holding the door for Marisa. Maylore entered the main room behind her.

"Have you eaten yet?" Marisa asked, looking at them. "The sun has risen, and we can start our tasks."

"Come in, Marisa," Jendrin said. "We can discuss the day's schedule inside."

"I believe I can," Marisa said, entering the room. "The council has voted to accept you as guided refugees so I can enter huts when asked."

"I thought we were already accepted," Jendrin said, sitting at the table.

"You were permitted to stay in Olona temporarily as a refugee," Marisa replied. "This is the next step to becoming a citizen."

"How many steps are there?" Jendrin asked.

"The next step is accepted," Marisa said. "The last, which is being allowed to own a home," Marisa said. "Only women are allowed to own a home. If granted home ownership, Airalee will decide if you live here or elsewhere."

Both men looked at Airalee before she smiled.

"You two had better watch it," Airalee said.

"If she tosses us out, where would we go? I assume we would be citizens, too," Jendrin asked.

"You could use an empty hut or cave or build your own," Marisa said. "You could choose to become a baby-mate, child mate, or a life-mate to a woman in the village who accepts you."

"We should start looking for a tree to live in, Maylore," Jendrin said, looking at Maylore.

"No," Airalee said, "if ownership happens, you both stay here. I won't accept breaking up this companionship. Assuming you two don't cause me trouble, especially you hero."

"I have never considered causing you any trouble, Airalee," Jendrin said with a stern look.

"This trio needs all of its legs to work together," Maylore said. "If we damage one leg, the whole trio will fall to ruin, destroying each of us. You have no concern about me, Airalee."

Airalee's posture straightened as if they had removed a stone from her shoulders.

"Thank you," Airalee said. "I did not anticipate starting the day with a heavy situation, but I feel much better." Looking toward Marisa, she changed the subject by asking, "Do all villagers rise this early?"

"Well, no," Marisa said, "I am anxious to help you get started. You can help yourselves gain full citizenship by being self-reliant and cooperative citizens. We can start by gathering wood and food for ourselves and the kitchen. Cooking for yourselves and gathering with a group is even better." Looking at Airalee, she said, "You and I may help Mirtha or Kai with her group tasks. Jendrin and Maylore's guides will be here soon with their tasks. I suggest we all start with firewood for cooking," she said as she turned to the door.

"Maybe we can start with a latrine stop," Maylore said.

"I agree with that," Airalee said.

The four accomplished that morning task before gathering wood on their return.

"We can gather several bunches each and help clear this path to the village," Marisa said as she started snapping off branches. Gathering large armloads each, Marisa led them back to the kitchen

102

and dropped their wood at the end of the pile. "Grab a dry load from the front for us to use," Marisa said, motioning for Jendrin to grab a dry load. Walking to their hut, Marisa pointed to trees growing near the brush patch. Long pods hung from it even longer than the bush beans they had gathered the night before. "The pods on this tree have beans inside them. They are edible, cooked or not. They taste better cooked." Walking to a tree, she pulled down a fist-long pod. Splitting open the pod revealed a series of large, waxy brown beans. She popped one into her mouth, chewed, and swallowed. "Not much flavor, but they fill you up and will keep you alive," she said, motioning for the others to gather some pods. Jendrin put down his load to help the others gather the beans. They quickly had enough for several meals. Gathering the wood again, they continued to their hut.

"There is a small area next to their hut to store the wood," Marisa said as Jendrin placed it inside the indicated cove. "Time to cook breakfast," she announced, gathering a few pieces of wood and returning inside the hut. "We do it the same way as last night, only with different beans," she said, handing the wood to Maylore. Maylore broke up the branches and built up the fire.

"We can open the pods and fill the pot," she said, looking at Airalee and Jendrin. "The remaining ones we save for another day." The three quickly shelled the pods and were ready to cook as Maylore finished building the fire. "Add water and put the pot near the fire for dinner. We will finish last night's beans for breakfast and eat lunch in Kai's kitchen. Today, Airalee and I can gather fresh vegetables, herbs, and greens to add variety," Marisa said as Jendrin put the pot near the fire. "Eat your breakfast, and we will start the day." The group ate and exchanged chatter with each other.

"Dad, did you really see a blue rock yesterday?" Airalee asked, looking at Maylore.

"Yes, it had a blue glow," Maylore said. "You all say you saw nothing?"

"It was just a black rock," Jendrin said between bites.

"That is what I saw, too," Airalee said. Marisa kept quiet and listened to their discussion.

"I may need an eye adjustment," Maylore said, eating his beans. The chatter continued until they finished their breakfast. Jendrin took all of their bowls and left the hut to wash them.

"We will start at Rendal's hut," Marisa said. "Maylore may visit with Rendal today. We next visit Latel's to allow Jendrin to work with him. You and I will go to Mirtha's hut to work with her. Kai is not gathering today, so you can work with us, Airalee," Marisa said, opening the door. "We will wait for Jendrin, then continue," Marisa said. Jendrin quickly returned, placing the bowls into the hut before joining their group. The trio followed Marisa into the already busy village. Villagers smiled at the group as they walked through the village and arrived at Rendal's odd-looking hut. As they approached, Rendal met them at the door. "Beacon, good morning," Marisa said as they arrived.

"Good morning, all," Rendal replied. "Maylore, are you here to join our work group?" Rendal asked.

"Yes, if you will have me," Maylore replied. "I would be pleased to join."

"Good, good." Rendal replied, opening the door wider." Looking at the other two, he added, "I believe you will be good additions to our village. Marisa will help you get started. Thank you, Marisa." he said with a smile. The three waved and turned toward Latel's hut. "Please come in," Rendal said, bidding Maylore to enter. Three chairs were set near the small fire with the rock in the center. Throc stood near one of the chairs and nodded to Maylore. "We were discussing area lore and possible treaty changes for visitors. Throc added interesting points to those potential changes. He will be an exemplary village Beacon someday." The discussion of lore caught Maylore's attention.

"How much of this lore is written down?" Maylore asked.

"Some, not too many since it takes time and the writing materials are scarce," Rendal replied. "We have a few who help transcribe the stories, but only Throc and I are willing to do the research."

"I would be glad to help with research when you think I can help," Maylore said.

"That would be welcome," Rendal said. "Throc and I also watch for villagers or visitors who show any ability."

"I can write," Maylore said, "but have no crafting ability. I am sure I will learn."

Rendal looked at Throc with a pleased expression on his face.

"We are bid to look for those with abilities beyond everyday life," Rendal said.

"What abilities are you looking for?" Maylore asked.

"We look for those who can use the energy around us," Rendal said.

"I can start a fire with flint and iron stone. Not much of an ability, however," Maylore said, starting to look dejected.

"Look at the rock in the center. What do you see?" Rendal asked.

"It is a beautiful rock with shimmering blue colors," Maylore said.

Rendal looked sharply at Throc before replying, "We suspect you can see Almora's energy. Do you see anything else unusual about this rock?"

"Did someone put you up to a joke?" Maylore chuckled. Looking closer at the rock, he saw a single blue spark jump from the rock to the ground. "What was that spark?" He asked, glancing back toward Rendal. Throc took a step back in amazement before Rendal continued.

"There are some who would be interested in knowing you can see the blue field, Maylore," Rendal said.

Maylore looked confused, saying, "Doesn't everyone see this?" he said, remembering his companions saw only a black rock. "Airalee and Jendrin said it was a black rock. Is it black to you two also?"

"Yes, black obsidian," Rendal said as Throc nodded. "It was a test set up by a sorcerer seasons ago to find people who could see the planet's energy. He built this hut to be on top of a ley line."

"Is that person in the village?" Maylore asked.

"He disappeared long before I was born," Rendal said. "I carry on testing every newcomer like the Beacon before me."

"Who is the person who would be interested in this?" Maylore asked, his questions tumbling out in rapid succession. "What do I do with this supposed ability? Do I hide it from everyone? Do I look for other things that glow blue? Can it be removed?"

Rendal interrupted him. "Please, Maylore, I understand it is a shock to you. It is still a shock to us. You said you saw a blue shimmer yesterday but today confirms it. We want you to avoid telling anyone about this, including your companions."

"You said there was one person to avoid," Maylore said. "Who is that person I should avoid?"

"He does not live in Olona," Rendal said. "We do not know where he lives," Rendal replied. "He calls himself the master. He does not seem to have a name and rarely comes to Olona. He seems to have a network of spies. We believe one is in Olona."

"The master," Maylore said, "perhaps an ego problem?"

"We will not discuss him further," Rendal said.

"The person is a man then," Maylore said. "Helps eliminate a few people."

"I believe he is who he says he is," Rendal said, looking at Throc.

Throc looked to Maylore before replying.

"As discussed yesterday, Beacon, I defer to your decision," Throc said. "I do not know if he is a spy or a true refugee. I have heard enough from him now to believe he is a true refugee who does not know the master. I suspect we will find out too late if he is a spy."

"A spy?" Maylore asked, looking abashed. "I would be a terrible spy for anyone."

Rendal noticed his reaction and visibly relaxed.

"I did a poor job setting a trap," Rendal said. "I do not believe you are a spy, but I could have better disguised my objective."

"I am a simple man who humbly seeks a home," Maylore said, sitting in a chair.

"Excellent," Rendal said, "let's be done with that and turn to your experiences yesterday. You told us you saw Almora's energy running, turning the rock blue."

"I see the glow of the rock and a few new sparks," Maylore said, looking closer at the rock. "Where did you find a special rock to show this?"

A visible smile parted Rendal's lips as he reached down and picked up the rock. "It is just a rock," he said, giving it to Maylore. "It does have a crack down the middle, interrupting the energy flow, causing the sparks to jump." Maylore examined the black piece of obsidian before passing it back to Rendal. Rendal placed the rock back into a hollow spot carved into the floor. Rendal put a cushion on the floor in front of the stone. "Please sit, Maylore," he said as Rendal sat beside Throc. "Look closely at the rock and tell me what you see."

Maylore sat on the cushion and looked at the rock glowing softly again. A spark appeared at the base of the rock and traveled swiftly to the center, disappearing into the center. Another appeared on the other side and raced to the center. As he watched, more sparks appeared on all sides of the rock, making their way to the center and diving down into the rock.

"I see many sparks appearing at the edge of the rock, racing to the center and then disappearing," Maylore said.

"Good," he heard Rendal reply. "Tell me if you see anything different," Rendal added.

"He may have a small talent," Throc said.

"We will see," Rendal replied. Their voices became distant to Maylore as they continued their discussion. Their voices became a dull noise then faded away entirely as Maylore continued to observe the sparks. Two sparks appeared to travel in tandem—one pushing the other or being pulled by the first. Three, four, five at a time emerged from the edges and ran to the center. Maylore sat entranced as the sparks continued to flow.

"I do not think he hears us," Rendal said. They continued to discuss what they could do for Maylore as time passed. "We will need to find the written word about testing him. I do not remember much about it."

"We should ask Gilriel to work with him," Throc said.

"Yes, I forgot about Gilriel!" Rendal said. "He would certainly know far more than I do about this," Rendal said.

"It would expose Gilriel if Maylore or his companions are spies," Throc said.

"Yes, true," Rendal said. "I will consider that possibility and talk with Gilriel before suggesting it to Maylore."

"He has been watching the light for quite a while, Rendal," Throc said. "The sun is nearing its peak. We should interrupt him so he does not get lost in his mind."

"Yes," Rendal said, "it is time we roused him and asked him what he saw." Rendal placed his hand in front of Maylore's eyes and touched his shoulder. Maylore roused from his observation and looked to Rendal. "What did you see, Maylore?" he asked. Maylore slowly shook his head to clear the images from his eyes before replying.

"Small blue sparks traveled from the ground along the rock before disappearing into its center," Maylore reported. "At first, just a few joined, and then a train of sparks began to flow. It was fascinating."

"I am becoming convinced you see the planet's energy," Rendal said. "I have heard and read about it, but that is all. I understand this kind of mental work can make you hungry. It is time for the mid-day meal if you would like."

"I do feel hungry," Maylore said as he stood.

"All right, " Rendal replied, "Throc will walk you to the kitchen. I will make some notes about your work. Keep secret what you saw," Rendal said in a warning voice. Throc touched Rendal's elbow and turned slightly toward him. "Please wait outside for a few moments, Maylore," Rendal said. Maylore nodded and left the hut.

"Are we going to report this?" Throc whispered after the door closed.

Rendal stood silent momentarily before answering, "No. I want to see if this is a short-term event or if we have a new sorcerer in our midst."

"Yes, Beacon," Throc said before following Maylore out the door.

Airalee and Jendrin followed Marisa on the short walk to Latel's hut. Marisa knocked before opening the door.

109

"Welcome," Latel said, looking up from his work. "Glad to see you both again," he said, nodding to Airalee and gesturing for Jendrin to sit in a chair near him. "I will work with Jendrin this morning and help him get started crafting. Thank you, Marisa." Marisa waved as she and Airalee left the hut.

Setting aside the vest he was working on, Latel turned his attention to Jendrin. "You may not remember any skill you had before you arrived, but what do you think would help the village?" Latel asked.

Before speaking, Jendrin considered what to say.

"I would like to build things," Jendrin replied. "Develop ways to ease the villagers' lives. I may not make much of a tailor," he said, looking at the vest Latel was making. "I believe I could help with procuring materials for you."

"I am fortunate to have two other full-time tailors making clothes for our village and trade," Latel said. "I would not turn down another, but your offer to do multiple trades would be most welcome. A person who can develop ways to ease our village life would be beneficial."

"I also seem to know military options and can teach villagers how to defend the village," Jendrin added.

"We have not had a raid in several lifetimes," Latel said. "The sentinels give us a good warning to allow us to hide. We can discuss it with the Beacon later if you wish."

"Where would you go if you had a raid?" Jendrin asked. Latel considered before answering, "You are new to our village," Latel said. "We will discuss what you should know with the Beacon."

"Of course, a wise response," Jendrin replied, looking slightly abashed. "Let me attempt to help you before I look to other tasks," Jendrin said as Latel picked up his work.

"This robe needs leather thongs inserted to close around the wearer," Latel said, pulling a robe from behind him.

Jendrin spent the next few hours cutting leather, making holes in the robes, and inserting the cords to close around the wearer. "I fear this is not the task for me," Jendrin said as he finished another one.

"Being a tailor is not for everyone," Latel said. "My associates and I already have a good inventory of clothes. Your talents may lie elsewhere. I suggest we take a walk through the village," Latel said. "Let's see if there are areas that would interest you." Latel stood and led the way out of the hut.

"Let's start at the far end of the village at the garden," Latel suggested, walking toward the far end of the village. They stood near the large garden. "This garden my mother tends has rich soil and can grow many different vegetables," Latel said, pointing at different vegetables.

"Where does she get the water?" Jendrin asked.

"Over the slope toward the sea, the creek flows alongside the village," Latel said. "The creek's location is a major reason she chose this site for the garden."

"She carries water from the creek to the garden?" Jendrin asked.

"Yes, she and several others carry water daily to different parts of the garden," Latel replied. Jendrin considered if he could help her with the watering.

"Perhaps we can create a way for the water to be delivered here," Jendrin said, looking at the rocky slope.

Latel looked at the rocky climb toward the creek. "She would welcome that if you could do it," Latel said.

"Let me put that on my list," Jendrin said, considering the work involved.

"Wonderful idea, if you can do it," Latel said with a smile.

"Let's continue through the village," Latel said. They walked along the creek side of the village, arriving at a large hut with clay pots sitting outside. "We did not visit the pottery area before. It too may be of interest."

"Where do they get the clay?" Jendrin asked.

"Beyond the forest, the river forms a bog on the mountainside. There is a clay pit, and we dig clay to make the pots," Latel said, pointing back the way they had come.

Two men carrying a litter came toward them on the path. "Coming through," a voice said as they saw a litter filled with lava rock.

"Are you expanding or building a new hut?" Latel asked the lead man.

"Expanding," he replied. "My baby-mate decided she wanted to stay in this hut. Just add room for children."

"Good," Latel replied before looking toward Jendrin as the men continued. "We must have a new baby on the way," Latel said, waving toward the two men. "We have several girls approaching the age of wanting children. We may have several more children running between the huts," Latel said. "Let's continue our walk." They walked past several homes and a path leading toward the ocean.

"Where do these paths lead?" Jendrin asked.

"There are more crafting areas," Latel replied. "We may visit those areas another day." They ended up on a cliff overlooking the ocean. "This is where we gather on fish collection days," Latel said, pointing down the cliff. A pair of knotted ropes sat coiled to one side.

"Your people climb down the cliff to fish the ocean?" Jendrin asked.

"Yes," Latel replied. "Usually, the same villagers use these ropes to go down to the shore. Another gathering group lowers baskets over the edge to haul the fish back up. It is difficult work, and several villagers get injured each season." Jendrin noted that there were no rollers or pulleys to ease the work.

"I can envision a way to help our villagers here," Jendrin said.

"We will have another fishing day in a couple of sunrises. You can join the gathering," Latel said as he turned back toward the village. Jendrin nodded, making mental notes of the cliffside trees and boulders as he followed Latel. The twin suns were directly overhead as they emerged back into the village. Passing the companion's hut, they walked to the rock hill behind the childcare area. The same two men were loading more lava rock onto their litter. Jendrin noticed a giant jumble of granite on the mountainside. To the ocean side, he saw a glimmer of black stone.

"Is that obsidian over there, Latel?" Jendrin asked.

"Yes, we collect and shape a few pieces for knives," Latel replied. "You will need to make your knives and tools for yourself. You could collect material here to make sharp tools." Jendrin made another mental note of its location and the many uses for the sharp edge it could provide.

"Let's visit the rest of the village before we visit the kitchen for lunch," Latel said as he returned to the village.

Life in the village looked simple to Jendrin. He made mental notes of things and processes he believed he could improve upon as he followed Latel to the kitchen.

Airalee

Marisa and Airalee left Latel's hut and arrived at Kai's hut. Marisa knocked on the door as they heard Kai call out for them to enter. Kai sat at a table examining dried herbs.

"Good morning, girls. Sit," Kai said, pointing to two chairs. "We can find out what Airalee may already know," Kai said. Airalee and Marisa sat in chairs facing the table laden with herbs and mushrooms.

"Do you recognize any of these herbs or mushrooms?" Kai asked Airalee.

Airalee stared at what looked like a pile of weeds and toadstools. "No," Airalee said before a particular plant caught her eye. "This is rosemary," she answered, pushing the pile around. As she gazed at the plants, more and more names popped into her head. "Thyme, basil, dill," she named several others before Kai stopped her with a laugh.

"Very good," Kai said. "Tell me how to use them."

Airalee felt a trickle of botanical information enter her mind from somewhere. "Most of these you can use for cooking," Airalee said. "You can enhance meat with these," she said, holding up a group of herbs. "Starch-based foods work well with these," she added, holding up a different group. "These mushrooms add a nice flavor to almost anything. I believe these are poisonous toadstools best left alone," she said, pushing them aside. Airalee was unsure where the sudden rush of plant names came from, and it left her head spinning slightly.

"I am glad your mind was not completely wiped," Kai said. "You may be useful to us already. These toadstools have a useful purpose, which you may learn about later. Marisa will explain them when the time comes," Kai said.

Airalee saw pink mushrooms with white spots, a light yellow one, and bright blue ones. "I will store these mushrooms while you two take herbs to Mirtha and store the rest," Kai said. Has the council accepted Airalee?"

"Yes, as guided," Marisa answered. "All three have been granted guided status."

"I hope they are not acting too quickly," Kai said. "They have proven little so far. Show Airalee where to store these herbs." Looking at Airalee, she said, "Go prove yourself, girl! Drag those two men along with you! We could use more young help." Kai said, waving a dismissive hand at them. Kai gathered the mushroom as Airalee and Marisa left the hut.

"She is a forthright woman," Airalee said as they walked.

"Kai has been like that for many seasons," Marisa replied. "We always know what she thinks, and she tolerates little nonsense. She is dedicated to healing and compassionate when needed."

They arrived at the kitchen to find Mirtha examining a pot of stew. "Mirtha," Marisa said, "we have some fresh herbs."

"Nice," Mirtha replied. "I will take some of each," she said, taking some from their outstretched hands. "Thank you. Are you helping guide Airalee again today, Marisa?"

"Yes," Marisa replied, "I can have Airalee help us if you need help today."

"No," Marisa replied, "I have a lot of help today. Feel free to get Airalee going."

"We will add these herbs to the storage area and turn the drying stock over," Marisa said.

"Good," Mirtha said, adding different herbs to other pots. "We went herb hunting a few days ago," Marisa said. "Tomorrow, we will go foraging again for whatever else we can gather. Kai or Mirtha will go with us to verify that we have all gathered useful items and left enough of the plants to keep growing. You should join us for a fun day."

"I look forward to it," Airalee said, smiling.

"Marisa, would you collect some seagrass for our lunch?" Mirtha asked.

"Yes," Marisa replied. "It would be a good time to show Airalee our seashore."

"Good idea," Mirtha replied. "Please check our storage hut for old herbs if you have time."

"We will do that first," Marisa said, standing and bidding Mirtha farewell. They walked a short distance and entered the storage hut.

"Now, we will inspect the herbs and toss any old ones," Marisa said, "Be sure to turn each over to keep it from molding."

The room was large and contained shelves from the floor to the ceiling. They took time to inspect the contents of each basket and discard old or molded items. The process took the rest of the morning, and the discard baskets were full when they finished. Airalee had noticed a small door at the back of the hut with a large red branch keeping it closed. She decided now was the time to ask about it.

"What is in the room at the back?" Airalee asked.

"This is our dangerous item area," Marisa replied. "Kai stores the medicinal items and other things we find on our trips. The door makes a loud noise when it opens to alert others that it is being opened. Kai will decide when you are ready to learn about them, assuming you continue to learn with her."

"I plan to learn as much as I can from her," Airalee said. "Are any of these items written down?" Airalee asked, indicating the entire room.

"No, but it is a good idea," Marisa replied. "I started doing that but didn't get far. We always had too much work to do or ran out of bark paper to write on. Kai told me she knows what she has and what they do. She claims we don't need to write them down."

"Until Kai is unavailable, then what do we do," Airalee said.

"She told me she is not going anywhere until her students learn everything she knows," Marisa replied. "When I suggested bad things happen, she merely scoffs at me."

Airalee started devising how to organize a book of these items.

"It should be a short book about herbs and their uses," Airalee said. "We could start another book about mushrooms and other botanicals. Between the two of us, it should not take too much extra effort."

Marisa smiled at the idea and agreed to help.

"Let's gather and dispose of the discarded herbs before we walk to the sea cliff. The seagrass Mirtha wants is easy to gather and will not take us long," Marisa said.

"I would like to see the seashore anyway," Airalee said. They walked back toward the bathing pool and continued to the cliff overlooking the sea. Marisa picked up the stored climbing rope and tossed it over the edge.

"There are a few steps down the slope," Marisa said. "It is an easy climb but daunting the first time."

Airalee looked over the side at the slope leading to the beach.

"Dauting may be an understatement," Airalee said.

"Follow me," Marisa said, grabbing the rope and starting down.

Airalee watched Marisa start down the rope before gathering her courage to follow. The slope had enough footholds dug into it for her to feel comfortable going down. "The seagrass grows all along the waterline," Marisa said, pointing from sunrise to sunset. "We will walk sunrise along the waterline." Marisa led the way to the shoreline and followed it sunrise. Airalee followed her, looking at the calm sea.

"The sea is very calm," Airalee said as she touched the water with her foot. "Cold, too," she said, pulling her foot back.

"It is nearly flat unless there is a summer rainstorm or a winter snowstorm," Marisa said, bending down to pick up seagrass.

Airalee moved next to her and bent to pick up more seagrass. Her foot stirred the water when she noticed a bright blue stone near her foot. The stone seemed to jump onto her sandal and wedged between her toes.

"That's interesting," Airalee said, bending down to take the stone from her sandal. Her fingers tingled when she pulled out the stone. She started to drop the stone, but it stuck to her fingers.

"What did you find?" Marisa asked.

"A pretty blue stone that stuck to me," Airalee said, showing it to Marisa.

"It is a pretty rock," Marisa remarked.

"It is unusually oval and has a white streak running through it," Airalee said, examining the stone.

"I don't think I have seen any blue stones here before," Marisa said, looking at the stone. "It is beautiful."

"I will adopt it," Airalee said, putting it into her pocket.

The two women collect a satchel full of sea grass before returning to Mirtha's hut.

Jendrin and Latel were sitting at the lunch table when Airalee and Marisa arrived. Jendrin waved to Airalee as she filled a bowl with the hearty soup. Waving back, Airalee sat across from Jendrin. Marisa gathered two bowls and placed hers next to Airalee, saying, "I will take this bowl to Kai and return."

"Should we wait for Marisa to return?" Jendrin asked.

"You mean like you waited for me, hero?" Airalee said with a smile.

Jendrin paused with his spoon in hand.

"I didn't know you were coming," he replied. "I will refill my bowl so we can start together," he said with a smile as he rose to refill his bowl. Airalee and Latel talked as Maylore and Throc entered the kitchen. Airalee waved heartily to him.

"Come sit next to me, Dad," Airalee called.

"Dad?" Throc said, stopping and looking at Maylore. "She knows you were a baby-mate to her mother?"

"Her idea of a joke," Maylore replied. "I am not her dad, baby-mate, or anything else except a companion," he said, waving to Airalee.

Maylore filled a large bowl and brought some of the bread to the table as Marisa returned. Light conversational banter between the group ensued. Even the reserved Throc joined in on the conversation.

As the meal ended, Airalee looked toward Marisa.

"Marisa, are we headed back to training?" Airalee asked.

"We don't work all the time," Marisa said. "We usually work or train in the mornings. We use the afternoons for our activities. If you are finished eating, we will help clean up the kitchen." The group followed her lead and helped clean up the kitchen. Marisa introduced them to more villagers as the group returned to the companion's hut.

"We will see you in the morning," Marisa said as the guides left them at their hut.

"Domestic time," Airalee said to her companions.

"I will get more water," Maylore said as he took the empty pot and left the hut.

"I will get more firewood for tomorrow," Jendrin said.

"I will open more bean pods while you two are gone," Airalee said.

The men returned from their duties, and the conversation centered on the day's activities. Airalee discussed the herb storage seagrass collection and showed them the blue stone she found. Jendrin discussed his ideas for the village. Maylore discussed the politics and lore of the area. He kept seeing the blue energy to himself, convinced it was a tired man's illusion.

119

Council Meeting

Rendal sat in the empty council hut. Worry nibbled at him, telling him he may have made a mistake pushing too hard, making the newcomers as guided.

Marisa, Throc, and Latel arrived, and without a preamble, he started his questions.

"How is Airalee doing?" he asked, looking at Marisa.

"I believe Airalee is doing well," Marisa said. "We met with Kai, and Airalee identified many herbs on the table. Kai seemed impressed with her."

"How about Jendrin?" Rendal asked, looking toward Latel.

"Jendrin appears to have some good ideas for helping the village. He is not interested in being a tailor. He is interested in helping with village operations. He also expressed interest in starting a militia in the village. I suggested he discuss it with you, Beacon."

"A militia," Rendal said. "There is more tension in Olona and the valley. Perhaps we will discuss it sometime. Let's put that aside until he shows his true colors. Throc and I spent most of the morning with Maylore. Do you have anything to add, Throc?"

"No, Beacon," Throc replied. "We ate lunch with the group, and I saw nothing extraordinary."

"Did anyone see anything that made them suspicious?" Rendal asked.

"No," the group replied at once.

"Excellent," Rendal said, feeling a wave of relief. "I asked the Tocor if they had noticed a problem. They told me they had not. Let's hope it continues. I see no reason to call a full council meeting. I will meet with them in a few sunrises anyway. Thank you all for your reports. I will see you all tomorrow night."

CHAPTER 9 - TRAINING CONTINUES

Jendrin arose and quietly left the hut to satisfy his body's needs. He considered using the empty bathing pool as he passed it but decided to bathe after breakfast. Returning to the hut, he gathered herbs, beans, and water they had prepared the previous night. Combining the items into a pot, he set them near the fire. He was putting their bowls on the table when Airalee entered the room.

"Nice," Airalee said. "Is the hero being domestic, or is he trying to earn my favor to avoid being tossed out?"

"My good deed for the day," Jendrin said as Airalee smiled and left the hut.

"Good morning, Jendrin," Maylore said, poking his head through his curtain.

"Good morning, Maylore," Jendrin replied. "Our little breakfast is cooking."

"I will join you after I visit the latrine," Maylore said, opening the door.

Airalee and Maylore returned to join Jendrin in their morning meal. They were finishing their meal when they heard the sound of heavier footsteps approaching.

"Doesn't sound like Marisa," Airalee said as a heavier knock sounded at the door. Jendrin opened the door to find Throc standing there.

"Good morning, everyone," he said with a slight bow. "The Beacon would like Maylore to come to his hut if possible."

Maylore rose and picked up his bowl as Airalee interrupted.

"I will take care of your dishes, Dad," Airalee said, reaching for his bowl.

Maylore gave her a resigned smile.

"Thank you, Airalee," Maylore said as he left the hut with Throc and followed him to Rendal's hut.

"Good morning, Maylore," Rendal said as they entered his hut. "I hope you rested well."

"Yes," Maylore replied. "Thank you, Beacon."

"Excellent," Rendal replied. "I have read Parthwen's training text and would like to explore your potential ability."

"I was thinking we would discuss different agreements within the villages," Maylore replied. He took a seat in a chair near Rendal. The rock was in its exact position but now surrounded by the three chairs.

"I ask for your forbearance this morning," Rendal said. "We will look at those items in the future. Today, I would like to investigate if you may have a latent ability. Throc will need to take over this session since I have more travelers to greet shortly. I will help you start, and Throc will take over when I leave. Ready?"

"I am ready," Maylore replied. He looked at each of them, not sure this was what he expected or wanted to do.

"I want you to concentrate to determine if you can control the energy flow," Rendal said as he pointed to the rock. "What I mean by concentrate is to block out the noise around you but leave your ears open to the world around you," Rendal said, reading from the notes. "You will focus on the energy source, but your ears are open to alert you if dangers are approaching. If you are fortunate, you may someday learn to open a portal in your mind. This portal would allow you to see the world's energy without using your eyes."

"What?" Maylore said, looking at Rendal with a look of disbelief. "I know nothing of portals or whatever else you just said." Looking down at the rock, he added, "I believe today all I see is a black rock. Shall we consider treaties or other written texts I could study?"

"I do not want to waste the possibility to explore a latent ability," Rendal said. "If you can expand on this ability, it would be valuable to Olona and, indeed, Almora.

Maylore looked at Rendal as if he were perpetuating a joke. 'He seems serious,' Maylore thought, looking at him. 'Am I about to make a big mistake?' Maylore wondered. 'I should ensure this test fails,' he thought. Realizing that an unknown ability could reveal his deception, he decided to find out what they could be to ensure he suppressed them.

"This is almost as confusing as waking up on that desert floor," Maylore finally said aloud, rubbing his head. "Perhaps I should go back to bed and try again."

"If you try to bring forth your ability and if there is nothing there," Rendal said, "we will discontinue trying in a few sunrises."

"A few sunrises," Maylore said, looking down. "All right, Beacon, I will try," Maylore said.

"Excellent!" Rendal replied. "Let's see if Parthwen's notes lead to a good conclusion for you."

'Basrah, I may have trapped myself,' Maylore thought.

"Portals, you were saying?" Maylore asked, looking back at Rendal.

"Yes," Rendal said. "We will fully discuss portals another time. Let's proceed one step at a time to see if you are successful. We may add to your training with the aid of another person or go another direction if we fail."

"Is that person the village sorcerer?" Maylore said.

"He is not a sorcerer," Rendal said, "He has insights none of us possess. He can be difficult and does not want people to know about him. If we are successful, I will contact him.

"Another mysterious man," Maylore said in a soft voice.

123

"Yes," Rendal replied, realizing he had failed again to conceal what he preferred to hide. "Shall we proceed?" he said as he pointed at the rock. "What do you see this morning?"

Maylore looked at the rock as it resumed its blue color. It took longer for the sparks to appear and even longer for them to start flowing.

After a while, he said, "The sparks are flowing again from the outer edges to the center."

"Good," Rendal said with a hint of relief. "I want you to reach out with your left hand and try to pull the energy away from the rock."

Maylore started to laugh but decided to try. The energy flow did not change.

"Nothing happened," Maylore said after a few tries.

"Try to imagine a string from your palm to the center of the rock and pull the energy up the string," Rendal instructed, scanning the text.

Maylore could easily envision a string from his hand to the rock, and he pulled on the string repeatedly but to no avail. Maylore shook his head but kept trying.

"This may take time to do, Maylore. Keep at it," Rendal said encouragingly. One of the sparks started up this string, which surprised Maylore. It fell immediately back down when he lost concentration. Refocusing his attention, he tried to pull the energy again. This time, several sparks started up the string.

"I have several starting up the string," Maylore said aloud.

"Excellent!" Rendal almost shouted. "See if you can get the energy to flow up one arm and down the next."

Maylore saw the sparks slow to a stop and slide back down.

"No. The energy starts to flow but slips back down," Maylore announced, looking up at Rendal.

Maylore noticed Throc's slight look of amazement, which quickly disappeared when Maylore looked at him.

"Sounds like a good start," Rendal said. "Keep trying."

Returning concentration to the rock, Maylore picked up on the energy flow quicker this time. Spreading his hands apart above the rock, he envisioned the strings again. A few sparks traveled up a little farther before slipping back down again. Maylore continued to try to pull the energy up his arm. He was getting a little farther each time before the sparks drained away.

"Maylore," Rendal said after some time had passed, "What do you see?"

"I can pull the energy flow from the rock nearly to my fingers," Maylore said. "It drops away before it reaches any further," Maylore said, sounding a little frustrated.

"Let's try something a little different," Rendal said. "Take off your left sandal and place your bare foot near the rock. We will ask the energy to flow to your foot, then up to your hand. Tie the string from your hand to your foot." Maylore nodded, removed his sandals, and began concentrating on the rock. Sound from the outside world dissipated as he concentrated. Slowly, the sparks gathered at his foot, forming a line on the string flowing past his knee before falling back to the ground. Maylore felt he had accomplished a small victory and must have smiled.

"He has a small smile, Beacon," Throc said. "Perhaps he is doing it."

"Perhaps," Rendal replied. "Let's leave him to practice a while." A knock sounded on the door. "Enter," Rendal said. Marisa peeked in, informing Rendal that the visitors were ready for him.

"Thank you, Marisa," he answered. "That was short. Throc, I want you to take these notes and coach Maylore on gathering energy and transferring it to each hand. Please note what happens." Throc nodded as Rendal left the hut.

Airalee

Marisa walked from Rendal's hut to the companions' hut and knocked on the door. Jendrin answered, asking her to enter. Marisa noticed the table was clear, and Airalee sat at it.

"Have you not eaten yet?" Marisa asked.

"Yes," Airalee answered. "We finished breakfast shortly after Maylore left. Are we ready to go gathering?"

"We are," Marisa said. "Kai has asked Mirtha to have you help gather roots and nuts. We are searching the sunset side of the forest today. I don't think it has many edible roots or nuts. Ready?"

"Later, hero," Airalee said as she left with Marisa. Jendrin waved to her as the door closed.

Mirtha was waiting outside her hut as the two women approached.

"I find we are running short of a few vegetables," Mirtha said. "There is some in the drying hut, but we should gather and plant more. Before we go into the forest, have you warned Airalee about the wildlife, Marisa?"

"We have discussed it, but I will remind her now," Marisa replied, looking at Airalee. "Most of the creatures we may see are not dangerous. The boars attack if you get too close, but only some have tusks. Go the other way if you hear one of them. The blood wolves will ignore you unless you are bleeding. The fierce wolves attack as a pack. If we see them, we will climb a tree. Bears usually ignore you but move downwind from them if you see one. The other animals only eat plants and know you won't try to eat them, so they ignore you."

"Good," Mirtha replied, "We will be walking to the river to show you what we want to gather. This sunset meadow is the safest area to gather."

Two more people joined their collecting group as they passed through the village and arrived at the garden.

"I don't see any vegetables we need growing in the garden," Mirtha said, looking over the garden. "We will help plant more another day. We will see what the forest has for us." The gathering group walked past the garden and through the bamboo forest. Mirtha stopped at the edge of the meadow.

"We usually gather from here to the road on the mountainside, over to the seaside, down to the river at the end of the meadow," she said, pointing in each direction. "We will walk together today to allow Airalee to learn what we gather and how much. Marisa will talk, and I will fill in what she may miss. Next time, you may be going on your own. So, Airalee, learn quickly."

Mirtha walked a short distance before stopping and looking at Marisa.

"What do you see we can take?" Mirtha asked.

"Some onion, cooking herbs, and the chicory is blooming," Marisa said, scanning the area.

"Let's gather some of each," Mirtha said.

Marisa showed Airalee how to gather, leaving some of each to propagate for the future. The group gathered as they walked until the end of the first meadow. The trees pinched into the meadow, forming a shallow closure.

"Here are a few brown mushrooms," Marisa said. "There are also some brightly colored mushrooms. Bright colors like those generally mean to watch out. We are poison!" Marisa warned, holding up one hand. "We will leave those alone. Let's gather some brown ones to cook with our vegetables and meat."

Airalee bent down to look at the bright-colored mushrooms. Bright red, blue, yellow, orange, and white mushrooms grew in the shade. She saw a group of white mushrooms with blue spots hiding behind a tree trunk.

Mirtha diverted her attention by pointing at a few berry bushes growing at the edge of the next meadow.

"There aren't enough triangle berries for a meal here," Mirtha said, "but we can share these," motioning for the others to join her. Airalee put a few in her mouth and noticed the sweet, juicy flavor invigorated her mouth.

"These are very good," Airalee remarked.

"They give you their energy, allowing you to continue working," Mirtha said, finishing the few berries before her. Looking at Airalee, she said, "We are entering the next meadow with the swamp on the mountainside and the river ahead of us. Let's be on our way."

The group walked and gathered until they heard a faint roar of rushing water touch their ears.

"We have reached the edge of the meadow," Mirtha said. "Just past those trees, the river rushes toward the ocean. Birsha's group inhabits the land beyond it." Mirtha said, pointing to the sunset. "We don't want to be seen, even though they are unlikely to try and cross the fast river."

Airalee tried to see the river through the remaining trees but could not.

"Can we move close enough to see the river?" Airalee inquired.

"We can," Mirtha said. "It isn't too dangerous," Mirtha replied after a short pause. "Leave your baskets here with the rest of the group. We will walk through the brush." The sound of the river grew louder as they made their way between trees and brush. Mirtha pushed aside a final branch, revealing a fast-moving river. The water crashed against large boulders as it swept past them. Marisa and

Airalee moved beside Mirtha as Airalee admired the strength of the flowing water.

"Down!" Mirtha urgently said as she pulled back the branch. The women sank to one knee as Mirtha pointed to the opposite bank. A burly man appeared behind a boulder, walking down the opposite riverbank. "It's that devil, Oleg," Mirtha said, watching him intently. Oleg did not notice them and continued down the riverbank.

"I saw him with Birsha talking to the Beacon when we first arrived," Airalee said.

"He is Birsha's lieutenant and a bad man," Mirtha said. "Stay away from him."

"The way he looked at me that first day, I think that is sound advice," Airalee said, stepping back.

"We will gather our baskets and continue toward the ocean side before returning to the village," Mirtha said as they returned to the group. The group walked toward the meadow's ocean side, approaching an area of torn-up vegetation.

"The wild pigs have been here," Mirtha said, looking over the deserted area. "Let's start back toward the village," she said, turning back. Airalee approached the uprooted area, noticing an oblong object sitting on the ground. Picking it up, a flash of recognition hit her.

"These are potatoes!" she exclaimed, looking for more amongst the uprooted plants.

"What are potatoes?" Marisa asked, following her lead. Airalee pulled up a small white potato to show Marisa.

"This is," Airalee said. Marisa and Mirtha merely looked at her.

"Isn't pig food poisonous?" Mirtha asked. Airalee looked from them to the potato before replying.

"No," Airalee replied. "They make a good meal by themselves or mixed with other food. Besides, pigs wouldn't eat them if they were poisonous."

Mirtha looked at her sideways before replying.

"You eat them for a month," Mirtha said. "If you live, we will consider them. Gather them in a separate bag so they do not poison the other foods you have gathered," Mirtha said. She watched Airalee gather a few potatoes into a new bag before they continued. The women started down the oceanside slope, picking up more green leaves before returning to the garden.

Levyna was tending the garden when the group arrived.

"Airalee," Mirtha said, "show Levyna the item you found."

Airalee retrieved a potato and showed it to Levyna.

"Levyna, have we used this for food before?" Mirtha asked.

"Pig food?" Levyna remarked. "No, I have heard it is poisonous."

Airalee began to doubt her discovery but thought the pigs were eating them.

"I will risk eating them for a month," Airalee said. "If I live, I will tell you about them."

"You may wish to ask Kai if she has a poison remedy first," Levyna said with a smile.

"I may do that," Airalee said, putting the potato back into her bag.

"Levyna, we gathered fresh herbs if you need some," Mirtha said to change the subject.

"I see you have some basil. I could use that," Levyna said.

"Enjoy," Mirtha said, passing her a bunch still with roots. "Do you need any other help while we are here?"

"The crew has almost finished their tasks, thank you anyway," Levyna said. The women bid each other goodbye and returned to Mirtha's hut.

"Place the baskets on the table," Mirtha said, setting her basket on the table. "It's time to examine what we gathered and remove mistaken items. We will distribute the greens and store the other items. Airalee, I want you to leave your potatoes outside and remember to take them with you after we finish."

Airalee smiled as she piled her items onto the table and put the potatoes outside.

Jendrin

Jendrin finished his cleanup duties before venturing outside the hut to find Latel. He noticed villagers hauling water from the creek for their gardens, gathering wood beans, and chatting with their neighbors. He walked past storage huts half full of dried fish and other supplies. 'The village will not starve,' he thought as he walked. Jendrin knocked on Latel's hut and stood to the side. Latel called for him to enter.

"Jendrin, please sit," Latel said, pointing to a chair near him. "I am trying to finish this vest this morning, but I want to hear from you. Have you considered what would be a good village project for you to do?"

Jendrin considered for another moment before replying. "I would like to build a village water delivery system," Jendrin said. Latel stopped sewing the vest and looked toward Jendrin.

"That would be very welcome," Latel said, "especially by my mother. How would you do it?"

"I saw a large bamboo stand beyond your mom's garden," Jendrin said. "I could use that hollow wood as a source for the piping."

"We always considered bamboo a nuisance with no value except to create doors," Latel said.

"We need long pieces that end with small diameters to fit into the next piece large diameter," Jendrin said.

"Many bamboos are 20 sticks tall and up to ⅓ stick wide at the tough base. How do you plan to cut them down?" Latel asked.

"We need a long-handled cutting tool," Jendrin replied. Latel looked at his knife, considering what he said.

"We don't have chopping tools like that," Latel replied, looking back at him. "Each person makes their tools. You can try to make one," he said.

"I will go back to the obsidian flow and see if I can find a rock that I can shape into a chopping tool," Jendrin said.

"Obsidian is too fragile to use for chopping," Latel replied. "It works well as a slicing tool like a knife."

"Do you know of a stout rock I can shape"? Jendrin asked.

"There is a dark, shiny rock that is shapeable," Latel replied. "I know of a hillside near the clay pits. We can travel there sometime if you wish."

"That would be good," Jendrin said. "I will check the bamboo patch to see if we could use any down pieces. I also need to find a strong branch for the chopper handle."

"There is an ironwood tree on the other side of the road," Latel said after a moment of thought. "The branches are tough to break, so we don't use them. The sentinels use the small straight ones for their arrows."

"Good, I will start with that," Jendrin said, rising from his chair. "Did you have something you wanted me to do before I go?" he asked.

Latel shook his head.

"No," Latel replied, "It sounds like you have a good project. I will inform the Beacon of your choice. I am sure he will be pleased."

Jendrin nodded as he left the hut and returned to Levyna's garden. He waved to her as she carried water from the creek with two others. He walked to the rise above the creek that flowed below. A waterfall came over the hill from the forest side down to a series of pools before continuing past the village. The rocky bank was over one stick above creek level with a path cut by the gardeners to the water. Looking back up the creek, Jendrin noticed the last water pool was higher than the bank's edge before the waterfall dropped down to the low creek bed.

"If I can make a pipe that starts at that pool," Jendrin said aloud, "I could create a pipeline over the bank and down to the garden. The water could gather at the garden and perhaps flow in a new pipe to the rest of the village," he pointed where each piece would go as he talked.

The sound of moving brush across the creek caught his attention. A large wolf was staring at him. Jendrin started backing slowly away as the wolf moved toward him. Jendrin saw the women were returning for more water.

"There is a large wolf here," he loudly warned. "Move to safety while I distract him." The three women started to laugh and continued toward the creek.

"The wolf is thirsty," Levyna said. "Leave him be, and he won't bother you." The wolf walked to the creek's edge and bent down to drink. The three women arrived, filling their buckets. The wolf continued drinking while watching them.

"You aren't dead yet," Levyna chided him. "He will have no interest in you. Here is a bucket; fill it and help us water the garden." Jendrin filled the bucket and carried it back to the garden. Levyna was watering plants and traded him her empty bucket. He returned to the creek to gather more water, noting the wolf was gone. He spent time carrying water to the garden before Levyna called a halt.

"Thank you, Jendrin," Levyna said. "Take these vegetables to the kitchen or eat them yourself if you wish," she said.

Jendrin nodded, gathered the vegetables, and walked them to the kitchen. He returned to the edge of the bamboo forest.

"There are a few downed ones that might work," he said aloud. Many had cracked or splintered when they fell. "I need a way to cut these trees," he said. "Perhaps I can burn the tree to the size I need." He grabbed a downed, undamaged seven-stick section of bamboo and dragged it back to the kitchen. Latel entered the area as Jendrin approached.

"This may be the first section of pipe," Jendrin told Latel. "I will burn off the small, narrow end to create a bigger opening for the next piece. I may have to burn off sections until I can make a chopping tool." Latel nodded as Jendrin stuck the small diameter end into the fire and placed a rock where he wanted it to stop burning.

"Shall we go look for a handle?" he asked, looking at Latel.

"Sure. Back toward the village entrance," Latel said, pointing the way.

The Beacon was standing by the road as they approached the village entrance.

"Beacon," Latel said as they stopped near him.

"Latel and Jendrin, I hope your day is going well," Rendal said, looking up.

"Yes, thank you," Latel replied. "Jendrin wishes to build a pipe to carry water into the garden and the village. I hope you approve."

The Beacon stopped, and a smile appeared on his lips.

"Yes!" Rendal said. "That would be very welcome by many. It is not far from the creek, but all villagers would appreciate water delivered into the village."

A group of humans emerged from the visitor's hut.

"Who are they?" Jendrin asked in a low voice.

"Traders," Rendal said. "They travel the valley swapping what one village has for what it does not. We traded our large fish supply for new rope, berries, pitch, and hides. Their carrier will pass by soon. We must gather the fish and bring them to the carrier."

"We will help when you issue the call, Beacon," Latel said.

"Excellent. Where are you two going next?" Beacon asked.

"Jendrin is making a chopping tool," Latel said. "He needs a strong stick for a handle. I was taking him to the ironwood tree across the road before we looked for an obsidian stone to make his knife."

"Good," Rendal replied. "Obsidian does not make a good chopping tool. What are you planning to use?" looking at Jendrin.

"Latel tells me there is a pile of shapable stone near the clay pits," Jendrin said. "It is probably flint. I can turn that into an axe head."

"Perhaps," Rendal replied. "I wish you good fortune with it. I will bid these men farewell before returning to my hut to work with Maylore. Good day to you both." he turned toward the traders.

"Good day, Beacon," they replied as they walked away. "Let's continue up toward the mountain." They passed the cave from which the trio had emerged. Jendrin looked up, trying to spot the sentinel.

"Sentinels are small, and they hide well in these trees," Latel said, smiling. "He may not even be in any of these trees."

Crossing the road, they arrived at a small grove of stocky-looking trees. Jendrin surveyed the downed limbs, spotting several candidates.

"This one looks like it will work," Jendrin said. "I wonder how strong it is?" He picked up the three-stick long limb and pounded it on the ground. "It barely wiggles, let alone breaks. I can burn a hole in the large end. It will easily support the axe head," Jendrin said while examining the limb. "I will burn off the short end when we return to the kitchen. Interested in joining me at the obsidian flow to find a suitable piece to build a knife?" Jendrin asked.

"Yes," Latel said. "There may be several slices left that will work, or you can create your own," Latel said.

They walked back through the village, greeting villagers as they walked. Jendrin placed one end of the ironwood stick in the fire to burn off one end. The next stopped at Latel's hut to retrieve a long piece of leather. Walking past the companion's hut, they climbed the lava ridge to the obsidian flow.

"Many others have used this flow to create their slicing tools," Latel said. "There are some good slices here already, or you can slice a rock for yourself," he said, pointing in different directions. "Have you made a knife before?"

"I don't think so," Jendrin answered after a moment. "I generally understand how to do it."

Latel pointed to a nearby flat rock under a tree.

"Let's sit under the tree and start knapping it," Latel suggested. "I recommend you make a cutting knife about half the length and width of your hand to allow you to sharpen it repeatedly. There will be a lot of glass shards from the knapping. Do all that work here, not in the village where someone may get cut on a shard. You will ruin many pieces, so don't worry when it cracks and falls apart as you learn."

Latel handed the leather piece to Jendrin as he sat on the rock.

"Put this piece of leather over your leg to keep the shards away from your leg as you work," Latel said. "Use a palm-sized rounded rock to strike the obsidian at an angle and flake away the rock you don't want."

Jendrin spent half a sun cycle knapping and turning the obsidian into pebbles. Latel stayed with him to suggest how he could improve his striking technique. Slowly, obsidian pieces remained whole and gained some sharp edges.

"Good start," Latel said. "You can continue your work on your own. Let's return to the village for lunch."

Jendrin and Latel returned to the trio's hut, where Jendrin had retrieved the group's bowls. Before leaving the hut, he added some wood to the fire.

"I will get my bowl and join you in the kitchen," Latel said, walking toward his hut. Jendrin continued to the kitchen, setting the bowls on a table. He examined his axe limb and bamboo pipe in the fire.

"Are those your trees in my work fire?" Mirtha asked, glaring at him. Jendrin stopped, realizing he had put both pieces in a spot that interfered with her work.

"My apologies, Mirtha," Jendrin said, pulling both out of the fire. "I should have asked if I might use your fire," he said, looking at Mirtha.

"Yes, you should," Mirtha said, her expression softening. "If you are finished playing with my fire, I have to finish lunch," she said, lifting covers from two pots. Another cook added the freshly chopped vegetables Jendrin had brought to each cooking pot.

"Is there a place I could burn off the ends of these pieces without getting in the way?" Jendrin asked.

"On the other side of the fire toward the wood pile," Mirtha replied. "No one walks on that side," she said as she checked other pots.

"Thank you," Jendrin replied, placing both pieces on the other side of the fire. "I tend to forget how I impact others' work when doing my projects," he told Latel sheepishly.

"Jendrin, would you gather drinking water?" One of the cooks asked. Jendrin smiled, picked up the pot, and headed to the creek. He

137

followed a trail to the top of the bank. A small waterfall created an ideal filling spot. Looking first for any wolves in the area, he filled the water jug and walked back to the kitchen area. Latel was examining the pieces burning in the fire.

"It has a long way to go," Latel said.

"I will check it later before someone throws the whole thing into the fire'" Jendrin replied with a grin. He looked up to see Throc and Maylore entering the kitchen area. Maylore looked fatigued as Jendrin walked to meet him.

"Are you all right, Maylore?" Jendrin asked.

"Yes," Maylore replied, smiling at him. "I'm just tired. Is the soup on?"

"I believe it is," Jendrin replied, following Maylore to a table, ready to assist if needed. Maylore sat at the table as the others joined him.

Airalee and Marisa finished sorting the herbs after Mirtha left the hut. They found just a few items to toss.

"We will tie these herbs into small bundles and store them in the drying rack," Marisa said. They were tying bundles when they heard a commotion outside. Mirtha was unhappy with someone about the cook fire. They decided they did not need to see what was causing the stir and continued tying. Placing items into baskets, they left the hut for the storage area. The storage hut had several matching items already drying as they added new bunches to the racks. They finished racking the fresh herbs and gathered the empty baskets to leave.

"I will get my bowl and join you at a table," Marisa said, starting toward her hut. Airalee nodded and returned all the baskets to Mirtha's hut. Airalee walked to the kitchen and noticed the growing number of villagers gathering there. She saw Jendrin, Maylore, Throc, and Latel near one of the tables.

"Hi, Dad, hero, Latel, Throc," she said as she approached. "Shall we eat?" They all greeted her unanimously as they stood to fill their bowls. Maylore stood with a wobble, which Airalee noticed.

"Dad, do you not feel well?" Airalee asked.

"Just tired," Maylore replied. "I need to teach you that my name is Maylore," he said, smiling at her. She smiled back at him without indicating she was committing to a change. Jendrin gave Airalee her bowl, and the group filled theirs with the rest of the villagers. Marisa returned and joined the group after filling her bowl. They sat together, discussing village life before retiring to their huts.

Maylore took the afternoon to bathe and rest. Airalee considered how to write a journal of plants and mushrooms as she planted potatoes in her new garden. Jendrin removed his wood pieces from the cookfire and returned to work on his knives.

Rendal decided to visit each guide individually instead of waiting for them to gather that night.

"Is all well with Jendrin?" Rendal asked as he stopped Latel.

"Yes, Beacon," Latel said. "He is in the process of making his tools and beginning the water pipe."

"Nothing seemed out of the ordinary?" Rendal asked.

"No," Latel replied, "Marisa and I ate lunch with them. They only seemed interested in fitting into village life. Jendrin has a more wanderlust spirit but still wants to stay."

"Excellent," Rendal replied, "I will have good tidings to report to the council tomorrow. Thank you, Latel," he said as he left to search for Marisa.

"Marisa," Rendal said, finding her talking with a neighbor. "May I speak with you?"

"Of course, Beacon," Marisa said, excusing herself from her neighbor.

"Is Airalee doing well?" Rendal asked.

"Yes, Beacon," Marisa replied. "She joined Mirtha and me as we gathered herbs and greens today. She found a root the pigs eat, which she said was a potato. Mirtha allowed her to collect it but banned it from our food. She told Airalee to eat it for a month, and she would consider it if it didn't kill her."

"Wise choice," Rendal said. "Anything else that seemed out of the ordinary?"

"Nothing, Beacon," Marisa said.

"Throc and I spent the day with Maylore," Rendal told her. "I know what he was doing. Throc told me Maylore seemed tired at lunch, but nothing else seemed suspicious. Thank you, Marisa," he said as he walked away.

Chapter 10 - Practice Practice Practice

Ten sunrises had passed, and the companions continued their morning routine. The first to rise visited the restroom and gathered wood for the hut's fire. The second person collected beans and water, while the third set the table and ensured breakfast was warming before heading to the restroom. Jendrin and Maylore bathed on alternating days after breakfast. Airalee preferred to bathe at night when the pool was empty.

Rendal had paused the village work schedules since the storehouses were full. Marisa, Throc, and Latel visited the companions daily to help them adjust and monitor for potential problems. The companions had several sunrises to prepare for their new life in Olona.

Jendrin created several knife blanks and many more shattered pieces. The ironwood branch had burned through in the kitchen fire, and several sections of the bamboo water pipe were also burned. He used coals from the fire to burn a hole through the large end for a future axe head to fit into.

Airalee started an herb notebook using berry ink and the papery skin of the breadfruit tree. She maintained her new potato garden and added a few greens she liked. Airalee noticed that Maylore seemed to be wrestling with something he kept to himself. She grew concerned about Maylore's refusal to listen to her concerns.

"I am fine, Airalee," Maylore would say. "I am considering new things, which takes a lot out of me, especially as I am getting older."

Airalee looked at him sideways before deciding not to pursue it with him but to talk with Marisa about it.

A knock on the door drew their attention. Airalee opened the door to find Throc standing there.

"Good morning," Throc said with a slight bow. "The Beacon requests Maylore join him this morning."

"Good morning, Throc," Maylore said, approaching the door. "Let's see what he wants. Goodbye, all," he said as he left.

"Goodbye, Dad," Airalee said as she and Jendrin waved. Maylore had accepted her calling him dad but still found it odd.

He followed Throc to Rendal's hut. Rendal met him at the door and bid him to enter and sit in a chair.

"We have not met in some time since I have been busy with travelers, council duties, and trying to understand researching notes," Rendal said. "I assure you have spent some time working with the blue energy?"

"Yes," Maylore replied, "several times a day."

"Excellent," Rendal replied. "I would like to continue our discussion of energies and portals," Rendal said.

"I have been considering the results of our last meeting," Maylore said. "I am not sure I am ready to research it further."

"I understand," Rendal replied. "We are only interested in determining what ability you may have."

"I would prefer to join you and Throc in lore and treaties," Maylore replied.

"You will have that when the council fully accepts you," Rendal said. "The task of joining Throc and me in negotiations with other villages and traders will be there. Research of any ability would be a secondary task. We can work on this secondary task until the council approves you to assist us with treaties."

"All right," Maylore said, resignation coming to his face. "What ability do you think I may have?"

"I would like to know the strength of your ability and if you can detect an ability in others," Rendal said.

"What do we need to do?" Maylore asked.

"It is a tradition," Rendal said, "that the Beacon evaluates potential villagers for any ability they may have. Finding those with possible skills is an advantage to you and the village. There are very few on Almora who have any ability. We would keep any ability you have a secret."

"Why keep it a secret?" Maylore asked. "I found it difficult not to discuss it with my companions already."

"We believe there is a spy among us looking for those with any ability," Rendal said. "You do not know your companions' backgrounds. They were strangers to you until recently. I suggest you keep this a secret for now. The future may prove they are trustworthy and potentially good members of Olona."

"I do not consider them strangers," Maylore said. "It is true I have not known them very long. I do have faith in both of them, however."

"Excellent," Rendal replied. "I find that refreshing. I hope to develop the same faith. Shall we continue?"

"Yes," Maylore replied, looking resigned.

"Throc and I have been studying the ability evaluation notes left to us by the original sorcerer," Rendal said.

"Is that Gilriel you spoke of before?" Maylore asked.

"No," Rendal replied, "Parthwen developed these notes long ago. I do not know if they are correct. I read what he wrote."

"Let's begin," Maylore said.

"All people have seven major portals," Rendal said, reading the text. "Each portal may have several smaller portals. Some portals have a dome over them, which allows the person to use power within the portal. We understand several portals and how they connect, but not what all portals do. Most people do not know about their portals, and even fewer can consciously use them. A person's conscious recognition of a portal may occur spontaneously or through using certain mushrooms. When a portal first opens, it sounds like a person's ears popping."

Looking up from the text, Rendal asked, "Did you hear a popping noise?"

"No," Maylore replied. "I may not have noticed anyway since the planet energy absorbed my attention."

"I am going to skip down to sections that may pertain to you," Rendal said, looking down and resuming reading. "Almora's energy is not the only energy one can use. Subjects may draw energy from fires, water, wind, and twin suns. Most subjects are limited to one or two sources."

Looking up, Rendal pointed to a water bowl sitting on his table. "I do not know if it means moving water, hot water, or what kind of water. Try collecting energy from the water."

Maylore turned to the water bowl and drew it over to him. He concentrated on finding the water's energy, asking it to flow along his fingers. He used the same techniques he used for ground energy, but after some time, nothing occurred. Maylore realized his ears were closed to any sound around him. He consciously reopened his ears to listen. He continued to ask for energy from the water, but nothing appeared.

"Maylore, Do you see anything?" Rendal asked.

"I do not see a thing," Maylore replied. "I have not concentrated very long. Perhaps it takes more time."

"You have been staring at the bowl long enough," Rendal said. "I should have stopped you sooner." Pointing to the fireplace, Rendal said, "Let's try fire. Look at the fire in the fireplace. Use the same technique you used for Almora's energy and try to pull the fire's energy to you."

Maylore moved his chair nearer the fire. He tried to pull the energy up his leg. The fire quivered slightly, and Maylore saw a different energy move from the fire to his foot. This energy was clear and moved quickly but did not burn his foot. He thought he heard a soft murmur from the clear energy as it progressed. Maylore tried to move closer to the sound to try and listen to what it might be whispering. A hand grabbed his shoulder as he moved.

"Maylore! Enough for now!" the Beacon said, pulling him back from the fire. "My guess is you saw the fire energy."

"I believe so," Maylore replied, his head feeling hot. "It was clear and seemed to whisper something. I could not understand what it whispered or get it to flow past my toes," he replied, feeling a little dizzy.

"Beacon," Throc said before Rendal raised a hand for him to stop.

"Perhaps you have more ability than I thought, Maylore," he said. "You appear to be dizzy. We will stop for today and continue another day. Lunchtime is approaching, and you should eat and then rest for a few hours. Throc will ask you to do it another day. Can you walk?" Maylore stood a little shaky, but it quickly passed.

"Yes, Beacon, thank you," he said.

"Excellent. Get some food and rest, then we will see you again." Rendal said. Maylore nodded to them as he pushed past the door, looking for lunch.

"Still think he is a spy, Throc?" Rendal said to Throc after a few moments.

"No, Beacon," Throc replied. "We must report this to the master that he can use the energies, or we may be the next to go missing."

"I know you follow his instructions, but I am wary of the master's intentions. We will keep Maylore's secret." Rendal said. "Let's see how much of any ability Maylore has before we do any reporting. He may only see the energy, not use it."

"Yes, Beacon," Throc said, nodding.

Airalee

Airalee wandered to the food storage hut, where she knew Marisa would be working. After exchanging greetings, Airalee grew more serious.

"Maylore seems more tired these last few days," Airalee said. "He seems to start each day well but is tired after training with the Beacon. He does not say what training he is doing, but I worry it is wearing him down. Do you know what training he might be doing?"

"I do not know, Airalee," Marisa said. "He is training with Throc and Rendal on treaties, village law, and other agreements. Perhaps it is wearing him down."

"Perhaps," Airalee replied. "I was hoping we had something to help him recover quicker."

"We could ask Kai if she can help," Marisa suggested.

"It would be nice if she can help," Airalee said.

"She will probably say he needs to go outside and eat more often," Marisa said. "I will not second-guess her. She is experienced in health matters and worth listening to."

"I am still hoping to work closer with her as an apprentice," Airalee said. "I assume she tends to the whole village."

"Yes," Marisa replied. "She tends to our village and helps other villages when asked. Most of her healing centers on pains, cuts, scrapes, and a few broken bones. She also delivers babies and makes our pregnancy prevention medication. I use her medicine and have not been pregnant yet. My baby chamber still stirs each period, reminding me it is ready for a child. I am not yet ready for it to be filled. Not yet, anyway," Marisa said, grinning.

"Well, I don't need it," Airalee said. "Living with dad, an adopted brother, and a strong club should keep me safe," she sighed. Marisa laughed at Airalee, assuming she was joking. Marisa quieted, seeing Airalee was serious.

"Help me finish searching for rotted items," Marisa said, changing the subject. "We will both visit her."

Kai was looking through her medicinal herbs and mushrooms when Marisa and Airalee knocked on her door. "Enter," she called, not looking toward the door.

"Greetings, Kai," Marisa said as they entered.

"Marisa and Airalee," Kai said. "What brings you to my home?" Kai asked, turning toward the door. Kai's young apprentice appeared from behind her.

"Gilda!" Marisa exclaimed, "Are you working with Kai now?"

"Yes, I turned 15 and was allowed to help someone. I asked Kai if I could assist her," Gilda said. Kai nodded and pointed to the chairs around her table.

"Welcome to you both," Kai said, inviting them to sit at her table. "Are you girls feeling well?" she asked, sitting in one of the chairs.

"Yes, thank you," Airalee said, sitting down.

"I am well, too," Marisa said. "Airalee asked a question I thought best answered by you."

"Yes, I was hoping you could help me with a problem," Airalee said.

"I will try," Kai replied. "Let me guess your situation. You are living in a large hut with two men. Do you need a pregnancy preventer?" Kai asked.

The question knocked Airalee back a bit before she regained her composure. "Oh, no, not that!" she said, red-faced.

"I do not judge you," Kai replied with a smile. "It appears I guessed poorly. How might I be able to help?"

Marisa was grinning as Airalee formed her question.

"Maylore is fatigued later in the day," Airalee said. "I was hoping you had something to help him recover quicker."

Kai studied her a moment. "Maylore is the older man, I believe," Kai replied. Airalee nodded. "He is probably too old to keep pace with you. I can make a potion to enhance his libido if you wish," Kai said, a grin growing on her face.

Airalee felt a blast of heat hit her face, but she kept her composure.

"No, Kai," Airalee said. "I treat him like he was my dad, not anything else. He has become more than just a traveling companion, but not that. Before you ask, Jendrin is a mild irritant but an adopted brother. He is nothing else," she said.

Kai retained her smile.

"Does Maylore eat, drink, and stretch every few hours?" Kai asked.

Airalee looked at Marisa.

"I do not think so," Airalee said.

"Since you are concerned about him," Kai said, "fill a bowl of bean soup, vegetables, and simple water for him every few hours. Then, push him out the door for a few minutes of fresh air. I can make a drink to help with fatigue if you wish. I even have all the herbs I need for it. Sit here while we make it," she said, turning to Gilda. "Gilda, pick out some Holy Basil, Ginseng, and Ashwagandha for me."

Marisa was still grinning at Airalee as Gilda started gathering items.

"You were right, Marisa," Airalee said, ignoring Marisa's smile. "Let's see what she comes up with."

Gilda returned, giving the herbs to Kai. Kai verified they were the correct items and then measured each into the grinding dish. Airalee felt she recognized each of the herbs but could not determine why.

"Gilda, please rough grind these," Kai said, passing the herbs to Gilda. Gilda ground the mixture and poured it into a small clay pot. "Thank you, Gilda," she said, turning to Airalee, "There should be enough for a week's worth of tea. Make a large pot after he finishes a day or for dinner. It will help him feel stronger and sleep better, too."

"Thank you, Kai and Gilda," Airalee said. "I will start using this tonight."

"Kai," Marisa said. "Mirtha asked if you needed supplies; we could gather for you."

"I could use more ginseng and peppermint," Kai replied. "The Beacon was looking for blue-spotted mushrooms a few days ago. Gilda and I did not find any in our storage area. We could use those if you can find them."

"I saw a few of those mushrooms on our last gathering trip," Airalee said. "I believe I can find them again."

"I am sure the Beacon would appreciate it if you could," Kai said.

"I will look the next time we go into the meadow," Airalee said.

"Good," Kai replied as Marisa and Airalee turned to leave. "Airalee, please return my pot when it is empty."

"I will, thank you, Kai," Airalee said as they left the hut.

Jendrin

Latel walked to the obsidian flow to find Jendrin busy knapping his knives.

"Jendrin, I see you may have finished your knife blade," Latel said, standing nearby.

"Yes, very close," Jendrin replied. "I am knapping the end of the blade to create slots for sinew to fit in. I have already broken off several blades doing this, but I think I can finish it now," Jendrin said as he held up the irregularly shaped blade.

"I think that will work," Latel said. "It looks good. I have fashioned a handle for you from a spare wooden blank I had. I also brought some sinew I saved from making clothes and knives. Are you ready to put your blade into a handle?"

"Yes," Jendrin said, smiling up at Latel. "I was thinking about making a handle. Your handle will shortcut the process. Thank you, Latel," he said, reaching for the wooden handle. One end of the handle had a slot cut to hold the blade. The blade had a ring cut around the handle to hold the ligament and allow tightening of the blade onto the handle.

"I will create a couple of replacements for you since I need a few for my knives," Latel said. He gave Jendrin a scrap of leather to wrap around the knife handle. Jendrin smiled, satisfied with his first knife.

"We need to collect a few pieces of flint to create my ax," Jendrin said as he stood up.

"That is what I thought we would do today," Latel replied. "I created several knife sheaths in the past. I brought one for you," he said, passing the sheath to Jendrin.

"Thank you again," Jendrin replied, putting the new knife into the sheath. Jendrin and Latel walked back to the companions' hut as Airalee and Marisa approached.

"Finish your knife, hero?" Airalee asked as she approached. Jendrin pulled his knife from his pocket.

"As a matter of fact, yes," Jendrin said, showing her the knife.

"Great," Airalee said, raising her hands in mock surprise. "A man with a knife is what I need," she finished with a grin. Turning serious, she added, "I am worried about Maylore, Jendrin. He seems very tired in the evening. He sometimes sits in the hut, mumbling to himself. Kai says we need to give him food and water and force him to take to the outdoors from time to time. Would you help me do that?" Jendrin could see she was serious, so he agreed to help. "We can start tonight," Airalee said.

"Latel and I are going to a flint deposit so I can make an ax head," Jendrin said.

"Marisa and I will see to Maylore," Airalee said, starting toward the kitchen. "I will see you tonight," she said.

"Lead the way, Latel," Jendrin said.

"We will go through the bamboo forest to the river," Latel said as he started walking. "We will pass by the mud pit to the stone slope," Latel said, pointing in a general direction. Entering the bamboo stand, Jendrin kept his eyes open for downed bamboo that may work for the piping. Many were split or too short to be helpful.

"Here is one that may work," Jendrin said, picking up a section. "This one has a curve that would help change the direction of the water. I will set it aside and collect it later."

They continued through the forest, walking along the edge that skirted the meadow. They passed the mud pits, arriving at the rockslides. The first rocks Jendrin found were disappointing shale. It crumbled too quickly when picked up. They searched farther along the hill.

"There," Jendrin said, pointing up the hill. "The black-colored rock is what we want," he said, moving toward it. A large bank of flint stuck out of the hillside in front of them. "Let's see if we can find some pieces I can use for an ax head," Jendrin said, searching through the rock rubble. Many were too small, some too big. Gathering a few of the larger ones, Jendrin used his new cleaving skills to slice off the large ones using a smaller piece. Several cleaves created sharp pieces, but he wanted something else. "Here is one that is solid with no cracks in it," he said, hefting the rock. "This section also looks good. Would you mind carrying one?" he asked Latel. Latel agreed and picked up the wedge-shaped rock. "I hear fast-running water nearby," Jendrin said. "May we see it?" he asked Latel.

"This way," Latel said, going toward the river. "We may see bandits on the other side. I prefer they did not see us," Latel said as they approached brush alongside the roaring river. Pushing aside the brush, they saw three women on the other bank. Two stood while the third was bent over, collecting something from the river. "One captive is a Tocor. The second is a human I don't recognize. I believe the third is Calel from our village," Latel said in amazement. "She disappeared several seasons ago. I am pleased she is alive and will inform her mother." Frowning, he added, "She may be too old for the bandits," he said. Calel stood up, showing she was near-term pregnant. "Oh, she will be returned to us soon," Latel said. "I will tell Kai to expect Calel and to warn her of her condition."

"What happened to her?" Jendrin finally asked.

"Calel disappeared while collecting with other villagers," Latel said. "When we searched for her, we found a torn cloak and a basket but no sign of her. We guessed she was killed since there was blood on the nearby bushes. It appears the bandits abducted her after a fight," Latel said, lowering the branch and heading back toward the meadow. "Another reason for Olona to consider a militia," Jendrin said.

"Let's return to the village," Latel said.

Airalee and Marisa found Maylore sitting in the kitchen, eating soup.

"Dad, are you doing well?" Airalee asked as they approached.

"Yes, thank you," Maylore replied, looking up. "It was a tiring session this morning, but I will recover," he said with a smile.

"Are they using you as a punching bag?" Airalee asked.

"No, it's mental things they asked me not to discuss," Maylore replied. "Maybe I've said too much already. I'm poor at keeping things from people."

"I worry about you, Dad," Airalee said.

"Dear girl, no need to worry about this old man," Maylore said with a chuckle.

"You're not old," Airalee said.

"Perhaps not. I just feel older at times," Maylore replied.

"Marisa and I visited Kai today," Airalee said. "She suggested you develop regular eating, drinking, resting, and outside time."

"That sounds like good advice to me," Maylore replied. "I advise you not to worry about me."

"All right," Airalee said. "Marisa and I are going mushroom hunting. We'll be back later."

"Thank you, Airalee," Maylore replied. "I'm going back to the hut to rest."

"We should check with Kai before we go into the forest," Marisa said. "She likes to know where we go if we are needed."

They knocked on Kai's door, and Gilda opened it. "We are going into the meadow to find the blue-spotted mushrooms Airalee saw," Marisa said.

"May I join them?" Gilda asked Kai.

Kai silently considered for several moments before answering.

"Stay here, Gilda," Kai said. "You will assist me in verifying the mushrooms when they return." Gilda nodded and listened to their talk.

"The mushrooms were near the pigs," Airalee said. "It shouldn't take long to do this."

"If you see any other colored mushrooms," Kai said, "gather one of each, using a stick to gather them. Don't take them all, and put them in a separate pot," she added, passing Marisa an empty pot. "Put the blue-spotted ones in this pot," she said, giving another pot to Airalee. "The blue-spotted ones are not poisonous but will make you crazy if eaten raw," she said with a severe smile. Both women smiled and left the hut.

The two women started toward the meadow, passing Levyna's garden and the bamboo forest before entering it. Airalee spotted some Holy Basil, while Marisa found some Ginseng near the bank leading up to the creek. They also searched for any mushrooms that may be growing. Airalee spotted a familiar rotting tree and went to investigate it. The sight of a blue-spotted mushroom caused a sudden flash of recognition in her mind. The blue stone in her pocket felt warm as she bent to examine the mushroom.

"This is a psychedelic mushroom," she said, her mind swirling a little as she thought about it. "People use it in small amounts to open their minds to others and themselves," she said without thinking. She reached into her pocket to find the blue stone was indeed warm.

"How do you know that?" Marisa asked.

"I don't know," Airalee said. "It just came to me when I saw these mushrooms this time," Airalee said. "The red one is toxic and causes a coma lasting for days. It's deadly if you consume too much," she said, pointing to the solid red mushroom.

A noisy commotion started behind them as the women discussed the mushrooms. They saw a large, tusked boar attacking two smaller pigs. Snorting and huffing, the tusked boar hit one of the smaller pigs with his snout, sending him flying. Whirling around, he sank a tusk into the other pig and tossed it into the air. The pig sailed in their direction, landing with a heavy thud. The boar noticed the two women and started in their direction.

154

"Run to the tree!" came a voice from up the meadow. Both women ran back toward nearby trees.

Jendrin and Latel were well into the meadow when they saw Airalee and Marisa discussing something and the sudden boar altercation. Jendrin yelled as the two men started toward the boar. The boar gave chase as the two women ran. A small arrow suddenly shot down from the trees, hitting the boar in the rear. The boar whirled to see what was attacking him. Seeing only Jendrin and Latel, it started in their direction. The two men halted their advance and prepared to run to a tree when another arrow struck the pig's rear. The pig whirled again, seeking its attacker. The boar circled several times before deciding to flee. It finally turned back toward the creek and ran with its tail high in the air. Jendrin felt relief and looked into the trees but did not see anyone with a bow. Latel was eyeing the gored pig a short distance from them.

"Let's gather the pig before the blood wolves arrive," Latel said, looking toward Jendrin. Realizing Jendrin was looking for their savior, he said, "One or more of the sentinels shot the pig. You won't see them. We were lucky they were watching us or perhaps you. Otherwise, we may be running for a tree. Let's carry that pig back to the village for our dinners," Latel said, moving toward the pig.

"Looks like the boar killed both smaller pigs," Jendrin said. "This one through the middle and that one through the neck." A wolf's howl broke the quiet of the meadow, followed by several others joining in.

"Quickly," Latel said, "grab the front legs while I take the rear,"

"Won't the wolves follow us?" Jendrin asked, gathering the front legs.

"If we leave one, the wolves will eat it and leave us," Latel said. The men took off at a jog. The pig did not slow the two men, weighing just over one stone. They could hear the howling as the wolves got closer. They jogged to where Airalee and Marisa stood, watching them.

155

"You got the boar?" Airalee asked as they approached. "It looked much bigger than that," she added.

"No, this is one it killed," Latel replied. "That boar weighed about eight stone. We are fortunate that the sentinel's arrows scared it away. Otherwise, we would all be sitting in a tree right now."

"Thank you, sentinel!" Airalee said, looking into the trees. A single IB bird call echoed out from an indistinct source in the forest. "Well, I will take that as you are welcome," she said.

Examining the pig, Latel noted that a small amount of blood still dripped. "We must pack the neck with mud to prevent blood from seeping out. We don't want the wolves to follow us," Latel said. The two men quickly packed the neck with mud. "They will follow the blood here and probably stop since there won't be any more blood to follow."

"Probably?" Airalee questioned.

"Yes," Latel answered, picking up the hind legs again. "Let's go," he said to Jendrin. Jendrin grabbed the front legs, and they all jogged back toward the village.

CHAPTER 11 - NEW LESSONS

Arriving in the village, Latel stopped outside a creek-side hut Jendrin had not noticed before.

"Jendrin and I will work with Dirdin to cut up this pig," Latel said, looking at Airalee and Marisa. You two are welcome to join if you wish."

"No, thank you," Marisa said, raising both hands. "We have duties to attend to with Kai and Mirtha," Marisa replied. "I don't mean to speak for you, Airalee. Are you staying?"

"I believe we are needed elsewhere," Airalee replied, nodding. The two women started toward Kai's hut as Latel opened the door with his foot. The room contained a concave table and ropes strung through the ceiling joists. Several buckets lined the walls, some filled with water.

"If you clean off the dirt and wash the pig, I will find Dirdin," Latel said. "Dirdin is our lead butcher and tanner," he remarked as they placed the pig in the center of the table.

"Will do," Jendrin said, picking up a water-filled bucket. As Latel was leaving, he started cleaning the dirt off the pig. Water ran down the table and out the side of the hut along a channel made of river rock. Examining the table, he saw short ropes attached to the table and long ropes strung above. Large sea sponges lay in each bucket he used to clean off the pig. Jendrin needed more water and grabbed several buckets to refill them. The trip to the creek was short, with the hut near the stream. Filling two buckets, he started back up the bank to the hut. Latel was approaching the hut with a large man Jendrin did not know. Jendrin had seen him several times but did not know what he did in the village.

"This is Dirdin," Latel said as he approached. "Dirdin, this is Jendrin. He is one of our new arrivals," he said, opening the door.

Dirdin nodded to Jendrin and entered the hut. "Have you done this before, Jendrin?" Dirdin asked.

"No," Jendrin replied. "Time to learn another skill."

Dirdin moved to the head of the table, inspecting the pig.

"This should be easy since it is a small pig," Dirdin said, pulling out his knife.

"I asked Dirdin to help since he made a special knife with a hook with a sharp edge to cut the hide," Latel said. "It is duller to separate the hide from the meat."

"Sometimes it is easier to pull the hide off than use the knife," Dirdin said. Dirdin used a slight cut around each leg, then used the hook end to cut along the hide to the neck and down the other leg. Sliding the knife under the skin, he pulled the front section down to the chest. "Let's rope him up," Dirdin said. They tied each leg to separate ropes hanging from the rafters. Hauling up the pig, Dirdin cut and pulled down the skin on the backside. Hauling the pig off the table, they tied the short ropes to each leg to prevent the carcass from swinging as he cut.

"This should be a nice hide for clothing once we process it," he said, putting the hide into one of the buckets. "Get your knives out, men. Let's chop him up for dinner," he said, looking at the other two. "Jendrin, you cut through here," Dirdin said, showing him how to cut. "Then cut over here. Latel, you do the other leg," he said, pointing at the other leg. The three men finished cutting up the pig quickly under Dirdin's guidance. "I will take the hide and start processing it," Dirdin said. "Join me in a few days, and I can show you how to process it," he said, looking at Jendrin.

"Jendrin has only been given guided status," Latel said. "I anticipate he will achieve accepted status soon."

"When he is accepted, you can join our group," Dirdin said.

"I will be glad to do that," Jendrin replied. Dirdin took the bucket with the hide and bid them a good day. "I am surprised I have not met him before."

"We were not allowed to visit Dirdin since he uses a process the village considers a secret," Latel said. "The council wishes to keep village secrets from non-members. I believe the council will soon grant you accepted status. Then we can discuss the village secret processes."

"They still think I am a spy?" Jendrin said with a sour look.

"The council is cautious," Latel said. "At times, they see spies under every rock."

"Why are they so cautious?" Jendrin asked.

"The village was infiltrated by a spy in the past posing as a refugee. He caused harm to our village. That was long ago, but the council has a long memory. They will likely approve the three of you before the hide is ready for processing."

"We are not spies," Jendrin said, looking directly at Latel.

"Are you sure of your companions?" Latel asked.

"I am," Jendrin affirmed.

"I believe it is true," Latel said. "We should visit with Mirtha next," Latel noted, changing the subject. "Mirtha will want to cook some meat and salt the rest for storage."

Airalee

Airalee and Marisa tapped on Kai's door.

"Come in, you two," Kai said. "Sit." she directed, pointing at two chairs. "Gilda and I were discussing medicinal herbs when you interrupted us. You can listen in," Kai said, turning back to Gilda. "We were fortunate to get some Stoneseed and Jack root from the traders. You and I can now make more pregnancy preventers in a few sunrises. We will store them in the closed-off area of the storage hut,

159

away from healing herbs." Kai continued sorting more healing herbs they had received or gathered. Airalee's mind suddenly lit up when she saw what they had.

"You have some Calendula, Meadow Sweet, Witch Hazel, and Dang Gui," Airalee said. She realized she had spoken out of turn and had no idea where the names came from.

"That's correct," Kai said, looking at her askance. I did not know you knew about the healing herbs."

"I don't," Airalee replied, shaking her head. "The names sprang into my mind," she said, looking perplexed. The blue stone was warm again as she reached into her pocket to check it.

A short silence filled the room before Marisa spoke.

"Just like you knew about those mushrooms we found?" Marisa queried.

"Yes," Airalee said, "that was strange too," as she watched three faces stare at her. "Where did you find these medicinal herbs?" Airalee asked, attempting to change their focus to the herbs. Gilda started to answer when Kai held up her hand to stop her.

"Perhaps we will discuss that someday, but not today," Kai said. Airalee nodded in acceptance. "Well then, apparently, you found a few things for me?"

"Yes," Marisa said, placing the basket down. "Two blue spotted mushrooms and a red mushroom, which Airalee says is dangerous. We would have gathered others, but there was a wild boar fight. The boar killed two small pigs and then charged at us. A sentinel wounded the boar twice with arrows, causing it to run off. Jendrin and Latel happened to be in the meadow and brought one pig back to the village."

"That is quite a tale," Kai said, leaning back in her chair. Turning to Airalee, Kai asked, "Tell me what you think the red mushroom does."

"I don't remember the name," Airalee said. "If eaten, it causes a coma that lasts for days. If they get too much, it is deadly."

"Interesting," Kai replied. "I was trained to leave them be. The one with blue spots Gilriel and Rendal use for reasons I don't care to understand. Leave the basket here. Gilda and I will take care of them. Thank you both." Airalee and Marisa turned to leave, and Kai added, "Airalee, I see no need to wait for the council's approval since you know what these items are. I want you to join Gilda and me in collecting mushrooms and medicinal herbs someday."

"Thank you, Kai, I would be glad to," Airalee said.

"Good. It will be sometime before Gilda and I go again, but I will find you," Kai said, returning to her sorting. Marisa and Airalee left, heading for the companion's hut.

Maylore was sitting by a small cooking fire when Airalee and Marisa entered the hut. Noting their arrival, he continued to concentrate without looking up. Finishing his latest attempted energy pull, he turned to the two women.

"I see you have returned," Maylore said, standing up. "I was worried I wouldn't get Kai's tea," he said, grinning at them.

"Tea?" Airalee said. "I will make some now. We were delayed by running from a boar," Airalee told him.

"Boar?" he questioned. "The kind with tusks?"

"That's the kind," Airalee replied. "Lucky for us, a sentinel intervened. Otherwise, we would have all been climbing trees," she said.

"All?" Maylore asked.

"Yes, Jendrin and Latel were there too," Marisa said.

"Oh my. Glad I wasn't there," Maylore replied. "Tree climbing is not a strength anymore at my age. Is there more to this story, or do I have to guess," Maylore continued.

"A little more," Airalee said, smiling. "The boar killed two small pigs. Jendrin and Latel got one before the blood wolves arrived. They brought it back to the village and are preparing it to become our dinners."

"That sounds good. Don't remember eating pig," Maylore said, moving to the table. "Shall we have some tea?" Airalee finished making the tea and poured a cup for each person. The three discussed the weather, gathering activities, and gossip about minor village activities.

"What have you been doing today, Maylore?" Marisa asked.

"I had assumed I would start learning the history and lore of the area," Maylore said. "It appears my interests will be delayed."

"What did he want you to do instead?" Airalee asked.

"The Beacon asked me not to discuss it," Maylore replied.

"Does it have something to do with that black rock in his hut?" Airalee asked.

"Yes, the blue rock has something to do with it," Maylore said. "It is mostly mental exercises, but that is all I can say for now."

A knock at the door caused Marisa to open it.

Airalee's face turned to a look of determination.

"Maylore," she started to say as Throc's voice interrupted her from outside.

"The Beacon requests that you join him in his hut, Maylore," Throc said from outside the hut.

Maylore looked at Airalee and smiled. "Saved by the bell," he said, standing up. "I will ask the Beacon if we can discuss it tonight," he told her.

"All right," Airalee replied, "I will take care of the dishes. Marisa and I will gather wood and food for dinner and breakfast."

"Thank you, ladies," he said, rising from the table.

"Lead on, Throc," Maylore said, opening the door.

"I would leave the use of the mushrooms to you, Gilriel," Rendal said as they returned from Kai's hut to his. Fortunately, she found a dried, blue-spotted mushroom while drying the new ones.

"I would prefer not to deal with him or anyone else," Gilriel said as he opened the door.

"I have no skills to assess any possible ability," Rendal said, sitting down.

"You were able to help me long ago," Gilriel replied, sitting across from him. "The master himself tested you."

Rendal leaned on the table with a severe expression on his face. "I believed he may have been trying to get rid of me. The master advised me how to do the assessment using a blue-spotted mushroom. He failed to mention that the mushroom that awoke your ability could kill me."

"That was many seasons ago, Rendal. I believe you can handle it better this time," Gilriel said.

"I think not," Rendal replied. "You have done several assessments since then, finding those with abilities."

"We tested those born here of refugee parents," Gilriel said. "There were a few successes, but some disappeared. I suspect they went insane and died in the wilderness," he added.

"I suspect not," Rendal said, sitting up. "I believe the master may have arranged their disappearance."

"Why would he do that?" Gilriel said after pausing a moment. "Most of them had some energy transference, communication, object movement, or illusion ability, but were many hours of practice from being able to use them effectively. None of them would have become sorcerers."

"I suspect he wanted to get rid of them in case they could develop into sorcerers," Rendal said.

"I agree with you," Gilriel said. "It would be consistent with other mysterious disappearances. The few remaining people with skills have become adept at hiding from him."

"I will not tell him if Maylore is a candidate," Rendal said.

"That would be wise," Gilriel said, smiling. He was silent momentarily before continuing. "Kelkalyn told me the master has killed most of the sorcerers on Almora."

"He has not told me that story," Rendal said. "It is all the more reason to keep Maylore's a secret."

"If there is anything to be kept a secret," Gilriel said, turning to the task. "My only ability is to use a mushroom to see what portals people may have. I have occasionally been able to open a portal. I assume the master uses me to find those in other villages with an ability. I would not be a real threat to him." Gilriel's posture changed from one of confidence to one of doubt. "I should have your suspicions of testing strangers to see if they are spies. I will test Maylore. If he has portals to open, I will help him open what he wishes to use. It could easily take many seasons to develop any ability."

"Excellent," Rendal replied. "How shall we handle his investigation?"

"Maylore is unlikely to handle too much in each session," Gilriel said. "Perhaps I should say I may not be able to handle too much in each session," he said with a smile.

"We need to keep what we learn today a secret," Rendal said. "I will let no one else be privy to what we find."

"Good," Gilriel said. "I believe I will secretly start an investigation of the master using my contacts."

"You must be careful, Gilriel," Rendal said, his expression growing grim, "he is suspicious of all and has many spies of his own."

"Yes, I know," Gilriel said, nodding.

A knock at Rendal's door drew their attention.

"Enter!" Rendal said. Throc entered but stopped in the doorway when he saw Gilriel. Gilriel was wearing his cloth tunic with the orange village slash. He had an additional decoration of a blue radiating star on his left shoulder.

"I brought Maylore as you requested, Beacon," Throc said as he moved aside for Maylore to enter.

"Good, thank you, Throc," Rendal said. "We will meet privately with Maylore so you may have the day for your activities."

"Yes, thank you, Beacon," Throc said, leaving the hut.

"Maylore, this is Gilriel, our local scholar," Rendal said, indicating a chair for Maylore to sit in.

"Gilriel will assist us in a test to determine your abilities," Rendal said.

"Is he a healer?" Maylore asked. "Do you suspect I am diseased or can jump high?"

"No," Gilriel said, cracking a smile. "I assume Rendal discussed portals with you?"

"A little," Maylore replied. "It was very confusing, and I put most of it aside."

"I understand," Gilriel replied. "Most of it is a murky subject to me, too. I have a slight ability to see if people have any portals they could use. I do not know what many of those portals do." he said, looking Maylore in the eyes. "I do understand they can be used differently by each person."

"Oh my," Maylore said, "the adventure continues."

"Indeed," Gilriel replied. "We will see how big an adventure it is."

"I thought I was getting beyond the days of adventure," Maylore said, looking slightly resigned.

"You could be correct," Rendal said. "Please sit while we prepare."

Gilriel noted Maylore's size and pushed a cut of the smaller dried mushroom to him.

"We will each eat one of these dried mushrooms," Gilriel said. The smaller mushroom should be the correct amount for you. I will use the other piece."

"What will this mushroom do?" Maylore asked, examining the mushroom.

"It will open your mind to allow me to see what portals you may have," Gilriel said. "You will sleep and not know what is happening."

"It appears to be a white mushroom with a few blue spots on it," Maylore said, examining the mushroom.

"It will not taste good, but eat it anyway," Gilriel said. "Rendal tells me you may be using one portal. We can see if I can expand it and look for other portals." Gilriel put the mushroom in his mouth and chewed it. Seeing Gilriel had eaten his, Maylore followed his lead.

"There are beds to lie on back here," Rendal said, moving to the back of the hut. "Choose one and lie down," he said, looking at Maylore. Maylore chose one, and Gilriel lay on the other. Rendal moved a small table between the beds and continued. "Place one arm on the table and the other at your side. I will tie one end of this sash to each of you. I will remain here with both of you during this test."

"What is going to happen?" Maylore asked, placing his arm on the table and looking at Gilriel.

"You should not feel anything throughout the test," Gilriel answered. "You may sleep through it or be conscious but find yourself looking inward. You may notice a slight buzzing sensation in your mind as we progress. If I find a portal I can open, you may feel a popping sensation and perhaps a flow of energy as it opens. There are many unknowns, and we will face them if they occur. You will come out of this unharmed but tired." Gilriel finished.

Maylore relaxed, deciding he had to have faith in these two and hoping to wake up alive and well. A short time elapsed before Maylore drifted into a peaceful rest. He felt himself floating in the air, with nothing but blackness around him. He drifted upwards until a wall above him stopped his climb. He could see the ceiling thinning until it burst, and he floated through. He could see a spider web of strings extending in all directions around him. Different colored pulses zipped along those strings in all directions. Maylore marveled at the sight before he attempted to follow one series of pulses to their end. Most ended at a black wall while others bounced back the way they came.

Maylore sensed a change around him. He looked in the direction he thought the disturbance was coming from. A large pulse of energy had entered the area with a blue star appearance to it. It jumped from one string to another, heading in the opposite direction from Maylore. Maylore willed himself to follow the blue spark and found he could move swiftly and efficiently on the strings. He caught up with the blue spark and followed it briefly before it stopped and started spinning in place. A surprised, disembodied voice spoke.

'You are here,' the voice said. 'No one has found me before.' Maylore recognized Gilriel's voice as he continued. 'Perhaps you have the same ability that I do.'

Maylore was still trying to figure out what to say.

'Are you Gilriel?' he simply thought.

'Ah, you can communicate too. Yes, this is I,' Gilriel said. 'You can join me as we check for portals inside your body. Let us first check the port that allows communication,' he said, starting upward. Maylore easily kept up as they traveled along one quiet string. They arrived at its end with a string connected to a dark wall.

'This is the outside of your communication portal.' Gilriel said. 'It has a string to power the portal, but it does not go through the wall into the portal. If I can open it, you may be able to communicate with others. I have heard of someone who can use this portal to examine others without using mushrooms. It may also have uses I don't know about. Do you wish me to open it?" he asked.

Maylore could see what looked like a cut string near the portal.

'Yes,' he thought, unsure of what would happen. One edge of Gilriel's blue spark sharpened into what looked like a knife. It quickly cut the portal to the size of a string. He pressed the loose end of the string into the portal.

'In time, the energy string will grow through the entire portal,' Gilriel said. If you are fortunate, it will open a dome on top you can use for communication and searching.'

Maylore noted that energy was already traveling to the end of the string. Reaching the end, it turned back the other way.

'Let's find the energy transfer port,' Gilriel said. 'Perhaps we can determine what is slowing your gathering its energy. Lastly, we will look for as many other ports as possible before the mushroom wears off.'

Gilriel started back up the string as Maylore followed. They traversed the seemingly endless array of strings, moving from one to another as a string ended. Maylore thought they were moving downward, but he decided there was no up or down here.

'There,' Gilriel said, moving to a new string. 'The red energy on these strings will lead us to our goal.' The red sparks continued on fewer and fewer stings until they merged at a portal wall. Gilriel seemed to be surveying the string's entry into the portal wall. 'The external entry is open. Some kind of dead-looking energy material fills most of the portal. I have seen this in other refugees, and I can not clear it most times.' Gilriel considered if he should even try after so many past failures. 'Let me try anyway,' he said. Gilriel's blue energy formed a knife as he struggled to slice through the blockage. He changed tactics to using a chipping motion at the blockage. He was able to clear some small pieces from the dead particles. 'This will take too much time, I am afraid. Let me try and chip a larger path around the string.' Slowly, he could clear a small area around the existing string. Maylore observed Gilriel's method and decided to try helping. Maylore attempted to create his knife from the spark he was in. The result looked more like a small ice pick than a knife, and he tried it anyway. He chipped outside the area Gilriel had already chipped, creating even smaller pieces but making the portal a little wider. Gilriel reached the end of the portal and saw the energy dome extending outside the portal. He turned to Maylore, saying, 'The channel is mainly blocked, but more energy flows along the string. The energy portal's dome is open so that you can collect or see the energies. The future will tell if your energy transfer improves.'

Moving up the string, Gilriel said, 'The time the mushroom provides us is short. Let's check as many other portals as the time allows.'

Gilriel's spark started moving back up the string. 'We will look for the orange energy this time.' Maylore spotted a flash of orange just above where they started.

'There,' Maylore said. Gilriel changed directions as he saw where Maylore pointed. Traveling along the new string, they reached the end where the orange sparks entered and exited a wall.

'This energy is used only by your body,' Gilriel said. 'It does not have a portal or an accompanying dome to the outside world. I can not do anything with this one. Onward we go. This time, look for green or yellow energy sparks.' Gilriel said as he started again. Sparks of yellow soon filled their view as they continued upward. Yellow sparks entered and exited a portal as they followed the yellow strings to its end.

'There is a portal here, but it does not have an outside portal dome,' Gilriel said. "We can not create a dome, so we move on." They traveled a short distance before spotting green-colored sparks traveling up and down another string. 'Green energy,' Gilriel said as he started following the green sparks. The number of strings carrying the green energy merged into fewer and fewer strings. The strings ended at another wall. 'This is no usable portal here either,' Gilriel said, pausing to think. 'I know of only two more portals. One is light and the other dark blue. Let's see if we can find them,' he said as he started again. They quickly found the light blue energy and followed it to the wall. 'There is a portal here and a dome. There is no energy flowing inside the portal, but I may be able to open a source,' Gilriel said, peering at the string from the outside. Creating his energy knife, he cut the string from the portal and cut a hole in the portal wall. He pushed the string into the portal hole and watched as the portal sealed itself around the string. 'I don't know what this portal does,' Gilriel said. 'You may find out one day,' Gilriel said. 'One more.' Gilriel said, starting again.

The dark blue and light blue sparks seemed to be sharing strings. The dark blue became more prominent as they moved upward. The dark blue sparks congregated at their portal wall as the two arrived. 'This portal is completely sealed,' Gilriel said as they stopped at the wall of the portal. Maylore could see black energy particles stuck to each other, filling the portal and its string. 'I won't be able to help here either,' Gilriel said. 'There may be more portals I am not aware of...' Gilriel started to say before he vanished.

Maylore was briefly mystified before recalling Gilriel telling him they would be thrown out when the mushroom's drug ran out. Maylore decided to see what else he could find before his time ran out. He found he could move faster on the strings than Gilriel. Sparks of different colors, sizes, and speeds were traveling in each direction along the various strings as he moved with them. Maylore spotted what he thought were other portals, only to find they were areas where the strings came close to the wall before continuing somewhere else. Maylore spotted yet another likely portal and started that direction when he felt his energy body disintegrate in all directions. Maylore awoke on the bed to find Rendal watching him from a chair.

"Welcome back, Maylore," he said, offering him a cup of water. "I am pleased the mushroom did not harm you."

Maylore started to sit up, but his head spun, so he laid back down.

"He gave me a mushroom that could harm me?" Maylore thought he said.

Rendal only heard Maylore make grunting noises.

"Gilriel said if you awaken with a spinning head, you were to sleep here tonight." Maylore nodded and turned to the empty bed Gilriel had been in. "Gilriel has done this process many times and has no ill effects. He left a long while ago."

"I was just with him," Maylore thought he said, but Rendal only heard more grunts.

"I will have Throc tell your friends you are staying here tonight," Rendal said. "Throc or I will be here when you awaken tomorrow."

Maylore thought he said thank you, but it came out as another grunt. Maylore closed his eyes and slept.

Council meeting

Rendal met with Marisa, Throc, and Latel inside the council hut.

"Thank you all for joining me," Rendal said. "Have you seen a reason why we should not grant full acceptance to Airalee, Jendrin, and Maylore?".

171

"I have seen no reason not to accept them," Marisa said. "Airalee seems to recognize plants and some of their uses. Mirtha is skeptical of her new foods but will let Airalee and her companions verify they are not poisonous."

"Jendrin continues to work to integrate into village life. I believe he will be a craft leader of some type," Latel said. "He is still interested in forming a village defense group."

"Yes," Rendal said. "I will bring up the idea tonight with the council. It is likely to be a contentious subject. What do you say about Maylore Throc?"

"I believe Maylore is who he claims to be," Throc said. "He will be a welcome steady addition to Olona."

"I agree with you all," Rendal said. "Gilriel examined Maylore's portals today and tells me he is like other refugees he has reviewed. Maylore can potentially use a few portals, but others are blocked or non-existent. The sentinel leader, Olach, had his Tocor following each refugee. Olach reported that they saw no suspicious activity. Do you three vote for full admittance?"

"Yes," they all voiced at once.

"Excellent," Rendal said. "Thank you all. I will meet with the full council tomorrow morning."

CHAPTER 12 - DISCLOSURE

Council Meeting

Rendal asked the council members to gather in the council hut early the following day. As Gilriel entered the hut, all of the members were seated.

"Gilriel is here?" Baruo said, smiling. "This must be an important meeting for our cave dweller to attend." Gilriel ignored him and sat in a chair near Rendal.

"Good, we are all here," Rendal said. "Indeed, this is an important meeting. It is also time we vote on granting full acceptance to Airalee, Jendrin, and Maylore. We have been keeping secrets about our village, and it is time they learned the details of Olona."

"You have finally realized they are no threats to us?" Baruo said, smiling at Rendal.

"They are not a threat," Rendal said, looking at the group. "I did ask you to keep some secrets from them until they passed the agreed upon ten days. I was fearful that the master or other outsiders had planted them as spies. We do not want the locations of our food stores known to others who may take them. We have a crafting process to keep from prying eyes."

"They need to know the bandits steal from us, you mean," Argila said.

"We should reveal to them that the bandits abducted our young," Katiana said.

"They need to learn about the agreements we have with the bandits that keep us safe," Caudra said.

"Yes," Rendal said, "those and others."

"We should inform them where we hide our young when trouble comes. Airalee may decide to have children and must have that knowledge," Avahairiel said.

"Living with two men," Katiana said, "I believe she has already decided to have children."

The council members chuckled with her. Rendal waited for calm to return before he continued.

"There are a few village traditions and other secrets we don't mention to outsiders," Rendal said.

"You mean the traditional Lemidge visit?" Katiana said.

"Yes," Rendal sighed, "that is one. Shall I continue?"

Katiana and the other women smiled at him as he continued.

"Yes," Baruo said, "we all have secrets, Rendal. Outsiders can easily determine most secrets."

"True," Rendal replied. "If they were spies, we needed to determine what information they were looking for. I now believe the newcomers were not looking for information for others. They would have pushed harder to find information and then left Olona."

"Agreed," Baruo said. "We would have missing items or raided by now." The murmur in the room seemed to agree with him.

"My last worry about them," Rendal said, "is the master finding out about villagers who have any ability. We know the master wants to eliminate anyone with a usable ability." The council members murmured agreement and nodded. "Gilriel tested many of the villagers born here in the past," Rendal said. "He found a few who showed potential, but just a few gained use of those abilities."

"The ones I know of decided they did not need them," Avahairiel said.

"Records from the past say some had strong abilities before they lost their minds and disappeared," Baruo said.

"We never saw them again," Caudra said. "I sometimes wonder if the testing caused them to go crazy."

Gilriel sighed but didn't say anything.

Rendal interjected, sensing a battle may occur. "We have tested everyone in the village at some point, and they are still here."

"True," Caudra said, nodding. "My son tested with a small latent ability. He is now 20 seasons old with no ability I know of."

"We want to track down how the master found out about those with abilities," Rendal said. "We are due to test several more villagers. I suggest we keep test results secret to prevent the master from finding out about those with abilities. I propose that the council, Gilriel, and I, and I would be the only ones to know about them. The council will decide if and when the villagers are to be informed. It may allow our villagers to remain hidden from the master."

"Unless the spy is in this group," Katiana said. A short discussion ensued, but all agreed to the idea.

"Good," Rendal said. "We have several villagers past their 15th season and should be tested. We also found one of the new arrivals to be able to use planet and fire energy." The council buzzed before quiet returned.

"Who has this ability?" Nenaias asked.

"Maylore," Rendal replied.

"The older man?" Nenaias said. "He seems too old and calm to be a budding sorcerer."

"We can hope his age brings enough wisdom to avoid destruction," Gilriel said.

"Did the other two have an ability?" Katiana asked.

"We have not tested them yet," Rendal said. Maylore could see the planet's energy on the rock, so we tested him. The other two saw it only as a rock."

"I want to know what kind of ability Maylore has," Nenaias said. "Should we be concerned about it?"

"Let's ask Gilriel about that," Rendal said, looking at Gilriel. Gilriel cleared his throat as all eyes moved to him.

"I found he has two portals he may be able to use," Gilriel said. "One portal gathers energy from the planet or fire and may learn to transmit it where he wishes it to go. He also has a communication portal. It could allow him to locate people and communicate with them. It is difficult to tell how much of either skill he will learn to use. He may never develop skill in either ability, but the potential exists."

"We have had others who had greater abilities and were never a problem for us," Caudra said.

"We never really found out since they wandered away," Nenaias said. Caudra nodded and fell silent.

"Let me finish my analysis of Maylore," Gilriel said as the chamber quieted and looked his way. "I found dead energy partially blocking his energy portal. He may still be able to teach himself to gather energy from fire, water, and the planet. Dead energy nearly blocked his communication portal, too. I was able to open it partially. We will have to wait to find out what he can use."

"Will he go mad and wander off like the others?" Nenaias asked.

"We hope to keep him in the village," Rendal replied. "I suspect the disappearances are the result of the master's work. We will help Maylore stay safe."

"Directly accusing the master could result in your disappearance," Nenaias said.

"If I do," Rendal replied, "you will know his spy is in this room. I hope none of our esteemed citizens are his spies." Heads turned to look at each other in silence.

"Let me finish with Maylore, too," Rendal said, changing the subject. "Maylore may develop an ability similar to Gilriel to search for portals within a villager. If Maylore can find others with abilities, it would free Gilriel from that responsibility in our village."

"That would be most welcome," Gilriel said, realizing what Rendal was saying.

"Gilriel still has to travel with the master to each village to test their citizens," Rendal said. "That was the master's choice we could not avoid."

"Do you tell the master if the person has an ability?" Baruo asked.

"I keep those with latent or unused abilities to myself," Gilriel said. If the village seems aware of someone's skills, I must tell the master, or he will be suspicious of me. I keep many to myself and monitor them on the next visit."

"Are you going to test Airalee and Jendrin?" Katiana asked.

"It may be a good idea to verify if either has an ability," Rendal replied. After Gilriel returns, we should test them both."

"We will need to find more blue spot mushrooms," Gilriel said.

"I will ask Kai to hunt for more of them," Rendal said.

Looking at the council members, he spoke loudly.

"Shall we take a vote on full membership?" Rendal asked.

"Before we vote, do the companions have ways to help support themselves and help Olona?" Caudra asked.

"Yes," Rendal said. "Jendrin will build us a village water system. Airalee is quickly learning about cooking and healing herbs. Maylore will work with Throc and me on diplomatic missions and record keeping."

"Good," Caudra said. "They could be more help to Olona than many of our residents."

177

"All those in favor of raising Airalee, Jendrin, and Maylore to accepted status, raise your hand." All of the council members raised their hands. "I see no reason to ask for those opposed."

"I suggest we do not need to be suspicious of them and believe they will be valuable residents. I propose we also change Airalee's status to permanent home ownership," Rendal suggested.

"Basrah," Baruo said. "It only applies to women. The men would not be any better off."

"It is a village status title," Katiana said.

"I have no objection," Baruo said.

The rest of the council voiced approval and no objections.

"This vote grants Airalee ownership status of their hut. Any disagreements?" The council members looked silently at each other before Rendal continued.

"Excellent," Rendal said. "I have information and one more subject I would like to revisit. Kai and Gilda will try to find more mushrooms after the Lemidge visitors have departed. When Gilriel returns, we will test Airalee, Jendrin, and the remaining untested villagers."

The council all nodded their understanding.

"I have one more subject," Rendal said. "Jendrin has offered a possible method of avoiding subjecting our girls to bandit servitude."

All of the council members looked at Rendal with interest on their faces.

"And what is he proposing?" Caudra inquired.

"He believes we could develop a group to successfully defend ourselves from the bandits' preposterous demand for our young girls," Rendal said.

"Does his plan avoid harm or killing anyone?" Nenaias asked.

"I have not heard his plan, only that I would ask this council about developing a plan," Rendal said.

"If it does not include attacking another village, killing, or harming others, we could listen," Caudra said.

"I am unsure," Nenaias said.

"We need to do something," Katiana said.

A quiet discussion followed that grew louder as time passed. Rendal allowed the arguments to continue briefly before standing and raising his hands.

"Thank you, everyone," Rendal said. "I will ask Jendrin about his intentions for us to consider. I believe that is all for this council meeting."

Gilriel pulled Rendal's sleeve, silently asking him to wait until the others had left.

"You did not tell the council I was investigating the master," Gilriel said.

"I see spies behind every bush, I guess," Rendal said. "I didn't see a reason for them to know the additional reason for your travel with the master. I believe the council is trustworthy, but I am unsure."

Gilriel nodded and pushed the door open so Rendal could leave.

Airalee and Jendrin awoke a little later than on prior days. They each attended to their human needs and settled at the table for breakfast.

"It seems odd not to have Maylore here this morning," Airalee said.

"I am sure he is well in the Beacon's care," Jendrin said.

They each filled a bowl with the herb-soaked beans Airalee had made the night before. Their good-natured ribbing continued but was much less pointed than when they arrived in the village.

"Hero, could you make me a short knife for cutting up herbs?" Airalee asked.

"Only if you promise not to stab me with it," Jendrin replied, looking at her.

She looked at him with an evil smile.

"No guarantees," she said.

"I should dull the tip," Jendrin said, slowing his eating. "I have several obsidian slices that would make good herb tools. I need to make several handles, one for your knife and one to repay Latel."

"I can try to help make the handles," Airalee said in a helpful tone. "I would like to use my hands to make something today."

"Good," Jendrin said, nodding. "We can start on that today if you wish."

Airalee thought for a moment about her commitments for the day.

"I have no training session today since Mirtha, Kai, and Marisa are busy," Airalee said. "I need to help gather wood and some water for the cookfire. We can start after I do that."

"I can help you with both," Jendrin said. "Then, you can help me carry the new sections of water piping to their starting points. Latel and I will add them to the pipeline later."

"Mirtha is excited about the water pipe," Airalee told him. "Do you plan to have it carry water to the cooking area?"

"That is my plan," Jendrin said. "I found two more bamboo sections we can carry to the end of the last one near the garden. My new axe is nearly complete, so I can cut down the size of the tree I want. I won't have to use Mirtha's fire to create my desired lengths. I still need to determine how to split the water in different directions."

They finished their breakfast and cleaned up quickly. Wood was plentiful around the area, so they quickly gathered what they needed. Jendrin helped Airalee carry water for the cooking area and one back to their hut.

"If you grab those two ends, we can carry these two pieces to the garden area," Jendrin said, hefting the two larger ends. Airalee picked up the other two ends and carried them to the garden. Setting them down end to end, Jendrin showed Airalee where he planned to split the water off to serve the garden, cooking area, and several points for the huts. "The last one is near our hut before the overflows run back into the creek. It doesn't save us much effort, but the huts on the far side will have less of a trip for water," he said, pointing in different directions.

"Looking good, hero," Airalee said. "Shall we return to the hut and create some knife handles?"

Traveling back to their hut, they passed by the cooking area. Several women added more vegetables, meat, water, and herbs to the cooking pots. Groups of villagers were leaving the area as Rendal stepped down from a table and headed toward Kai's hut.

"It appears there was a public announcement we missed," Jendrin said as they continued.

Several men smiled at Airalee as she walked past the pots.

"That's odd," she said. "The village men generally ignore me. Do I suddenly have holes in my tunic?" she asked, looking down. Seeing no holes, she looked at Jendrin.

"Pretty women always gather glances," he said with a smile.

"Shut it, hero," she said.

"They may be aware you are in line for a hut," Jendrin said. "If you choose one of them for a mate, they will have a new home."

They passed several more men who also smiled at her as they passed.

"Something has changed," Airalee said. "These men ignored me up to this point.

I will ask Marisa when I see her," Airalee said as they approached their hut.

Kai, Mirtha, and Rendal sat around Kai's table discussing village affairs.

"Did Airalee notice if there were more mushrooms?" Rendal asked.

"Airalee said there were just the two full mushrooms," Kai said. "There may be some more later, but not yet," Kai replied. "I have found them before in a meadow beyond the Lemidge village of Liqua. Gilda and I can hunt them in a few sunrises. It would be a good experience for her to get farther from the village."

"Good," Rendal said. "It could take several days and lead you past the bandit camp."

"We must travel off the main road," Kai said. "I believe we can do it."

"I assume you will rest a night near Liqua?" Rendal said.

"Perhaps in the village, if we are welcome," Kai said, smiling.

"Bringing a gift from each of you will increase your odds," Rendal said, chuckling.

"Speaking of the Lemidge," Rendal said, "A traveling group of Lemidge will be coming here. I believe they will be visiting shortly after the master leaves. I request you, Mirtha, or Marisa speak with Airalee about them."

"I would leave it to Marisa, but she would melt doing it!" Mirtha chuckled. "Kai, would you like to handle it?"

"Airalee is no giggly girl," Kai said. "If you wish, I will explain to her and any other girls of age. I would like to send Gilda," Kai said. "We may still be mushroom hunting during that time."

Rendal considered for a moment.

"I would not deprive you or Gilda of the visit," Rendal said. "I believe the master is going sunset with Gilriel to visit the other human villages. He is likely to be gone ten sunrises or more. You will likely complete your task before he returns. It is your decision if you wish to wait."

"Thank you, Beacon," Kai said. "I have had the pleasure of their company before, but Gilda has not. I will ask her what she wishes to do when we meet with Airalee."

"Good," Rendal replied. "As you know, we expect Birsha to arrive in two sunrises. He will likely demand his share of food, crafts, and serfs. We have enough dried fish, meats, and vegetables to meet his demands without causing us hardship. He may expect us to provide a female with an appropriate age for his village. If we are fortunate, he will find none here and look for his servant in another village. Remind villagers to listen for the sentinel's signal and immediately have the older girls move to the cave."

"I will help pass the warning," Mirtha said.

"Jendrin has offered to teach us warrior skills," Rendal said, changing the subject. "At another council meeting, I would like Jendrin to discuss how our village could defend itself. I present it now so you can consider the option. I would like both of your support."

"You know you have my support," Kai said. "This old woman would be a poor warrior, but I support the idea."

"I, too, support the idea," Mirtha said. "Even if I could only throw vegetables at them!"

Airalee and Jendrin had returned to their hut. They were discussing how to make knife handles when someone knocked.

"Come in, Marisa," Airalee said.

"How did you know it was me?" she asked as she entered.

"You quietly knock four times," Airalee said.

"Oh, I see," Marisa replied. "The Beacon wants you two to join him in the council hut with Maylore," she said, recovering quickly.

"Maylore remained at Rendal's hut last night," Airalee said. "We can get him and then go to the council hut."

Maylore awoke to see Throc sitting at the table, making notes in a large book. Throc noticed he had awakened and passed him a cup of water.

"The Beacon has gone to a council meeting," Throc said. "I will help you with your meal then Rendal wants to meet with you and your fellow travelers."

Maylore sat on the bed, feeling dizzy as he drank the water. "I am surprised Gilriel could leave so soon after we finished."

"Rendal requested I not ask any questions but simply watch over you," Gilriel said. "I can tell you that Gilriel has told us before the process wears off quickly for him. A mushroom is not needed for the tested person. He was testing you to judge your ability to use the blue-spot mushroom. Apparently, you passed."

"Good for the guinea pig," Maylore chuckled.

"I have meat and bread on the table," Throc said, offering to help Maylore stand. "Eating will help you regain strength and settle your mind."

Maylore rose steadily on his own and walked to the table. He noticed the twin suns were shining through the window, telling him it was still morning.

"Would you join me for breakfast?" he asked Throc.

Throc smiled for the first time.

"Yes, thank you," he said as he sat in an opposing chair. Maylore started eating and took the opportunity to question Throc.

"You mentioned villagers before me," Maylore said. "Have many in the village been tested?" Throc realized he may have trapped himself into revealing information meant to be kept secret.

"Villagers have been tested, that is true," Throc said. "The results are known only to the council and the master. I, too, was tested, but I have no special ability. Gilriel told me I would make a good statesman. That is why I work with the Beacon."

Maylore looked up, and before he could say anything, Throc continued.

"When I turned 15, I was tested and then allowed to work with the Beacon," Throc said. "The Beacon continued my education, teaching me how to create trading agreements, village censuses, notes from visitor's meetings, and records of births and deaths. I started accompanying him on visits to other villages when I was about 18." Throc smiled, hoping what he said would distract Maylore from questions about other villagers.

"You looked to be in late in your twentieth season now," Maylore said, finishing his meal. "Twenty-seven," Throc replied. "I hope to start taking over more statesman tasks so Rendal does not need to be involved in mundane details."

A tapping on the door sounded.

"Enter," Throc called out, relieved at the interruption of the questioning. Marisa stepped in the door.

"Good, you are awake, Maylore," she said.

"Yes, I was having breakfast with Throc," Maylore replied.

"The Beacon would like you all to gather in the council hut for a meeting," Marisa said.

"Of course," Maylore said. "Thank you for watching out for me and providing breakfast," Maylore told Throc as he stood to leave.

Throc bowed as they left the hut.

CHAPTER 13 - NO MORE SECRETS

Airalee, Jendrin, Latel, and Beacon Rendal were already seated in the council hut when Marisa and Throc arrived with Maylore.

"Dad!" Airalee said as he entered. "I'm glad you are well!" she said, walking over to hug him.

"Thank you, Airalee. It's good to see you, too," he replied, thinking how odd it was for her to hug him. She had avoided contact or touching him up to this point. "I was gone, what, one night?" he said with a smile.

"Yes, but I got so used to seeing your snarling face," she laughed.

"Snarling?" he questioned. "I didn't know I snarled," he said.

"Not so much anymore," Airalee said, smiling and returning to her chair.

"I will need to check myself each morning to prevent it," Maylore finished.

Rendal's face maintained a serious expression throughout the greetings. He stood as everyone stayed seated.

"We have many subjects to discuss today," Rendal started. "These include citizenship, Maylore's test, village secrets, bandits, skepticism, traveling visitors, and other subjects we have not disclosed to you until today. I will review the list and answer questions at the end."

"I should get my book and take notes," Airalee said.

"No," Rendal replied, "These are subjects we do not want written down. A few subjects are sensitive for some of us."

"Oh my," Maylore said, settling back into his chair.

"I will begin with good news," Rendal said. "The council has agreed to allow all three of you to become accepted citizens of Olona. Airalee has been granted ownership status. She now owns the hut you are staying in and will determine who will live there."

Airalee grinned widely at her companions.

"Don't worry," Airalee said, "You will remain in our hut."

"It explains why so many men were smiling at you this morning," Jendrin grinned.

"You may be correct this time, hero," Airalee replied.

"We will have a little presentation for each of you at the end of this meeting," Rendal said, ignoring their comments.

"Thank you, Rendal," Maylore said. "I look forward to a place to settle." His two companions echoed his sentiments.

"Next, I would like to address the reason for our skepticism you may have felt," Rendal said. "We have one man who oversees all of Almora. He calls himself the master. He is human but doesn't seem to have a name. He travels with a small group who seem to be his guards. He visits all the villages regardless of whether they are Tocor, Lemidge, or humans. The Tocor say someone calling themselves the master has been here since the first humans came to Molia. No one knows where he came from or where he lives. He wears a hooded cloak, and they never see his face. The Tocor says a different person replaces him every twenty seasons or so. He is tracking people who have extraordinary abilities. We suspect he eliminates some of them."

"It seems you would be suspicious of him instead of us," Jendrin said.

"The master seems to have spies everywhere," Rendal said. "We do not know who the spies are, but we believe he has several. Some of his spies masqueraded as refugees, so we suspected your group."

"I hope we removed your suspicion," Airalee said.

188

"Indeed," Rendal said. "We believe you three will be a benefit to Olona."

"What raised your suspicions in the first place?" Jendrin asked.

"We became suspicious as the master had information about everyone in the human villages. He told us a group would soon arrive in Olona during his last visit. Your arrival the same day made us suspicious. I asked that a sentinel be assigned to each of you and for them to follow you everywhere. They slept in shifts above your hut each night, moving from tree to tree. I doubt you had any idea they were following each of you."

The three companions looked at each other and shook their heads.

"I thought not," Rendal said. "You found them around when two sentinels shot arrows at the rampaging boar. Usually, sentinels do not go that far from the village except when asked."

"I suspected they helped us," Airalee said. "Are they still following us?"

"They reported to us that they never saw suspicious activity," Rendal said. "I have informed the sentinels that they no longer need to follow you. Your guides also watched for deceitful behavior," Rendal said, indicating the three guides. "They consistently reported no problems and believed you three would be good citizens."

"You were spying on us thinking we were spies?" Maylore asked.

"I would say we were guiding you to becoming welcome citizens," Marisa said.

"I don't think she answered my question," Maylore said. "I understand why and accept Rendal's explanation. Is she part of your diplomatic training program?"

"No," Rendal said, "but I must consider it. I usually know her to have a sharp edge to her tongue. She must have been wearing her nice attitude when she was with you."

Marisa smiled a big grin and kept quiet.

"Impressive, Marisa," Rendal said before continuing his explanations. "The council originally asked our villagers to keep Olona's secrets to themselves. They may have been courteous but did not engage with you too much. I have informed our citizens they may be more forthcoming with you."

Looking toward Jendrin, he continued, "Jendrin mentioned at our first meeting that you could be prisoners here. You were never prisoners, and we would have accepted your moving on to avoid the possibility of spying. However, we would all be unfortunate if you were to leave now. I offer no apology for our skepticism or the monitoring. I am very pleased that there was no betrayal, and I welcome you all to Olona."

The three companions looked at each other with a look of how they could suspect us.

"I accept the explanation," Airalee said. "I am pleased to have the opportunity to become a stronger part of your community."

"I am pleased to have a home," Maylore said.

"I will stay with my companions," Jendrin said. "This is a good village and can be a good home."

"Excellent," Rendal said. "Let me move on to Maylore's test. You may remember Maylore could see the blue energy on the rock in my hut."

"You mean the black lava rock in your hut?" Airalee asked, cocking her head at Rendal.

"It is indeed black to me, too," Rendal replied. "Gilriel says it sits on a conjunction of ley lines of Almora's energy. The planet's energy looks blue to those who can see it. We had a few others who could see the rock as blue. Gilriel remains with us and can find what abilities others may have. When the master discovered his ability, he conscripted Gilriel to help him find others with abilities. We thought the master was arranging for those with strong abilities to disappear. However, he was never near when they disappeared. We still suspect he arranged their disappearances but cannot prove anything. We would also like to test Airalee and Jendrin to see if you have any hidden abilities."

"I have no objection to that," Airalee said.

"Nor do I," Jendrin said. "Do many of the villagers have an ability?"

"We have a few villagers with small latent abilities," Rendal replied. "None have shown any strong ability."

"What are these abilities?" Jendrin asked.

"There are several types of abilities," Rendal said. "Collection of energy from the planet, fire, wind, or air. Some can collect and direct that energy wherever they wish. Ivar could collect energy from fire and direct it to another place. He used to light the village torches from the cook fire for practice. He showed he could create a wave of fire and send it to ignite something large. Hawnele could see across great distances. He told us of the large Lemidge villages in the mountains far to sunset. He spoke of many Tocor villages going sunrise. He told of large mountains and the tunnels within them. He also claims there are monstrous animals toward the sea from the Lemidge village of Liqua toward the sea. We were unsure of anything he said since we had no direct knowledge. We do know lava tunnels spread throughout the mountains. We do not explore the deep tunnels since the eurg live inside them. We considered his stories to be just stories. Gilriel's testing showed that both men might be able to develop those abilities and several more. Instead, both men disappeared into the mountains a few days after the master visited us."

"I hope Maylore doesn't get the wandering disease," Airalee said.

"We are trying to keep him within the village," Rendal said. "He does not show any significant ability yet, so we believe he is safe."

"Good," Airalee said. "We need to keep Dad around."

"Could you explain more about this master you keep talking about?" Jendrin asked.

"I hate to admit we know little about him," Rendal said. "He appears in Molia during the summer and then disappears during the winter. No one knows where he comes from, where he goes, or how he gets there. The Tocor tells us he first arrived in a Tocor mountain village, and it was sunrise from here. He walks along Olona with three tough-looking men who never speak. He speaks pleasantly to us when we meet, only asking about new villagers, travelers, and news we hear. He does not enter the villages, and after eating and using our entertainment hut, he walks away."

"What does he look like?" Airalee asked.

"I glimpsed him once as he left the entertainment hut when a strong wind blew his hood back. He is a medium-sized bald human in his late fifties with greying dark hair," Rendal replied. "I did notice he has a star on his left temple. He replaced his hood so quickly, I couldn't see anything else that would distinguish him."

"That is more than I have ever heard about him," Marisa said.

"I did not remember that much until Jendrin asked," Rendal said. "Even that much information could be trouble for those that know it. I suggest keeping it to yourselves."

"Does he seem to be in command?" Jendrin asked.

"He carries himself with authority and seems to command respect from his associates," Rendal replied.

"Does he carry weapons?" Jendrin asked.

"Not that we know of or have seen," Rendal replied. "He probably thinks his associates would handle any problem he may run into. The bandit village does not seem to give him any trouble either."

"Does he exhibit any ability?" Maylore questioned.

"Not that I have heard any," Rendal said. "Gilriel tells me others with abilities avoid contacting him. Gilriel said he would avoid him too if he could."

"Well, sounds like we should keep him at a distance," Airalee said.

"Agreed," Rendal said. "I would like to continue with Maylore's testing if you have no other questions."

The companions said they didn't and looked at Rendal to continue.

"Gilriel will use the same process on both of you," Rendal said. "He will use part or all of the rare, blue-spotted white mushroom."

"I found a few of those," Airalee said.

"Yes," Rendal replied. "When those dry, we will put them to use. We will need several more to finish testing our young ones."

"I will be glad to help Kai and Gilda find more of them," Airalee said.

"Excellent," Rendal said. "I will explain the plan to Kai after we finish with Maylore's test." Airalee nodded and sat back to listen.

"Gilriel gave Maylore and himself a piece of a mushroom to eat. The person being tested does not need to use a mushroom, but Gilriel wanted to verify that Maylore could survive." Rendal said.

"It could have killed dad?" Airalee said, giving Rendal a stern look.

"Unlikely," Rendal said. "Gilriel gave him a tiny piece, which made me sick. I have not tried again. Kai believes it would kill me to use another one. I will not test her theory. The good news is that Maylore could follow Gilriel inside his own body. He now knows he can use the mushroom to inspect others."

"Seems like a risk, but I am glad Dad survived," Airalee said, looking at Maylore.

"I accepted the risk," Maylore said. "I am unsure what happened after that, however."

"Gilriel was nearby as the mushroom unlocked his body's ability to search a person," Rendal said. "The other person must be in contact so he can enter and look at specific spots for portals. Gilriel will note if the portal is open, closed, or does not exist. He moves on to the next portal if a portal does not exist. If it is closed, he will try to open it. If it is open, he looks for a dome outside the portal. The dome indicates a power portal the person can use with the outside world. Gilriel found Maylore had a choked energy-gathering portal, which he could open slightly wider. I asked Maylore not to tell either of you what he was doing until we could decide on your new loyalty."

Jendrin and Airalee looked toward Maylore, who nodded.

"I am glad there was a reason for you being so worn out," Airalee said. "I feared you were coming down with a disease."

"Maylore also has a clogged communication portal," Rendal continued. "Gilriel managed to open it partially. We currently don't have anyone else with that ability. Gilriel's book says people with this ability may be able to locate and talk to others. We hope Maylore can learn to use this someday." Looking toward Airalee and Jendrin, he said, "We strongly ask you to keep information about his abilities secret from all others."

Airalee and Jendrin nodded in agreement as Airalee squeezed Maylore's hand.

"Let me return to the mushroom hunt before I get into other subjects," Rendal said. "Kai and Gilda plan to search in a far-away meadow, which Kai knows near the village of Liqua. They will pass the bandit's village en route and must avoid detection. Kai is far too old to be of interest to the bandits, but Gilda is near the age they seek to serve them."

"Serve?" Airalee grimaced at him.

Rendal's face grew long, and his body sagged in response. He continued in a more sullen tone. "The bandits require all villages in Molia to contribute what they feel is their due. Citizens must contribute food, clothing, trinkets, and prizes from each village. One of those prizes is for young women. They prefer human girls ages 16 to 20 but will take Tocor or Lemidge girls. They consider other girls too young or too old. The girls are generally treated well but will likely return pregnant, injured, or after they reach their 21st season."

"Barbaric! Giving away our young girls is wrong!" Airalee said with rage building in her voice. "Why is that allowed to happen?"

"The villages need to stop them from kidnapping them," Jendrin said, bristling.

"We did try in the distant past," Rendal sighed. "Years ago, we tried to fight them. We built weapons but quickly found we were not warriors and could not effectively wield them. The bandits train to fight and would quickly kill the parents or other villagers who tried to stop them. The bandits would then simply take the girls anyway. We asked the Tocor to have their sentinels watch for the bandits and notify us when they see them. They notify us with a loud whistle like the IB bird. The sentinels use the bird's sounds to communicate from one sentinel to another throughout Molia. They do it to protect their villages. We just benefit from their watchfulness."

"Our village sentinels use a different whistle to warn the village and our young girls to run to the council hut," Rendal continued. "We hid the cavern entrance behind the grass wall behind you."

The group looked at the back wall. Jendrin walked back to the wall and brushed it aside.

"There appears to be a cave entrance here, all right," Jendrin said. "Where does it lead?" he asked.

"There are a myriad of tunnels back there," Rendal replied. "We have explored a small section to find a side cave where we can safely hide from bandits. You must have lit torches with you since eurg are

195

furious beasts who will gladly eat anyone they find in the caves. The eurg do fear fire since their long hair burns quickly and would kill them. We have not heard of any eurg in a long time, and they avoid us when we carry a torch. The bandits don't know where the caves are, and the sentinels warn us with time for most young girls to hide before they arrive. The location of the caves would bring our young girls into harm's way. A few girls were captured when they did not hear the sentinel's signal. It was traumatic for them, their parents, and the village," he said, looking down. "Thanks to the sentinel's warning, there are no girls for the bandits to see when they arrive. They gather what food and clothing they want and move on to the next village without any of our girls."

"I am surprised they did not kill villagers until the girls were produced," Jendrin said.

"In the past, the bandits did kill parents when appropriate girls were not given to them," Rendal said. "Birsha quickly stopped the practice when he took command from his deceased father, Malin. He told his bandits they were killing his little people. How could they produce goods for them if they were dead?"

"We must determine a way to prevent any more abductions from occurring," Airalee said.

"I believe I can train your villagers in weapon use," Jendrin said. "We need to make some first. I can help with that, too."

"I discussed the idea with the council," Rendal said. "The majority are opposed to harm or killing, even bandits. The current method is working at great expense to our families. I have noted the idea and invite you to the council meeting when members are ready to discuss it."

Jendrin conceded the topic with a sour look on his face. Airalee still looked angry but finally sighed and shook her head.

"Do they take boys too?" Maylore asked.

"Not often," Rendal replied. "They have enough men to support the village, and only when one dies do they look for a replacement."

"What happens to the pregnant girls?" Airalee asked.

"They return to their village," Rendal said. "The village welcomes them back. The girls give birth to their children and raise them in their village. Our village will treat the child like any other village child. I assume other villages do the same."

"That is some good news," Airalee said.

"Speaking of good news," Rendal said, "Latel was gathering flint with Jendrin near the river when he spotted a girl we thought was dead. When she disappeared, she had been gathering berries and roots with two other village women in the forest. Her gathering group went to find her when they had finished, but all they found were shredded, blood-stained clothes. A wide trail of bear prints was in the area, so we thought a bear got her. That seemed odd since bears make lots of noise and would have attracted the attention of the gathering group. They told us she was some distance away but would have heard a bear attack."

"It is nice she is alive, but her servitude is not good news," Airalee said.

"True," Rendal said. "The point is she is alive, and since she is pregnant, she will return soon to Olona."

"I see," Airalee said as she looked at Marisa. "I am surprised you accept this situation."

"It has been that way since before I was born," Marisa said. "I am unhappy about it and would gladly see it changed."

Airalee considered the conversation before sighing.

"What of the injured ones from their camp?" Airalee asked.

"The injured are brought back at night by the younger bandits," Rendal said. "Healers tend to their wounds and counsel them with their mental wounds. They are fortunate in one respect. The bandits do not want them back after they heal."

The three companions stared in silence.

"We have other topics we need to discuss before we adjourn," Rendal said.

The companions gathered themselves and sat up to hear the next topic.

"Travelers and tradespeople. We are close to the main road that traverses Molia beneath the mountains. Humans, Tocor, Lemidge, and animals travel the road. The animals give us little trouble and merely pass through. Humans travel trading for food, trinkets, adventure, and information. We usually have a group come through every few sunrises in the summer. The Tocor are concerned with trade. They want dried fish, trinkets, and a chance to visit with the Tocor staying in the entertainment hut. They create ropes from the mountain nottoc trees and trade them with us. We use them to climb the sea bank. We unbraid the ropes into threads to create soft fabric clothes when they wear out. We also make tunics and robes from old nottoc ropes."

The companions looked at their tunics before looking at Rendal again.

"Latel's group may have made your tunics from flax," Rendal said. "Long ago, we created trade treaties stating what value goods made by each village would have to each other. We have very few trade disagreements. Throc and I work with traders to establish a fair deal if a conflict arises."

Rendal paused to see if they had another question. When the room remained silent, he launched into his next subject.

"The Lemidge are another group that travels Molia's road," Rendal continued. "They trade their skills for foods, trinkets, and rare items like honey, special mushrooms, and flowers." Looking at Airalee, he continued, "The Lemidge men trade a natural skill that

198

human women find extremely alluring. It intoxicates nearby human women. Village women look forward to their late summer visits. I suggest you discuss it with Kai and Mirtha."

"All right," Airalee replied. "I am surprised Marisa has not mentioned it," looking at Marisa.

"Now that you are accepted, she may discuss if you ask," Rendal replied, looking at Marisa. "You are new to the village, and I asked your guides not to discuss many subjects. She is occasionally discrete."

"I will gladly talk about it," Marisa said, grinning from her chair.

"Please, not here, Marisa," Rendal said.

Marisa continued to smile but kept quiet.

"A Lemidge woman travels with their traders to keep track of their rewards," Rendal said. "They do not have a skill that attracts human males."

"Unfortunate," Jendrin replied.

"Human men do not need that encouragement anyway," Rendal said, smiling.

"That covers what I wanted to talk with you three about." Looking toward Marisa, Latel, and Throc, he asked, "Anything you want to add?"

"I look forward to having you three as permanent members of Olona," Marisa said. The two men nodded their heads in agreement.

"Latel?" Rendal said, standing.

Latel stood and produced three orange-colored sashes.

"The color orange is Olona's village color," Rendal said as Latel passed a sash to each companion. "Many villagers wear them as belts or across the chest. You do not have to wear them at all if you wish. It is easy to identify other villagers if you leave Olona."

The three companions put them to use as a belt.

"Thank you, Latel and Rendal," Airalee said as the two men echoed her appreciation.

"I hope my discussion has not dissuaded you from staying," Rendal said. "You may now be known as Airalee, Maylore, and Jendrin of Olona.

"We have a home," Maylore said, smiling at his belt.

"A society we can fit into," Airalee smiled.

"Indeed, a beginning point to explore," Jendrin said.

"Thank you for joining us," Rendal said as he rose to leave.

CHAPTER 14 – SOMETHING FISHY

Latel knocked on the companions' door just as they finished breakfast.

"Come in!" Airalee said, sitting at the table with the other two.

"Jendrin, it is a fishing day, and we could use your help," Latel said as he entered the hut. "Good morning, Airalee and Maylore," he added.

"Fishing?" Jendrin questioned. "I have not tried that yet. I look forward to learning how the village does it," he said.

"The Beacon believes the approaching traders will want fresh fish, crab, and sea grass," Latel said. "The weather is good, so Finhile decided we should go fishing."

"Who is Finhile?" Airalee asked.

"Finhile is our fishmonger," Latel said. "He decided today is the day to restock our supplies."

"That was probably him inspecting the stored dried fish," Jendrin said.

"I saw him once when Throc pointed him out on our walk to the Beacon's hut," Maylore said.

"You are both welcome to join us atop the cliff," Latel said. "We can always use more help pulling up the catch."

"I would be glad to join you," Maylore said, rising to his feet. "I could use some physical activity."

"I can carry the catch to the drying racks," Airalee said.

"I will finish the breakfast cleanup then join you," Maylore said, gathering the dishes.

The top of the sea cliff was close to their hut. They arrived to find a dozen people already gathered. Two villagers were throwing ropes over the cliff's edge as they arrived.

"I will go down first," Finhile said as he grabbed the larger rope and started down the slope. The slope was climbable with a rope but difficult otherwise. The seasons of use have created crude stairs. Another person started down the rope as Finhile reached halfway.

"Do they use both ropes?" Jendrin asked.

"The second rope hauls the collection basket," Latel said. Pointing to the left, he added, "We move that rope over five sticks toward the waterfall. It is mostly vertical there, and we can pull the catch basket back up without hitting the side of the hill."

Four men went down the rope to the rocky beach below. Mirtha appeared from the crowd and grabbed the climbing rope.

"Mirtha!" Airalee exclaimed, "May I accompany you?" Airalee asked.

"Yes," Mirtha replied after considering for a moment. "I could use help with the sea grass," she said with a smile.

Airalee followed Mirtha down to the rocky beach below.

"Marisa is not with you?" Airalee asked as they reached the bottom.

"I asked her to prepare the drying racks for the sea grass and the cut-up fish," Mirtha replied. "Usually, the sea grass is plentiful, and I can quickly gather all we need," she said, walking toward the sea.

The sea was calm, with only a slight ripple disrupting the water's surface. The men had retrieved long poles with a hook carved on one end and a short rope attached to the other. Jendrin selected a pole following Latel's lead.

"My guess is we are going spearfishing?" he said, following Latel down the beach.

"Yes," Latel answered. "We will follow Finhile to the starting point."

Finhile stopped a few steps later and looked down. The water appeared deep and full of seagrass.

"I hope there are plenty of fish so we don't have to do fish too long," Finhile said.

Two men thrust their spears into the water as he spoke. They each pulled back a large silvery fish with black backs.

"That's what we want, sabb," Finhile said. "They will fill the racks quickly."

Jendrin looked into the water but only saw seagrass.

"Latel, what are they looking for?" Jendrin asked as Latel speared his first.

"Look about two hands' width below the surface," Latel said. "If you see a black line above a silver line, it is a sabb. Spear it quickly and lift the fish onto the beach." Latel told him. Walking a few steps up the beach, Latel pointed into the water.

"There is one," Jendrin said. Staring at the water, he saw two lines move a little. Raising his spear, he started forward just as the sabb darted away.

"The spear is long, so they don't see you approaching," Latel said. "Stay back from the edge and look ahead for another."

Jendrin watched as the other men crept along the beach, thrusting their spears into the water. They often came up empty, but several fish soon lined the bank.

"The spear's entry into the water scared off nearby sabb," Latel said. "They return quickly to the edge to hide from the large anut who swims in the channel just beyond the seagrass."

Jendrin saw another sabb swimming back to the edge as its silvery body revealed its position. He moved nearer the fish and thrust his spear at it. The spear missed above the fish, and it swam off again. Jendrin pulled his spear back as the surface erupted, and a large silvery fish broke the surface with a sabb in its mouth.

"That was an anut." Latel said, "He just ate your lunch." He added with a smile.

The four men continued up the beach as Mirtha and Airalee reached the seashore.

"All the seagrass is good to eat," Mirtha said. "If we see some red sea grass, we want that for its softer flavor," Mirtha said, bending down on one knee. She quickly pulled up a large amount of seagrass. She added her gathering to a basket. Airalee followed suit, quickly filling their baskets.

"We will take these baskets to the cliff and send them up," Mirtha said as she led the way back. Mirtha tied both baskets to the smaller rope. The villagers atop the cliff pulled up the baskets and sent two empty ones down.

"We will start again closer to the fishermen," Mirtha said, picking up an empty basket. "We may be able to find some red sea grass where they are," Mirtha said, starting in their direction.

Airalee looked up the cliff to see the creek's water cascading over it a short distance from the collection point. It created a new creek on the shore that flowed to the sea.

"Usually, the red sea grass grows where the creek enters the sea," Mirtha said as they crossed the creek. "Here is some," Mirtha said, reaching into the water. She retrieved a large amount of red sea grass and added it to her basket. Airalee spotted another patch a short distance away. She sank to one knee, and a large eye appeared below her hand as she reached into the water. It glared at her before it disappeared into the darkness below. Shocked, she pulled her hand back.

"What was that!" Airalee exclaimed, standing up.

"What did you see?" Mirtha asked.

"It was an eye as big as my hand!" Airalee said.

"You may have found a squid," Mirtha said. "You didn't catch it?" Mirtha asked.

"No," Airalee said, "I am glad it didn't eat me."

"If you were a fish, it would have tried." Mirtha laughed. "They catch the small sabb for food. They also taste good if we catch one."

The men had already gathered a group of fish. Finhile stopped fishing and started cleaning them where the creek entered the sea.

"This is where we may be able to catch crab," Mirtha said as she moved toward Finhile. "Finhile cleans the fish here so the water will carry the innards into this rock basin on the shore. The crab will come up here to eat the scraps as the scent of the fish drifts into the sea. We will wait by Finhile so the crabs will not see us as they enter the basin. Most of the crabs move slowly enough that we can catch them. We don't need more than 10 to 12. A large population of crabs live in the sea, so there is more than enough to keep the population going. We will return these two baskets to the cliff and ask for the crab basket." Mirtha said, starting back toward the cliff. The women exchanged the baskets for a crab basket and returned to the crab basin.

"Lots of crabs," Mirtha said as they got to the basin. The crabs saw shadows above them and slowly walked back toward the sea. "Open the basket, Airalee," Mirtha said, picking up a large crab by its back. The crab struggled to reach its captor but could not as it landed in the basket. Mirtha grabbed twelve more before stopping. "That is enough to have a large meal," she said, closing the top of the basket. "We will take these to the rope, then help the men carry the fish to the cliff."

Finhile was making quick work of the catch. Mirtha and Airalee returned to the site where he had already cleaned and beheaded the fish.

"Grab two fish and carry them to the rope," Mirtha said. The women grabbed two each and walked back to the rope. Mirtha created a loop in the rope and tightened the loop around the tail of each fish. Villagers on top pulled the four fish up as the women returned for more.

The men continued up the coast, occasionally casting their spears into the water. Near the end of the beach, Latel turned to Jendrin and pointed to a shelf a short distance above them.

"This is where we collect salt when the storms push the seawater onto this shelf," Latel said. "After it dries, there is usually enough for our village to use and some to trade. Let's see if it is salt harvest time," Latel said, starting up the slope. Dried salt clung to rocks where the water had evaporated. "Seawater remains at the bottom of the shelf. We have several weeks before the rest of the water evaporates. We will make a trip down the rope in the future to collect the salt," Latel said, gesturing toward the shallow trough.

"Let's gather the speared fish and take them back to Finhile," Latel said, leading Jendrin back with the fish for cleaning. The process repeated itself until Finhile called a halt to fishing. They had collected twenty fish weighing about two small stones apiece.

"This should be enough for the village and our traders," Finhile said as others joined him in cleaning the fish.

"Enough people are helping Finhile clean the fish," Mirtha said, looking to Airalee. "Let's walk in the other direction and look for colorful shells or stones for our crafters." The two women walked along the beach, picking up small shiny shells and colorful rocks.

"Are you planning to meet with us to discuss the Lemidge travelers?" Airalee asked.

"Yes," Mirtha replied without looking at her. "Kai will gather the younger girls, and I will bring you and Marisa to the meeting."

"Are these travelers dangerous?" Airalee continued.

"Why would you think they are dangerous?" Mirtha asked, looking surprised.

"Rendal would not discuss them. He told me to ask you or Kai about the Lemidge," Airalee said. "I wondered if they were dangerous."

"No," Mirtha replied. A smile slowly crept onto her face. "Perhaps some human men would consider them threatening in a way, but they are very peaceful people. We will discuss them later."

Airalee noticed a white object in the sand before her as they walked. She bent down and pushed the sand aside, revealing a white stone about the size of her thumb. Picking it up, she held it between her fingers and felt a slight tingle that quickly disappeared.

"The rock made my fingers tingle," Airalee said, showing the rock to Mirtha. "It reminds me of the blue stone I found," she said, pulling it from her pocket.

"Interesting," Mirtha said. "It is a pretty blue. I have not seen a blue stone like that before. Add the white one to your collection." Airalee put it in her pocket with the shells she had collected. Stirring the sand, she found two clear stones. Picking both up, she showed them to Mirtha. Mirtha took one of the stones and looked into it. "I don't think I have seen clear stones before," Mirtha said. "You have found stones I have never seen on this beach. Lafrea is our jewelry maker. Perhaps she has seen them before." Mirtha returned the stone to Airalee as they continued their search. The women gathered a few more shells and rocks before returning to the ropes.

Airalee and Mirtha were the last ones on the beach. Martha looped the rope under her arms and told Airalee to do the same with the remaining length. "We will climb together. Just follow my lead," Mirtha said, starting up the slope. The villagers on top helped pull them back up the slope as they climbed. Maylore and the other villagers had been carrying baskets of the sea bounty back to the village as they arrived at the top. Maylore returned as Jendrin helped pull the two women over the top of the cliff.

"Thank you, hero," Airalee said as she unwound the rope around her. "It's good to see you are being helpful."

"Helpful is my middle name," Jendrin replied, smiling at her.

Stopping in her tracks, Airalee tilted her head.

"I'm sorry. All this time, I thought your middle name was 'Arrogant,'" Airalee said, smiling as she bent to pick up a full basket.

"Your time is coming," Jendrin said, pretending to scowl at her.

"Now, you two be nice," Maylore said in a parental voice.

"I was being nice!" Airalee said in mock surprise. "I said thank you!"

"True, she did," Jendrin said. "I was being nice not to push her back off the cliff," he smiled as he wound up the climbing ropes.

"They are fortunate to have one adult in the group," Mirtha said, looking at Maylore. Maylore chuckled and followed the villagers with the last of the bounty.

Latel and Jendrin remained behind to store the climbing ropes.

"She holds affection for you, my friend," Latel said.

"She has an odd way to show it," Jendrin replied. "She feels more like a younger sister to me. I think we have normal bantering between siblings."

"As you say," Latel said, shaking his head slightly.

"Do you see how much the ropes are wearing pulling them over the cliff?" Jendrin said, purposefully changing the subject.

"That's how it has always been," Latel said, nodding. "We trade for new rope sections from the Tocor," Latel replied matter-of-factly.

"We can help change that," Jendrin said. "Remember how we created a roller for the water pipe to sit on? We could run a stick through a bamboo section so the rope would roll over the bamboo instead of grinding against the cliff."

"It should help save rope and make pulling easier for our people if we can build your roller," Latel said.

"I believe we have enough supplies to build one," Jendrin said as they returned to the village.

"We will have time to build the roller since we won't fish for many sunrises," Latel said. "It could be longer if we get another boar or a woca."

They arrived at the kitchen work center as others were cutting and getting the fish ready to store. "Let me show you how they cut, salt, and dry the fish," Latel said. "We will finish quickly today since there are so many villagers helping. Those who help cut and salt the fish for storage will take fresh fish home for dinner," Latel said, pointing to the various work areas. "Finhile cleaned the sabb as he and others cut the fillets off before tossing the bones back to the sea. Villagers are cutting the fillets into small steaks. We will then salt and move the fillets to the dryer." Latel said as he moved to the end of a line to pick up salted steaks. "Grab that basket of fillets, and we will take them to the dryer," Latel said, starting toward the drying hut near the pig slaughter hut.

Jendrin grabbed a full basket and followed Latel. The door to the drying hut was open when they arrived. Finhile was inspecting the steaks to ensure they would dry correctly. "More salt," Finhile said, sprinkling more salt onto the fillets. "In they go," He said to both men. Marisa was inside, pointing to the next space to place the fish. Jendrin nodded to her and followed Latel's lead in setting each steak on the angled drying rack. Latel signaled Jendrin to follow him outside and around the side of the hut.

"We will have a small smoky fire built here to put smoke and some heat into the hut to smoke and dry the fish. It could have been pork, woca, or whatever we want to preserve. Finhile and his helpers will watch the fire during the drying process." Jendrin noticed a young man was intent on the smoky fire.

"Are you excited about doing this job?" Jendrin asked.

"Yes, I am," the young man replied. "I won't let it get too hot or have all the smoke run out. I have lots of elppa chips and water to keep it smoky inside," he said proudly.

"Good," Finhile said, coming up behind him. "It is an important responsibility." The young man smiled and continued to set up his smoke pit under the side of the hut. Latel and Jendrin shuttled a few more baskets from the kitchen area to the smoke hut.

"How much fish remains?" Marisa asked as Jendrin and Latel arrived.

"This is the last of them," Latel said.

"Good, I will return to the kitchen," Marisa said. "You two can rack up the last fish," Marisa said as she waved and started back toward the kitchen. The two men racked the last of the fish and closed the door to the smoking hut.

"The fish have been racked, Finhile," Latel said.

"Good," Finhile replied. "Start your fire," he said, looking toward his young helper. "I will close the heat vent until the temperature inside is right," he said as he entered the hut.

"Now that you are a full village member," Latel told Jendrin. "I will show you where the cold food storage cave is. Do not tell anyone outside the village about it since a raid would leave us without food for the winter. Follow me to the potty area," he said, starting in that direction.

"You keep food in the potty?" Jendrin joked as they arrived. Latel stopped and turned toward him with a smile growing on his face.

"Yes," he replied. "If you look down that hole, you will see what is left of our food."

Jendrin stared at him a moment before starting toward the potty.

"If you can joke, I can too," Latel said, catching his shoulder. Jendrin felt slightly silly, realizing what he meant by 'what is left.' He chuckled aloud.

"You win that round!" Jendrin laughed. Latel smiled and pointed toward the waterfall behind them.

"An ice cave entrance is underneath the waterfall above us," Latel said, smiling. He started moving up the path toward the waterfall. They came to a small crack in the wall behind the waterfall. "This opening is too small for the large animals and is difficult to find unless you know its location," he said as he turned sideways to slip into the crack. Jendrin followed him and found a large cavern of ice inside.

"I didn't bring a torch since I am just showing you where it is. There are mostly meats and root vegetables in here. We can survive long winters from this store if we need to. We have supplied other villages when they run short of supplies during the winter snows." Jendrin felt the frigid air touch his body as he looked around the cave. He spotted a row of large leaves lying on the rocks near him. He picked one up and peeked inside it to find a frozen cut of meat. "That is part of the boar we recently cut up," Latel told him. Jendrin put the meat back as Latel said, "We use the same rope system to raise and lower baskets down here. Now that you know of this, you can help us maintain it." Jendrin nodded in assent as Latel turned to leave. "It is cold here, and I am ready for lunch," Latel said, exiting the cave.

Marisa arrived at the kitchen as the last of the villagers were leaving with their portion of the catch.

"Marisa!" Airalee said, "Good to see you!"

"Good to see you!" Marisa replied, smiling.

"Are you ready for lunch?" Airalee asked.

211

"Actually," Marisa replied, "I talked with Mirtha, and she asked for our help drying the seagrass. She told me you helped with the harvest. We could work together to set up the seagrass drying racks. We can grab some bread if you can help us." Airalee looked at her fish-slimed hands. "As soon as I clean up, I will join you," Airalee said. The two washed up and grabbed some bread before they walked to Mirtha's drying racks. Mirtha was hanging the first batch of seagrass on the sunny drying rack as Airalee and Marisa arrived.

"Good," Mirtha said. "If one of you will wash the grass, we can quickly finish hanging it out." The three women chatted as they cleaned and hung the baskets of grass. "Marisa, will you check the rack daily to see when they are dry?"

"I will, Mirtha," Marisa replied.

"Good," Mirtha said. "We will then move it to storage." Looking at Airalee, she said, "Airalee and I have seashells and beautiful stones to deliver to Lafrea's hut. We caught a crab that, perhaps, Lafrea will trade for some of her jewelry. I would like you to join us, Marisa."

"I would be glad to," Marisa replied.

Mirtha picked up the basket with a crab and started toward Lafrea's hut. The women arrived at the jeweler's hut, but before they could knock, a voice came from inside, bidding them to enter. Mirtha opened the door as Lafrea smiled and sat at her table.

"Ah, nice to see you three," Lafrea said, moving toward the door. "You have the smell of the sea, but you are still welcome," Lafrea said.

"My apologies," Mirtha said. "We were part of the fishing crew this morning." Lafrea waved her hands dismissively.

"I am pleased you are here," Lafrea said. "Is there something I can help with?" she asked. Mirtha pulled shells and stones from her pocket.

"I was hoping to trade seashells, stones, and a crab for a few pieces of your jewelry," Mirtha said, putting the basket onto the table.

"A crab will get you almost anything," Lafrea said, laughing. Airalee and Mirtha pulled the rest of the sea treasures from their pockets and placed them on the table. "These shells and rocks are already the right size. I won't have to do much to turn them into necklaces, rings, or bracelets," she said as she picked up the white stones. "These white stones deserved to be necklaces," she said, examining each stone.

"I also found a blue stone at a previous gathering," Airalee said, pulling the stone from her pocket.

"This blue stone is beautiful," she said, looking up at Airalee. "I don't remember seeing a clear blue like this. I can see it belongs around your neck as an amulet, Airalee," Lafrea said in a quieter tone.

"Thank you. I would be pleased to wear it," Airalee said. "I did not expect such a gift."

"It will be my pleasure to make it," Lafrea said. "I will start on the necklaces today," she said.

"I would like to keep the blue stone with me," Airalee felt herself say as she wondered why she said that.

"I will measure the stone and add it to the amulet when you return," Lafrea said.

"Thank you, very generous," Airalee said, still wondering why she suggested keeping the stone.

Lafrea measured the shape of the stone with her string and noted the size of each area.

"Did you notice the cuts in the stone?" Lafrea asked, pointing them out to Airalee.

"I did not," Airalee said, looking at the minor cuts in the stone.

"It may have been jewelry lost in the past," Lafrea said. "It will serve a new master now."

"That will make it all the more interesting," Airalee said, putting the stone back into her pocket.

"Would you each take a gift of something I have already made?" Lafrea said, pointing to the side table. Marisa and Airalee browsed through the many pieces of jewelry on the side table. The pieces were all made from strong breadfruit silk woven between rocks, shells, and dried berries. Marisa and Airalee each picked out a bracelet. Mirtha chose a woven ring with a green stone in it.

"Thank you, Lafrea," Mirtha said.

"You are welcome," Lafrea replied, looking pleased at their choices. Airalee and Marisa said their thanks and put their bracelets on.

"I feel we got the better of this deal for only one crab," Mirtha said, opening the crab basket. Lafrea waved her hand dismissively again as she picked up the crab and placed it into her basket. "We thank you for the crab. My family and I will certainly enjoy it."

"It seems a good trade for all of us," Mirtha said, nodding.

"Thank you again, Lafrea," Mirtha said as she approached the door.

"If you find any more blue or white stones, I would be pleased to get them!" Lafrea said, raising her hand. The three women waved to her as they closed the door and started toward the kitchen.

"Do not get attached to the bracelets," Mirtha said. "They will be gifts from you to the Lemidge visitors when they arrive."

Marisa stopped in her tracks, her face gaining a big smile.

"The Lemidge are nearing Olona?" Marisa asked. "I am finally going to be in one of their ceremonies?"

"Yes," Mirtha replied. "Along with Airalee and some village girls."

"There is that name again," Airalee said. "Are we going to discuss that soon?"

"Yes," Mirtha replied, "Kai said we will meet in the council hut tomorrow. I will accompany you two, and she will gather the young girls." Mirtha said as she continued to the kitchen. Airalee noticed the smile on Marisa's face.

"Since you are smiling," Airalee said, "I guess they are not unwelcome here."

"No," Marisa said, moving closer to her. "It will be my first time experiencing their ceremony."

"I look forward to seeing what this mystery is all about," Airalee said.

"We will both learn about this village tradition," Marisa said. "I have heard about it, but not firsthand."

"We should help Kai visit some of the sick villagers after lunch," Mirtha said. "Several villagers are already helping with the sick, but we should visit to help keep their spirits up," Mirtha said as they approached the kitchen area.

Maylore had just finished washing off fish odors as he walked to the kitchen. The smell of the soup and cooked fish made his stomach grumble. He had brought the three companions' bowls and set them on the table. He scooped out some fragrant soup with the freshly cooked fish into his bowl. He sat at one of the tables and chatted with other villagers. The villagers were more talkative and forthcoming since the notice of their full acceptance had gotten around.

"Maylore," Finhile said, looking toward him. "You finished your first fish catch. I hope you enjoyed it!"

"Yes," Maylore replied. "It was good exercise. I need to do more activity like that."

"I will ensure you get word of our next fishing day!" Finhile laughed. "You will have plenty of exercise!" he said as he started eating his soup. Small talk of the weather, fishing, and other subjects continued up and down the table during the meal.

"Hey, dad!" came a familiar voice.

"Must be Airalee," Maylore said as others chuckled.

"May we join you?" Airalee asked, sitting beside him before he could answer.

"Apparently," Maylore said with a laugh. "I brought your bowl and Jendrin's, too," he said, pushing her bowl to her. Maylore greeted Mirtha and Marisa. "The fish is excellent."

"Thanks, dad," Airalee said, taking her bowl. Mirtha and Marisa filled their bowls and returned them to the table.

Pleasant small talk continued throughout the meal.

"Maylore," came a voice from behind him.

"It looks like I am popular today," Maylore said, turning around to see Throc standing there.

"Could you join us for a discussion?" Throc asked.

Maylore considered for a moment.

"Of course," Maylore replied as he rose from the table.

"This is getting to be a habit," Airalee deadpanned. "I will take your bowl and see you tonight," she said.

"Thank you." Maylore smiled and followed Throc toward Rendal's hut.

"Maylore," Rendal said. "Please come in and be comfortable."

"Thank you," Maylore said, noting Gilriel was seated at the other end of the table.

"Throc, please stay a moment," Rendal said, motioning for Throc and Maylore to sit at the table.

"Yes, Beacon," Throc replied, sitting down.

"Maylore, as you may have guessed, Throc and I are statesmen and politicians," Rendal said. "We learned from Gilriel and the writings of others about what to watch for in those we encounter. I cannot see what Gilriel can see in people, and I would like you to work with Gilriel to determine if you can," Rendal said. "If you decide to work with Throc and me later, you will be welcome."

Maylore tried to determine if this was an offer or an order.

"I had thought of becoming a scholar and statesman until recently," Maylore said. "Experience with the mushroom has piqued my interest in that area, too."

The room was silent while they waited for Maylore to continue.

"I would like to explore what abilities Gilriel can help me build," Maylore said.

"I suspect you may not have any real abilities," Gilriel said. "I could still use an assistant since I am approaching my 80th season," Gilriel said. Throc looked sharply at Gilriel before quickly returning his gaze to the table.

"Throc," Rendal said. "Since you no longer need to monitor Maylore, you can return to our tasks of diplomacy and being a statesman. Maylore will start working with Gilriel. We thank you for your help." Rendal finished. "Please return to the writing of the new Lemidge agreement."

"Thank you, Beacon," Throc said as he nodded to the others and left the hut.

"Throc knows you do not want any assistant, Gilriel," Rendal said.

"Yes, I am sure he does. I hoped to prevent him from learning what we plan for training and testing of Maylore," Gilriel said. "The fewer people who know, the better."

"Do you still suspect him to be a spy?" Rendal asked.

"I suspect everyone," Gilriel said. "I believe my small skills are the most the master will tolerate. I have the testimony of a survivor who pointed their finger directly at the master."

"Are you the survivor?" Maylore asked.

"We will not discuss them," Gilriel said firmly, looking toward Maylore. "We will discuss what I hope you can do to help all of us."

"What could I do to help?" Maylore asked.

Softening his tone, Gilriel continued. "I have been attempting to read notes from sorcerers long gone about what abilities they had seen. I believe you may have communication, energy transfer, and perhaps illusional abilities. I have not found anyone with communication and illusion skills before. We will need to work together to see what you can do."

Maylore sat dumbfounded for a time. "Are you sure it was me?" Maylore said. "I don't believe I am anyone special. I thought you said I didn't have any real abilities."

"I said you were not special to prevent Throc from hearing what he should not. Perhaps you are not special. We will have to find it out." Gilriel said. "Tomorrow, I want you to come here. We will walk up to my cave, where we will meet until I leave." Maylore looked at Gilriel.

"May I tell Airalee and Jendrin what is happening?" he asked.

"Tell them you are training to be my assistant in researching cryptic texts. We have already told them the generalities," Gilriel said.

"We don't suspect your companions." Rendal said, "However, we want to keep information from getting to the wrong ears." Rendal looked toward the door. "Something is fishy about how our secrets leak out. I am hoping you may develop a skill to help us find the leaks."

Maylore nodded in understanding.

"How far away is your cave, Gilriel?" he asked. Gilriel pointed toward the mountains.

"It is in the cliffs just above the road," Gilriel said. "It is a short walk up the hill. You may want to bring some food since I have little except berries, beans, and roots." Maylore nodded again while he considered his options.

"I believe this is a good option for me," Maylore announced. "I will be here tomorrow after breakfast."

"Excellent," Rendal said with relief in his voice. Standing up, Rendal said, "Thank you, Maylore. We look forward to a good future."

Maylore stood and smiled at both of them before leaving the hut.

"I wish we had more of the blue spot mushrooms," Gilriel said, watching Maylore leave. "It could speed the process. I assume we have not found any more purple mushrooms." Rendal shook his head.

"They are rarer than the blue-spotted ones," Rendal said. "Do we need to give him a truth mushroom?"

"I do not detect any deception," Gilriel said. "A second method to verify the first would be welcome."

"You sound as suspicious of strangers as me, Gilriel!" Rendal said.

"I am suspicious of everyone," Gilriel said, looking toward the door. "I just hide that suspicion, most of the time."

Chapter 15 - Let me tell you about

Mirtha and Marisa met Airalee as she walked toward Mirtha's hut the following day.

"Good," Marisa said upon seeing Airalee. "We don't have to get you out of bed this morning!"

"I was on my way to shake you awake!" Airalee replied.

A short round of good-natured ribbing occurred before Mirtha stepped in.

"All right, girls, let's go to the council hut," Mirtha said. "The rest may already be there." Mirtha carried a small basket of herbs Airalee recognized to be used to prevent pregnancy.

"Who are we meeting with this morning?" Airalee asked.

"The group who will soon meet with the Lemidge for the first time," Mirtha said as she led the way.

"There are the mysterious Lemidge again," Airalee said. "Who are they?"

"They are a traveling group who perform a special ceremony," Mirtha said. "We will explain to the group when we get inside."

"Group? Who is going to be there?" Airalee asked.

"We gather all the girls who have not heard the true story about the Lemidge," Mirtha said. "Sometimes girls from other villages join us, but not today. We will have four village girls, ages 14 to 18, who are part of the ceremony, plus you two. Other women may sit in the background during the ceremony but won't attend this meeting," Mirtha said as she opened the hut door.

Gilda and three other girls were seated around the table chatting as Kai rose to greet the newcomers.

"Please sit at the table," Kai said, indicating the two remaining chairs as Mirtha moved to stand beside Kai.

"I will start today," Kai said. "Mirtha will join the discussion as we go along. You must understand the meaning of our conversation today. You are free to ask questions." Kai said, surveying the table. They all seemed to be listening.

"Let me begin with village customs many of you may already be aware of," Kai said. "When you decide it is time for your child, the women of Olona are free to choose any partner or group they wish. You may choose a seeding group or one man to create your children. You may select another person to be your baby's partner, another to raise them to adulthood. You may choose another to be a life partner as you age. You may select a different person to be a retirement partner. A partner you select may accept or refuse any role, but many already know what role they want to fulfill." Kai looked at the group, then Airalee, expecting questions. The girls were already familiar with the tradition, and Airalee seemed content to listen.

"Seeding party," Kai started. "When or if you are ready for a child, most women use a seeding of four men to create their child. If you choose that option, you will have no problem finding one man to seed your child."

"Why would we choose a seeding party instead of someone we love?" Airalee asked.

"In past times," Mirtha said, "many of the men of Molia were, for unknown reasons, infertile. The Tocor and Lemidge were having the same problem. The village populations were small, and they found themselves facing severe inbreeding. Village leaders from each race gathered to discuss ways to avoid the situation. A solution they agreed upon was to send four males from each village to offer their services to each village in Molia. Tocor, Lemidge, and humans traveled throughout Molia during the late summer. They found the Tocor travelers produced no children in humans or Lemidge women. They were successful in creating children in other Tocor villages.

Human men were rejected by Lemidge women but welcomed by Tocor women. No children came from those meetings either. Human women did create children from human travelers, and our population stabilized. All races accepted the Lemidge travelers. The human women especially welcomed their visits."

The girls around the table all giggled at the last statement. Airalee could only stare at their amusement.

"The Lemidge did not produce any children except with Lemidge women," Mirtha continued, speaking over their giggling. "The custom of traveling groups stopped for all except the Lemidge."

"To finish on Airalee's question," Kai said, "it is your choice. The seeding group continues in our village to ensure that someone in the group is fertile. It also avoids directing jealousy at one man from other men. Some men are braggers, and their crowing at seeding a child can be difficult."

"Thank you," Airalee replied.

"I will continue with tasks you will be assigned now that you are of the correct age," Kai said. "We will ask you to begin with nursery or elder duty. We will help train you to care for a baby in the nursery. This duty gives you the experience to determine if you want to have children. Some women choose to have none of their own and assist others with childcare. Some choose to help older people. Mirtha and I decided not to bear children and decided to do other tasks for the village. When you participate in the nursery, care for the child will be directed by the baby's mother. She will decide everything for the baby. If the mother is not available, her baby partner will decide. Do you have any questions for me before we move on?"

The girls were quiet as Kai looked at each one.

"All right, next subject," Kai said. "The council assigns a hut to a woman. You are all near the age of having your own hut. You may remain where you are, assume another hut, or build your hut. Airalee is our newest accepted member, and she was also granted permanent status. She can ask a partner or group to leave at any time. She can also ask another person or group to live in her hut. Refrain from being too erratic. You will find none will be your baby or life partner."

"I do not plan to change anything," Airalee said. "Who builds the huts?"

"Men and some women work together to build huts," Kai said. "We have a small group who like building and repairing homes. Sometimes, a baby-mate will build a home for her children. Unattached men and women may live in a new hut or one of the mountain caves. The turnover of homes has balanced with new families being created and elders passing."

"If someone builds a home, does the council take ownership of the home anyway?" Airalee asked.

"No," Kai replied. "The builder owns the home they build. When the builder and their family leave or die, it becomes the council's concern to be assigned." Kai looked at the other members before saying, "This is a quiet group. No one else has a question yet?"

The group shook their heads no.

"The things we discuss now are not easy subjects," Kai said. "You need to be aware of what could happen. Most parents have discussed these subjects with you, but we want to reinforce them. Be wary of all strangers. Bandits, in particular, view young women as prime candidates for slavery. We have lost a few recently due to vigilance. We suspect other villages have lost more. We thought Calel had perished, but she was seen in the bandit camp. She appears to have been captured while gathering. Women who return to us tell us the bandits choose young women since they are prone to domination. They tell us they are likely to obey when commanded to do a task. The bandits do not want older girls because they develop their own will and become uncooperative. Bandits view young girls' bodies as village property to be used by any man in the village. Bandit leaders claim the pretty girls and rarely share them. The few women living in the bandit village fear being beaten if they interfere.

Bandit village women are secretly pleased to have attention go to another girl."

"Barbaric," Airalee said, turning red on her face.

"I fear it gets worse," Kai said. "Bandits do not see the connection between using the girls and the resulting pregnancy. They will refuse to raise children and will force the pregnant girl to return to their village as broken. They believe the girls were sent to them damaged."

"Damaged?" Airalee said indignantly.

"These men are not interested in the welfare of others, especially women," Kai said. "Their ego sees a pretty toy that is now deformed and will soon deposit a burden on them. That is why some bandits choose a Tocor female who is far from pretty but functional until she is too old."

Airalee sputtered, but her anger produced no recognizable words. The rest of the group had heard pieces of the story before, but this part was different.

"It is worse than I have heard," Marisa said.

"The women who return will not speak of their time in the bandit's camp," Kai said. "Only after I gently prod them many times about their experiences will they relate some things to their healer."

The two youngest girls started to cry. Airalee put her arm around the nearest one to try to comfort her.

"We must do something to stop this," Airalee said, hugging the younger girl.

"We agree," Mirtha said.

"Do I tell you these things to scare you?" Kai asked. "Yes, I do. If you hear the sentinels whistle, run to the caves to hide. If you cannot get there quickly, find a hiding spot. Wait for the sentinels to signal the clear signal before you come out."

"Birsha has not sought to collect a new girl in a while," one girl said. "I hope he stays away."

"Birsha recently told Rendal he requires a new girl," Kai said, looking at Airalee. "Oleg had selected Airalee."

The gathering hushed as they looked at Airalee.

"No chance," Airalee said, her teeth gritted.

"Birsha told him you were too old," Kai said. "I would not trust Oleg to follow Birsha's order. Be quick to hide if you hear the sentinel's warning."

"I will be quick with my knife," Airalee said.

"I will be there to join you with my knife," Marisa said.

The rest of the group sat silently with dread and fear in their eyes.

"We hope you will not face that situation," Kai said.

"Does anyone have a question before we continue?" Kai asked.

"My sister has already served in the bandit camp," one girl said sheepishly. "She will not speak of it but tells me I am safe under their village agreement. Is that true?"

"The agreement they signed with us says they will not take more than one child from a mother," Kai said. "Even if your sister has served, do not trust them to honor the agreement. Hide anyway. I understand some mothers have discussed who would serve with girls near the same age. Did your mother discuss this with you?"

"I," she shuddered, "do not know. My sister stared at me when someone else mentioned it before. She would not speak to either of us about it."

"It would be difficult for her or your mother to tell you about," Kai said.

The girl's shoulders slipped, and she fell quiet.

"This has to change," Airalee said, working hard to control her voice.

"Agreed," Kai replied, seeing someone else find the concept unsavory. "We are open to ideas. Passivists run this council and control the guilds. They will not allow any form of force. They have built solid political associations to prevent any offensive force from being built in the village. Most villagers have fallen in line with the council's thinking, becoming sheeple. Do you have an idea of how to change that?"

"I will work on it," Airalee said evenly.

"Let me help, too," Marisa said.

"Join me in my hut when you start developing your plan," Kai said.

The rest of the group was silent. Some shrank back in their chairs at the talk of rebellion.

"If this old woman can help, count me in," Mirtha said.

"Good," Kai said, looking at the girls. "You are no longer children and must know the world's realities. Do not face them with fear. Face them with knowledge and plan what you can do to deal with them." Looking at the sad faces around the table, she took a more conciliatory tone. "Discussing this subject is very distressing to me, too. It is time to move on to other matters we must discuss."

"Thank you," one girl said.

"I assume you have had desires by being attracted to boys or men," Kai said. "You need to know I have herbs to prevent or stop a pregnancy. It would help if you were unafraid to come to me for the herbs before you start. Mirtha has brought a basket of herbs. Take some with you when you leave. Brew them in hot water and drink it daily. It must be your decision when you have a child. I have herbs to comfort you during your pregnancy when that happens. Some of you may have already had experience with village boys. I hope he took precautions, too."

All the girls at the table sat stone-faced except Marisa, who smiled broadly.

"I know you need no encouragement to use the herbs, Marisa," Kai said.

"They work well," Marisa said, smiling.

"The herbs work most of the time, but not all the time," Kai said, looking directly at Marisa.

"I understand," Marisa said, her smile fading.

"Good," Kai said before returning to look at the group. "Rendal has talked with young boys to emphasize leaving their seed outside the girl's body. We all want you to enjoy your body but remember that children are a lifetime commitment not to be taken lightly."

"Next subject," Kai said. "Many of you have heard or have seen the Lemidge, but I will tell a little about them for those who have not. The Lemidge are a race similar to the Tocor but differ in appearance, customs, abilities, and talents. The Lemidge are generally taller, stronger, and thinner than the Tocor. They lead simple lives living in villages similar to ours. They make homes from the wood of fallen trees and use woven grass for the thatched roofs. They avoid contact with other races except when trading their services to others. They act more stoically than the Tocor, except for festivals. I understand their festivals are wild affairs held seasonally in their mountain home." Kai scanned the table to see if there was any reaction. Seeing no reaction, she continued.

"What do they mean to us?" Kai asked. "They are the last of the traveling seeders. A few of them will leave their travel village of Liqua and travel to other human villages in Molia. They particularly like jewelry, leather clothing, or sweet foods. Human women find a Lemidge man irresistible when they are near. They have a natural odor that makes human women swoon. Women cannot resist them and become open to their advances if they get close for long enough. Women are fully aware of what is happening and welcome their actions. The effects last a few hours after the Lemidge has departed. You would be wise to avoid leaving the group hut until their effect wears off. Human men are unaffected by the Lemidge and will offer their services to you. Conception occurs more frequently after a visit by the Lemidge. The village men do not resent Lemidge's visits; instead, they look forward to the aftereffects they may be able to enjoy.

When the Lemidge group arrives, we will ask you to decide what you want to do. We will meet with them in a hut where they will walk among us and offer additional service if you pay extra. Their effect on women fades after a few visits by the Lemidge. Their effects become fainter each time until you are unaffected. Mirtha and I have been through this several times and are unaffected by their presence. We will have a few of the other village women join for the pleasure they bring. Eventually, they will lose Lemidge's effects and not return. Does anyone have questions before we move on?"

Most girls around the table already knew what Kai was talking about. Airalee was surprised but unsure what to think.

"I am not sure what to say," Airalee said. "Are all girls required to attend the meeting?"

"No, but you will enjoy it," Kai said. "If you have had no experience or only with human men, it will be a frenzy you should not miss."

Airalee could not decide what to say. Marisa and the other girls were smiling, so she relaxed.

"We will gather you all together again when the Lemidge arrives," Kai said. "Back to work with you," Kai said, indicating the door.

Jendrin

Jendrin gathered his work in progress and walked to Latel's work hut. When he arrived, Latel was hard at work creating a large vest of leather and stone beads. "Good morning, Jendrin," he said, looking up.

"Good morning," Jendrin replied. "Do we have something going on today that I can witness?" he asked.

"Tanning," Latel replied. "We will visit with Dirdin later today. He is preparing to tan our pig hide. I asked if we could learn the process."

"I will continue to work on my axe and knives until then," Jendrin said. "Find me at the kitchen fire when you are ready. Mirtha may put me to work helping with lunch, but I can handle that too."

"Mirtha and Kai are hosting a meeting this morning with the girls," Latel said.

"Just the girls?" Jendrin asked.

"Yes," Latel replied. "The Lemidge will be visiting Olona soon. They meet with the girls who have not been around them before. They reinforce village customs and what to expect when they are near the Lemidge."

"Are they dangerous?" Jendrin asked.

"No," Latel laughed. "They have an aphrodisiac effect on human women. The village elders want them to be aware of and take advantage of the visit. Before you ask, Lemidge women do not affect human men."

"That's too bad," Jendrin replied. "That would add a little spice to life if they did." Jendrin chuckled. "I will work at the kitchen fire until Dirdin is ready," Jendrin said, holding up his project bag.

"I will be a half day with this, then I will join you," Latel replied, smiling. Jendrin nodded and walked to the kitchen area. When he arrived, Several villagers added vegetables, meat, and spices to the growing stew.

"Jendrin, would you add wood to the fire?" one villager asked. Jendrin waved and retrieved some wood from the drying pile. Adding the wood to the fire, he ensured it would not overheat the cooking pots.

Jendrin retrieved his projects from the bag he carried: two axe heads, one mostly finished stick for the axe, and a smaller one to make a hatchet. He noticed that the butcher did not have a hatchet to cut the meat. Dirdin is a powerful man who could cut most meat, but others who cut meat could benefit from a hatchet. Jendrin decided that if he cut meat, he would need a chopping tool.

Jendrin inspected the ends of each stick that flared out at the top. It would allow him to push the wedge-shaped axe heads through the handle near the end. He had already removed some of the handle's wood and used a small burning coal to make a hole for the axe head to fit through. He lined up coal from the fire along the line on the handle he wanted burned through. Lightly blowing on the coal, it brightly glowed as it burned the wood away. The burning process took time, but he could do both handles simultaneously. Finally, the coal burned through the axe handles enough that he could push his knife through to widen the hole. He pushed the head's unsharpened end through and tied it on the opposite side of the handle.

"Jendrin," a voice said approaching him. "Are you ready to visit with Dirdin?" Latel asked, stopping near him.

"Yes," Jendrin replied. "I can finish this axe later," he said, dousing both handles with water to prevent further burning. The two men started walking toward Dirdin's work area, near the smoking hut and the flat near the creek. Dirdin saw them approaching.

"Ah, two more volunteers," Dirdin said. "Let me get the pig's hide from the pool in the creek." Several other men and women were working on various stages of hide processing.

"Where did these hides come from?" Jendrin said, looking at the multiple stages of hide processing. "I thought the village did not hunt animals."

"They gathered them from the death pit in the foothills above us," Latel said. "One is a bear, and the other two are young blood wolves." The sound of heavy boots announced Dirdin's return bearing the pig's hide.

"We think the blood wolves smelled the bear's death," Dirdin said. "We believe the young wolves tried to go down the near vertical sides of the pit, fell, and died with the bear. Blood wolf tracks were around the top, but they were larger, and they knew they could not get down the sides. We leave ropes to get down into the smelly pit. The meat was no good, but we could still gather the hides."

Dirdin finished the story by tossing the pig hide over a slanted skinning post. Spreading out the hide, he picked up a long, straight flint rock with a slight edge.

"Your job is to scrape off the last of the meat and fat on the skin, leaving just the white hide below it," Dirdin said as he started to scrape the hide with the rock. He turned the hide on the post to show the men what to do, then handed the stone to Jendrin. "It will probably take you the rest of this day to finish this. Tomorrow, we will continue the process," he said, waving to them as he checked other processors. "Looks like I will start," Jendrin said, smiling at Latel.

"Be my guest," Latel replied.

CHAPTER 16 - MAYLORE

Maylore waved to Airalee and Jendrin as they left the hut that morning. He set out toward Rendal's house, not waiting for Throc to come for him. Rendal opened the door to his place before Maylore could knock and invited him inside. Gilriel sat at the table as he arrived.

"You are late," Gilriel said, pointing to the chair opposite him.

"Good morning to you both," Maylore said as he moved to the indicated chair. He noticed that the glowing rock was missing. "The rock is gone?" he asked, looking toward Rendal.

"Yes," Rendal replied. "The test of who could see the energy is over. We do not expect more visitors, so I put it out of the way. If we receive additional travelers, I will set it up again," he smiled, sitting down.

"I hope you did not get too many questions from your companions," Gilriel said.

"No," Maylore replied, "They both heard you say to keep the information secret."

"What are they doing today?" Gilriel asked.

"Jendrin is learning to tan hides," Maylore replied. "Airalee is meeting with Kai and Mirtha about women's stuff."

"Ah yes," Gilriel chuckled. "The Lemidge are visiting, I hear."

"Lemidge?" Maylore quizzed.

"The Lemidge are seasonal visitors to human villages," Rendal replied. "They usually look to trade for items of interest to them."

"Why would just the women care about them?" Maylore asked.

"The Lemidge men have an undetectable scent that drives human women wild," Rendal replied. "Their scent does not affect men."

"Perhaps they must bring their women with them," Maylore smiled.

"They do," Rendal replied. "The Lemidge women start the process in the Lemidge men. Unfortunately, Lemidge women have no special effect on human men."

Gilriel turned his head to look at Rendal.

"Men are men and will accept any woman," Gilriel said, drawing a sharp look from Rendal. "All right, Beacon, I will be silent."

"Why be silent about what is true," Maylore said with a laugh. Gilriel chuckled with him, but Rendal didn't join them.

"All right, gentlemen, let's move on to our task," Rendal said. "We would like you to accompany Gilriel to his hut to learn what if any, ability you may have. Have you tried to gather energy this morning?" Rendal asked.

"No," Maylore said, "it was a short night, and I came here this morning as instructed."

"Good," Rendal replied, "Gilriel will evaluate and train you. He will be leaving with the master when he visits Molia's villages. I hope he can help you learn how to use the abilities you may have. Gilriel will not be able to train you completely. You must experiment and practice each area as you discover it."

"Would it be better if I move to the cave also?" Maylore asked, looking at Gilriel.

"I value my privacy," Gilriel replied. "Years ago, when my tutor Ivmar left the cave, I moved from this hut to the cave. I do not enjoy the constant noise of village life when I come here."

"I see," Maylore replied. "My companions might miss me if I don't show up each night."

"I believe they would," Rendal said. "Airalee seems to view you as a substitute father figure. Jendrin, I believe, sees you as an older brother."

"Perhaps," Maylore replied, "at least they don't see me as just the old man," he smiled.

"You are not old," Rendal said. "I believe you to be mid-50s." Maylore realized again that he had no idea of his birth date, where he was born, or how old he was.

"I would agree with that," Maylore replied.

"I was 30 summers when I became Beacon following Beacon Savrin's death." Looking toward Gilriel, he started to speak, but Gilriel cut him off.

"Let's say I am near your combined ages," Gilriel said. "I qualify as an old man," he added with a straight face. "I would prefer to slip away into the arms of death on my terms than burden village youngsters to tend to me."

"Nonsense, Gilriel," Rendal said, sounding annoyed. "You would not be a burden to the village. We take care of our own here."

"To wile away the time in an elders hut waiting for death is not living!" Gilriel said. "I hope to go out with a blaze!"

"Well," Rendal replied, "It is not nearly that time yet. Many of our elders contribute to the village in other ways. Many have the patience to teach younger villagers skills they can pass on to the younger generation."

"You mentioned a key I do not have: patience," Gilriel said.

"You sell yourself short," Rendal said. "You have much more patience than you had in the past. Someday, you may be ready to slow down and help in other ways."

"You have more faith in me than I do, Beacon," Gilriel said.

"Be that as it may, let's take up Maylore's training," Rendal said. "Are you two ready to begin?" Rendal said, looking at the two men.

"Yes," Maylore replied. Gilriel nodded and stood up.

"Have any more blue spot mushrooms been found?" Gilriel asked, looking toward Rendal.

"Airalee found a few that are drying," Rendal said. "Kai and Gilda plan to go hunting above the Lemidge's village after the Lemidge leave our village."

"I thought Kai would be immune to the Lemidge effects by now," Gilriel said.

"She is," Rendal replied. "She is shepherding Gilda, Marisa, Airalee, and the other girls through the experience."

"I see," Gilriel replied. "I hope they return from their trip before the master arrives. I will need to take the few remaining dried mushrooms with me."

"That is our plan anyway," Rendal said, nodding.

"Come Maylore, I will lead the way," Gilriel said, standing and walking to the door. Maylore looked to Rendal, who nodded.

"Thank you, Rendal," Maylore said. "I will do the best I can," he said as he followed Gilriel outside.

Gilriel walked quickly for an older man, forcing Maylore to move quicker than he would normally. They walked toward the mountain, passing the cave where the companions emerged. They crossed the road near the visitor's hut and climbed into the hills. Gilriel pointed up the side of a tumble of granite boulders.

"This way," Gilriel said, starting between the boulders. A nearly invisible path led up between the granite rocks to a slightly flatter area 70 sticks uphill. Maylore thought he could hear the sound of running water but did not see water anywhere.

"Is there water flowing nearby?" Maylore asked, looking at the dry hillside.

"There is an underground river flowing beneath us," Gilriel said as he continued to the top. Looking down, Maylore wondered how far down the water might be before following Gilriel again. Boulders gave way to a large, flat area. Gilriel stopped and spread his arms.

"If you can find the opening to the cave," Gilriel said, "I will pick you a bowl of berries. If not, you pick me a bowl."

Maylore suspected he would not find the opening. He started looking for a path or any indication of a gap in the granite. Looking at the jumble of boulders continuing up the mountain, he suspected the cave was before him. He looked toward the ground for a worn path, but the gravel showed no sign of travel. He started walking toward the rock wall before him. He was looking behind the rocks, above and below him. Walking to the left and right did not reveal any sign of an opening.

"I don't see any cave opening here," Maylore said, returning to Gilriel.

"Exactly!" Gilriel exclaimed. "That is why Savrin chose this cave after he found it. It provides excellent defense from casual intruders. My tutor, Ivmar, inherited it after Savrin disappeared. It also protects against dangerous animals since they are too large to fit through the cave opening."

Moving to the right, Gilriel pointed to a large rock in front of another stone. Turning to his side, he slipped between the rocks and disappeared. Maylore followed him to the rock and followed him. He came face to face with a granite wall, appearing to be the end.

"This way," he heard Gilriel say to his left. Maylore followed his voice as the wall curved, hiding the cave entrance. Maylore followed the wall as it opened into a small cave. Sunlight filtered in from a small hole in the top of the cave.

"Come, come, don't stand there," Gilriel said. "You have berries to pick for my breakfast!" Gilriel chuckled.

Maylore could make out his outline as Gilriel moved down a much broader and taller tunnel. The sound of water grew louder as he followed Gilriel down the tunnel.

A sudden scream stopped Maylore as he involuntarily squatted down.

"Yes, I know IB," Gilriel said, waving his hand above him. "There is a stranger in the cave. Thank you." Turning to Maylore, he added, "I neglected to inform you about the Intelligent Bird living here. It chooses to serve as my watcher in the event something manages to wander in. Usually, the intruder is a small animal that scurries away when the bird screams. He will probably be quiet now. Follow me," Gilriel said. Turning, he continued down the tunnel. Maylore looked up but only saw a dark wall. Standing up, he followed Gilriel through the tunnel.

"What is an intelligent bird?" Maylore asked Gilriel's back.

"They are large, intelligent birds with black feathers and orange wing tips," Gilriel said as he walked. "They live where they want, and I hear they quickly learn tasks. I have not tried to teach this one a task. This one sounds an alarm when it sees a stranger in the cave. That is a huge benefit to me. These birds know people, and some animals are dangerous. They will hide quietly in trees, caves, and any other place that will conceal them. I have heard they will even hide underwater." Gilriel explained as he walked.

"Why is it just called IB," Maylore asked.

"No one came up with a good name," Gilriel said. "The birds learn tasks quickly and keep their mouths shut. Keeping to themselves made them seem intelligent, so the convention became IB." Gilriel said as the tunnel opened into a large round area. Rocks and boulders were strewn about the floor of the cavern. The area before him was clear of stones, and a crude wooden table occupied the center. The sound of water emanated from the right side. Maylore noticed two blue ley lines crossing the floor. The lines meet at the water source on the other side of a rock ledge.

"Do you see something?" Gilriel asked, noticing Maylore's looking toward the water.

"There are two ley lines here," Maylore replied, pointing at each line.

"Correct," Gilriel said, "I believe that energy drew Savrin to this cave. Ivar told me his tutor, Savrin, was a powerful sorcerer who could see and disperse energy sources anywhere. He could gather immense energy from two lines very easily." Waving his hand toward the cave, he added. "Let me show you my home."

Maylore moved to stand beside him near the table.

"This is my study table," Gilriel said. "Behind it is my bed, and to the right is my water supply," he said, waving his arms in different directions. "Light comes in from holes in the ceiling, letting out smoke from the fire."

Maylore looked up to see a large hole in the ceiling facing the sunrise. A thick brush surrounded the hole. Maylore turned and walked to the sound of the water. A small pool of water bubbled up from the bottom. It exited the pool to his right, disappearing into the mountain's depths.

"Let's go out the back of the cave, where you will find my breakfast ready to pick," Gilriel said. They weaved between the tumble of rock to the opposite side. Gilriel turned sideways again and disappeared behind the rock wall. Maylore followed suit and, after a short shuffle, emerged next to Gilriel in the bright sunlight. A bread tree grew before him, surrounded by berry bushes and other fruit trees. "Prior generations lived here planting trees and bushes," Gilriel said. "Ivmar told me he replaced a few of the trees that died and added a few berry bushes. He told me before he left to care for the trees and plants, and they would take care of me. I have trimmed dead branches for firewood and diverted water for the plants. I find I need little else. You may explore the area after our lessons if you wish." Gilriel pointed to a berry bush and a basket near it. "Fill the basket, and I will meet you inside," Gilriel said, returning to the cave.

Maylore picked up the basket and started picking the large blackberries. As he worked, he noticed a small stream of water. The water flowed alongside an assortment of trees. Flowers of different types grew around the area.

"I wonder where the water comes from?" Maylore said, looking at the cliffs surrounding the garden. Maylore followed the stream up the garden incline. The water bubbled up from the rocks and flowed alongside the garden. Maylore noted that many different flowers and vegetables appeared to be planted in groups in the garden as he worked his way back to the berry bushes. Maylore quickly filled the basket and returned to the cave's center.

Gilriel was adding wood to a small fire.

"Good," Gilriel said as Maylore returned. "Set the basket on the table, and we can start our first discussion."

Maylore set the basket down, curious about how the table was level on the rocky floor. Looking underneath it, he saw someone had cut the table's legs at different lengths so they would only fit into particular rock crevices. The legs of the two chairs were cut similarly, providing one level spot to sit. Gilriel filled a small pot of water and returned with wooden bowls. Setting the water and bowls on the table, he filled his bowl with berries and sat down.

"After we eat," Gilriel said, "let's try your energy-gathering skills to see if they are stronger here. It may not be stronger yet. The healing I did of your portal takes time." Maylore nodded, noticing a large book on the table. "Ivmar's book," Gilriel said, noticing Maylore's gaze. "It is more of a sorcerer's diary and valley history than a usable book. I believe others created the book, and Savrin left it for Ivmar. Ivmar told me he knew nothing about the book's authors. Ivmar discussed what ideas he could gather from the book. He added his notes on the later pages about using nature's energy and finding others with abilities. I added a few pages at the end as I learned different things. When you come to visit, look through it while you are here. Be careful; the page tears easily, and there are no copies." He opened the drawer at the end of the table and placed the book inside. "Be sure to put it back when you leave to avoid animals using its contents for nests," he said, closing the drawer. "You may want to hide it in a rock crevice once I leave. A table is a natural place to look for items if a stranger enters when I am gone."

Maylore nodded as he ate his berries. The two of them finished eating and set the bowls aside.

"Let's begin by testing your energy-gathering ability," Gilriel said. "I want you to concentrate on gathering but not lose track of your surroundings. If you ignore what is around you and are killed, you are useless to your group."

Maylore nodded, considering again how to concentrate and listen to the world around him.

"There is a small fire beside the table," Gilriel said, pointing down. "I want you to collect some of the fire's energy. This time, do not get close to the flame so that it burns you. I want you to bring the energy through your energy portal and out to your fingertips."

"Portal?" Maylore questioned. "Is this what we discussed before?"

"Yours was blocked," Gilriel said. "I was able to open a small portion, which should allow you to transfer energy."

"How do I use the portal?" Maylore asked.

"Imagine traversing via your string from the source to the portal and then to your fingers. The portal is located approximately here in your body," Gilriel said, pointing at his own body.

Maylore moved to the other side of the table and sat on a nearby rock. Using the same method he practiced before, he removed one sandal and stretched his arms along his lap with palms pointing toward each other. He imagined a string connecting from his portal to the small fire. The fire's energy started rising along the string and into his energy portal. He kept pulling the energy until it finally stopped coming. Maylore realized the little fire had gone out, and Gilriel was not in the cave.

"I didn't do a good job of staying aware of my surroundings," Maylore told himself.

"Indeed not," Gilriel said from behind him. "We will work on that after you prove you can control an energy source. What did you see during this exercise?"

Maylore recounted the fire energy moving from the fire up to his body before disappearing. Gilriel merely nodded as he moved in front of Maylore. "Is the energy stream larger than before?"

"It was slightly larger," Maylore replied. "There were usually two or three energy sparks at a time instead of just one."

"Excellent!" Gilriel said, sounding surprised. "You are making progress already. We only widened the portal a short time ago. I doubt the portal string has grown to the dome yet."

Maylore accepted Gilriel's analysis but was displeased that he could not gather the energy.

Gilriel pointed to the water pool.

"Try pulling energy from the crossing ley lines," Gilriel said.

Maylore moved to the rock but faced the pool.

"As you gather the energy, try moving the sparks to your palms," Gilriel said, sitting back in his chair.

Maylore concentrated on the spot where the ley lines appeared to cross. The sparks moved to him and seemed to collect in his energy portal as the energy from the ley line slowed, then stopped. No energy arrived at his palms.

"I seem to leak," Maylore said. "The energy comes to me, but nothing appears in my palms."

"I see," Gilriel said. "I suspect the leak is in your head! Do you believe you could do something others cannot? Do you believe you have no right to do this? Do you oscillate between thinking 'I can do this' to 'who do I think I am'?"

"True," Maylore said, a slow smile coming. "A few days ago, I was a typical human. I intended to live quietly in Olona before the blue rock ratted me out."

The comment caught Gilriel off guard, and he started laughing.

"I understand," Gilriel said, regaining control. "We are asking you to delay the quiet, scholarly life to determine what skills you may have. You do yourself a disservice by not exploring what was granted to you. If you are a true sorcerer, you could benefit Olona, Molia, and even Almora. I realize it is challenging to learn any new skill, let alone something you did not know existed!"

"I will try as long as I get my peaceful life in the end," Maylore said, returning to a chair facing the ley lines.

"I can promise nothing like that," Gilriel said. "The sorcerers I have heard about lived very peaceful lives."

"That is good," Maylore said, resuming his practiced position.

"This time," Gilriel said, "I want you to close your eyes and use your mind to look down at the energy portal. Demand it open the energy dome and let you pull the energy out to your hands."

"Ah, perhaps that is where I was failing," Maylore said. "I was concentrating on retrieving the energy into the portal, but not what to do with the energy after that."

"Form the energy into a ball between your hands," Gilriel said.

Maylore closed his eyes and requested that the energy from the ley line come to his energy portal. This time, he focused on his energy portal, demanding it open to the outside world. Maylore could sense a popping sensation as a tickle of energy left the portal and rose through his arms. The feeling of the power entering his arms excited him. Maylore pushed the energy to his palms and formed a circular ball of sparks between his palms. The sparks moved into a circle, made one circle, and then dropped to the ground. Maylore started drawing and forming the ball several times for what he thought was a short time. Someone shook his shoulder.

"Maylore!" Gilriel was saying. "You have practiced long enough for one day."

Maylore could see the cave was much darker, and a fire burned behind him. A bowl of berries and fruit sat on the table.

"I want you to tell me what you saw," Gilriel said, offering him the bowl.

Maylore took the bowl, realizing he was starving. Eating a few of the berries and fruit, he started recounting what had occurred.

"I heard the energy portal pop, and I could get the blue sparks to form a small ball," Maylore said. "I completed a circle before they would drop to the ley line again. I continued to work on getting the ball larger and keeping the sparks going around. I got them to circle a few times before they fell away but did not get a larger ball," he finished.

"That is excellent for one day," Gilriel said, smiling. "Evening approaches, and I promised you would return to Olona at the end of each day. Let us return."

Gilriel turned to go as Maylore attempted to stand. His knees felt locked in place, and he took a little time to stand. Gilriel noticed he had not moved and returned to offer a hand-up. Maylore accepted the help and followed Gilriel through the cave. The bird made a few soft noises when he saw Maylore but otherwise remained quiet. Gilriel was also silent as they made the quick trip back to the village. He stopped in the kitchen area and faced Maylore. "Can you find your way to the cave tomorrow?"

"Yes," Maylore replied. "It is a simple route once shown."

"Good," Gilriel replied. "Join me there tomorrow morning, and we will continue." Gilriel turned toward Mirtha's work hut and walked quickly away.

The kitchen was empty, but a pot of soup was available. Gilriel reappeared with a large cut of cooked fish in his hand.

"Mirtha spared us some of this excellent fish," he said, passing half to Maylore. "Good night," he said, starting back to his cave.

The smell of the fish turned his hunger wild, and he sat at one of the tables and devoured the large chunk. His hunger was soon satisfied, and he turned toward the companion's hut. Maylore could feel the start of a headache as he walked the path to the hut. Opening the door to the hut, he saw Airalee and Jendrin sitting at the table. Airalee wrote notes on bread tree paper, adding notes of herbs and mushrooms to a new book. Jendrin worked to complete the slot in his ax handle for the new ax head.

"Greetings all," Maylore said, stepping through the door.

"Hi, dad," Airalee said, looking up from her writing.

"Maylore, welcome back," Jendrin replied. "Airalee said I had to wait for you to return before discussing our day. I would like to hear what Mirtha and Kai had to say to the women," he said, looking toward Airalee. Maylore was tired but decided to sit and hear what his companions had been doing.

Airalee recounted information about village customs, the bandits' demands, and the future Lemidge visit.

"The bandit's practice needs to stop," Jendrin said. "We are the ones who can start this change."

"Marisa, Kai, and Mirtha are willing to work on a plan to effect change. You and dad are welcome to join us."

"It would be my pleasure to join," Jendrin said. "We need to convince the council and villagers of the need to fight back. The passive attitude of the council is where we should begin."

"We can also try to recruit the women who were forcefully taken in the past," Airalee said. "Few will discuss their past, but we must try."

"Agreed," Maylore said.

"Shall we move to lighter subjects before we try to sleep?" Airalee asked. "What did the hero do today?"

"I'm working on tools I can use," Jendrin said. "The hatchet is complete, and the ax is nearly complete. It's not as exciting as what you were doing, but useful," he said.

"What was dad's activity today?" Airalee asked, looking at him.

"I worked with Gilriel on mystical stuff," Maylore said, unsure what to tell them. "I practiced in his hideaway cave not far from here. He seems to want to keep its location a secret."

"He can keep it a secret as far as I am concerned," Jendrin said, continuing to work on his ax.

"I suspect I wouldn't understand the mystical stuff even if you try," Airalee said with a laugh.

"I don't understand it either," Maylore said. "According to Gilriel, it is part of the problem. It is far from the quiet life I was expecting."

"You could stop," Jendrin suggested.

"It is a challenge I would like to explore for now," Maylore said. "Rendal promised to allow me to study with him after I finish."

"Don't let it run you over, dad," Airalee said. "If it wears you out, you won't be able to study."

"Speaking of wearing out, I am ready for sleep," Maylore said. "See you all in the morning."

"Good night, Dad," Airalee said as Maylore entered his room.

"Enough documenting herbs and mushrooms for now," Airalee said. "Good night, hero," she said as she stood. Closing her book, she pushed through the reeds to her room.

"Night, Airalee," Jendrin replied as he cleaned up. He smiled at his completed tools and turned to his bed.

CHAPTER 17 - VISITORS

The three companions awoke the following day to a now familiar pattern: a visit to the privy, gathering beans for breakfast, wood for the fires, clean up, and alternating baths. Airalee continued her nightly bathing but became comfortable with Marisa and the other women in the pool. Maylore's headache from the day before continued, but he picked up his share of wood and took it to the village woodpile. Airalee built their cooking fire and placed the pot of beans Jendrin had prepared near the fire.

Opening the door, she tossed her fist-sized lava rock into the bushes. "I do not need you any longer," Airalee said, re-entering the hut. She retrieved the club from the side of her bed and took it to the fire pit. "Thanks for your reassuring presence," she said as she placed it into the fire. "My companions are my friends, and I do not fear them."

Jendrin and Maylore returned to the hut, and light conversation between the companions filled the air as they ate breakfast. Maylore was pleased to hear Airalee and Jendrin had stopped bickering with each other in the mornings. His consistent pressure "to be nice" seemed effective, although he suspected other forces might be at work. Jendrin cleaned the dishes while Airalee tidied the hut and banked the fireplace. A knock drew their attention to the door. Jendrin opened the door to find Marisa smiling at him. Beyond her, he saw Latel coming up the path. Latel stopped and waved for Jendrin to join him.

"Good morning, Marisa," he said, exiting the hut but holding the door for her. "Goodbye," he said as she entered.

"Bye, Jendrin," Marisa said, moving to the table.

"Bye, hero," Airalee called.

Jendrin jogged down the path to join Latel, who had already turned toward the tanning area.

"Where are we headed?" Jendrin asked, catching up with Latel.

"Dirdin has started the tanning process on our pig hide," Latel said. "Now that you are an accepted citizen, we have been invited to continue the process."

Latel and Jendrin arrived at the tanning area to find someone Latel had not seen before.

"Ah, you two are finally here," Dirdin said. "I was just about to introduce Gulstan, a tanner from Forsba. Forsba is a village several sunsets from here," he said, looking at Jendrin. Turning to the small group, he added, "He will show us the methods their village uses for tanning."

The gathered crew was well aware of the laborious tanning process. The team was happy to see anything that could speed up the process.

"The first hide we will do is a pig hide," Gulstan said. "We will want to remove the hair from this hide," Gulstan said. "The second is a wolf hide. We want to keep the hair on that hide. We will first soften the wolf hide using water. Water softening the hide can take quite a while. Dirdin tells me you use natural tannins from the cedar trees and others to tan the hide."

"True," Dirdin said.

"We will use ash from our hardwood fires for the pig's hide," Gulstan continued. "It will remove the hair much quicker. Take the ash from your smoking hut and add water to it. Soaking the hide in that water makes the hair ready to be removed much faster." Gulstan pushed the pig hide into a pot with a stick.

"Jendrin may be ready to scrape the hair off tomorrow or the next," Dirdin said, looking at Jendrin.

Jendrin nodded, acknowledging his new assignment.

"When you remove it from the pot," Gulstan said, "be sure the water does not get on your skin, or it will burn you. Rinse the hide completely before you start scraping the hair off of it," Gulstan said, moving toward the wolf hide. "This wolf hide will not be soaked in that solution since we want to keep the hair. We will clean the hide of fat and muscle and create a solution from the wolf's brain and some soap weed."

The gathering looked at each other as he spoke but kept quiet.

"We will crush the animal brain in water and add a small amount of soap weed," Gulstan said. "Work the solution onto the hide, ensuring we do not get it on the hair side of the hide. It will take quite a bit of time to work it in," he said, scanning the group. "Roll up the hide and store it in a dry area for a few sunrises." Gulstan looked at Dirdin before continuing. "It sounds like you use the same hide stretching and softening methods we use. Are you smoking the hides to add color and preserve them?"

"The wood tannins do that for us," Dirdin answered.

"Good," Gulstan replied. "I can show you the smoking method if you wish."

"We are open to other ways," Dirdin said.

"Let's create the softening solution," Gulstan said. "We don't have the wolf's brain," Gulstan said. "We do have the pig's brain to create our solution." Gulstan crushed the pig's brain into a workpot until all the pieces dissolved into the solution. Adding some soap weed, he continued his teaching. "We will put the hide on a flat surface and work the solution into the wolf hide. The process will take a quarter sun cycle, and usually, several people trade off doing the job."

"I will take the first session," Dirdin said. "Latel and others can join in later." Dirdin laid the hide on a flat rock and started working the solution into it. Gulstan commented as he worked, and the rest of the crew observed.

Jendrin took ownership of the pot with the pig hide and stirred the hide in the solution. Setting the pot near the stretching post, he joined the rest of the group.

Airalee

Marisa took a chair opposite Airalee after Jendrin left the hut with a smile on her face.

"The Lemidge from Liqua arrived this morning," she said. "I saw the Beacon greeting the five in the roadside visitor's hut. One was a woman who led the four men to the council hut. In the past, they met with our villagers in there."

"What did they look like?" Airalee asked.

"They were all one and a half sticks tall, with long dark hair and a slender, wiry build," Marisa said. "They looked like taller Tocor with dark hair. Let's go to Mirtha's hut and wait for her to call the group together. Get your Lemidge gift, and let's go."

Airalee walked back into her room to get the gift bracelet. Marisa held the door for her as they started toward Mirtha's place. A voice from behind her made her turn to see who hailed her. Maylore was returning from his bath and was waving goodbye to them. Airalee said goodbye as they waved to him and continued on their way.

"It looks like most of the group is here," Airalee said as they arrived at Mirtha's hut. A few older women had joined the group and were chatting with each other. The young girls from the prior discussion were standing near Mirtha. Mirtha saw them approaching and waved them over to the group.

"Is Kai and Gilda here somewhere?" Mirtha asked, looking around at the gathering.

"Marisa," Mirtha said, not seeing them. "Would you see if you can find them?"

Marisa started running toward Kai's hut when she saw them approaching her. Waving to them, she returned to the group.

"They will be here soon," Marisa said.

Mirtha nodded, then directed comments to the older women present.

"I am sure you are aware that the effects of the Lemidge diminish each time you are in their presence. If you are expecting excitement like the last time you were with them, it will be much less, if at all. I have led these groups for many seasons, and the Lemidge no longer affects me. Sad to say, really," she smiled. "The Lemidge will still require your contribution to be in the hut with them even if they do not affect you. It is their requirement, and our village respects it."

Kai and Gilda joined the group just as she finished. Gilda stood next to Marisa and shyly took her hand. Marisa looked at her and saw a look of askance on Gilda's face.

"Good to see you, Gilda," Marisa said, squeezing the younger girl's hand. Gilda smiled and moved closer to Marisa as Mirtha started speaking to them.

"Girls, the Lemidge are peaceful people and will not harm you," she said, noticing Gilda's anxious behavior. "They are soft in their approach, unlike our men, and give you a chance to decide what is right for you." Looking softly at the younger girls around her, she said, "If you choose to have them deflower you, you must provide an additional offering, or they will ignore you, assuming you do not want their attention." The girls showed their second offerings of jewelry and clothing. "I remind you that you cannot get a child from the deflowering. Your body is too different from theirs to support building a child inside you." Mirtha looked at the girls around her to verify they understood.

"Deflowering?" Airalee said. "I didn't know that was the purpose of the ceremony."

"It is not, really," Marisa said. "That is a tiny part of it. It is an enjoyable experience."

"I am not sure I want to be deflowered," Airalee said.

"You do not have to," Marisa said. "The effects of the Lemidge are not as powerful, but enjoyable. Besides, Kai and Mirtha will not let any harm come to you."

Airalee looked at Kai and Mirtha, thinking Marisa was correct. Her mind wavered on what she should do.

"When we enter the council hut," Mirtha said, "you will sit or lie on the mats while the others sit behind you in chairs. Spectators only need to be near the Lemidge to be affected. The process will start when the Lemidge woman has collected the offerings and verified who participates in the ceremony. She will lead the Lemidge men into the room, and they will stand at the front of the mats. You will feel your muscles relax, fears slowly fade, and other worries dissipate. The Lemidge have performed this ceremony for many seasons, and they know when you are ready. One will ask you to verify that you want him to proceed. I can tell you, as time passes, you will find it extremely difficult to deny him. If you answer yes, he will ask you to lie on the mat and complete the ceremony. You will feel nothing except extreme pleasure and blissfully rest on the mat. The rest of the group will be intoxicated and euphoric but will not feel the blissfulness of the participants. The Lemidge will leave immediately after all the participants are complete." Looking at the faces in the group, she continued, "Kai and I will be there at your sides to ensure everything happens as you intend. Even an older woman like me is strong enough to force Lemidge away if needed. Does someone have a question before we go?" she asked.

The younger girls didn't know what to expect, so the group had no questions.

Mirtha approached Marisa and Airalee and gave each a small pot. Airalee peeked into the pot and saw herb-spiced honey.

"Is this for me?" Airalee asked.

"It is your gift to the Lemidge," Mirtha said. "You may have been deflowered in the past, but you should have the full Lemidge experience."

"Thank you, Mirtha," Airalee and Marisa both smiled.

"Deflowering?" Marisa said quietly. "Does she just mean today?" Marisa grinned.

"Speak for yourself," Airalee said. "It will be new for me."

"Sure," Marisa said, with an unbelieving look.

Mirtha smiled at Airalee before shifting her attention to the gathering.

"Let's move to the council's hut," Mirtha loudly said.

The group walked the path from Mirtha's home to the council hut. The female Lemidge met the group at the door.

"Welcome," the short woman said, straining with their foreign language. "I will collect your offerings."

The observers placed their offerings in the basket and sat in the chairs on the side. The five participants put one offering in the basket and sat on the floor with the second one.

"Thank you," the Lemidge said, closing the door. "I will have the men join us," she said, walking to the back of the hut. She disappeared behind the reed curtain as the villagers waited.

"Ready," she said, emerging with a torch and four small dark-haired men. Each wore a sort of dress as they entered the room. The women in the room could immediately detect something in the air. Kai and Mirtha were unaffected as they stood beside the girls on the mat.

The Lemidge walked from the back to the front of the room and faced the girls on the mat. They watched the girls before them as the female Lemidge approached the hut's door. Airalee could feel some kind of quiet euphoria coming over her. Her muscles relaxed, and her curiosity about the men faded to desire. Gilda stared at the Lemidge before her, squeezing Marisa's hand harder. Marisa's hand still felt relaxed and calm, allowing Gilda to calm herself.

"We will begin our ceremony with the men humming a traditional ceremony song," the Lemidge woman said. The men began a low hum that rose higher before starting again. After several iterations of the song, they began to sway in place. The female Lemidge watched the girls and the onlookers, looking for signs of surrender.

Gilda suddenly felt a strange calm come over her as her muscles relaxed and her body became attuned to the sounds around her. Her fears dissipated to the point that she felt afraid of nothing. Gilda let go of Marisa's hand, who lightly let go of her.

"Complete," the Lemidge female said. The men stopped humming and swaying. "Begin the ceremony," she said.

Gilda saw the Lemidge in front of her move quietly toward her. Slowly, she felt a greater calm and strong desire overcome her.

"Is it your wish to contribute your gift to continue the ceremony?" the Lemidge man said in a practiced singsong. She felt herself standing up straight and offering her gift to him. The Lemidge stood still quietly, saying, "Is it your desire to be deflowered?" Gilda felt herself smile widely.

"It is," she said, almost yelling. The Lemidge accepted her gift and passed it to the Lemidge female behind him.

"Lie back on the mat," the Lemidge man said. Gilda felt as if she floated down onto her back and let her arms drift to her sides. She felt a slight weight upon her as serenity completely engulfed her. The sounds in the room faded just before an explosion of color, sound, and smells rocked her body. She closed her eyes and felt her body shaking from head to foot. The euphoria had taken over her body, but it slowly calmed, allowing her to lie quietly. It seemed a very short time before someone was calling her name. She considered ignoring the voice, but the sea of giddiness she was riding was fading. Looking up, she saw Kai offering her hand to pull her up.

"You have been resting quite a while, Gilda," Kai said, pulling her to her feet. The Lemidge were gone, and the women behind her had left. Marisa and Airalee talked with Mirtha as they helped the other girls rise from the mat. Gilda pushed her short robe down and arranged it to hang straight.

"Your experience is yours to keep secret or share as you see fit," Kai told the girls. "You may sit and talk until you regain your composure. Leave when you are ready." Kai said to them all. "I will remain here until the last one leaves. I will try to answer your questions." The group moved the chairs into a circle to chat.

Maylore

After bathing, Maylore returned to the hut as Airalee and Marisa left.

"Goodbye, ladies," he called, waving in their direction.

"Bye, Dad!" Airalee said, waving back. Maylore felt clean, but his head continued to ache. He decided a headache would not stop him from learning with Gilriel. Maylore gathered some dried fish, bread, and beans from the hut before leaving for Gilriel's cave.

He waved and chatted with a few villagers as he walked to the edge of the village. Rendal was leaving the visitor's hut when Maylore reached the road.

"Good morning, Maylore," Rendal said as he stopped near him.

"Good morning, Beacon," Maylore said, pausing before him.

"Are you on your way to Gilriel's cave?" Rendal asked.

"Yes," Maylore replied, "I want his help while he is available."

"I trust Gilriel will do what he can," Rendal said. "We could use more people skilled in the mystic arts."

"I hope not to disappoint," Maylore said. "I wish you good fortune," Rendal said as he turned and waved goodbye.

Maylore nodded and turned toward the road. Crossing the road, he started up the hill toward the cave entrance. Looking up the mountain, he saw a flash of red near the top.

"Who might that be?" Maylore said. "I doubt Gilriel has any red cloth in his wardrobe."

It took him some time to wind his way to the cave entrance. Upon entering, he heard the expected squawk of the IB somewhere near the top of the tunnel.

"Didn't scare me that time, bird," Maylore said, looking in the direction where the bird might be. Maylore could hear the quiet conversation as he continued along the tunnel. Entering the cave, he saw Gilriel talking to a man cloaked in red leather with his back to Maylore. Maylore watched them until Gilriel waved him closer.

"This is Maylore," Gilriel said as Maylore joined them. "This is the man I was telling you about. He will join me for the next few days until I leave with the master on his usual journey." The visitor looked in his direction, but the hood of his cloak hid his face in shadow. Maylore could not tell if it was a man, woman, or beast. The visitor merely nodded to Maylore and turned to leave.

"I hope to have more for you the next time you visit," Gilriel said as the visitor left.

"Who was that?" Maylore asked as the man in red left.

"The man in red," Gilriel said after hesitating. "He occasionally travels the valley checking on activity."

"He has no name?" Maylore asked.

"I shall call him the man in red," Gilriel said. "I suspect the name he told me many summers ago is not his true name. For some reason, he wants to remain in the shadows. I decided long ago to respect his wishes."

257

"Living in the shadows breeds distrust, especially nameless shadows," Maylore said. "There seem to be many mysterious individuals in Molia."

"Indeed," Gilriel said. "Many more you will never meet. Some will make themselves known when you prove to be trustworthy."

"Perhaps I would prefer to remain unknown," Maylore said.

"Molia is not so large that people will not see your actions and reactions," Gilriel said. "Even those who try to hide are known by what they do."

"How is the man in red known?" Maylore said.

"He is a quiet man with some ability to control energies," Gilriel said. He trusts very few and avoids contact with humans. He has a good rapport with the Tocor and visits their villages near his home."

"Where is his home?" Maylore asked.

"He lives sunrise from here near the end of the valley," Gilriel said. "I have not traveled that far. The master visits the human and Tocor villages near him but not with him. I suspect the man in red is cautious about avoiding the master.

"You mention the master often," Maylore said. "What else do we know about him?"

"There is very little beyond what we have told you before," Gilriel said. The master does not explain who he visits or when. He does not answer questions about his travels and merely ignores them. I learned to follow his direction and keep to myself to avoid complications," Gilriel said.

"Perhaps it is best to avoid him," Maylore said.

"Yes," Gilriel said. "I will point him out to you the next time he is in our village."

"Thank you," Maylore said.

"Today, let's continue with energy gathering and see if you can use the other portals we found with the mushrooms. Have you noticed changes in what you see, feel, or sense?"

"I have had a headache since yesterday," Maylore said after considering a moment. "I have been exhausted after our sessions."

"Perhaps the ports are expanding," Gilriel said. "It is difficult to say. It could just be a headache." Gilriel moved toward the table. "Sit, and let's start," he said. Maylore sat in the chair and set his supplies on the table.

"Try gathering energy from the ley lines," Gilriel said, sitting in the other chair. Maylore decided to stay in the chair and extended his arms, palms up toward the center of the ley lines.

When he touched the ley line, the blue energy immediately started up the string. It circled through the portal and gathered in his palms. Maylore remembered Gilriel wanted him to form the energy into a ball between his hands. Maylore mentally directed the energy to flow right to the left, creating a circling ball of energy.

"Stop!" Gilriel said as the ball continued to grow in his hands. Maylore's head suddenly felt like it was exploding. A wave formed under his chin and rapidly pushed past the top of his head. Maylore found himself standing on his feet as the energy disappeared. "You were glowing blue," Gilriel said with a surprised look. "What did you see?" he asked. Maylore recovered for a few moments before he sat and tried to explain.

"The energy had formed into a ball between my hands and grew when you said stop. It had nowhere to go, so it flew over my head."

"Excellent!" Gilriel said. "You formed an energy ball, and you heard me speak. Which way did the ball turn?" he asked.

"It was going right to left, between my hands," Maylore said.

"It's a destructive ball," Gilriel said. When you learn to unleash it, it will unwind what it hits. If it spins left to right, it will push or build upon what it hits. You must learn both, but the left to right helps develop and push. Practice here so you will limit the chance of destroying something important. I want to see you develop your abilities, but not if others can see you or be injured."

"I understand, trust no one," Maylore said.

"You are learning," Gilriel smiled. "Your companions may be trustworthy, but they could slip when the wrong ears are listening," Gilriel said. Standing up, he put a rock atop a boulder near the water pool. "I want you to form a ball to push the rock off this boulder. After you form the ball, turn your thumbs inward to push the center outward. Try that while I watch."

Maylore sat facing the ley lines again and tried pulling the energy along a new string. The energy did not follow his string as it had in the past. It jumped immediately to his left hand as Maylore pushed it to his right. The ball formed quickly, circling left to right as it grew to the size of a small rock. It stopped growing, so Maylore aimed the ball at the rock and pushed the center of the ball with his thumbs pointed down. Maylore could see the ball slowly leave his hands, accelerating to push the rock off the top of the boulder. The energy ball continued to the back wall, where it dissipated.

"Wonderful!" Gilriel exclaimed. "I could see a blue ball move from your hands and push the rock away. You will get even stronger and faster as you practice. Try using fire and water energy when you practice. Right-to-left fire energy will put a fire out, and left-to-right fire energy will cause an explosive fire. Making anything useful takes lots of practice. I wish for you that luxury."

Maylore felt like part of his stomach went with the energy ball. He quietly sat as he regained his composure and listened to Gilriel's words. He wanted to try Gilriel's concepts but felt his body would severely object.

"I suspect you feel tired using energy," Gilriel said as Maylore nodded. "Let's try a different portal to see if you can use it. Eat some of your food, and we will try that," Gilriel said, pushing food toward him and pouring water into his cup. The food and water settled Maylore's stomach and allowed him to regain focus.

"I am ready to try," Maylore finally announced.

"The throat portal we visited using the mushroom is your destination," Gilriel said. "I want you to close your eyes and project your thoughts through your throat portal. You won't use your voice, but you will visualize talking through your throat."

"I remember visiting the portal," Maylore said. "It had a dome over it."

"Yes," Gilriel said. "If you find your way to the portal, we will attempt to use the dome. I will remain here to see that unexpected events don't harm you while you do this. I don't expect fireballs or lightning to hit you, but you may get lost in concentration, and I will pull you back."

Maylore resettled in his chair and closed his eyes. He started projecting his thoughts through his throat. Maylore waited but did not sense that anything was happening. Reversing the process, he tried pulling thoughts from his throat. This time, he saw a black dome with a few white spots. One was quite large to his left. Maylore concentrated on this spot, considering what it might be.

'What happens is if I try to move or squeeze it mentally,' he thought, gazing at it. Maylore felt he spent considerable time trying to move, squeeze, or otherwise affect the dot to no avail.

"Maylore," came Gilriel's voice from nearby. "Time to break off," he said. Maylore felt the black dome and its dot disappear as he opened his eyes. It was growing dark again inside the cave.

"Was I concentrating that long?" he asked aloud.

"Yes, quite a while," Gilriel said, standing up. "You did quite a bit of staring up and moving your arms and hands. What did you see?"

"I saw a black dome with white spots on it," Maylore said. "I was trying to touch, move, and squeeze the dots. Nothing seemed to happen, but it was interesting," Maylore said.

"I remember reading a bit about that in Ivar's book," Gilriel said, standing straighter. "I interpreted it to say the dome is the area around you, and the dots were intelligent minds." Looking back at the book, he said, "You are the first person I have found who can see the dome. I will try to find what little was in the book tonight. I may have to translate the near gibberish the authors use to hide what they found. It is a slow process, but I can do it. We will discuss what I learned about the dome tomorrow and show you how to use the book. Later, we will determine if you have other abilities I did not find. We will need more blue-spotted mushrooms to do that search. Kai told me she would be looking for more mushrooms. I will need to take the ones Airalee found with me. We will need new ones to fine-tune your abilities. Kai will find some if we are fortunate and return in a few sunrises."

Maylore listened, but his mind was still foggy. Black domes and white dots swirled around his vision.

"You have made excellent progress today. You are progressing faster and further than I thought could happen," Gilriel said, steadying Maylore as he stood.

"I will welcome some food and rest before learning more about these abilities," Maylore said with a smile.

"The learning may be slow, but practice will ease your use," Gilriel said as Maylore started back down the tunnel. As he passed through, a soft cawing sound came from the side of the cave.

"Good night, bird," Maylore said, waving in its general direction.

Returning to the companions' hut, he opened the door to find Airalee and Jendrin finishing the dinner preparation.

"Greetings all," Maylore said as he closed the door.

"Dad, welcome back," Airalee said.

"Good timing, Maylore," Jendrin said, setting the cooked pork and beans on the table. Airalee added the greens she had picked as she sat down. Maylore sat next to her as Jendrin questioned him.

"You look tired, Maylore," Jendrin said. "What happened during your day?"

Maylore decided he would trust his companions. He discussed gathering energy but left out how to use it. He also discussed the black dome with white spots, which drew several questions from the other two. Maylore honestly admitted it was a mystery to him, too.

"What was your day like, Jendrin?" Maylore asked.

"Dirdin had a visitor discuss that village's tanning process," Jendrin said. Jendrin discussed the tanning process he was learning and the possible clothing results. He omitted the details of using a pig brain.

"You had a visitor too?" Maylore said. "I encountered a man in hooded red clothing in Gilriel's cave. He said nothing, and Gilriel told me he was just a visitor."

"It was a day of visitors," Airalee said before realizing she would try to avoid discussing her day.

"Oh, whom did you see today?" Jendrin asked.

Airalee decided to discuss the group gathering in the council hut without discussing what happened there.

"Five Lemidge were visiting from Liqua today," Airalee said. They left a good impression on the women gathered there."

"What did they discuss?" Jendrin said, eating his pork.

"They demonstrated techniques Lemidge uses in their village that interest women," Airalee said.

"Their techniques would not work for humans, but they were exciting." She hoped they would not question her further. The two men gave her a sidelong look, knowing a little about the Lemidge, but kept comments to themselves.

The meal finished with quiet discussions before Maylore arose and gathered his dishes. "I will clean the dishes, dad," Airalee said. "Marisa and I are meeting for an evening bath."

"Thank you, Airalee," Maylore said, "I am tired, and sleep would be welcome."

"I will clean the hut," Jendrin said, standing up. Airalee left the hut, and Maylore went to bed. Jendrin cleaned the hut and finished his day working on a little project.

Chapter 18 - Adventure with Kai

Kai awoke the following day, remembering yesterday and considering today's travel. She recalled talking with Gilda for quite a while as she came down from the Lemidge spell.

"Just remember, Gilda," Kai told her, "your experience with our village men will unlikely be so uplifting. Our men do not have the special ability the Lemidge have to create euphoria."

Gilda claimed she understood, but Kai was not entirely sure she really did. Kai suspected Gilda was claiming to understand even though she did not have the experience to gain understanding. Kai decided that future experiences would be Gilda's best teacher.

"You are welcome to seek me out to discuss life, men, and children," Kai told her. "Your mother is a good woman who will discuss your questions."

"Thank you, Kai," Gilda replied.

The seasonal process of the Lemidge visits had been the same for many sessions with new girls each time. The difference this time was that Gilda was her charge, and Kai developed a genuine affection for the girl. Gilda's giving attitude and helpfulness were a refreshing change from the recent trainees she had tried to work with. Kai spent time with each of the prior candidates only to be disillusioned. Many had only a passing interest in being a healer and moved on to other areas when learning needed to be combined with compassion.

Kai had discussions with Gilda's mother, but those discussions made Kai suspicious. Gilda's mother seemed to concentrate on Gilda's younger sister and let Gilda go her own way. A cold thought of long-past agreements between mothers and the bandits seeped into her mind. Mothers would have two or more girls, with the first girl sacrificed to serve with the bandits.

"That cannot be what Gilda's mother intends," Kai said aloud. She glanced at Gilda's nearby empty bed and called, "Gilda?" Gilda pushed aside the small curtain separating the living area.

"Yes?" Gilda replied.

"Good, you are here," Kai said. "We need to get ready for our journey this morning."

"Yes," Gilda said, smiling broadly. "I couldn't sleep, so I made breakfast. I will be ready to leave after you eat, Kai."

Kai got out of bed and was inwardly pleased with her apprentice as she wore her travel clothes.

"I am excited to go since I haven't left the village in a long while," Gilda said, returning to the table.

"Let's eat some of your breakfast then," Kai said.

The first sun was just over the horizon when the two left the hut with lightly loaded travel bags over one shoulder and gathering bags over the other.

"I told the Beacon and several others we were leaving this morning," Kai said. "I told them to expect us to return late tomorrow. Did you tell your mother you were traveling with me today?" Kai asked.

"Yes," Gilda replied, "She seemed sad to see me going but said she knew I was ready." Kai patted her on the shoulder as they walked by the visitor's hut to the road leading up to the hill toward sunset.

"You have not traveled this road before?" Kai asked her.

"No," Gilda replied. "I walked with gathering groups in the forest but not on this road. I was told it was too dangerous to walk this road, especially alone."

"That is true," Kai nodded. "There are many creatures we may need to hide from today. The most dangerous are the two-legged ones! Tell me if you hear any noises I miss. We will get off the road and hide," Kai said, pointing to the bushes along the road. "Usually, few travel this road, so we may travel quicker if we do not need to hide."

"I look forward to seeing different sights," Gilda said, studying the area.

"It is less than a quarter sun to the bandit's village," Kai said. "Be wary of them until we get past their area. A half sun should put us well past them."

The two women climbed the slight wooded slope to a roadside fork. One road led into the mountains and the other continued sunset.

"Up this road, there are two human villages and one Tocor village," Kai said, pointing up the mountain road. "Some of our Tocor sentinels and traders came from those villages. We trade for their wood, edible mushrooms, and other items. They usually visit our village every few months for fish, vegetables, and healing herbs. They do not have a healer, so I give them what healing herbs I can spare," Kai said as she continued walking. "The human villages have traders who occasionally visit and trade their woodwork for fish."

The rocky road continued upward toward sunset between the trees and brush until it finally leveled off into a clearing.

"We may collect herbs in this meadow on our return," Kai said, pointing to the mountainside. "No one else gathers anything from here, so we should find an easy harvest."

The women continued to walk when Gilda suddenly stopped.

"Do you hear that?" she asked.

Kai did not answer as she dashed into the brush.

"Behind the trees," Kai said, moving behind large bushes. They sank to their knees behind the brush near a large tree. She turned to Gilda.

"What do you hear?" Kai whispered.

Gilda's eyes searched the road and the brush alongside.

"It was a rumbling sound with a rustling in the brush, I think," Gilda said.

Kai half stood to look up the road but saw nothing.

"I don't see anything," Kai said. "Let's just wait," she added, squatting back down.

A loud popping noise preceded a large bear emerging onto the road from the seaside. The brown boar sniffed the air and looked in all directions.

"We are fortunate we are on the downwind side of it," Kai said. "It would be quite happy to make a meal of us." Looking at the thick brush around them, she continued, "It can outrun us, and this brush will not slow it down. It climbs trees far faster than we can," Kai said, lowering her head. Gilda watched the bear finish sniffing and started across the road into the meadow.

"It is not coming our way," Gilda said as Kai looked for a potential escape route. "It is headed into the meadow."

"We will wait for it to get far away before," Kai said, interrupted by an eruption of snarling wolves jumping and biting the bear as it entered the meadow. The wolves' razor teeth tore at the bear's thick hide as it tried to fight off the pack of fierce wolves. Loud growling, snarling, and animal bodies hitting the ground filled the air. Kai felt her muscles limp, realizing they could have been the wolves' next meal.

Gilda was fascinated as she watched the struggle until she saw Kai's face lose all color and sink onto her bottom. Gilda started to ask what was wrong when she realized why Kai had suddenly sunk to the ground.

"Should we move away from here, Kai?" Gilda asked as her shoulders slumped.

Kai sat a few seconds longer before replying.

268

"Child," Kai said, "we should thank the bear for saving our lives. The wolves now have a much bigger meal than we would have been. They may leave us alone since they have such a large meal. We should not test them, however." Kai stood to see the carnage when they heard the blood wolves howl. "The blood wolves will chase away the smaller fierce wolves," Kai said. "Fierce wolves usually avoid the road. They may have been crossing over when they heard something approaching. It could have been us they heard or the bear. The rustling you heard was probably the wolves setting their trap."

Gilda considered what Kai was saying as she noticed the battle before them was over. There appeared to be ten or more wolves snapping at the carcass as each sliced off a chunk and moved away. The feasting continued until the air filled with the sound of the approaching blood wolves. The feasting wolves looked up before feeding, knowing they did not have much more time. The howling grew louder as time passed, and several blood wolves suddenly appeared. Most of the fierce wolf pack ran, but a few thought to fight the much larger blood wolves. Snarling as they approached, the blood wolves knocked them aside to get to the kill. One wolf got up to attack a blood wolf and was killed with one snap from the blood wolf's jaws. A few of the pack had been standing a short distance away, watching their pack mate. Seeing their pack mate was so quickly dispatched, they turned to follow the rest of the pack into the mountains. Kai found it difficult to stand, taking a couple of attempts to rise to her feet.

"Come, Gilda," Kai said, "we are safe for now. Let's move close to the blood wolves in case the other wolves are nearby." Gilda rose to her feet and looked at Kai.

"Are you sure they won't harm us?" she asked.

"They will not," Kai said, "They are carrion eaters and won't bother with us unless we attack them. We should not try that."

Gilda returned a weak smile and followed Kai back onto the road. They walked near the blood wolves who looked at them between bites and ignored them. Kai scanned the meadow but did not see any remaining fierce wolves. The blood wolves were finishing their meal, and a few had walked past the two women heading off the road headed seaside. The blood wolves were nearly half her height as they walked past them. Gilda froze until the large animal had disappeared into the brush.

"Come, Gilda." Kai said, "We should leave in case the fierce wolves return for leftovers or perhaps to have us for dessert." Kai said, starting up the road.

Gilda followed but glanced behind her several times to see if anything was following them.

The two women continued on the road, walking toward sunset. They arrived at the crest of the hill overlooking a valley.

"There is the river that runs on the sunset side of our forest," Kai said. "This side of the river is the bandit's village. The meadow below the village has many usable raw materials."

"It looks like a small village," Gilda said, surveying the area.

"It is," Kai replied. "It is small because Birsha does not want a large population he would have to handle. We should be glad since they steal enough from the villages around them. Slaving freeloaders, I call them."

The road dipped into the valley before rising again. Kai pointed up the hill.

"We will leave the road here and create a path above the road," Kai said. "We could stay on this road since they are unlikely to see us, but why take the chance."

Kai led the way into the thicket, away from the road and into the mountain. Passing above the road, Gilda tried to see the bandit camp as they passed, but trees and brush hid it. They walked between brush and trees for quite a while before Kai declared, "We can join the road again now."

Gilda was pleased to leave the face-slapping branches behind for the clear road. Walking for another quarter-sun brought them to the entrance to the Lemidge village of Liqua. Two Lemidge guarded the entrance. The guards watched the women as they passed. Kai and Gilda waved in their direction and continued up the road. The road started climbing another hill when Kai pointed into the meadow.

"We will enter the meadow just as the road starts to climb the mountain," Kai said, pointing toward the hill. "We will search for our mushrooms and herbs from that point to the other side of this meadow."

"Did they only want the blue-spotted mushrooms?" Gilda asked.

"Gilriel and Rendal are keen on us finding blue-spotted mushrooms," Kai said. "If you see any other colored mushroom, let me know. If you find herbs we can use, gather them."

"Where are we likely to find the blue spot mushroom?" Gilda asked, surveying the meadow.

"They grow near the tree line," Kai said, pointing to the trees on the far side. "I am also interested in finding therapeutic, pregnancy-preventing herbs or any mushroom."

Gilda nodded, thinking of what those herbs looked like. The twin suns were past midday as the women started their search. They were several paces apart, with Kai leading the way. Gilda found several herbs they needed, and a few were already in ample supply. Kai was pleased Gilda found the herbs even though she had spotted them sooner.

"You will be valuable at gathering for our village, Gilda," she said. Gilda smiled and kept walking. Halfway through the meadow, the women stopped before a patch of shin-high dry grass. "This is a nice patch of grain," Kai said, sweeping the patch with her hand. "If we had time and bag space, we would collect it." The women turned to continue their search when a rustling in the grass came from

271

behind them. Both women turned in the direction of the sound. The rustling stopped, but a few of the grain stalks moved anyway.

"Wolf?" Gilda said, looking anxiously toward Kai.

"It would be a small one," Kai said. "It would still be dangerous." The rustling sound came again as the women saw it moving parallel to them. "When I say run, you run and climb that tree," pointing slightly to one side. "I will ensure it doesn't chase you and then follow you up a tree," Kai said, dropping her shoulder bag. Gilda dropped hers and got ready to run. The rustling sound came again as a large, orange-tipped blackbird burst into the clearing, wings flapping and jumping around. It stopped, cocked its head at them, and squawked a "Haww Haww Haww!" sound before taking wing into a tree.

"An intelligent bird," Kai said. "It looks like this IB was playing a joke on us, Gilda," Kai said, sounding relieved.

"Stupid bird!" Gilda cried, her body shaking in relief. "Do you think it saw what happened to us with the wolves today?"

"It would not surprise me," Kai said, picking up her bag. "IBs are known for their intelligence. They seem to have a sense of humor, too."

"Haww Haww Haww!" came the bird call from somewhere in the trees ahead of them.

"It could have been following us for a long time," Kai continued. "It may well follow us until we leave its meadow."

Gilda picked up her satchel and continued to the meadow's edge. Fallen trees, branches, and various leaves covered the ground.

"This is a good location to find mushrooms," Kai said. "We will search from here to the edge of the rock wall on the seaward side. Then, follow the wall, looking for what we need. Grab a branch and use it to sweep away leaves," she said, picking up a bushy branch. The women swept and overturned rotted logs, looking for mushrooms. They found many bugs, worms, and edible mushrooms but nothing they needed. Overturning yet another log, Kai glanced back to see motion behind them. The IB was gobbling down a worm as Kai looked at it. The bird cocked its head and snapped up another bug and another, always watching Kai.

"The bird is using us to find its dinner!" Kai laughed. Gilda turned to look at it and tried to shoo it away. "Don't bother, Gilda," Kai said, "We can forgive the jokester," Kai chuckled. "If you want to help us, bird, show us where the mushrooms are," Kai shouted at the bird. The bird appeared to shake its head and continue eating worms and insects from the overturned leaves. Gilda did not see the humor in it but returned to the task. Sweeping a few steps more, she saw a few red mushrooms on the ground.

"Red mushrooms," Gilda said.

"Good," Kai replied. "They are poisonous when improperly used. Use your stick to gather them. Leave at least one to keep them producing." Gilda used another stick to spear four of them and put them in one of the small pouches of her satchel. Kai spied a group of blue mushrooms nearby. She added them to a pouch in her satchel using the same technique. They continued walking toward the rock pile, finding more blue and red mushrooms. Gilda continued onward until a large group of boulders blocked her path. Looking up, she saw a mountain of boulders above the treetops.

"This is an odd pile of boulders," Gilda said.

"The story I have heard," Kai replied, "is there are large dangerous animals on the other side of this rock pile. I have not gone there, and I suggest you do not either."

"I have already had enough of animals today," Gilda replied, following Kai along the rock wall. Kai walked a few steps when she saw a mushroom sticking out between two boulders. Reaching down, she picked up a blue-spotted-white mushroom.

"Success!" Kai said, turning to Gilda. Kai picked up two of the four mushrooms and put them into her pouch. The IB bird saw her excitement and hopped over to see what they found. Gilda watched it straighten up and caw twice before flying to a nearby tree. It cawed again, pointing its beak toward the rocks.

"I think it wants us to follow. Let's see what it is pointing at," Kai said, motioning Gilda to follow.

"It is probably a wolf," Gilda said as she followed. The bird flew higher into the tree as the women approached. Bending down to where the bird seemed to be pointing, Kai saw a group of blue-spotted-white mushrooms growing on a log between the rocks. Twenty mushrooms were growing in a row along the log.

"Leave one on each end and t take the rest," Kai said. "We will call our mission here finished."

"Caw Caw," a sound came from above them. Looking up, Kai saw the bird twisting its head left and right as it looked at them. Kai smiled at the bird.

"Thank you, IB," Kai said as she waved in its direction. "It would be nice if you could find us some other rare mushrooms and herbs!" The bird was silent but watched as they prepared to leave. "Let's go back along a different route along this line of trees. Different mushrooms grow under piles like these," Kai said, starting along a sunrise direction. The two women casually brushed away leaves, looking for mushrooms or herbs in the rich soil.

"There seem to be many more bugs and worms going this way," Gilda said as she casually swept away leaves and twigs. She stopped suddenly when different-colored mushrooms appeared. "Here are orange-spotted black mushrooms. Do we want these?" Gilda asked.

"Yes," Kai said, coming over to look. "We have not had any in a long time. They will help a person be more astute. They disappear from inventory when villagers find out we have them," Kai said.

"I can gather them with my hands?" Gilda asked.

"Yes, quite safe," Kai replied. Gilda gathered six mushrooms into her pouch, leaving several to continue developing. When the women finished searching the forest, the twin suns had moved lower in the sky. They walked back through the meadow, searching for any additional herbs. The IB continued flying overhead and occasionally cawed at them.

"Tell us if you see a wolf pack, bears, or whatever else may attack us, bird," Gilda called up to it. The bird appeared to look at her and kept circling them. The grass gave way to rocks and sand as the women caught sight of Liqua. The women had dropped their sweeping branches and scanned the ground for herbs and mushrooms.

"Some mushrooms thrive in the sun and poor soil," Kai said. "Keep an eye out for them," Kai said as they walked amongst the rocks and sand. A flash of yellow caught Kai's eyes as she spotted a few green-spotted yellow mushrooms growing in the poor soil. "These could be useful too," Kai said, picking up several with a stick.

"What do those do?" Gilda asked, walking up to Kai.

"These are wandering mushrooms," Kai replied. "Whoever eats one temporarily loses their mind and wanders. The Beacon and I thought some people with abilities were eating these and wandering off. We closely counted all these mushrooms; none were ever missing. We will replace the old ones in our storage with these since nobody uses them."

Looking up, Gilda pointed to feathery plants growing nearby in a large group.

"That looks like something Mirtha has in her storage area," Gilda said, touching the feather leaves.

"Yes," Kai replied. "Bird feathers she calls them. She uses them as a bittering agent if the food needs balance. She has a good amount, but let's gather some anyway," Kai suggested. Gilda gathered some into her pouch. They rejoined the road going sunrise. They arrived at the entrance to Liqua as the two suns were on the horizon. Kai spoke to the guards.

"We ask to use your visitor's hut for this night," Kai said, pointing first to herself and then to the nearby visitor's hut. The guards looked at each other as one held his hand up and the other jogged toward the village.

"Perhaps we will be allowed to stay if the village Beacon allows it," Kai said. "Otherwise, we may be sleeping by the road," Kai smiled.

A short time later, a small bald man appeared near the gate, looking at the two women. The bald man returned to his village as the guard returned to his post. He nodded to the two women and pointed to a grass hut near the guards and outside the village entrance. Kai nodded to them and walked to the indicated hut. Inside were four grass beds, a table along the back wall, and an unlit firepit in the middle of the hut.

"Claim a bed, Gilda," Kai said. "We will rest a bit before our dinner," Kai said as she sat on a bed near the table. Gilda took the bed on the opposite side of the table and lay back on the soft fabric grass.

They rested for a short time before someone knocked on the door. Kai opened the door to find two young Liqua girls carrying water and a food basket.

"How generous!" Kai said. "Please come in."

Gilda stood up as they approached the table.

"Thank you, girls," Kai said as they set the food and water on the table. The two smiled and started to leave when Kai asked, "Do either of you understand the human tongue?" The girls stopped, with one pointing to the other, who nodded.

"Some, yes," she said.

"Wonderful!" Kai said. "I am Kai, and this is Gilda. May we know your names?" she asked.

"I am Nuae, and this is Irriel," Nuae said. The other nodded when she heard her name.

"Thank you, Nuae and Irriel," Kai said with a slight bow to them. "Would you ask your leader if we may visit your village?" Nuae looked to be translating to Irriel.

"Visit Liqua. Yes, Irriel will ask," Nuae said as Irriel ran out the door. Kai and Nuae had a brief, halting conversation until Irriel quickly returned. Irriel quickly spoke to Nuae before Nuae turned to Kai. "Visit now. Follow me," she said, beckoning to them. Kai and Gilda followed the girls out the door and into the village. The guards noticed but merely smiled.

Tall grasses lined the sides of the building, and thatched roofs of tightly woven grass kept the rain out. Several rows of huts lined the outskirts of the central plaza.

"Women separate grain for storage and dinner," Nuae said, pointing to a large group chatting and filling wooden grain containers in the center of the village. The activity stopped as the group entered the plaza. The women started at the newcomers. Men carrying food and minding the ovens stopped to watch. Kai bowed to the group.

"Mae," Kai said, using their word of greeting. The villagers seemed satisfied that these two were no danger and returned to work.

"You speak our tongue?" Nuae asked.

"No," Kai replied. "Just the greeting 'mae,' and departing word, 'kesa.'" Nuae smiled, then stepped back as a woman emerged from the group and approached them.

"You have visited Olona many times," Kai said as the women approached.

"Yes. My name is Firlia, and I speak the human tongue. I travel to the human villages, negotiate with their Beacons, and prepare our men for their ceremony," Firlia said.

"There were many happy humans when you visited us, weren't there, Gilda?" Kai smiled at Gilda. Gilda smiled sheepishly and lowered her head, not knowing what to say.

"I am pleased," Firlia said, smiling at Gilda. "I remember you were in the ceremony," she said, looking at Gilda. Returning to Kai, she said, "Few humans visit our villages except for the one they call master. What brings you here?" Firlia asked.

'When the day ended, we had been collecting herbs and mushrooms in the forest and meadow," Kai said. "We asked to stay in the visitor's hut to avoid this old woman sleeping on the ground."

"You should be allowed," Firlia replied. "All peaceful visitors are welcome. Humans are sometimes dangerous, so few are allowed here," Firlia said as she glanced at someone approaching them behind Kai. "Mae Baralas," Firlia said. Kai turned to find a stern-faced bald Lemidge man two hands shorter than her staring at her. Baralas carried a load of wood but appeared to be judging the two women. Looking back at Firlia, he spoke to her in the Lemidge language. Firlia replied to Baralas as he looked harshly at Kai and Gilda. He talked to Firlia again and walked away with his load of wood. Firlia bowed her head to him as he left. "Baralas decided you were not a wolf or a bear in hiding. He said I could talk with you."

"Is he the village leader?" Kai asked.

"Yes," Firlia replied. "He has proven his leadership and wise decisions many times. We all attend to what he says."

Kai watched him disappear into the village.

"Baralas," I will remember that name," Kai said. She looked at the workers and asked, "What are they doing in this group?"

"They prepare dinner and breakfast," Firlia replied. "Some will prepare the vegetables, others add meat or grains, and the men cook the food in the ovens. Everyone helps prepare food, including Baralas." Kai nodded as Firlia explained. Kai noticed it was a small population of Lemidge.

"Is this the entire village population?" Kai asked.

"Nearly all," Firlia said. "Some are traveling to human villages to barter as we did. We travel with about 100 at a time from our home village."

"This is not your home village?" Kai asked, "Where is your home?"

"Our home is in the mountains," Firlia said, pointing to the sunset. "We will be home in less than 20 sunrises. The next group of Lemidge will arrive here after we leave. We will all meet at our mountain home before the winter season arrives."

Kai could tell Firlia was uncomfortable answering questions about the Lemidge movements and changed subjects.

"May we visit your hut?" Kai asked.

"Yes," Firlia replied. "It is at the end of this row. My hut sits on the edge of the hill overlooking the floodplain." Looking at Nuae and Irriel, she spoke to them. The two girls smiled and joined the women sorting grain. Firlia, Kai, and Gilda walked to the end of the gathering area where the men were tending the ovens. Most of the men nodded as they walked past. Two of them smiled broadly at Gilda as they passed. Gilda felt self-conscious and smiled weakly at them.

"Why are they smiling like that?" Gilda asked, looking at Kai.

"They were part of your ceremony," Kai said. "You won't remember since you were under their influence and unaware of what was happening." Gilda turned and smiled at the two men as they continued walking.

Baralas was frowning. He held a combination of a scowl and a questioning look as he watched them pass. Firlia opened the simple door to her hut and held it for Kai and Gilda to enter. The spartan room had two beds, a cabinet, and a small firepit. The back of the room had a small window where the women gathered. The hut sat atop a three-stick drop to the plain floor. Firlia pointed out the window.

"The spring waters flood this plain," Firlia said. "It gives life to the seeds and plants that grow here. Our people gather berries, flowers, herbs, grain, and fish. We carry them back to our mountain home. The grain is ready now, and we will gather what we can carry home. The last group will gather the last of the grain and berries." Gilda looked around the inside of the hut, noticing grass sheets and wood stuffed inside the rafters. Two dresses hung nearby. A fabric and leather satchel lay on the bed. Gilda pointed to the dresses.

"Do you make your clothes?" Gilda asked.

"I do," Firlia replied. "The redberry-colored one and the blackberry-colored one. The grass I use grows here and near our mountain home. The breadfruit thread creates a soft chest covering. It is a good project at night. I carry some of the material with me to make clothes at home when the winter blows snow around." Gilda touched the edge of the dress, finding it pliable and soft.

"You put a lot of work into creating these," Gilda said.

"Yes," Firlia replied. "It is nice you noticed," she said. "Shall we see if the food is ready?" Firlia said, turning to the door. Gilda and Kai left the hut to see a long line of cooked food on a long log. "Let's get three cooked dinners and return to the visitor's hut," Firlia said, walking toward the ovens. One of the men was removing food from the stove as Baralas stood near him. The man held out servings to Firlia as she passed one to Kai and Gilda. Firlia gathered one for herself and started toward the visitor's hut. Kai stopped and whispered to Firlia.

"How do I say thank you in Lemidge?" Kai asked.

"Wanici," Firlia whispered. Kai looked at Baralas.

"Wanici," Kai said as she bowed her head. Baralas almost smiled but merely nodded and turned back to his work. Firlia smiled at Kai and led the way back to the visitor's hut.

Firlia lit the lone candle as the three sat eating warm, spiced food at the table. Firlia seemed extremely relaxed after Kai showed gratitude to Baralas. Gilda felt brave and asked personal questions.

"Do you have children?" Gilda asked.

"I do," Firlia said without hesitation. "My son and daughter are at our permanent village. I look forward to seeing them soon."

"Are they with your chosen mate?" Gilda asked. Firlia considered for a moment before replying.

"My mate is with another group visiting human villages as I did," Firlia said. "My children are with their teaching group, which cares for village children. I will rejoin the teaching group when I return. My mate will help the children even if he is not their father." Gilda looked at Firlia questioningly.

"Does the father also help with the children?" Gilda asked.

"I believe so," Firlia said, smiling. Women do not know who creates the child. Child creation happens during the Fetru ceremony each season. Is that different from your village?" Kai interrupted before Gilda could answer.

"The women of our village choose a group of seeders, or just one if they choose," Kai said. "Any one of them could create the child. Each child could be from a different group. She may also choose a different mate to raise the children and another to live life after the children are grown. Sometimes, a woman chooses one mate for all situations. It is up to her and her mate," Kai finished. Gilda felt relieved having Kai explain.

"I see," Firlia replied. "It is similar but different. Perhaps it is different for each village."

"The human villages I know of are generally the same," Kai replied. "Some may still use traveling seeders. Olona does not."

"I have heard that story before," Firlia said. "It appears what the Lemidge do now is a form of how it used to be for all villages. Thank you, Kai."

"When you get to my age, you have heard many tales of history," Kai said, nodding. Firlia could see Gilda was bursting with questions she wanted to ask.

"You have another question, Gilda?" Firlia asked.

"How old are your children?" Gilda asked.

"My daughter is 13 summers, and my son is 11 summers," Firlia said.

"Are you going to have more children?" Gilda asked.

"Gilda," Kai warned, "you are asking too many personal questions."

"I am sorry," Gilda said.

"I do not plan more," Firlia said. "Instead of participating, I will help prepare for the Fetru celebration."

"How do you prepare for a Fetru?" Gilda asked.

"We are already preparing for the next Fetru party," Firlia said. "The grain we gather here is taken to our village where it is added to boiling water and mashed with herbs and berries to create Reeb. The reeb cools for a few days, then rests until it stops bubbling. We remove the grain and herbs from the reeb and bake it into bread for the party. The reeb is ready when the elders declare it is crazy water. The village elders then organize a Fetru party for women who want to have a child and men who want to produce one. Those participating drink the reeb with the baked bread and a lot of bad singing and dancing. I remember very little from my last participation, but I did have a child. My mate was not part of the celebration since he helped prevent participants from injuring one another. My task in the following seasons has been to help prevent problems during Fetru."

"Wanici Firlia," Kai said. "I welcome education of any kind."

"A story for a story," Firlia said. "It is a fair trade to each show a part of our way of life." The women finished their meal with quiet chatter. Gilda listened intently, contemplating what she heard. The meal ended, and Firlia collected their plates as Gilda looked up with a smile.

"Wanici," Gilda said.

"Deesi," Firlia replied, nodding her head.

"I could have you two speaking Lemidge in short order if you were not leaving," Firlia laughed. Kai and Gilda laughed with her as Firlia stood up. "I leave you now, but Nuae will check later to see if you are comfortable." Firlia smiled at them as she left the hut. Kai and Gilda sat at the table and recounted the day's adventures.

"The day ended well," Gilda said. "We were fortunate to avoid the bear's fate. We were almost wolf food."

"Yes," Kai said, "We were also fortunate to find the mushrooms and herbs we were tasked to find," Kai said, smiling at Gilda.

"I am also glad we lost that IB bird. It was annoying." Gilda said, smiling back at her.

"Caw?" A bird call came from the door. The women looked at the door and saw the IB bird hanging upside down, looking at them through the crack in the door. Kai chuckled, and Gilda stared in amazement.

"We have a new friend," Kai said.

Gilda didn't feel as charitable.

"Go away, annoying bird," Gilda said.

The bird climbed back up the hut and was silent.

"Thank you," Gilda said.

Kai and Gilda finished the fruit the girls had left them when a voice sounded outside the door.

"Are you both all right?" Irriel was asking.

"Come in," Kai said. Irriel opened the door as Kai waved to her to come in. "Yes, Thank you, Irriel."

"Good night," Irriel said, waving and closing the door.

The hut was dark even with the lit candle.

"We should get some rest. Tomorrow is a long walk," Kai said.

"Yes. Good night, Kai," Gilda said as she put out the candle and lay on the bed.

"Good night, Gilda," Kai replied, sinking into the bed.

CHAPTER 19 - MEANWHILE, BACK AT THE RANCH

Maylore was the first to awaken. He dressed and accomplished his routine of using the bathroom and gathering firewood. He returned to the hut as Airalee and Jendrin were getting started. Airalee was inspecting the pot in the fire pit.

"The beans and pork I set last night are ready to eat," Airalee said. "Dad, grab the bowls and spoons, and let's eat."

Jendrin left for his morning duty as Airalee and Maylore sat down.

"Are you working with Gilriel again today, dad?"

"Yes," Maylore replied. "I hope to have many more training sessions to determine the extent of my abilities."

"Can you tell us what your dilemma is yet?" Airalee asked as she smiled at him.

"If I understood it better, I would gladly tell you," Maylore said in a half-truth. "It is still a jumble for the most part. Are you and Marisa going to gather today?"

"We are going to investigate the marsh near the clay pits," Airalee said. "I hope we can find some useful herbs or food growing there."

Jendrin returned and sat beside Airalee with his bowl of beans and pork. Maylore was a little surprised she allowed him to sit near her. In the past, he would sit near her but not beside each other.

"Good morning, all," he said, eating.

"What is the hero's plan for the day?" Airalee asked.

"I hope to finish cutting bamboo for the water pipe," Jendrin said. "Latel and I will check on the tanning of our pig hide and see if Dirdin needs help. Wood and food gathering, normal stuff."

"Kai and Gilda are leaving to find special mushrooms," Airalee said.

"Hopefully, they find what we need," Maylore said, looking up without elaboration. Maylore finished his breakfast and stood up from the table. "I am off to Gilriel's cave. I plan to return tonight, probably after your dinner," he said as he started toward the door.

"Goodbye, dad," Airalee said. Jendrin waved between bites as Maylore left the hut.

Maylore chatted briefly with several villagers as he made his way out of the village. He found Rendal and Throc discussing something as he approached them on the road.

"Good morning, Maylore," Rendal said. "Are you going to see Gilriel this morning?" he asked.

"Yes," Maylore replied. "I hope to make more progress while he is here."

"Excellent," Rendal said. "I hope for the best," Rendal said, not wanting to elaborate in the open air. "Throc and I were drafting a new letter of understanding with Gulstan's village Forsba. Gulstan's visit showed our tanners methods, which we did not know. It made us realize we did not have an understanding between us for trade. Dirdin told me Gulstan's methods are valuable to us and that he wants to repay them somehow."

"I am sure we can come to some reasonable agreement with their Beacon. I wish you success." Maylore said. "Good day to both." as he started toward the cave. Rendal and Throc wished him well as they restarted their conversation.

The climb to the cave seemed shorter with each trip. Maylore entered the cave and wound his way through the tunnel. He heard a soft cawing sound above him.

"You must be getting used to me already, bird," he said in the general direction of where the bird might be.

"Come in and sit, Maylore," Gilriel called as he neared the table. "I have found more about energy collection and usage that we can discuss today. There is a bit more about communicating through the portal dome, too. Perhaps your skill can do that, so I will show you where it is in the book and how I understand it. Come, sit here," he said, pointing to the chair opposite him. Gilriel pushed the book across the table and placed it before Maylore. The thick tomb was open to a page written in a symbolic language that Maylore thought looked like a child's scrawl.

"Where did this book come from?" Maylore asked.

"We don't know who started this tomb," Gilriel said. "Scholars through the ages have read and added to it during their lifetimes. My predecessor, Ivmar, got it from another scholar named Esteren. She disappeared soon afterward. Ivar suggested she stole this tomb from someone. He did not know who but stressed that I must not reveal I had it. The Beacon and I believe you are trustworthy, and I tell you now, do not reveal to anyone we have this book! Not even your companions!"

Maylore felt a little overwhelmed but nodded in agreement.

"My days as the village scholar may soon end with the passing of my 85th season," Gilriel said, calming his voice. "It seems you will one day become our village scholar."

"Me?" Maylore said, sitting back in his chair. A shocked look spread on his face.

"One day in the future," Gilriel said. "We know of only two sorcerers in the valley. You and the red scholar."

"The one I saw here?" Maylore said, looking up.

"Yes," Gilriel replied, "Neldor trusts very few."

"Neldor," Maylore said, "Today I can be trusted with his name?"

Gilriel realized he made a mistake but kept a straight face.

"I believe it is a false name," Gilriel said smoothly. "Keep it to yourself anyway."

"I will," Maylore replied.

"He came to trust me only because of the seasons we have known each other," Gilriel said. "I did help him by using this tome. I did not intend to tell him about the book, but he was suspicious when he told me of a problem, and the next time he visited, I had a possible answer for him. He has no patience to interpret the book but knows a few symbols, so he repaid me by adding them to the translation key Ivar started. He warned me not to reveal I had this book, especially to the master."

Maylore glanced between the book and Gilriel as he listened to him talk. The symbols on the page made no sense, and the notes on the sides were of little help.

"Where is the key for these symbols?" Maylore asked. Gilriel pulled a small folder from inside the drawer and opened it to its beginning.

"This key describes what we know about those symbols. Ten pages cover just a few of the total number of symbols." Gilriel pulled out a few more pages. "Long ago, I decided to create new pages for my translations rather than change other scholars' work. I suggest you do the same." Maylore looked at the gibberish on the pages.

"You think I will be able to do that?" Maylore asked.

"Of course," Gilriel said. "It will take time and experience. It took me several careful passes through this book using the key and Neldor's help to generate what I have. My meager skills are in the book, and I could determine what the symbols meant based on what I could do. I found another person I thought might be a sorcerer. He was reluctant and pretended he knew little of what they meant. I persuaded them to translate a few symbols I copied from the book. He answered so quickly I suspect he knew much more than he would admit."

"I hope you are right," Maylore said, sitting back in his chair and sighed. "It looks way beyond me."

"That is what I thought in the beginning, too," Gilriel said. "It took me seasons before I seriously worked at learning a few symbols. The long winter seasons are here on these few pages," he said, touching the key pages. Looking up, he added, "I became concerned my work would be destroyed or stolen. I decided to move the book to a few different spots. I chose different rock hollows inside the cave." Gilriel pointed in several directions within the cave as Maylore followed his hand. "If I forget, the IB will find it for me," he said, pointing to the IB bird sitting on the back of the empty chair. Maylore had not noticed the bird as it turned its head left and right and softly cawed at him. The bird's feathers were black with orange tips. It had black eyes and a beak to match. It had two orange feathers on its black head, which ran on each side of its beak.

"Does the bird have a name?" Maylore asked.

"I do not think so," Gilriel replied. "I have never asked him," Gilriel said with a grin.

"You can talk to the bird?" Maylore asked, looking at him.

"No," Gilriel said chuckling. "It is chatty enough without me adding to it."

Gilriel's face turned serious as he leaned on the table.

"Let me tell you what little I found in the book last night," Gilriel said. Maylore straightened to listen to him. "Energy can come from any living or nonliving thing. The ley lines we see have the most easily available energy to tap. Fire has significant energy, water, air, and finally, rocks. Lightning is difficult to direct but has significant energy. I don't know of anyone who can direct lightning. The book suggests that the caster imagines a string from the energy source to you and your target. It gives a path for the energy to travel along. It suggests that the more you practice, the less you need this idea and can push the energy directly."

"Do I need to learn special hand movements or speak a special word sequence to direct the energy?" he asked.

"No," Gilriel replied. "The book's authors used hand gestures when they started. They say they are unnecessary after practice and become a hindrance. Hand gestures, words, and special objects slow you down. One author used a stick with hand gestures and became discouraged when concentrating too much on the mechanics, not the energy transfer. The book says he used the stick to walk but no longer waved it around."

"I will continue to use my hands for now," Maylore said, considering what he was hearing.

"By all means," Gilriel replied. "I am sure the book's authors spent many hours practicing before they came to this conclusion. Let me tell you now about what I learned about communication skills."

"Yes, this too should be interesting," Maylore said, leaning forward as he listened.

Gilriel pulled the book over to him and carefully opened it to a specific spot.

"The dots you see on the portal dome are living creatures," Gilriel translated. "Most will be human, and a few will be intelligent animals. It suggests imagining a string drawn to the dot you want to communicate with. Animals communicate using pictures, while humans can use words or images. Imagine your words or pictures going down the string to the dot. If the animal is capable of listening, they may respond to you. The book says you must practice to determine who belongs to each dot. I am unsure if that means you can learn to associate a dot with a person or animal. Perhaps you can try it now." Gilriel said, looking at Maylore.

Maylore closed his eyes and tried to ignore most of the sounds in the cave as he concentrated on his throat portal. The black dome appeared with a few white dots near and far from him. He attached a string from him to the nearest one and sent a greeting to it. He waited, but nothing happened. He attached a string to the larger dot and sent the same greeting.

"Did you send me a greeting?" Gilriel asked. Maylore opened his eyes and smiled.

"Yes, I did," he said.

"Amazing!" Gilriel exclaimed. "I felt a bump on my throat. Let me try and send a reply this time."

Maylore closed his eyes and tied a new string to the larger object. He sent the same greeting.

"I felt something touch my throat. This is truly amazing!" Gilriel said. "Did you hear a reply from me?"

"Sorry, I did not," Maylore replied.

"Regardless, you may be genuinely gifted, Gilriel said. "I do not believe I have the communication skills, so you not receiving me is unsurprising."

Maylore thought for a moment, unsure of what to say.

"It would be useful to communicate with others without using words," Maylore said thoughtfully. "It would make confidential communication much easier." Maylore's face took on a more somber look. "I hope this proves useful and not an invasion of others," Maylore said.

"The burden may be with you for now," Gilriel said. "I suspect the other person must be willing to participate for the communication to succeed. We will practice to see what is possible." The smile returned to Gilriel's face as he said, "Try connecting to another dot and see if it works."

"I tried the small dot near me but received no reply," Maylore said.

"Perhaps the dot was the bird," Gilriel said, looking toward the bird. "Our language is probably nonsense to it. Try sending it a picture this time."

Maylore repeated the process by tying a string to the smaller dot. He sent a picture of the table with cheese on it. He heard a small squawk and saw a return picture of an empty table. Maylore laughed out loud and stood up.

"What happened?" Gilriel asked.

"I sent it a picture of cheese and received a picture of this empty table," Maylore replied.

"Incredible!" Gilriel said, dancing a few circles, then leaning on the table.

The IB ruffled its feathers but stayed on the chair's top.

Maylore reached into his bag, pulled out a small piece of cheese, and tossed it toward the bird. IB jumped down, ate the cheese, nodded three times to Maylore, and returned to its perch.

"Communication may be your best skill," Gilriel said. "Perhaps you can try others to see if they respond."

Maylore sat at the table and looked for the black dome again. He saw the dots had moved since he last looked. The dots for the bird and Gilriel were larger and still in the exact location. Maylore selected a dot in the direction of the village and tied a string to it. He sent a greeting and a picture of him waving. He waited quite a while before untying the string and trying a new dot. No response.

"I wonder if the ability has a distance limit," he said. "I didn't get a response to the two dots I tried."

"Perhaps," Gilriel said, looking thoughtful. "It could be that they could not receive a message or just ignored it, not knowing what it was."

"Perhaps," Maylore replied, leaning on the table. "Let me try more of the dots to see if I get a response." Maylore spent half a sun cycle trying each dot. He received no responses but eventually noticed the two dots closest to him had moved. He opened his eyes to see the bird, and Gilriel had left the room. "If I can find a way to determine who the dots are in the void, I could be a tracker," Maylore said aloud.

"That would be very useful," Gilriel said, entering the room from the garden. He had berries and fruit, which he laid on the table. "If you can identify a particular dot, you can see where people or animals are. Very useful indeed." Maylore nodded. Looking at the fruit, he realized he was ravenous. Gilriel pushed the fruit to Maylore, who ate some of the berries and the fruit.

"Did the book mention a way to do that?" Maylore asked.

Gilriel shook his head.

"I could not translate any more of the symbols on communication," Gilriel said. "There are a few symbols left, which I will work on tonight. You have accomplished much today. Daylight grows short, and you will need rest very soon. You can practice this skill with others around you since they will only think you are resting. Work on it when you can and tell me the results," Gilriel said.

"I will," Maylore said standing. He did feel tired as he started toward the entrance. Rounding the corner where the bird seemed to live, he received a picture of a bird flying away. Somewhat startled, Maylore stopped for a moment to consider what happened. "I did not disconnect your string, did I, bird?" Maylore said, looking in the direction where the bird might be. Smiling, he sent a picture of himself waving and disconnected the string. He left the cave and climbed down the hill, speaking to a few villagers as he returned to the hut.

His companions were absent, but he was pleased he did not have to explain what happened that day. He pushed past the reeds covering his room, intending to rest briefly, but fell asleep.

CHAPTER 20 - AIRALEE MEETS THE ELDERS

Airalee waved goodbye to Jendrin as she left the hut that morning. She was walking toward Mirtha's hut when she met up with Rendal.

"Good morning, Airalee!" he called as he approached.

"Good morning, Beacon," she replied.

"I was going to ask Mirtha, but would you help with Kai's duties while she is traveling?" he asked.

"I am not sure what her duties are," Airalee replied.

"She makes daily visits to the elderly, sick, and the children," Rendal said. "I don't expect you to know what herbs they need, but the elders would know what they used. Perhaps Marisa may be able to help."

"I would be glad to help," Airalee said. "I could use Marisa's help doing this."

"I will ask her," Rendal said. "She is very familiar with the elderly, having assisted Kai occasionally."

"What would I need to do?" Airalee asked.

"Most of them need a kind voice and food to satisfy them," Rendal said. "A few may ask for a steady hand to move to the bathroom and back or perhaps take a short walk. If you find they do not want visitors, verify they have food, water, and wood for their fire, then check the next person. Would you help do that for the next two days?"

Airalee did not need to consider before answering.

"Yes," Airalee said. "If Marisa helps, it could be a fun task."

"Excellent," Rendal replied. "Let me ask Mirtha if she can spare Marisa," he said as they walked toward Mirtha's hut.

Rendal started to knock on the door when he heard Mirtha call out.

"Come in, Rendal," Mirtha said. He opened the door to see Marisa at the table with a 'what do you want' look on her face. Airalee followed him into the hut and smiled at Marisa.

"Good morning, Mirtha," he said as Mirtha nodded toward him. "I asked Airalee to tend to Kai's duties for two days. I was hoping Marisa could help her."

"I assumed you were here to ask me to do Kai's tasks," Mirtha said. "I would be pleased to have the girls assume her tasks. I have three more people to help me today than I need, and I was afraid you wanted me to find jobs for more." Turning to Marisa, she said, "Marisa, do you mind helping Airalee?"

"I would be glad to," Marisa said, rising from the table.

"Good," Rendal said. "I am off to find Throc," he said as he left.

"Do you know what Kai does with her day?" Mirtha asked, looking at Airalee.

"Rendal told me she tends to the sick, elderly, and young," Airalee said.

"That is concise. Any details?" Mirtha asked.

"He told me to look after their food, water, herbs, and firewood," Airalee said. "He also said I may need to help them move around or accompany them on a short walk."

"I have known all of the elders since I was small," Marisa said. "We will help the ones who want or need help. Many have family in the village and only want a new voice to hear a story. It should not be a big task for us," she said, looking at Airalee.

"The elders were independent people in the past," Mirtha said, looking toward Airalee. "If you do not try to take that away or insult them, you will be welcome. Some do not take to being served, even though some can no longer fend for themselves. They insist on living alone in an elder's hut with only their families helping. If the family is there when you arrive, check to see if they have the necessities, but do not interrupt them. Some will want to talk, some will ignore you, and a few may need help to move around. A few can be challenging to engage, but I will not try to bias you with my opinions."

"Rendal said I should visit the sick, too," Airalee said.

"I don't know of any illness," Mirtha said. "You should check in at the children's area. If they want to play or talk, they will come to see you. Some will watch you, while others ignore you. Their eyes will tell you whether they want to be approached. There are usually many helping with the children, so your time there could be short.

"It is a good opportunity for me to meet villagers I have not met before," Airalee said.

"When you finish, walk to the marsh and collect soapweed," Mirtha said. "Do you have any questions?"

"I understand what to do. I will follow Marisa's lead," Airalee said.

"I can be the boss again! Let's go," Marisa said.

Airalee and Marisa left Mirtha's hut and gathered fruit, bread, fish, and a water container. The two walked toward the elder huts on the cliffs above the fishing area. The path from the fishing area to the huts was well-worn, with old straw to ease foot traffic from the bathrooms to the huts. Ten huts were spaced several steps apart and built with heavy rock along the cliff overlooking the sea.

"We have six huts to visit today," Marisa said. "Let's start with Melronna's hut. She had no children, and her mate passed. She chose not to have another life-mate. 'Someone to clutter my thoughts,' she has told me. She seems quite happy here, just lonely. We will visit with her until she tires of us, and then we will move on."

A lady sat in the hut looking out the window to the sea beyond as they arrived at the door. She waved to them as they passed the window. Marisa tapped on the door and then opened it.

"Good morning, Melronna," Marisa said as they entered.

Airalee noticed two beds, a small table with fruit, and a firepit in the back with wood on both sides.

"Good morning, lovely ladies," Melronna said, smiling. "Do you have time to visit today?"

"We do have time to visit," Marisa replied. "I brought Airalee to meet you today. Airalee, this is Melronna, one of our younger elders."

"Greetings, Airalee," Melronna said. "Where is Kai?"

"Kai is away gathering in a distant area," Marisa said. "We are helping her today."

Melronna seemed satisfied with the answer as Marisa sat in a nearby chair.

"We brought some fruit, bread, and fish for you. Do you need anything else?" Marisa asked.

"Water and conversation are about all I need," Melronna replied.

"I will gather the water," Airalee said, walking to the table.

"Such a tall, fair girl," Melronna said, looking at Airalee.

"Thank you, Melronna," Airalee replied, picking up the pitcher.

"You have one child. Do you plan more?" Melronna asked, her face acquiring a blank look.

"I have no children," Airalee replied.

Melronna's eyes blinked.

"I believe you will be a mother soon," Melronna said, staring past her. "I see one little girl standing behind you who looks like you. Her hair is light, and her heart shines."

Airalee looked behind her and saw nothing.

"I have no children or mate," Airalee said as she approached the door.

"You may have fought them off so far, but you will choose one for the child soon," Melronna said, her blank face following her to the door.

Airalee looked at Marisa with a look of 'what do I say?' on her face.

"I will fetch the water," Airalee said as she left the hut.

Melronna's eyes followed Airalee as she left but returned her gaze to Marisa.

"Marisa, what happened to your arm?" she asked. Marisa looked at her arm as Melronna continued, "It is crooked. Did you break it?" The door slammed closed, snapping Melronna back to the present.

"No. My arm is fine," Marisa said.

"Your arm?" Melronna questioned. "It looks whole to me. Why did you mention your arm?"

Marisa was stunned and did not know what to say.

"No matter. Talk with me a while," Melronna said, seeming to forget her prior comments. Marisa sat confused but decided to ignore what had happened.

"Do you need anything else besides water, Melronna?" Marisa asked.

"I have fruit and bread from yesterday," Melronna said. "I can walk to the bath and toilet alone." Marisa continued the small talk with Melronna until Airalee returned with water. "Thank you,

Airalee," Melronna said. "Place it on the table and sit with Marisa." The three women continued with small talk until Melronna appeared satisfied talking to them and grew quiet. Marisa decided it was time to move on.

"Airalee and I need to visit the other elders," Marisa said. "We will be back tomorrow to check on you," as they stood up.

"Thank you for visiting with me, girls," Melronna said, sitting back in her chair. Airalee and Marisa left the hut and started toward the next hut, which was a few sticks away.

"Does she have the ability to see the future?" Airalee asked.

"Not that I know of," Marisa said. "She spent her working life talking and creating clothes for the village. Melronna was generous with her time and helped others with their tasks. Age changed her hands to where she could not create clothes, and she despaired about losing her life-mate. The Beacon moved her here, noting her lifelong village support, and it was her time to rest."

"She made an odd comment that I would soon have a daughter," Airalee said.

"Perhaps you will," Marisa replied.

"I do not plan it anytime soon," Airalee replied.

"You might decide to join a baby seeding group like I plan to do," Marisa said.

"I think not," Airalee replied.

"We will see," Marisa chuckled. "While you were out, she asked me how I broke my arm."

"When did you break your arm?" Airalee asked, looking at Marisa's arms.

"I have never broken an arm or anything else," Marisa replied.

"I think we should talk with Kai about this," Airalee said. Marisa nodded as they continued walking the short distance to the next hut.

"Who lives here?" Airalee asked.

"This is Selakiir's hut," Marisa said. "He was our village builder and helped others with their building projects. His mate died several seasons ago, but his children see to his needs daily. He was injured building a large hut and had trouble moving independently. He may need our help moving to the bathroom, but otherwise, he manages." The door to Selakiir's hut opened just as Marisa reached for it.

"Hello, Marisa, Airalee," a voice said as she left the hut.

"Hello, Lulth. Is your dad doing well?" Marisa asked.

"He is doing well enough," Lulth replied. "He could use more fruit and bread, but he seems fine now."

"Good," Marisa replied, "we will greet him and refill his pantry."

"Thank you," Lulth replied, holding the door for the other two to enter.

"Greetings, ladies," Selakiir said from his chair near the window.

"Hello, Selakiir," Marisa replied. "We took over Kai's duties while she was on a gathering trip." Motioning toward Airalee, she added, "This is Airalee, Selakiir. She is working with Mirtha and me. Meet elder Selakiir, Airalee," she finished, indicating Selakiir.

"Pleased to meet you, Selakiir," Airalee said as Selakiir extended his hand.

"Greetings, Airalee, please sit," he said as Airalee shook his hand and sat in a table chair. Marisa added fruit and bread to his pantry as Selakiir talked with Airalee.

"Are you new to our village?" Selakiir asked.

"Yes," Airalee said. "My companions and I have been here for some time now."

"Are you a refugee or from another village?" Selakiir asked.

Airalee recounted coming to the village with her companions and their adjustment to life here.

"Young people are needed here. Our young learn our old skills, but different ideas would be useful," he said with a smile. Airalee listened and then asked what he did when he was young. "I built things," he replied. "I built many of the village huts with my crew of workers. I supervised the creation of these elder huts when my mother reached the age. Kai's idea was to create these huts so the village would know the people in them deserved extra care. My daughter, several villagers, and my old mate came to visit. I am pleased they do."

"You developed our fishing spears too, Selakiir," Marisa said as she returned to sit on the bed near Airalee.

"Yes," Selakiir chuckled, "It was an accident. We used to use a short pole with a string and bait. One day, I caught nothing, while others caught several fish. Frustrated, I threw the pole at a fish near the surface and speared it. I realized it would swim away with my pole and did not want to lose it, so I grabbed the line just before the fish swam away." Selakiir laughed. "It was small, but I got a fish that day! That accident made me decide I could do better with a spear than bait. I worked on several ideas for a long pole and decided a thin spear with a hook end and a retrieval line worked the best. Others saw I got more fish, so they built their own with my help. They still use that to this day!"

Airalee laughed while Marisa smiled, having heard the tale before.

"Your life's work is everywhere in this village, Selakiir," Marisa said, continuing her genuine smile.

"Yes," Selakiir said, smiling. "I hope the work serves for many more seasons."

The three continued small talk for a time before Marisa determined it was time to move on. The two women wished him well and waved as they left his hut.

"Who is in the next hut?" Airalee asked as they walked another short path to the next hut.

"Phaerl and her mate Adandir," Marisa said. "Phaerl made baskets and worked with children as she raised her own. Their daughter, Grena, lives in the village. They lost their son Qiuven to the sea. Adandir made cooking pots and helped with the fishing group. They both have joints that sometimes freeze on them and need help doing daily things."

Phaerl was sitting in the window when she saw the two women walking toward the door.

"Come in, Marisa," Phaerl called as Marisa reached for the door. Adandir was sitting at the window on the other side as Marisa opened the door.

"Hello, Phaerl and Adandir," Marisa said as they entered the hut. She introduced Airalee and explained the reason for Kai's absence.

"You are both welcome here," Phaerl said as Adandir agreed.

"Do either of you need to visit the bathroom?" Marisa asked.

"Grena was here and helped both of us. Thank you anyway, Marisa," Adandir replied. Airalee filled their water jug and added more bread and fruit to their pantry while they talked.

"Would either of you like some food or water?" Airalee asked.

"Yes," came the reply as Airalee filled their cups and took them to each person.

"Are you both doing well?" Marisa asked.

"Well enough," Adandir answered.

"Grena is also faring well?" Marisa asked.

"She is," Phaerl said. "She still mourns her child's passing this day many seasons ago." Looking toward Airalee, she added, "Grena was taken by the bandits when she was 16. She returned to us two seasons later, heavy with her child. The child was born but did not live. Grena believes she did something wrong, but the baby was destined not to live."

Airalee had heard a similar story of abduction from other village women. They accepted the situation, but it upset Airalee. Phaerl continued her story as Airalee stewed.

"Her next attempts at seeding did not produce any children," Phaerl said. "She decided it was her task to pick a life-mate and work with the children of others."

"We will probably see her today when we visit the children," Marisa said.

"She is usually there," Phaerl said as she looked at Airalee.

"I know Marisa has not chosen yet," Phaerl said. "Have you decided on children or a mate, Airalee? I understand you live with two men. Are they part of your plan?"

Airalee had become used to explaining her living situation and repeated what she had told others about her companions. When she wanted to change the subject, she spoke to Adandir.

"Adandir, I understand you made pottery in the village?" Airalee said.

"I did," Adandir replied. "We traded many of them to other villages for rope and supplies. Our son Qiuven and I gathered and helped with the fishing crew. His leaving was a blow to all of us."

"I do not wish to bring back bad memories, but what happened to Qiuven?" Airalee asked quietly.

"It was a sad memory," Adandir replied. "He had an idea of how to fish for the larger anut which swim farther out in the bay. He built a raft of logs along the shore and an old rope we had traded for. He paddled out to the current and speared large fish. The current was strong and pushed his raft out to sea. He tried to paddle back, but his paddle broke, and the current swept him out to sea. Our hopes for him sank, helplessly watching him drift away. I thought I should go after him, but I don't swim, and I would have joined him in his fate."

"Each time he tells that story," Phaerl said, "I remind him he was right to stay here with Grena and me even if Qiuven did not."

"It is a sad tale," Airalee said. "I regret asking you to recount it."

"It no longer hurts me to tell the tale," Adandir said. "I view it as a teaching tale to younger folk to consider what their actions may bring."

"It is a sad story, but it was long ago," Phaerl said. Phaerl smiled at the two girls, eager to change topics. "What news do you bring?"

Marisa and Airalee talked about their activities and recounted the village news. Phaerl and Adandir listened to the stories until the two women decided to move on.

"Thank you, both," Adandir said as the two women stood.

"We will return to see how you fare," Marisa said as they opened the door.

"Please do," Phaerl said, waving to them. Marisa and Airalee waved back as they started toward the next hut.

Airalee considered what herb could help them with their frozen joints. She could not recall anything Kai had that could help them.

"The next elder we may see is Sharaera," Marisa said as they walked the path. "Kai says she is near death and sleeps most of the time. Kai told me that if she sleeps, she should be left alone. Put food and water on the table and go to the next hut. If she is awake, help her to the potty and back. We may have to carry her if she cannot go that far." The two saw Sharaera asleep in a window chair as they approached. A heavy blanket had slipped to one side. Airalee opened the door and pulled the blanket back over her shoulder. Sharaera opened her eyes.

"Hello, sweet one," Sharaera said in a weak voice before she closed her eyes again.

"Sweet dreams, Sharaera," Airalee said. She refilled the water jug and put bread on her table while Marisa waited outside. Airalee closed the door and rejoined her.

"Kai says she is beyond our help," Marisa said as they started toward the next hut.

They approached the next hut when Marisa stopped and touched Airalee's shoulder.

"Werloth lives here and is Sharaera's son," Marisa said. "He wished to be near her to help, but she insisted she live alone. Werloth is a young elder in good health. He was our last villager to hunt animals for food. He lost his left arm to the woca firebird on one of his hunting adventures. I will warn you, he is a dirty old man. Stay out of arm's reach to avoid being pinched or touched." Airalee nodded as they turned toward the door. The door burst open as she prepared to knock. Werloth came out a few steps and then looked toward the mountain. He finally noticed the two women standing behind him.

"Hello, lovely ladies," he said. "Do you hear the woca firebird coming?" He turned his attention back to the mountain. Airalee and Marisa looked at each other but heard nothing.

"I don't hear a thing, Werloth," Marisa said, following his finger. Werloth pointed further to sunrise.

"There!" he said.

The two women followed his finger again but only heard the sound of the wind in the trees. A soft buzz came from the sunrise side a few moments later as the woca firebird appeared carrying a dead woca in its claws.

"There it goes!" Werloth said with a satisfied smile on his face. They watched the firebird fly over the sea and drop the woca into the water. Werloth turned back toward the volcanic cliff over which the firebird had just passed. "There are the blood wolves!" he said, pointing to a pack standing at the cliff's edge. "You didn't get it either!" he yelled, taunting the wolves. Shaking his fist at the wolves, he returned to the two women. "Old competitors," he said. "I don't begrudge them the woca, but I rarely got a chunk of one before they arrived. They never bothered me but wouldn't let me take more. Did you notice they didn't howl? They know the woca firebird drops the dead ones in the sea, but sometimes it loses its grip and drops one on the land. That's why they follow for the chance of getting one." Looking toward Sharaera's hut, he asked, "Is my mother still sleeping?"

"She is," Marisa replied. "We left her more food and refilled her water cup."

"Good," Werloth said. Opening the door to his hut, he held it with his left shoulder. "Please come in. I was hoping to talk with Kai about more herbs for Mom. Perhaps you could ask her for me?" he said, motioning with his right hand for them to enter. Airalee entered the hut but felt a hand caress her bottom. She started to complain but realized she had been warned.

"Hand down Werloth," she said as she moved toward the chair. Werloth feigned innocence as he gestured for Marisa to enter.

"You first," Marisa said. Werloth smiled and moved to the chair opposite Airalee.

"Besides putting your hand where it is unwelcome, what else keeps you busy here?" Airalee asked.

"I get dinner for many elders and visit them during the day. I keep track of my mother and check with Kai to keep her pain under control. I suspect Kai sent you two to see that I am keeping up with the other elders."

"She didn't tell me anything like that," Airalee said.

"Nor to me," Marisa said. "I did wonder why most elders seemed to have quite a bit of food in their pantry. Perhaps you do have redeeming qualities."

"Thank you, I think," Werloth said. "Since I can no longer hunt effectively, I can still help others."

"You are the only one I have heard of that hunted," Airalee said. "What did you hunt?"

"Woca, bears, boar, deer," Werloth replied. "I used to climb the mountains and try to get one of the woca to leave their valley. The Tocor managed to entice a few away in the past. The woca seemed to be bred to be dumb and would simply follow you. That is how they have milk and cheese to trade for our goods. I never got one since the fierce wolves were waiting for one to leave the protection of the woca firebird and then attack the woca. If attacked, the woca would let themselves be killed. I would wait for the blood wolves to arrive to chase off the fierce wolves, then cut a piece off before they returned. Most times, I got a good amount."

Marisa had heard enough of this subject.

"You have two beds here," Marisa said. "Why don't you have a mate?"

"I wear them out," Werloth said with a wry smile. "When I was in my 20s and 30s, I volunteered many times to join seeding parties. I traveled a few times to other human villages in seeding groups. Breeding has never been a problem for me and sometimes helped several a day." he beamed at Marisa.

"Oh," Marisa replied.

"Once my arm got cut off," Werloth continued, "I didn't receive any more requests. That seemed odd since the firebird only cut off my arm," Werloth chuckled. "I had several mates after that, but they said I was too much for them. Their loss." he finished casually.

Marisa looked to Airalee with a look of 'I asked the wrong question' on her face.

"We should check on the last elder," Marisa said as they rose.

"I will see you to the door," Werloth said, starting to rise.

"No," Airalee said, a little firmer than she intended. "We will see ourselves out."

"Come visit again," Werloth called as they left. A few feet away, Marisa spoke to Airalee.

"Kai told me a story about Werloth," Marisa said. "When she was younger, she had seen through his bravado and decided to call his bluff. She sat close to him and allowed his advances. When he realized he was no longer in control, his bravado stopped, and he moved away." Marisa laughed. "I don't think we should tempt him, but he may be all bluff now."

Airalee smiled as they continued to walk.

The two women approached the last inhabited hut and saw a man in a white robe on the cliff staring out to sea.

"That is Kelkalyn," Marisa said, indicating the man. "He says he came here from another village many summers ago and often leaves for half the season before reappearing again. He rarely comes into the village except for festival day. Gilriel, the Beacon, and Kai are the only ones he allows to visit him. He sometimes has difficulty controlling happiness and sadness, which scares others away. Kai gives him an herb to help, but she doesn't think he uses it. He told her the herb 'makes him a bore.' Let's check his pantry and leave him be." Airalee agreed but felt compelled to speak with him.

"I will go check on him," Airalee said as she approached the cliff. Marisa shrugged and went into the hut.

"I do not know you or your companion," Kelkalyn said without turning around. "Why do you bother me?"

Airalee paused, thinking they did not make that much noise for him to notice them. Walking up to his side, she introduced herself.

"I am Airalee. My companion's name is Marisa. We came to check on your comfort," she said, looking out to sea. Seeing nothing, she looked back at Kelkalyn. He glanced at her but returned his attention to the sea.

"Pretty women do not visit me," Kelkalyn said. "Beauty visits a selfish ego or intent of only their own interests. Which brings you?" he asked, staring out to sea. Airalee was surprised but determined not to be deterred by him.

"Neither," Airalee said, starting to bristle. "I ask if you could use our help with food or companionship."

"Neither," Kelkalyn said. "I gather my food and tolerate Rendal, Gilriel, and Kai, who visit too often." Looking at Airalee, he added, "You need not," stopping his tirade, his expression changed to surprise. "You have a burnt heart. Are you the one who tried nonverbal communication with me?" Airalee stepped back, wondering what he was talking about.

"Burnt? Communicate?" Airalee stuttered, staring at him. Kelkalyn's face snapped back to expressionless. Standing tall, he stared at Airalee. Kelkalyn suddenly burst out laughing and pointing at her. Airalee stepped back again, wondering what was happening now. Kelkalyn continued to laugh, crouched over, as he started walking sunrise on the cliff. His maniacal laugh blared along the ridge as he straightened, stooped, and staggered away from his hut. Airalee was confused as she watched him move away. Marisa ran from the hut to her side.

"What happened?" Marisa asked.

Airalee considered for several moments.

"I think he made a mistake," Airalee said. "He is now using his madman laughter to cover it up."

"Why do you say that?" Marisa asked.

"He said I have a burnt heart," Airalee said. "He asked if I tried nonverbal communication with him. I don't know what that means. He seemed shocked that he told me anything." They watched Kelkalyn, who was still laughing until he disappeared behind a boulder. "I suspect he is not ill and doesn't use Kai's herbs because he does not need them." Airalee surmised.

"Kai says he is morose most of the time," Marisa said. "She doesn't think he is dangerous."

"I think it is an act," Airalee said, looking at her. "I suspect he is a very intelligent old man who has things to hide and wants to keep them private."

"Be that as it may, I finished stocking his hut," Marisa said. "We should return to the village and inform Kai. We should first check on the children's care area."

CHAPTER 21 - MUD'S THE NAME

Jendrin was the last to leave the hut. Before leaving, he cleaned the hut, banked the small fire, and filled the dinner pot with more beans and spices. The air was still cool as he walked along his recently completed water pipeline. A villager approached carrying a pot of water from the pipe's new outlet.

"Did you see any leaks in the pipe?" Jendrin asked.

"A couple," he replied. "I walked the pipeline as my pot filled and saw a few leaky joints." The man pointed in different directions. Jendrin thanked the man and walked to the village kitchen to retrieve the pitch pot near the fire. Mirtha was directing several villagers on tasks as he approached.

"Good morning, Mirtha," he said, gathering the pitch pot carrier.

"Good morning, Jendrin," Mirtha said. "Airalee just left if you are looking for her."

"No," Jendrin replied. "I was going to patch leaks in the water pipe." He placed the warm pitch pot in its carrier. Mirtha looked toward the bamboo water line on the other side of her hut.

"I don't see any leaks here," Mirtha said.

"Good," Jendrin replied. "There are some further down the line." He waved to her as he started his walk toward the water line. Mirtha waved and went back to her business.

There were a few leaks at the jointing of one bamboo pipe to the next. The leaks were slow enough that water soaked into the ground, making a small pile of mud. The pipe ended near the companion's hut with a pot receiving a trickle of water. Jendrin made sure the overflow from the pot was still draining away from the village down into a crack in the rock. He carried the pitch pot back to the kitchen fire as Latel carried firewood to the woodpile.

"Jendrin," Latel called, "Let's check on how well our pig's hide is tanning," he said, stacking his load onto the pile.

"I will be right there," Jendrin said, adding another chunk of solid pitch to the pot. He replaced the pot near the fire and joined Latel in the walk to the tanning area.

This morning, the crafting area was quiet. Dirdin was stirring several pots when he noticed the two men approaching.

"Good morning," Dirdin said. "If you want color, I suggest adding it to your tanning solution. I have some orange bark there if you want to use it."

Jendrin stopped beside the pot, looking at Latel.

"Do you have a plan for the hide?" Jendrin asked him. Latel looked at the hide, considering what he could make with it.

"It would make a good satchel for gathering," Latel said. "Do you have an idea?"

"I was only interested in learning a bit about tanning," Jendrin said. "I leave it to you and Dirdin to decide."

"The satchel Kai is using is very worn," Latel said. "I would like to create a new one for her."

"Good choice," Dirdin said, with Jendrin echoing his response.

"Let's add the orange bark to denote our village," Latel said. Dirdin picked up a few large pieces and handed them to Latel.

"Break them up so the color will reach the hide quicker," Dirdin said. "It will still be a week before it is colored."

"What happens after that?" Jendrin asked.

"We will dry it, then stretch it," Latel replied, "it will fit nicely into my work schedule."

Breaking up the wood, they added it to the pot. The three men discussed the recent visitor's works and how his ideas would help the village.

"I had two young boys and one girl who wanted to join a workgroup," Dirdin said. "I will start them by having them help with tanning hides. We may have them join the hide-gathering group to look for or trade hides. One of them wants to help create clothes with you, Latel."

"Good," Latel replied. "I have three working now, but I can ask if they want to create clothes as they age. Perhaps I can convince one of them to help with creating fabric. The two doing it now are getting older and would probably like help processing the breadfruit webbing and soft grasses."

Jendrin and Latel finished adding and stirring the orange bark into the solution. A young boy approached the group as Dirdin smiled at him.

"Haryk is one of the boys who wants to learn the craft," Dirdin said. "He will stir all the hide pots for several days and tell you when we are ready to remove the pig hide from its pot."

"Thank you, Haryk," Latel said, nodding to him. "Your help is appreciated." Two more children approached the group. "This is Daena and Toross. They will be helping with hide preparation and stretching."

"Good." Latel said, "If either of you would also like to try being a tailor, let me know."

"Wait!" Dirdin said, holding up one hand. "No stealing my help!"

Latel looked at the children and leaned in their direction.

"If you remain undecided," Latel said conspiratorially, "I will try bribing you when you get older," he said in a loud whisper.

"What will you offer?" Dirdin asked in a loud whisper. "If it is good enough, I may join instead!" he said, chuckling. A short round of light-hearted bantering occurred before Dirdin looked at them with a big smile. "You two leave," he said, pointing to Latel and Jendrin. "I will put these three to work before you steal my staff."

"Thank you, Dirdin!" Latel called as he turned back toward his hut. Dirdin waved to them as Jendrin followed Latel back into the village. "I have a vest to finish today," Latel said, looking toward Jendrin. "What is your plan for the day?" he asked.

"I asked the council to consider training some villagers to defend our village," Jendrin said as they walked. Latel paused and looked at Jendrin.

"You know the council will not allow any killing or permanent injury to anyone," Latel said.

"Yes, I know," Jendrin replied. "I need to decide how we can accomplish it," he said as Latel started walking again. "I plan to wander through the mountainside forest looking for inspiration," Jendrin said. "I also plan to bring back some colored bark for Dirdin's tanning solutions."

Latel smiled and bid him farewell before walking toward his hut. Jendrin waved to his friend and returned to the kitchen area. Mirtha was directing the beginnings of lunch as he approached.

"Need help with anything, Mirtha?" he called.

"I have plenty of help, thank you," Mirtha replied. Jendrin waved as he started toward the mountain.

Jendrin began considering how to defend Olona. He knew the sentinels were in the trees but could never spot them. 'Perhaps I could convince them to assist us in defending the village,' he thought as he walked.

'The Tocor are too small to defeat a human intruder,' he thought, discarding that idea. 'The bow and arrows they shoot sting more than injure,' Jendrin reasoned as he walked. 'They could be a good distraction. Perhaps we could develop a better warning system.

Maybe an improved relay of tree-to-tree signals would be understood by all villagers. Sentinels already have an IB call they use to warn of the danger approaching, but it is sometimes too late for all villagers to find shelter. I will ask Rendal about it.'

Jendrin walked to a large rock near the road running by the village. He sat on the rock to ponder his options. Looking at the ground, he considered another option. 'A trap of some kind?' Information about traps flooded his mind from some unknown location.

'Not sure where this information came from, but we could dig holes for traps, build a tripwire trap or a snare. How would I ensure none of our villagers fell into one of the pits or sprang an action trap? Even if they were all told, someone would forget and be hurt. I think it would cause more trouble than help us,' he concluded.

Jendrin wondered what else his mind was hiding as he stood looking at the trees. Rather than ponder where the information came from, he continued his defense planning to see what else may come out.

'Could we modify our fishing spear to help?' he thought. Another stream of military information jumped to the forefront from the depths of his mind.

'Range weapons, perhaps? Spears, throwing weapons, bow and arrow, slings, rocks. It takes a lot of practice to become an effective range fighter. These would be effective but likely kill, too. The council will not agree to that,' he thought.

'Clubs?' he thought as more information flooded his mind. 'Melee weapons instead? Swords, ax, knives, sticks, staffs, clubs, flail or a whip.' He considered each option to eliminate those ideas which would kill rather than defend. A sword or ax would kill. Whips and flails would also be challenging to use in close quarters. Sticks, clubs, or staff may work. A club is hard to use as a defense-only weapon. Sticks would do better at that. A quarterstaff would be effective as a defense and offense weapon.

'I could train a villager fairly quickly to use a quarterstaff. I should be able to train them for defense or offense. The other options would take too much training to become proficient. Villagers would not need to become proficient to defend with a quarterstaff,' Jendrin reasoned.

"Yes. A quarterstaff would be the better option," Jendrin said aloud. As he spoke those words aloud, the methods to build the weapon surged into his mind. "My thanks to wherever that information comes from," he said aloud, looking into the sky.

"What else is stored in my mind that I am unaware of? Perhaps how to build one of those flying firebirds?" he asked loudly. He waited, but nothing came to mind. The only sound came from the buzzing insects. He waited a little longer before sighing and staring off into the forest.

'How do we make a quarterstaff?' he thought. 'Not too long or short. Not too heavy or light. Straight as possible.' he thought as he walked. His first stop was the ironwood tree he had used for his ax. He found a piece long enough to be a quarterstaff, but it would be too heavy to wield quickly.

Tossing it aside, he continued looking. Thoughts came to him as he considered how to create the quarterstaff. 'It should be about the height of the wielder's chin. Heavy enough to deflect weapon attacks and light enough to be used quickly by the average villager.' Using this as a base premise, he considered many of the trees and bushes in the area. He spent a quarter sun cycle trying out different thicknesses and types of wood. None seemed to be suitable for him in this mature forest.

He found himself skirting the village as he wandered sunset. He had already walked through the meadow's edge and approached the river. The marsh was in front of him as he walked toward the mountains. He came across dead trees and spotted orange bark that would be right for tanning. 'At least I found one item I wanted,' he thought. He started to gather up the bark when the marsh insects went silent.

Jendrin crouched down, knowing something was causing the marsh to go quiet. He looked to the nearby marsh but didn't see anything. 'Did I cause them to go quiet?' he thought. Looking up to the top of the rockslide spilling into the marsh, he saw a large figure quickly picking its way through the brush. 'Friend or foe?' Jendrin thought as he considered following the person. 'They have too much of a lead for me even to consider catching them,' he thought.

The person seemed to sense they were being watched and stopped. They turned toward the swamp and pulled a white object from their belt. Jendrin crouched down even further as the person scanned the swamp. Jendrin could not tell if it was a man or a woman. The distance made their features indistinct. Jendrin continued watching as they finally replaced the white object and fled the swamp. Jendrin considered following them anyway, but the swamp would slow him too much as he slogged through it.

'Gather what I can and return to the village,' he thought. Jendrin waited a few more minutes to see if the figure would return. When they didn't, he gathered the orange bark and started toward the village. He occasionally glanced behind to verify that nothing was following him.

Dirdin waved as Jendrin dropped his load near the other orange bark in the tanning area. Jendrin decided to return to the marsh to continue his quarterstaff search. First, he needed to retrieve his axe from his hut if he found a suitable quarterstaff branch. He was walking back toward the kitchen when he heard a familiar voice.

"Hey, Hero!" they said as Jendrin turned to see Airalee and Marisa coming from the fishing area.

"Ladies," Jendrin said as they got closer to him.

"I want you to join us in visiting the children," Marisa said as they stopped before him.

Airalee looked at Marisa with a questioning look.

"Sure," Jendrin replied, wondering what this was all about. "Do they need a strong talking to?"

"No," Marisa replied, "If they needed that, I would be doing the talking, not you."

"I see," Jendrin replied with a smile. "Airalee is beginning to rub off on you."

"Perhaps," Marisa replied, "Have you visited with the village children yet?" she asked.

"No," Jendrin replied. "I have seen several in the village but did not visit with them."

"Join Airalee and me as we check up on them," Marisa said. Jendrin shrugged and followed the two women to an area near the council hut where several children were playing. As he entered, Jendrin set his ax against the tree to avoid frightening anyone. Three older women and one younger woman watched two babies and six older children. The children appeared to be 2 to 8 seasons old. They were listening to one of the women teaching them something. Jendrin and Airalee recognized all of the adults as they greeted them when they arrived.

"Are you doing Kai's rounds this morning?" one of the women asked.

"Yes, Airalee and I are checking to see if anyone needs food or help," Marisa said. "Jendrin is here to help, too," she finished.

One little girl got up from her spot near the teacher and took Jendrin by the hand.

"You may sit with me," she said. Jendrin smiled at her, took her hand, and sat beside her.

"Marisa, would you and Airalee hold the babies while we walk to the potty?" one woman asked.

319

"Of course," Marisa said, taking one child as Airalee took the other. The teacher restarted her discussion while Marisa and Airalee held the babies, and Jendrin listened. Marisa walked around the area to check the food and water supply. Airalee followed her as she checked.

"What are you up to, Marisa?" Airalee asked.

"I am checking the food and water supply," Marisa said. "The children all seem to be in good health."

"No," Airalee said. "Why did you want Jendrin to join us?"

"Don't you wonder if he would make a good baby-mate?" Marisa asked.

"I had not considered it," Airalee replied.

"You should," Marisa replied. "I am considering asking him to join my seeding group when I am ready for a baby. I have already picked a baby-mate to raise the baby and a retirement mate."

Airalee stood blinking at her, unsure what to say.

"You are thinking way ahead," Airalee said.

"You should be, too," Marisa replied, "I am testing various mates to find the ones I think would be best. Perhaps Jendrin would create a kind, intelligent, independent child. I hope it will help its mother when I age like the children of the elders we saw today." Airalee was surprised at Marisa's honesty and calculating thought pattern. That thinking had not entered her thought patterns.

"You and I are thinking of life in different directions," Airalee said.

"We get several chances in life at many things," Marisa said, "but having children does not wait. If I delay too long, I may not have a healthy child or find my desired baby-mate. I do not want to be so old and can't keep up with my children." Marisa said as she started back toward the group. Airalee hugged the baby tighter and followed Marisa.

"That's my brother!" the girl sitting with Jendrin said.

"He is?" Marisa said. "Would you like him to be near you while you listen?"

"Yes," the little girl replied.

"Jendrin, you hold the baby," Marisa said, handing him the baby. Jendrin took the child as if he had childcare experience. The little girl leaned over and talked to the baby as Jendrin held him. Marisa stepped back to Airalee's side, saying, "He did not object, and he held the child correctly. He may be a good child-raising mate after all." Airalee looked between Jendrin and Marisa.

"Have you tested other possible mates?" Airalee asked. Marisa continued to watch Jendrin before replying.

"I have tested several this way," Marisa said. I may not want children yet. I just want to know who a good candidate would be. I have tried several girls who would work well, too, but I think a man would suit me better." They observed Jendrin and listened to the storyteller until the two childcare women returned.

"Thank you for watching the babies," the older woman said. "It is my turn to tell the next story about our fishermen," she said, standing next to Marisa.

"I will gather supplies for the children, then listen to your story," Marisa said.

"I am going to ask Jendrin to help me carry the heavy pottery mud from the swamp to the village," Airalee said. "I hope to find a few fresh herbs and vegetables for dinner tonight, too."

"I will walk with you as far as the storage huts," Marisa said as she returned to reclaim the baby from Jendrin. "You have rested enough, Jendrin. It's time to go back to work."

"I want Jendrin to stay," the little girl said, looking up at Marisa.

"Sorry," Marisa replied. "Jendrin has important things to do today. You get to stay and listen to the story," she said, picking the baby out of Jendrin's arms. "I will get lunch for everyone, then come listen and eat with you." The little girl relented but was not happy. "It looks like you have a new friend, Jendrin," Marisa said.

"Apparently," Jendrin said, standing up. "Thank you for letting me sit next to you," he said, speaking to the little girl. She smiled and waved to him as he left. Marisa returned the baby to one of the women as Jendrin rejoined Airalee.

"Hero can handle a baby," Marisa said lightly.

"It is a natural talent," Jendrin looked at her.

"Do you have enough talent to help me carry pottery mud from the swamp to the potters?" Airalee asked.

"I do if you have eyes to help me find wood for a quarterstaff," Jendrin replied as Marisa joined them, walking toward the kitchen.

"I would if I knew what a quarterstaff was," Airalee said. Jendrin explained what a quarterstaff was and the type of wood he needed. Villagers were eating lunch as the trio arrived in the kitchen area.

"Let's have some lunch before we forage," Airalee said, indicating a spot for all of them. There seemed to be more people helping than eating today. One woman handed each one a community bowl filled with hearty stew. Thanking the woman, they sat at the table.

"I want to talk about what we heard this morning," Airalee said, taking a bite.

"Dirty old man?" Marisa teased.

"Just one dirty old man propositioned you?" Jendrin asked, looking at Airalee.

"No," Airalee replied, hesitating for a moment. "I mean, there was only one. I put him in his place. I think." Believing that was not probable, she changed the subject. "I want to talk about what happened to Grena."

"We all would like a solution to that," Marisa said. "It has been that way for a long time."

"What happened to Grena?" Jendrin asked, eating his stew.

"The bandits took her, used her, and sent her back to the village heavy with child," Airalee said. "She suffered from time spent in the bandit village. When she returned, she lost her baby. Her mother says she will not discuss it. I assume the experience was beyond appalling."

"None of the girls who return will discuss their plight," Marisa said. "We get bits and pieces of their ordeal by asking indirect questions. Some start to answer before suddenly going quiet. All those girls think it was their fault and deserve what happened to them. Beacon, Kai, and their mothers were unable to convince them otherwise. They eventually put it aside when their baby was born or busy themselves with other work."

"There must be a way to stop it," Airalee said, clenching her jaw.

"It has been tolerated for a long time," Marisa said, "If we try to stop them, the bandits claim they will kill us."

"I understand," Airalee replied, sighing. "I wish we had a way to stop them anyway." Jendrin waited until she stopped to interrupt.

"I believe we can teach a few of these villages how to defend themselves," Jendrin said.

"You do?" Airalee asked. "Is this the quarterstaff you were talking about?"

"Yes," Jendrin replied. "I can teach them how to defend themselves and the village using the quarterstaff."

"I heard you describe a quarterstaff, but the council will not agree to a weapon that kills," Marisa said.

"I believe we can defend without killing," Jendrin said. "The attacker could press an attack and force them to kill an attacker. I suspect most bandits are not looking for a fight and will look for easier targets."

Marisa looked at Jendrin for a short time.

"It seems possible," Marisa said. "The bandits I have encountered seem full of bluff instead of action. I will help you talk to the council."

Airalee felt her spirit lift with the discussion.

"What do we need to do, Jendrin?" she asked. Jendrin started to answer before realizing she called him by name.

"You do know my name," Jendrin said, looking at her.

"Yes," Airalee said. "This is your chance to be a real hero instead of a hero in name only."

"I hope to prove myself worthy," he said, collecting his thoughts. "We can start by looking for sturdy limbs to make a staff. We then arrange a meeting with the council to get their blessing to develop a training class. If they approve, it will take time to make the quarterstaffs and train people to use them."

"I will ask Beacon Rendal to arrange the meeting," Marisa said. "You find what you're looking for, and we will discuss what to say to the council."

"Thank you, Marisa," Jendrin said.

"I promised your new little friend to listen to a story," Marisa said, "I will keep that promise," Marisa said, getting up. The woman who brought them the stew took their empty bowls and left before Marisa could thank her. "I will meet you again tomorrow for Kai's rounds," she said to Airalee as she walked toward the children's area.

"Well, hero," Airalee said, "let's see if we can find your quarterstaff."

"I see I have fallen back to being a hero in name only," Jendrin said, standing up.

"You have to earn it now," Airalee said, smiling at him. "Let's get the clay collection basket, then go to the marsh." Picking up his axe, Jendrin followed Airalee to the potter's area to get the basket.

"Argila," Airalee said as she spotted the lead potter working her trade. "We will gather more mud for your group if we can borrow the basket."

"Yes," Argila answered. "We are running low, and more clay would be appreciated," she said, looking at both of them. "Jendrin could carry it fully by himself, I suppose, but take the two-person basket there," she said, pointing to a nearby basket. They each picked up a handle on the basket and started toward the marsh. "Thank you!" Argila called after them.

Entering the forest on the mountainside, the two looked for different things. Jendrin stopped on occasion to examine a branch as a potential quarterstaff. They all bent too quickly, were too thick or thin, or broke with any pressure.

"Keep looking, hero," Airalee said as he picked up his end of the basket. The forest thinned as they moved into the swamp.

"Let's try this direction," Jendrin said, pointing more toward the mountain. The duo walked another 30 steps when Airalee suddenly stopped.

"Why are those leafy plants glowing?" she asked.

Jendrin looked to where she pointed but saw nothing glowing.

"I don't see anything glowing," he said. "The sun is beyond the point of shining into this part of the forest. It can't be sunshine." He set the basket down and walked toward the plants. Airalee felt transfixed by the sight and watched as Jendrin approached the plants.

325

He had gone a few steps when the glow faded, and the plants blended into the background.

"Stop!" she said. Jendrin stopped and looked back at her. "They stopped glowing. Walk back this way," she said. Jendrin retraced his steps back toward her. Airalee let out a soft gasp as the plants resumed their soft glow. "They are glowing again," she said in quiet amazement.

"Glowing plants, huh," Jendrin said in disbelief as he turned back toward the plant. Airalee saw the glow fade and stop as he moved away.

"They stopped glowing again," Airalee said.

"Why would they stop glowing?" Jendrin said with a suspicious look on his face.

"Perhaps they dislike you and go into hiding when you approach," she said, setting down her end of the basket. She started walking toward the plants.

"I suspect you ate the wrong mushroom," Jendrin said.

Airalee ignored him as she walked toward the plants. A few steps closer, the glow started again.

"They glow again," Airalee said, looking back at Jendrin. Jendrin simply smiled and walked away. The glow from the plants faded and then disappeared. "Come back this way again," she said.

"What for?" Jendrin said, turning around.

"The plants stopped glowing again. Come back here," Airalee demanded.

"Yes, master," he said, walking back toward her. Slowly, the plants started to glow again as Jendrin approached.

"Don't you see that!" Airalee exclaimed, "They are glowing again!"

Jendrin looked at the plants, then at Airalee.

"They aren't glowing, Airalee," he said. Airalee looked at him and tilted her head, thinking, 'Why doesn't he see it? Am I the only one who can see it? Perhaps it takes both of us to cause the glow effect. How do I find out which it is?'

"Walk a few steps away," she said. Jendrin walked back several steps, and the glow faded with each step. "It takes both of us for me to see the glow!" she said excitedly, facing him.

"As you say," Jendrin said, deciding just to humor her. Airalee turned back to the plants, which had started a soft glow again as he approached.

"Glowing again," she said. "Walk back with me a few steps," as she walked away from the plants. Jendrin followed beside her until the glow faded, and then she stopped. "Walk a few more steps away." Jendrin took another two steps, and the glow stopped. "Stop. Give me your hand," she said, watching the plants. Jendrin reached for her outstretched hand as she watched the glow return. "We need to be near each other for me to see the glow!" she said, facing Jendrin. Jendrin stared at her, unsure if he should laugh or worry about her. Deciding he should do neither, he sighed.

"Oh, my, as Maylore would say," he said. Airalee ignored him and tightened her grip on his hand as she pulled him toward the glowing plant. She dropped his hand when they stood above the glowing plant. Bending down, she touched the leafy plant.

"This is Lamquart," Airalee said with a flash of recognition coming to her mind. "We don't eat it for some reason. It grows everywhere and has a pleasant flavor." Airalee was unsure where the information came from as the blue stone in her pocket warmed. She gripped the warm stone before reaching down with that hand to pick several bunches. She added them to her satchel. The glow of the plants faded as she picked them. Standing up, she knew that, having identified the plant, it would not glow for her again as the warm stone cooled. "We have this growing behind our hut. This plant will make it even easier for food gathering," she said. Jendrin looked at her.

"Who will eat it to prove it is safe?" he said.

"I will," she said. "After a week, you can join me, too." Jendrin nodded, thinking to himself to be sure Kai was nearby in case it was poisonous. "We have not gathered together before. I wonder if this glow occurs when we search near each other." Airalee said, not looking at anything.

"I will walk with you if you help find a glowing tree for me," Jendrin said with a grin.

"Do we eat trees?" she asked.

"Let's find out," he said, returning to the basket. They continued toward the swamp, with Jendrin searching trees and bushes as Airalee stayed near him, looking for herbs and anything glowing. They entered a small clearing where they could see the swamp. Airalee stopped again, rising to her full height.

"There," she said, becoming stoic. She pointed to a Ficus tree. "The roots growing down from the branches of that red tree are what you need," she said.

"Are they glowing?" Jendrin asked.

"Yes. A few branches are," Airalee said as she walked toward the tree. Jendrin followed until she stopped again before a root that grew downward. "There is the beginning of one quarterstaff. These are strong roots and will serve you well," she said, pointing to a few of the closest roots. The long root was intriguing and caught his attention as he looked at them.

"It may work," he said, feeling the root.

"These three and several over there," Airalee said, pointing to the other side of the tree. She bent down to pick up some mud and marked two spots on five roots. She walked to the other side and marked several more. "There are several more trees over there if you need them," she said, returning to him. Her expression changed as she stood before him.

"Oh, you found wood for a quarterstaff?" Airalee inquired.

"How did you know this would work for a staff?" he asked.

"Know what?" she asked with a questioning look.

"You said this root would make a good quarterstaff, and they will serve us well," Jendrin said.

"I did?" she said. "Not that I remember," she said, looking quizzical. "I think you ate the wrong mushroom."

Jendrin looked at her briefly, wondering what he had fallen into. Deciding logic would not suffice, he put it aside and chose to feel glad to find a source for the quarterstaffs.

"Yes, I think this may work," he said, raising his axe. Airalee stood back as he started cutting the root. The axe bounced off the root like it hit a rock instead of wood. He changed his cutting point to match the mud Airalee had painted onto the root before his axe bit into the wood. He had to repeat the process on the top cut until he found a spot to cut through the wood. The root dropped to the ground with a ringing sound instead of a thud. Picking up the chopped root, it felt light in his grip and reached from his chin to the ground. "This already seems to balance fairly well," Jendrin said, looking at the nearly straight piece of wood. "I may have to shave off a little to balance it."

"I hope a stick can help defend Olona," Airalee said dubiously.

"Once I determine how to use this, I can train a group of villagers to turn away most invaders," Jendrin said as he tied the five roots together with solid grass.

"I hope you are right," Airalee said, picking up the other end of the basket.

"Let's get the mud," Jendrin said as he hoisted the roots onto his shoulder and picked up one end of the basket.

They started toward the swamp as insects sang their lone songs. The brush thickened as they approached the edge of the noisy marsh.

"The brush will thin out if we enter the marsh near the river," Jendrin said, pointing toward the sunset. They skirted the marsh's edge until they reached the spot Jendrin had previously searched for quarterstaff wood. Jendrin stopped and pointed past the marsh toward the mountain. "I saw someone up there this morning trying to creep. I don't think he was one of our villagers. He was dressed in leather and seemed nervous as he walked."

"Let's hope you don't need to try out your new staff already," Airalee said, touching the knife in her pouch.

"I am sure he is far away," Jendrin said as they continued toward the river. They had taken a dozen steps when the marsh went silent.

"Down," Jendrin said, crouching down. Airalee followed his lead as they scanned the marsh. Nothing was moving, and they did not see anything unusual. "I am not surprised some insects went quiet as we approached, but the whole marsh?" Jendrin said, rising. Airalee followed but continued to scan the area. Suddenly, the sound of hundreds of wings filled the air as flocks of IB birds swept down from the trees from various corners of the marsh. Cawing loudly, they landed and scooped up bugs, worms, and small fish around them. Jendrin and Airalee involuntarily ducked as the birds flew near their heads. "I didn't know the birds were there," Jendrin said, watching the birds.

"Good thing we aren't bugs, or we would have been dinner," Airalee said with a stress-relieved laugh. They decided the birds were no threat to them and continued the walk along the marsh toward the river.

Airalee spotted cattails with glowing sprouts at the base of each plant.

"The bottom of those cattails are glowing," she said, pulling them toward her. She bent down to touch the base of the cattail. "These new cattail shoots are good to eat. Help me gather the new shoots," she said to Jendrin. Drawing out her knife, she started cutting new shoots and putting them in her pouch. Jendrin put down his load and started cutting the shoots. They had collected shoots from several dozen cattails before her satchel was full.

"I don't think I have ever eaten these before," Jendrin said as they finished.

"Nor I," Airalee said, putting her knife away.

"Another coarse weed I will be forced to endure?" he asked.

"No, a delicacy you will have the privilege to enjoy," Airalee replied, picking up the basket.

"I see," Jendrin replied, unsure if his stomach would welcome another unknown item. "The mud pit is just around the edge by the stone pit," Jendrin said, picking up the basket.

The clay, like mud, took time to gather into the basket. Jendrin used his axe to cut into the wet mud and put it into the basket. "This may be enough weight," Jendrin said, eyeing the basket. Airalee picked up one end of the basket.

"It isn't too heavy yet," Airalee said. Jendrin eyed the basket again.

"By the time we carry it back to the village, it will be heavy," Jendrin said. Airalee shrugged, looking between the basket and Jendrin.

"If it gets too heavy, I will carry your end, too," she smiled.

"I will welcome it," he replied. They started back toward the village, following the river's edge to the end of the marsh. Airalee watched for other items they could use when she spotted soapweed growing at the marsh's edge.

"Hold up, hero. We need to gather some soapweed for the bath area," she said, putting down her end. "I am going to gather some with roots attached to see if we can grow it near the bath," she said, digging the soapweed with her knife. She quickly gathered what she wanted and added it to the mud basket. She picked up her end of the basket, and they continued. They had walked about a third of the way back when Airalee felt her arm straining. Halfway back, it felt like it was going to fall off.

"Hold up, hero," she said, setting the basket down. "I think my end is heavier than yours." Jendrin looked at the basket, noting that his end had more mud than hers.

"Do you want to trade ends?" he asked.

"Yes," she said, walking around the basket. Jendrin shrugged and picked up the other end. "Off we go," she said. After they had walked another quarter of the way, she felt the other arm was tired. "Do you need to rest?" Airalee asked.

"No," Jendrin said, lifting the basket even higher.

"Good. You take this end too," Airalee said, pushing the other end toward him.

Jendrin laughed and took both ends.

"You take the axe and the roots, and I will carry the basket," he said, passing the roots and axe to her.

The basket was now heavy for him as they trudged through the forest. As Jendrin's arms ached, they arrived at the village potter's area. Argila saw them approaching and pointed to where she wanted the basket. Argila looked into the basket.

"You brought back much more than we normally get," she said with a smile.

"Yes," Airalee said, "I had to force him to stop gathering the mud, so I allowed him to finish carrying it."

Jendrin looked at her.

"I was fortunate," Jendrin said with a smile.

"I will talk to Mirtha about the new food if you plant the soapweed near the bath area," Airalee said, giving him the roots, axe, and soapweed. "I will meet you back at the hut, then cook these for our dinner," she said.

"Can't wait," Jendrin replied, taking the items from her.

"Goodbye, hero," Airalee said. "Goodbye, Argila!" she said as she walked away.

"Thank you, Airalee!" Argila said. "And thank you, Jendrin."

"You're welcome," Jendrin said. "Off to the bath," he said as he started in that direction.

CHAPTER 22 - COUNCIL PLANNING

Maylore awoke with a fuzzy feeling in his head. "I know I didn't drink Dirdin's brew last night," he said aloud as he sat up in bed.

"Time to get up, dad," Airalee called out as he stood up.

Pushing open his curtain, he saw Airalee and Jendrin preparing food. Jendrin spooned beans.

into the bowls while Airalee tore up Lamquart leaves and added them to her bowl.

"Are those the leaves you picked up yesterday?" Jendrin asked.

"They are," Airalee replied. "I will eat them to prove they are not poison."

"Is it dinner time?" Maylore asked, looking at the food preparation.

Airalee looked at him with surprise on her face.

"It's breakfast time," Airalee said, "You slept all night, dad."

Maylore remembered lying down to take a nap in the late afternoon.

"Oh my," Maylore said, shaking his head. "I can't believe I slept that much."

"Come join us for breakfast," Jendrin said. "We need your wisdom to prepare for a council meeting."

"Wisdom?" Maylore asked, looking at Jendrin. "I don't believe I have heard that before," he said with a slow grin. Airalee grabbed his arm and pulled him to the table.

"Sit by me and add your comments," Airalee said as she sat down. Maylore sat with them and started eating the large breakfast they had prepared.

"I wanted both of you here to tell you about my encounter with our elders," Airalee said, gathering her breakfast.

"I knew we had elder huts on the cliff, but I have not seen any of them," Maylore said. "Why did you venture to their huts?"

"The Beacon asked Marisa and me to assume Kai's duties while she's away," Airalee said. "He wanted me to help with basic food, herbs, and visitation. Some have difficulty moving around and need help doing basic tasks. I asked if Marisa could accompany me since she had previously helped Kai with the elders, and Mirtha agreed to let her help."

"What did you find out?" Maylore asked, starting to eat.

"We visited six huts," Airalee said. "The first elder was Melronna. She lives alone with no children or mates. She told me some odd things."

"Odd?" Maylore asked, "Like what?"

Airalee looked at Maylore before continuing.

"She said I have one child and will soon have a daughter," Airalee said.

Both men stopped and looked at her while Airalee stared at Maylore.

"Don't look at me!" Maylore said.

"I was not accusing anyone, dad," Airalee said. "I wanted both of you to hear why I thought she was odd. Melronna also asked Marisa how she broke her arm. Marisa said she had never broken an arm."

"Indeed, that is odd," Maylore replied, returning to his breakfast. "I have not heard Rendal or others mention any ability like that."

"Do we have an intuitive in the village?" Jendrin asked.

"I asked Marisa if Melronna had shown that ability," Airalee replied. "She had never heard of her or any other villager with an ability like that."

"Odd is right. Melronna is imagining things," Jendrin said, returning to his breakfast. "Did other elders seem normal?"

"Yes, most of them," Airalee said.

Jendrin chuckled but did not comment as he continued to eat.

"The next hut we visited belonged to Selakiir," Airalee said. "He lived alone and was a former builder for the village. He designed and helped build many of the huts."

"Did he show any abilities?" Maylore asked.

"No," Airalee replied. "He just seemed lonely but satisfied.

"Ah, a normal person I can identify with," Jendrin said.

"Normal? Questionable hero, questionable," Airalee said.

"Who did you see next?" Maylore said, deflecting the taunting.

"The next hut had two elder mates living in it," Airalee said. "Phaerl and Adandir made pottery and baskets for trade. He was part of the fishing crew but lost a son to the sea many seasons ago."

"Oh dear," Maylore said. "Did he get pulled into the sea by an anut?"

Airalee explained what happened to their son before continuing.

"Their daughter was taken by bandits when she was 16 seasons old," Airalee said as she clenched her jaw.

Both men looked at her as she fell silent.

"We need to correct that situation," Jendrin finally said. "The council seems to believe it is acceptable to lose one to protect the rest. I do not think we should sacrifice anyone to keep the peace."

336

"Thank you, Jendrin," Airalee said, looking at him. "It is nice to see we continue to agree on something."

Jendrin looked at her without speaking before returning to his breakfast.

"I want to discuss it further, but I need to finish relating the rest of my visit," Airalee said. "I can relate one interesting thing from that visit. Adandir accidentally developed the fishing spear you use."

"Accidentally?" Jendrin questioned.

"He told us he was not catching any fish as the rest of the crew caught several," Airalee said. "He said he threw his pole at the fish in frustration, spearing one of the fish. He experimented with developing a longer spear with a hook at one end and a longer line to pull the fish in. He learned to spear more fish than the others were catching. The other fishermen soon switched to using a spear instead of a fishing pole."

"We are fortunate that the fish hide near the surface, or a spear would not work too well," Jendrin said.

"I am surprised the fish didn't pull you into the water anyway, hero," Airalee smirked.

"They are strong, but not that strong," Jendrin replied. "I would not want to swim in that water since a passing anut might mistake me for a fish."

"I wouldn't worry," Airalee said. "They would spit you back out for being sour," Airalee replied with a grin.

"Possibly, or too sweet to pass up," Jendrin replied.

"Unlikely," Airalee quipped.

"Now, you two," Maylore interrupted. "Who else did you visit?"

"Next was a hut belonging to Sharaera," Airalee said. "She is a lady near death who was asleep when we arrived. Her son Werloth lives in the hut next to her. He was the last villager who hunted. He lost an arm to the woca firebird, which ended his hunting. You may want to talk with him, Jendrin. He may be a good reference for wildlife around here."

"I may do that," Jendrin replied, looking up. "I have enough to keep me busy for some time. I would like to hear more about that firebird someday."

"Kelkalyn uses the last hut," Airalee said. "He is another odd one. He acts like he wants no contact with anyone and tries to push Marisa and me away. I think he is just a lonely man who is hiding something."

"Why do you say that?" Maylore asked.

"When I asked him questions, he told me to leave him alone without even looking at me. He finally looked at me angrily and suddenly assumed a shocked look before saying, 'You have a burnt heart.'"

"Burnt heart?" Maylore questioned. "I wonder what that means?"

"I don't know," Airalee said. "He also asked if I was the one trying to communicate with him non-verbally."

Maylore nearly choked on his breakfast as he sat straight up with a sheepish look. Airalee noticed the look on his face.

"Dad," Airalee questioned, "Do you know something about that?"

Maylore regained his composure before replying.

"I have heard Gilriel mention that ability," Maylore said. "I would like to talk with him. Where is he?"

"The last hut along the cliff," Airalee replied. Her expression said, 'What are you hiding?' "He will act morose and unwelcoming. You have to ignore his off-putting demeanor to get him to converse. He told me he only talks to Kai, Gilriel, and the Beacon. Perhaps you can join one of them when they visit."

"I will ask the Beacon the next time I see him," Maylore replied. "What did Marisa say about him?" he asked, trying to deflect her from asking questions. Airalee filed away Maylore's reaction to her communicating comment for later inquiry.

"Marisa knew little about him," Airalee said. "He spends little time at his hut and avoids people. He is hiding something, so he puts on an act of appearing insane when he knows what he is doing."

"They all sound like interesting people," Maylore said. "Did you determine anything else from your visits?"

"Yes," Airalee replied. "Kai provides herbs for some of the elders to lessen pain. We should expand our herb gathering to find other possible medications. Less stiffness in their joints would help many. I want Jendrin to accompany me on the next herb gathering trip."

"I would be glad to go with you again," Jendrin said. "Even if I didn't see anything glowing."

"You started glowing?" Maylore asked.

"Jendrin and I searched for wood sticks for him and plants for me," Airalee said. "We approached a plant in the swamp when I saw it start to glow."

"The plant glowed? It was indeed a day of odd things," Maylore said.

"It got more odd," Airalee said. "We found Jendrin needed to be nearby for it to glow."

"I bring out the best in all things," Jendrin said. "I just have to get close for plants and wood to glow."

"So you say," Airalee said.

"You were the one who pointed to a tree root, saying it was good material for a quarterstaff," Jendrin said.

A familiar knock on the door interrupted their talk. Looking toward the door, Marisa entered the hut.

339

"Good morning, everyone," Marisa said, closing the door. "I talked to the Beacon this morning. The council will meet after Kai returns. He has agreed to allow us to talk with the council." She sat close to Jendrin as she spoke. A coy smile crossed her face as she looked at Jendrin and scooted closer to him. Jendrin ignored her.

"We will have to start planning soon," Jendrin said.

"We?" Maylore said. "Do I need to meet with them?"

Airalee gave Marisa a 'Knock it off look' before turning to Maylore.

"I would appreciate your support if you would attend," Airalee said. Maylore nodded in agreement and returned to breakfast. Looking again at Marisa, she said, "I told them about our visits with the elders yesterday."

"You have already told them about the dirty old man grabbing you as you entered his hut?" Marisa said, grinning.

"I did not," Airalee replied. "I did threaten to punch him if he tried it again."

"You did," Marisa said, nodding. "He acted like you had burned him."

Maylore and Jendrin were grinning at her.

"Not a word from you two." She said, looking at both of them. Both men continued to smile but kept quiet.

"We were going to plan our meeting with the council before someone brought up something else, Marisa," Airalee said.

Marisa's smile vanished.

"Forgive me, Airalee," Marisa said. "It is a serious subject, which I know inflames you."

"Yes, it does," Airalee said as the room's mood turned serious. "The village acceptance of the forced slavery of Olona's young has been gnawing at me for some time. The village needs to prevent them from being taken. The story Phaerl and Adandir told us has pushed the subject even more for me."

"They did not finish the story," Marisa said. "Birsha and two of his men found her before she could get to the safety of the caves. Several villagers stood with her but did not stop them as they led her away. The villagers were unhappy, but they followed the council's pacifist doctrine. It has been that way since before I was born, but it makes me sad each time."

"The village needs to defend itself from bad people, whether they take objects or people or kill us," Jendrin said.

"I am with you all," Marisa said, bowing her head.

"We need to plan how to do that," Airalee said with stiffness in her voice.

"I suggest we use a slow push approach," Maylore said softly. Three heads turned to look at him.

"What was that, dad?" Airalee asked.

"Olona's people have become pacifist to the point many will run instead of defend themselves, their children, neighbors, or their home. We should approach them with a plan that begins with passive resistance. They could begin by approaching an aggressor with a strong bluff and no weapons. I suspect using verbal opposition will allow many villagers to approve a beginning plan. Loud noises from the whole village can help prevent a less determined attack. A village of people yelling may be enough. The pure pacifist in the group may not go along, but their presence increases the size of the group, signifying strength may be enough."

"Do you think it will work with the council?" Jendrin asked.

"It should help," Maylore smiled. "Those members who believe in no aggression may go along with it. Some members will want a plan to defend with more force. You will not find any to agree to an aggressive war."

"I think he is right," Marisa said in a small voice.

"We can start with a nonaggressive option," Jendrin said. "We could progress to a stronger defensive option if needed."

"How many members do we need to make this defensive force work?" Airalee asked.

"A small force," Jendrin said. "Four to ten villagers trained to use a quarterstaff could repel a small group of aggressors."

"One on the council will suggest using force to attack the bandit village," Marisa said. "Are you suggesting we do that?"

"No," Jendrin said. "We do not war on any village. The council and village team members are unlikely to support that anyway. We will be fortunate to get the council to allow a defensive group."

"Agreed," Maylore said. "Olona has been under the sway of a pacifist group for too long to allow any action like that. I would not support aggression on any other village."

Silence filled the hut as the group pondered the suggestion.

"It seems to me," Marisa started, "that it may push the council to some action. Some council members will not agree to the defensive force, but bandits have victimized some council members' families who are likely to approve."

"How does Olona's council make decisions?" Maylore asked.

"The council works on a majority-rule basis," Marisa said. "Even those who oppose a plan will begrudgingly accept the group's will."

"How did they get on the council?" Maylore asked.

"Council members change every five winters, but some new members decline to serve, and the old councilor serves in their place.

This council is currently split between those who want to stay with the old ways and those who want change."

"We must ask the council to change the village charter to allow a defensive force," Marisa said. "It will be challenging to make it happen."

"This seems like a good starting point," Airalee said. "What do you think, dad?"

Maylore nodded along with the rest of the group.

"Jendrin could discuss his idea of a defense force and how it would help Olona," Airalee said. "Dad and I will try to fill in what we can and perhaps calm the water. Comments, anyone?"

"It seems a good general plan," Maylore said. "The council may reject it all, so we will need to create a new plan."

"Marisa, when do they plan to meet with us?" Jendrin asked.

"They want to talk with Kai when she returns," Marisa said. "It could be the day after she returns."

"Good," Jendrin said. "It will give me time to start work on the quarterstaff."

"I want you to help me gather new plants and herbs, hero," Airalee said.

Jendrin nodded in agreement.

"Airalee, you and I have rounds to make this morning," Marisa said.

"Yes," Airalee said, standing up. "It should be a quick trip."

Marisa followed Airalee out the door as the two men finished their breakfast.

"I will wash her dish," Jendrin said, gathering the bowls. "Let me wash yours too, Maylore."

"Thank you," Maylore said, passing him his bowl.

"Are you going to Gilriel's cave this morning?" Jendrin asked.

"Yes," he replied. "I will return early in the afternoon for the meeting if it happens. I will council her before I leave."

Jendrin nodded and started out the door with the bowls as Maylore followed him. Jendrin cleaned all three bowls, checking the water flow from his bamboo pipeline. Jendrin was returning when he saw more lamquart growing behind the hut. He gathered several handfuls and returned to the hut. Maylore collected hognut beans for another meal and returned to the hut. Maylore was busy storing the beans as Jendrin entered.

"This looks like the lamquart plant Airalee was adding to her breakfast beans," Jendrin said, holding up the plants. Airalee said it would grow everywhere. I will leave it to her to decide if she wants to use them, assuming she does not fall ill from the first group. I wonder what this lamquart tastes like?" Jendrin cautiously ate one leaf and looked surprised. "It tastes good. It has an earthy and minerally flavor."

"I will attend the funeral for you and Airalee being given to the sea and sing the song of passing loudly," Maylore smiled.

"Thank you," Jendrin smiled back.

"She was right about the potato," Maylore said. "Potatoes are a good addition to beans and stews."

"I can agree with that," Jendrin said.

"She said she wanted to gather more potatoes from where the boar killed those pigs," Maylore said.

"I will join her this time," Jendrin said. "I will plan escape routes in case the boar shows up."

"Airalee said she planted a few potato fragments in our sunny area," Maylore said. "I should see if they grew when I leave."

Maylore loaded his satchel with some fruit and bread. Jendrin picked up a potential quarterstaff leaning against the wall.

"Listen to this," Jendrin said as he tapped the wood on the stone wall. The staff rang with a muffled sound.

"Wood that rings?" Maylore asked.

"I was surprised, too," Jendrin said. "I cut it from what Airalee called a Ficus tree. Did she tell you the story of the glowing wood?"

"No," Maylore said, "She said she saw glowing plants."

"After we collected the lamquart," Jendrin said, "I asked her to help me find suitable wood for a quarterstaff. We walked until she stopped and stared into the wilderness. Raising her hand, she pointed to the Ficus tree root. She told me it would serve me well and seemed oblivious to my presence. She marked several roots with mud, saying I should use the roots she marked. She turned to face me and returned to being herself. I did not see anything glowing and kept quiet in my confusion."

"Keeping quiet and observing seems like the best idea," Maylore said. "There seemed to have been quite a few odd happenings. Perhaps we are best served remembering the incidents and going on our way."

"Seems like good advice to me," Jendrin said. "I am curious about what will happen on my next trip with her."

"I wish you the best," Maylore said, preparing to leave.

"I will start work on this wood until Airalee returns," Jendrin said, opening the door.

They bid each other farewell as Jendrin went to his crafting area behind the hut. Maylore verified that the small potato plants were growing before starting his trip to Gilriel's cave.

CHAPTER 23 - BUSY DAY

Maylore followed the now-familiar route through the village and up the path to Gilriel's hut. Loud roaring sounds greeted Maylore's ears as he approached the top of the hill. Moving to the side of the trail, he crept up behind rocks facing the cave entrance. A large bear was clawing at the cave entrance. The boulders were close together and showed no sign of allowing the bear passage. The bear did manage to wedge its head between the rocks. Unable to go forward, it roared in frustration and sat back. Pawing the air several times, it finally relented and wandered off to the other side. Maylore watched as the bear disappeared into the brush. He waited a little longer before starting toward the cave entrance. Maylore watched for the bear until he slipped past the boulders and into the cave. He wound through the cave, hearing the IB greet him with a soft caw. Maylore waved in its general direction as he walked. He stopped when a picture of him waving at the bird entered his mind. Maylore thought about what he had just received.

"Smart bird or dumb human, whichever," he said as he continued into the main chamber.

"Welcome, Maylore," Gilriel said as Maylore entered the main cave.

"Greetings, Gilriel," Maylore said as he sat down. A fire burned nearby, giving the area a pleasant warmth. "A bear was waiting outside to see you. The bear looked disappointed he couldn't get through the entrance."

"Yes," Gilriel said, "I heard him roaring. Lucky for me, he is too big to get between the rocks."

"I also got a mental picture from your bird as I walked past him," Maylore said.

"Picture?" Gilriel exclaimed. "I know they are intelligent birds, but that is more than I would expect. The fact you received the message without concentration is impressive, too!"

"Powerful bird brain," Maylore said casually.

"By the way, it is not my bird. It just lives here," Gilriel said.

Maylore smiled, shifting in his chair.

"I understand," Maylore said. "Animals live where they will."

"Indeed," Gilriel said.

"I heard some news that may interest you," Maylore said.

"What is it?" Gilriel asked.

"My companion Airalee made an interesting discovery visiting with the elders," Maylore said. "She told me a man living in an elder's hut accused her of trying to communicate with him telepathically. I did a poor job of hiding my surprise at her announcement."

"Interesting," Gilriel said, looking thoughtful.

"It would have been about when I was attempting to communicate with the various dots on my communication dome. I denied knowing what the man could be talking about, but she seemed to know I was less than truthful."

"Your companion is an intelligent woman," Gilriel said. "Beauty and brains are a good combination for her, not others. How did you dissuade her inquiries?"

"Poorly, I fear," Maylore replied. "I managed to change subjects enough until someone knocked on the door to change the focus. I could see she is now suspicious of me, too."

Gilriel leaned on the table as he listened.

"Did she say who this man was?" Gilriel asked. Maylore thought for a moment.

"Kelman?" Maylore said.

"Kelkalyn, perhaps?" Gilriel asked.

"Yes, that's what she said," Maylore said.

"I thought as much," Gilriel said. "It seems he has returned. Kelkalyn is a good man with secrets who spends little time in one place."

"Airalee said he was hiding something," Maylore replied.

"Indeed," Gilriel answered. "He is a very private man who hides from most people. Rendal and I visit with him a few times when he is here. He tells us little except about his travels to other villages and the cave he lived in. I think it is time we visit again if he remains here. I will suggest Kelkalyn talk with you when I see him. He may or may not agree, especially when talking with strangers. The positive side to her news is that Kelkalyn received your knock. He has proven that you can request communication. I have suspected Kelkalyn was more than he seemed. Did anyone else mention your knock?"

"Airalee said she felt a tap on her throat," Maylore said. "She was surprised but ignored it."

Gilriel looked at him, tapping his fingers on the table.

"She may be able to communicate nonverbally," Gilriel said.

"Something else Kelkalyn told her seemed odd," Maylore said. "Kelkalyn finally looked at her as he accused her of attempted communication. He stopped and said she had a 'burnt heart.' Kelkalyn recoiled after he said it, perhaps realizing he should not have said anything. She said he began acting eccentrically. He doubled over, laughing and dancing away like a madman. Airalee told me she saw an intelligent man who was putting on an act."

"Interesting," Gilriel said.

"Does a burnt heart mean something?" Maylore asked.

Gilriel blinked in surprise as he thought.

"Indeed," Gilriel said. "It tells us Kelkalyn can see people's portals without using a mushroom like I do. A burnt heart is a portal plugged with dead energy. It is the same as your plugged energy portal." Staring into the distance, Gilriel said aloud, "Kelkalyn is a surprise. He did not want anyone to know about his ability, even if Airalee was unlikely to know what he was talking about. Portraying a madman was an effort to convince her to ignore him. I wonder if the master knows about him? Could Kelkalyn be our spy?" Gilriel said, thinking out loud. He focused on Maylore, saying, "We will keep his secret. I will inform Rendal, but no one else."

Maylore agreed to keep the secret before looking directly at Gilriel.

"Can we repair Airalee's burnt heart?" Maylore asked.

Gilriel sat back in his chair for several moments.

"My abilities are meager at that job," Gilriel said. "If the two of us had enough blue spot mushrooms, we could repair some of it in a full summer. The heart portal is large and uses the sun's energy. It has power far beyond what we have been trying to use with fire, ley lines, and water. I regret we will have to leave her as she is. If she asks again what a burnt heart means, I suggest you say you have no answer for her."

"And that would be true," Maylore said, nodding.

Gilriel leaned forward.

"I would like you to try telepathically contacting Kelkalyn again," Gilriel said. "He felt you call but refused to answer. He may have wondered who has the communication gift. If you try again, he may answer. If not, Kai returns tomorrow, and if she has blue spot mushrooms, we may be able to work together to determine to whom the portal dots are attached."

"Could I take a mushroom and work on my own?" Maylore said, sitting a little straighter.

"Yes," Gilriel replied. "I did it often, looking for portals in arrivals like you. Use half of a small mushroom to start. If you use too much, you cannot connect to the person you are working with. You will instead see colors and shapes of things that do not exist. Use too much, and it kills."

Maylore nodded as he listened.

"I understand," Maylore said. "I would prefer your help, but if you are unavailable, I could work independently."

"True," Gilriel replied.

"Let me try to contact some of the communication dots now," Maylore said. "I did promise to help my companions with a council meeting later. I will go back to the village midafternoon to be available."

"Of course," Gilriel said, "I do not envy your having to talk with the council. It is something I avoid."

"I understand," Maylore said, chuckling. "I will try and contact Kelkalyn. Before I do that, I want to do another test." Pulling a small piece of food from his satchel, he placed it on the table. He concentrated on his communication portal dome and saw two dots near him. Sending a picture of the food to the smaller dot, he heard a flutter of wings, and the IB flew to the back of the empty chair. The IB grabbed the food and flew back to its hiding place. "There are two dots near me," Maylore said. "The IB has a smaller dot on the portal. The larger one is probably you. It may be that simple to tell animals from people."

"Excellent," Gilriel said, watching Maylore. "If you can eventually determine a way to identify each dot, you would make the skill even more valuable to you."

Maylore spent half the sun cycle tying a string and sending a picture and verbal request to each dot on his portal. Maylore felt most of his requests bounce off the dot. A few dots absorbed the request, but he did not receive a reply. Maylore eventually tired and willed himself out of using the portal. He roused to see a fruit bowl on the table before him. The IB was looking at him from the top rung of the chair. Gilriel was filling a water jug from the water pool. Turning back to the table, Gilriel saw Maylore was looking his way.

"Ah, you are back," Gilriel said. "Did you make any contacts?" Maylore shook his head.

"I noticed most of the requests seemed to bounce off the dot," Maylore said. "A few others seem to absorb the request. I wonder if the ones absorbed are people who can communicate but do not. I guess the ones bouncing off do not have a communication ability."

Gilriel sat at the table and pushed the fruit and water toward Maylore.

"That seems like a reasonable theory," Gilriel said. "Now eat and drink some water. We will then practice sending energy at the targets I set on the rocks," he said, pointing to the far exit.

Maylore ate the fruit and drank the water while looking at the distant target. He began to remove his sandals when Gilriel spoke.

"Try gathering energy with your shoes on," Gilriel said. "You will need to be able to do that when there is no time to remove shoes. You will find you do not need to do arm or hand motions in the future. You may continue to do the hand motions for now to help you concentrate."

Maylore nodded as he began pulling the energy from the nearby ley line. It was getting easier to do each day he practiced. The blue energy flowed to his energy portal and onto his hands as a ball formed. He rotated his hands to the right as the energy ball grew significantly more. Maylore pushed his arms forward with his thumbs going down as the energy ball flew toward the first target. The ball hit its target, spinning the fruit to the right and off the rock.

"Excellent!" Gilriel said. "You are progressing rapidly. Try a left-spinning ball to unwind the fruit." Maylore started collecting the energy, forming the ball, and spinning it to the left. He pushed his hands outward, sending the ball toward the second fruit. The ball struck the fruit, and it unwound on itself and disappeared.

"Where did the fruit go?" Maylore asked in amazement.

"The energy is the opposite spin of its matter," Gilriel replied. "It unwound the fruit's structure. It becomes part of the air. If you smell the air where it was, you will still smell it."

"That is dangerous to whatever it hits," Maylore said, shaking his head.

"Indeed," Gilriel replied, "Use it cautiously when there are no other options. Now practice pulling energy from the fire, forming balls left and right." Maylore pulled energy from the fire in a right-spinning ball and sent it at the next fruit. The ball missed, but a small fire lit on the fruit before burning out. Maylore formed another ball, spinning left and pushing it toward the same fruit. This ball struck the fruit, sending it flying backward as it burned in a fiery streak.

"Good," Gilriel said. "Now try forming a ball of air." Maylore found compressing the air into a ball was more difficult. A left and right spin merely pushed the fruit off a rock. "Left-spinning air does not disintegrate the fruit," Maylore said.

"You currently do not have enough strength to create a dangerous right-spinning ball of air," Gilriel said, nodding. "Someday, you may be able to create a force strong enough to destroy a target.

"I will need to be careful," Maylore said, talking to himself.

"You will learn control as you practice," Gilriel said. "I remind you not to practice where others can observe. In the future, we will see what transpires."

"I understand," Maylore nodded. Looking up, he noticed the twin suns were moving toward late afternoon. "I will go back to the village to fulfill my promise. Thank you for your teachings, Gilriel," he said as he rose on wobbly legs.

"Of course," Gilriel said. "I have read and listened to others to tell you what they did. I do not have those abilities, so I feel the honor is mine."

"I would have been helpless determining how to do any of this," Maylore said. "Then again, I would have been satisfied living a quiet life as a scholar."

"It is difficult to learn something you did not intend to pursue," Gilriel said. "Kai may return soon, so perhaps we will have more time to enhance your abilities."

Maylore nodded, gathered his pouch, and turned to leave. The IB was still sitting on the chair back. Maylore sent the bird a picture of him walking away. The bird quickly returned a picture of him flying away. Maylore chuckled and made his way back to the companion's home.

Airalee

Airalee and Marisa arrived at the bathing pool, finding no one else in the water.

"Jendrin planted the soapweed, I see," Airalee said, examining the area. She had recently decided she could bathe in the daytime as long as Marisa was there and no one else.

"There is quite a bit of soapweed floating in the holding area," Marisa said, removing her robe, unconcerned about who may be present. She lay her clothes on a bush and walked into the bath. The water in the pool was always comfortably cool but not cold like the creek running nearby. Airalee looked around before placing her robe on a bush and entering the pool. The two slipped into the water, sitting on strategically placed rocks.

"Our visits with the elders will be short today," Marisa said, passing some soapweed to Airalee. "Most of the elders seem to be doing well. I want to verify that Sharaera is awake while we are there. I will check with Werloth about any additional care she may need."

"I will be sure to avoid his reach this time," Airalee said, soaping her hair.

Marisa chuckled.

"The older women in the village regard him as quite skilled in satisfying them."

"When I get older, I will still avoid him," Airalee said, rinsing her hair. "I would like to speak with Melronna about her visions," Airalee said as she started soaping her body.

"I wonder if there is any way to verify what she has seen in the past," Marisa said, rinsing her hair. "I asked the women at the childcare yesterday if they had heard of her foreseeing things. They had not heard of her saying things like that before."

Airalee got out of the water and walked to the drying fire. She found a dry community towel just as three men approached the pool. Modesty was not an issue in the village, but Airalee immediately stepped into the bushes to dry. The three men greeted the women as they removed their robes and entered the pool. Marisa had no modesty streak as she rose from the pool and chatted with them. Airalee walked through the bushes to put her robe back on with her back to them. She returned to the fire to add a few more pieces of wood as Marisa joined her.

"Doesn't it concern you to have them see you without clothes?" she asked Marisa.

Marisa looked at Airalee like she was being odd.

"No," Marisa said. "It has always been this way. No one in this village will attack me. If someone tried, I could defend myself, and a village full of others would help me. We would banish anyone from the village who did that. Besides, I am quite proud of my body." She finished with a smile.

Looking at the men, Airalee saw they were chatting with each other and not looking in their direction. Marisa finished drying, hung the towel by the fire, and put her robe back on.

"Are you ready to do our rounds?" Marisa asked.

"Yes," Airalee replied, moving beside Marisa.

They started up the village path to gather food and water. Mirtha greeted them as they arrived at her hut.

"Have you visited the elders already?" Mirtha asked.

"We are gathering food to take to them now," Marisa said.

"Good," Mirtha replied, "I have too many helpers again today to have anything for you two to do. I may have no help tomorrow, so I don't complain."

"Mirtha," Airalee started, "have you tried Lamquart?" She asked, holding out a sample.

"I have not," Mirtha replied, looking at the plant.

"I saw this yesterday and knew it was a plant to eat," Airalee said. Mirtha examined the plant before looking at Airalee.

"If you can eat it for twenty sunrises without dying," Mirtha said, "I will consider it."

"I had some this morning," Airalee said, smiling. "I will let you know in 19 more days."

Mirtha nodded sharply.

"The villagers often request the potato you found," Mirtha said. "I added a few more for them today," she said, gathering a pot to fill with soup for the elders. "See if you can get them to eat some soup today and return empty containers," she said, handing the carrying rope to Airalee.

"We will," Marisa said, gathering a few pieces of bread. The two women walked back to the elder's huts. "Let's start in Melronna's hut," Marisa said as they approached her hut. Melronna was standing near the edge of the cliff overlooking the sea. "Melronna, how are you?" Marisa asked as they stopped near her. Melronna turned to them.

"Well, I think," Melronna said, turning toward her. "The ocean, however, seems restless. Perhaps a storm is approaching."

"You seem to have a connection to nature," Airalee said as Melronna turned to her.

"Greetings again, Airalee," Melronna said. "Yes, I think I have always had some connection. It is stronger now that I have more time to think about it."

"It has not always been that way?" Airalee asked.

"No, only the last few seasons has it come to me," Melronna answered. "It never happened when I was younger, but I was always busy then and did not take time to observe."

"Perhaps it comes when needed or necessary," Airalee replied. She suddenly realized it might pertain to her, too.

"Perhaps," Melronna answered.

"Would you like to go back into your hut?" Marisa asked. "We are checking to see if you are doing all right. We do not intend to intrude," Marisa said.

"No villager is an intrusion," Melronna said. "I welcome visitors." She turned and walked toward her hut. "I will welcome your mate too when he comes to visit," Melronna said without turning to look at either of them. Airalee and Marisa stopped and looked at each other in surprise.

"Who was she talking to?" Marisa said. She started to call after Melronna, but she was already entering her hut. "I don't think I want to know," Airalee said.

356

"I want to know," Marisa said as she returned to Melronna's hut. Knocking on the door, Melronna opened quickly. "Back already?" Melronna said, causing Airalee to laugh.

"I wanted to ask you who you were talking to about their mate coming to visit?"

"Mate?" Melronna said, perplexed. "I did not say anything about your mate."

"We heard you say you would welcome our mates when he visits."

"I did say I would welcome all visitors," Melronna said.

"You did," Airalee said, nodding at her. "Mirtha sent you some soup with potatoes. Would you like some?"

"Yes," Melronna replied.

Airalee poured some soup into her bowl as Marisa collected empty containers. The hut was tidy, and she had ample other necessities.

"If you don't need anything else, we will be on our way," Marisa said, smiling.

"I have everything I need," Melronna said. "Thank you, girls," she said, opening the door for them.

They said their goodbyes and continued to the next hut. Knocking on Selakiir's door, they got no answer.

"Selakiir, are you here?" Marisa called. No answer came, so Marisa opened the door. No one was inside, but the table had new fruit and a full water jug.

"It looks like he is out," Marisa said, closing the door.

The two girls started walking toward Phaerl and Adandir's hut when they saw Lulth helping Selakiir hobble along the path toward the village.

"There is Selakiir," Marisa said. "His daughter is helping him." They continued to Phaerl's hut and could hear voices inside. Knocking on the door, Phaerl opened it.

"Greetings, ladies," Phaerl said. "Our daughter Grena is visiting, but you can come in if you wish." Airalee and Marisa could see the small hut was already full and declined the offer.

"We were checking to see if you need anything," Marisa asked.

"We have what we need," Adandir said. "Thank you, ladies."

"You are welcome to visit anytime," Pearl said.

Airalee and Marisa waved to them as Phaerl closed the door.

When they arrived, Sharaera's hut door was open. They could see her propped up on her bed, looking out the door. "Hello, sweet ladies," she said as they approached the door. Werloth sat beside her with a small pot of mashed fruit he offered her.

"Come in, ladies," he said, indicating the chairs at the table.

"Thank you," Marisa said, staying by the door. "We came to see if your mother was awake and needed anything. You have already taken care of that."

"Yes," Werloth replied, "we have already visited the privy, and I am trying to get her to eat more fruit."

"Werloth," Sharaera said. "I am sure they are not interested in those subjects."

"We are interested," Marisa said with a smile.

"Oh my," Sharaera replied, looking at Airalee, "I saw you yesterday. Are you taking Kai's place?"

"No," Airalee replied. "Marisa and I are helping while Kai is away."

"I see," Sharaera replied. "Is Marisa here too?"

"Yes, Sharaera," Marisa said. "I am glad to see you."

"I can at least hear you, Marisa," Sharaera said before looking at Airalee again. "Kai, Marisa, and my son work hard to keep me going," she chuckled, which turned into coughing. Her coughing quieted as she studied Airalee's face. "You have a kind as well as a lovely face. You would do well to learn from Kai."

"I would welcome that as well as working with Marisa and Mirtha," Airalee said. She could see Sharaera was tired and should eat more before sleeping again.

"We will leave you to eat peacefully and check on Kelkalyn," Airalee said. Sharaera tried to wave but failed to raise her arm. She smiled and whispered her goodbyes. Airalee and Marisa waved and closed the door.

Kelkalyn sat at his table, looking out the window as they approached. He saw them as they came by his window.

"I am doing fine," Kelkalyn said. "You do not need to check on me." He said with a stony voice. Marisa shrugged her shoulders and turned back toward the village. Airalee stared at him before deciding to open his door. Standing in the doorway, she stared at him for a moment.

"I see through your disguise, Kelkalyn," Airalee said. "I will find what you are hiding someday," she said, closing the door and following Marisa.

"I fear you may," Kelkalyn said softly, watching her depart.

Marisa and Airalee returned to the village, arriving at Mirtha's hut.

"Has Kai returned?" Marisa asked Mirtha.

"Not yet," Mirtha said. "I hope she arrives before dark."

"It is hours before sundown," Marisa said, turning to Airalee. "Are you going to gather with Jendrin or help tend the children?"

"I want Jendrin to help me gather," Airalee said, taking the nearly full satchel of food off her shoulder.

"All right," Marisa said, "Let's put the food back into storage first."

Chapter 24 - Kai's Return

Kai and Gilda awoke the following day to a knock on the door. Gilda arose quickly to answer.

"Good morning," Ireel said, standing next to Nuae. "We brought you breakfast at Baralas' request. He wishes you a good journey and asks you to return when we come next season."

Kai arose from her bed as Ireel spoke.

"Please tell Baralas Wanici," Kai said. "We plan to return."

Ireel and Nuae smiled and waved as they returned to their village.

"I think we established a connection we did not have before," Kai said as she looked at Gilda. "In the past, Firlia and the Liqura men left Olona immediately after the ceremony. She may now pause to talk with me."

"Why have they not talked with us in the past?" Gilda asked.

"It appears they were following Baralas' decree," Kai said. "I believe Baralas' mistrust of us prevented further contact. It was only the old tradition set by his forebearers of traveling baby seeders that he allowed any interaction. Beacon Rendal and I have discussed this in the past. You saw how mistrustful Baralas was when we met with him yesterday. Perhaps the greeting in their language and courtesy persuaded him to reconsider. Ireel and Nuae would not have been allowed to make such an offer unless he approved."

Kai motioned for Gilda to sit at the table. "Shall we enjoy our breakfast before we depart?" The two women sat and ate fruits, grains, and small breads as they discussed the day's activity plans. "We will be careful going back up the road to the clearing. The wolves are likely far into the mountain hunting grounds. We need to avoid detection by going around the bandit's camp again. They are usually uninterested in who walks the road, but we do not need to risk it."

Kai and Gilda finished their breakfast and returned to their beds to pack.

"We should check our supplies and be off," Kai said. She opened her satchel and retrieved two small shell bracelets. "Place this on the table where you sat. It is a gift for the Lemidge who care for the hut." Kai saved the remaining food into their pouches. They cleaned up the hut and started toward the door. Gilda opened the door to see Firlia approaching the hut.

"Halie." Kai said in her language, "It is nice to see you again."

"Halie," Firlia replied with a wave. "Your greeting in Lemidge is nice. I wished to see you off this morning. You made a good impression with Baralas, who seems to like you. He is never clear on who or what impresses him, but I will be allowed to visit with you next time we visit."

"That would be very welcome, Firlia," Kai replied with a big smile. "I often wondered why you left so quickly."

"We were forbidden to communicate with anyone beyond doing our ceremony and leaving," Firlia said. I will have more options now. I say goodbye to you both, and have a good journey."

"Wanici Firlia," Kai and Gilda said as Firlia turned back toward her village.

"Halie," Gilda said as she waved.

"Caw!" came a cry from the top of the hut.

"The bird stayed here all night?" Gilda said, looking up at the IB.

"I don't believe I have seen any IB remain near people," Kai said.

"Lucky us," Gilda said surly. The bird cawed at her and flew to a tree near the road.

The two women left the hut and joined the road toward Olona. They climbed the hills and returned to the point overlooking the bandit's valley.

"The twin suns are past half day," Kai said. "We will stop by the trees and watch for activity while we eat," Kai said quietly. "We will leave the road here to bypass the bandit village."

The IB flew into the tree above Gilda's head. It looked at Gilda and cawed quietly.

"Hello again, bird," Gilda said, retrieving food from her bag. The two women ate quietly, looking for signs of trouble ahead.

"I don't see any sign of trouble," Kai said, finishing her lunch.

"I don't either," Gilda said.

"Caw," the bird said, looking down at them.

"We will be back in Olona by sunset," Kai said. "Let's be on our way." Cawing, the bird took flight when it saw the two women stand. "Caw, Caw!" it cried as it flew up to another tree. The two women left the road and walked into the brushy trees. The IB flew from tree to tree ahead of them as they walked. Looking down, they could see their improvised path skirting the road below. Trees and brush hid them from the road, but the noise of their passing was unmistakable.

"We should be near the entrance to their camp," Kai whispered to Gilda. "Try to be as quiet as possible." The grass softened their footfalls, but the brush made noise as they lightly pushed past it.

"Caw, Caw!" The IB called as it reappeared ahead of them. The bird jumped up and down on the ground, less than three sticks ahead of them. Both women ducked down, trying to quiet the bird.

"It is a noisy bird," Gilda said. "I hope they don't hear it."

"Let's move on," Kai said with chagrin. They started walking again, with the bird taking flight and circling them. It cawed at them as they walked. The bird suddenly flew near their faces, cawing.

"Go away, bird!" Gilda said, trying to shoo the bird away. The bird suddenly stopped cawing and landed on Gilda's satchel.

"That bird is wise, and you should have heeded him." A large man said, stepping into their path. Two other men stepped in from each side as the man spoke again. "I feared you would heed the bird's warning and hide in the brush. It would make it troublesome for us to find you."

"We want no trouble with you," Kai said, trying to sound confident.

The large man laughed at her.

"Birsha wishes to talk with you," he said. "You will walk with us to the village," He said, turning toward the main road.

"We have no interest in seeing Birsha," Kai said as the two women stood their ground.

"It matters not what you want," he said. "You will follow." He signaled the two men. One man took Kai's arm, and the other took Gilda's. Kai tried to resist, but the man was far too strong for her to defy him. She glanced back to see Gilda's shoulders sag as she allowed the man to lead her. They weaved their way through the brush back to the road. They continued until they reached a fork leading into the bandit's village. There were no visible guards nor any structures to denote the village entrance. The village looked like a wide circle of stone and wood huts lining the perimeter leading to a large wood and stone hut at the far end. Two bonfires were in the circle's center, with several men tending the fires. The large man leading their little group followed the line of huts leading to the other end. He stopped outside the large hut.

"Wait here," he said. "Birsha will call when he wants you," he said as he entered the hut. The two women looked at each other as the men released their arms. A sad smile came to Gilda's face.

"I'm here already," Gilda said. "I was hoping to learn from you for a while." She finished, looking down at her feet. Kai stared at her in wonder.

"You knew you were coming here?" Kai asked.

Gilda shook her head no.

"Not this day," Gilda said sadly. "I understood one day I might be sacrificed. I was hoping not today." Looking up again, she said, "The only good thing is my sister will not have to endure this camp."

Kai took Gilda's hand, squeezing like a mother who may lose a child.

"Gilda, you jump to an unwarranted conclusion," Kai said. "Birsha asked to see me, not you. We do not know what he wants. My hope is you will not be involved in any of this."

The door to Birsha's hut sprang open as Birsha pulled a girl behind him.

"Calel!" Kai exclaimed on seeing the girl. Calel looked at them without a smile.

"Greetings, Kai and Gilda," Calel said meekly. "I am sorry you had to come here."

"I am pleased to see you," Kai replied. "I heard someone spotted you one day. We thought a bear killed you on your gathering trip seasons ago." The pregnant girl returned a small smile as Birsha began speaking.

"Quiet!" Birsha said. "She is yet another defective female from your village. She developed this affliction after being my servant for several seasons," he said, pointing at her swollen abdomen.

Kai looked at him in disgust with the bandits having no concept of men's usage of women to produce babies. To the bandits, it was unrelated to them and was a defect of the women who came to their camp. Kai knew trying to teach him they became pregnant because of them was hopeless.

"Your abuse of our girls produces the baby!" Kai shouted. "She is not defective!" her voice rising as she spoke. Birsha stared at her before he spoke.

"She is broken," Birsha said. "Why else would we have four others who never got this sickness? They will return to their Tocor village because they are too old," he said almost calmly. Kai could see she would not convince him and sighed.

"We will take Calel back to Olona," Kai said. "Like the others, we will help her with her 'sickness,' as you call it."

Birsha gave a sharp nod and rose to his full two-and-a-half stick height.

"This one will take her place," Birsha said, pointing at Gilda.

Realizing what he said, Kai could feel a motherly instinct roar up in her.

"No!" Kai shouted. "You can't take my girl!" she said as she stepped between Gilda and Birsha.

Birsha stared down at her.

"You have no children, Kai," Birsha said, pushing her to the side. Kai tried to get between them again, but something hit her in the knee and collapsed her to the ground. Calel and Gilda managed to pull her back to her feet, but Kai could only stand on one foot. Kai's anger was now even greater, but she knew she could not physically resist them.

"She is my charge, and she is nearly my child!" Kai yelled, standing as tall as she could.

"Foolish woman," Birsha replied, "I know who her mother is. Her younger sister will not have the honor to live here if she is first," he said, reaching for Gilda's arm. Gilda quickly removed her pouch and passed it to Calel. Gilda allowed Birsha to lead her as tears appeared in her eyes. Birsha led her into his hut, closing the door with a conclusive bang.

Kai collapsed to the ground and started to cry. Calel knelt beside her and tried to console her. The two men behind them walked away, leaving the two women with tears.

"I lost her," Kai cried. The pain in her chest pushed up her body and spilled more tears onto the ground. Kai realized Calel was beside her and reached out to embrace her.

"She's gone. Dead, gone," Kai could hear herself saying. She repeated it several times before Calel's voice came through to her.

"No, Kai. She will return to us," Calel said. Calel repeated it several more times before Kai realized what Calel was saying and that she may be right.

"Not dead," Kai finally said. "Stolen, not dead," she repeated as she could feel the heavy weight of loss start to move aside. She knew the weight would remain with her before she could lift some of it from herself. It reminded her of the weight set upon her after her mate passed. That weight was great and lasted a long time. It was a sad reminder. "I will see her again," she said, looking at Calel.

"We will," Calel said. Kai started to rise, but her knee refused to allow it.

"I will help you," Calel said, supporting Kai's damaged side. Kai finally stood but could not put any weight on the damaged leg. Looking at her knee, Kai could not see any real damage. A large red area covered her knee.

"I will have a big bruise on that knee soon," she said, looking at Calel.

"I am afraid you are right," Calel replied.

"Are you allowed to leave with me?" Kai asked, realizing she may lose her too.

"Yes. Pregnant women are broken and could infect others," Calel said, shouldering the satchel.

"You would infect others?" Kai said sarcastically.

"Let's leave this camp," Calel said.

"Of course," Kai said. "I am pleased to see you, but it hurts to lose Gilda."

"I understand, Kai," Calel said. They started the slow walk back to the camp gate. Kai began to walk, putting light pressure on her leg.

"I seem to be able to walk with your help," Kai said, "but you are in no condition to help me for long, Calel."

"We will go as far as we can, then rest," Calel replied.

The few villagers who were out watched as they passed by. They reached the village entrance as a young woman ran up to Calel, giving her a wooden stick with a woven covering on the top of it.

"Thank you, Mosis," Calel said as Mosis hugged Calel and quickly ran back into the camp. "One of my friends brought a crutch for you," she said, putting Kai's arm over the crutch. "The bandits will not trouble us again."

"Will she be punished for helping us?" Kai asked.

"No," Calel replied, "She must make a new crutch before someone else needs one. She has friends who can do that for her. She can make the covering but is not allowed cutting tools to make the crutch. Shall we try this to see if it helps you walk?" Kai nodded and shifted her weight to her other leg. The crutch fit well under her arm but was short for her size. Kai pulled a piece of clothing from her pouch and wound it around the top of the crutch.

"This will do," Kai said as she slowly walked again. Both women could see that progress would be slow, especially up the hills. They started climbing the hill outside the bandit's valley when the IB landed on a boulder and glared at Kai.

"Yes," Kai said, looking at the IB. "I would have heeded your warning if I spoke IB. I still thank you for trying to help us." The bird seemed to understand, ruffled its feathers, and stood straight. "Would you watch over Gilda for me, bird?" Kai asked. The bird bobbed its head and took flight toward the bandit's camp. "I wish the bird could tell me what is happening to her, but perhaps I am better off not knowing," Kai said in a low voice. Kai refused to let Calel carry her satchel as her knee swelled twice its size.

"Would you like to rest, Kai?" Calel asked after walking a while.

"No," Kai replied. "I would like to return to Olona before dark. Do you need to rest, Calel?" Calel didn't need to rest. The women of the bandit village were expected to work even as their 'disease' progressed. Calel decided Kai should rest, so she pointed to a nearby boulder.

"Yes, a brief one would be nice," Calel said. Kai seemed grateful to lean on the boulder. Calel considered pressing Kai to rest her knee for a day but remembered Kai was hard-headed once she made up her mind. Calel decided to see how far the two could go before one or both decided it was enough. "What brought you past the bandit village, Kai?" she asked.

"We were searching for blue-spotted mushrooms near the Lemidge village Liqua," Kai replied, flexing her sore knee. "I found them growing on the sunset side of their meadow in the past. We found several growing there and then asked the leader of Liqua to stay the night in their guest hut. We were fortunate to make a diplomatic connection with them and were allowed to revisit them. We were returning to Olona when Birsha's men captured us," Kai said, looking at Calel. "I was so concerned with Gilda and my aching knee that I didn't inquire about you in that camp. How did you survive your time there?"

Calel drew a deep breath before starting her story.

"I was captured by one of Birsha's men near the swamp while gathering food. I tried to fight back, but he laughed and hit my head.

369

I lost my cloak and left blood from my bleeding head on the ground. I thought he was going to assault me, but I think my bleeding head put him off it. He pulled me up and took me back to their camp. Birsha decided I should be given back to him. I had to learn how to mend clothes, tend his hut, cook his food, and attend to his nightly desires. Birsha trusts no one, so he made me sleep beside him on the side facing the door. I tasted everything before he ate or drank anything. He particularly liked the reeb one of his lieutenants made but would not drink it until I had drunk it first."

"You have been gone three summers?" Kai asked. Calel nodded.

"Almost four," Calel said. "I used to track sunrises but stopped long ago. I did make friends with many of the women in the camp. We would do our chores together to help speed up the day. The bandits assigned to watch us preferred we stay in a group since it made it easier for them to keep track of us."

"Did anyone escape?" Kai asked.

"None that I know of," Calel replied. "A few tried, but the bandits are expert trackers and could find us wherever we went."

"They probably found Gilda and my tracks even though we left the road," Kai said, looking down.

"Birsha said his trackers followed your tracks and saw you when you entered the Lemidge camp," Calel said. "He told them to wait until you returned so you could take this 'defective one' back to Olona," Calel said with a sad smile. Kai shook her head at their ignorance.

"You were Birsha's girl for that long before getting pregnant?" Kai said.

Calel touched her stomach.

"Birsha is impotent," Calel said. "The women in the village say he has never gotten any other human girls pregnant. They would get too old and leave the village."

370

"Someone else then," Kai said, looking at Calel. Calel nodded, rubbing her abdomen.

"Late last summer, the firebird dropped a woca near the camp," Calel said. "The men got to it before too many blood wolves arrived. There was a big feast, and a lot of reeb was drunk. I served Birsha sitting with his four lieutenants as he ate and drank too much. One of them looked at me, asking Birsha if he was willing to share his bounty. Birsha looked at me drunkenly, saying he could share this one night. The men were gleeful to share their leader's girl. Some returned several times before the night was over. They left me with enough seed to create many babies."

Kai felt a tear form in her eye.

"I am sorry that happened to you," Kai said.

Calel nodded before she continued.

"I learned long ago how to let my mind escape somewhere else and not feel what was happening to my body," Calel said. "Birsha did not allow them to get rough with me, so I would hardly notice him or them."

"I am sorry, Calel," Kai said. "We must develop a way to stop this." Kai pushed herself to her feet as Calel finished. "Let's leave those memories here, Calel," Kai said, pointing at the ground. "We may discuss those things later if you wish. Leave them here if you can."

"I leave them on this rock," Calel said, placing her hand on the boulder."

Kai gathered her satchel as Calel gathered Gilda's.

"I have some cloth in my pouch to wrap my knee," Kai said. "Would you help me with it?" she said, hoping to distract them from the horror of Calel's story.

"I will," Calel said. Finding the cloth, she wrapped Kai's knee.

"Thank you, Calel," Kai said when she had finished. "Let's be away from this source of sadness," as she stood and hobbled up the road.

Kai's climb out of the bandit's valley was challenging. Calel helped support her at times but was tired herself. They passed the meadow where the wolves had attacked the bear without incident.

"We are sorry travelers today," Kai said with a smile. "We are both hobbled." She pointed slightly ahead and said, "There is another good resting rock. Let's use it." Kai said, shuffling toward it. "We are near the top of this hill. We will start down into our valley soon." Kai said with a sigh of relief. "Returning to my bed and resting this knee will be welcome. You will reunite with your mom. That will be welcome, I am sure."

Calel could feel her face cloud up as she started crying.

"I had not considered how welcome that would be," Calel said, sobbing. "Freedom from the bandits contrasted with sorrow for Gilda, and your welfare had filled my thoughts. Seeing my own family and friends will be very comforting," she said with her head in her hands. Kai could see relief pouring over Calel. She decided to remain quiet as the best idea as she touched Calel's arm. Calel leaned into Kai as she started to calm herself. "I didn't realize how much relief I would feel getting away from there and returning home."

Calel finally quieted as Kai patted her arm.

"Let's finish this trek before both suns go down," Kai said, pushing herself off the rock. The walk up and over the hill proceeded with no problems. Walking down the other side was almost as complex as the climb. The crutch took most of the weight off her leg, but her knee still complained about being used when damaged. The two approached the curve near the marsh when an IB bird call erupted above them.

"Ah, the birds are here," Calel said as they walked.

"It was probably a sentinel," Kai said, "He was informing the village we are approaching. The tone of the call was one for friendly visitors. Two more short calls came from the trees as they walked. "I don't know what that means." Kai said, "It could be an actual IB."

They approached the last turn down the hill when they saw five village men running up the hill. Four carried the rock litter, and the fifth was Rendal. The five stopped before the women as Rendal realized Calel was with her instead of Gilda.

"Calel!" Rendal said. "I am pleased to see you! Where is Gilda?"

"We will discuss that later, Beacon," Kai said as the litter was set on the ground. The village men were helping Kai into the litter when she pushed them away.

"I don't need you four to help me into the litter," Kai said. "I can do that part on my own. I appreciate you all coming to get us, however," she said, sitting in the litter. "Do you want to sit with me, Calel?" Kai asked.

"Thank you, Kai," Calel said. "I can walk the rest. I am extremely pleased to see you, Beacon, and glad this brings me closer to my family."

"They will be more than pleased to see you, Calel," Rendal said, "Shall we proceed back to the village?" He motioned the men to start walking.

On the walk back to the village, Calel peppered Rendal with questions about the village. Rendal told her about the three new villagers, babies born, and the deaths of a few elders. Arriving at the village entrance, Rendal turned to Calel.

"Your mom lives in the same hut. We told her you were alive when spotted in the bandits' camp," Rendal said. "Would you like one of us to accompany you?"

Calel considered for a moment before answering.

"No, thank you, Beacon," she replied. "I hope I am not too much of a surprise for her."

"I think not," Rendal said, smiling. "Remember, the village will support you and your baby when it arrives."

"I know, Beacon," Calel said. "It has always been that way." Calel kissed Kai on her hand, saying, "Thank you, Kai. I am sorry about Gilda's sacrifice."

"Thank you, Calel," Kai said. "She seemed to know already what would befall her. I will miss her almost as much as her own family. I am confident she will return to us just as you have." Calel and Kai hugged as Calel turned toward her mother's hut.

"Rendal, let's discuss what happened to Gilda in my hut," Kai said. "First, we will go to the storage hut for herbs to reduce the swelling and allow me to sleep."

"Of course," Rendal replied. "Men, to the storage hut."

Kai exited the litter at the storage hut and thanked the men for helping her. She hobbled into the hut and picked up herbs to help with swelling and one to allow her to sleep.

"Join me in my hut, Rendal," she said. "We need to discuss the trip."

The two spent a lot of time discussing the trip to gather mushrooms, improving their relationship with the Lemidge, Gilda's abduction, Calel's experiences in the bandit camp, and the return to the village. The herbs slowly took effect on Kai, and as her story concluded, Kai fell asleep.

CHAPTER 25 - FACE THE COUNCIL

The three companions had just finished breakfast when Marisa burst into the hut.

"Kai is back!" she exclaimed. Realizing she had just entered without asking permission, she looked down. "I am sorry, I should have knocked. I was hurrying to let you know Kai returned and forgot my manners."

"You are almost one of us anyway," Airalee laughed. "Come sit and tell us about Kai."

Marisa sat at the table close to Jendrin. Grinning at him, she looked at Airalee.

"I fear she also brought bad news with her," Marisa said. "Birsha's men captured them as they were returning to Olona. Birsha forced Gilda to become his servant and told Kai to remove Calel, telling her she is broken."

"Broken?" Maylore said.

"She is pregnant," Airalee said.

"Basrah," Maylore said.

"Yes," Marisa said. "Calel is in Olona now, but Gilda is lost to us."

"I wager Kai put up a fight for Gilda," Jendrin said.

"Kai did," Marisa said. "One of Birsha's men injured Kai as she tried to prevent Gilda from being taken. She tried to protest through the pain, but Birsha was indifferent to her and took Gilda into his hut. Kai cried for Gilda along with Calel until Calel could help Kai hobble back to Olona."

"We should see if we can help Calel this morning," Airalee said.

"Calel returned to her birth mother's hut," Marisa said. "Rendal informed Gilda's mother of her capture."

"I would imagine Gilda's mother was devastated," Airalee said.

"I have not seen the Beacon to ask," Marisa said. "I assume Calel was just pleased to be back in Olona."

"Calel," Jendrin said, "That is the girl Latel saw on the other side of the river."

"How injured was Kai?" Airalee asked.

"She has a sore knee," Marisa replied, "but her temper is even stronger. We all knew she felt very close to Gilda. The bandits have taken girls in the past, but she had not experienced the loss herself."

Airalee looked at Jendrin.

"This adds more fuel to the fire to convince the council we need to be able to defend our villagers," Airalee said.

"I am ready to meet with them today," Jendrin said.

Marisa looked up at the group.

"Kai may be bedridden," Marisa said, "but I believe she could fly to the council." Her comment brought smiles to their faces as they continued to discuss their options.

"That would be one powerful voice in our favor," Jendrin said.

"She would be an advocate for us," Maylore said. "Unfortunately, the council votes in secret and may fear an attack on Olona if we respond. They are unlikely to allow a rescue attempt to gain her freedom."

"I am afraid that is true," Marisa said. "We will be fortunate if they allow resistance to the bandits or others in any form."

"Perhaps we have other paths to try," Jendrin said, looking at each one. "Calel may provide the information we could use to sabotage their ability to plunder and kidnap others."

"In what way?" Airalee asked, "We can't poison or attack them."

"I agree, and we cannot do anything that puts suspicion on Olona," Maylore added. The room was silent while the group considered their options.

"Maybe we can enlist the other villages to help," Jendrin suggested.

"Perhaps we could try to teach the bandits to be self-sufficient," Marisa said.

"We should teach them how babies are created," Airalee growled.

"I believe we need to talk with Calel to see what we can do," Jendrin said. "Right now, we need to meet with the council to provide them with our concerns and solutions."

"Well done, hero," Airalee said, "We can talk for hours in our hut and not gain action." Perhaps Marisa could ask the Beacon when the council will meet?"

"I will ask him today," Marisa said. "It may depend on Kai since her harvest trip interests them."

"Good," Airalee said. "I wanted to talk to Jendrin and Maylore anyway."

"I didn't do it," Jendrin said, holding both hands in a child's reaction.

"You will have to prove that to me, hero," Airalee said. "This time, you didn't cause any problems. I want to tell you a few things about the elders we visited." Looking toward Jendrin, she said, "Werloth, the hunter, said he knows how to get to the area where the firebird guards the woca." Jendrin looked at her and sat up.

"I understood there was no way to get there," Jendrin said.

"He knows a route," Airalee said, "but you need to climb, and he finds it difficult with one hand missing."

"I must be careful to avoid the firebird," Jendrin said. "It is still too bad he lost his hand."

"Yes," Marisa said. "He almost lost his other hand testing the cloth Airalee was wearing," she laughed.

"I put him in his place," Airalee said, moving on to other subjects. "I believe we can find herbs to help more of the elderly. Jendrin has agreed to go with me on a few gathering trips to see if we can find some."

"Of course," Jendrin smiled at her. "I would be glad to find something when I don't know what I am looking for."

Ignoring him, Airalee looked toward Maylore.

"Kelkalyn is the other elder we should learn about," Airalee said. Do you have any new ideas about what the burnt heart might mean, Maylore?"

Maylore considered whether he should disregard Gilriel's comments or keep quiet.

"I may learn something if Gilriel can convince Kelkalyn to discuss it," Maylore said. "Kelkalyn is said to be a very secretive man."

"I would welcome any news," Airalee replied. "I felt a knock on my throat twice in the last two days. Do you know what that means?"

Maylore considered again what Gilriel told him and merely murmured.

"Are you learning to strangle people?" Airalee asked with a smile.

"No, nothing like that," Maylore said, looking at her.

"So, you are doing something," Airalee said.

Maylore felt trapped by what he had already said and decided to answer more truthfully.

"I am trying to communicate without words to those who can receive it," Maylore said. "Perhaps you may be able to communicate without words. I don't know yet. Gilriel told me to keep quiet until I learn about it."

Airalee nodded, satisfied she had learned something.

"We will keep it to ourselves until you inform us otherwise," Airalee said, indicating the other two. Jendrin and Marisa nodded, although they did not know what they agreed to. "I have talked long enough. Does anyone else have something to say?" Maylore was concerned he had already said too much. Jendrin indicated he had nothing to add.

"When I leave here, I will ask the Beacon what the council agenda is and where we fit into it," Marisa said.

"I guess we wait for the council to call for us," Airalee said as the group arose from the table.

Time slowly passed as they waited for Marisa to return. The rain had fallen, forcing the companions to work inside their hut. Airalee wrote about the plants she found in her book. Jendrin worked on his first quarterstaff, shaving off wood bumps and polishing the long staff. Maylore continued to work on energy transfer and tried to decide which dot belonged to what person in the communication dome. The splash of running footsteps drew their attention to the door. The footsteps stopped, and a gentle knock came from the door. Jendrin had already started toward the door and opened it before the knocking stopped.

"Come in, Marisa," he said as he opened the door. Marisa smiled as she entered and moved toward the table. "Beacon says we will meet with them soon. He asks us to come to the council hut and wait outside." The three companions gathered what they needed and followed Marisa outside.

"At least it stopped raining," Airalee said, looking up. They walked the short distance to the council hut and stood near the entrance as a bit of sunshine peeked through the clouds. They could hear a slight murmur inside the hut, but nothing distinct.

"I will see if Kai needs help walking here," Marisa said as she walked toward Kai's hut.

"Do you want help?" Jendrin asked.

"Sure!" Marisa said, smiling. "I could use your company." Jendrin followed Marisa as she grinned at Airalee. Airalee grimaced at her but said nothing.

"What was that about?" Maylore asked as they moved away. Airalee sighed as she faced him.

"Marisa believes Jendrin would be the perfect seeder for her baby," Airalee said. "She seems to think I am competing against her or want to prevent it from happening."

"Do you want to prevent it?" Maylore asked.

"No," Airalee chuckled. "I feel like the big sister looking after her brother. I am not sure he realizes what she wants."

"Jendrin is a grown man," Maylore replied. "He may ignore her signals, but he knows she is up to something. I am not sure he wants to help raise a child quite yet."

"She has already picked out a baby-mate to help raise the baby," Airalee said. "She just wants him to help create the baby."

Maylore chuckled.

"Any man would be willing to do that, even old men!" Maylore said with a grin.

Airalee looked at him sharply.

"Dad! You can't be serious!" she said.

Maylore cocked his head at her.

"I'm not dead yet!" Maylore laughed. "She is an attractive girl who draws attention. I doubt she would choose a man of seasons for the task. I will certainly not suggest it to her."

Airalee took a step back as Maylore noted her reaction.

"What's wrong, Airalee?" he asked.

Airalee considered momentarily, deciding the truth was the best answer.

"When we first met in the cave," Airalee said softly, "I had a vision of being attacked by a faceless man. When I awoke, I saw two strange men by the fire. I lay thinking, where am I? Who are these men? Did they capture me for their pleasure? Have they already had their way with me? I felt sure I had not been attacked yet, but how could I defend myself from two men? I thought I could stop you, but not Jendrin. The two of you would be impossible for me to stop."

As Airalee spoke, Maylore's face grew pale, and his head drooped.

"I carried a rock in my fist and the little club. I kept both by my bed for some time before disposing of both. I hoped the village people would help defend me if I called for help. It was also possible they could have been worse."

"Oh, no, Airalee!" Maylore replied with a quiver in his voice. "That would never happen! We were three strangers thrown into a dangerous situation we knew nothing about. We needed to stick together, and we still do! Something like that would have split us apart, destroying any chance of cooperation. Jendrin and I have felt protective of you and each other since the beginning. That is all we had! Those thoughts never crossed my mind!" Maylore felt a small tear forming in his eye as he raised his arms to hug her but realized that would not be appropriate, so he took a step to the side, watching her reaction. Airalee saw the tear in his eye and walked toward him.

"Thank you, dad," she softly said as she wrapped her arms around him. She could feel the pent-up dread pour out of her in her tears as she tightened her grip. The old suspicions in her mind drained to the ground. Maylore wrapped his arms around her in a fatherly grip.

"Thank you, Airalee, for telling me," Maylore said. "You do not need to fear harm from me. You are more important to me each sunrise. Even though you are not my daughter, I would have been proud to call you daughter." Maylore hugged her for a few more seconds before releasing her. Airalee hung on for a little longer before letting go.

"Is it okay if I still call you dad?" she asked.

"Of course!" Maylore laughed. "Sometime in the future, I would consider it an honor to be called grandpa too!"

"Let's not rush things," Airalee said, wiping tears away. "I have not considered finding a baby seeder or a baby-mate, but now I have a grandpa!" she said, looking up at him.

"You do!" Maylore said. "The other pieces may come when you want them." Airalee stepped back as they heard others approaching. Marisa and Jendrin walked beside a determined Kai as she hobbled to the council hut. Seeing tears on Airalee's face, Marisa rushed to her.

"Why are you crying?" Marisa softly asked. Airalee wiped the rest of her tears away.

"Dad and I had a private heart-to-heart conversation," Airalee replied.

"You are not hurt? Marisa asked.

"No," Airalee replied. "I feel much better." Kai glanced at Airalee.

"Dry your eyes, girl, before we meet with this group," Kai said, waving toward the door. Looking toward Maylore, Kai said, "I assume you are responsible for her tears?"

"I fear you may be right," Maylore replied.

"No!" Airalee almost shouted. "Dad helped me release old worries I had been carrying around." She grabbed his arm and briefly laid her head on his shoulder.

"A father figure," Kai grunted. "You are good for her," she said, looking at Maylore. Looking at Airalee again, she said, "Stay out here or at the back of the group until your eyes are clear. We do not want this council to be distracted by your tearful emotions."

Kai started to open the door.

"Aren't we to wait for them to call us Kai?" Marisa asked.

"Wait? Wait for what?" Kai said, reaching for the door. "They can argue the lack of stored nuts later," she said as she opened the door. The front part of the hut was empty as they entered. The room divider was closed as Kai opened it and entered the back room.

"Kai," Beacon Rendal said as she entered. "I was about to ask Throc to request you join us. You have saved him the trip."

Kai grunted again, looking at Rendal, who was seated at the head of the table.

"You can give this cripple your seat, Beacon," Kai said. Rendal did not look surprised as he stood and offered her his chair. Rendal continued to address the council.

"I would like to recap what we discussed before Kai starts her comments," Rendal said. "We have a surplus of food and other supplies on hand. The master will be arriving in a few days. Birsha and Oleg are coming to claim their share of our supplies. We will set the next fishing day when our surplus has been drawn down. Onto other business, we cheer the return of Calel and Kai. We are all sad at the loss of Gilda to servitude. Kai will relate the story of her trip. Jendrin would like to discuss setting up a defense group." A low murmur came from several council members on the last point. "We will start with Kai. The council would like to hear about your adventure," he said, returning to an empty chair. Kai did not arise as she looked at the council members.

"My original purpose was a foraging trip to gather blue-spotted mushrooms. I know they grow in a forest beyond the Lemidge camp. I brought my apprentice, Gilda, to train her in travel and gathering. Things first went wrong as we approached the first meadow." Kai then related the story of the bear who had walked into a trap the wolves had set for Gilda and herself. She reported their travels after the blood wolves chased the fierce wolves from their prey. Kai recounted leaving the road to trudge through the thick brush above the road to avoid the bandit camp. She told of Gilda's encounter with an IB, attempting to convince them it was a small wolf. She looked to Rendal, describing their request to stay in a Liqua guest hut, which was granted.

"We asked to visit Liqua and were escorted by Firlia, the woman who brought the Lemidge men to Olona," Kai said. "We met Baralas, the Lemidge group leader. We learned a few polite words of Lemidge, and by using them with Baralas, we seemed to have gained his trust. He will allow Firlia to visit us the next time a Lemidge ceremony is held in Olona.

"A visit with the Lemidge would be most welcome," Rendal said with surprise. "I have tried many times to convince Baralas to allow the traveling Lemidge group to visit here with no success. I need to start calling you Kai, the diplomat," he said.

"Basrah," Kai said, "I can force myself when the need is great."

"That is wonderful news, Kai," Rendal said, nodding. Kai continued her tale of leaving Liqua and traveling up the mountain. She described the accompaniment of the IB and its antics. Her speech took a severe turn, telling of the bird trying to warn them of the bandits waiting for them in the brush.

"Three large men forced us to walk to the bandit village under the guise of Birsha wanting to speak to me," Kai said. "I assumed Birsha had a demand for healing he wished to discuss. Birsha emerged from his hut, pulling Calel behind him. He instead demanded Gilda replace the 'defective now broken' Calel." Kai's voice started to waver as she told her story of trying to keep Gilda from them, only to be struck in the knee by one of the guards.

"The injury hurt much less than my realization I could not protect Gilda from any of these men. I felt powerless for the first time in the many summers of my life as Birsha took Gilda into his hut," she said with a tear in her eye. Remembering what she had just told Airalee, Kai took several moments before deciding the story was important, not her emotions. Wiping away the tear, she continued. "Calel helped me gather myself enough to leave that cursed place. I was fortunate that Calel had friends who could help me by giving me a crutch. We left that sad place and walked back to the road." Kai continued relaying some of her conversations with Calel on the return trip. She deferred to Calel to tell them her story in her time. Kai finished by staring at the council members for comments. All of them were looking down at the table.

"I am glad Calel has returned," Rendal said, "but sad Gilda has been taken," Rendal said with most members nodding. Kai nodded sharply before speaking.

"I know this council wants to avoid conflict," Kai said, "but I believe Jendrin can help us learn to protect our villagers, avoid future conflict, and protect our girls from servitude."

Council members looked at Kai.

"Protection and avoiding conflict?" Caudra said. "I find that hard to believe."

"Yes," Rendal said, standing. "We have Jendrin's thoughts on our agenda. Jendrin, tell us your ideas."

Jendrin stepped forward next to Kai. He noticed four council members crossed their arms and sat back in their chairs. Two leaned forward to listen as Rendal sat. Rendal indicated to Jendrin to proceed. 'A slightly split council already,' Jendrin thought to himself.

"Greetings to all of you," Jendrin said. "I see you are all saddened by the loss of another one of our young women. It would be difficult for us to recover her without conflict, and I do not suggest it. My suggestion is for Olona to begin defending our own against kidnapping. It is possible that a passive show of force may be enough to deter them." The two crossed-arm council members started talking at once. Rendal interrupted them.

"Hold!" Rendal said. We haven't heard Jendrin's ideas yet. Let him speak!"

Nenaias was not to be denied.

"This man is too new to our village to know its past!" Nenaias shouted. "Our forefathers did try to resist the taking of our young, but they were slaughtered for their efforts. Their daughters were taken, and most did not return. At that time, the Beacon negotiated a treaty with the bandits' leader and agreed to lend a few in return for no violence. The village charter was developed to reflect the agreement and prevent more slaughter. We all must avoid any aggression or use of force in conflict against another."

"We must not support aggression," Caudra said, interrupting, "even from our villagers against another villager. It must be true, even for self-defense. Arbitration and compromise are our duty to prevent many from being harmed. If a villager is confronted, we must not stop possible harm to them from others. It is their choice for this life to absorb the harm from another. Death is preferable to violence or resistance." Nenaias nodded her head in agreement.

"We must not kill nor prevent others from being killed," Nenaias said. "No good can come from aggressive actions. We must prohibit our killing of anyone!"

"That goes too far, Nenaias," Baruo said, crossing his arms. "I believe there is the sanctity of life allowing self-defense. Killing is indeed unconditionally wrong. Our village must allow one to protect oneself and others from aggression. If Olona's are attacked, we must capture and restrain the aggressor. No one is to kill another. We must

386

allow protection of ourselves and others from those who would harm us. If the aggressor is killed unintentionally, that may be allowed. We also must prevent a war against other villages. Innocent people have the right to peace with no violence done to them. If you can help protect the innocent, then you must do so. If you do not help the innocent, you are helping the aggressor."

"We should indeed avoid aggression and war," Katiana said. "One must protect oneself and others from aggression. The defense of a village or individual should be allowed. No good can come from aggression or war and is thereby prohibited."

The council glared at each other.

"We must find a peaceful solution to every conflict, even those with aggressors," Arguil said.

"Aggressors lose the right to peaceful solutions if they attack Olona first," Katina said. "If our villagers agree to the idea they should not defend themselves and then are killed, who continues our village?

"I believe bad behavior will flourish where good villagers do nothing," Baruo said. "If a villager is suffering, we must find resources to correct the problem, even if it comes from aggression against another person or village. Passive resistance will not be effective in stopping aggression and protecting the innocent. It would be time to use might to protect ourselves and other villagers from aggression. Those who can fight must protect the innocents. If you stand by, you help murder the innocent and are as guilty as the coward who willfully killed."

"We must remember the emotional trauma it causes the victim's loved ones," Katiana said. "Pacifism has no place in the face of extreme evil. Worse than war is the killing of the human spirit of the population because of the evil of the victors." Katiana finished as the council members all spoke at once. Rendal leaned back in his chair, waiting for the tide of words to subside. Eventually, the council quieted to a murmur. Rendal spoke as the council quieted.

387

"We have a real diversity of opinions here," Rendal said.

Nenaias interrupted again.

"Throc has the written village document," Nenaias said. "I ask that you read it for our enlightenment."

Rendal nodded to Throc.

"Please read the portion on dealing with disagreements and contentious outsiders," Rendal said. Throc stood with the document already in hand and read aloud.

"Peaceful rather than violent methods are to be used by all villagers," Throc read. "Villagers may not attack or kill one another or any outsider who confronts them. Villagers must not defend others even if it means a loved one is lost to them. Belligerence is to be avoided by those who govern the village when dealing with other villages. The village must migrate to a new area if the confrontation cannot be peacefully resolved." Throc finished and sat down again.

Heads turned as the last part was read.

"I propose we remove the part about migration from the document in the face of unresolved confrontation," Baruo said. "We have built a good village over the seasons since it was written. We should not give it to usurpers. Most heads nodded at his comment."

"I will agree," Avahairiel said. "If we change it to read, we share the village with the others."

All heads nodded in agreement.

"Throc," Rendal said, "Please remove the last part and replace it with 'travelers will be welcomed into the village with help accommodating them from all villagers.' Looking toward Jendrin, he added, "I would still like to hear what Jendrin is proposing before the council makes any decisions."

Rendal held up one hand to stop comments and signaled Jendrin to proceed. Kai and Airalee were visibly upset, but Kai grabbed

Airalee's arm to hold them in check. Jendrin still stood before the council and gathered himself as he spoke.

"Council members," Jendrin said. "I have heard the result of the kidnapping of your young to be used by the bandits. The pain abduction causes individuals, families, and the entire village must be avoided. I suggest we develop a group of people to defend our village and its young from those who raid Olona."

With arms crossed, the same two council members started to argue when Rendal raised his hand again.

"Council," Rendal said. "Let Jendrin have his say; we have heard your arguments and should hear what he has to say." Rendal again pointed to Jendrin to continue as the hut quieted. Jendrin spread his hands before continuing.

"I agree with your village doctrine to the point that we should not purposely kill others," Jendrin said. "Olona should not attack any other village, nor should we harm others we disagree with. I propose to teach a small group of villagers how to use a quarterstaff to defend themselves and others without killing anyone. I believe this would be best for us to support each other."

"Weapons?" Caudra said. "No weapons!" she shouted as the room erupted again in loud disagreements. The same points expressed earlier echoed inside the hut. Kai slumped slightly in her chair, realizing they were unlikely to win the council over today. Airalee, standing at her side, seemed ready to go to war on the council itself as Kai pulled her arm to shout in her ear.

"We will not win the battle today, Airalee," Kai said. "They are focused on how things are currently done. They fear change will make it worse. That fear is greater than seeing how terrible it is for our young."

When Kai touched her arm and spoke into her ear, Airalee stared at the council, ready to join the fight.

"Do not speak harshly to them now, or you will harden them further," Kai said. "We will work on methods to convince them to change their minds. I hope that it does not take a catastrophe for them to see the need for change. Now, help me up, girl." Kai said, starting to stand. Airalee helped her up and walked to the door with her. Airalee told her companions what Kai had said and suggested they keep quiet, even though Airalee could feel the top of her head lifting off with anger.

"Stay and render moral support for Jendrin," Airalee said. "I will help Kai back to her hut."

Jendrin could feel the hot blast of words directed at him as some of the council raged on. Maylore and Marisa moved beside him as the council began to rage at each other. Disagreement slowly began to lose intensity as council members seemed to run dry. The Beacon finally held up his hand.

"I will call for the council to vote on Jendrin's motion after guests have left," Rendal said. Rendal invited Jendrin and his companions to leave. "I will inform you of the results," he said as they closed the door.

The group stood outside talking for some time before Rendal emerged from the hut.

"The council has voted four to two to disallow your request, Jendrin. I suspect one member is close to changing their mind in your favor. Time will tell." Jendrin looked at Rendal.

"Seven are on the council. Who did not vote?" Jendrin asked.

"I only vote when there is a tie," Rendal said. "I do, however, have some powers outside of the council. I can ask for special tasks that do not violate the council's previous decisions. I ask you to do a special task now. I want you to develop a demonstration of your quarterstaff and your training methods. You will review it with me when ready. I have already informed the council of my decision, and I am receiving a result similar to what you got. It is within my power as Beacon to ask for these things, and I want to see what you can do to develop a defensive skill. I remind you, do not teach it to others and limit it to defense."

Rendal turned to Maylore.

"The master is due here tomorrow," Rendal said. "Gilriel and I will meet with him when he arrives. Gilriel will be leaving with him when the master leaves. Perhaps you should visit with Gilriel before he leaves."

Maylore nodded to him as Rendal turned to the group.

"Birsha usually follows behind the master on his trips here to 'collect his due,' as he calls it," Rendal said. "The council and I are setting aside his tithes." Rendal looked for Airalee but didn't see her. "Tell Airalee Oleg travels with him. She needs to avoid the reception hut when he arrives."

"I will inform her Beacon," Maylore said as Rendal returned to the hut.

"The only good news is he wants you to develop a defensive demonstration, Maylore said.

"It will take time to determine how to make it work for defense anyway," Jendrin said.

Airalee returned to the group with a determined look on her face.

"What was the decision?" she asked as she approached.

"The council voted to reject my proposal," Jendrin said. "The Beacon has asked me to demonstrate defensive skills and let him review it."

"They wish to continue the enslavement of our girls?" Airalee said, her tone matching her stormy appearance.

"I will not defend the old ways," Marisa said, looking down. "I spent many hours hiding in the caves when the bandit gathering party came to our village. It was just the way we lived. We were fortunate the sentinels would warn us of their approach so we could hide. If the bandits did not find one, they moved on to the next village. I would like to see the practice stopped since the fear of being taken hurts." Airalee took Marisa's hand to console her.

"We need a plan to do more," Airalee said, hugging Marisa.

"Agreed," Jendrin said. "At least we have a starting point. The Beacon asked us to warn you of Oleg coming to Olona. He said you should avoid the visitor's hut."

"I will do that," Airalee said. "Not because I fear him, but we don't need more problems for Olona."

"I need to attend to Kai and some duties for Mirtha," Marisa said. "Are we going to meet tomorrow?"

"Yes," Jendrin said. "Come to our hut tomorrow, and we can do some planning."

"Since Gilriel is leaving, I will visit him," Maylore said. I will meet you back at the hut."

"I will help you, Marisa," Airalee said as the group went in different directions.

Marisa and Airalee arrived at Kai's hut to find Kai in her bed.

"Marisa, would you replace the compress on my knee?" Kai asked.

"I will do that instead if you want to check on Mirtha," Airalee said. Marisa looked to Kai, who nodded.

"I will see you both tomorrow," Marisa said as she left the hut.

"Marisa is a good girl," Kai said. "Mirtha depends on her as the senior to direct the younger girls in food preparation, cooking, and spicing our food." Kai looked at Airalee as she removed the old poultice. "Now that Gilda has been taken from me, I need another apprentice. It would be nice to find several, but even one would be helpful. Are you interested in learning the healing arts, Airalee?"

Airalee did not need to think about it before answering.

"Yes," Airalee said. "I would like to do that." Kai smiled and studied Airalee's face and her movements.

"You may be a little old to be an apprentice," Kai said, "But I think you would do an excellent job as a healer."

"Even at my advanced age," Airalee said with a smile, "I can learn new things!" Kai chuckled with her.

"Good," Kai said. "Marisa has been staying here at night. I will tell her she has one less duty after tomorrow. I do not need anyone to stay in my hut with me. You should sleep with your men." Airalee looked sharply at her.

"I do not sleep with the men," Airalee said firmly. "We just all sleep in the same hut."

"I see," Kai said with a crooked smile.

CHAPTER 26 - EVIL APPROACHES

At sunrise the next day, all three companions arose at once. The familiar morning routine of using the bathroom, gathering for breakfast, and cleaning up had become a split routine among the three of them.

Maylore practiced his communication skills at the table, using Airalee as the test subject. Jendrin continued to smooth and oil his first quarterstaff. Airalee looked to Maylore as he asked her to practice communication with him.

"Yes, that is me you are tapping on, Dad," Airalee said. "I feel the pressure on my throat as you try to communicate. I don't hear or see anything, though."

"I don't seem to be able to send you a message or a picture," Maylore said. "I will consult with Gilriel today to see if he has any suggestions. Do you feel anything, Jendrin?" he asked as he switched to the nearest dot. Jendrin stopped what he was doing and waited to see if he felt a knock on his throat like Airalee suggested.

"Sorry, Maylore," he said.

"Basrah," Maylore said. This time, in frustration, he kept pushing down on the dot. He finally stopped pushing on the string, and to his amazement, the dot turned over. "Jendrin," Maylore said for an unknown reason. The word "Jendrin" appeared on the dot he had been holding.

"Yes, Maylore?" Jendrin said, hearing his name. Maylore sat back in shock at the words on the dot.

"Oh my!" he said. "Your name is now imprinted on the dot!" Jendrin did not know what to think but felt happy for Maylore.

"Congratulations?" Jendrin said. "I believe it is a good thing."

"Yes indeed!" Maylore said, looking up. "Let me try with Airalee," he said, tying a string to Airalee's dot. He pushed and held the dot before releasing it. The dot turned over, and he said, "Airalee." Her name appeared inside the dot. "Yes!" Maylore shouted as he stood, looking at Airalee. Both of his companions sat back in their chairs at his outburst.

"Congratulations?" Airalee said, not understanding the importance of the process.

"Thank you!" Maylore said. "Now I just need to find someone or something to communicate with," he said, sitting back down. "Perhaps Gilriel will have an idea about that, too. I am off to his cave," he announced. "I will return later," he said as he hurried out the door.

"Bye, Dad!" Airalee said as he disappeared.

"That is the fastest I have seen Maylore move!" Jendrin said with a laugh. "I don't understand what just happened, but I am happy for him," he added with a shrug.

"I am too," Airalee said. "I can tell he is trying to communicate with me, but nothing happens. I am glad to let him practice on me if I can help." Looking toward Jendrin, she asked, "I was hoping you would help Marisa and me talk with Kai. There must be a way to help Gilda and perhaps other villagers slow or thwart the bandit camp."

"I would be glad to help," Jendrin quickly replied. Airalee felt relieved that Jendrin would readily agree to help her. "You may be slogging through the muck again."

"I have been muddy before," Jendrin replied. "I can handle it," he said as he resumed oiling his quarterstaff.

"Let's go to Kai's hut," Airalee said. "Marisa was staying there while Kai recuperated her leg." Jendrin set his nearly finished quarterstaff against the wall and followed Airalee out the door.

Marisa opened Kai's door as Airalee knocked. "Come in," she said as she moved aside to let them in. Kai saw them enter and sat up on the side of her bed. Marisa moved to help her up but stopped when Kai held up her hand.

"I am not helpless, girl," Kai said. "I am just going to claim a nearby chair at the table." She stood and hobbled to the table. "I assume you are here to discuss yesterday's meeting?"

"In some ways," Airalee said, claiming a chair beside her. "I hoped we could develop a plan to stop the bandits from claiming our girls." Kai winced with pain before speaking.

"We heard the council reiterate that we may not attack the bandits," Kai said. "We may not defend our girls if they come to abduct more. I would love to hear any plan you may have," she said, turning to Marisa. "Marisa, could you get a new compress for the knee pain?" Marisa immediately went to gather the premade pain compress. "Marisa is a good nursemaid. She has been a big help to me." Kai said. Marisa brought a new compress for Kai's knee. The herbs in the compress gave Airalee an idea.

"Could we develop a combination of herbs to slow or stop the bandits?" Airalee asked.

"Possibly," Kai said after a long pause. "What would we want it to do?"

"I am not sure," Airalee said.

"We could develop a method to prevent our girls from getting pregnant," Marisa said. "The bandits would not come here as often for a replacement."

"Possibly," Kai said. "We already have a formula that works. How do we deliver it to the girls in that camp?"

"I believe we could work something out," Jendrin said. "Perhaps I could deliver something to Gilda."

"I don't want you killed trying something, boy," Kai said, wagging a finger at him.

"Perhaps I could get Gilda's IB to help deliver it to her," Kai said. "That would help Gilda, but not enough to help the other women." The room was quiet before Airalee's face brightened.

"Instead of preventing pregnancy," Airalee said, "what could we do to prevent the men from having any interest in mating with them?"

"Preventing the abuse would be a better solution," Kai replied, "I don't know of any potion for men. The men in Olona would never use it. How would we get the bandits if we could determine a concoction to do this? They certainly would not want to use it if they suspected what it was." The hut was quiet as the group privately considered possible solutions.

"We need to add the solution to their food or drink so they don't realize what it is," Marisa said.

"We could add it to the food they collect from us," Jendrin suggested.

"Perhaps," Kai replied. "It must be a combination that does not change the taste of the food."

"Drink?" Airalee asked.

"Calel told me on our way back that all men drink the ale they produce in the camp," Kai said.

"I suspect it already tastes bad," Marisa joked as the group chuckled.

"We could add it to their ale and get all his men," Kai said. "How would we add it to their ale?" looking at Jendrin.

"Am I now expendable?" Jendrin questioned.

"No," Kai said, "but perhaps we can dress you so you can enter the camp and add the potion without being noticed. On our return trip, Calel pointed out the vat they use for brewing, which is close to the road. You may be able to add it to the vat without being noticed. If someone saw you, you would be dressed like them and unlikely to raise an alarm."

"I would prefer we not put anyone at risk," Airalee said.

"It seems we are developing an empty plan," Kai said. "No one knows if we can make such a potion." The group looked at each other, but no one spoke. Kai considered it a little longer before saying, "My guess is there is something we could make."

"I seem to be able to find things if Jendrin is with me," Airalee said, looking toward Jendrin. Marisa and Kai looked quizzically at her. "He was with me when he asked for wood to make a quarterstaff. He told me I pointed to a hanging tree root, telling him it would create a quarterstaff. I was unaware of saying anything to him."

"Why do you think Jendrin was needed?" Kai asked.

"I don't know," Airalee replied, shaking her head.

"When you, Marisa, and I gathered hunting herbs and mushrooms in the same area, I saw nothing unusual about the plants. When Jendrin was with me, some plants I did not know would glow. I instinctively knew they were edible or what use they could be." Kai and Marisa looked toward Jendrin.

"Do you power her talents, Jendrin?" Kai asked.

Jendrin stuttered before answering.

"I don't know how to answer that," Jendrin said. "I am not aware of anything like that."

"I have heard stories of such before," Kai said. "An alliance of two or more people could create a new ability if each has a piece of it. I have not heard of anything like it in Molia for many summers. Do you need an object to use with this?"

Airalee considered for a moment before replying. "I had my gathering satchel and my lucky stone with me at the time," Airalee said. Kai looked between the two. "The method I have heard," Kai said, "is you lock your mind on a plant, animal, or thing for the result you are after." Looking toward Jendrin, she added, "Stay close to her. If needed, carry her around to get the result."

Jendrin smiled as Airalee spoke up.

"He would probably drop me in the mud," Airalee said. "I held his hand briefly when I saw the glowing plants, but it did not seem to improve the finding."

Kai smiled at Jendrin. "Having to stay close to a pretty companion?" Kai said. "I am sure it will not hurt your feelings."

"I am pleased I do not have to carry her," Jendrin said. "I suspect my muscles would eventually grow tired of the weight."

Airalee grimaced at him. "I am also pleased," Airalee said. "If you carried me, you would be too tired to walk back to Olona, and I would have to carry you back."

Marisa laughed as the two continued to banter. Kai interrupted their banter.

"You two are welcome to start searching now," Kai said. "I will tell Beacon Rendal of our possible plan. I will relay how Airalee and Jendrin will look for candidate herbs. I won't mention we don't know what we are looking for. I wish you both great success in finding a solution for us." Kai started to stand before the pain in her knee reminded her she needed help. "Jendrin," Kai said, "help this lady back to her bed." Jendrin rose and supported Kai as she hobbled back to her bed. "Take care of Airalee and yourself," she softly said. "If she has the skill I think she has, you two are even more valuable to our village. Now, off you go," Kai said as she laid back on her bed. The group bid Kai farewell as they closed the door behind them.

Maylore

Maylore arrived at Gilriel's cave to find him packing a travel bag.

"Ah, Maylore," Gilriel said. "I am glad you are here. I am leaving with the master in a quarter sun, and I was hoping you would visit. How are your studies progressing?"

"Well, I believe," Maylore replied. "I found I can identify the dots on the communication dome and add a name to each dot."

Gilriel stopped packing and looked at Maylore.

"Why, that is amazing," Gilriel said. "That suggests you may be able to track people by looking for their dot. Do you think you can tell the distance?"

"I am not sure yet," Maylore replied. "I only learned of this ability this morning while trying to communicate with Airalee. She says someone has been knocking on her throat and pushed me to reveal it was my doing."

Gilriel started packing again.

"She is an intelligent woman," Gilriel said. "She knows to keep it to herself. Did anyone else hear this?"

"Jendrin was there at the time," Maylore replied.

"I believe we are safe with him," Gilriel replied. "See if you can identify me on your dome." Maylore sat at the table and tried to visualize the communication dome. The dome opened quickly, and he saw two dots near him. He attached a string to one and tapped on it.

"Squawk!" came a complaint from the IB sitting on the chair back.

"Ah, that is the IB," Maylore said. "I am going to ask if it has a name." Maylore sent a picture of him with his head cocked and his hands in a questioning stance. The IB seemed to understand and returned a few images that appeared to spell Bert. "Bert?" Maylore said aloud. The IB seemed to laugh but ended with an affirmative squawk. "Bert, it is," Maylore said as he held down the dot. He said

"Bert" when the dot turned. "This must be you," he said, holding down the dot near Bert. Maylore said, "Gilriel," and closed the dome.

"I suspect the string into your portal, which I added, may have grown near its end," Gilriel said. "You may be more effective in communicating with others. I plan to use the blue spotted mushrooms and find what abilities we have in common. I would also like to find out what abilities other villagers may have. When I return, you and I will test your companions and a few other villagers." Gilriel said.

"Is one of them Kelkalyn?" Maylore asked. Gilriel slowed his packing before replying.

"I suspect he will detect us and not allow it," Gilriel said. "Why do you ask about him?"

"Airalee met him," Maylore said, "and he told her in the heat of an argument that she had a burnt heart. She still questions me on its meaning."

"Burnt heart," Gilriel repeated. "The heart holds immense power to attack and defend a person. It appears he can see her heart portal without using a mushroom. You can tell her we will be unlikely to clear the blockage, which would be much bigger than the blockage in you. It appears he retained a few more capabilities than he has let on, Interesting."

"Yes," Maylore said, "He is becoming increasingly interesting."

"Any other surprises you have for me?" Gilriel asked. Maylore thought momentarily before replying.

"No," Maylore said, "I just have so much yet to learn."

"I have lived here my entire life, and I still learn daily," Gilriel said. "Now, before I go, I found what I think is a masking spell in the book. It has something to do with bending light and air. I marked it with a piece of cloth for your study. The book is behind the rock over the chair, and the key is with it."

"I will look at it another day," Maylore said.

"Good," Gilriel said. "If you can determine what more symbols mean, add them to the key. If you would also check in at my home when you can, I prefer the animals not take it over while I am gone." Picking up his travel sack, he turned to leave. Maylore followed him as Gilriel said over his shoulder, "The master does not know who you are or your abilities. I suggest you return to your hut without getting near the visitor's hut." Maylore nodded and followed him down the mountain, stopping in the brush near the road. He watched as Gilriel disappeared into the guest hut. Maylore circled away from the guest hut before crossing the road and returning to the companion's hut.

Jendrin, Marisa, and Airalee stood outside Kai's hut as they met with her.

"Kai tells me you will help her as an apprentice," Marisa said, looking at Airalee.

"Yes," Airalee replied. "She asked me last night to take Gilda's place in learning healing skills. I didn't mean to take your job, Marisa."

"I already have an apprenticeship with Mirtha," Marisa laughed. "I like my job and don't want to be a healer."

"I am pleased to hear you say that," Airalee said, smiling. "I am drawn to the healer role but didn't want to interfere with you."

Marisa grabbed her arm.

"You are welcome to it," Marisa said pointedly.

Jendrin was listening as the women finished their discussion.

"Does anyone know what we are looking for and what direction it might be?" Jendrin asked. Airalee dropped a small bag, and as she picked it up, she pointed to sunrise.

"That way," Airalee said. Jendrin and Marisa both looked in that direction.

"That way, not toward the meadow?" Jendrin asked. Airalee straightened and looked at him.

"That way, what?" Airalee asked.

Jendrin and Marisa both spoke at once.

"You pointed toward sunrise saying that way," they said. Airalee looked at them, confused.

"I did not point anywhere," Airalee said.

"You did point that way," Marisa replied. "It appears you and Jendrin are using your ability to find things."

"I am beginning to sound like Melronna," Airalee sighed.

"It is as good a direction as any since we don't know what we are looking for or where it is!" Jendrin said.

"Let's gather our collection tools and bags and go that way," Airalee said. Marisa bid them good luck and started toward Mirtha's hut. Airalee and Jendrin gathered their tools and bags and started toward the road.

"We have not gone sunrise on this road since we arrived," Jendrin said as they walked.

"True," Airalee said. "We were underground in that cave," as they passed the cave entrance. They passed well away from the visitors' hut and could see the hill where Gilriel's cave was located. They joined the road, walking sunrise as the road slowly descended out of rocks and trees and onto a desert landscape. Rocks were plentiful, but trees and plants became scarce. As they walked the deserted road, the twin suns rose near a 45-degree angle.

"Do you feel like someone is watching us?" Jendrin asked. Airalee scanned the area, looking for threats as Jendrin quickly said, "What direction is the medicine we seek?" Jendrin said, seeing her attention was diverting. Airalee's hand raised and pointed further sunrise before it dropped. "Onward we go," he said.

"I don't feel like anyone is watching us," Airalee said, unaware she had raised her arm, "but I see a plant useful to us." She walked above the road to a glowing plant on the bank. "It is Desert Lavender," she said, examining it before adding it to her gathering bag. "We can use it to help stomach ailments and nausea." They continued on the road as plants and trees became scarce.

"I hope we are going in the right direction."

"I believe we are," Jendrin said.

"What is that large spike plant?" Airalee said. She approached the plant, and it started glowing. She touched the waxy spike. "It is an Agave plant. We could use it to prevent infections; if you cook it, the syrup is sweet." Seeing she was distracted again, Jendrin asked her again.

"Which way to the medicine we seek?" Jendrin quickly asked. Airalee raised her hand, pointing to sunrise.

"This plant is too large for us to gather," Airalee said, "but I know what we could use it for."

"All right," Jendrin said, "sunrise we go."

"Are you sure, hero?" Airalee said. "We have walked half the day finding little."

"We will find it," Jendrin said as he started down the road. Airalee sliced off a piece of the agave and followed him.

The sun was high overhead when Jendrin saw a well-worn path leaving the road and heading into the desert.

"Do you see any plants that may be interesting?" Jendrin asked. Airalee looked near and far at the trees and bushes around them. Noticing Airalee was again occupied with her search, he asked quietly about the medicine. Airalee still seemed unaware that her hand was now pointed toward the ocean.

"There is a cactus I have been meaning to get a closer look at," Airalee said, moving to the prickly bush. Touching an area with no thorns, she said, "It is a prickle pear. We could use it to heal burns and wounds. It is also edible after cooking it," she said, looking up. "That tree has a slight glow," she said. Walking to a branch, she saw large thorns with narrow needle-like leaves hanging from the branches. She touched one of the long pods that hung from a branch. "It is a Mesquite tree. We could make an antiseptic if we boil the branches. These pods have seeds we can grind into flour. I don't see any flowers, but they can be brewed as tea. I will take a few of the pods to examine when we get back to Olona. Any idea which way we go now?"

"We go toward the ocean," Jendrin said. This time, she did not question the direction as she followed Jendrin along the path into the desert. A short time later, they saw a distant group of trees growing in the middle of the desert. The trail led to trees and bushes surrounding a large pool of water.

"Should we try the water?" Jendrin asked. "It should be good to drink."

"You first," Airalee said as she looked at the trees and bushes around the pool. Jendrin scooped up and drank some water from the pool as Airalee noticed a nearby bush was glowing. "This bush is glowing," she said as she touched the shrub. "These are Chaste bushes," she announced, moving to examine the vase-shaped bush closely. "See the last purple feathery bloom and the small berries forming behind them? We can use the leaves and flowers to lessen menopause in women. The hard berry is also called lone man's pepper and lowers a man's libido." Airalee turned to Jendrin with a smile, realizing what she said. "We found what we were looking for!"

"I knew you would lead us to it," Jendrin smiled.

"You did?" Airalee asked. "I had no idea where to find what we needed."

"I had faith," Jendrin said with a broader smile.

"Let's gather what we can from these bushes," Airalee said as they collected berries and a few leaves until their bags were packed. "We have a good amount of the plant we can use. Come with me to search the pool for other plants." Jendrin followed her around the pool, noting a few animal tracks but little else. They completed their circle but found no other valuable plants.

"Let's eat, then get back to the village before dark," Jendrin said as he moved to sit beside the pool.

"I believe I will drink the water I carry," Airalee said. "If the hero lives, I will fill my container from the pool," Airalee said as she sat near him. They ate the dried fish and bread and discussed the pool in the middle of the desert. The water seemed to bubble up near the center and spread into the trees and bushes around it. As they finished their lunch, Jendrin filled his water container from the pool and packed it into his bag. He stood up as Airalee repacked her satchel.

"It appears the water from the pool didn't kill you," she said as she rose. Jendrin smiled at her when he suddenly started to waver and slowly collapsed to the ground. Airalee stood in shock momentarily before yelling, "Jendrin!" and kneeling by his side. He looked at her as he lay on his side.

"I don't feel well," Jendrin said. "Guess you will have to carry me back."

"I can't carry you!" Airalee shouted, looking at him in alarm.

Jendrin opened both eyes.

"Well," Jendrin said, "I guess I will have to walk back," as he got up. Airalee leaned back as he started to rise, then, in anger, hit him on the chest with both hands.

"Don't scare me like that!" Airalee yelled. "Some hero you are!" as she rose, glaring at him. Jendrin got to his feet with a smile on his face.

"The joke is on you!" Jendrin said. "You said before we left that you may have to carry me back. I wanted to see if you would try."

Airalee could feel the anger dissipate, replaced with relief.

"I could have done it if I had to," Airalee said.

Jendrin dropped his bag.

"All right, let's see if you could," Jendrin said. Airalee dropped her satchel.

"Lean on my back, and let's see," Airalee said. Jendrin leaned on her back as she leaned forward to lift him off the ground. She managed one step before she felt her knees buckle under his weight and set him down. "I would have had to drag you up the road on your back. Do you think the rocks would cause you any problem?" she asked slyly.

Jendrin laughed.

"My hide is tough," Jendrin said. But I will avoid that trial and call it a draw."

"If you wish to give up, that is all right by me," she said with a relieved grin. Jendrin laughed again and picked up his pack.

"The water in the pool is good, by the way," Jendrin said. "The constant inflow of water would wash any poison out quickly." He handed her satchel to her and started back up the trail. Airalee filled her water container and followed him. The trip back was quiet, but Airalee felt they were being watched after they reached the main road.

"I feel as if someone is watching us," Airalee said, looking into the trees.

"This is Tocor's homeland," Jendrin said. "They could be in these trees, and we will not see them." They continued to walk side by side as the road skirted the mountain foothills. The granite hill rose before them as they left the outskirts of the desert and started the climb back to Olona. They reached the top of the hill and tried to see if they could spot Gilriel's cave. The entrance was hidden behind brush and boulders, not allowing them any view. As they traveled down the hill, they rounded the corner leading into the village to see a group of people standing near the road by the visitor's hut.

"It looks like Birsha and his crew have arrived," Airalee said aloud.

"We should leave the road to avoid them," Jendrin asked, looking toward the group of four bandits and several others with packs. Rendal was trying to finish the conversion so they would take their share and leave.

"I don't trust any of them," Airalee said, standing to Jendrin's right.

"We can go around them through these bushes," Jendrin said, pointing to the side.

Oleg looked up to see Airalee and immediately started walking toward her. The rest of the group followed him until he stood before her.

"Birsha, I want this one," Oleg said, pointing at Airalee, who looked shocked.

"I have said many times before she is too old for you," Birsha replied.

"She is not defective," Oleg said. "I will have her," Oleg said as he started in her direction. Jendrin stepped in front of Oleg as Airalee took a step back.

"No," Birsha said. "She is not for you," he said with a firm voice. Anger flashed in Oleg's eyes as he suddenly drew his knife and lunged at Airalee.

"If I can't have her, no one will!" Oleg shouted as he raised his knife. Airalee froze as Jendrin slid in front of her. Oleg's knife plunged into the right side of his chest. Birsha showed his deceptive

408

speed and grabbed Oleg's shirt. Oleg pulled his knife free and prepared to strike again. Birsha pulled him back and down as the blade sliced Jendrin's right thigh. "No!" Oleg screamed, "She must die!" Birsha tossed Oleg to the ground behind him. Rendal, Throc, and Airalee rushed to Jendrin as he fell. Birsha looked at Jendrin and turned to Oleg.

"You hurt one of my little people!" Birsha yelled. "How can they make things for me if they are injured!" Kicking Oleg's knife away from him, he said, "I will decide your punishment later." Looking at the three guards, he said. "Tie his hands. He is no longer your commander!" Looking back toward Rendal, he said, "We will collect the rest of our tithe another time." Birsha showed no concern for Jendrin as he turned and led his group back up the hill.

"Jendrin!" Airalee exclaimed as he lay crumpled on the ground. Blood was slowly flowing from his chest wound. Blood from the leg slice flowed more freely. Throc and Rendal rushed to his side. Rendal removed his yellow scarf and tied it around Jendrin's leg wound. Airalee was pressing on the stab wound as Throc removed his scarf and gave it to Airalee to push into the wound. "Let's move him back to our hut," Airalee said as she moved in front of him. Throc and Rendal got under each arm as Jendrin struggled to walk toward the hut. Other villagers heard the commotion and ran to see what was going on. "Get Kai and have her come to our hut!" Airalee shouted at the group. Several of the villagers ran toward Kai's hut as Jendrin continued toward the hut. The group was near their hut when Marisa appeared out of the crowd.

"They said Jendrin was dead!" Marisa said, panic on her face and in her voice. "I am glad you are not!" she said, tears flooding her eyes.

"Not dead yet," Jendrin said, looking at her.

"Out of the way, fools!" came Kai's voice as she hobbled through the crowd. "Get him onto the bed!" she ordered when she arrived with a medical bag. Marisa opened the hut's door as the group led him in.

"Put him on my bed," Airalee said, pointing to her area behind the curtain. Throc and Rendal pushed aside the blankets and laid him on the bed as Kai took charge.

"You two keep the crowd out or tell them to go home," Kai told Throc and Rendal. She opened her bag and started crushing leaves in her hands.

"This will slow the bleeding," she said as she pointed to his tunic. "Open his tunic, Airalee, and I will press these into the wound." Airalee did as instructed, exposing the knife wound. Kai pressed the leaves onto the wound. "Airalee, hold the leaves down," Kai said. Airalee pressed on the leaves as Kai pulled up his robe to expose his leg wound. Kai took little time examining the leg wound. "Marisa, cut some fabric into wide sections. Maylore boil water to sterilize the materials."

Kai was crushing more leaves as she looked at the scarf holding the leg wound together.

"It appears you are lucky," Kai said. "None of the major bloodlines were cut. I doubt we could save you if they had been." She laid the crushed leaves on the side of the bed as she untied the scarf. Blood started to flow in a slow stream from the wound. Kai pressed the leaves onto the length of the wound as she looked at Marisa. "Marisa, hold the leaves in place while I tie this scarf. Marisa climbed onto the other side of the bed and pressed down on the leaves. Kai unwound the scarf and spread it to become a broad bandage. She wound it around his leg as Marisa moved her hands to allow the scarf to be tied on top.

"Do I need to press on it?" Marisa asked.

"No," Kai answered. "You could get blankets and cover him. He will be cold soon." Looking at Jendrin, she said, "I will use a sleep draft to force you to rest," as she retrieved a bottle from her bag. "It will take a while for the leaves to stop the bleeding. Can you hold them a while longer, Airalee?" Kai asked.

"Yes, Kai," she answered.

"Good," Kai replied. "Jendrin, drink the sleep aid so you rest, and I can stitch your wounds." Kai held the bottle to Jendrin's lips for him to drink. "Your breath seems good. You are fortunate that your breath is not leaking out the wound. You are in little danger for now. I will return with my wound needle and string to close the two wounds." Looking at Airalee, she said, "He should be asleep soon and will not feel the needle. We will then apply healing herbs and watch for infections. Marisa, take the herb bag back to my hut. We will start to make the healing compress." Kai hobbled to the door, saying, "Everyone else, go home!" she said as they exited the hut.

"Do you want me to come back and help Airalee?" Marisa asked.

"He will sleep soon," Kai smiled. "The two of them need to discuss what happened with none of us present." She grabbed Marisa's arm and added, "Help me get back to the hut, girl. My leg still hurts."

The two walked back to Kai's hut, passing Maylore and Mirtha boiling cloth in water over the cooking fire. "Hang those to cool, then come to my hut, Maylore. We will create bandages and a chest wrap for Jendrin's wounds."

Maylore removed the cloth from the pot after a short amount of boiling. He and Mirtha spread them on a nearby rack. The cloth cooled as he joined Kai and Marisa in Kai's hut. Kai instructed him to cut long sections to wrap the chest and many short pieces to cover the leg wounds. Kai and Marisa started creating a healing paste and more sleeping draught while Maylore and Mirtha cut the cooled fabric and hung it near the fire to dry.

Jendrin was in pain as Kai, Maylore, and Marisa left the hut. The pain from his injury began to sink deeper, causing him to look at the stab and slice areas.

"I need to move faster," Jendrin said, lying back down.

"You didn't need to be a hero," Airalee replied with a small voice.

"It was a reaction to an attack on one of my companions," Jendrin replied. "I would have done the same for Maylore, Marisa, or Latel. It is built into me," he said without raising his head.

"I am grateful you were there to help me," Airalee said just above a whisper. "I was shocked Oleg would attack me and froze where I stood. He most certainly would have stabbed me in the heart if not for your quick action. I am sorry you were injured, Jendrin," she said with tears coming to her eyes. Jendrin raised his head to speak but saw the tears in her eyes and reached for her free hand. He lay back down as Airalee started crying. The two sat for some time as Jendrin held her hand, and Airalee cried. A short time later, she realized he was holding her hand and gripped his hand tighter. She willed herself to stop crying and look at both wounds. The blood had slowed and was already drying around the lesions. A knock on the door was immediately followed by Latel rushing into the hut. Seeing Jendrin on the bed, he moved near Airalee as Jendrin looked his way.

"I am glad you are alive, Jendrin," Latel said. "People running by my hut said Oleg had killed you." Jendrin smiled without letting go of Airalee.

"I am still here for now," Jendrin said, his voice thinner. "I am pleased you came so quickly."

Latel laughed in relief.

"I am pleased to be able to talk to you," Latel said.

The hut's door banged open again as Marisa entered carrying a small jar. She stopped behind Airalee and looked at the two wounds.

"It looks like the leg wound has stopped bleeding. Is the chest wound still bleeding?" Airalee lifted her hand and checked under the leaves. "It has slowed," she said, placing her hand back over the leaf.

"Kai wants you asleep," Marisa said. "She thought the potion she gave you was insufficient. Drink this knockout potion so you sleep, and she can sew up your wounds."

"I would argue, but Kai is meaner than I am," Jendrin said, smiling and reaching for the jar.

"You are learning," Marisa said. Seeing the tears on Airalee's face, Marisa bent over her and wrapped her arms around her neck. "I am sorry Jendrin was injured, but I am happy you are alive."

"Thank you, Marisa," Airalee replied, reclaiming Jendrin's hand.

"Kai will be here soon," Marisa yelled as she turned and ran out the door. The three exchanged light banter, avoiding the topic of the attack until they heard voices outside the hut. Maylore carried Kai into the hut and set her down behind Airalee.

"Latel," Kai said, "I want you to find a chamber pot and cut a hole on the other side of the bed to put it under. Jendrin will not be moving from the bed for some time." Latel smiled and bid the group farewell as he went to fulfill his task. "Maylore, brew us all some tea while we wait."

Maylore was pleased to make the tea while the women fussed over Jendrin. Maylore returned shortly with the tea and could see Jendrin was asleep.

"Ah, tea," Kai said, taking a cup from Maylore. "We will wait a while to be sure he is completely out before I begin. I should say before Airalee begins since she accepted being an apprentice."

CHAPTER 27 - REFLECTION

The day slipped into the night as Kai instructed Airalee to close both wounds with her needle and string. Marisa and Airalee learned to clean and stitch the wounds as Airalee progressed. They finished by applying healing salves on a clean cloth to all the wounds.

"We will need Jendrin awake to apply the chest wrap," Kai said. "I fear he is too heavy for us to move. If we tried, we could cause the wound to bleed again."

The two girls wrapped his leg as Kai issued directions. Maylore passed them more wrappings as needed. Kai inspected their final work before nodding approval.

Jendrin moaned and opened his eyes slightly.

"You should not be awake yet," Kai said, looking at his eyes.

"I don't think I am," Jendrin said. "I feel like I was thrown down and kicked," as he looked at the people around him. "Ouch, I was stabbed, wasn't I," he finally surmised, trying to sit up.

"Yes," Kai said. "Sit up while we wrap your chest."

"Sure," Jendrin said, weaving slightly.

"Wrap him like I showed you doing his leg," Kai told them.

Airalee and Marisa wrapped his chest quickly, earning Kai's approval.

"Jendrin, lie back and try not to move too much," Kai told him.

"No problem," Jendrin said, lying back on the bed.

"I want someone to stay with him to catch any problem that may start," Kai said, surveying the room. "I assume Airalee is one. Marisa and Maylore, are you going to take a shift?" Both agreed they would help. "Good. I will visit him and the rest of our sick and injured tomorrow. Maylore, if you will gather dinner for Airalee and yourself, Marisa will help me hobble back to my hut for dinner. Maylore will watch him tomorrow while I train Airalee to create the healing salves."

Kai turned to Marisa.

"I have kept Marisa from Mirtha too long, so she will assist Mirtha with the noon lunch. After lunch, you can help watch Jendrin."

Kai's matter-of-fact speech left no room for debate as all three nodded that they understood.

"Maylore, you can carry the healing supplies to my hut as Marisa helps me," she said as the two helped her out the door.

Airalee realized she felt drained of energy as the hut door closed. She slumped slightly as she blankly watched Jendrin fall back asleep. The door opening snapped her out of her stupor as Maylore returned with food for them. Maylore placed food and water near her as he sat in the chair next to her.

"Do you want to talk about this?" Maylore asked.

"No, dad," Airalee said in a small voice. "I would prefer to sit quietly." Maylore sat with her as they ate their dinner. Airalee ate a small amount, keeping her thoughts to herself.

"Do you wish to do your evening routine first?" Maylore asked.

"Yes, thank you," she said. Realizing she had to go, she arose and left the hut. Maylore gathered a few craft things she liked to do and laid them by her chair. After Airalee returned, he did his evening routine and went to bed. Airalee took the chair next to Jendrin and watched him sleep.

Maylore awoke the following day to a quiet hut. He found Airalee had fallen asleep in her chair, her hand on Jendrin's chest wound, and her head lying on the edge of the bed. As she continued to sleep, he checked that Jendrin's wounds were secure.

"Airalee," Maylore said as he softly shook her shoulder. She bolted upright, staring at him, but didn't seem to see him. "Are you all right?" he asked.

"Dad," Airalee said as her eyes focused on him. "I was dreaming Jendrin was killed," she said as her head sank. Maylore sat in the chair next to her.

"I was angry with myself for not trying to defend him as he did for me," Airalee said. "I should have insisted we run from Oleg."

"We are fortunate Oleg didn't kill him," Maylore said, taking her hand. "You were Oleg's target, and if you had tried to help, we would now be mourning your death," he said, patting her hand. She did not seem to hear him as she stared at him.

"Birsha stopped Oleg," Airalee said. "I am not sure why."

"Birsha sees all of us as his little people," Maylore said. "He believes we are only here to serve his needs. Birsha, seeing Oleg trying to kill his workers, saved both of you."

"He still leads a bad group of men," Airalee said.

"Agreed," Maylore said. "You are likely to suffer bad dreams for many summers before they completely fade away," he said softly.

"I hope they go away sooner," Airalee said, nodding. "I didn't get much sleep and probably won't until he is well." Maylore patted her hand again.

"It is our job to help him get better," Maylore said. "You do your morning routine while I stay with him. Here is a fresh robe to put on after your bath," he said with a smile. Airalee nodded blankly, looking at Jendrin before leaving.

"Jendrin, my boy, you do not need me to watch you sleep," Maylore said, looking at him. "I will make all three of us breakfast.

You may be hungry when you awaken." Maylore made a hot breakfast from the beans, herbs, greens, and meat gathered from the meat storage. He moved the table near the opening to Jendrin's bed chamber and placed their breakfast on top. Airalee returned, but Maylore pointed to the chair at the table, saying, "You need to eat before you fall over. Kai wants you to learn to create salves, and I want you to have the energy to do it." Airalee smiled and sat at the table, heartily eating as she watched her unmoving companion. Airalee finished and washed their dishes as Maylore stayed with Jendrin.

She collected a few things in her satchel and checked Jendrin's wounds. Satisfied that he was doing well, she turned to leave the hut.

"I'll be back soon, dad," she said as she closed the door.

Maylore decided to examine the wounds himself.

"If I were a healer, perhaps I would know what I was looking for," Maylore said, sitting in the chair. "I will instead work on my skills while on my watch."

Maylore decided he would start by trying his tracking dome. He looked inward at the now familiar tracking dome. He could see Airalee was close. Gilriel seemed to be on the sunrise side. Bert the bird looked to be near his cave. Maylore sent Bert a picture with his hand on his eyebrow in a 'looking for you' signal. Bert returned a picture of bread and fruit on Gilriel's table. Maylore smiled at the bird's response. He changed focus and started looking for nearby ley lines, fire, and wind energy. He spotted a ley line of planet energy flowing near the hut. Fire energy emanated from their hut fireplace, but there was no wind movement.

"What would happen if I asked Almora's energy to flow over his body?" Maylore said aloud. "Would it help his healing?" He gathered the blue energy and asked it to flow over Jendrin's body. The dancing energy flowed over Jendrin's body in an amount greater than Maylore had gathered before. The stream flowed in and out of his closed wounds. Maylore watched the flow as he tried to gauge the

417

depth of each wound. The knife wound appeared deep, and the leg wound somewhat shallow. The energy going into the chest wound came out looking the same. The energy coming out of the leg wound had a slight pink tinge. "I wonder what that means, if anything," he said aloud. "Almora's energy does not seem to affect his wound. I suspect it is safe for me to use the energy to inspect his wounds." The opening of the hut door broke his concentration as Latel entered the hut.

"I got a chamber pot for him," Latel said. He carried a clay pot with handles in the middle and a length of rope attached to each handle. "I will cut a hole on the other side of the bed and put the pot under it. We can use the rope to adjust it and pull it out to empty," he said.

"He may awaken," Maylore said, nodding, "but that is good since he needs to eat." Maylore moved into the main area, allowing Latel access to the bed on the opposite side of Jendrin. He cut a hole in the bed, matching the size of Jendrin's bottom. Maylore pushed the pot under the bed, and Latel positioned it under the hole. He added supports on the top and bottom of the new hole to support Jendrin when he used the chamber pot.

"I believe that will work," Latel said.

"Me too," Maylore said. "It would be a mess if it doesn't."

Kai was ready for Airalee when she arrived at her hut.

"Our patient survives?" Kai asked, stating it as a fact rather than a question.

"He sleeps," Airalee replied.

"Good," Kai said. "I want you to follow me to the storage hut to see which herbs and plants we use for the healing salve," Kai said, gathering her crutch. "You will make the salve. Tonight, you will gather the stored herbs and plants without my help and assemble the salve as I watch. I will make the pain and sleep potions for now. You will learn to make those later. Ready?" Kai said, leaving without waiting for an answer. Airalee could see Kai was already walking better this morning.

"Is your knee feeling better, Kai?" Airalee asked.

"Yes," she replied. "In a few more sunrises, I will be ready to gather more herbs and healing plants. I will want you to join me when I next gather."

"I will be ready," Airalee said. "Jendrin has other people who can watch him." Kai stopped and turned to her.

"He does not need watching all the time," Kai said. "He will either heal or not, regardless of us watching him," Kai said as she started toward the storage hut. Kai smiled as she walked, saying, "He is pretty enough to be watched, but his wounds will not heal faster."

"I worry about him," Airalee said as they entered the storage hut.

"Be concerned for him, do not worry," Kai said. "Worrying makes you stressed. Concern keeps your mind on action and problem-solving," Kai replied. "We need problem-solving if infections occur. We also need to keep him from getting out of bed too soon and tearing his wounds open." She turned to face Airalee and said, "You have your own wounds to heal, girl." Kai said as she began to recite her list of concerns about Airalee. "The shock of the attack will affect you. The guilt of Jendrin taking a wound meant for you. The sadness of his nearly being killed. Anger at Oleg for attacking you both. The trauma caused by this violence will come to you for many sunrises. Taking care of him will help to close your wounds in time."

Airalee took in her words, thinking Kai must have looked inside her to know that was what she was feeling or overheard her talking with Jendrin. Kai watched Airalee for a few moments before continuing.

"I have been through many injuries and how they affect the people around the injured. The relatives of the injured generally react the same way each time," Kai said as she turned to walk into the hut. "Come, girl, let's gather the supplies so you can return to him." Airalee followed Kai into the hut as Kai pointed to the plants and herbs she wanted to use.

"Gather some turmeric, marshmallen, pennywort, and neem from their baskets," Kai said. "We will need to gather more from the forest soon."

Airalee recognized each of them from a distant memory she did not know existed. She gathered a few of each and added them to a basket.

"We will grind them at the workbench," Kai said, moving to the workbench inside the hut. Airalee did most of the chopping and grinding until Kai told her they were ready.

"I want you to apply the salve to clean linen strips and apply them to the wounds," Kai instructed. "When you change the dressings, you must burn the old strips to avoid spreading disease. Be sure to keep him in his bed. If he moves too much, add a few drops of the sleeping potion to his pain medication." She looked at Airalee, waiting for questions. When none were forthcoming, she turned to leave the hut. "I will walk to your hut and see how he progresses."

Jendrin was awake and talking to Latel and Maylore when Kai and Airalee arrived. Jendrin started to wave to them when the movement caused him to wince in pain.

"You need to remain still for the foreseeable future," Kai ordered. "I don't want you to tear your wounds. Airalee and Marisa do not want to repeat their skin-tying skills, and I may not give you any

420

sleeping tonic, so next time you feel the pain." Kai said, giving Jendrin a stern look. Jendrin merely smiled as Kai looked toward Maylore, saying, "I see you made him breakfast. Be sure you eat Jendrin." Kai instructed Jendrin. "Can you feed yourself, or should one of us help you?" Jendrin raised his left arm.

"I can use my left hand without straining the wounds," Jendrin said. Maylore passed the breakfast bowl to him as Jendrin started to eat. Kai noticed the chamber pot and said, "You accomplished your task, Latel."

"Yes," Latel said, "We discussed how to use it before you arrived. I will also take care of disposal and bed repair even though Jendrin didn't like the idea."

"You are a good man, Latel," Kai said. "Airalee, you may begin your task." Airalee moved to the bed, carefully unwrapped the wounds, and removed the strips from each injury. She applied new dressings and passed the old ones to Maylore.

"Dad," Airalee said, looking at him, "Please burn these." Maylore took the dressings to the firepit while Kai examined the wounds as Airalee progressed.

"The wounds look good for now," Kai said. "We need to watch to catch any infection. Jendrin, you must sleep to allow your body to repair itself. You should start being awake more during the day as time goes by. Airalee will administer your sleeping and pain potions, and we will all watch for infection." Kai looked at Latel and waved him toward the door. "Latel and I will depart to allow quiet time for Jendrin."

"I will attend to things we discussed," Latel said, nodding to Jendrin. "I will return tonight," he said, moving to the door and holding it for Kai.

"I am not far away," Kai said to Airalee as she left the hut. Airalee and Maylore tended to Jendrin the rest of the day. Several villagers dropped in to visit with Jendrin throughout the day. A few council members, except Caudra and Nenaias, visited with him too. All of them expressed their pleasure that Jendrin survived the attack. The council members noted they had been updated about the attack since Rendal had been present. Airalee portioned out Jendrin's pain tonics and chased visitors from the hut as Jendrin tired. Night's arrival stopped visitors from coming as Maylore and Airalee prepared dinner and other nighttime activities. Maylore and Airalee ate their dinner when a knock came on the door. Latel and Marisa entered at Maylore's request and greeted everyone. Latel moved to Jendrin's bed.

"I managed to find what you asked about this morning," Latel said as he passed a leather-cased object to him.

"Thank you, Latel," Jendrin said, taking it with his left hand.

"I must not stay long," Latel said. "I have tasks to do for my family. I wish you continued improvement." Latel said as he moved to the door. "Good night, everyone," he said as they all wished him good night.

"I, too, have other tasks to finish," Marisa said. "Now I want to know what Latel was searching for this afternoon. He said it was up to Jendrin to discuss."

"It is no secret," Jendrin chuckled. "I asked him to try and find the knife that stabbed me. He heard from Rendal that Birsha had kicked it aside, and no one reclaimed it." Jendrin pulled the white bone knife from the case and showed it to everyone.

"I see," Marisa said, sounding unimpressed. "I don't know why you would want that. It is no good for anything except stabbing someone. You should toss it into the sea."

"It is a reminder of how quickly death's agents can seek us," Jendrin said. Marisa grimaced at him before changing the subject.

"You seem to be doing well," Marisa said. "I will visit more tomorrow." She hugged Airalee and left the hut. Airalee looked at the knife like a dangerous animal being set loose.

"Do you need to keep that knife?" she asked.

"I do," Jendrin answered, "It is what almost ended me, and instead, I have it," he said. He put it back into its sheath and laid it beside the bed. "I need to use my new chamber pot before I sleep," Jendrin said.

"Maylore will help you slide over," Airalee said. "While you help him move, dad, remove the dirty robe and use the blanket beside the bed." Airalee moved back into the main hut and started making new healing poultices while the two men worked. Maylore helped Jendrin remove the top part of the robe before holding the bottom part as Jendrin slowly slid over to the other side. Jendrin finished as Maylore handed him a lid for the pot. Jendrin slowly made his way back, and Maylore covered him with the blanket.

"That was very tiring," Jendrin said as he settled in. Airalee returned with the new healing salves and examined each wound. Both wounds looked undisturbed as she replaced each bandage. "I will get your pain and sleep potions to let you rest," Airalee said. The hut was silent as she prepared the potions. She returned to find Jendrin already asleep and Maylore adjusting the blanket. "I will keep this potion close. He will be in pain when he awakens," Airalee said, sitting in her chair. Maylore sat in the chair near Jendrin's knees.

"Since you did not sleep last night," Maylore asked, "should I take this watch?"

"No, dad," Airalee replied. "I will stay with him since he is sleeping in my bed anyway."

"I will lend you my bed while I watch him," Maylore said. "You could use his bed instead."

"Thanks, dad, I will sit here," Airalee said.

"I will stay with you until you fall asleep," Maylore said, sitting back in his chair.

"You would be welcome to," Airalee said. "You should instead sleep so you are fresh tomorrow. I plan to pass the time by adding the plants we found in the desert to my book," Airalee said, retrieving her chronicle of plants from the shelf.

"I will sit with you and Jendrin a while longer," Maylore said, settling in his chair.

Maylore decided he would quietly continue practicing his skills. He looked again at the wounds and asked the planet's blue energy to flow through them. To Maylore, the chest wound looked the same, but the leg wound had more pink in it.

Jendrin shifted in bed as Airalee lifted the blanket to check the chest bandage. It had moved slightly, so she pushed it back into place, touching the stitches to be sure they had not broken. Maylore saw a small flow of green drops begin moving into the wound as he watched the blue and green energy flow.

"What's this?" Maylore said aloud as he remained focused. "Green energy is flowing into his wounds." Airalee reacted by pulling her hand back. The flow of green energy immediately stopped. Maylore dropped his focus to look at Airalee. "Green energy was flowing into his wound. It stopped suddenly. Did you touch his wound?"

"I was checking his stitches," Airalee said.

"Interesting," Maylore said. "Try putting your hand on it again after I start watching." Maylore concentrated and gathered blue energy as he watched the wound. A small stream of green energy suddenly appeared. Maylore dropped his concentration and saw Airalee touching the wound with her fingertips. "Amazing," Maylore said. "You seem to be creating a stream of green energy. I don't know if it is helpful or harmful." Airalee removed her hand, unsure what to do. Maylore considered for a few moments before continuing. "I want you to leave your hand on the wound while I try to see what is happening." Airalee thought it strange but put her fingertips on the wound. Maylore focused on the injury and saw a single file of green energy dots flowing from her hand down into the wound. It did not flow back out of the wound like the blue energy.

"Where did it go?" Maylore muttered aloud. He concentrated on following the green energy to the end of its trip. The energy flowed into the wound, briefly glowing as the flesh absorbed it. "Is it poison or repair?" Maylore said as he pulled his focus back and saw a single file of blue energy still going into and out of the wound. The green energy did not seem to cause any harm, nor did it seem to help.

"The green energy dissipates when it arrives at the end of the wound," Maylore said. "I cannot tell if it helps or harms the wound. I need to determine how deep the injury is to find if it helps or hurts." Airalee listened as Maylore considered his options. "I will try to count the pulses of energy, and if tomorrow fewer numbers are going to the end of his wound, then it is helping.

Maylore concentrated and counted how many pulses it took to fill the wound. He fixed the count in his mind and dropped concentration.

"I can't tell if your energy is helping or poisoning the wound," Maylore said. "I counted the depth of energy units going into the wound. Tomorrow, I will see if it is less or more."

"You can see energy flowing from me?" Airalee asked.

"I assume it is," Maylore said. "It starts to flow when you touch the wound. I don't know what it is or what it does. The blue energy I summon flows beside it as a natural energy. My guess is that it is helping his body rebuild. However, I don't know that."

"If it helps," Airalee said, "I can rest my hand on the wound while we all sleep."

"As you will," Maylore said. "If you want relief, I can sit with him while you are gone."

Jendrin stirred and opened his eyes.

"I don't know which is more painful, my shoulder or my leg," Jendrin grimly said. Airalee got the pain and sleep potions and mixed them in a mug.

"Kai's special drink should help you," Airalee said, passing him the cup. Jendrin did not protest and immediately drank its contents. He rested on the bed with his eyes open and not speaking.

"Kai believes the best thing for you is to sleep for several days," Airalee said.

"This time," Jendrin said, "I think she is right." As he closed his eyes, Maylore gathered a blanket and some water for Airalee.

"I wish you good dreams," Maylore said. "I will see you in the morning," Maylore said as he moved toward his bed.

"Good night, dad," Airalee said as she laid her hand on Jendrin's wound. She tried to write in her book, but fatigue won over. She lay her head on the side of the bed and fell asleep. Her dreams were not good. Visions of being attacked flooded her mind as she froze each time Oleg stabbed Jendrin. In another dream, she was the aggressor, taking Oleg's knife and killing him. She was angry in several other dreams and then extremely sad. She awoke several times, shaking and confused as to where she was. "That's enough of that," she said aloud, reaching for Kai's sleep medicine. She took a small amount and checked Jendrin's condition before falling into a dreamless sleep.

CHAPTER 28 - SICK DAYS

Airalee's head popped up as Jendrin stirred the following day. Daylight had not yet begun as he moaned and opened his eyes. He finally focused on Airalee, who was watching him. "I see my nursemaid is still here," he said with a small smile.

"Where else would I go?" Airalee said. "You are sleeping in my bed, hero," Airalee chided with much less force than usual.

Jendrin examined the bed he was lying in. "I didn't notice before how large this bed is," Jendrin said. "I need to move over to the other side."

"You don't need to on my account," Airalee said. Jendrin removed the top of the chamber pot.

"Well, not for your benefit," Jendrin said as he slid. Jendrin grimaced as pain roared in his leg when he tried to slide it over. He didn't notice the short bark of pain that escaped his throat. Airalee and Maylore heard it.

"Your leg is in pain?" she asked as he stopped mid-move.

"I think Oleg's knife is still in the wound," he grimaced, waiting for the pain to subside. Maylore rushed into the chamber as Airalee moved the blanket to look at the leg wound. It was pink and slightly swollen compared to yesterday.

"That doesn't look good," Jendrin said, looking at the wound.

"No, it doesn't," Airalee said. "Maylore, if you help him slide his leg over, I will push his hips. Ready?" she asked Jendrin.

"No, but let's go," he replied. Airalee counted to three, and they pushed and slid him together. Jendrin was ready for the pain this time and suppressed outward signs. As he settled into the new spot, a small bead of sweat appeared on his face. "I don't think I will try that again for a while."

"I will find Kai to get her ideas," Airalee said as she slid off the bed. "I am sure I can give you the pain medication before I go," she said, pouring a small cup and passing it to Jendrin. He didn't stop to look at the cup and drank it down quickly. She left the hut as Latel was coming up the path. She barely acknowledged him as she hurried toward Kai's hut. Latel entered the hut to find Jendrin in obvious discomfort and Maylore standing at the foot of the bed.

"Jendrin?" he asked, moving to the bed.

"Latel," he said as the pain lessened.

"Pain is greater this morning?" Latel asked.

"Yes," Jendrin replied, "I moved to the chamber pot, and my leg decided it was a bad idea," he said, trying to smile.

"I see," Latel replied, looking at the pink edges of the leg wound. "I am no healer, but I believe that wound needs tending."

"I would say the knife is still in there," Jendrin said. "It feels sharp to me." Latel tried to make small talk with him, but Jendrin was in no mood.

"I will switch the chamber pots and let you rest," Latel said as he bent to pull the rope attached to the pot. Undoing the ropes from the first pot, he tied them onto the second pot and pulled the pot back under the bed. "I will return later to switch them again," he said, looking at Jendrin.

"Return sooner if you will," Jendrin said. "I welcome your presence even if I don't speak it."

"I will," Latel said with a smile. He took the chamber pot and left the hut.

Maylore sat in a chair observing Jendrin.

"You and Airalee are my closest allies," Jendrin said, looking at Maylore. "If I speak ill to either of you, I do not mean offense. It will be the pain talking and not me."

"I understand," Maylore said. "We three have already undergone enough challenges to glue us together for many seasons. I look forward to many more adventures with you two."

Jendrin smiled with a look of relief on his face.

"I believe the medicine is already starting to work," Jendrin said. "Let's not move back to the other side of the bed," Jendrin said.

Marisa pushed open the hut door and moved to bed without acknowledging either one.

"Good morning to you, too," Jendrin said.

"You are not well?" she asked, pushing aside the blanket on his chest. She carefully removed the coverings on the wound and examined the chest wound. "Kai will be here soon to examine the wounds," she said, pushing aside the blanket covering the leg wound.

"Hey, a little privacy if you don't mind," Jendrin said.

"I am here to prepare you for the examination," Marisa said. "Kai is the healer, and she expects Airalee or I to remove coverings. I arrived first, so she expects me to prepare for her arrival."

"I still have a little modesty even with her around, let alone with you," Jendrin said.

"Modesty?" Marisa asked. "You and Airalee talk of being modest when there is no need for it in this village. When the days are hot, we often go without clothes. It is no problem for anyone here."

"I suspect many hide age and injury behind the coverings even when it is hot," Jendrin said. "You may go without if you wish, but I doubt you do," he said with a painful grin.

"It is warm, and I have nothing to hide," Marisa said as she slipped out of her robe and folded it into the chair.

"I didn't mean now!" Jendrin said. "It is still cool this time of season!" Maylore averted his eyes but noticed the beauty in her form.

"I see. Did I win your challenge?" Marisa said, picking up her robe.

Kai and Airalee entered the hut as Marisa picked up her robe. Kai barely noticed as she moved to the bed.

"Marisa!" Airalee exclaimed, "What are you doing?"

"You and your companion have the same strange concept of modesty," Marisa said calmly, sliding the robe back on. "I told him the custom here is that the weather determines what we wear. If it is hot, we leave clothes in our huts. When it is cold, we wear more."

"Is our hut too warm for you?" Airalee asked.

"Jendrin suggested I would not go without clothes when it was warm," Marisa said. "This sounded like a challenge since it was warm. I accepted his challenge, but he objected when I did, so I put them back on."

Kai interrupted them with a stern voice.

"You two stop and look at this wound with me," Kai said. The two women quickly surrounded Kai as she removed more poultice from the wound. Jendrin tensed as she lifted one corner away. Kai pointed to the exposed portion of the leg wound. "It is becoming infected. He may not yet be in great pain, but he soon will be. We need to stop the infection while we can." Kai lightly touched the stitches, and Jendrin reacted by tensing the leg muscle. "It is warm, swollen, and painful. When he sleeps again, you two remove the rest of the poultice, wash the wound, and apply a new poultice. We may have to remove the stitches and allow it to drain and redo our work with stitches and more healing potions." Looking at the chest wound, she said, "This is the one I thought would be infected. Is this painful?" Kai asked, looking at Jendrin as she pressed lightly around the wound.

"It feels injured but not painful," Jendrin replied.

"We are fortunate there," Kai said. Looking at the two women, she said, "If you see an oozing around the wound, come get me, and we will remove the stitches and clean the wound. In the meantime, he needs medicine, food, water, and sleep. Has Latel emptied the chamber pot?"

"Yes," Maylore replied.

"He is a good man," Kai said, nodding. "He will see to his duties." Looking at Airalee and Marisa, she said, "The next time he sleeps, you two will bathe him with water and soapweed. Make sure he eats and drinks water. It would be no good to have a patient survive the illness but die from starvation. I have other villagers to attend to. And will return tomorrow," she said as she turned to leave. "Marisa, you need to return to your duties after you help with the wash. See to your tasks," Kai said as she grabbed her crutch and pushed out the door.

Airalee made enough salve to redo the wounds. The three looked at Jendrin, who looked at each of them, unsure what to say.

"I think I would like some breakfast," Jendrin said as the pain returned to a low level. "A nice cup of strong reeb would be nice, too."

Maylore retrieved the breakfast he had made and set it next to Jendrin. He placed a cup of water on the bed.

"I believe Dirdin has some brew left," Maylore said. "I will check with him."

Airalee poured a larger dose of sleeping potion.

"Healer's orders for you to sleep," she said, pushing the cup into his hand. Jendrin drank the potion with no comment.

"I will gather the soap and sea sponges from the bathing pool to wash him," Maylore said as he rose and left the hut.

"I will heat the water for his sponge bath," Marisa said. "Even though he won't notice, I don't want to be cold." She gathered the water pot and left the hut. Airalee looked at Jendrin, and the slight smile on her face faded to sadness.

"I am sorry you are still injured," Airalee said.

"Me too," Jendrin replied, attempting to sound upbeat. Airalee looked down,

"I still feel responsible for your injury," she said.

"Did you hold the knife that struck me?" he asked. Airalee shook her head as she looked up.

"I could have tried to strike back," she said.

"Oleg is a trained fighter and was intent on killing you," Jendrin said softly. "We were fortunate that Birsha stopped Oleg's attack, but if you attacked Oleg, he most certainly would not have stopped Oleg from killing you."

"Maylore said similar things," Airalee said. "You proved yourself a hero this time," she said with a small smile. Jendrin relaxed but realized this was not the end of her misery either.

Jendrin started eating breakfast and drinking water as he talked with Airalee about subjects unrelated to the attack. Jendrin was growing sleepy as Marisa returned with a pot of warm water. The three continued with small talk as Maylore returned with soap and sea sponges.

"Welcome back, Maylore, I hope," Jendrin started to say before falling asleep mid-sentence.

"It appears he sleeps," Maylore said, setting the soap and sponges beside the bed.

"Yes," Marisa said. "Be careful around the wounds. We do not want to injure the wound by washing it too vigorously."

"I will wash the blanket covering him since we three cannot fit around him anyway," Maylore said.

"Good idea," Marisa said as she lifted the blanket covering him. A foul body odor struck their noses as she pulled the blanket away. Marisa rocked back from the smell as she passed the blanket to Maylore.

"It smells like you have a big task ahead of you ladies," Maylore said as he left the hut. Airalee took one of the sponges and started washing his face toward the chest wound. Marisa started at his feet and washed upward to the leg wound. Peeling off any old remaining poultice, they pressed on each to see if any oozing occurred.

"I don't see any oozing on this wound," Airalee said as she started washing the rest of his chest.

"There may be a problem here," Marisa said as she pressed the wound. "It feels like a liquid under the wound. We may want to cut a stitch and see if it oozes. You should touch this, Airalee, to know what it feels like for the next patient." Airalee slid down the bed to press lightly on the wound.

"Doesn't feel right," Airalee agreed. "Should we find Kai before we cut it?"

"Probably," Marisa replied. "Let's finish washing him before we try to find her." They cleaned their sponges and continued their job. Marisa dried the wound before moving up his torso and washing it. "Jendrin has a woman-pleasing baby maker," she said in an observational tone as she cleaned and started on his other leg. Airalee sighed and continued washing.

"Do you have any more considerations about having a child?" Marisa asked. Airalee had been thinking about it since Melronna told her she already had a child.

"Yes," Airalee answered, "I have been considering it. I have not decided when, but perhaps soon. I feel settled here; there is shelter and plenty of food for us."

Marisa stopped washing and looked at her.

"That is a change," Marisa said.

"Yes," Airalee replied. "I feel it may be all right now. Have you decided?"

"Yes," Marisa replied, "I would like to fill my baby's chamber next winter." She wiped the soap off his leg. "Have you chosen a group of baby seeders?"

"No," Airalee replied, finishing the other side of Jendrin's torso. Marisa started washing Jendrin's foot.

"I will probably follow tradition and use a baby-seeding group," Marisa said.

"I am considering several baby seeders but have not decided. Jendrin would create strong children," she said, scanning his physique. "Gobelben has already agreed to be my baby-mate when the baby is born."

"I think of Jendrin as an adopted brother than anything else," Airalee said. "I am not sure I want more than one baby seeder," Airalee said.

"It has been the tradition in Molia for a long time," Marisa said.

"It just seems odd to me," Airalee said.

"It is your choice," Marisa said, shrugging her shoulders.

"Let's turn him this way and wash his back," Airalee said, pointing to her right. The two women turned him on his side and balanced him as they washed and dried his back. "Back you go," Airalee said as she and Marisa rolled him back onto the bed. She looked up and noticed Marisa looking at him. "Marisa, do you have to stare at him?" she said with embarrassment.

"He is pretty," Marisa said, breaking her stare. "But I am looking at this wound again," she said, pointing to the leg wound. "It is oozing around the end of one stitch. I will go find Kai," Marisa said, sliding off the bed and running out the door.

Airalee looked at the wound and saw a small break beside one oozing stitch. She retrieved a fresh blanket and covered Jendrin except for the leg wound.

Kai arrived, followed by Marisa, who was carrying her medical bag. Airalee watched as Kai sat on the bed and examined the leg.

"Oh my," Kai said. "It appears his body could not hold back the poisons. Marisa, find us some water that has boiled but is not hot enough to burn him," she said, waving to Marisa.

"This pot has boiled water," Marisa replied. "We used it to wash him." Kai nodded, then looked at Jendrin.

"He appears to be sleeping soundly," Kai said. "We will remove the stitches to drain and clean the wound." Kai retrieved her knife from her bag and started cutting the first stitch before she abruptly stopped. "Airalee, you need to practice," Kai said, passing the knife to her. Airalee sat on the bed, cutting each stitch and pulling it out of the wound. The oozing increased as she cut and removed each stitch.

"I have seen worse," Kai said, examining the wound as Airalee cut. "Wash water into the wound and collect it on these scraps of cloth," Kai said, pointing to the center of the injury. They continued pouring water and wiping the result until the water ran clear. "Pour a little of this reeb extract to stop the flesh rotting," Kai said, passing the bottle to Airalee. She poured a small amount along the wound and dried the edges. The extract was clear and had a strong odor. Kai handed her the needle and string. "Redo your stitching." Airalee restitched the injury as Kai monitored her progress. "Good," Kai said. "We will make a healer of you," as she examined the stitching. She turned to both women with a serious look on her face. "I fear we still may lose him if the rot spreads. I don't want you to lose your first patient, Airalee, but you should know it is possible." Looking at Marisa, she said, "You may return to your tasks as Airalee will stay with our patient. We can only hope we just improved his chances for survival." Kai said as she gathered her tools and left the hut. Marisa hugged Airalee, wishing for Jendrin to recover, and left the hut.

Airalee created new poultices and placed them on his chest and leg wounds. Touching his forehead, she noted he felt a little warm.

"All right, hero, time to fight back," Airalee said, settling onto the empty side of the bed.

The day turned to midday as Maylore returned with the washed sheet and a small jug.

"Dirdin said we could have all the reeb and its extract we want," Maylore said. "I told him this small jug of each will do fine," setting them on the table. Draping the blanket and sheet near the fire to dry, he returned to Jendrin's bed. "I wanted to see how Jendrin was doing. It appears he sleeps." He said, looking at his quiet form.

"He does," Airalee said. "Kai saw the leg wound was more infected than she liked, so we removed the stitches and cleaned the wound. I practiced stitching him up again. We hope he improves."

"How is his chest wound?" Maylore asked as Airalee moved the blanket so he could inspect it.

"Kai said it looked good," Airalee said. "She thought the chest wound would be the one to be infected." Airalee replaced the blanket as Maylore checked the leg wound.

"Yes," Maylore said. "This does look infected," he said, replacing the poultice and covering. "Remember I saw green energy flow from your hand when you rested it on his chest wound?"

"Yes, any new idea of what it does?" Airalee asked.

"I believe it was slowing the infection and speeding his healing," Maylore said. "I want you to touch his leg wound while I watch." Maylore moved to the foot of the bed. Airalee did not question him. She slid down the bed and placed her hand near the wound. Maylore concentrated on the injury, blocking out everything else. A short time later, he saw a small stream of green energy marching from Airalee's hand into the wound. The energy seemed to stop at the stitches as it burst on contact with the pink energy on top of the wound. Maylore requested the blue energy to flow over Jendrin's body. The energy flowed quickly and penetrated the injury to its depths. The wound seemed deeper than last time and had more pink energy. Maylore stretched the blue energy to the chest wound. He measured its depth compared to the previous time, noting it was not as deep; however, a small area of pink energy formed at the top of the stitches that was not there before. Maylore stopped concentrating and returned his awareness to the hut. Airalee was watching him as he focused on her.

"The leg wound is full of pink energy," Maylore said. "To me, that means it is infected. Your energy is small but destroys the pink energy where they collide. I believe your hand on his chest has slowed or stopped the infection. I suggest you place your hand on his chest wound to keep it from getting worse. Airalee slid back up the bed and slid her hand under the blanket over the chest wound. "You may not be able to reach the leg wound with your other hand. Let's try placing your knee near his leg injury to see if energy will flow from another point." Airalee uncovered her knee and placed it near his leg wound. Maylore concentrated again, watching the energy from her hand flow to the chest wound and destroy the pink energy near the stitches. He shifted concentration to the leg wound. A small stream flowed from her knee but ended short of the injury. Rather than lose concentration, Maylore pushed her leg up to get it closer to the wound. The green energy started flowing into the leg wound, destroying the pink energy it had encountered. Maylore monitored both injuries for a time before dropping concentration. Airalee was lying awkwardly on her side in a very uncomfortable position. "You may feel silly laying there, but your healing energy flows to each wound when you are that close." Airalee nodded and noted how she was lying next to him.

"This position is unseemly and very uncomfortable," Airalee said. "I can move up to ease the discomfort, but I will get little sleep. I am willing to do it for his sake." She rose and adjusted her robe as they moved to the table.

"You may now be his greatest chance to beat the infection," Maylore said, sitting at the table. "I believe he may not survive without your healing energy." Airalee noticed Maylore had the most thoughtful look on his face since she had met him.

"I will visit the privy, then return," she said. Marisa knocked on the door as Airalee retrieved a fresh robe from her store.

"I brought some food for all of us," Marisa said as Airalee met her at the door.

"Thank you, Marisa," Airalee said. "Would you mind staying while I bathe?"

"I would be glad to," Marisa said as Airalee smiled and left. Marisa placed the food on the table and went to check on Jendrin. "He will awaken soon. I will make a bowl for him," she said, returning to the table.

Maylore built up the fire and placed the water pot near it. He helped Marisa prepare the food and set the table.

"Kai worries the infections may cause him great harm. I have seen enough injuries to understand she is right," Marisa said.

"We hope Kai's healing skills and Jendrin's will to live will prevail in this battle," Maylore said. Marisa nodded and sat near Maylore as they watched Jendrin sleep.

Airalee returned, looking refreshed and carrying her wet-washed robe. "I see he still sleeps," Airalee said as she dried her robe near the fire.

"His body will do a lot of sleeping while the poison remains in the wounds," Marisa said. "Let's have some food and drink before I need to return to help my mother." Marisa pointed at a spot for Airalee. The three discussed what else could be done for Jendrin when he stirred.

Jendrin felt like he was looking through a fog as his eyes opened. He could not stop the groan that escaped his throat as he felt the pain in his leg. Three heads suddenly appeared in his view as he tried to quell the pain. "My nursemaids appear," he said, trying not to sound sarcastic.

"Your wounds have become poisonous," Marisa said. "We have removed the stitches and cleaned the wounds. The new poultices may help your body fight the poison. We will give you more medicine after you eat and drink water."

Jendrin felt hungry despite the pain.

"I could eat a woca leg if you have one," Jendrin said.

Three faces smiled as Marisa disappeared.

"You slept most of the day," Airalee said. "No wonder you are hungry." Marisa returned with a bowl of stew.

"You will need to sit up a bit to eat," Marisa said. Jendrin pushed his way up, feeling the pull on his wounds. He pulled down the blanket to look at the chest wound.

"Nice stitching job," Jendrin said. "It does not hurt like the leg jabbing daggers at me," he said as he pulled up the blanket.

"Thank you," Airalee said. "It was my second time with a needle and string." Jendrin smiled at her.

"You had a sharp object aimed at me?" Jendrin said. "Glad I was out of it for that."

"I am, too," Airalee replied. "I couldn't have handled the yelling and crying while I stitched you."

Marisa looked at Maylore.

"Do they still fight all the time?" Marisa asked as she passed the bowl to Jendrin.

"Yes," Maylore replied, "Just not as often as they used to."

"Do you have any more of Kai's pain potion?" Jendrin asked as he started eating. Airalee disappeared but quickly returned with a small cup. She pressed it to his lips between bites. Jendrin drank the potion and continued eating. Jendrin finished and handed the bowl back to Marisa.

"Thank you all," Jendrin said, "that tasted good."

"Your body will force you back asleep as the pain potion starts working," Marisa said. "We will change your poultice when you sleep."

Maylore appeared with a cup in his hand.

"Dirdin sends his regards," Maylore said, passing the cup of reeb extract to Jendrin.

"Cheers to Dirdin and all of you," Jendrin said as he drank it.

"How long have I been laying here?" Jendrin asked.

"It has only been a few days," Marisa said. "It will be many more before you feel right again. You have us and the village behind you to help you get well." The group traded small talk until Jendrin felt tired and ready to sleep again. He returned the empty cup to Maylore and slid down in the bed again. He mumbled something about being warm as his eyes slid shut.

"The pain potion will allow him to sleep for quite some time," Marisa said. "We should prepare another dose of pain and sleep potion for him to take when he awakens." Airalee poured two small cups and gathered more poultice material. The two removed the old poultices and applied new ones as Maylore burned the old ones in the fire.

"I will leave and help my mother but will visit tomorrow," Marisa said as they finished their jobs.

"Thank you, Marisa," Airalee said, hugging her.

"Good night," she said as she left. Airalee and Maylore cleaned up the hut and prepared for another day. They sat at the table, reflecting on the day and what was to come. The day had worn them both down, and they could feel sleep was approaching.

"I suggest you sleep near him tonight and let your healing energy work for him," Maylore said. Airalee agreed, gathered the two potions, and set them near the bed. She laid down near him and placed her hand on the chest wound. She raised her knee and put it near the leg wound. Maylore moved her leg over his calf where he had seen the healing energy flow before.

"That still looks uncomfortable," Maylore said. "I will gather some cushioning material for support around and behind you." Maylore gathered some blankets and robes from their belongings and created cushions for her.

"Thank you, dad," Airalee said. "This will work," she said, laying her head on a robe beneath her head.

"I will check the green energy is flowing," Maylore said. He sat at the foot of the bed and concentrated on the energy flow. Airalee's energy was flowing to both wounds as Maylore watched. "Your energy is flowing to both wounds," he said, looking at Airalee.

"I hope it helps," Airalee said.

"Me too," Maylore said. "Good night, Airalee," he said as he went to bed.

"Good night, Dad," Airalee replied.

Airalee lay near Jendrin as thoughts from the day ran through her head. They seemed to swirl around and start over again as she tried to relax and let herself go to sleep. She finally arose and grabbed the sleeping draft potion. There was enough in the jar for several people for several nights. Airalee followed Kai's recommendation that Jendrin drink only a small amount.

"I want to be sure I awaken before he does so I can explain why I am touching him," she said to herself. Laying back down, the swirl of thoughts eventually slowed to a stop. Her vision faded to black as she fell asleep.

Jendrin awoke to a silent, dark hut. His head was swimming in confusion, his eyes refusing to focus as he tried to see in the darkness. Something had trapped Jendrin's right arm. He turned his head to see what was holding it down and saw someone sleeping beside him. His eyes focused enough to see it was Airalee. She had her hand draped on his chest. Jendrin pulled his arm free from beneath her as she moaned and moved to lay her head on his shoulder. Jendrin raised his arm and put it around her shoulder, pulling her closer. "Airalee?" he questioned, turning his cheek to her head. An unintelligible response came from her lips as she threw her arm across his chest and snuggled closer. "I would enjoy this more," he said, "if I knew this wasn't a fever dream." Jendrin's enjoyment was brief as his head spun even more. Stars appeared before his eyes as he slipped back to sleep.

CHAPTER 29 - EXPLORING ENERGY

Jendrin awoke as the twin suns were rising in the sky. His head felt clear, and Airalee was indeed sleeping near him. He did not want to disturb her since he enjoyed contact with her.

"I guess I wasn't dreaming," he said quietly.

"Dreaming about what?" Maylore said, standing by the table. Jendrin turned his head to see Maylore watching him.

"I dreamed Airalee was sleeping with me," Jendrin said. "This morning, I find she is."

"I am afraid looks are deceiving," Maylore said. "We found she has healing power if her skin touches an area near a wound. She was supposed to keep her hand on your chest wound as you both slept. Her robe prevented skin contact, so we must do it again."

"I am all right with that," Jendrin said, grinning. Maylore smiled back, looking toward the leg wound.

"Her knee is still near your leg wound," Maylore said. "It may have helped with healing last night. We will check it later." Jendrin looked down to see her knee on his leg.

"The leg hurts so much I didn't notice her leg was there," Jendrin said, laying his head back down. "I am surprised she did not awaken while we were talking."

"I believe I see why she sleeps," Maylore said, shaking the empty sleeping draft container. "There was enough for two nights in here last night."

"Airalee," Jendrin said, softly shaking her. Airalee awoke, taking a few seconds to realize where she was. She bolted upright.

"What are you doing!" Airalee demanded, looking at Jendrin.

"What am I doing?" he answered, "You were sleeping on me, and I woke you up."

"I was not!" she said, looking around.

"You were, Airalee," Maylore said from behind her. Airalee turned to see Maylore still looking at them. "You were supposed to keep your hand on the wound, not an arm across his chest," he said with a cheery voice.

"Oh, yes," Airalee said quietly. "I failed my task," she said as she climbed out of the bed.

"I don't think so," Jendrin told her.

"Be quiet, hero," she said quietly. Jendrin started to laugh but stopped when his leg sprouted loud pangs of pain with her leg movement.

"This leg aches as much as yesterday," he said, trying to resettle his leg. Airalee retrieved more pain potion and poured him the correct amount.

"You haven't had any pain potion yet," Airalee said, passing the cup to Jendrin. He gulped it down and settled back into his bed.

"I will look at it after my morning routine," Airalee told him. Looking at Maylore, she said, "I will return soon, Dad," as she left.

Latel arrived as Maylore prepared some breakfast.

"I see you are awake," Latel said, bringing a clean chamber pot.

"Yes," Jendrin replied. "I hate to see you have to clean up after me, Latel." Latel waved it off.

"Kai seems to prefer me to do this task. I have done it many times, just like she tends to the sick and injured," he said with a half-smile.

"What have you been doing these past days?" Jendrin asked.

"We managed to get the hide of a bear yesterday," Latel said as he retrieved the pot's rope from the far side of the bed. "We brought it to Dirdin to tan, and he gave me two hides to create overcoats or leggings. I have to see what my little group can make with them," he said as he pulled the pot from under the bed and untied the ropes.

"I hope to join you in doing those things soon," Jendrin said.

"Me too," Latel replied as he pulled the replacement pot back under the bed. When someone knocked on the door, the three men were discussing tanning, fishing, and tailoring activities. Marisa entered and walked toward Jendrin.

"I see the men's group is having a meeting," Marisa said, bringing more supplies into the room. The three of them greeted her. "Kai's leg is improving, so she should be here soon." As Jendrin removed the blanket from the two wounds, Marisa moved to the bed. "You are learning," she said, examining the chest wound.

"I just didn't want to expose more of myself than needed." Jendrin smiled.

"You're too late," Marisa said, cutting stubborn pieces of the poultice from the wounds. "Airalee and I gave you a full sponge bath yesterday," she replied straight-faced.

"I hope nothing important got cut while you were doing that," Jendrin said with a shrug.

Marisa moved to the leg wound.

"We had to cut a few rotting things off after your sponge bath," Marisa said. "An unfortunate slip of the knife may have cut an area we did not intend to. Kai will be here to discuss it with you. It was an unfortunate occurrence," she said, removing the poultice. "Don't worry; you weren't using it anyway," she said cryptically.

Jendrin grimaced with pain as she pulled it. The hut door swung open as Kai entered.

"Move aside," Kai said as she pushed past Maylore and Latel. Airalee followed her with newly made potions and poultices for Jendrin. "You are awake," Kai announced. "Good, you can tell me if there is pain here," she said as she pressed along the sides of the chest wound.

"There is one spot that aches near the shoulder," Jendrin said.

"Very good," Kai said, nodding. "It seems to be healing." Looking toward Airalee, she said, "Let's put one more day of poultices on this." She moved to the leg wound. The wound was still red but not as swollen as the day before. She pushed the sheet further to verify that the infection was not spreading. "The skin looks good even to the torso. A slight improvement." Kai looked up at Jendrin as she said, "I had Airalee do some cutting yesterday." Jendrin looked concerned as she continued. "She cut the stitches on your leg as she and Marisa drained the infection from it." Jendrin's face changed to a smile. "Did I worry you about what she cut?" she asked.

Marisa started to chuckle.

"I told him we had to cut something off he didn't need after we gave him a bath," Marisa said. "He assumed we cut something we didn't touch!"

Kai simply smiled as the rest looked on.

"My leg pain is enough to cover any wound she may have inflicted," Jendrin said. "I was afraid to look."

"Airalee stitched up the wounds again," Kai said, smiling. "She did fine work. I do not see any leakage. I believe you when you say your leg is in pain. Airalee will continue giving you pain potions. I want you to sleep half of the day and all night. You appear to be healing, but it will be long unless the infection stops soon. Do you have a question for me?" Kai asked.

"No," Jendrin said, "thank you for your help."

Kai stood up to leave, but Maylore stopped her.

"May I have one of the small blue spot mushrooms?" Maylore asked. "I believe I can learn from its use," Maylore said, looking her in the eye. Kai returned his stare.

"Gilriel told me you should be allowed access to them," Kai said. "We have not allowed others to use them so quickly in the past, but I believe you will use them correctly. I see no reason to go against his wishes. I will have Marisa bring you one." Looking at the two girls, she said. "You two are doing well by Jendrin, even if you tease him," she said, smiling as she left the hut.

"I'll be on my way, too," Latel said as he took the pot and followed her out of the hut. The four of them talked and finished their breakfast.

"I will get the mushroom now if you wish," Marisa said as she stood with her bowl.

"I would like that," Maylore said. "It needs to be the smallest mushroom."

"I will bring the smallest mushroom from storage and wash all the bowls," Marisa said as she left.

"I will do my morning routine while she is gone," Maylore said, gathering his spare clothes and heading for the bath. Airalee started sorting the herbs and potions and creating two new poultices. She ordered the potions for the day and that night's use. She took the next poultice to his bed and placed the first one on the chest wound.

"I am sorry I slept on you last night," Airalee said. "I intended to follow Maylore's healing directions and failed in my job."

"It was enjoyable after I realized what was happening," Jendrin grinned. "I thought it was a fever dream when I awoke last night with you near. I was pleased to find it was true this morning."

"I will try harder to do the job correctly next time," Airalee said, her face flushed.

"I thought you did well," Jendrin said, continuing to grin.

Airalee looked at the leg wound before covering it.

447

"The wounds do look better today," Airalee said quietly. "We will check it later," she said as she finished applying both poultices.

Airalee felt a little embarrassed but warm inside, remembering how good it felt to be physically close to someone. She had no memory of physical contact with anyone. Putting the thought aside, she pulled the blanket over the wounds and returned to the table. She exchanged small talk with Jendrin as she stored the herbs and potions in the small storage area. A quick knock at the door announced Marisa's return.

"Kai gave me several small mushrooms," Marisa said, showing Airalee the small bag she carried. "Where is Maylore?" she asked.

"He is doing his morning routine," Airalee said. "I am sure he will return soon. Let's sit near Jendrin while I explain why Maylore wants the mushroom." Marisa nodded as they moved back to the bed. Airalee sat at the foot of the bed, where she could see both of them at once. "Maylore has learned he can see some energy fields surrounding us. He was examining Jendrin's wounds when he saw green energy enter Jendrin's wound. We experimented and found it occurred when I touched a wound. We found that I needed to have close skin contact with the injury for it to work. I was supposed to sleep with my bare hand near his chest wound and my knee near your leg wound. Sometime during the night, I moved my robed arm across his chest, which stopped the energy flow. Maylore hopes the leg wound is better since I kept my knee near the injury." Jendrin's face showed a slight sadness for the logical reason she was near him. Airalee noted his change in expression.

"You're a sorcerer!" Marisa said in amazement.

"No," Airalee laughed, "Maylore may be, but not me. I may have a previously unknown ability. We shall see. That is the reason Maylore wants the blue spot mushroom. Maylore is new to this possible energy and hopes the mushroom will enhance his ability to determine its source. He believes it may come from inside me or from my surroundings."

Marisa looked at Jendrin.

"Are you a sorcerer too?" Marisa asked. "Am I surrounded by amazing people?"

The story and Marisa's question took Jendrin aback.

"I am no sorcerer," Jendrin said. "I am fortunate to be alive."

Airalee smiled as she tried unsuccessfully to answer anxious questions from Marisa.

"This is why Maylore did not want this information to get around too quickly," Airalee said. "The uproar it may cause would not help any of us. I decided you should know since you are involved in Jendrin's recovery." Marisa stopped her questioning and nodded her understanding.

"I understand," Marisa said. "I can keep my mouth shut if I need to," she said, smiling.

"That's good," Airalee replied. "When Maylore returns, I want you to stay and watch."

"I would be glad to," Marisa answered.

"Guinea pig says he will stay, too!" Jendrin said, pushing himself up in the bed.

"You will not know anything is happening," Airalee said as the door to the hut opened. Maylore entered to see three faces looking at him. He stopped short with his freshly washed robe.

"What is wrong?" Maylore asked. "I did take a bath." He watched amusement spread on their faces.

"No, dad," Airalee said. "I was explaining your discovery of seeing green energy. I told the group what you said about possible healing energy and why you wanted to use the mushroom."

Maylore looked at Airalee and Jendrin before fixing his gaze on Marisa.

"Marisa is practically our fourth companion," Maylore said. "She will keep quiet about this, right?"

Marisa nodded as Maylore relaxed and dried his robe near the fire. Maylore moved to the bed, and Marisa passed him the small bag of mushrooms. Maylore sat in a chair at the foot of the bed and opened the bag. Several mushrooms were in the bag, ranging from very small to medium size. Maylore ate the smallest one and closed the bag, setting it aside.

"Perhaps you could explain how it works and what you see," Airalee said. Maylore considered what to say for a moment.

"I disregard most of the outside world and look inside myself at the energy dome," Maylore started. "I can see various energy flows from different origins. Almora has ley lines that have blue energy flowing from point to point. Fire has red energy. Air contains a light blue energy. I have been practicing using these different energies but I still have much to learn. I was using blue energy to probe the depth of Jendrin's wounds when I saw a small green energy flow from Jendrin's skin into the wound. We determined Airalee was touching his wound when I saw the energy start. It would flow a short distance anywhere her bare skin touched his wound. It would stop when she moved too far away." Maylore looked up to see three faces intently listening to what he was saying.

"That is incredible, sorcerer Maylore," Marisa said.

Maylore felt as if he had grown another head in her eyes.

"What will the mushroom do, Dad?" Airalee asked.

"I hope it will extend my view to the source of your green energy," Maylore replied. "It will take some time to affect me and will not last long. After it wears off, I must eat and sleep. I hope I used the correct amount."

"We do not know of any remedy if you use too much," Marisa said.

"I will be ready," Airalee said. "How do we proceed?"

"I will again send the blue energy into Jendrin's wounds to see how deep they are today," Maylore said. "When I raise my finger, I want Airalee to place her hand near the chest wound. When I raise two fingers, Airalee will remove her hand, and Marisa will put her hand near the wound. Ready?" he asked.

Both nodded, and Maylore started his process to close off the world and look inside the energy portal's dome. He requested the blue energy to flow to the leg wound, which returned with a pink tinge all along the wound. The stitches looked better than the last time. Shifting his focus to the chest wound, he sent more blue energy into the wound. It returned with a pink tinge near the outside of the wound but was not as deep. Maylore raised one finger and saw green energy flow into the wound in seconds. Most of it flowed to the infection site, destroying some pink energy. Some of it flowed to the bottom and seemed to speed healing. Maylore raised two fingers, and the energy flow stopped. The healing sites returned to a slower pace, and the infection held its spot. Maylore watched for a few minutes before returning to the world.

"I could see healing energy flow from Airalee's touch but nothing from Marisa's."

"It means I am not a sorcerer like Airalee," Marisa said with a playful pout.

"Not yet anyway," Maylore said.

"Is there hope?" Marisa asked.

"There is always hope, Marisa," Maylore said. "You may have a talent yet to be detected." Marisa chuckled but did not comment further.

"What did you see, Maylore?" Jendrin asked.

"Ah," Maylore said, "Both wounds look better. The chest wound is healing but has a small infection on the outside edge. The leg

451

wound is still infected and will require more attention. Things are looking up for you, Jendrin." Jendrin smiled with a look of relief as he listened.

"The mushroom's power may take effect soon," Maylore said. "When it does, I won't be able to talk with you until I awaken from my sleep. This mushroom is small, so perhaps I will not sleep long." Maylore stood up and moved to Jendrin's bed. "Gilriel had us lie down the first time I ate a mushroom. I will be your bunkmate for a short time, Jendrin," he said as he lay down on the other side. "Airalee, place your hand on the wound. I also need a physical connection to Airalee. Do we have a short rope we both could hold?"

"I will hold your hand, Dad. Wouldn't that be easier?" Airalee asked.

"Yes," Maylore said. "I suspect Gilriel didn't want to hold hands, so he used a rope." Maylore reached over to take Airalee's waiting hand. Maylore relaxed as the others talked amongst themselves. Slowly, their voices faded, and his awareness turned inward. He quickly passed through the barrier in his mind and found himself amongst a tangle of connections. He couldn't determine where he was, so he said to himself, 'I need to find Airalee.' He zipped down and around the links as he effortlessly moved to another location and stopped. He knew this was not his body and that he was near her communication portal. 'She has a communication portal, but it is incomplete. How did Gilriel fix my portals?' he thought to himself.

'I will need to study the book and try this again. Move to the heart portal,' he thought. He started zipping down the connections. He quickly found himself facing her heart portal.

'Dead energy completely blocks this portal,' he thought as he examined the portal. 'This must be what Kelkalyn saw when he looked at Airalee. I wonder how he knew that? I will have to visit with him to find out.' Looking at the rather large portal, he decided to see how packed the dead energy was by forming a pick and attacking the blockage. His pick managed to break off a tiny piece.

'I would be at this for months with my meager power. I will ask Kelkalyn about this too,' he thought. 'Where is the healing energy coming from?' he thought. Maylore didn't move.

'Is Airalee touching Jendrin? I need to go to Airalee's hand on Jendrin,' he thought. He started moving again, stopping at a narrow spot where Airalee's skin touched Jendrin.

'There is the green energy,' he said as he watched a small flow leave Airalee's hand. Looking back at the threads, he saw the one with the green energy flowing along it.

'There!' he said, following it back to its origin. The twists and turns of the threads led him back to the opposite side of the heart portal.

'Interesting!' he exclaimed, looking at the exit point of the energy. The portal was small and mostly blocked by the same dead energy plugging the rest of the heart portal. Looking beneath the emerging green energy, he saw another large thread entering the portal. This thread carried a pearl-white energy.

'What is this?' he thought. 'Perhaps this pearl-white energy is converted to her green healing energy in the portal?' he reasoned. 'Where does the pearl-white energy come from?' he thought, looking back at the large thread entering the portal. Maylore started following the thread back, but it split into hundreds of smaller lines going in different directions. Maylore picked a larger one and followed it. The line eventually ended at her skin. The pearl energy penetrated her skin and entered a thread in her body.

'It is an outside energy, but from where?' he thought. Maylore considered it for a time but could already feel the warning signal that the mushroom's power was running out.

'Find another thread and follow it back,' he thought as he followed the pearl energy to a more significant junction. He followed that line to its source, which was also the skin.

'She may only receive the power from outside herself and not through a portal like I do,' he thought. Suddenly, he was thrown out of her body and into complete darkness.

Maylore awoke, still lying on the bed. Sitting up, he turned to see the women gone and Jendrin asleep. He stood up, looked out the door, and saw that most of the day had passed. Both suns were in the last quarter of their day, and villagers moved about finishing their daily tasks.

"My stomach is growling," Maylore said. "It is time to eat." Someone had left dried fish, fruit, and bread on the table. Maylore sat at the table and devoured the meal. He cleaned his bowl and added wood to the fire as Airalee returned.

"You are awake, Dad," Airalee said, setting down newly picked beans, herbs, potatoes, and greens.

"Yes. It looks like the day is nearly over," Maylore said. "Last time I used a mushroom, I slept most of the night. A few hours is an improvement! I will need to use another mushroom to further my search."

"Kai says one mushroom per day," Airalee said. "She says it is dangerous to use more than one. Some have died using a small one. You are fortunate there."

"Gilriel told me a similar story," Maylore replied. "Besides, if I sleep that much, I could only use one daily anyway."

"That is true," Airalee said. "Do you need anything else to eat?" Airalee asked, putting her supplies on the table.

"Yes," Maylore replied, "I will help you make dinner."

"If you fill a pot of water, we can start dinner and discuss what you learned," Airalee said.

"Good," Maylore said. "I will visit the potty, gather water, then return," he said, smiling at her. Airalee cut up the various ingredients and put them into their cooking pot. Maylore returned as she moved the pot near the fire. Maylore added the water to the pot and saved the rest for drinking.

"Let's sit at the table as you tell me what you have seen so far," Airalee said, moving to the table. Maylore sat on the same side so they could both watch the sleeping Jendrin.

"Should we wait for Jendrin and Marisa?" Maylore asked.

"Probably, but I can't wait," Airalee said. "You can repeat it when they are here."

"Good," Maylore said. "A second telling may bring other details out."

"We saw you relax on the bed, and you seemed to be in a trance," Airalee said. "What did happen?"

"I wasn't sure where I was when the mushroom took effect," Maylore started. "I saw long, thin strands with energy running in all directions. I was pretty sure I was in my body. I asked to move to your body. I quickly moved along the twisting strands and into your hand. I saw different energies running along the threads. I stopped at your communication portal in your throat. It was not connected to any energy strands, so you could not use it. Gilriel knows how to connect it, but I do not. I will ask him to help me connect it the next time I see him."

"Will I be able to talk to you if it is connected?" Airalee asked.

"I believe so," Maylore said. "You could feel my trying to talk to you when I tried."

"I felt a bump," Airalee said.

"I believe there is a small connection I didn't see," Maylore said.

"Can you communicate with anyone?" Airalee asked.

"Only Bert, the IB in Gilriel's cave, can communicate with me now," Maylore said.

"Animals can talk?" Airalee asked.

"Animals talk by sending and receiving images," Maylore said.

"This bird has a name?" Airalee asked. Maylore smiled.

"I asked him his name, and I thought he said Bert," Maylore said. "The bird chuckled, saying that would do. I suspect the bird has a name we can't pronounce."

"Ask Bert to come visit us," Airalee said with a smile. "We would all like to meet him." Maylore chuckled at the thought of Bert willing to visit humans.

"I will ask," Maylore said. "He prefers to stay close to his home in Gilriel's cave and avoid people."

"Did you find anything else?" Airalee queried.

"Yes," Maylore replied, "When I decided I couldn't connect to your communication portal, I asked to move to your heart portal. I saw you have a large heart portal completely clogged with dead energy. I tried to remove some of it but only chipped off a small piece. It would take a power far greater than mine to clear it."

"Is this what Kelkalyn meant about me having a burnt heart?" Airalee asked.

"Yes," Maylore replied. "I need to talk with him about what he saw. I also wonder how he knew it without using a mushroom. Even if Kelkalyn had used a mushroom, how did he know just by looking at you? I have to follow energy threads to see the damage."

"Kai told us he is strange and mysterious," Airalee said.

"Indeed," Maylore replied. "Perhaps he is a real sorcerer. I hope he can tell me what a normal heart portal looks like."

"You talk about portals," Airalee said. "What does a portal look like to you?" Airalee asked.

"I have little experience with portals," Maylore said, "but they appear cup-shaped with a dome. Gilriel told me most people do not have portals. Perhaps you and I are fortunate or cursed. I am not sure which."

"I would say, special perhaps," Airalee said with a laugh. "What else did you see?"

"Your particular heart portal appears to have a clear dome on it," Maylore said. "It has a large group of disconnected threads that do not reach the bottom of the portal. It might do something if we could clear out the dead energy and connect the threads. I don't know what the heart portal does. Perhaps Kelkalyn knows."

"Interesting," Airalee said. "My interest grows to find Kelkalyn and ask what he knows."

"Yes," Maylore said. "He may have all our answers or be an eccentric old man who thinks your heart is wounded. We will have to find out."

"Did you find anything about healing energy?" Airalee asked.

"Yes," Maylore replied. "I asked to be taken to where your hand was touching Jendrin. When I arrived, I saw the green energy leaving your hand and entering his skin. I found the thread that carried the green energy and followed it back to its source. It was on the other side of your heart portal. It could be a less damaged part of your heart portal. I saw pearl-colored energy entering the portal and leaving it as green energy. The pearl-colored threads were far more numerous than the existing green threads. At this point, I could feel the mushroom's power starting to fade, but I wanted to know the source of the pearl's power. I followed one of the pearl threads from your heart portal to your skin. The pearl energy appeared outside your body and funneled onto a thread. I backtracked the tread to another branch and found It began at your skin, too. I guess you receive pearl energy from a source outside yourself and convert it to healing energy in your heart portal. It is a wild guess and may not be accurate. I intended to investigate further, but the mushroom's power ran out, and I woke up on the bed."

Airalee sat quietly, thinking of what Maylore had told her.

"That is amazing," Airalee said. "You have kept this ability a secret from us for a long time. I worried you were very ill when you would sit and stare at the fire or some unseen object. I don't know what to think about your revelations, Maylore."

"I understand," Maylore replied, "I am sorry it caused you to worry. Gilriel and others thought it best to withhold the information. They thought I could become one of the missing they talk about."

"I assure you," Airalee said, "we will keep your secret to ourselves."

"Thank you. I want to be around for a long time yet," Maylore said.

"Do you have any more you want to tell me about your investigation?" Airalee asked.

"I know very little more than what I told you," Maylore said. "I thought my studies were already full of studying planet, fire, and wind energy. Adding this new field of interesting study will keep me very busy!" A groan from the bed announced that Jendrin was waking up.

"Jendrin needs to eat and drink before I give him a nightly sleep potion," Airalee said. "Will you help get dinner ready, dad?" she asked as she moved toward the bed.

"Of course," Maylore replied, preparing the pot of food.

"How are you feeling, Jendrin?" Airalee asked as she got to the bed.

"Hot," Jendrin replied as he pushed aside the blanket covering him. Airalee touched his forehead, finding it warmer than she expected.

"You may have a small fever," she replied. "Can you eat a before your sleeping potion?"

"I feel hot but hungry," Jendrin said. "I smell something good cooking."

"Airalee put together a stew a while ago, and it does smell good," Maylore said as he handed the bowl to Jendrin.

"Thank you both," Jendrin said as he started eating. Maylore and Airalee sat at the table, eating their dinner. The group was lost in their thoughts until Jendrin finished his dinner.

"Before I went to sleep," Jendrin said, "Maylore was going to try to find the source of Airalee's energy. Were you able to find out?" Maylore first looked to Airalee.

"You should tell him the whole story, dad," Airalee said. Maylore moved to the side of the bed as Airalee prepared the sleeping draft. He started telling Jendrin what he told Airalee. He explained what he knew of portals and how his and Airalee's looked. He included the story about Bert, which drew Jendrin's chuckle.

"Bert?" Jendrin said, "The bird should indeed come to visit us." Maylore continued describing Airalee's burnt heart portal and finding the healing energy coming from the back of her heart portal. He finished by telling the pearl energy coming from outside of her body.

"Fascinating!" Jendrin said. "Do you guess where the pearl energy originates?"

"I don't know where it comes from," Maylore said, shaking his head. "I suspect it comes from living things such as trees, plants, or animals, but that is a guess. It could even come from the stars!" he said, sitting back in his chair. Airalee brought the sleeping draft to Jendrin.

"Storytime is over," Airalee said. It's time to go back to sleep," she said as she passed him the bottle. Jendrin drank the contents without commenting.

"I will be dreaming of portals and power threads, I think," Jendrin said, passing the bottle back to her. "Assuming it doesn't get too hot in here," he said, laying back on the bed.

"I didn't think it was hot," Maylore said, looking at Airalee.

"It looks like he has a small fever," Airalee said, putting the bottle back on the table.

"I am still tired from the mushroom adventure," Maylore said, nodding. "I will do the evening routine and go to bed." Maylore bid Jendrin good night and left the hut.

It was dark, and most villagers were in their huts already. He finished his evening tasks and returned to the hut to find Airalee sitting on the bed. Jendrin appeared to be asleep as she wrote more notes in her book. "Good night, Airalee. Make sure you have skin contact with his wounds tonight," Maylore said, going to his room.

"I will," Airalee said. "I will be careful to touch his wounds tonight. Good night, dad." Airalee said. She added more notes about the plants they had found before feeling sleepy. She put the book aside and lay next to Jendrin. "This time, I will remove the robe from my arm and leg to be sure I have contact with him all night." She laid her bare arm and leg on him and slowly drifted off to sleep.

Hours later, Jendrin was sweating from the fever, causing her to sweat from his body heat. She pulled off her robe and let it fall on the floor. She resumed her position but found him too hot to be that close. She pushed herself back from him to allow cool air between them but kept contact with her hand and knee. She eventually returned to sleep.

CHAPTER 30 - MENDING

Airalee awoke before the twin suns rose. She felt freezing as she sat up in bed. Touching Jendrin's forehead, he felt cool, signaling the fever was in retreat. Casually gathering her robe from the floor, she slipped it back on. She retrieved the blanket from Jendrin's feet and covered him to keep him warm. She quietly rebuilt the fire and pushed in the water jug to warm it for later. Looking out the window, she found no one was stirring in the village. It appeared to be some time before dawn. She returned to sitting on the bed, peeking at the chest wound under the poultices. It seemed the same as yesterday. The injury was not swollen, and the skin seemed to mend beneath the stitches. She looked at his face, which appeared free of pain's distress.

"You appear to be getting better," she said aloud. She really studied his face for the first time. "Marisa is right," she sighed. "He is pretty and would likely make pretty children," she said, looking up. "Am I being influenced by Marisa, being jealous, protective, or am I considering my future?" Looking at Jendrin, she added, "I considered you an annoying brother to be tolerated by our circumstances. You are proving worthy of notice, a hero, and perhaps more. I must be sure that Marisa's notice of you does not color my choices." Airalee stood facing Jendrin. "Marisa is a calculating woman but shows wisdom in her planning." Looking at her hands, she said, "We would miss you if you did not survive." She shook her head after a few moments. "This is no time to think of such things," she reprimanded herself. "I will consider it further after you recover, and we have dealt with Oleg and the bandits."

Airalee decided that more sleep would help them both. She laid down on her side, covering herself with her robe. Rolling up her sleeve, she stretched her arm across his chest under the blanket, laying her hand on the wound. She placed her bare leg along his leg below his wound. She snuggled up to him and laid her head on his shoulder. A slight smile came to her lips as she drifted off to sleep.

"Are you comfortable, Airalee?" Maylore said as he entered the room sometime later. Airalee didn't react this time when his voice awoke her.

"Yes, I am, Dad," she replied, staying where she was. The sound of her voice awoke Jendrin, who noticed she was lying there.

"Good morning," Jendrin said. "I have a pretty bed companion again."

"You were supposed to stay asleep," Airalee said, sitting on the edge of the bed. "Now I have to get up," she said as she rose from the bed.

"Don't get up on my account," Jendrin said with a smile.

"My nightly healing time of you is over," Airalee said, finding her shoes.

"I should have kept my mouth shut," Jendrin said, slowly sitting up.

"I agree," Airalee replied. "You sometimes talk too much," she said, putting on her shoes. Jendrin chuckled as he adjusted the pillows and blanket.

"Dad," Airalee said, "His fever has broken, so we can leave him alone if you want to start your morning routine," she said to Maylore.

"I will gather some food for breakfast and meet you back here," Maylore said.

"All right," she replied, "I will do my morning routine and be back."

"I will be right here!" Jendrin said as they left the hut.

Maylore was preparing breakfast as Airalee returned with wood for the fire and healing herbs. She finished making new poultices as Maylore was ready to serve their breakfast.

Latel arrived to change the chamber pot and was invited to stay for breakfast. A knock came at the door as Marisa let herself in.

"Good morning," she said with a smile for everyone and moved to the bed. "Kai will be here soon, and I am here to prepare you," she said, pushing the blanket off the wounds and removing the chest poultice.

"I am getting used to you being forward," Jendrin said with a slight smile.

"Forward?" Marisa questioned. "You have yet to see me be forward. I have no trouble being forward to those who interest me."

"I do not doubt you," Jendrin said as Marisa removed poultices.

"Airalee," Marisa called. "This wound is looking better," turning to look at Airalee.

"I agree," Airalee said. "I examined both this morning and thought they looked better. We will see what Kai says."

Marisa moved to the leg wound and removed the poultice there.

"There is less swelling and no redness to the skin," Marisa said. "Much better today. I would guess we can remove the chest stitches soon, but the leg stitches will be a while," she said, standing.

"That would be nice," Jendrin said as he lay watching. "Maybe I can leave this bed and do a few routine things alone."

"We would all welcome that," Airalee said. There was a quick rap on the door, and Kai entered, walking without a crutch. Moving purposefully to the bed, she gave no greetings, only looking at the two wounds.

"This chest looks good," Kai said aloud to no one in particular. "We should remove the stitches soon. The leg will require more time." She looked at Jendrin's face. "You have no fever?" she asked, touching his forehead.

"He did," Airalee injected. "It broke last night." Kai looked over at Airalee.

"He lost his voice last night?" Kai asked, returning to look at Jendrin.

"I did have a fever, but not now," Jendrin replied.

"Good," Kai said. "Voice is back, too." Looking at Airalee, she said, "He is making a remarkable recovery. Keep changing the poultices. He may yet recover. Let him be awake more today and allow more visitors to see him. They will wear him out, and when they do, push them out so he sleeps." Kai stood and looked toward Latel.

"Latel, I could use some help with the next patient." Walking to the door, Kai said, "Airalee, we must look for more healing herbs today. Find me when you are ready. Jendrin will be fine while we are searching." Airalee nodded as both Kai and Latel left.

Jendrin flexed his shoulder slightly, trying to determine how much pain there would be. He found he could move it well enough to be useful. He started to move his leg to the side of the bed but stopped when the pain rang high.

"Would you find me weights to lift, Maylore?" Jendrin asked. "I need some physical activity to keep me from going nuts. Even a weight I can bounce up and down would help."

Marisa moved closer to Airalee with an evil smile on her face.

"I know of a weight he could bounce," Marisa said quietly to Airalee.

"His leg would not stand that pressure, Marisa," Airalee replied quietly. Marisa's face showed mock surprise as she stepped back.

"How did you know what I might be thinking?" Marisa said.

"I am beginning to know how you think," Airalee said. "You will have to wait a while longer."

Marisa laughed as Jendrin looked at them.

"What is so funny?" Jendrin asked.

"She does not think you can lift any weight," Airalee said. "I told her to let you try arm weights." Jendrin looked sideways at them.

"I hope Maylore doesn't bring back two large rocks," Jendrin said, looking at his right hand.

"If you found them too heavy, I would hold your rocks," Marisa said, laughing again. Jendrin looked at Airalee.

"She has been taking lessons from you," Jendrin said, looking at Airalee.

"I believe she is far ahead of me," Airalee said, smiling. "Besides, I am more discreet," she added, looking sternly at Marisa.

Maylore returned with a large and small rock. He handed them to Jendrin as he reached the bed.

"Try the large one in your left hand and the small one on the injured right side," Maylore said. "I found other weights if you prefer a different one."

"Thank you, Maylore," Jendrin replied, taking each rock. The light rock caused pain on the injured shoulder, while the left side felt good as he lifted the stones. "These will do fine. I will be wary of the right side to avoid overtaxing the stitches," he said, slowly lifting each rock. His right hand felt weak, and the rock bounced off the bed each time. Maylore stepped to the end of the bed.

"I would like to check the wounds before I set out for Gilriel's cave," Maylore said. Jendrin set the rocks aside as Airalee sat on the bed. Airalee placed one hand near the chest wound and the other near the leg wound. Maylore sat in the chair and concentrated blue energy onto the two injuries. Three sets of eyes watched him as he stared at the wounds. Maylore found it easier each time he used the blue energy to check the wounds. He did not take long before looking back at them.

"The chest wound has no infection," Maylore said. "It looks to be healing quickly. The leg wound has a small infection, but much less than yesterday. A few more days, and he should be much better."

"That is reassuring. Thanks, dad," Airalee said with relief in her voice. Marisa and Jendrin nodded but said nothing.

"When will you tell Kai about Airalee's healing ability?" Marisa asked Maylore. "She is suspicious of Jendrin's recovery from normally fatal infections."

Maylore looked at Airalee.

"That is up to Airalee to decide," Maylore said, standing. "If she decides to inform Kai, I will gladly add to the conversation." He looked around the room for his traveling pouch, then said, "I will gather a few things and go to Gilriel's cave. I want to see if he has returned and ask for his advice. I will also check the bird's status and try to contact you, Airalee."

"Understood," Airalee said, nodding. "I will help Kai gather herbs today. I will note when you try contacting me."

"I will tell the villagers that they can visit with Jendrin and chase them away when he tires," Marisa said.

"Hearing from others would be welcome," Jendrin said.

Maylore

Maylore walked the familiar path toward the cave, greeting villagers as he walked. Climbing up the path from the road, he watched for bears or other creatures that may be near the cave entrance. He saw no other animals as he entered the cave. He waved at the location where Bert may be sitting. The bird responded with a soft squawk and rustled his feathers.

466

"Hello, Gilriel," he said as he approached the central part of the cave. Silence greeted him as he scanned the cave. The furnishings looked to be untouched since his last visit. Dust gathered on the table, thick enough to leave a smear when he touched it. "Guess he is not back yet," he said as a rustle of feathers announced Bert's arrival. Bert sat atop his usual chair back, cocking his head each way, looking at Maylore. "Let's see if I can read anything new from the book," he said, looking at Bert. He retrieved the book from its hiding place and opened it to an arbitrary page.

"I would like to find information about healing, what portals a person may have, connecting a broken portal, cleaning fouled ones, and whatever else I can find here," Maylore said, setting the open book on the table. He looked for symbols he recognized from Gilriel's key. He found nothing in the key about healing and few references to portals. "Communication portal," he said aloud, looking at the book. Bert hopped down from his perch and tapped his beak on a symbol written on the page. "Why thank you, Bert," he said with amusement. Maylore's amusement faded as he said aloud, "You have probably seen these pages many times before with Gilriel and perhaps others. They do not refer to you as an intelligent bird without reason. You may understand far more than humans give you credit for." Looking at the rest of the keys, he did not see a symbol for the communication portal. "Gilriel said I was one of the few who might be able to use that portal. Since he could not, that may be why there is nothing in his key." Looking at Bert, he said, "I wonder if you understand some of our language? It would not surprise me." Bert watched him from the table.

Maylore decided not to dismiss Bert's tap as being arbitrary. He started to add notes to Gilriel's key but stopped short. "I do not know if the translation is correct. I could be wrong and corrupt this key," Maylore said, looking around the cave for an empty book to write in. He found blank scrolls, which he decided would accomplish the same thing.

"How do I want to create this?" he asked himself. "I think I will write it in our common language. Everyone could read it, but others will not have the skills to use it." Laughing aloud, he added, "I suspect the sorcerer society would not approve of me giving away their secrets. If I translated correctly, that is."

Maylore used the same format as the book and Gilriel's key. He copied the communication portal symbol and pictures onto the new scroll, added a standard language description, and ended it with a black square. "My first scroll entry," he said, looking at the single symbol on the new page.

"Let's see if Bert knows of other entries," he said, looking at Bert. "Heart portal?" Maylore asked. Bert sat quietly, looking at Maylore. "Let me try a picture," he said as he sent an image of him pointing to his heart to Bert. Bert looked at the page and shook his head. He tapped on the pages farther in the book. Maylore opened the tome to a point near Bert's tap. Bert looked at the page and tapped farther back. Maylore repeated the process until Bert tapped a symbol on the page. "Let me add that to my new key," Maylore said, copying the symbol onto his new page. Staring at the arcane words around it, he said, "What do you suppose the words and symbols around it mean?"

Maylore studied the lettering, trying to guess what they could mean. A few words matched Gilriel's key, allowing him to guess their meaning. "I think the next three symbols say power, shield, then weapon," he said as he looked from the key to the book. "I think that would be a good combination," Maylore said as he wrote: "heart portal, power, shield, and weapon ending with a black square."

Maylore started to ask Bert another question when the bird suddenly jumped back. Bert looked into the distance and flew out of the cave. Maylore called after him to return, but he was gone. Maylore sent him a picture of outstretched hands signaling, 'Where are you?' Maylore received a picture from Bert of a flock of birds finding a cache of their favorite worms for food. "The stomach calls," he said.

Maylore looked at the key to see if the word healing was attached to any other symbol. The symbols in the book and Gilriel's key are related to physical forces such as wind, fire, and planet. "Perhaps this book is for people like me. It is meant for those with physical energy use abilities versus internal abilities like Airalee's healing and plant identification." Maylore made some notes about it on his scroll and put them aside. "I will wait for Bert to return to see if he can ease my use of this book." The twin suns were already past halfway as he considered practicing communication and energy skills.

"Alright, Airalee, let's see if you hear me," he said as he looked inward at his communication dome. He saw that Airalee was not far away, so he sent a picture and a verbal greeting. As expected, he did not receive a reply. He looked for Gilriel's dot on the dome but could not find it. "Perhaps there is a limit to the range I can talk," he said. He looked for Bert's location, which appeared to be near Airalee. Maylore sent him a picture asking what Bert saw. He promptly received a picture of worms.

Smiling to himself at one success, he practiced using earth, fire, and wind energy. He used destructive twists and additive forces. With each practice session, he could tell he had improved his ability to control the forces.

"What if I combine two forces at once?" he thought. He gathered fire energy into a ball and assembled the planet's energy around the ball. He threw the ball at the opposite wall. The fire stayed compacted in a ball until it hit the opposite wall, where it burst into a bright blast of fire. Surprised at the result, he repeated the experiment several times, getting similar results. Looking at the sunlight coming through the holes in the ceiling, he noticed it was late.

"I should return to the hut soon to help Airalee," he said aloud. "One more session before I move on," he said as he lined a group of small sticks on his practice rock. He placed a piece of animal hide with holes as his target across the room. 'Gather wind and follow it with fire,' he thought as a new test. He pushed the wind onto the sticks, aiming it at the hide. He followed that with a fire burst. The

469

sticks stuck into the hide as the fire charred the sticks. "Perhaps that could be useful," he said as he approached the target. Pulling on the sticks, he found several would not come out. Looking at the hide, he saw the stick appeared to be glued to the hide. "Somehow, the stick is attached to the hide," he said, looking at the penetration sites.

A flurry of feather noise announced Bert's return. The bird landed somewhere in his usual area and was silent. Maylore sent him a picture of a greeting and received an image of Bert asleep with ruffled feathers. Maylore chuckled, saying, "Good night, Bert," as he cleaned the area. He gathered fruit from the cave's protected area and returned to the hut.

Airalee

Airalee walked to Kai's hut as Kai returned from her morning rounds.

"Airalee," she said as they met on the path. "Get two gathering bags, and we will start collecting." Airalee nodded and went to the storage hut to pick up two bags. She returned to find Kai at the door of her hut.

"We will search the mountainside meadow today. We have gathered what we should from our sunset meadow and must let the rest grow," Kai said as she started toward the road. "Now that Jendrin is getting better, I would like you to join me in visiting with our elders and sick people daily. Most days, I complete the round within an hour. Most elders just want someone to listen to them as they complain about their ills. We will listen, check their health and supplies, then move on."

"I will be glad to help," Airalee replied as they crossed the road toward the meadow.

"We need to collect more of these pain-reducing plants," Kai said as she spotted a group growing nearby. "Sharaera appears to be near death. Her pain increases daily, and her son worries about her pain. He knows his mother will die. He just doesn't want her to be in pain.

470

If we give her too much more, the potion will kill her first." Looking at Airalee, she asked, "Jendrin should be using less each day. How much does he use now?"

"He asks for it at night so he can sleep," Airalee said. "He prefers to be awake during the day even if it is painful."

"He is recovering remarkably well," Kai said. "I feared the infections would claim him." Kai started moving again.

"Yes," Airalee said, following along. "Maylore believes I have a healing touch," she said as Kai turned around.

"Why does he think that?" Kai asked.

"Maylore can see energy flows when he looks from within himself," Airalee said. "He says he sees a green energy flow from my skin to Jendrin's wounds when I am close to them." Kai straightened up with a surprised look on her face.

"We have a sorcerer and a healer in our camp?" Kai said in amazement. "I heard Maylore could see the planet's energy but did not know he could control it. If you have a healing ability, you would be the only human with it still alive. It is excellent news to me, Airalee," Kai finished with the first big smile Airalee had seen on Kai's face. Airalee felt herself sigh.

"I was not sure how you would feel about it," Airalee said. "I thought you might feel I was intruding on your work."

Kai's face showed shock as she threw her hands in the air and cackled.

"Girl, I would welcome help from a Tocor if they could help heal our villagers!" Kai laughed. Composing herself again, Kai said, "I will not live forever. I would one day like to move to an elder's hut and live in their silence and peace. It is not yet my time, but I am planning on others like you to take my place someday."

"Perhaps someday I will be worthy of your job," Airalee said with a smile.

Kai laughed again, somehow erasing the age lines on her face.

"I have experience, that is all," Kai said. "I hope to teach you and perhaps a few others what I know and create better healers for all of us."

"I hope to be up to the challenge," Airalee said.

"Let's gather as we talk," Kai said, walking again. Airalee spotted some healing herbs and added them to her pouch. She followed close to Kai.

"I was concerned about Jendrin," Airalee said. "He seems to be better this morning, however."

"He did," Kai replied. "It made me suspicious of his quick recovery from such a serious infection. I have seen many villagers die of infection rather than the accident they had suffered. I wondered if you had some secret knowledge of healing infections you kept from me."

"I did not know about it until Maylore discovered it," Airalee said. "We were both surprised at what he found."

"The ability to touch and heal someone is amazing," Kai said. "Do you touch the person once, or how often do you need to touch them?"

"I must touch the wound constantly to help heal," Airalee replied. "Maylore says the green energy flow from my skin is minimal and absorbs an infection's energy or is absorbed by the healing area once the infection is gone. I have to sleep next to him with my hand and leg near his wounds to give him my energy."

"The healing you can do would apply to dire circumstances," Kai said. "To have you spend whole nights with patients is a huge undertaking. I am sure the men would be pleased to have a pretty woman touching them, but it is not the best for quick healing." Tilting her head slightly, Kai added, "You have become close to Jendrin since the attack. I realize he saved your life, but you are just

472

his nursemaid. That is enough payment. You do not owe him your body as payment," she finished with a wag of her finger.

"I understand, Kai," Airalee replied. "I owe Jendrin for his assistance, but I am repaying him as my adopted brother's nurse. I do not feel I owe him anything else. Should other situations confront me, I will choose actions as I see fit."

Kai continued to face her, expecting Airalee to have more to say.

"Marisa is considering children," Kai said. "Has she spoken to you about it?"

"Marisa and I have discussed her having children several times," Airalee said. "I considered it a possibility for my distant future but have recently changed my mind. If I am to have children, I should do it while I am young to handle the task. Marisa seems intent on having a child soon. I now would welcome the idea of raising them together."

Kai wagged her finger at her again.

"Do not let Marisa's decision affect your choices," Kai said. "I find it hard to believe you would let that happen."

"She did influence me, that is true," Airalee said with a smile. "I have not decided yet, but I am seriously considering it now."

"Do you know the custom for baby seeders in Molia?" Kai asked.

"I have heard women choose who seeds their babies," Airalee said.

"True," Kai said. "Come, sit with me, and we will discuss the history of Molia and Olona," she said, sitting atop a nearby downed tree. "You must know the history if you become our new healer."

"In the distant past, the population of Molia was small," Kai started. The human population was too small to prevent inbreeding within a village. Some of the men and women even became sterile. The Tocor and Lemidge had larger populations but had similar problems. Beacons, Lemidge, and Tocor leaders gathered to consider the situation. Their solution was to send a small group of seeders from each village to other villages. They determined four men from each race would travel to each human, Lemidge, and Tocor village in Molia. Each of the four men would seed the same women to ensure they received sufficient seed and prevent knowing who created a child. It seemed a good plan until things didn't go as planned. Tocor women accepted all groups but only created children from visiting Tocor. Lemidge women were not interested in human men and rejected their advances, although the human men were willing. They accepted the Tocor men but did not produce children. Only visiting Lemidge men created their children. Human women accepted all groups but could not make children from the Tocor or Lemidge seeders. Visiting human men did create human children. The human women, however, found the Lemidge men's mating scents caused them to lose self-control and hallucinate. The women would rejoice in their visions and ask the Lemidge to send their seeders each summer. You experienced their visit not long ago."

"Yes, I did," Airalee replied with a large grin. "It was relaxing and extremely pleasant. I didn't even see his face during seeding. Instead, I saw a burst of colors, sound, and exhilarating joy rush from my middle to my head. I remember laying on my back with visions and colors swirling around me. It seemed like a short time to me before my head cleared. I remember the Lemidge and the women in chairs were gone.

"Were your men surprised with your encounter?" Kai asked.

"I did not tell my companions any of this," Airalee said as Kai smiled.

"It is the same for all human women," Kai said. "After a few sessions, the scents no longer affect you. I attend the sessions to keep the activities orderly since they do not affect me. If you continue in the healer role, you will organize and monitor the sessions when I retire."

"I can do that," Airalee said. "Do seeders still travel the valley?"

"They do," Kai said. "The Tocor send four seeders to other Tocor villages. The Lemidge has two festivals each summer. Large groups of Lemidge men and women congregate at their mountain homes twice each season.

"Do we have immigration from other villages?" Airalee asked.

"We have a few leave our village each season," Kai said. "A similar number replaces them. You and your companions are examples of that."

"I wish we knew something about where we came from and why we are here," Airalee said. "We have been here for many sunrises and still have no idea of our origins."

"I wish I knew something to help you," Kai said, smiling again. "I was born here. It is all I know."

"I am content here," Airalee said. "Maylore is happy to stay, and Jendrin seems to put aside his desire to travel the valley."

"He is developing an interest in you, which is why he put it aside." Kai chuckled. "He has attracted the attention of others who have requested him to be one of their baby seeders."

"He has not said anything about that," Airalee said.

"I have not discussed it with him yet," Kai replied. "When multiple women want the same baby seeder, they come to me to arrange the seeding order. I will visit with each man who optionally accepts or rejects being in a seeding group. I will inform him he may have to be in a group multiple times before the baby starts. No man is asked to seed more than four women at a time."

"I doubt they see it as an arduous task," Airalee said with a crooked smile.

"They do not at first," Kai said. "Some women reject all of their seed even after thirty attempts. By then, the men feel drained of all seed, and I stop the seeding."

"Who selects the men? "Airalee asked.

"Most women choose one to four to seed her simultaneously," Kai said. "That allows one or more men to be infertile and still produce a child. The village is more likely to assist with the child since no one knows who the original seeder was. If they wish me to choose the traditional four-man seeding party, I will gather four to perform the task. Marisa has asked for specific seeders, and I have arranged all except one. Jendrin has not been asked, but Marisa has another in mind if he rejects her.

"Does Jendrin know about this process?" Airalee asked.

"No," Kai replied, "I will inform him of the requests when he is well. You may tell him of the request and the process if you wish. Marisa and two others have already asked for his seed."

Airalee was not surprised by Kai's information but wondered how Jendrin would feel about it.

"I believe you should inform him," Airalee said.

"I will do that," Kai replied. "Someday, your task will be to align the women with their seeders. You would also be charged with forming the traveling seeder group. It is not a difficult task since many women choose not to have children. I did not want children and others to have chosen the same path. It becomes challenging when women from other villages request one of our seeders."

"Your position in the village is more challenging than caring for the sick and injured," Airalee said.

"I like my position," Kai said. "Time teaches you how to handle tasks without losing your mind," she said, ending with a smile. "Shall we continue our gathering?"

Airalee nodded and pushed herself off the log. The two gathered full bags before returning to the village. The twin suns had reached midway in the sky, and villagers were gathering for soup.

Kai entered the storage hut and stood by the sorting table, where she indicated a chair for Airalee.

"I want you to sort our collection while I watch," Kai said. "I hope to leave this task solely to you shortly." Airalee separated the plants into piles along the table. Some were for healing, another pile was for pain wound clotters, and another was for plants she did not recognize. Kai watched with a half-smile as Airalee completed the sorting.

"Good," Kai said. "You even sorted the weeds I added to test your knowledge." She pointed to the storage bins and said, "Add them to our storage bins, then we can eat lunch. After lunch, you can make new pain potions for our village and Jendrin."

Airalee stored the plants and then joined Kai at a table for lunch. As Airalee arrived, several villagers chatted with Kai.

"Airalee will be helping me with healing duties," Kai told people at the table as Airalee sat down. "We will work together on village ills until I feel she can do it alone. Then you may see only her at your side instead of me," Kai said, smiling. Airalee and Kai ate while chatting with several groups as villagers came and went. Kai repeated her talk with each new group about having Airalee do healing tasks.

"Airalee, it is time we create new potions and poultices. Good day to you all," Kai said, looking at the villagers and rising from the table.

"That is the largest number of villagers I spent time talking to," Airalee said.

"I wanted the largest number of people to know you are working with me," Kai said. "It is the reason we sat here so long. I wanted to be sure many crafting heads were here so they would spread the word quickly." Kai rose from the table as she led the way back to the hut.

Kai and Airalee spent the rest of the afternoon creating more potions and poultices. It was very late afternoon when Airalee returned to the companions' hut.

Jendrin

Jendrin watched his companions leave, wishing he could go himself. There was much he needed to do, but he realized if he moved his leg, he would require pain medication to calm it this time. He sighed, causing Marisa to turn to him.

"Too much pain?" she asked.

"No," Jendrin replied. "I feel trapped on this bed when I have many things to do. I would like to be awake enough to help plan how to handle the bandits and perhaps rescue Gilda. I must create a defensive weapon and convince the council we need a defensive force. I would like to fish, build, and hunt animal fur. I would even welcome cleaning and tanning hides!" he said, waving his arms.

Marisa thought for a moment before replying.

"I could bring you a few of those poles you made to cut on if you wish," Marisa said.

"Good suggestion!" Jendrin said, brightening. "I can carve on those sitting here."

"I will also pass word for people to visit you as Kai suggested," Marisa said. "They worry about you too."

"Excellent ideas!" Jendrin said. "Thank you, Marisa," he said, smiling at her. Marisa smiled back as she left the hut. Latel soon arrived, followed by Rendal and Fenhild. They stood chatting with Jendrin, who visibly enjoyed the company. Marisa returned, carrying two poles for Jendrin to work on as the visitors stood near the table. Marisa pushed past them to set the poles near the side of the bed. She sat in the chair beside the bed. The three men stopped talking as Marisa entered the room.

"My guard for the day," Jendrin said, smiling at Marisa.

478

"You finally figured it out," she said, looking at him. The three men chuckled and resumed their conversation with Jendrin. Other villagers replaced the three men as the morning wore on in a steady stream of men and women. Jendrin found himself answering the same questions each time but was pleased to see others come to visit. Marisa paid close attention to him, watching for signs of fatigue. Midday came, and Marisa left the hut to get lunch from the kitchen. When she returned, two men from the fur tanning group chatted with Jendrin. They discussed using the new techniques Gulstan had taught them for tanning. She could see he was interested in what they were saying, but she could tell he was tired. She waited for a break in their conversation before interrupting.

"Visiting time is over for now," Marisa said. "Jendrin needs to eat and sleep," she said, moving into the bed chamber. The two men nodded and wished Jendrin well as they left.

"It was good to see all of them, but I am tired," he said, accepting the food bowl from her. Marisa sat on the chair and ate with him as they recounted the visitors' conversations. Finishing their meal, Marisa gathered the bowls and went outside to wash them. She returned to find Jendrin asleep. Sitting at the table, she rested her head and fell asleep.

Maylore returned to the companion's hut to find Marisa sleeping with her head on the table. Looking into the adjacent room, Jendrin was stripping bark off one of the poles.

"Greetings, Maylore," he said in a low voice.

"Are you feeling better?" Maylore asked, entering his room.

"As long as I don't move the leg too much, I am good," Jendrin said with a smile.

"Good," Maylore replied, setting his satchel on the table. He added more wood to the fire as Marisa raised her head.

"Maylore," she said, stretching her arms. Looking at Jendrin, she said, "I see you are awake."

"I have been awake for quite a while," he said, working on cleaning the staff.

"I will leave Maylore on watch while I attend to other duties," she said, standing up. Looking to Maylore, she said, "Jendrin had many visitors today. He should eat, drink, and sleep more to improve his leg. I will return later to check on him," she said as she walked out the door. Maylore waved goodbye to her and sat down at the table.

"I can offer you some delicious fruit from Gilriel's garden," Maylore said as he emptied the fruit onto the table.

"That would be very welcome," Jendrin said, looking at the fruit on the table. Maylore cut the fruit and took a bowl to Jendrin as Airalee opened the door.

"Hello, dad, hero," Airalee said as she walked to the storage area. She put the new potions and poultices on the shelf.

"I see you were busy making potions," Maylore said as he continued cutting the fruit.

"Yes," Airalee replied. "I joined Kai for herb gathering and made potions and poultices afterward. Have you been looking after Jendrin all day?"

"No, Marisa was here all day," Maylore said. "I just arrived as she left to attend to her needs."

"Marisa has been a big help to all of us," Airalee said, moving to the table.

"Indeed," Maylore replied as he passed her fruit.

"Thank you," she replied as she ate the ripe fruit. She sat on the bed, looking at Jendrin's wounds. "It looks good," she said, looking at Jendrin. "Is there any fever?" she asked. Jendrin set the staff aside.

"No," Jendrin said. "I feel good, except my leg complains," he said while eating a bite of fruit.

"He complains. He must be getting better," Airalee said as the door opened, and Marisa entered with a stew pot.

"Dinner," Marisa said, setting the pot on the table. Airalee rose and helped fill bowls and pass one to Jendrin. They sat at the table and recounted some of their day. Maylore gathered the bowls from everyone as they finished and took them outside to wash.

I bit you all good night," Marisa said as she stood.

"Good night, Marisa," Airalee said. "Thank you for staying with Jendrin."

Marisa waved as she left the hut.

"I will put new poultices on your wounds, and then we all can sleep," Airalee said, gathering her supplies.

"I look forward to the day I can be independent again," Jendrin said, laying back in the bed. Maylore returned as Airalee finished the new poultices and tossed the old ones into the fire.

"Dad," Airalee said, "Would you recheck his wounds tonight while I get his sleeping potion?"

"Of course," Maylore said, moving to a chair at the end of the bed. Maylore looked inward and asked the blue energy to enter Jendrin's wounds. Airalee returned with the sleeping dose as Maylore looked up. "He still has a small infection on his leg, but the chest wound is near to complete healing," he said, sitting up in the chair. Jendrin started to resist the potion but accepted it when Airalee insisted he take it.

"I will ask Kai if we can remove the chest stitches," Airalee said as she returned the empty bottle to the table.

"I will do my nightly routine, and then you can go," Maylore said, standing up.

481

"I will go with you, dad," Airalee said. "Jendrin will be asleep soon and does not need watching."

"Alright," Maylore said as they left the hut. When they returned, Jendrin was asleep, and Maylore bid her goodnight as he went to his room. Airalee removed her robe and used it as a blanket as she lay next to Jendrin, her arm across his chest and knee on his leg.

CHAPTER 31 - HAMMER TIME

Sunrises sped by as activity in the village continued as before. Marisa worked with Mirtha to integrate the new foods Airalee had proven safe to eat. The new foods expanded the palettes of the villagers and allowed existing foods to last longer. Fewer fishing days were needed, and trading with other villages for meat decreased. Marisa continued to help Airalee with Jendrin's care, but Jendrin required less daily care. Airalee had removed Jendrin's stitches at Kai's direction. The stitch removal hurt, but he would not let her see it. The wounds still needed more healing but no longer required poultices.

Jendrin was able to return to his old morning and evening routine. He washed in the bath area independently and helped haul wood for its heat. He continued to work on the quarterstaff, removing some of the outer bark and smoothing the rigid inner core with oil.

Maylore trekked up to Gilriel's cave each day to find it empty. With each empty trip, he felt sadness and worry for Gilriel's safety. He continued practicing his skills with planet, fire, and air energies as his skills improved with each. He practiced using the communication portal, but only Bert would answer him. Airalee would inform him she felt the knock on her throat when he returned to the village hut, but discreet questions to others saw no result.

Airalee continued to learn from Kai's teaching. She helped gather herbs, mushrooms, and food plants. Airalee conspired with Kai to devise a potion to slow the bandits' libido, but no men in the village were willing to try it. She started a more extensive herb garden, planting healing and pain-reducing plants. Kai sent her to a few villagers when they requested healing. Many were strains requiring pain medication or cuts needing cleaning and stitches. Quiet times would find her adding entries to her book on plants and herbs. She would prepare their meal most nights while Jendrin or Maylore would clean up afterward. At bedtime, she asked Maylore to check Jendrin's wounds with her probing the area. He would verify they were healing until one night, he told her they were healed. Airalee continued to sleep next to Jendrin. When Maylore arose lately, he would find Airalee was just putting her robe on when she entered the common area.

A chill wind greeted this new day as Airalee arose and slipped on her robe. She built the fire and looked for a warmer tunic in the hut. Putting on the tunic, she stored the shorter robe inside the storage area. Maylore appeared at his door.

"The snow must be coming soon," Maylore said. "There is a definite snap to the air."

"I am afraid so, dad," Airalee said. "Mirtha says the village has plenty of supplies for the snow time, but it will still be cold."

"Ah, the crisp air," Jendrin said, entering the room. Jendrin lost the odd feeling he had about sleeping with his companion as his wounds dramatically improved with her healing powers.

"Your turn to collect breakfast," Airalee said as she passed him the cooking pot.

"Be right back," Jendrin said as he took the pot and left the hut.

"What do you have planned for the day, dad?" she asked, sitting at the table.

"I was going back to the cave to see if I could get Bert to look for Gilriel," Maylore said. "I also hope to add more information to my scroll. What is your plan?" he asked.

"I told Kai I would help her tend to the elders," Airalee said. "She wants to check my solo healing. Jendrin does not require us to help him, so time with Marisa would be welcome. We plan a late afternoon bath and a visit with Lafrea to see what jewelry she has." The door opened as Jendrin returned with a sloshing pot he had placed near the fire.

"I got us some fish, mushrooms, plants, and beans," Jendrin said. "I added some herbs you normally use to the pot and hot water from the kitchen."

"Sounds good," Maylore said as he moved to the table. The companions cleaned up the hut and set the table while they waited for the breakfast to cook. Stirring the pot, Airalee announced it was ready to eat. The companions shared small talk as they ate their breakfast.

"I will wash our dishes," Airalee said as she gathered the empty bowls and went outside.

"It looks like there are several more meals in this pot," Jendrin said as he moved it back near the fire. He added more water to ensure the pot didn't go dry.

"I am off to Gilriel's cave," Maylore said as he stood up.

"See you tonight?" Jendrin asked.

"I plan on it," Maylore replied as he gathered his satchel. Waving farewell, he left the hut. Jendrin waved to him as he gathered the five quarterstaffs he was working on. Choosing one, Jendrin tried to see where he should start on it. Airalee returned, placing the bowls on the table. She walked over to the row of quarterstaffs and absently picked one in particular.

"This is your staff," she said, presenting it to Jendrin. "You must remove all the outside wood to the clear wood underneath. Use the oil from your body to condition it for you; let no one else use it," she said with a blank look and a distant stare. She collected the bowls from the table and walked to the storage hut to put them in their place.

"Why should I remove all of the outside wood?" Jendrin asked as she turned back around. "Would it not be easier to grip if I left some inner bark on it for handholds?" Airalee looked at him with a quizzical look on her face.

"Remove what?" Airalee asked.

"You said I should remove all wood to the center from this quarterstaff and oil it," Jendrin said.

Airalee looked confused.

"I didn't say anything," she replied. Jendrin didn't know what to say, so he dropped the subject like he had done with her in the swamp.

"This one is slightly longer than the others," he said aloud, attempting to deflect any additional comment. Airalee looked at him like he was hearing things and gathered her satchel.

"Back tonight," she said as she left.

"Goodbye, Airalee," he said, watching her go. He sliced farther down to where the clear wood began on the staff. "There is a lot more wood to be removed," he said as he started cutting the staff.

Airalee

Airalee joined Kai as she was cleaning her hut. Looking up to see Airalee enter, she picked up her medical pouch.

"Good," Kai said. "We will get started on our rounds." Kai stored a few items in the bag. "If you would resupply your bag with pain potions and bandages, we will be on our way." Airalee added the requested items to her bag as Kai finished her cleanup.

"Would you carry the bag for me?" Kai asked.

"Of course," Airalee replied, picking up the medical bag as they left the hut. They visited several villagers that Airalee had helped with injuries. All of them told Kai they were happy with Airalee's healing efforts. After leaving the last hut, Kai smiled, hearing that the villagers were pleased. They started up the rise to the elders' huts when the zephyr hit their faces at the crest of the slope.

"We must roll down the insulating layers in their huts soon," Kai said. "Today will still be warm for them, but we will roll down the window coverings for them," Kai said, pulling her robe closer. "We will start with Melronna. She was in good health two days ago and seemed to know the snow was coming soon." Kai knocked on her door as Melronna called to them.

"Come in," Melronna said. The two entered the hut to find Melronna weaving a complex design into cloth as she sat at the table. Looking up, she said, "Welcome, Kai," as Airalee stepped up beside Kai. "You brought Airalee, too. Welcome, Airalee." Melronna seemed to stare past her as she said, "Your daughter doesn't follow you now. She has moved to your baby chamber. She will be a great addition to the village." Melronna's focus faded, and her gaze returned to them. Kai looked surprised and looked at Airalee.

"You will bear a child?" Kai asked.

Airalee looked somewhat surprised.

"No," Airalee said. "I don't believe so."

Melronna looked again at Airalee.

"You are with child?" Melronna asked in surprise.

Kai looked at Melronna.

"You just said she was with child," Kai said. "What makes you say that, Melronna?"

"I didn't say that. You just did, not I!" Melronna said. Kai and Airalee looked quizzically at each other before Kai spoke.

"We will discuss it later," Kai said. Melronna pointed to the two chairs.

"Please sit and visit," Melronna said. "The snow will be here soon, and it may be too cold to leave." Kai and Airalee sat as Kai scanned the room.

"Are you feeling well, Melronna?" Kai asked.

"Yes, very well," she replied. "I worry about getting wood for the fire when the snow arrives."

"Beacon has already organized for young villagers to bring wood and food to all our elders," Kai said. "If the snow becomes dangerous, he will move you all to the council hut. You don't need to worry." Melronna felt a wave of relief on her face.

"That is good news," she said. "The snow will start in ten sunrises, and the air will be colder this season. I can feel it is coming in the wind."

"You have gained prophecy?" Kai asked.

"No, but living alone allows me to concentrate on natural things," Melronna said. "The wind seems to whisper its intentions to me."

"Is this why you think Airalee is with child?" Kai asked. Melronna looked at Airalee.

"I did not say she was with child," Melronna said. "You asked her, and I wondered if it was true." Kai chuckled and decided to drop the subject.

"If you feel lonely," Kai said, "Meliniel is living alone and wants to move to an elder's hut."

"I know Meliniel!" Melronna said, brightening. "She is quiet; we got along well in the past. She would be welcome to the other bed," she said, pointing at the second bed across the room. "Please invite her to move here." Kai nodded. The rest of the visit was small talk of new foods, Jendrin's recovery, and other village subjects. The conversation continued until Melronna appeared to tire.

"It is time for us to visit the rest of the elders," Kai said. "I will tell Meliniel of your invitation. We will see you again in a few days." Melronna smiled as they stood to leave.

"Visit anytime," Melronna said as the two left the hut. Selakiir's hut was the next one to visit. The hut was quiet as they approached. Kai knocked softly on the door in case he was resting.

"Come in!" came a quick response. Kai opened the door to find Selakiir alone in the hut, slicing some fruit at the table. "Welcome, ladies, please sit," he said, putting aside the fruit.

"Are you doing well?" Kai asked as she sat.

"Yes, very well," Selakiir replied. "My son was just here and left me some fruit. He stocked my wood pile, leaving me with few worries."

"Good." Kai said, "We will prepare the elder huts for snow season soon. Melronna believes snow will be here in 10 sunrises." Kai then repeated the Beacon's plan for food, wood, and evacuation if needed. Selakiir nodded as she talked. "You appear to be doing well."

"I am for an old man," Selakiir said with a smile. "I am fortunate to have family visit each day. I am now due for a walk along the cliff to stretch my legs."

"Would you like to join us?" Kai asked.

"I did not mean for you to leave," Selakiir said.

"We have many to check on today," Kai said. "We will go outside with you as we move on to the next hut," Kai said, standing up.

"Thank you for stopping," Selakiir said, rising from the table. The two women followed Selakiir out the door as he walked toward the sea, and they moved onto Phaerl and Adandir's nearby hut. Their knock on the door went unanswered. Opening the door, Kai saw the hut was empty.

"Many days, they help with the children in the baby care area," Kai said, looking toward Airalee. "I suspect that is where they are now," she said, closing the door. "They have plenty of wood and food."

They continued to Sharaera's hut as the gentle breeze blew over them. Airalee knocked on the door.

"She cannot come to the door any longer," Kai said. "She may be sitting or sleeping." She opened the door to find Sharaera sitting at the table.

"Ladies," Sharaera weakly said as they approached the table. As Kai and Airalee came near, she pointed to the chairs. The desire to speak was on her face, but she could not form words.

"We stopped to check on you, not to disturb you, Sharaera," Kai said. Sharaera shook her head and pointed to her mouth and then Kai's.

"You want me to speak?" Kai asked. Sharaera nodded as Kai recounted the Beacon's plan and some village gossip. Sharaera tried to smile, then pointed to Airalee. Airalee told her she had joined Kai's group in collecting herbs, plants, and mushrooms. She related the general story of tending to Jendrin and a few other villagers. Sharaera's face slowly turned sad as she pointed to her bed and held her hand out for help. Both women jumped up, with Kai taking her hand and Airalee readying the bed. Sharaera lay on the bed as Airalee covered her with her heavy blankets. Sharaera whispered something as her eyes closed. Werloth opened the door, surprised to see the two women there.

"I was just coming back to help her into bed," Werloth said. She usually sits briefly for water and fruit, then sleeps again. Please come to my hut so she is not disturbed," he said, opening the door and moving to his hut to hold it. Kai entered the hut as Werloth held the door for Airalee. Airalee stopped, indicating he should go in first.

"You don't trust me?" he asked.

"No," Airalee replied simply. Werloth laughed and entered his hut as Airalee followed him. Werloth sat on his bed as Airalee and Kai sat in chairs.

"I fear Mother will not last this snow season," Werloth said, looking at Kai. "She rallies some days and spends others sleeping. She refuses the pain potions but uses the sleep potion many nights. I lowered the window coverings since the wind's bite would not help her. She is unhappy since she cannot see outside. Late today, I will take her outside and wrap her in blankets so she can watch the sunset. It seems to be one of the few things that make her happy.

Kai indicated to Airalee to open the bag of potions.

"How many sleep potions do you have?" Kai asked.

"One," he replied. "It is nearly empty," he said.

"Pass him two more potions, Airalee." Kai said, "We will take the extra pain potions from you," she added.

"Well, there is only one," Werloth said. "I use it to slow the pain in my mouth."

"Pain in your mouth?" Kai questioned, pulling a small flat stick from the bag and moving it to his side.

"Open your mouth," Kai instructed, brokering no argument. Werloth opened his mouth as Kai looked inside. "Yes, there is at least one infected tooth. Airalee, come see if you spot it." Airalee took the stick and used it to search his mouth. One tooth was dark compared to the others.

"Is this one you mean?" Airalee asked.

"It is," Kai replied. "We will have to remove it. Do you see others?" Airalee's hunt for the problem had distracted her from realizing Werloth was stroking her hip. Instead of jumping back this time, she hit the bad tooth with the examination stick. Werloth's face went white as he almost howled from the pain.

"I told you before," Airalee said, "keep your hand to yourself," she said, staying where she was. Werloth's hand dropped to his lap.

"I will give him the sleeping potion," Kai said, getting a bottle from the bag.

"No, I will do it," Airalee said. "The bottle serves as a hammer for those who misbehave." Werloth seemed shaken by her threat and watched her wide-eyed. "He will not attempt that again today," she said, taking the bottle from Kai. She waited for him to calm down before saying, "Be good and drink a third of this so we can pull your tooth."

Werloth drank the amount she suggested before looking toward Kai.

"Kai, would you pull the tooth?" Werloth said. "I fear Airalee will want revenge."

Airalee laughed aloud at his, believing she would try to harm him physically.

"I would find other ways to exact revenge, not that way." Airalee said. Kai smiled as Werloth shrank back on the bed. Werloth was soon asleep as Kai got a long, thin rock and a small hammer rock from her bag. Kai gave the tools to Airalee.

"Put the small rock near the middle bottom of the tooth and hit the rock with the hammer until the tooth breaks loose," Kai said. Airalee did as she suggested. She needed two small taps to break the tooth free. Kai swabbed the tooth stub to stop the bleeding. She examined his mouth to see if more work was required. "It looks like only that tooth was bad. The rest of the area looks good. He is fortunate we caught it now." Airalee nodded and placed the rocks that needed cleaning in the satchel's outside pocket. "You handled him well," Kai said. "He will think harder next time before he touches you."

"I have finally grown accustomed to hugging and friendly touches from my companions and friends," Airalee said. "I no longer jump when touched. A severe reaction to his unwelcome touches seems to reinforce his need to do it again," she said. "Perhaps calmly using a large stick will dissuade him."

"Good girl," Kai said, "Remember, any man or woman in this village will come to your aid if you yell for help." Airalee nodded as she picked up the satchel. "He will sleep for a time and have a sore mouth," Kai said. "I will leave him this pain medication."

"Kelkalyn is our last stop," Kai said as she opened the door. The two women approached the last hut as its door suddenly opened. Kelkalyn stood in the doorway looking out to sea. He saw Kai and started to walk in her direction. He took a step and then saw Airalee was with her. He turned around and ran away from them.

"He is an odd man," Airalee said, watching him run.

"We will check his hut, then go back to the village," Kai said, smiling. They found the hut was well supplied. Kai left only one herb for him to use. "He appears to be using the quieting herb since only a small amount remains. Some people still seem to worry him," she said, smiling at Airalee.

"I seem to spawn fear in several men," Airalee said with a slight smile.

"Kelkalyn is fearful of strangers," Kai said, "especially women with big stones," she said with a chuckle.

"He has not reproached me," Airalee said. "He has nothing to fear from me. He seemed frightened of me from our first meeting."

"You should not be over-concerned about Kelkalyn," Kai said. "He mistrusts most people."

"I would like him to talk with Maylore," Airalee said. "I think Maylore could learn from him."

"I will ask Rendal to arrange a visit," Kai said. "Kelkalyn will likely allow the visit if the Beacon is with him. Let's return to the village."

"If you don't need me," Airalee said, "I told Marisa we would sit in the bathing pool and relax today."

"Good idea," Kai said. "Do you plan to tell anyone about what Melronna said?"

Airalee shook her head.

"I don't think so," Airalee said. "I don't think Melronna foresees the future."

"I have not known Melronna to do it in the past," Kai said as they walked. Marisa approached them as they descended the slope toward the village.

"Ready for a soak?" Marisa asked. "I have built up the water-warming fire enough to warm the pool."

"I am ready," Airalee replied as they waved goodbye to Kai.

Maylore

Maylore traveled to Gilriel's cave to discover that he had still not returned. Bert was not in the cave, but everything else seemed untouched.

"I wonder if I should just move up here," Maylore mused aloud. "When Gilriel returns, I could move back to the hut or remain with him. I would still be able to visit with my companions but would have more space here to practice."

Maylore sat at the table and concentrated on his communication portal. He found Bert's dot and requested that Bert return to the cave. He rotated through the other dots on the dome, sending a picture and words of greeting. He did not expect any answer and did not receive any. Bert arrived at the cave with a squawk and landed on the back of the chair.

"Welcome, Bert," Maylore said. The bird cocked its head at him as if to listen. Maylore sent a picture of Gilriel, attempting to ask if he had seen him. The bird shook his head and sat up on the chair rim. Maylore sent him two pictures to request that he look for Gilriel. Bert returned a picture of him flying at sunrise. Maylore extended his palm upward and bowed his head to say thank you as the bird took wing.

Maylore took a small container from the shelf and removed one small blue spot mushroom. "Today, I will try half of a small one to experiment on myself," he said aloud as he cut the small mushroom in half. He ate the mushroom, followed by spring water, and lay on the bed. He rested quietly for several minutes as he felt himself rise to the ceiling of his mind. The door flew open, and he used that as his signal to look within. "I want to go to my communication portal," he said aloud. He traveled quickly downward and slid along the tangle of threads inside him. He stopped at his communication portal. Several new threads were waving alongside the main thread connecting the portals. The original thread he had seen on his first trip was still attached to the communication portal. Maylore grabbed the end of one of the new threads and pushed it against the portal wall. It was long enough but would not stay attached.

"How do you get it to stay attached?" he said, looking at the waving thread. "Did Gilriel cut a hole to push it through?" Maylore decided to try using a fire spark to cut a hole in the portal. "It is better to find the process to use on myself than ruin someone else," he thought. Summoning a fire spark, he used it to cut a hole in the portal wall and push the thread through it. The hole immediately closed around the thread, showing no sign of damage to the portal wall. Grabbing the other thread, he repeated having two new threads join the existing one into the portal. "I wonder what this does to me?" He watched as the threads started carrying power to the portal.

'Travel to the heart portal,' he thought as he started moving along the lines to the heart portal. The portal seemed to exist but was very small and had no connections to it. He looked at the back of the portal where Airalee had a healing connection but found nothing there. 'Apparently, I cannot heal,' he thought. Turning to the front side, he looked for a thread he could use to connect the heart. He examined the bundle of threads running past the heart portal. He saw one dark thread. 'Is it inactive, disconnected at the source, or waiting to be used?' he thought. 'What do you suppose happens if I try pushing a loop of the thread into the heart without cutting the thread? Will the heart portal reject, accept, or ignore it?' Maylore considered for a time as he pulled on the inactive-appearing loop to make it long enough to reach the heart. "I hope it doesn't kill me," he thought. He summoned a fire spark and created a hole in the heart portal. He pushed part of the loop into the cut as it quickly closed around it. He watched the connection for signs of activity as the thread remained attached to the portal. "I don't see any activity on the thread," as he continued to watch. Suddenly, he seemed to explode as the mushroom's power ran out. Maylore awoke to the sound of water running in the spring and an otherwise quiet cave. He felt famished as he moved to the table, eating fruit. He looked at the sun's shadows on the floor from the cracks in the ceiling. It appeared to be late afternoon. Remembering what he had done, he said, "I did not kill myself." He patted his upper body to verify he was whole. He walked into the garden and devoured a few more pieces of fruit. "Another day. I hope I accomplished something," he said as he walked back into the cave. Sitting at the table, he concentrated on the communications portal. The dome seemed grander than before, and many dots appeared to be moving. He saw the dot labeled Bert, which seemed to be coming in his direction.

"This is new," Maylore said of the moving dots. Airalee appeared to be stationary in the village.

Other dots moved like Bert, which he guessed were birds. He sent a greeting picture to a few and received a response questioning, 'Who are you?' He sent an image of himself to them but received no response.

"Bert will be here soon," Maylore said. "If I am reading the portal correctly. I'll gather some fruit, berries, and nuts for his trouble," he said, returning to the garden. Arranging his collection on the table, he sat and waited for Bert. He was eating a few more pieces of fruit when he heard Bert fly into the cave. Bert landed on the back of his chair and shook his head. Maylore received a picture of Bert shrugging his wings as he ate the nuts. "Thank you, Bert," he signaled as Bert ate. Maylore gathered more fruit and berries into his satchel. He sent a goodbye picture to Bert and walked back to the companions' hut.

Jendrin

Jendrin sat outside the hut, cutting away the outer bark down to the clear wood beneath it. His attempts to cut into the clear wood proved futile.

"How did I cut this off the tree?" he asked himself as he looked at each end. The clear wood did not extend to either end. He cut back each end until he found clear wood underneath. "It looks like I was fortunate to cut in the right spots," he said, examining the end. He spent his morning clearing just half of the wood from the staff. The knife needed frequent sharpening, and now his hunger was sharp.

Returning to the hut, he spooned a bowl of the morning stew and ate while examining the staff. He noticed the clear wood glowing a light yellow where he touched it. Surprised by the sight, he rolled his hand over the clear wood. The yellow glow expanded to the size of his hand and slightly beyond.

"Glowing wood?" he said aloud.

Forgetting his hunger, he went back outside in the stronger light. The yellow glow was gone, but he suspected it was there. Cupping his hands, he could see the wood glowing.

"Incredible," he said, watching the glow, "I wonder what it means?"

Astounded by the discovery, he resumed cutting the outer bark from more of the staff. The twin suns were approaching the last quarter of the day when he stopped to sharpen his knives again. Hunger was pulling at him to eat the rest of his lunch. He glanced at the other quarterstaffs lining the wall. "Do the other quarterstaffs have a clear wood center?" he asked. Grabbing one of the other quarterstaffs, he cut a hole in the center of the staff. It, too, appeared to have clear wood at its center. 'Intriguing,' he thought, setting it back against the wall. "I will clean it like Airalee said and see if she can explain it." He returned outside the hut and continued cleaning the remaining bark from the staff.

Maylore returned to the hut as Jendrin finished removing the last bark on the staff.

"What beautiful wood," Maylore said as he stood beside Jendrin. Jendrin stood and placed the end of the staff on the ground. It was not straight and curved like a growing root would in and out.

"I agree," Jendrin said as he looked at the staff from top to bottom. "What is amazing is the staff glows where it is touched," Jendrin noted, moving the staff toward Maylore. The brightness of the day had passed, and Maylore could see a slight yellow glow near Jendrin's hands.

"Incredible," Maylore said, looking at the glow. "I wonder why it does that?" he asked.

"I don't know," Jendrin replied. "I was hoping Airalee could explain it since she told me to remove all the bark to the clear wood center. She also said I should rub oil into the wood to condition it. You hold it and see if it glows in your hands." Jendrin passed the staff to Maylore, who held it like Jendrin had.

They looked closely at the staff, but it did not glow.

"I think it doesn't like me," Maylore said with a smile. Maylore returned the staff, and the soft glow returned near Jendrin's touch. Maylore patted Jendrin on the shoulder.

"I need to do some physical activity," Maylore said. "I will gather more meat, plants, and herbs and fill our cooking pot again. I have fruit and berries we can all share," he said as he entered the hut.

Airalee returned to the hut as Maylore stirred the refilled cooking pot. Jendrin sat at the table, running his hands over the smooth quarterstaff. Airalee's hair was wet, so she moved to the fireplace to dry it.

"I managed to get all the bark off of the quarterstaff," Jendrin said, holding it up.

"Good," Airalee said, sounding unimpressed.

"Why did you want me to clean off this particular staff?" he asked.

"I didn't say anything about your staff," Airalee said, perplexed. "Why do you ask?"

Jendrin looked at Maylore, deciding to change the subject.

"Come look at it," he said, holding it for her to examine. Airalee saw a mostly crooked staff with pretty clear wood as she approached the table. Then she saw a light yellow glow around his hand where he held the staff.

"It glows around your hand!" she exclaimed, looking closer.

"That is what I hoped you could explain," Jendrin said.

"I wish I knew," Airalee said, stepping back. "If I could, I would be a sorcerer," she said with a smile. Jendrin knew he would not learn an answer to his question, so he set the staff aside and made a suggestion.

"It's dinner time," Jendrin said.

Chapter 32 - The Reveal

Ten sunrises passed as the snowfall Melronna had predicted came to the valley. A light coating covered the village, filling the slopes of the mountains with much more. The sun was shining this morning, and the temperature was cold. Villagers had switched to their winter clothing and were doing their everyday tasks as Jendrin peeked out of the hut's door. Maylore had already made breakfast as Airalee and Jendrin cleaned the hut and set their table. The companions had been busy with their projects in the past but found each morning an excellent time to plan their day.

"Snow," Jendrin said as he returned to the table. Airalee looked up sharply at the mention of snow. She had not told anyone about Melronna's prediction of the weather nor her comments about Airalee.

"Snow," Airalee said softly, mentally counting the days since her visit with Melronna. 'Ten,' she thought to herself as a mix of trepidation, curiosity, and anxiety filled her thoughts.

"Latel said the weather on Almora alternates from heat to periods of snow," Jendrin said. "I guess it is the snow's turn. Latel told me the snow ranges from hand height to elbow depth."

Airalee sat down with the other two as she considered Melronna's second message. Jendrin continued discussing the weather, but she did not hear him.

'I don't feel any different,' Airalee thought to herself. 'My 30 sunrise blood flow did not happen as it should have.' She counted through the previous days before realizing something was amiss. 'I will talk with Kai, but it has been a short time,' she reasoned.

"It was a good thing you and I have been busy helping repair roofs and huts for the coming snow," Maylore said.

"We need to help with the elder's huts today," Jendrin said, nodding. "I hear we will finish all of them today. I have not been working on my quarterstaff since we started hut repair. I still have not decided how to use it for defense without killing someone. I need to develop a plan to present it to Rendal."

"I have not been back to Gilriel's cave while we did this," Maylore said. "Manual labor wears me out as I age."

"Labor wears on you no matter your age," Jendrin said.

"Thinking of the cave," Maylore said, "I asked Bert to send me a message if Gilriel returned. He has not contacted me." Looking at Airalee, he said, "You are quiet this morning, Airalee. What do you say?"

Airalee looked up at the mention of her name, trying to remember what he asked of her.

"I was thinking about the task I am doing with Kai," Airalee said, covering her honest thoughts. "She wants me to write down the food, herbs, mushrooms, and healing plants she uses. Kai was interested in documenting each plant and how to use it. She wants to pass the information on to other healers."

"I thought she asked you to take over the healer role," Maylore asked.

"She has," Airalee replied. "She would like her experience with plants written for others to use."

"Smart woman," Maylore said.

"We have already written about many of them," Airalee said, "but there is still much to do. I could spend the entire snow season adding to the book's depth," she groaned.

"You are a natural for the task, Airalee," Maylore said.

"Thanks, dad," Airalee said.

"Congratulations if that is what you wish to do," Jendrin said.

"It is, I believe," Airalee said. "We have also been working on a formula to slow the bandits' desires for women. We have developed a potion using the monk berries we found but have not found any man willing to try it."

"I suppose that is not surprising," Jendrin said with a chuckle.

"Let me try it," Maylore said. "If it contributes to lessening the abuse of our girls, I will help."

"Dad," Airalee said, "We have not been pushing it since we don't know how much to use or what will happen."

"Let's start small," Maylore said, looking at her. "I might be able to see what happens if I use a mushroom."

Airalee was silent for a few moments.

"I do not want to experiment on anyone," Airalee said. "Especially one who is dear to me. I would accept using a bad person like Oleg, but few others."

"Start small," Maylore said. "If the potion affects me, I will let you know."

Airalee considered for a short time but did not look convinced.

"I will talk with Kai about it," Airalee said. The companions finished their breakfast as a knock came on the door. Jendrin opened the door to find Latel standing there.

"Are you two ready to work?" he asked, looking at Jendrin and Maylore.

"I will do cleanup," Airalee said. "Off with you two." The two men left as she cleaned up and did her morning routine. Returning to the hut, she found Marisa sitting at the table.

"We said days ago we would visit Lafrea to see what jewelry she would trade to us. Are you ready today?" Marisa asked.

"It sounds more fun than writing about plants," Airalee said. "I will check with Kai first to be sure she doesn't mind." The two women visited with Kai, who was willing to do other activities and asked them to look for a small piece of jewelry for her.

The two walked to Lafrea's hut and knocked on her door.

"Come in!" Lafrea said upon opening the door. "I am pleased to see you both," she said, returning to her table. "Please sit. What can I do for you two?" she asked.

"We would like to see what kind of jewelry you may be willing to trade," Airalee said.

"I have three special pieces I have been saving for you," Lafrea said. "I was asked about them many times but decided you would have the first chance," she said, walking to the back of the hut. She retrieved three pieces from a closed box and presented them to Airalee. Two were chokers with lace-weaved white threads surrounding a white stone. The other was a simple amulet awaiting its center stone.

"These are the stones I found on the beach long ago!" Airalee said.

"Yes," Lafrea replied. The polished stones deserved to be made into simple chokers. I surrounded each with a broad white weaving of bread silk."

"They are beautiful, Lafrea," Airalee said.

"Thank you," Lafrea said. "Let me mount your blue stone inside the amulet; it will be complete, too."

"It has brought me good luck, I think," Airalee said, pulling the stone from her pocket. "May I wait for it to be mounted?"

"Yes," Lafrea said. "I have mounted many stones through the seasons, and this one is already cut for mounting." Lafrea quickly mounted the stone into the center of the wolf fur center, tying it so that the thread barely showed.

"Let me tell you how to put it on." She passed the blue stone amulet to Airalee. "Put it around your neck with the stone in back. You attach three hooks on the end to the other side of the weaving. Spin it around so the stone is in front." Lafrea instructed as she watched Airalee complete each step. The blue stone with white lacing complemented Airalee's color and face structure. "Beautiful. It matches you well," Lafrea said.

Airalee felt undeserving of the amulet.

"What could I trade to you to justify such a piece?" Airalee asked.

"You treated several of my workers for their injuries," Lafrea replied. "You brought me several stones for other pieces. I am satisfied with the trade," Lafrea said, smiling. "If you happen upon more stones or things I can turn into jewelry, I would welcome that."

"Thank you," Airalee said. "Do you have someone in mind for the white stone?"

"No, girl, that is your choice," Lafrea said, passing the choker to Airalee. Airalee unhooked the white stone choker and spoke to Marisa.

"Turn around, Marisa," Airalee said. Marisa turned around, and Airalee hooked the white stone choker onto her neck. Airalee admired the choker as Marisa turned back around.

"Thank you, Airalee!" Marisa exclaimed with obvious delight. "It is a wonderful gift," she said with a small tear coming to her eye.

"Please keep the last one for yourself, Lafrea," Airalee said.

"I had hoped I might keep one," Lafrea said smiling. "They look beautiful on you two. It makes me proud to have made them." Airalee reached across the table and hugged Lafrea.

"Kai asked if you had a small piece for her," Airalee said.

Lafrea stood and stepped into the back room.

"I do," Lafrea said. "I know Kai's taste and made this for her long ago," she said, reaching into the shelf. She pulled out a leather bracelet with shells that sparkled within it. "She wears little jewelry, but I believe this will work for her," Lafrea said, handing the piece to Airalee.

"It is beautiful too, Lafrea," Airalee said, looking at the bracelet. "I will see to it if she gets it. Thank you again," she said as she turned toward the door.

"Thank you, Lafrea, and you too, Airalee," Marisa said, following Airalee out the door.

"That was so much more than I was hoping for," Airalee said as they walked toward Kai's hut.

"Very much so, since I expected nothing!" Marisa said.

"Do you think we could hunt stones on the shore today?" Airalee asked.

Marisa thought momentarily before replying.

"This snow will likely melt before too long," Marisa said. "Going down the rope to the shore will be no problem. I used to climb the rope before but had no problem during snowtime. We should inform Kai where we are going." Marisa said as they reached Kai's hut. Kai noticed the choker and amulet as soon as they opened the door.

"Those are beautiful," Kai said as they entered.

"These are the stones I found on the shore long ago," Airalee said.

"Lafrea does wonders with ordinary rock and string," Kai said, looking at each one.

"Lafrea sent this for you," Airalee said, passing the bracelet to Kai.

"Oh," Kai said as she looked at the piece. She finally put it on her right wrist. "It is beautiful. I will be sure to thank Lafrea when I next see her." Kai said, watching the sparkles from the shells.

A loud caw interrupted them.

"Basrah, what is this about?" Kai said as she opened the door. "Caw! Caw!" came a call from just above their heads. Kai looked up, noting the IB bird had two red feathers between its eyes.

"That is Gilda's bird," Kai said as the bird bounced its head up and down as if acknowledging what she said. "This IB followed us from the meadow where Gilda and I gathered mushrooms. It later tried to warn us of the bandit's presence in the woods, but we didn't understand the warning. I wonder why it is here?"

The bird slipped down to a lower branch near Kai. The three women started walking toward the bird as it flew high into the tree. Cawing loudly at them, it sat watching.

"Perhaps it would allow me to approach it, but no one else," Kai said, looking at the two others.

"We can test that by going back toward the hut," Marisa said as she turned. Airalee followed her, standing near the door. The bird flew back down to a branch near Kai's head and stuck out its leg. There was a note attached to it. Kai slowly reached up, untied the note's string, and pulled it off the bird's leg. The bird immediately flew off in the direction of the bandit's camp. Kai went back into the hut to read the note.

"It may be a note from Gilda," Kai said, unrolling and reading it to them. "I am a slave to Birsha – protected from others. Make food and clothes, clean, and serve. Not with child, Gilda." Kai felt tears coming to her eyes and passed the note to Marisa as she went into the back. "I am happy she is alive."

"We should leave Kai to her grieving," Marisa announced. "I am glad she still lives too, Kai. We will stay if you wish. Otherwise, we will leave and attend to our business."

"No, you can leave," Kai replied, facing them.

"Marisa and I are going down to the shore to try and find stones for Lafrea," Airalee said. "We plan to be back before the sun's third quarter."

"I will come looking for you if you are late," Kai said.

"We will be sure to check in with you before then," Airalee said.

"If you find some blue seaweed, bring it back," Kai said.

"I will," Airalee replied, closing the door. "Let's get our satchels and meet at the top of the rope."

"See you there," Marisa said as she headed for her hut. Airalee walked back toward their hut but suddenly felt a sickness in her stomach. Stopping beside the path, she lost her breakfast in the bushes.

"I hope I am not getting ill," Airalee said aloud before continuing to the hut. Gathering her satchel, she waited for Marisa to arrive. The climb down the rope with Marisa was less daunting than Airalee remembered. Walking the beach, they found more stones and shells after the recent storms. Walking the length of the beach, they found small shells that would fit into bracelet weavings and a few white and green stones.

"These are not as good as our stones, but they will still make nice jewelry," Airalee said. Kicking aside several large shells, Airalee spotted a clear rock peeking out from the sand. "This is interesting," Airalee said, pulling it out and showing it to Marisa. They dug around the sand but found no more clear ones. They started back to the rope when Marisa spotted some blue seaweed. She dipped her hand to collect it when a large fish surprised her. It jumped out of the water and then swam away.

"I think I just missed catching our dinner for the night," Marisa said, standing up. The two girls approached the rope up to the village.

The trip back up the rope was an easy climb. The first snow had melted from the path, allowing easy footing.

Returning to Lafrea's hut, they gave her the shells and the white and green stones. Airalee pulled the larger clear stone out last.

"Oh!" Lafrea exclaimed, "You found a power crystal!"

"I did?" Airalee said.

"Well, the story is that clear crystals have special powers," Lafrea said. "No one knows if it is true, but that is the story." Lafrea ended with a chuckle.

Perhaps you will find out, Lafrea," Airalee said with a smile.

"Perhaps so," Lafrea replied.

"I hope you feel like you made a good trade with us," Marisa said.

Lafrea's face softened.

"We already made a good trade," Lafrea said. "I do not like going up or down that rope to the sea. Your gifts allow me to create new things without scaring myself on that rope!" she exclaimed. Both girls chuckled, recognizing their past fears of using the rope.

"We need to check in with Kai before she sends out a search party," Marisa said, looking at Airalee.

"Yes," Airalee replied, "We do not want her to worry."

The two said their goodbyes and traveled to Kai's hut.

"Blue seaweed," Marisa said, showing Kai the seaweed.

"Excellent!" Kai said. "Please give it to Mirtha to add a different flavor to our dinner."

"Maylore told me he is willing to try our libido potion," Airalee said.

"Brave man," Kai said, picking up a small container. "Suggest he drink half of it tonight, and if he is well the next morning, drink the rest."

"I only hope it will not harm him," Airalee said, putting the container in her pocket.

Looking at Airalee, Kai cocked her head to one side.

"You don't look quite right, girl. Are you feeling all right?" Kai asked.

Airalee thought for a moment before replying.

"I did lose my breakfast in the bushes this morning," Airalee said. "I feel fine now." Kai looked sidelong at her.

"I have seen many women when they start carrying a child," Kai said. "You look like one of them."

"I don't know," Airalee replied, stammering in her speech.

"You may yet prove Melronna has foreseeing," Kai said, looking up.

"You didn't tell me?" Marisa loudly said with a smile on her face.

"I don't know if it is true," Airalee replied, looking down. Marisa jumped to Airalee and hugged her with glee.

"I am glad for you!" Marisa said, hugging her tighter. Releasing her, she continued. "You decided on seeding without speaking of it? Did you form your own seeding group?" Airalee looked up, but no happiness was on her face.

"I didn't plan it," Airalee said. "It was slow developing, but I have only been with Jendrin." Marisa continued to smile, a small tear of happiness forming in her eye.

"I have a way to test for a child," Kai said. "Would you try it?"

"I would like to know. Let me try it." Airalee said.

"You both sit here," Kai said, pointing at the chairs. She walked to the back of the hut and returned with a small pot.

"This mixture in this jar is safe to eat. Women who are with children throw it up. Those that are not keep it down." Kai scooped a spoonful for each into a cup of water.

"Here is one for you and one for Marisa," she said, watching them swallow the concoction.

"We will sit at the table and soon know one way or the other." Kai put a wide-mouth pot on the table as both girls sat and talked. She asked them to tell her about their stone-gathering trip. They shared the tale of gathering shells, stones, and white crystals and returning them to Lafrea.

Marisa told of their return to Kai's hut when Airalee grabbed the jug and threw up the concoction. Kai was not surprised, and Marisa merely grinned. Airalee did not know what to think and looked sheepishly at the jug as she set it on the floor.

"Do you feel sick, Marisa?" Airalee quietly asked.

"No," Marisa answered, "just happy."

"Marisa shouldn't throw up," Kai said. "She has been using my potion to prevent this problem for many seasons."

"I enjoy my activity with men," Marisa said defensively. "I don't intend on giving it up."

"I should have sought you out sooner, Kai," Airalee said.

"That is like saying you should have patched the roof now that the puddles are on the floor," Kai smiled. "You will make an excellent mother, Airalee. Let's discuss what to do next."

"All right," Airalee said. "It appears I will again learn first what to do to pass on to others."

"Indeed," Kai said. "You don't need to change any of your activities. Continue your normal tasks until the baby is ready to be born. Be aware that food, smells, and the actions of others will affect you differently. The village will help you, but you may want to pick a baby partner to help raise the baby."

"My companions will help me if I need it," Airalee said, looking back toward her.

"As will I," Marisa said. Airalee smiled compassionately at her.

"I know you will," Airalee said. "I was hoping my men would agree."

Kai interrupted them.

"Those two men love you dearly, Airalee," Kai firmly said. "They will fight wolves to support you, I am positive. You also may come to me to discuss what will happen with the baby. I have helped many women throughout this process. I suggest you tell your men about your condition so they can adjust to the new Airalee that is coming."

"New?" Airalee asked.

"Yes." Kai said, "You may be suddenly annoyed or angered by small things that wouldn't typically bother you. They must be ready for that. You may be anxious, worried, sad, or depressed. Other times, you will feel joy, especially as the baby progresses and you begin to feel it move and kick."

"Oh my," Airalee said, "It sounds like my old carefree life has ended. I must work to avoid becoming a burden to all and raise my child simultaneously."

"Don't worry, Airalee, you can depend on all of us to help you," Marisa said, hugging her again.

Jendrin

Dirdin had taken the lead in repairing the village huts for winter. He was now working with two other villagers on Melronna's hut. He had assigned Jendrin, Latel, and Maylore to Selakiir's hut. Most of the work was the same for each hut: replacing missing lava rock on all sides, replacing rotted ceiling joists, roofing material, and fireplace rock. Selakiir's hut was in good shape but needed a few repairs. They lowered the internal insulation and replaced the missing window insulation. Selakiir helped where he could and offered water to the men as they worked.

"You've built strong huts for the villagers over the seasons, Selakiir," Jendrin said, taking a drink of water. "Most need minimal repairs," he continued, passing the water to Maylore.

"It's the best part of using rock," Selakiir said. "It's abundant here and stable. It's difficult to work with and harder to modify an existing structure. In the past, our forefathers lived in the caves behind the meeting hut, but the eurg lived in the caves too. The eurg constantly threatened their lives if we were not vigilant. Our ancestors had to keep fires and torches burning to keep them away. Eventually, they started building homes outside the caves but still burned fires and torches."

"The eurg don't come out of the caves at night?" Jendrin asked.

"They used to," Selakiir replied. "They would hunt the mountains and valleys for anything they could find. They are skilled at hunting deer, bears, wolves, blood wolves, or people. They avoid the village since we have fires in the kitchen and torches burning in the village."

"Does anyone know what they look like?" Maylore asked.

"There have been a few glimpses over the seasons," Selakiir said. "The eurg hides to catch something but is surprised by the torchlight. The eurg have long, fine fur that will easily catch fire. The eurg know this and run from fire."

"Do they still live in these caves?" Maylore asked.

"Yes, a few," Selakiir said. "We believe most of them have moved into the mountain tunnels as our village has grown."

"Abandoning the caves was a good idea," Jendrin said.

"We didn't completely abandon the caves," Selakiir said. "When the bandits come looking for young replacements, the sentinels recognize their intentions and sound a warning. The young run to the council hut and use a hidden passage to hide from the abductors."

"Aren't the young in danger from the eurg?" Jendrin asked.

"The hidden tunnel has light coming in through a crack in the ceiling," Selakiir said. "There is a torch at the entrance the children use to light several torches in the hidden cave. The noise of the children may draw the eurg, but the fire from the torches keeps the eurg away."

"The bandits don't search the caves?" Jendrin asked.

"Long ago, they tried," Selakiir said. "Birsha's grandfather Laico sent a few men to search the caves even though they had not seen anyone enter them. The bandits outside would hear a low growl before the voices of their men ceased. The bandits were frightened when their companions did not return and refused to enter the cave. We believe they decided the caves meant death, and no villager would enter them anyway."

"I am surprised the bandits didn't force villagers to reveal the children's location," Jendrin said.

"They used to try," Selakiir said. "They tried to force the parents to reveal their location, but they simply said the children were scattered in the forest and rocks. The bandits also tried to force them to call them back, but the parents used a call that warned the children that the bandits were still in the camp. Laico used to harm or kill a parent, but the parent would die before revealing any information. Birsha's father, Malin, witnessed Laico's maiming and killing, deciding it achieved nothing but to remove one of the little people from his workforce. He taught Birsha that killing the little people depleted his workers and should never be done."

"Village history," Latel said. "I did not know some of the stories. We should add new storytelling to our 'Summer Returns' festival. A collection of short village histories would be good for everyone."

"I would be glad to contribute if asked," Selakiir said.

Dirdin and two crewmen passed as Latel's crew talked.

"When you finish here, move onto Werloth's hut," Dirdin said. Latel waved in acknowledgment as they all stood up.

"Thank you, Selakiir," Jendrin said.

"Thank you, three," Selakiir replied. "I shall be comfortable while the snow blows."

Latel, Maylore, and Jendrin moved to Werloth's hut. Werloth was already outside, replacing missing rocks.

"Greetings!" Werloth said as they approached. "I am glad to see you all. Would you help me replace some ceiling wood?"

"That is what we will do," Latel said as he climbed the outside rock wall. Werloth looked at Jendrin and Maylore.

"I believe you two live with Airalee," Werloth said. Both men nodded as he continued, "Your lovely companion visited me and removed a bad tooth. It is still painful today, but Kai was right to see it removed. I was fortunate to be asleep while she hit me with rocks."

"It does not sound like Airalee to hit someone with rocks," Maylore said.

"She knocked out the bad tooth with a rock," Werloth laughed. "I was fortunate she did not smash anything else."

Jendrin and Maylore smiled at him, understanding what he was talking about.

"Be that as it may, would you help me repair the rock on the fireplace?" Werloth asked. The hut needed minimal repairs, and the ceiling beams were quickly replaced. Resting near the front of the hut after they finished, Jendrin turned to Werloth.

"I understand you were a hunter," Jendrin said.

"Yes," Werloth replied with pride. "I was one of the last of this village to hunt for food. Villagers found it too difficult to hunt animals. They would gladly eat what I caught but not kill an animal. I was glad to hunt and found it exhilarating. Now, I race the blood wolves for woca that the firebird drops."

"Marisa told me they sometimes trade for woca milk from the Tocor," Maylore said.

"The Tocor once managed to capture two young woca," Werloth said. The woca turned out to be female and provided milk for them and to trade. Once, I attempted to capture a female woca to provide milk for our village. However, the woca firebird spotted me and sliced off my arm with a fire bolt."

"A firebolt?" Jendrin asked.

"Yes," Werloth said. "I thought the firebird was distracted by the wolves harassing the herd, so I put a rope around the neck of a beast and started leading it away. The firebird spotted me and shot a bolt of fire that sliced off the arm! My arm did not bleed as I ran, but I feared the firebird would pursue me. The firebird stopped when the woca turned back toward the herd. I lost my arm as well as the woca that day. I did not return to try again!"

"That is sad," Maylore said.

"Indeed," Werloth said. "It was seasons ago, but I still have nightmares about it. I could not hunt with one arm but adapted to scavenging."

"Could you show me the way there?" Jendrin asked.

"I will," Werloth said. "The woca will be gone now that the snow is here. They will return when the next summer comes."

"Where do they go?" Jendrin asked.

"I don't know," Werloth answered. "The Tocor in the village near their valley say a huge shiny bird comes and takes them away. I have not seen it, so I don't know. The firebird has not taken dead woca out to sea for the several sunrises, so I assume they are gone."

"Perhaps you could teach me some of your hunting skills," Jendrin said.

Werloth looked delighted.

"I would be glad to!" Werloth said. "It pleases me someone else is willing to learn the hunting trade." Werloth stopped when he noticed Dirdin and his crews were approaching Sharaera's hut. "I need to ensure mother is not overly disturbed when they start working on her hut. Please excuse me," he said as he hurried away.

Maylore, Latel, and Jendrin moved onto Kelkalyn's hut as they discussed what Werloth said about hunting and wocas. Kelkalyn was outside his hut as the trio approached. He started to walk away along the cliff when he stopped and returned.

"Latel," Kelkalyn said, "could you fix the water leak from the fireplace? It has become a nuisance with the last snow." He came within a few paces of the men. He suddenly stopped and pointed at Maylore. "You! You are the one!" he almost yelled. Maylore stopped and stared at him.

"One what?" Maylore replied with a perplexed look on his face. Jendrin and Latel moved to stand next to Maylore as Kelkalyn strode steadily to Maylore.

"I must speak with you!" Kelkalyn said. "Walk with me to the rock ledge." Looking at Jendrin and Latel, he added, " I assure you, men, I will not harm him," as he started walking away.

"Let me talk with him," Maylore said. "I will join you when he finishes." Jendrin and Latel nodded and walked toward the hut to start repairs. Maylore walked to where Kelkalyn stood.

"You have the communication portal that keeps bothering me daily," Kelkalyn said.

"You received my call?" Maylore asked. Kelkalyn nodded.

"I do not reply to distance calls," Kelkalyn said.

"My apology," Maylore said. "I recently learned I have this skill but do not know how to use it. I did not realize there would be protocols to follow."

"If someone does not answer you, do not hit them again!" Kelkalyn said.

"Perhaps you could send a simple do-not-disturb notice," Maylore said. Kelkalyn grumbled at the suggestion but eventually replied.

"Assume I do not wish to be contacted unless I contact you," Kelkalyn said.

"You can send a message?" Maylore asked. Kelkalyn looked down and mumbled before replying.

"I do not have the skill to send messages," Kelkalyn said.

"Let me find your dot on the dome and mark it as you," Maylore said. "I can then know not to send you messages."

"You see people on your portal?" Kelkalyn said in amazement.

"Yes," Maylore said. "I see people and a few animals, such as IB." Kelkalyn stepped back and leaned on the rock.

"You are a tracker!" Kelkalyn exclaimed. "I have not heard of one for many seasons." Suddenly standing upright, he pointed to Maylore, saying, "Do not tell anyone else about being a tracker, especially the master!"

"Only a few know," Maylore replied.

"Tell no one else. I hope it is not too late for you," Kelkalyn said as he turned and hurried away.

Maylore felt shocked at his sudden departure but decided their first encounter had been primarily successful. He rejoined his team to help with repairs on Kelkalyn's hut.

"What did he say?" Jendrin asked when he arrived. Maylore repeated the story to both men as they replaced rock and wood on the structure. Maylore asked them to keep the information secret to avoid exposing Kelkalyn to danger. As they finished, the twin suns were starting their descent. Dirdin was happy with the day's work and asked them to join him tomorrow to repair the visitor's hut.

"It will be a short job with the men we have today," Dirdin said. Maylore, Jendrin, and Latel decided a bath would be the next task and joined a small group already in the pool. The conversation was light as the bathers finished and left one by one. Maylore and Jendrin were the last to finish. They dried off and dressed in the same clothes. They returned to the hut, picking a few mushrooms and edible plants along the way.

Airalee sat at the table, writing in her book. She touched her new amulet and looked at it, considering what to say to her companions. "I should tell them of my condition, but when? Now is as good a time as any," she said aloud.

The door of the hut opened as the two men entered. She greeted them with a smile. "The working men return," she said, closing her book and standing up.

"We come bearing gifts," Maylore said, placing the mushrooms and plants on the shelf. "We can add them to the pot later since it is ready," Airalee said, stirring the pot again.

"You have a new amulet," Jendrin said, looking at the stone.

"It is beautiful indeed," Maylore said.

"Lafrea created this amulet to hold the blue stone I have been carrying around," Airalee said. "She created a white stone choker for

Marisa to wear." Moving back to the table, she invited them to sit. "Do you two have any news to share?"

"We have stories to tell from our visits with the elders," Jendrin said as they sat down.

"Good," Airalee replied, "I will add my news after yours," she said, looking at him with a much broader smile.

Jendrin relayed Selakiir's story of village ancestors living in the caves, the bandits hunting the village young, and how villagers diverted them from being found. He also mentioned the dangerous eurg still living in the caves and their vulnerability to fire.

"The village has a festival at the beginning of each summer," Jendrin said. "Selakiir suggested they add a retelling of the village history each time. He suggested telling short stories so villagers didn't feel lectured. It would be a reminder to some and new to others like the young and ourselves. We can ask Rendal about it the next time we see him."

"We also met your friend Werloth," Maylore said with a smile.

"My friend?" Airalee said with a sneer. "What did he tell you?"

"He told us you knocked his teeth out," Jendrin said, smiling.

"True," Airalee laughed. "He is lucky it was only one bad tooth I smashed," she said, grimacing at them. "Did he tell you he likes to test the fabric softness of women's clothes?" she said, looking sideways at him.

"No," Jendrin said. "Is that really how he lost his arm?" he smiled. "Did Werloth tell us an untruth? He told us it was a fire bolt from the firebird."

"The firebird beat me to it," Airalee said, grinning. The group chuckled before Jendrin continued.

"He did say he would lead me to the woca valley next summer," Jendrin said. "He can't be all bad."

"He isn't," Airalee said seriously. "He helps all the elders and cares for his mother next door. His manners just need a little tuning. I will teach him better manners," she smiled.

"We also met Kelkalyn," Maylore said, looking at Airalee.

"You did?" Airalee said. "Kai said he avoids contact with everyone. What did he say?"

"He correctly accused me of distant communication through the portal," Maylore said. "He appears to avoid portal communication for fear of being identified and reported to the master. He inferred the master prefers to dispose of anyone who can use a portal. The good news is he could respond to me through the portal if he chooses to! He told me he would not answer unless he decided it was important."

"It seems you made a good contact," Airalee said.

"He was not pleased to see me," Maylore said. "Now, what news do you have, Airalee?"

"I have the libido potion for you to try," Airalee said, pulling the bottle from her robe. "Kai said you should drink half before you go to bed. Then, if you feel well the next day, drink the rest."

Maylore took the bottle and drank half its contents.

"Foul flavor," Maylore said, setting the bottle on the table.

"I hope there are no other adverse reactions," Airalee said.

"I will tell you in the morning," Maylore replied. "Any other news?"

Airalee decided that she would tell them in a simple answer.

"I am with child," she said.

Both men stared at her for a few moments before Maylore replied. "I am happy for you," Maylore said. "A young one is welcome if you choose it."

Jendrin rose from his seat and hugged her. "May I be your baby-mate?" he asked sincerely.

"Yes," Airalee said. "I just had not asked you."

Chapter 33 - Snow Fall

"I believe your child is halfway to joining us, Airalee," Kai said, poking Airalee's abdomen to examine the child. "I believe the child is developing well. I assume you have left the morning sickness behind?"

"Yes," Airalee replied.

"You should continue to make the ginger tea even if it has stopped," Kai said. "It is a good herb for many things."

"Actually," Airalee replied, "I like to drink it."

"Have you been eating properly for the baby?" Kai asked.

"Except for the fresh greens, I eat what I can for both of us," Airalee answered.

"Are you staying inside to avoid snowstorms?" Kai asked.

"I was very pleased to stay inside during these many sunrises while the snowstorms raged outside!"

"Good," Kai said. "Do you have anything else for me?"

Airalee considered for a moment whether to speak of her dreams.

"I sometimes feel I have been through this before," Airalee said. "I have an odd feeling that I have created children before. I sometimes feel Melronna could be right."

Kai looked at her without blinking.

"You came to this village from a place you don't remember," Kai said. "Others like you who came to the village tell me similar things. They tell of a fleeting impression of something that burns away in a flash. Do you remember something?"

"No," Airalee replied, "It is like a memory the body has, but my mind does not."

"Well," Kai said, smiling at her, "I am here to listen if you want to talk."

"Thank you, Kai," Airalee replied.

"I still have nightmares of Jendrin being stabbed," Airalee said. "They happen less often as time passes, but still haunt my dreams."

"I fear they may be with you for many more seasons," Kai replied.

"Seeing Jendrin daily helps banish the thoughts," Airalee said. "I believe they will disappear sometime."

"Speaking of Jendrin," Kai said, "I have another subject that concerns him. I know you understand the valley tradition of baby seeders," Kai said as Airalee nodded. "We have discussed Jendrin being requested to be a baby seeder. I have four girls who want Jendrin to be one of the baby seeders for their group."

"Marisa has told me, who are the others?" Airalee asked.

"Ah, Marisa told you," Kai said. "I do not tell the names of the requesters. You have no say in the matter, but since he is your baby-mate, I wanted you to know he may sometimes be tired." Kai finished, smiling.

"I understand the need to share," Airalee laughed. "Jendrin is a wonderful man, and many miniature versions of him would suit our village."

"He will be part of a four-man baby seeding group," Kai said. "He may not create the children."

"I understand," Airalee said, smiling. "Do you wish me to tell him?"

"No," Kai replied, "I will visit with each seeder to arrange the first meetings. Some women prefer a group setting, while others prefer a private setting. They usually seed two in one day, then the other two the next. When one begets a child, they concentrate on the remaining group."

"Sounds tiring to me," Airalee said.

"I have yet to find a man who rejects a quick seeding with a willing woman," Kai laughed. Airalee chuckled as she stood to go.

"With that, I will visit with our patients," Airalee said.

"Be wary of the slippery snow," Kai said.

The snow outside had long ago refused to melt during the day as Airalee left the hut. The twin suns may occasionally appear, but the snow builds up as the days pass. Today, the clear sky allowed the villagers to trudge through the snow to collect stored food. There was no fresh fruit or vegetables, but meats, potatoes, dried vegetables, and herbs kept the villagers fed. Boredom was sometimes a problem. Villagers would occasionally meet in the kitchen between storms just to converse.

Airalee made rounds of the sick and elderly on days Kai didn't. Melronna didn't make any new pronouncements other than belatedly noticing Airalee was with child. Selakiir was generally in good spirits since his children would visit several times a week. Phaerl and Adandir used a chamber pot to avoid forcing their creaky joints through the snow. Airalee would empty the pot for them if their children had not visited that day. Airalee would chat with them before moving on to the next hut.

She walked toward Sharaera's hut, but as she got closer, she felt a sudden heaviness fill the air. Pausing at the Sharaera's door, she listened for sounds inside the hut. She heard a soft rustling noise and called, "May I enter, Sharaera?" Airalee asked.

"Come in, Airalee," Werloth answered. Airalee opened the door to find Werloth sitting in a chair, looking up at Airalee.

"Mom passed away last night," he said simply.

"I am sorry to hear that," Airalee replied. Werloth looked back down at his mother.

"I have been expecting her to leave, but it still pains me to find she is gone," Werloth said. Airalee hugged him and sat in a chair at his side. Werloth did not move and continued to look at his mother's hand.

"She was a traveling healer for many seasons," Werloth said. She visited many of the villages from sunrise to sunset. She also helped many people and some Tocor using the skills she learned. I learned to hunt from the villagers where we stayed. We were always welcome since she had skills every village could use."

Airalee listened as he recounted a few of his mother's memories. He eventually seemed to wear down as he turned and laid his head on Airalee's shoulder. He shed a few quiet tears as Airalee hugged him. He finally straightened.

"I am sorry I cried on your shoulder," Werloth said. "I knew this was coming, but I am unprepared."

"I am glad I could be here to help," Airalee said, smiling. "Do you wish me to help handle arrangements?"

"No," Werloth said. "Mother and I arranged what was to be done long ago. She wishes her body to be placed on the death slide and given to the sea. It is a tradition Olona has used for many seasons. I already had a linen cover made for her eternal sleep. If you would help me, we will wrap her in it. The next clear day, we will let her go," he said, moving to the cabinet. He searched the bottom of the cabinet and found the large brown and golden-colored wrap. An orange ribbon with the healer symbol was woven into the fabric. Sharaera was a petite woman, and the two of them wrapped her body to the head quickly.

"Traditionally, we leave the head uncovered for all villagers to see who is being given to the sea," Werloth said. "The head wrap will be added just before she slides into the sea."

Werloth showed Airalee the hood and placed it along Sharaera's body. "I will go inform Rendal and Kai of her passing," Werloth said. "Thank you for being here, Airalee," he said, hugging her and leaving the hut.

"I wish you peace," Airalee said, looking at Sharaera's face. Airalee quietly closed the door as she continued to Kelkalyn's hut.

Knocking on the door, she got no response. She noticed there were no footprints in the snow.

"Kelkalyn, are you here?" she asked. She heard no response, so she opened the door. The fireplace was unlit, and the food on the table was uneaten. She reasoned he had not returned since the day Maylore had talked with him about portals and the master. She saw no reason to leave food or water. She closed the door and looked at the sunrise where he had hidden before. Snow covered the ground along the ledge, and she did not expect to see him anyway. She returned to the village to the children's care area to check the caregivers before returning to Kai's hut.

Werloth was closing the door of Kai's hut when Airalee arrived. He silently hugged her and trudged back toward his hut. Kai opened the door as Airalee watched Werloth leave.

"Is there any help we can offer him?" Airalee asked.

"Only listening to him and allowing him to grieve will help," Kai said. "He told me he appreciated your listening and helping him with the shroud."

"It seemed so little compared to his grief," Airalee replied.

"It is the little things we can do that help," Kai said. "I will visit with him tomorrow and bring chamomile tea. We will trade days as usual to see his spirits not start falling. You return to your hut so you do not get too cold." Airalee nodded and walked back to her hut.

Jendrin

Jendrin's quarterstaff was complete, and he had several coatings of oil from plants and his hands on them. The staff was light in weight and easy to swing. The wood was translucent and glowed under his hands as he wielded it. The staff sang its light song when it struck something or dropped onto the floor. The wood was not straight and had a slight wave pattern to it. He practiced outside, moving the staff in different combinations without any real idea of how to use it. He knew that by simply holding and swinging the quarterstaff, he would know how to use it in time.

He saw Latel crunching through the snow to stand near him.

"You look dangerous," Latel said.

"I am dangerous," Jendrin said as the quarterstaff fell to the ground, "to me! I don't know how to turn this stick into a quarterstaff. I will be a danger to me and those around me," he said, picking up the stick and smiling.

"Quarterstaff?" Latel asked.

"Yes," Jendrin replied. "I somehow know this is a weapon called the quarterstaff. I don't know how to use it, but if I practice swinging it, I will be given that knowledge."

"Where does that knowledge

come from?" Latel asked.

"I do not know that either," Jendrin said. "It will seep into my head as I work with this stick."

"Once it gets through your thick head," Latel said, "I will gladly join your training session."

"I promised Rendal I would not involve others until he approved of my methods for village defense," Jendrin said.

"You believe a stick will be able to defend us?" Latel asked.

"I believe the proper use of a quarterstaff will be a good defensive weapon," Jendrin said. He turned the staff in his hand and struck his leg, making him wince with pain.

"You feel whole from your injuries?" Latel asked, watching him pick up the staff again.

"I no longer feel any effect from the attack," Jendrin replied. "It took a long time to be free from pain and have the strength to try this. I will soon know how to use this for defense and show Rendal a form to stop an attacker's aggression."

"Airalee's child will be here soon," Latel said. "I see why you would want Rendal's blessing before the baby arrives."

"That is a good reason," Jendrin said as he stopped and leaned on his quarterstaff. "I have to believe he will approve. I will only show him defense skills since he is looking for that. I will suggest I teach defense skills first and how to stop an attacker."

"I believe he will approve since Oleg attacked you and Airalee," Latel said. "However, the council may be harder to sell."

"Perhaps," Jendrin said. "They are more passive in their approach than I am."

"Since you are Airalee's baby-mate," Latel said, "I believe it is your task to help both of them. That includes defense against attacks. The council would not agree. I had not heard of an attack in the village before Oleg. He is still going to be a problem."

"I agree," Jendrin replied. "Oleg will likely return, and I want to be ready when he does. I plan to defend us and defeat Oleg regardless of the council's decision."

"We are of the same mind," Latel said, smiling. "I will be willing to learn the quarterstaff when you are ready to teach."

"You will be my first student," Jendrin replied.

"If he approves," Latel said.

The crunch of the snow announced another visitor to the hut. "Greetings, Kai," Latel said, seeing her approaching.

"Latel," Kai replied. "I need time to speak privately with Jendrin."

"Of course," Latel said. "I will see you tomorrow, Jendrin," he said, turning toward his hut.

"Let's go into your hut," Kai said. Jendrin held the door and set his staff inside the hut. Kai sat at the table, indicating that Jendrin should sit in another chair.

"I understand you were the only one to seed Airalee's child," Kai said. "That is not traditional in the human villages, and I advise you to keep it to yourself. Do not brag about it."

Jendrin was taken aback. Was he being reprimanded or given a healer's advice?

"I shall ask her forgiveness if you suggest it," Jendrin said. Kai waved dismissively.

"I don't question your male motives," Kai said. "Men have little control when a pretty girl is being suggestive. I do question Airalee's control of accepting you since you saved her from death."

Jendrin suddenly wondered, 'Did I take advantage of her mental state?'

"I did not come to question you or Airalee's choices," Kai said. "I came to ask you to join a seeding group."

"Seeding group?" Jendrin slowly said, confused by the change in conversation.

"Yes," Kai said. "You are aware women in Olona and indeed all of Molia can request certain men for their seeding."

"Yes, I have heard that," Jendrin said, sitting up straighter.

"I want you to join three others in a village seeding group."

Jendrin almost laughed, realizing he was not being lectured.

"I have yet to find a man who turns down a seeding group," Kai said, misreading his reaction. "You will be with three other men who will all seed the same four women. I will arrange it so that no man knows who the others are. The women know since they chose you."

"Why is it still done this way?" Jendrin asked.

"In days past," Kai started, "men and women claimed each other as lifelong mates, thus removing the virile men with desirable traits from availability. That method created a weaker population and jealousy among the women. We used to have men from other villages offer to seed, but the snow prevented that this time. We have enough desirable men in our village to do the task."

"I promised to be Airalee's baby-mate," Jendrin said. "I should discuss this with her."

"I have discussed it with Airalee," Kai said. "She has been made aware it is your choice, not hers. You will still be her baby-mate regardless of your choice. I suggest you accept since all four girls chose you. It becomes more of an obligation than an option."

"I am not sure it is a privilege or a command," Jendrin said. "Did they agree on all four men?"

"They did not," Kai said. "They agreed on two but were undecided on the other two. Tradition allows me to choose one or all of a group if the girls are undecided."

Jendrin felt torn between feeling privileged to serve and being required to join. He thought for a few moments before making a decision.

"When do we begin," Jendrin said.

"One girl is pushing the schedule," Kai said. "She wants to be seeded during snow time."

"Marisa," Jendrin said with a smile.

"It seems you and Airalee already know," Kai said. "I will not tell the names of the others. It is better for all if the baby's seeder is unknown. We will meet twice each week until each child has been seeded. I have a test to determine when the girl is successfully seeded. You will be released from duty when all the women are seeded."

"I am ready," Jendrin said.

"I bet you are," Kai smiled. "Do you know your responsibilities for being Airalee's baby-mate?

"We have not discussed it," Jendrin said.

"I will tell you our village custom," Kai said. "Most baby-mates will stay with the baby until the child is at least three summers old. It is the mother's choice. You may be asked to remain as her child mate. If you accept, it will be until the child is fifteen summers of age. I believe Rendal has spoken to you of this village custom before."

"Generally, not specifically," Jendrin replied.

Kai's expression turned even more severe.

"You recall," Kai said, "the village charter allows the bandits to select the firstborn female child to serve in their village. Most do not have to serve, but you should be aware of it."

"My child will not serve," Jendrin said firmly. "I would see the bandits destroyed first."

"Good," Kai said, sitting back, smiling. "I would welcome such a change. In the meantime, Airalee and I are developing a potion to stop the bandit's libido. If we are successful, we may slow their need for our girls and their abuse. Your brave companion, Maylore, may test it for us. If he reports a small decrease, I will strengthen the potion and ask him to try a new version."

"Perhaps it is already working," Jendrin said. "I believe his last visit to the pleasure hut was only for a hair trim," Jendrin said.

531

"Airalee offered to cut my hair, but the Tocor are quick and expert hair trimmers. I don't need the extra services they offer any longer."

"I see," Kai said. "I knew Airalee would one day claim you both."

"Just me," Jendrin said. "She views Maylore as her dad."

"I do not judge," Kai said. "It is a choice you all make together. Do you have any questions for me?"

"No, I understand what you ask of me," Jendrin said.

"If you feel reluctant to ask your lady healer," Kai said, "ask Rendal your questions. He is well versed in our ways."

"I trust you, Kai," Jendrin said, standing up. "I have no reservations about asking you anything." Kai nodded as Jendrin opened the door for her.

Maylore and Latel were standing a few feet away, deep in conversation. Kai walked to join them. "Latel," Kai said, "you can have him back now. Maylore, I will have a stronger potion to try if you are willing."

"I am glad to help," Maylore said. Kai smiled and walked toward her hut. Latel looked up at the sky full of dark clouds.

"It looks like a big snow is coming," Latel said. "I hope the wind stays light this time. I am going to gather some wood for Mom and her life partner. I will visit again soon." he said as he walked through the snow. Maylore waved and entered the hut to find Jendrin sitting at the table, apparently deep in thought.

"Jendrin," Maylore said as he approached the table.

"Maylore, glad you are back," Jendrin said.

"You appeared to be deep in thought," Maylore said. "Would you like to share?" Jendrin smiled and told the story of what he and Kai had discussed. "It sounds like an honor to me," Maylore said. "I assume you will join the group?"

"Yes, it just seems odd," Jendrin said as he stood up. The hut door swung open, and Airalee entered. A brisk wind pushed her into the hut.

"More snow," she said, latching the door closed. Both men greeted her as she removed her snow-covered wrap.

"Why is it so hot?" she asked. The two men looked at each other. "It isn't hot," Jendrin said before remembering small things could set her in a foul mood. Airalee felt an emotional storm rise and forced herself to stay calm. "The child keeps me very warm no matter the weather," Airalee said. Both men's faces relaxed at her reply, forcing her to smile.

"I can sometimes control my emotions enough not to breathe fire on you," Airalee smiled.

Both men laughed and invited her to sit at the table. Airalee told them of Sharaera's passing and her wish to be given to the sea.

"I fear we may lose a few more before summer returns," Airalee said. "I have not heard of anyone else approaching death, but it could change quickly. The villagers I visited seem healthy and are enduring the grey weather of the snow. I do not believe Kelkalyn has returned. The snow around his hut looks undisturbed, and I saw no fire in his fireplace."

Maylore had become adept at checking his communication portal without requiring preparation time.

"He is still nearby," Maylore said. "He appears to be inside a rock formation. I suspect he is in a cave near his hut."

"Amazing," Airalee said. "Do you see my dot nearby, too?"

"Yes," Maylore replied as he sent her a message.

"I felt that," she said with a smile. "Did you get a visit from Kai, Jendrin?"

"Yes," Jendrin replied. "She was here in her full healer responsibility." He relayed the same story he told Maylore. Airalee nodded as she listened to the recounting and smiled as he finished.

"You are accepting of this?" Airalee said.

"Yes," Jendrin said, "As I told Maylore, it just seems odd."

Airalee reached across the table to take Jendrin's hand. She next reached palm up to Maylore.

"Dad," she said. "Care to share anything?" she asked. Maylore took her hand.

"Kai said you two have developed a new potion she wants me to try," Maylore said. "I told her I am ready anytime."

"Did the first one have any real effect?" she asked.

"Some," he replied. "It needs to be stronger, I believe."

"If you feel ill," Airalee said, "you need to tell me," as she squeezed his hand.

"I will be sure to do that," he said.

Airalee could feel emotions bubbling up in her as she looked at them.

"I would be lost without both of you," she said as tears filled her eyes.

"We are here for you," Maylore said, taking her hand in both hands.

"I love you, Airalee, and will not be going anywhere," Jendrin said.

Airalee smiled at them through her tears, watching both of them.

"I believe you both," she said as her tears slowed. "Baby-making boils over my emotions very quickly."

Jendrin moved to her side and hugged her as her eyes dried.

534

"I'm hungry," she suddenly announced. "Shall we eat?"

They ate their dinner with a generous portion of light banter between them. The companions discussed the good times they spent together in Olona. Conversation slowed as they finished their meal.

"I do have a request for you," Maylore said, looking at Airalee. "I have two small mushroom pieces left. I would like to see how you are doing, if I may."

"Of course," she replied. "Do you want to start now?" she asked.

"I am ready," Airalee replied.

A light rap came at the door as they stood. Jendrin opened the door to see Kai standing in the snow.

"Come in, Kai," Jendrin said, standing aside.

"No," Kai replied, "I want you to join me for the start of the baby seeding," she started down the path, not waiting for him to respond. Jendrin turned to his companions.

"I will return later," he said as he left the hut.

Airalee sat as Maylore ate his mushroom piece and lay on his bed. Airalee took his hand in both hers and sat in a chair near his bed, waiting.

Maylore closed his eyes and chatted with Airalee until he felt the familiar opening of his mind's ceiling. He drifted up through the ceiling and immediately looked for the connection to Airalee through her hand.

"Take me to Airalee's communication portal," Maylore said. He moved quickly along the strings until he arrived at her communication portal. "It has more activity," he said, watching energy flowing through it. It was a small amount, but it still had an energy flow. He noticed two more strings waving near the portal. He cut a hole in her communication portal and added both strings. He could see some energy start up the new string and enter the portal.

He knew his time would be short, as he said, "Take me to her heart portal." Dead energy still clogged the portal, and the healing portal was quiet.

"I wonder why the healing portal is quiet?" He watched the other energy flow along the strings, which seemed normal. "It doesn't look like the baby's development has helped or hurt Airalee," he said aloud. He started to create a pick to remove some of the dead heart energy when he was suddenly aware that a new energy was rising behind him.

Turning around, he saw a rainbow-colored energy touching his hand. The energy led downward along the strings. Maylore followed the energy along its thread until it stopped outside the womb. A small area of the womb was translucent as he looked Inside. He saw a female child with crystal blue eyes facing him. The child slowly raised her hand and pointed to her head, telepathically telling him, "Ayare."

"Your name is Ayare?" Maylore sent her. "I am Maylore. I am pleased to meet you." He watched as the energy faded, and she closed her eyes. The walls of the womb became opaque, and he could no longer see her.

"I will tell your mother your name and that she has a daughter," he told her. Maylore knew nothing of what a pregnant mother's energy should look like, but the energy seemed normal with no hint of infection. "What a beautiful child," he thought as he watched. Realizing his time would be soon over, he said, "Move to the crown portal." He started upward, but his mind's ceiling snapped him back and abruptly closed.

CHAPTER 34 - WHO'S YOUR DADDY

Maylore awoke early the following day with hunger clawing at his stomach. He sat up on the side of the bed, noticing fruit and bread in the chair where Airalee had been sitting.

"Thank you, Airalee," he said quietly.

He was devouring the food when the excitement of yesterday's discoveries sprang into his mind. He stood and moved into an empty common area.

Looking out the door, he noted the sun was rising just above the treetops in a clear sky.

"Everyone will be awake soon," he said, "It is going to be a beautiful day." He noticed someone had already filled the food pot the night before. He stirred the pot and set it to warm by the fire.

Maylore left the hut to attend to his daily needs. The snow level was slightly more significant than the previous day.

"Tramping down the trails in the village will be more challenging today," he said as he walked toward the bathroom. He stopped at the bathing pool to ensure the fire would heat the water for use later.

"Good morning, Maylore," a villager said, already stoking the pool fire.

"Good morning indeed," Maylore replied. "It appears we will have a clear sky."

"Yes," the villager replied, "that is why I am building a fire so I can bathe later in the day."

"That is my plan as well," Maylore replied. The two chatted for a while as each gathered more wood.

"I need to finish my morning routine before my companions awaken," Maylore said. "Perhaps we can meet later," he said as he waved to the villager.

Maylore finished his morning routine before he returned to the hut. As he entered, Airalee and Jendrin were sitting at the table.

"Good morning, Dad," Airalee said with a big smile. "Jendrin was just telling me about his adventures last night. Have a seat," she said, patting the area beside her.

"There is not much to tell," Jendrin said. "I was telling Airalee we each seeded two last night. We will switch to the other two this morning. Kai says we will repeat this process for another session, then wait two days before starting again. She reminded us that we should repeat this until all of them are with the child."

"The men must hate it," Airalee teased.

"Well, not that I noticed anyway," Jendrin replied with a grin.

"I think I get the idea of it," Maylore said. "If we can leave that behind, I have news for both of you."

Both of them looked expectantly at him.

"Is this from your mushroom travel last night?" Airalee asked. "I hope you didn't find anything wrong," she asked with concern.

"Yes, it is about last night," Maylore said. "But I saw nothing wrong. I was able to add new connections to your communication portal."

"That part is good," Airalee said as she visibly relaxed. "What did you see?"

Maylore took her hand as he looked directly into her eyes.

"I met your daughter last night," Maylore said. Both sat, looking at him, trying to comprehend what he was saying to them.

"My daughter?" Airalee asked, tilting her head to one side.

"Yes," Maylore said. "I was examining your portals when an energy touched me. I followed the energy to its source in your baby chamber."

"Are you sure the mushroom didn't create the conversation?" Jendrin queried.

"I do not think the low dose of the mushroom could create that," Maylore said. "It was a brief encounter. She told me her name is Ayare."

Jendrin and Airalee both looked shocked.

"She has a name?" they both said at once.

Maylore laughed at their expressions and synchronized speech.

"Yes," Maylore said. "I noticed she had crystal blue eyes and seemed at peace. She tired quickly, only telling me her name before falling asleep."

Jendrin seemed overwhelmed by the news.

"Did she look normal?" Airalee asked. "Did she have all her fingers and toes?" Airalee rattled off several other questions, but Maylore simply smiled.

"I am sorry," Maylore said, "many of those details escaped my short visit with her. She looked very normal and did have fingers and toes. Perhaps I can plan a future visit with her and find those answers."

Airalee jumped up, hugging Maylore.

"That's okay, dad. I am happy with your news," Airalee said. Looking down, she said, "Hello, Ayare!" as she patted her baby bump. An amused look came to her face. "Ayare kicked hello!" she said, looking up at her companions. Jendrin stood and stroked the baby bump.

"Hello, daughter," Jendrin said. Airalee smiled at him.

"She gave me a strong kick," Airalee said. "I think she knows you."

"If not now, you soon will," Jendrin said, hugging Airalee.

"Her name is similar to yours," Jendrin said. "I hope we can keep them straight."

"I don't think we will tell everyone else she told us her name," Airalee said. "They may think we were eating the wrong mushrooms."

"I could tell them I gave her that name to avoid villagers thinking you were egotistical," Jendrin said.

"I doubt anyone will care," Airalee said, "however you may name her if you wish."

After filling their bowls, they gathered at the table. The talk centered on baby care and how their schedules would be changing.

"It will be a busy hut after Ayare arrives," Airalee said.

"I agree," Maylore said. "I will move to Gilriel's cave after the snow melts, assuming he does not return."

Both of his companions stopped eating to stare at him.

"No, Dad," Airalee said. "You don't need to leave. I was only saying it would be a busy hut, not that anyone should leave to make room," as she grabbed his arm.

Maylore patted her arm.

"I believe it will work better for all of us," Maylore said. "You will need room for Ayare, and I may be assuming Gilriel's job in the village. Whatever that is. I need to practice using energy powers where villagers cannot see. Besides, I will be here often to visit Ayare."

"All right, Dad," she replied, "As long as you don't think I am trying to get rid of you."

Maylore stood and kissed Airalee on the forehead.

"You will not be able to get rid of me," Maylore said. You, Ayare, and the hero are essential people to me. Together, we are just beginning our adventures."

Maylore collected the empty bowls and left the hut to clean them. Airalee's face began streaming with tears.

"He is not going away, Airalee," Jendrin said, moving next to her as he hugged her.

"I understand," Airalee replied. " Baby-making brings emotions I can usually suppress roaring to the surface. I can't stop them." She finished waving her hands in the air. Jendrin was learning to keep quiet, or he would make things worse. He continued to hug her until she regained control and returned his hug.

Maylore had finished washing their bowls when Rendal met him on the path.

"Maylore," Rendal said. "Will you tell your companions we will present Sharaera to the sea at half sun? They should attend since it is a village tradition," he said, stopping before him.

"I will do that," Maylore replied.

"Good." Rendal replied, "I have a few more groups to tell, then help prepare the site for her leaving," as he turned and left. Maylore continued to the hut. Opening the door, Jendrin was drying her eyes as they hugged.

"Should I come back later?" Maylore asked.

"NO," Airalee roared. Maylore stepped back initially but finally entered and closed the door. "Sorry, Dad," Airalee said. "I will regain control soon." Looking down at the baby bump, she said, "Easy on mom, please, Ayare. She is challenged enough already."

Maylore stored their bowls on the shelf before returning to the table.

"Rendal told me they will present Sharaera to the sea when the twin sun reaches halfway," Maylore said. "He wants us to be there."

"I certainly planned to be there," Airalee said. "Werloth needs all of us to support him today, even if he is a dirty old man."

A knock on the door caused Jendrin to open it.

"It is time," Kai said as she stood near the door. She waved Jendrin aside to enter the hut. "Are you doing well?" Kai asked.

"Yes. I plan to visit the ill today after Sharaera's ceremony," Airalee said.

"All right," Kai said. "Do not overdue. Take one of your companions with you today to help. Today, I want you to test the potion with Maylore."

"I will Kai," Airalee said.

"Tomorrow, I will attend to the villagers," Kai said. "I want you to rest."

"I can do that too," Airalee said.

"In three sunrises," Kai said, "I want you to help with the girl's baby-testing."

"I will be ready," Airalee said.

Kai nodded to Maylore and turned to leave the hut. "Come, Jendrin," she said as she trudged through the snow. Jendrin shrugged and followed.

Villagers gathered on the cliff outside the elder's hut as the twin suns approached midway. A long hollow log protruded from the cliff's edge over the sea. The companions arrived just as three men were spreading something inside a log. Most villagers were present, and a few more came as they watched.

At an unspoken signal, the door to Sharaera's hut opened. Four men emerged carrying the wrapped body. Werloth and Rendal each held an end of a sling with Sharaera's body in the middle. Two other villagers carried the sling at her feet. They walked silently to the log's opening and set the body beside it. Werloth uncovered her face and stepped back with the other men. The villagers walked past the body and formed a semicircle around her. Werloth waited for the last villager to see it was his mother's body, then covered her face again.

Rendal gave a quiet signal, and the men lifted the body into the mouth of the log. Almost in unison, the crowd began to sing a lively song of birth and death as the body slid down the log and was given to the sea. The song ended with villagers raising their hands to the sky and cheering. Airalee noticed Meliniel was holding Melronna's arm as the cheering subsided. Villagers each spoke a few words to Werloth and walked back through the snow to their huts.

"Looks like we have a song to learn," Airalee told her companions.

"I will teach it to you," someone said behind her. Airalee turned to see Marisa standing there. "Good to see you," Airalee said. "I would welcome the teaching," as she hugged her. "I will say a few words to Werloth, and then I can leave," she said as she walked his way. Marisa waited with the two men as Airalee spoke to Werloth, then returned. "Let's go learn a song," Airalee said as they started their return.

Before returning to their hut, they gathered wood, beans, and some frozen pork for dinner. Sitting at the table, Marisa taught them 'The Song of Leaving.' It was a simple song, and all three learned it quickly.

"It would be nice to stay in this warm hut," Airalee said, sitting back in her chair. "I have promised responsibilities to our villagers and should be about it," she said, standing up.

"I will do the rounds today," Marisa said. "I would like to do something besides attending to kitchen duties."

543

"Sounds good to my ears," Airalee said. "I was going to ask Jendrin to carry the medical bag and food. Perhaps he will go with you." She said, looking to Jendrin.

"I would be glad to," Jendrin said as he arose.

Marisa led the way out the door and toward the first stop. "I want to check on a few other villagers today to be sure they are doing well," Marisa said, knocking on a door. A man opened the door, greeting them both. "I was checking to see if you were well. Do you need a healer's aid?" she asked.

"No, thank you, Marisa. "I am doing well; I am just hiding from the snow," he said with a smile.

"I am glad to hear that," Marisa said. "I see you have firewood and food too."

"The Beacon sends youngsters around each morning with wood and food. I am thankful he does," he said, looking at the snow.

"If you do not need anything, we will be on our way," Marisa said, waving to him.

"Thank you, Marisa and Jendrin," he replied, waving to them as he closed the door.

They checked several more huts, finding the villagers in good health and well-supplied. "Let's start at the other end of the elder's huts this time," Marisa said as they continued to chat along the way.

"Kelkalyn's hut," she said, knocking on the door. No tracks were in the snow, and no one answered the door.

"Let me open it," Jendrin said, pulling on the door. The hut was empty and appeared to have been vacant for a while. "Maylore told us he was in a nearby cave and wanted to be left alone."

Marisa nodded, and they walked to Werloth's hut. Jendrin knocked on the door but got no answer. "Werloth, are you here,"

Marisa asked. There was no reply, so Jendrin opened the door. The hut was empty as they entered.

"It looks like he took packs, blankets, and hunting equipment," Jendrin said, looking around.

"He likely wanted to get away after his mother's passing," Marisa said. "I suspect he will return when summer returns."

Marisa turned to leave, and Jendrin followed her to Sharaera's hut next door. "Is anyone here?" Marisa asked, knocking on the door. She expected no answer and opened the door. The hut was very tidy and sealed from the storms. "It may be some time before someone moves into this hut," Marisa said. They picked up the remaining food and closed the door. Jendrin strapped the door closed as they departed for the next hut.

Marisa knocked on the door of Adandir and Phaerl's hut. "Come!" a voice said from inside. Marisa opened the door and saw the couple sitting by the fireplace playing an arcane game of rocks and sticks.

"Hello, Adandir and Phaerl," Marisa said. "I see you are playing the game that never ends. I found it boring after some time."

"Perhaps," Phaerl replied. "But we have lots of time to play it now," she said. Jendrin spotted a weaving and a partially completed pot. The weaving looked complicated, and the pot had an attractive shape.

"I see you are weaving something beautiful," Jendrin said, looking at Phaerl.

"Yes, thank you," Pearl said. "In the past, we never made things for decoration. When I finish, it will be an impractical wall hanging," she said.

"The pot you are making is interesting," Jendrin said, looking at Adandir.

545

"Thank you, Jendrin," Adandir said. "The decorative pot I am making will do nothing but look interesting when I finish."

"I think it is already interesting," Jendrin said.

"Thank you," Adandir replied. "I assume you are here to check on the old folk."

"We want to ensure you don't need a healer's help and see if you have food and wood," Marisa said.

"Thank you." Phaerl said, "The boys brought wood this morning, and Grena emptied the chamber pot and left us more food. We are doing well, just waiting for summer to return."

"Good," Marisa said.

"This appears to be a complicated game you are playing," Jendrin said.

"It is pretty simple," Adandir said. "One person has stones along one edge while the other has sticks. You move your pieces until you force your opponent's pieces off the edge. The piece forced off reappears on the other end. That is why it is called the game that never ends."

"I see," Jendrin replied, not seeing the sense in the game. "I will leave you to it."

"Kai will visit tomorrow," Marisa said. "If you don't need anything, we will move on to the next hut."

"Thank you both for stopping by," Phaerl said.

Jendrin and Marisa waved goodbye as they left the hut. They continued their walk to Melronna's home.

"This is Melronna's home," Marisa said. "She is the elder who foretold Airalee was to create a child. We didn't believe her, but now we know it is true. I wonder if she will tell us something interesting today?" She said as she knocked on the door.

Melronna opened the door, looking surprised. "I thought Meliniel was returning," Melronna said. "I thought it was odd she was knocking on the door," as she turned to the fireplace. "Come in, please, and sit. Meliniel will be back soon, but we can talk while she is out," she said, sitting down in her spot by the fireplace. Looking up, she pointed to a chair for Marisa to sit in. Looking over at Jendrin, her face suddenly went blank.

"Yours is the seed that settled in Airalee's baby chamber. The child's future is important for Almora," she said. Turning her blank face to Marisa, she continued, "You have the seed of many swirling within you. When your baby chamber is ready, the right seed will find its way." Jendrin and Marisa were stunned at her pronouncement.

"Melronna?" Marisa said. "How do you see this?"

The door to the hut creaked open as Meliniel returned. "Guests! How wonderful!" Millennial said.

Melronna's face snapped back to normal as she looked at Marisa. "How do you know this, Melronna?" Marisa asked.

"Know what Marisa?" Melronna asked with a quizzical look on her face. "Oh my, did I again say something interesting I don't know about? I may not let you in here again unless I get to know what I say!" Melronna teased.

"You implied I will be with a child soon, and Jendrin seeded Airalee," Marisa said.

"Oh!" Melronna said, clapping her hands. "That is exciting."

"Yes," Marisa replied, knowing she would not get an answer. Jendrin stood by with no expression on his face.

"How wonderful!" Miliniel said, moving to her spot near the fireplace. "Airalee appeared to be well on her way to bearing her child," she said as she sat down.

"Yes," Jendrin replied, unfreezing his tongue. She will be a good mother. She has granted me the honor of being her baby-mate. I look forward to the child's birth."

"Good!" Melronna said, clapping again. The group fell to light conversation as Jendrin and Marisa recovered. The two older women finally wound down on conversion as Jendrin spoke.

"I have other tasks to attend to," Jendrin stood up.

"Of course, don't let us keep you," Melronna said.

"I will come with you," Marisa said. "I will inform Kai that our villagers are doing well."

"Goodbye, Ladies," Jendrin said as he opened the door.

"Goodbye to you both," Miliniel said as they waved goodbye.

Airalee

Airalee watched as Jendrin and Marisa left the companions' hut to do the healer's rounds.

"I am pleased Marisa volunteered to check our village today," Airalee said. "I feel tired but would have done it. I am happier to stay here," she said with a laugh.

"It is also much warmer here," Maylore said. "I fear there is too much of the snow season left for my comfort," he sighed. "I want to return to Gilriel's cave to gather my last mushroom. I have one small one remaining. I would like to use it to check how you are progressing and try to open your communication portal."

"I think I would like that," Airalee said. "I don't know what it would mean if you can open it. Are you sure you want to hear what I am saying?" she grinned.

"I can close my portal if you get too noisy," Maylore said, laughing. "I did not get the opportunity to chip away any dead energy from that portal. Ayare's touch diverted my attention. I got the impression that Ayare wanted to know who was nearby. She probably wanted to ensure I did not invade her body since she closed the window to her home.

"It eases my mind that you can check on her," Airalee said. "Did she seem worried?"

"She did not seem worried or injured," Maylore said. "I also noticed you had no healing energy floating inside you."

"I don't understand where it comes from anyway," Airalee said. "I tried to heal injuries of villagers I tended to. They had minor wounds, but they did not recover quickly. Do you think only Jendrin can receive it?"

Maylore considered for a few moments.

"I can watch while you touch and heal someone else," Maylore said. "Bring them here. We can add a chair near my bed so I can monitor it when I use a mushroom."

"Deal," Airalee said, standing up. The blue stone in the amulet had a swirl pattern inside of it. Maylore quickly recognized where he had seen the color and pattern before.

"That is the same color as Ayare's eyes," Maylore said, leaning forward to look into the stone. However, I don't think her eyes had a swirl pattern," he said.

"A swirl would be unusual," Airalee commented as Maylore sat back.

"True," Maylore said. He felt a sudden tickle in his throat and coughed, but it didn't seem to be something in his throat.

"My throat tickled for a second," Maylore said, rubbing his throat.

"Let's hope you are not catching something," Airalee said.

"I don't need that," Maylore said as he looked inward at the communication portal. He attached a string to Ayare's dot on the communication dome.

"We will let you sleep outside if you catch something," Airalee said. Maylore sat up straight, realizing he had heard her through the portal.

"I hear you!" he said.

"I hope so," Airalee replied. "I am sitting across from you, dad."

"No, through the portal, just now," he said, standing up. "Say something quietly to see if I hear it." Maylore put his hands over his ears as she spoke.

"Ayare is my child," she said in a whisper.

"I heard you say 'Ayare is my child' very plainly!" he said, almost jumping up and down. Airalee sat in amazement for a time.

"Is it the blue crystal that allows that?" she asked. "I will take it off to test that. She quickly removed the amulet and then said, "Marisa is my friend." in a whisper. Maylore did not react.

"I am ready," Maylore said.

"I did try, dad," Airalee said. Maylore uncovered his ears.

"I didn't hear anything," Maylore said.

"I took this amulet off, and it stopped working," Airalee said. "Let me put it on again and go outside." Airalee put the amulet on and walked outside. She walked a few paces away, then said, "The snow is cold out here." She could hear a cheer inside the hut as she heard in her mind, "Come back in." She re-entered the hut to see Maylore with a big grin on his face.

"Success!" he said, waving his arms. Airalee wasn't sure which was more remarkable, Maylore dancing or the discovery of communication. Airalee decided both were important and did a little dance of her own. Maylore stopped and looked at the crystal. "Shall we try another test?"

"I think it swirled while you talked. Say something more," Maylore said, watching the stone. "It will be nice to talk with you more often, dad," she said.

"Yes." Maylore said, "It does swirl when you talk. Let's try a few more tests. I will walk to the garden as you talk. I would like to see how far away from each other we can communicate," Maylore left the hut and traveled to the garden at the far end of the village. He could clearly hear her talking to Ayare as he continued along the path. He reached the entrance to the garden and could still listen to her. "I am in the garden and can still hear you," Maylore said.

"This is wonderful," Airalee said. "I hear you like you are standing next to me."

"I am returning to the hut," Maylore said, walking in that direction. He reentered the hut to find Airalee removing the amulet.

"Let me change it to an armband to see what happens," Airalee said. The amulet was long enough that she could wrap it twice around her arm and hook it in place. "Is it working now?" she asked.

"No," Maylore said, shaking his head. "I only hear you with my ears."

"Good," Airalee said. "Now we know how to shut me up," she chuckled. Maylore looked at his communication portal and saw a string still attached to Airalee's dot.

"I still have a connection to you on my portal," Maylore said. "It appears the crystal helps your communication portal finish a connection."

"Two amazing discoveries in two days!" Airalee said.

"Indeed," Maylore said. "It would be nice if you wore it to notify me if you need help."

"Thanks," Airalee said. "I will wear it," she said.

She returned with a small bottle and gave it to Maylore. "This will seem like a punishment after what you have done for me," Airalee said with a crooked smile. "This is the bandit potion we want you to test. I suggest you drink half now and the other half tomorrow. Please tell me how it affects you in the next few days," she said, sitting down.

The door opened, and Jendrin entered the room. He smiled at Airalee and hung his outerwear near the door.

"The villagers seem to be doing well," he said, sitting beside her. "There was, however, an odd moment with Melronna." Airalee and Maylore looked at him. "She said I gave you the seed to create your child."

"She may be the only one who didn't know you were the seeder," Airalee said. "How did she look odd saying that?"

"Her face became blank, and she appeared not to see anything," Jendrin said. "She seemed to be staring through us into the distance."

Airalee nodded as he continued.

"She said the child will be important to us in the future," Jendrin said.

"I suspect her isolation has given her a form of seeing," Airalee said. "Marisa tells me it did not work for Melronna in the past, and she seems unaware of it."

"Even when it happened, she seems completely unaware of saying anything," Jendrin said.

"Did she say anything else?" Airalee asked.

"She said Marisa was full of seed," Jendrin said, "but her baby chamber was not yet ready."

"Interesting, too," Airalee said. "Marisa very much wants to have a child. I hope for her sake it is soon." A now familiar knock sounded at the door.

"Let's go Jendrin!" Kai called without stopping at the door.

"Duty calls," a smiling Jendrin said, leaving the hut.

CHAPTER 35 - BABY TEST

"Snowing," Jendrin said, opening the door to the morning. "Some things will not wait," he said, pushing himself out the door for his morning routine. Maylore followed him to the door and looked at Airalee.

"I will gladly walk with you during your morning routine," Maylore said. "If you are ready."

Airalee looked at him, wondering why she would suddenly need help, but she decided to allow him to accompany her.

"I don't need any help," Airalee said, "but I would be glad for the company, dad." She stood and joined him at the door.

"You misinterpreted what I was saying," Maylore said. "You can catch me if I start to fall in the snow," he said jokingly.

"I see," she said, grabbing his arm. "We will see who saves whom here." She laughed and went out the door.

They were returning to the hut from their routine when they saw Jendrin returning with wood and fish. He stopped before them.

"I am sorry I didn't offer to help you, Airalee," Jendrin said. "I didn't think you wanted help."

"I am helping dad, just in case he might fall," Airalee said, smiling.

"I just wanted a fair lady to walk with me," Maylore said.

Airalee smacked him on the shoulder and started walking. Jendrin smiled and followed them back to the hut. The breakfast and banter continued, just like many prior mornings. Airalee and Jendrin rarely picked on each other, with Maylore constantly feeling part of the group. Maylore was happy to see the cohesion in the group as a knock came on the door.

"Be right there, Kai!" Jendrin said, rising and waving goodbye to his companions.

"I am amazed he continues to face such dangerous duties," Airalee chuckled, looking at Maylore.

"He is a hale man, and he can handle it," Maylore replied, using a strong voice.

"Speaking of being hale, did you use the other half of the potion?" Airalee asked.

"I did," Maylore replied. "I'm not sure I can judge whether it is working correctly," he said.

"I could ask Marisa to display herself to see if you notice," Airalee said. "I suspect she would be willing."

"Don't tempt me," Maylore said, looking at her. "She has a beautiful shape, but I will pass."

"Alright, dad," Airalee said with a smile. "Perhaps it is working, or you want to avoid embarrassment. I will ask about the potion's effectiveness in a few days."

"Good idea," he replied.

A rustling of feathers stirred the outside air as a bird landed atop the hut. "Caw!" came a cry.

"A visitor?" Maylore questioned as he opened the door. "Caw Caw!" came the cry as the bird flew onto a branch near Maylore. "Bert! I think," Maylore said, looking at the black bird with two red feathers extending up his beak. Maylore felt a knock on his communication portal. "It must be Bert. Come in, Bert!" Maylore said, opening the door wide. The bird cocked its head and then hopped onto Maylore's shoulder. "That is a first," Maylore said, looking at the bird and closing the door.

"You have a friend?" Airalee asked, looking at the bird. Maylore sat in a chair as Bert cawed loudly and shifted behind Maylore.

"Oh my," Maylore said, looking at the communication portal. A picture of a greeting followed by one of a wolf came from the dot named Bert. Maylore laughed, saying, "He thinks you are a predator, Airalee, and he is hiding." Maylore returned a picture of a friend to Bert. The bird walked to Maylore's shoulder and looked at Airalee, his head moving side to side. "I think you are being judged," Maylore said.

"I hope I pass," Airalee said, sitting still. Bert finally ruffled his feathers and settled down, watching Airalee. He sent a picture of himself with his head cocked to one side. "It seems you are on probation. He sent a picture of you needing to be watched," Maylore said.

"I will be careful," Airalee said, smiling as she mimicked the bird by cocking her head. The bird seemed to chuckle and sat quietly.

"He has never shown any interest in approaching me before," Maylore said, picking up nuts from the table. He offered the nuts to Bert, who turned aside. Bert sent him a picture of the swamp, worms, and the twin suns at a third of their cycle. Bert sent another picture of being lonely. "Ah," Maylore said. "He is well fed, just lonely without Gilriel." Maylore sent him a picture of looking for Gilriel. Bert shook his head and returned a picture of an empty cave.

"Let's see what happens when I get up to clear the table," Airalee said as she rose. Bert watched her but didn't move. Airalee cleared the table and went outside to wash their dishes. The heavy crunch of snow announced another visitor as Jendrin opened the door. Bert rose, cawing at him as Jendrin abruptly stopped in the doorway. A picture of a wolf appeared to Maylore.

"An IB," Jendrin said, looking at Bert. "You are a man of surprises, Maylore." Bert continued to caw at him until Maylore managed to send a friend picture to Bert. Bert stopped cawing but was ready to fly as Jendrin held the door open. Bert eyed him with suspicion but stayed on Maylore's shoulder.

"This is Bert," Maylore told him. "He thinks you are a predator and is warning me to be ready to flee." Jendrin smiled and closed the door.

"Nice to meet you, Bert. May I come in?" he asked. Bert remained standing, watching as yet another stranger entered his world.

"Move slowly and sit," Maylore said. Jendrin moved slowly toward the table and sat in a far chair.

"This is the bird from Gilriel's cave?" Jendrin asked.

"Yes," Maylore replied, "It seems Gilriel has not returned, and the bird is lonely."

"Is he a hungry bird, I wonder?" Jendrin asked.

"He sent me a picture of recently eating worms in the swamp with the other birds," Maylore said.

"You can talk with him?" Jendrin asked.

"No, some animals communicate using pictures. Most animals do not communicate with others outside their species," Maylore said.

"He would be a welcome addition to our scouting force," Jendrin said.

"Do we have a scouting force?" Maylore asked.

"No, I don't believe so," Jendrin said. "If we start one, he would be a valuable addition."

"Perhaps," Maylore said. "He is an intelligent bird and is unlikely to cooperate unless it helps him too."

"Fair enough, a mutual benefit may be challenging to come up with," Jendrin said, standing to pick up his staff. "I believe I have figured out how to satisfy the council and train a defensive group. Latel and I are meeting in the council's hut to discuss a plan. There is enough room to conceive and practice skills to achieve that balance." He stood and collected his staff. "When Airalee returns, tell her I will see her tonight." Jendrin walked to the door, saying, "Nice to meet you, Bert. See you tonight, Maylore," as he left the hut.

"I will tell her," Maylore said, waving goodbye. Alone in the hut, Maylore looked to Bert, saying, "I need to move to the cave. Our hut will become too full when Ayare arrives and you come to visit. I will miss some of the daily activities, but a growing family needs space, and it is limited here. When the snow recedes, I will join you in the cave. If Gilriel returns, it is still large enough for us and then some." he sent a picture of the three of them sitting at the lunch table. Bert nodded his head up and down as if agreeing. Bert stood up and flew to the side of the door. Hanging onto the sides, he looked back from Maylore to the door. "Out, I assume," Maylore said, rising. He opened the door wide, and Bert flew into the sky. Airalee was coming up the path as Bert flew away.

"I was hoping to visit with Bert a little more," Airalee said, reaching the hut.

"He had more worms to catch," Maylore said, holding the door for her.

"That sounds wonderful," Airalee replied. "We will not be reduced to eating worms this season. There is still plenty of food stored for all of us," she said as she entered the hut.

"Good news for the birds, too," Maylore said.

"I passed Kai on the way back, and she wants to start testing the girls after the night session," Airalee said, stacking the dishes back in the cabinet. "She wants me to run the sessions so that I know how to mix and serve the potions."

"It seems like a good plan," Maylore replied, sitting at the table. "Jendrin said he and Latel would work on the defensive plan today. He believes he can convince Rendal and the council of the defensive abilities he can teach using the quarterstaff."

"If they can find a method to stop Oleg and Birsha's bandits from raiding, I am for it," Airalee said, returning to the table. "I would like to bring one of the injured villagers here to test for the healing energy while you watch."

"I will be ready," Maylore said.

A knock came on the door as he sat. Airalee opened the door to find one of the villagers with a gash on his arm, slowly bleeding.

"You helped us last time," the villager said, "I was hoping you could help me this time."

"Yes! Come in," Airalee said, holding the door wide. "I will get bandages. Sit at the table, and I will join you," she said, ushering him to the table. Maylore greeted him and retrieved a piece of fabric they created for Jendrin's injury. He laid it on the table underneath the villager's arm. Airalee returned carrying bandaging material and a potion bottle. "This will sting but prevent infection," Airalee said, opening the bottle. "The wound is not too deep." She cleaned off the wound and pulled the skin together. "Ready for the sting?" she asked. The villager nodded, and she poured a liberal amount onto the injury." The villager sat watching the process.

"What kind of magic is in this bottle?" he asked.

"Not magic," Airalee said. "It is from a Neem tree. We crushed the leaves and saved them into a container. It helps prevent infections." The villagers kept quiet and continued to watch. "Hold your skin together here while I wrap it," she told the villager. She started wrapping the wound with the strips of material, allowing the villager to remove his grip as she went. "Don't use this arm too much, and in two sunrises, return to me so we can add a poultice and wrap it again. We do not want it to become infected."

The villager nodded, said that he understood, and started to rise.

"Would you help us briefly," she asked him.

"What do I need to do?" he asked.

"Sit quietly with your eyes shut while I lightly probe the area around the injury."

"As Kai does?" the villager asked.

"Yes, like she does," Airalee replied.

"Alright," the villager replied.

"Good," Airalee said, nodding to Maylore.

He watched as her hand touched the villager's arm. He requested the planet's blue energy to flow into the wound. Maylore saw the blue energy flow into and out of the shallow damage. There was no sign of infection or healing energy from her touch.

Airalee saw Maylore signal her and knew this session was over.

"Thank you for your help," she told the villager after probing his arm.

"Is that all?" he asked.

"Yes," Airalee said, standing up.

"Did you feel anything?" he asked.

"I felt nothing out of the ordinary," she said. "That is good."

"Thank you," the villager said, standing and smiling.

The villager left as Maylore rested his head on the table.

"What did you see?" she asked.

"I didn't see any healing energy," Maylore said. "Perhaps the ability comes and goes."

Airalee was visibly disappointed.

"I did the same for the villager as for Jendrin," Airalee said. "Why does it work for him and not for others?"

"Perhaps the energy turns into healing energy from a different source," Maylore said, "I am afraid I don't know, Airalee."

"Thank you for trying, dad," Airalee said. "I will think about it while I work on the book the rest of the day."

"I believe I will practice my energy skills," Maylore said, moving to his bed.

Jendrin

Jendrin entered the council hut to find Latel making a fire in the fireplace.

"We need to build a fire in here occasionally to keep the insides from rotting," Latel said, standing up. "It won't be so warm that you get hot practicing with your quarterstaff."

"Good," Jendrin said, "Let's move the chairs away so I can attempt to develop ideas for defense skills." They moved the tables and chairs to the rear of the hut as Jendrin explained his plan. "Ideas seem to come to me as I talk. I will start by reviewing how I decided on the quarterstaff," he said, looking at Latel. "I considered what could be a defensive tool." Jendrin started a slow spin of his quarterstaff to keep his hand busy. "I knew edged melee weapons would not fit. Thrown weapons and other range weapons would not be allowed. Building traps would most likely hurt our villagers and are difficult to plan and use. The only things I believe would work are shields and handheld tools. A shield would protect us until it broke or the hand holding it tired. A club would work, except it does not protect a defender entirely. A long stick, or quarterstaff, is the only tool I think will work for defense."

"It still seems hard to believe a stick can defend us," Latel said. "The Tocor uses a bow effectively. Are you sure it will not work?"

"A range weapon is intended to kill the target," Jendrin said. "We are forbidden to use tools that kill."

"Yes, agreed," Latel replied, looking down.

561

"We could later adapt a quarterstaff for offensive skills," Jendrin said. "We could demonstrate offensive skills without practicing them."

"I would like to know it has offensive abilities even if we cannot teach them," Latel said. "How does it work for defense?

"I did not know at first," Jendrin said. "I sat considering how to use the quarterstaff to affect defensive skills. The concept slowly seeped into my mind as I played with this quarterstaff. I don't know where the ideas came from, but I seemed to know already how to use a quarterstaff." Jendrin said, grabbing the staff in both hands. Jendrin decided he needed a better stance and moved one foot back, pointed away from his attacker, and balanced slightly back of center and knees slightly bent. The stance allowed him to move forward and back without moving his feet. "This feels like a good stance," Jendrin said. "I can rock forward, back, and to each side. I can easily slide my feet forward, back, or to any side. I'll start with this."

"The stance makes you look dangerous," Latel said. "What is next?"

"The defensive part I will propose to Rendal is done with just a few ideas," Jendrin continued. "First, face away from an opponent and use a passive stance to show your presence. Second, If they continue, face your opponent, resting the quarterstaff at our feet as a bluff. If they advance, use a ready stance and spin the staff to make it look like we are prepared for their attack."

Jendrin started a slow spin, pointing in Latel's direction. He dropped the staff, attempting to speed up the spin, and settled again for a slow spin.

"If they do attack, we move to the third step, which is a block," Jendrin said. "We must hold the quarterstaff high to block their overhead swing if they attack with a hatchet, club, knife, or whatever." Jendrin held the quarterstaff high with one hand. "That's not going to be successful," Jendrin said. "They would knock the quarterstaff down if we use one hand." He changed the grip to hold it up with both hands. "This would work," he said, thrusting the quarterstaff upward. "They would hit my hands if I hold them too close," he said, spreading his hands shoulder-width apart. "I could catch the head of their club or hatchet between my hands."

"Would they break your quarterstaff?" Latel asked.

"Possibly," Jendrin said. "This quarterstaff is very strong," he said, swinging the staff to the ground. The quarterstaff made a slight musical tone as it heavily struck the ground, remaining whole. "It bends slightly but springs back quickly," Jendrin said, standing upright, ready to resume his demonstration.

"If they attack low, it would be a similar process, except we thrust downward to meet the weapon," Jendrin said as he thrust downward.

"How would that work for a knife attack or any weapon to the middle?" Latel asked.

Pushing the staff out to where a knife would be, the technique did not work.

"I could easily miss a small target like that," Jendrin said. "It also would allow them to press the weapon into my body since I would be too close." He considered momentarily before swinging the staff outward and sliding his hand down to meet the other hand. "Swinging the quarterstaff out, I can knock away any knife, hatchet, or anything else in the attacker's hands. Swinging down, I could prevent a kick from landing."

He practiced swinging out and down but lost the staff several times when it sailed beyond his intended stopping point. "I need a way to stop the staff where I want to," Jendrin said. He thought that his back arm would be pointing to the intended target so his quarterstaff would not need to go farther than that.

"If I pull the staff up to snap beside my trailing arm, I should be able to maintain control," he said, looking at Latel. He struck out at an imaginary knife, snapping the trailing end to his elbow area. The quarterstaff stopped at the imaginary hand where he intended. "This may work well," he said, sounding surprised. "My elbow may hurt temporarily, but the technique may work. "I need to do a lot of practice before I talk with the Beacon, but perhaps these base ideas will work for us," Jendrin said as Latel nodded.

"It will take time to learn your ideas," Latel said, "but they seem workable."

"Assuming Rendal and the council approve," Jendrin said. "If they disapprove, it will be just myself who attempts to create a deterrent," he said with a smile.

"I will be sure to join you, even if I have to train out of the council's vision," Latel said.

"Good man," Jendrin said. "If you will stand by the door and face me, I will stand far away and see how to work this defensive process," Jendrin said, moving to the back center of the room.

Latel moved to the door and faced Jendrin five steps away. Jendrin held the staff and stood straight. Jendrin started spinning practice again as Latel grabbed a stick and followed along. Time passed when they both heard Kai call, "Jendrin! It is time to do your duty!" she called from outside the hut.

"All right, Kai," he said as he gathered his belongings.

"I will set the hut right while you attend to your arduous duty," Latel said, grinning.

"Thank you, Latel. It is my contribution to the village." Jendrin laughed as he followed Kai through the snow. The short walk to the baby's birthing area allowed Kai to talk to him.

"Airalee and I will check your group's handiwork with the girls after this session," Kai said as they walked. "Tell her to come to my hut. I plan to have Airalee create the potions and run the process," Kai said, stopping suddenly and facing Jendrin. "I expect you to treat Airalee well," Kai said, poking Jendrin in the chest.

"I have every intention to treat her like she deserves, being a doting father," Jendrin said, slightly stunned she said it.

"I do not want to lose another apprentice," Kai said. "Especially one highly qualified. These old bones are telling me to retire soon. I plan to keep to their request." Kai turned and started walking. Jendrin felt at a loss but quickly followed.

Airalee and Maylore quietly played sticks and stones when the crunching snow outside announced a visitor. Jendrin opened the door and hung his outer cloak near it.

"Kai would like you to join her in her hut," Jendrin said as he filled his bowl. He hugged Airalee and sat beside her.

"Alright. I am off," Airalee said, standing up. She hugged both of them, gathered her cloak, and set off for Kai's hut. She saw Kai entering the storage hut and followed her in.

"Ah, good," Kai said. "I will show you how to mix the baby-testing potion," Kai said. "You need these four herbs and this one vegetable," Kai said, placing each on the sorting table. "Grind each one up and place them in the mixing bowl." Airalee ground each plant and put them in the bowl. "We add water and warm it to dissolve it into the water," Kai said. "When it becomes hot to your finger, bring it to my hut," Kai said.

Airalee carried the earthen bowl to the kitchen fire and warmed it. Airalee tested the bowl several times before she decided it was ready and returned to Kai's hut.

"Good," Kai said, testing the bowl and nodding. "The girls will be here soon." Kai poured the first small cup for testing, and both sat at the table. Airalee recalled her recent use of the baby-testing potion as they waited.

"I did not think I was with child when I drank this on my test," Airalee said.

"Most who come here are suspicious but unsure," Kai said. "Your skin seemed off-normal to me. You told us of your reaction to food, and you live with two men. It was not hard to suspect something."

"Only Jendrin," Airalee replied.

"We have discussed the wisdom of your choice before," Kai said. "I do not judge you and believe you will be a good mother."

A knock on the door diverted their attention.

"Come," Kai said as one of the village girls entered the hut. Airalee recognized her as one of Lafrea's assistants but could not remember her name. "Galaswen," Kai said, "Sit, and we will start your test." Galaswen sat at the table. "Drink this cup of herbs, and we can talk," Kai said. Galaswen drank the small amount from the cup. Airalee smiled at Galaswen and refilled the cup for the next person. Kai pushed the large earthenware pot to Galaswen. "If you get sick, empty yourself into the pot. While you wait, tell us what you are making with Lafrea."

Galaswen happily told them of the jewelry she was making.

There was another knock on the door, and Marisa entered the hut. Marisa hugged Airalee as she sat next to Galaswen. Airalee passed the cup to Marisa, who drank it and listened to Galaswen talk. Airalee filled the cup again as another knock came on the door. "Come!" Kai said as two more girls entered the hut. Marisa and Galaswen slid to the far end of the bench as the two newcomers sat and drank their portion.

The girls chatted with everyone as they waited for their test to finish.

Marisa suddenly jumped up wide-eyed and added her dinner to the pot. "I guess my baby chamber is ready," Marisa said, smiling and sitting. The three remaining girls laughed and congratulated Marisa. A short time later, the last girl to drink the potion grabbed the pot. The four girls chatted, waiting to see if the other two would follow.

"It appears we have answers for two of you," Kai said after more time passed. "The seeders will be sad two have finished, but they still have two more.

"I would be glad to continue," Marisa volunteered.

"I believe you would," Kai replied. "You would drain all four of them completely."

The girls all laughed as Marisa looked proud.

"Be that as it may," Kai said, "I will gather you other two tomorrow to continue your journey," Kai said, pointing to the two who were not sick. "I will soon gather all of you to discuss your motherhood journey. Now, all of you, leave so I may get some sleep." Kai said, shooing the group toward the door. Marisa was smiling as she hugged Airalee and left the hut. The other three smiled and bid them goodbye.

Kai poured the rest of the potion into a bottle and placed it on the shelf near the table. "Empty the large pot, Airalee, and we will do it again in two nights. I will visit our sick and elderly villagers tomorrow. You can do the next," Kai said.

Airalee nodded as she left the hut to empty and clean the pot before returning to her hut for the night.

Chapter 36 - Defensive Force

Sunrises went swiftly by as Airalee neared the end of her baby's development. More snow melted each day than fell from the sky, and clear skies became more frequent. The paths between village huts became visible, allowing villagers to travel easily between them. Villagers told the companions the snow would soon be gone, and summer would return. Clear skies brought more villagers out of their huts to meet in the bath and kitchen area. Some villagers had not seen one another since the snow grew too heavy to walk through. Many were joyous just to converse with someone. With heavy snow blocking the road, travelers had stopped coming but would soon return.

The companions continued their daily activities, which revolved around Airalee's baby and sharpening individual skills. Jendrin had long ago completed his duty with the seeder group. All of the girls were now with child. He continued to work out the details of his quarterstaff proposal and groomed his quarterstaff. Maylore grew assertive in his use of various energies and found it easier to communicate and monitor the location of dots on his communication dome. Airalee made rounds of the sick and elderly several days a week. Most patients did not require daily visits, allowing her to go every two sunrises. Marisa would take a few visits instead to enable Airalee to rest. Jendrin or Maylore would often accompany Airalee or Marisa on their rounds. Neither woman required any help, but each felt better with someone going with them.

Melronna made no new pronouncements other than forgetting that Airalee and Marisa were with child. Selakiir was generally in good spirits since his children would visit several times a week. After storms, Pearl and Adandir ventured out of their hut to view the calm sea surrounded by a new white coat of snow. Werloth and Kelkalyn had yet to return to their huts.

Traveling in the snow was becoming more laborious for Airalee, even with diminishing snow on the paths. Airalee made rounds alone this morning, briefly visiting each patient. She returned to the village children's care area, stopping to rest while talking with the children and caregivers. Gathering her strength, she returned to Kai's hut.

Kai noticed she looked tired as Airalee opened the door.

"Airalee," Kai said, "It is time to let me do the rounds again until your baby is here. Marisa can continue to help until she determines she cannot. Come sit here while I look at your baby's health."

Airalee happily sat in a high examination chair while Kai poked at her baby bump.

"It seems the child is getting ready to leave the baby chamber," Kai said. "You should remain alert to its birth."

"I am ready for her to come now," Airalee said, rubbing her back. "I think she is running up and down my spine."

"I believe the baby is turning to be born," Kai said. "You will not be genuinely comfortable until she has been born. When it is time, I want you to go to the birthing hut behind the children's hut. The women there will bring you to a birthing bed. They will notify me and help me bring forth the child."

"Are they going to birth her?" Airalee asked.

"They are skilled at birthing children, having helped nearly as many women through this as I have," Kai said. "I have set the room up with potions to ease the pain after delivery. I don't give pain potions before since it slows the birth process. My hope is I don't have to stitch you up afterward."

"That would be nice too," Airalee said, not considering there might be tearing.

"One key thing for all of our sanity," Kai said with a severe look. "Instruct your men to stay away! I don't want to have to deal with their distress over your birthing!"

Airalee laughed at that, but Kai remained severe.

"Those two men have become very close to you," Kai said. "Hearing you in pain will make them very irritable. We don't want to try to calm them and attend to you." Kai said, glaring at her.

"I will see to it they stay in the hut or somewhere else," Airalee said.

Kai nodded before continuing.

"You say you have not been through this before," Kai said. "Expect the process to last many hours to a day. Since this is your first child, it will take longer."

Airalee slumped a little in the chair as Kai continued.

"Do not be concerned," Kai said. "Many women before you created children, and all endured the process from beginning to painful birth. You will do well, too."

Airalee sighed and showed a little smile.

"If you have no objections, I would like all four recently seeded girls to attend your birthing," Kai said.

"I don't mind," Airalee said. "It would give them a glimpse of what is coming their way."

A knock on the door announced another visitor. "Come," Kai said as she helped Airalee down. Marisa opened the door and smiled at both of them.

"Ah, one of my four other baby creators," Kai said, waving Marisa in. Marisa's baby bump was plain, but she still moved quickly about.

"You look tired, Airalee," Marisa said, hugging her.

"I am," Airalee replied. "The snow is getting to me."

"Ah," Marisa replied, "at least the weight you carry with you is not slowing you down," she teased.

"Maybe a little," Airalee replied. "She is spinning around in there, making me dizzy."

"I can't talk," Marisa said, chuckling. "I will soon be in your situation."

"Do you have a complaint for me?" Kai interrupted, looking at Marisa.

"No," Marisa replied. "Just to ask you to check my baby and ask if you need help."

"On the chair," Kai said, looking at Marisa and then the baby. "I want Airalee to stop doing rounds and rest. If you would climb the hill to check the elders' huts, It would greatly help me. I will check the few patients in the village."

"I would be glad to do that," Marisa said. "Getting outside daily would be welcome unless there is a storm."

"Stay in the hut if there is," Kai replied. "The patients will be fine without us for a day or two." Kai turned again to Airalee. "I want you to watch my examination to begin understanding what to do for future baby makers,"

Airalee watched Kai prod different locations, asking Marisa questions as she went. She quickly completed her examination and spoke to Marisa.

"You and the baby seem fine to me," Kai said. "I expect the other three to arrive soon. I want you two to stay even though it is crowded. Stand in the back and wait for each exam. I will then remind you all about being a mom."

Just as she finished, a knock on the door announced another mom.

"Come," Kai said as two more girls entered. They all greeted each other and took their turn on the high examining chair. The last one arrived as Kai finished examining the other two and took her turn on the chair.

"Girls," Kai said, interrupting their chatter, "I realize many of you are long from your child being born, but I want to start telling you about birthing," she said, looking at each of them. Kai repeated what she told Airalee as their heads nodded in understanding. She finished her talk and asked for any questions.

"No questions?" she asked. They all shook their heads and waited.

"You will all attend Airalee's birthing when it happens. It will be a foretelling of your delivery." The room remained quiet, so Kai pointed to the door, saying, "Out the door with you all then. Come back in another week," she said as they all left.

Jendrin

Jendrin practiced using the quarterstaff while developing his plan to use it defensively. Ideas to use it effectively came slowly but steadily each day of practice. He practiced outside their hut when storms passed and did planning on stormy days. Today, he removed bark from the other four quarterstaffs and helped Airalee. He found that even though his staff was light, it still took new strength to wield it. Spinning the staff had built strength in his arms and wrists. It had become effortless for him to use either hand to spin and stop the staff effectively. He rarely dropped the staff, even when transferring the spinning staff from one hand to another. He recently learned to spin it over his head without dropping it. He considered each day how he would present a plan to Rendal on how to deter attacks. He knew it must range from passive resistance to defensive stances, ending with using force to defend oneself. He would suggest a plan to Rendal to teach the defensive force how to defend and do a counterattack. He held little hope that the council would allow a complete counterattack.

"Your form looks more impressive each time I see you," Latel said as he arrived and stood a safe distance away.

"Thank you," Jendrin said, turning to face him. "Today, I am working on what defensive techniques Rendal and the council would approve of for our defensive force."

"I would be glad to listen if you want to bounce the ideas off of me," Latel said.

"It does help to talk through it," Jendrin said. "The ideas seem to flow quicker into my mind that way."

"I am ready to listen," Latel said, leaning against a tree.

"I plan to start from the beginning and describe it as a series of steps the group would use if facing an opponent," Jendrin said.

"First, take a passive stance," Jendrin said as he demonstrated. "Face away from the aggressor, spread your feet apart, and hold the staff vertically with one hand, placing one end by your foot. Push the end of the staff to the ground."

"Why face away?" Latel asked.

"I hope it will appease the passive council to show our group is not aggressive," Jendrin said. "We could still see what the aggressor is doing."

"I see," Latel said. "What next?"

"If the opponent approaches and draws a weapon, use the second stance," Jendrin said. "Face the aggressor. Move one foot back but point slightly outward. Raise your quarterstaff to waist height. Place each hand one-third from each end. Center your weight between your feet. If they continue, we will add a little show by spinning the staff between your hands."

"It looked impressive when I arrived here," Latel said. "Do you think it will stop them?"

"A less determined aggressor may stop and move away," Jendrin said.

"What if they don't?" Latel asked.

"If they press an attack, go to phase three," Jendrin said, "stop the spin and bring the staff parallel to the waist. If they swing their weapon from the top, forcefully push your staff up to block the weapon. Hit it below the weapon head on the handle. Perhaps it will break a poorly made weapon and prevent damage to the quarterstaff." Jendrin was sure nothing would damage his staff, but he may not always have his staff. He may have to use a tree branch instead.

"If they attack low, forcefully push the staff down to block the weapon. If they attack from the center, thrust the end of the staff out to meet the weapon and bring the other end of the staff to stop alongside your elbow. If their weapon is not knocked away, thrust the elbow end of the staff out to hit the weapon away." Jendrin demonstrated by swinging the elbow end of the staff toward Latel. "We would repeat that process for each attack," Jendrin said.

"If they knocked my weapon away, that would stop me!" Latel said. "Do we need further steps?"

"I want to consider how to stop the attacks," Jendrin said as he stood quietly. "Perhaps a counterattack would force the opponent to stop and still be allowed by the council."

A vision came to his mind of a swinging staff that struck a weapon that could next hit the attacker in the ankle, knee, elbows, and hands or poke the end of the staff into their body.

"We could disable an aggressor by hitting them in an ankle, knee, elbow, or hand," Jendrin said. "I am sure that would convince them to stop simply from the pain. The council may approve of using the end of the quarterstaff to poke the aggressor in the torso. It would not cause permanent damage but knock them back for a while." Jendrin demonstrated by poking in the direction of Latel's torso.

"I would have stopped a long time ago," Latel said. "Knocking the wind out of me or smashing my joints would certainly do it."

"That is my hope," Jendrin replied. "The last step I am sure the council will not allow is an offensive attack to kill. The quarterstaff has a lot of power behind it and could easily kill. The tactics I will teach for defense counterattack will work for offense, too. It could easily put them down if we launch a strike to the head, throat, or body instead. What are your thoughts, Latel?"

"I believe you have a balanced method of defending us and getting the passive council to agree reluctantly," Latel said. "You will need to emphasize protecting our young and deemphasize the possible death of anyone."

Jendrin stood quietly, wondering if he could accomplish balancing that conversion.

"If our little group backs me up, I can do it," Jendrin said.

Moving to the center of the floor, he practiced spinning the staff with one hand and then the other.

"The thought comes to me that these are warm-up and practice exercises," Jendrin said. "I hope I am doing something useful," he said as he switched to a rowing motion. Jendrin spent quite a bit of time working through motions that began to flow smoothly.

"Impressive," Latel said. "How do you plan to train our little group?"

"I settled on first strengthening our arms and wrists by making these flashy quarterstaff spin moves," Jendrin said. "We start each session with a rowing motion, followed by spinning in one hand and a smooth transfer to the other. It will take a lot of time for them to be able to do that. We will finish with a transfer spin over his head to the first hand and planting the end of the staff on the ground."

"Good," Latel said. "I would like to try myself."

"I hope we can convince Beacon Rendal," Jendrin said, "and then you can be my first student. I can get around my promise to avoid teaching if you pretend to be a practice attacker. You would be instead teaching me to see if my plan will or will not work."

Latel's face showed caution as he considered.

575

"You may only have a stick," Latel said, "but you have proven to me it can kill anyone."

"I will not attack you, Latel," he said. "Use a long stick and pretend to strike from each angle and see if I can defend."

The two spent time practicing attack and defense. Jendrin could quickly stop attacks until Latel finally wore down and leaned against the tree again.

"It seems you can stop any attack," Latel said. "I think you should discuss it with Rendal.

"A few more practice sessions, and I would agree," Jendrin said. "I am beginning to feel I need to finish this development."

"Airalee's child will be here soon," Latel said. "I see why you would want to have Rendal's blessing before she arrives," Latel said.

"That is a good reason," Jendrin said as he leaned on his staff. "Oleg may return when the snow melts. I want to be ready if he does." Jendrin's face took on a stern look. "I plan to defend us from Oleg regardless of what the council decides."

"I concur," Latel said. "I believe most of the council will approve."

The crunch of snow signaled the arrival of another person.

"There you are, Jendrin," Rendal said as he stopped next to Latel. "I see you have a beautiful wood stick. Is it part of your defensive plan?"

"Yes, Beacon, it is," Jendrin replied, "It is called a quarterstaff, and I believe I have worked out a plan that will satisfy what you asked me to do."

"Good!" Rendal said. "Are you ready to show me what you propose?"

Jendrin looked at Latel before he replied.

"I believe I am, Beacon Rendal," Jendrin replied, looking back at Rendal. "I believe a four-step plan would work for us. Only steps one or two will be needed to prevent most attacks. If they attack us, we may need step three."

"Alright," Rendal said, "let's see what steps one, two, and three look like."

Jendrin stepped away from them and started his demonstration.

"First is a passive stance," Jendrin said, spreading his feet shoulder-width apart, he explained phase one. "I believe many less aggressive opponents will not push us. We will continue to watch the opponent and look passive. Step two is used when an opponent advances. Jendrin explained the second phase. "If they attack, go to step three." Jendrin stepped back and demonstrated step three. "I believe the more aggressive opponent will reconsider attacking us if it looks like we can defend ourselves."

Jendrin stopped and set the end of the staff near his boot. "The less aggressive attacker may be dismayed by the show and leave."

"Your demonstration looked dangerous enough to me," Rendal said, having moved back a few steps while watching.

"I am afraid not all attackers will be deterred," Jendrin said. "I recommend we teach the defenders how to stop an attack," Jendrin said, looking earnestly at Rendal. "Stopping an attack will prevent our people from being hurt or killed."

Rendal bowed his head, looking thoughtful.

"I want to hear all of your steps," Rendal said. "We will then discuss what to present to the council."

Jendrin nodded and explained and demonstrated the remaining steps of his plan.

Rendal listened and watched as Jendrin finished his plan. Rendal looked down again.

"I believe we could easily get them to agree to the first three steps," Rendal said. "The fourth, I suspect, will be a tie. I do not support the killing phase. No one on the council will support it either," he said, looking up again.

"I can teach the group phases one through three," Jendrin said. "We can consider phase four later. I can be ready to teach the steps when you are ready."

"Let's present this to the council first," Rendal said.

"Agreed," Jendrin said. "I can present the concept any time you are ready."

"Good," Rendal said, looking at the long, thin staff Jendrin held. "It seems hard to believe a stick could defend you against hatchets. Do you believe an attack with the quarterstaff would cause real damage?"

"I can assure you it can be deadly," Jendrin said.

"May I see your quarterstaff?" Rendal asked. Jendrin passed the staff to him as Rendal wondered. "It is made of beautiful, clear wood and is very light. Will it break easily?" he said, passing it back to Jendrin.

"It is solid," Jendrin said. "I cannot cut it with my knife," Jendrin said as he started bouncing the end of it on the hard ground. A soft, clear sound greeted their ears.

"I see," Rendal said. "It also sings," he finished with a smile. "I will arrange a meeting when more snow is gone." Rendal started to walk away when he said, "I believe Airalee's child is due soon. Tell her I wish her the best." Rendal turned and waved to them as he left. Latel and Jendrin waved back.

"It sounds like Rendal approved your training idea," Latel said.

"Yes," Jendrin replied, "I believe you will be my first recruit."

"I would be proud to be first," Latel said. "Will you help me find the makings of a quarterstaff I can build?"

"I have another staff Airalee picked out, and you may have it," Jendrin said. "I have already cleared the bark from it," Jendrin said, stepping inside the hut and retrieving one staff along the wall. "You need to finish clearing the outer wood, then smooth it with oil from your hands. You can also use some plant oil on it."

Latel looked very happy as he received the staff and gripped it with both hands.

"Thank you, Jendrin," Latel said, looking it over.

Maylore

Maylore saw that Jendrin was busy practicing with his quarterstaff as he exited the hut. Closing the door, he started walking toward Kelkalyn's hut. Maylore had seen on his communication portal that he was moving toward his hut. The snow didn't cover the ice beneath the path, making the climb up to the flat where the elder's hut was especially icy. Rendal's crew of boys were delivering wood and supplies to the elders as he passed behind the huts.

Waving at the now familiar faces, he walked to the end of the row, where he saw Kelkalyn standing in front of his hut looking out to sea.

"Kelkalyn," Maylore said as he approached. Kelkalyn was without expression as he turned and walked toward Maylore.

"Has the master been to the village?" he asked.

"No," Maylore replied. "I suspect the snow is too high for anyone to travel."

"I agree," Kelkalyn said as he walked toward his hut. "He will not return until all of the snows are gone. Come, let's warm up," he said, opening the door. Maylore followed him into the warm, sparsely furnished hut. "Sit," Kelkalyn said, pointing at the chair opposite him. Maylore sat as Kelkalyn started speaking. "I have

579

contemplated the danger you and Airalee pose and believe you will not betray my presence. I hope I have guessed correctly."

"If you want to remain here in secret, I will tell no one of your presence," Maylore said, nodding. Kelkalyn nodded in return.

"I will tell you of my past and how we can help each other in the future," Kelkalyn said, sitting in his chair. "I ask you not to spread the tale to anyone. Some will not approve and put the master on my tail again."

"Again?" Maylore questioned.

"A different name knew me in the past," Kelkalyn said. "When I was much younger, I unknowingly developed forbidden skills," Kelkalyn said, leaning back in his chair. "I was known as Esteren, a student of an ancient scholar named Parthwen. I trained with Neldor, now called the Red Wizard. Gilriel was part of a different training group under a lesser sorcerer. Parthwen and I developed greater abilities than the rest. Working together, we created some powerful spells we wrote into a book. We did not attempt to hide the book, and when the master found out about our work, he took the book and honored us with a feast to celebrate our work. He sat us at a table of honor above the rest of the group. We should have noticed he served the rest of the group from bowls different from ours. I later learned that our feast was full of yellow-spotted green mushrooms. I remember nothing after our feast. Gilriel told me he saw the master lead Pathwen and me out of the hall. I never saw Parthwen again. The sentinels of the Tocor village Nasin found me wandering the cliffs and saved me from walking off one of them. They tied me to a tree with a long rope so I could wander but a short distance. Days later, I recovered from the mushroom effects. I spent a few days with the kind Tocor as they fed and kept me warm. It became apparent that the master was not a good man and that I should hide my presence from him. I changed my name to Kelkalyn and stayed in the small human village of Sycros sunset from here. The master never visited, and I avoided other humans outside the village. I moved to Olona, where I heard Gilriel was living. Gilriel did not recognize me but knew my voice. He quickly overcame the shock of my being alive and promised to keep my secret. I want the master to continue to think Esteren is dead. Indeed, that name is dead. Now, it is your turn to keep the secret. I am getting too old to start over again, and my skills have fallen to rubble. I am afraid if I try to use them again, he will find and destroy me this time."

Kelkalyn stopped and looked at Maylore.

"I will keep your tale to myself," Maylore said. "Gilriel has not returned from his travels with the master."

Kelkalyn sat up with a concerned look on his face.

"How long has he been gone?" Kelkalyn asked.

Maylore considers for a moment before replying.

"Over 100 sunrises," Maylore said. Kelkalyn looked down.

"The master may have determined he was spying on him," Kelkalyn said. "My poor friend may now be one of the dead."

"I have not seen him on my communication portal for a long time," Maylore said.

"He allowed you to track him?" Kelkalyn asked.

"Yes," Maylore replied. "I can identify only you, Airalee, Gilriel, and Bert."

"Bert?" Kelkalyn asked.

"Yes, the IB from Gilriel's cave," Maylore replied.

"Bird?" Kelkalyn asked. "You named a bird?"

"Yes," Maylore replied.

"I didn't know birds had names, let alone could communicate," Kelkalyn said.

"I asked the bird what his name was," Maylore said. "He sent me a name that looked like Bert. The bird laughed at my attempt but accepted Bert for a name."

"I suspect your companion, Airalee, can also communicate," Kelkalyn said.

"She does after I added more connections to her communication portal," Maylore said. "She has a blue stone amulet to aid her ability to send and receive messages."

"You learned how to make new connections?" Kelkalyn asked.

"Yes," Maylore said. "I follow Gilriel's method of using a blue spotted mushroom and cutting holes in a portal to add a new connection."

"Amazing," Kelkalyn said. "You have gained more knowledge than I thought."

"Well, some," Maylore said. "It was enough to help Airalee communicate."

"It is likely you who have the full skill," Kelkalyn said. It is your skill to switch messages, while others can communicate when you are open to communication. I did not notice if she had a communication portal, only her heart portal."

"Her communication portal was present but lacking," Maylore said.

"I do not believe Gilriel has an open communication portal," Kelkalyn said.

"It may be there but is not fully functional," Maylore said.

"Gilriel needs to be careful," Kelkalyn said. "He needs to be more cautious when the master is near. He is not a good man."

"You have convinced me to avoid contact with the master," Maylore said.

"Good, that would be wise," Kelkalyn said.

"Did you discover anything about Airalee when you saw her burnt heart?" Maylore asked.

"No," Kelkalyn replied. "That was a potentially serious error I made. I was surprised when I saw a prominent heart portal. I blurted out statements I should have kept to myself. If she were a spy for the master, I would have exposed myself to danger again."

"We heard those concerns before," Maylore said. "I assure you, we are not spies for anyone. It took considerable time to convince the Beacon, and I am not sure he is completely convinced even now."

"Trust no one," Kelkalyn said.

"I believe most people are good," Maylore said. "The bad ones quickly reveal themselves through their actions. My companions are good people. Airalee is interested in meeting you."

Kelkalyn's face revealed he was suspicious.

"Why?" Kelkalyn said.

"Airalee is very interested in your story. She suspects you are much more than the eccentric old man you portrayed to her."

Kelkalyn chuckled aloud, his suspicious face remaining.

"She is perceptive and did not seem intimated by my act," Kelkalyn said. "I am afraid the only skill left to me is knowing what portals a person may have. I don't know how they use them or what they can do. I have some understanding of the communication portal you and I have, but I can't use it as you can. It suits me to remain hidden from the outside world."

"I was hoping we could exchange ideas and become friends," Maylore said.

"We shall see what the future brings for friendship," Kelkalyn said. "I do retain one trick I may be able to teach you. I can hide in plain sight.

"That would be a handy skill," Maylore said. "If you are willing to share, I would be glad to hear of it."

Kelkalyn straightened in his chair, wondering if he had said too much again.

"I can create an illusionary wall copied from objects behind me so that only the objects behind me show to a viewer," Kelkalyn said. "It seems to the viewer that I am not there."

"I would like to learn that skill," Maylore said with a smile.

"I may teach it someday," Kelkalyn said.

"Thank you," Maylore said. "Would you be willing to help me determine if other villagers have portals they can use?"

"I would prefer not to deal with others," Kelkalyn said.

"I could be the person the villager thinks they are dealing with," Maylore said. "You could stay silent behind a wall if you wish. The Beacon and I would entertain a few villagers while you examine their potential."

"I may help you," Kelkalyn said. "I have a favor to ask of you. Would you ask Rendal to have his boys leave me some wood and food? They do not think I am here and stop bringing supplies."

"I will do that," Maylore said. "Do you need supplies now?"

"Not yet," Kelkalyn said. "I have enough for another day. Then I will be cold," he said, smiling.

"I will visit with the Beacon next," Maylore said as he stood.

"Good," Kelkalyn said, watching as Maylore left.

Jendrin

"Jendrin," Rendal said as he saw Jendrin washing near the pool. Standing up, Jendrin greeted the Beacon with a smile. Rendal stopped near him.

584

"I am concerned Oleg may return this summer," Rendal said. "I am certain Birsha will return demanding more of our young. I have arranged for the council to meet to discuss your plan. I believe the sooner we start training the defense force, the better it will be for us to mount a defense. Are you ready?"

"I am," Jendrin replied.

"I suggest we show them the first three phases and ask for approval," Rendal said. "If they agree, I would ask them about adding phase four to the training. We should leave phase five out of it for now. I know counterattack will be a sticking point for some of them. You can explain if anyone asks about counterattacks and a killing situation," Rendal said with a severe look.

"Agreed," Jendrin said, gathering his supplies.

"Beware," Rendal said, "one or two of the council are complete pacifists. They disapproved of your interfering with saving Airalee's life. They believe it was her time to leave the living and the killer would face eternal consequences when they die."

"I find that logic difficult to understand," Jendrin replied, "It was fated I should stop the execution so she may accomplish greater works."

"You and I agree," Rendal said. "I warn you so you aren't ambushed by them when we meet."

"I appreciate the warning," Jendrin said, "I will get my quarterstaff and meet you at the council hut," he said as he walked with Rendal back to the village.

Jendrin waited outside the council chamber as a few unhappy voices filtered through the door. He couldn't understand who was saying what, only that a few were not happy. He moved a little farther away and instead considered how many would fit in his defensive group. He began to think about who may be willing to join.

"I hope someone besides Latel and I will be in our village defense force," Jendrin said as he practiced his movements.

"Jendrin!" came a call from the council hut as Rendal stood in the open door. "Join us for your presentation." Jendrin gathered his staff and walked to the hut. He entered the hut to see six faces. Three looked upset, and three wore small smiles.

"Greetings, everyone," Jendrin said, standing before them.

"As I was discussing with you," Rendal said, "Jendrin has developed a method to assist us in preventing abduction of our young. Please hold your comments until after he explains his ideas. Jendrin, please begin."

"I believe I have developed a process that will work within our village charter," Jendrin said. "I believe it will provide some defense from those that would harm our citizens."

Council members remained either stone-faced or actively listening to what he was saying.

"I am sure you remember Oleg's attack on Airalee. I was fortunate to have Kai's and Airalee's excellent healing, or I would not be here today."

"You should not have interfered," Nenaias said. The other members turned to look at her. "You prevented what should have occurred naturally."

"Your reckless actions put our village in danger from evil," Caudra said, looking at Jendrin. "You were wrong to stop the flow of nature."

"I could not allow the attack on Airalee," Jendrin replied. "She deserves to live peacefully with the rest of us."

"No," Nenaias replied, "She chose to escape this world, and you prevented her from achieving that goal!"

"On the contrary," Jendrin replied in an even voice, "I was chosen to prevent the loss of a valuable addition to our village. Airalee has helped many besides myself find new foods and ways of healing and is soon to be a mother."

"You may think so," Nenaias said, "She was intended to die to prevent attacks by the bandits. Her sacrifice would have saved us! They will soon descend on all of us, and you provided them the reason!" Nenaias shouted. Jendrin was surprised by the strong response but remained calm, realizing this was the same pacifist who had voiced similar opinions at their first meeting.

"No one needs to be sacrificed," Jendrin said. "We must develop a plan to prevent attacks on our village by bandits and the forced slavery of our young."

Nenaias looked unconvinced, sitting red-faced and turning her face away.

"Only through nonaggression can our village succeed in peaceful living," Caudra said.

"Sadly, our world contains aggressive people who feel they must push others out to gain power for themselves," Jendrin said.

"Those people will pay for their aggression when they leave this world," Nenaias said.

"We should not have to pay for their choices by dying," Jendrin said. "The aggressor chooses to live and will likely never receive a penance. We die and never have the chance to make choices of our own."

"Please Nenaias and Caudra," Rendal said. "The council knows your position. Let us hear what Jendrin has to offer our village."

"Basrah," Nenaias said, throwing her hands into the air. "I will not agree to what you will say, but others may listen." Jendrin nodded and was surprised at himself for keeping calm.

"Thank you, Rendal," Jendrin said. He intended his thanks for the interruption and the previous warning of their possible reactions.

"I believe we can create a small group of people to watch over the village," Jendrin said. "I will train them to use steps designed to dissuade invaders from violence. I will ask you to approve our new group to prevent future intrusions." Jendrin saw the same two scowling faces and four interested faces looking back at him. "I propose training a small group in the basics of defense using a new tool," Jendrin said, holding out his quarterstaff.

"A pretty stick will scare them off?" Nenaias sneered. Jendrin realized she was attempting to draw a strong reaction from him and kept calm. He chose to ignore her comment.

"Indeed," Jendrin said. "We begin by facing away from aggressors, passively standing side by side with the staff outside our foot. We would do nothing but watch for possible trouble. I call this phase one, and I believe this will be enough to prevent trouble from less aggressive foes."

"You are posing we add guards to the front of the village?" Nenaias said. "We have the Tocor sentinels toward our village."

"The Tocor are good people but too small to do anything except warn us of approaching trouble," Rendal said, "They have informed me they wish to return all but one sentinel to their village. They wish to leave one Tocor by the road to maintain the Tocor relay. They intend their relay to warn their village about approaching travelers and trouble. Olona is fortunate to have a relay Tocor, who additionally serves as our village sentinel. I have visited other villages with armed guards in front of them. We may need to do so soon. Jendrin fits nicely into a plan where the Tocor will signal each other, and we will hear the signal and send our group to meet a threat."

"I do not like the idea of guards at our village entrance," Nenaias said. "It appears to others we are prone to violence."

"The defense force will not be stationed at our entrance," Rendal said. "They will gather when our sentinel sounds their signal."

Nenaias settled back into her chair.

"I will not accept a group that attacks other villages," Nenaias said.

"I agree with you," Jendrin said as the rest of the room nodded in agreement.

"It must not use violence to retrieve our girls already in the bandit's camp," Nenaias continued.

"I agree with that, too," Jendrin said as all heads nodded again.

Nenaias and Caudra both sat back in their chairs with a look of satisfaction on their faces.

"I ask you to vote on establishing our defensive force," Rendal said. "We will discuss other phases of Jendrin's plan, but first, we need to replace the departing sentinels and consider protecting our villagers. I will ask Jendrin to leave the council hut while we vote."

Jendrin smiled and left the hut. He heard a quiet discussion from inside the hut, but there were no raised voices. Rendal called Jendrin back into the hut after a short time.

"The council voted four in favor and two abstaining," Rendal said. "We have approval for your team and at least the first phases, Jendrin," Rendal said proudly. "There is more the defense force can do for our village against more aggressive attackers. I would like Jendrin to inform you of those options. We will vote on those additional options after his explanation. Jendrin, if you please."

"Thank you for approving the beginning of our defensive force," Jendrin said. "It allows us the opportunity to repel the less aggressive invader. I want to present options to repel those with more insidious intentions."

Jendrin explained and demonstrated his plan's second phase. The council vote was the same.

Jendrin explained and showed how defending oneself in phase three would work. The two abstainers voted against the plan this time, but the other four voted favorably.

Jendrin knew the next phase might be problematic but showed how to counterattack to stop being attacked. The council voted four against and two for the option.

"Thank you for your presentation, Jendrin," Rendal said. "Please, follow me outside."

Jendrin thanked the council and followed Rendal outside the hut.

"I do not want to lose our people when they can defend themselves," Rendal said, looking at Jendrin. "I would like to revisit this at a later date."

"I understand," Jendrin replied.

"We will start with a force of six villagers," Rendal said. "You will be one of the six and teach the group phases one through four. Do you have any more comments?"

"Latel has asked to join," Jendrin said. "I have four more openings."

"Good," Rendal said. "The council will meet again after 30 sunrises," as he turned to reenter the hut.

Jendrin turned to find Latel sitting on a nearby stump as the council members departed.

"Did they approve?" Latel asked.

"Yes, partly anyway," Jendrin said. "I am not sure how you heard of this meeting. Rendal approached me as I was washing up."

"Word travels quickly in a small village," Latel said. "I heard there was a meeting, and you were in it. I assumed what the agenda might be."

"I see," Jendrin replied. "They agreed to allow a six-person force, which I will train. I can train them in phases one through three."

"No offense?" Latel said. "It is still a good accomplishment."

"I agree," Jendrin said. "It is a good start. We need to find four others to complete the group."

"I would like to join the group," said a voice behind him. Jendrin turned to see Councilwoman Katiana standing beside them.

"We have failed our young by allowing the bandits to take them for too many seasons," Katiana said. "I want to help stop that practice."

"We will not be going after the ones already taken," Jendrin said.

"I understand," Katiana said. "I want to stop future abductions."

"You are welcome to join our trial group to see if it fits you," Jendrin said.

"Trial group?" Latel asked.

"We will look for ten to try the concept and accept four," Jendrin said. "I hope we can find enough volunteers."

"When do we start?" Katiana asked.

"I will gather you and Latel in two sunrises. We can build our group from that point," Jendrin said.

CHAPTER 37 - GUESS WHO CAME TO DINNER

Airalee awoke to stabbing abdominal pain as Ayare was stirring more than usual in her baby chamber. Ayare seemed in a hurry, but Airalee was unsure she was ready.

"Stay calm, Airalee," she said aloud as she rubbed her baby bump. Jendrin awoke upon hearing her voice.

"Are you in pain, Airalee?" he asked.

"Not yet," she replied. "You will have to stay calmer than I do, hero. I may need your support soon."

The twin suns had risen enough to light up the village. Airalee could hear the crunch of snow as others walked outside. Maylore poked his head into the room, asking if she was all right.

"Yes, so far, dad," she answered. "I think today will be the day to visit the birthing hut. If you would ask Kai to visit me this morning, that would be helpful."

Maylore started toward the door when Airalee added, "Let's wait a while to see if Ayare decides to be born. My baby chamber often starts and stops, so I don't need help yet."

Maylore nodded and left to gather firewood to cook breakfast. Jendrin dressed and went to collect breakfast food. Airalee rubbed herself at the table, attempting to soothe herself or Ayare. Maylore and Jendrin returned, both staring at Airalee as they entered.

"I see why Kai told me to keep you two away from the birthing hut," Airalee said with a grin.

"Why is that?" Maylore asked.

"You two are already flying around when nothing is happening yet!" Airalee replied. "What would you do if Ayare was ready to be born?"

"I understand," Maylore said, relaxing. "It is difficult to stand by knowing you will be in pain, and we cannot help."

"Ah," Airalee replied, smiling. "You will both be helping me by knowing you are staying here to support us when we return."

"We both will support you," Jendrin said.

"Yes, but it is better when you say it," Airalee smiled.

Jendrin felt himself relax as he put the food on the table. "I am not hungry," Airalee said, "but you two should eat."

"I can make a light fish broth for you," Maylore offered.

Airalee decided it would keep him busy and that she might want some light soup later. "Good idea," Airalee said, "I will watch you work." Airalee found she could drink some of Maylore's broth while he and Jendrin ate the fish in the soup. The conversation was light, with both men looking at her when she made any sound.

"Relax, guys," she said. "I just need to move a little." Airalee's pains increased as the morning wore on until just before midday. "Maylore, would you ask Kai to come visit?" Maylore was already halfway to the door as she was speaking. Jendrin was sitting beside her, rubbing her back to comfort her.

Kai, Marisa, and Maylore returned to the hut in short order. "Your baby pains are getting stronger and closer together?" Kai asked as she stood beside her.

"Yes," Airalee answered, stretching her back.

Looking at the two men, Kai turned her attention to Marisa. "Marisa, you and I will help Airalee to the birthing hut," Kai said. "You two men stay here and prepare for the baby's arrival," she said, waving Jendrin away. Kai and Marisa helped Airalee to her feet and out the door to the birthing area.

"I believe we were dismissed," Jendrin said, looking at Maylore.

"Yes, I believe you are right," Maylore replied, chuckling. "Can we do anything to prepare for Ayare's arrival?"

"Nothing," Jendrin said with a smile. "Airalee told me Kai wanted to keep us busy and away from the birthing hut. She said we would only be in the way."

"Kai is right," Maylore said with a shrug. "I would only be a nervous wreck."

"I will occupy the time by continuing to develop our defensive plan," Jendrin said.

"If the snow is clear enough, I will travel up to Gilriel's cave," Maylore said. "Ayare will need room, and I need to practice destructive skills. The cave provides a good location for me to live and practice."

"You promised to visit us so Ayare will know you," Jendrin said. "Airalee and I need to keep up with your activities."

"Yes," Maylore replied, "I am not going far. I plan to prepare Gilriel's cave so I can live there. I plan to return tonight."

"Good," Jendrin said, "Airalee would be disappointed if you were not here when she returned. She knows you will soon move, but she might feel you abandoned her if you left now."

"You will need the room for Ayare, and now is a good time to start," Maylore said. "Remember, you are welcome to visit Bert and me in the cave."

"It is possible," Jendrin said. "As time passes, it may be difficult to keep Ayare from arriving at your door unannounced."

"She will be welcome," Maylore replied. "I will return to see how your stick swinging is progressing."

"Speaking of stick swinging, I will see if Latel can help me work on the class today," Jendrin said. "It will keep us busy while we wait for Ayare to appear."

"I would offer to join your group," Maylore said, "but I fear my swinging days are in the past if they ever existed."

"You could join us for the exercise," Jendrin said as he opened the door.

"I would likely smack myself with my stick," Maylore said, turning to collect his things.

Maylore gathered the few things he kept in his room and joined Jendrin outside, practicing his quarterstaff spins. "I will return to see if Ayare has arrived," Maylore said as he waved and started toward the cave.

"All right," Jendrin replied, "hopefully, the snow has cleared so you can get to the cave." Jendrin waved to Maylore and walked toward Latel's hut.

Airalee

Airalee let Kai lower her onto the birthing bed. She didn't need any help but decided to go along with Kai, fussing over her. Two other women were already at work setting up hot water, strips of cloth, blankets, and pain potions.

"Marisa," Kai said, "go collect the other girls so they can learn what will happen to them during childbirth."

Marisa hurried out the door as Kai covered Airalee with a blanket. Motioning to the other women, she looked at Airalee. "These women have helped me with many births in the village," Kai said. "You lay back, and let us track how you are doing. Are the pains continuing?"

"Yes, it feels the same," Airalee replied.

"They should start getting stronger," Kai said. "If not, we may be waiting for the baby to be born another time." One of the women offered Airalee a mint-smelling tea.

"This tea will help you relax without hurting the baby," the attendant said. "I am sorry, but we won't be giving you any pain potions until after the baby arrives. You will be feeling pain, dear," the woman said as she pushed a pillow behind Airalee's back. Airalee sipped her tea as Marisa and the three girls arrived.

"Sit at the back of the room and observe what happens," Kai said, pointing to chairs along the wall behind Airalee's feet. "It will be your turn soon enough." Kai didn't have to instruct the women who efficiently arranged the room and readied a small, lined bed for the baby.

"Can Marisa sit near me?" Airalee asked Kai.

"Marisa, bring your chair to Airalee's side," Kai said, pointing to Marisa. Marisa moved to sit beside her as Airalee reached for her hand.

"If you let me hold your hand," Airalee said, "I will hold yours when it is your turn."

"You don't have to ask," Marisa said, grabbing and squeezing Airalee's hand.

Her labor continued as time passed. Weak contractions turned to strong, closely timed contractions. Airalee did feel the pain increase with each contraction. Kai kept checking Airalee's progress, eventually noting the baby was ready to emerge. Kai looked first at Airalee, then the girls along the wall, as she warned.

"Airalee will probably have some screams for us," Kai said. "She will also lose some blood as the baby is delivered. Be prepared, girls. The same process will happen to you when you become a mother." One of the women brought a thick-looking mask near Airalee's head.

"If you wish to limit how loud the screams may be, you can wear this mask to soften the sound," she said. "You will be able to breathe through it easily." Airalee took the mask but thought she would prefer not to use it.

"You are proceeding quickly for a first-time mom," Kai said. "You may soon feel strong pressures and need to push the baby out."

The birthing process continued for a few hours. Marisa felt her hand go numb many times as Airalee squeezed it but did not let Airalee's hand go.

The increasing pressure surprised Airalee as more time passed. She suddenly felt it was time to push Ayare out. As she started, a fleeting thought floated up from her body, saying this process seemed familiar. A sudden wave of pressure erased that idea from her mind.

A soft cry announced that Ayare had arrived.

"Now that the baby is here," Kai said, "you three girls clean her up, then give her to mom." Kai turned to present the baby to the girls.

"I will take her," Marisa said, rushing to take Ayare from Kai's arms.

"Make sure the others help clean the baby, Marisa," Kai said, returning attention to sweating Airalee, "Congratulations, Mom. Take some pain potion, and I will see if you need more attention."

All four girls gathered around the baby, cleaning her with warm water and soapweed. Ayare cried very little. She simply watched the girls clean her off.

"She has such crystal blue eyes," Marisa said as Ayare opened and closed her eyes.

"Does she have a name, Airalee?" one of the girls asked.

"Yes," Airalee replied, "her name is Ayare."

"Hello, Ayare," another girl said. "Welcome to the Olona."

"Her name is similar to yours," the third girl said.

"I didn't choose her name," Airalee said. "She told me in a dream." Airalee was unwilling to tell how Maylore had visited with Ayare in her baby chamber.

"Her name, you can say it with one puff of breath, but my name needs three," Airalee said. The girls all nodded happily to see that the baby had been born, knowing their turn was coming. Ayare was getting tired of people fussing with her and started a soft scream.

"Bring her to me," Airalee said, stretching her arms. Marisa picked her up and took her to Airalee. Ayare quieted when her mom took her and snuggled up under her blanket.

Maylore

Maylore noticed that the snow and ice were diminishing each day. As he approached the road, the path out of the village had patches of grass and mud. As he expected, the path from the road to the cave was undisturbed. He waded through snow knee to waist high as he started off the road. He wound his way toward the base of the cave, where he saw much of the snow had melted away from the slopes. He could see the entrance to the cave was clear of snow and bears. He finally pushed to the entrance and sat on a rock to rest.

"The next trip will be easier," he said, breathing hard.

He entered the cave and wound his way to Bert's hideaway. Bert cawed softly and flew ahead of him into the main cave. Maylore followed him into the cave. Bert was perched on the back of a chair as he entered the main cavern. Maylore set his pouch on the table and examined the cave.

Gilriel was not there, and the cave looked like he had left it. Maylore had a sudden morbid thought.

"Did Gilriel die before the snow came?" he said aloud, looking at Bert. "You would have told me if he had, I think." Maylore decided. He turned to inspect the cave to see if a body was there. He didn't smell any scent of decay but looked behind rocks, cabinets, the creek bed, and outside in the garden. The garden had far too much vegetation to find anything. He noticed the snow did not stay in this garden. Maylore reentered the cave when he thought, 'Why didn't I ask Bert if Gilriel was dead in the cave?' Maylore sent Bert a picture of Gilriel as he returned to the table. Bert ruffled his feathers and shook his head, sending an image of Gilriel walking down the road. "Well, that is good if the last time Bert saw him, he was walking the road clear of snow."

Maylore sat at the table, looking around the dusty cave.

"If I move here," Maylore said aloud, "I will need new bed stuffing, a new bed blanket, and a broom to keep dust and grime off. Gilriel was not interested in cleaning anything, but I am." Looking back toward the garden, he said, "Did I see berries, gourds, and fruit growing in the winter garden?" He returned to the garden, looking at different berries and fruit. "I will return some to Mirtha to see if they are edible. I suspect Gilriel would remove poisonous ones, but perhaps not." He started picking various berries, vegetables, and fruits when he saw a tiny thread of steam. It rose beyond the end of the small trail Gilriel had used through the garden. Pushing aside vegetation, he walked a short distance up the bank to where the steam was rising from the side of the mountain. Pulling rocks out of the bank, he dug down a few lengths of his hand to find a small opening. Widening the gap, he saw water below that extended into the darkness of the mountain. Tossing aside more rock, he created an opening he could pass through. There appeared to be sandy mud below his hands and the water close enough to reach. Maylore reached down to touch the water briefly. "Warm, not hot," he said, pulling his hand from the water. "Would make a wonderful bath if the water is safe." He climbed through the opening and stood on the sandy shore. He looked in all directions, but the light was too weak to show the boundaries of the cave.

"I need a torch," he said as he climbed back out of the cave. Another small steam vent near the creek caught his attention. He aligned the stream source and the next vent and followed the line to the nearby stream. Looking into the water, he saw clear water entering under the surface. He reached into the water and felt warm water flow over his skin. "That answers my question of if the water is safe," Maylore said. "This stream is a source of drinking water for my predecessors."

Maylore returned to the cave to make a firebrand from the dry wood and pitch stored in Gilriel's cave. He returned to the watery cave and used the firebrand's light to examine the cave as he stood on the sandy ledge.

"Ten sticks high, twenty sticks wide," Maylore said aloud. The sandy ledge encircled the pool with enough room for him to stand and walk comfortably. He walked to the opposite side of the pool and noticed an orange glow emanating from the water. He looked into the depth of the clear water and saw bubbling water on the rocks far below. "Blood of the earth," he said. He could see water welling up near the far edge of the cave. "That must be cold water entering. Otherwise, this water would be boiling," he said aloud. He could not see any water exiting the cave. His firebrand was dimming, so he walked back to the entrance. A warm bath would be welcome since cool sponge baths had been the norm this snow season.

Maylore left the watery cave and looked beyond the end of the beaten path. He noticed large round balls growing from vines near another steam vent. He examined the balls, which were hand-width wide with a firm exterior. He gathered a few of them and turned to see large berries growing nearby. "Winterberries?" Maylore asked, recognizing them from Mirtha's early-season gathering. He collected a few of them and walked back into the main cave. He emptied his pockets of the berries and round balls onto the table. Bert immediately squawked and jumped down to eat all of the berries.

"Looks like the berries are good," Maylore said. Cutting open a round ball, he saw a pleasant pink-colored flesh surrounding tiny seeds. Bert hopped over, pulled one of the halves away, and ate the interior while Maylore watched. "I did not intend for you to be a food tester, but thank you, Bert. If you are alive the next time I am here, I will gather more for everyone," he chuckled. Maylore watched Bert for a time before turning to his next task.

'Time for skill practice,' he thought as he focused inward. Looking into his communication dome, he saw Bert nearby. Kelkalyn appeared in his hut, and Airalee was in the village. He connected a string to Airalee's dot. He heard a scream on the string, forcing him to drop the connection.

'Ayare must be on her way,' he thought. 'I am sorry for your pain, Airalee.'

Maylore decided to practice his other skills. He built a small fire and sat in a chair. The months of quiet practice in the village were paying off. He could gather energy much faster and push it out farther than before.

'Yay for me!' he thought after knocking over yet another target on the rock. He practiced left-spinning and right-spinning blue and fire energy. His drawing of the fire's energy had depleted the flames into tiny embers. He was adding more wood to rebuild it when he considered another idea. 'I wonder if I can start a new campfire or a firebrand at a distance from its source?' He let the fire rebuild as he created a new firebrand. He walked to the garden entrance and stood the firebrand against the wall. He concentrated on seeking the distant fire near the table. He sensed the burning fire and asked it to come to him. He felt the familiar energy arrive as he transferred it to the firebrand, which burst into flame. "Nice trick," Maylore said aloud as he dropped the transfer. The firebrand continued to burn as he carried it back to the table. "This one has a peaceful use," Maylore said, feeling he had accomplished something.

The day was nearing its end since the twin sun's light no longer shone from the holes in the ceiling.

"I need to gather more fruit since you ate those," he said, looking at Bert. Bert was picking at the remains of the other half of the gourd and ignored Maylore. Maylore returned to the garden to gather more berries and round fruit. Returning to the table, he found Bert had flown away.

"I will return tomorrow," Maylore said toward Bert's roost as he wound out of the cave and down to Olona.

Jendrin

Jendrin knocked on the door of Latel's hut.

"Is it time to practice?" Latel asked as he opened the door.

"Yes," Jendrin replied. "I see a broad practice area near your hut."

"There were supposed to be three more huts there," Latel said. "However, the village decided to leave it as a gathering area since it is near the kitchen."

"Let's practice there," Jendrin said. "It is a well-traveled area. A possible recruit may join us if they see our practice. If you would gather Katiana, we can start."

"Dirdin asked me to allow him to try out the day after the meeting," Latel said.

"Tanning master Dirdin?" Jendrin asked.

"Yes," Latel said. "He discussed it with his baby-mate and decided he should step up to protect their child."

"He would be a good addition," Jendrin said.

"Do you think the council sent Katiana to spy on us?" Jendrin questioned.

"Possibly," Latel said. "She has previously questioned the council about allowing raids on our village. I suspect they are serving their conscience."

"Good," Jendrin replied. "If you would gather both of them, I will get two more quarterstaff from my hut and set up for our practices."

"I will get my quarterstaff and join you," Latel said, closing the door.

Jendrin retrieved two more quarterstaffs and walked to the new practice area. He began his warm-up exercises, feeling his fingers and wrists stretch.

Latel returned, followed by Katiana and Dirdin.

"I have an unfinished staff for each of you to use for the time being," Jendrin said, giving Katiana and Dirdin a clear wood quarterstaff. "If you drop out of the group, I expect you to return it for the next member to use. If you continue, you must finish cleaning off the remaining bark and use your hands to add oil to the quarterstaff. These clear wood quarterstaffs are durable. I had not broken this one when I repeatedly struck the ground," he said, striking a nearby stone. The soft ring of the wood surprised the newcomers.

"Singing wood?" Katiana said. "I have heard of it but never seen it. Will my quarterstaff sing, too?" She tapped her quarterstaff on the rock but heard only a clunk.

"I suspect all of the bark needs to be removed," Jendrin said.

"I will see to it," Katiana said.

"I will first lead you through warm-up exercises," Jendrin said. "I use these exercises to strengthen my hands and arms to wield this tool better. After our warm-up, I will explain what the council allows our defensive force to use and how we will follow it."

"We heard what was accepted," Katiana said.

"I only explained the generality to the council," Jendrin said, "now we will learn the specifics. We will need many sunrises to accomplish all of the steps. I will review all of the steps today. Then, we will implement those steps in the coming sunrises. Let's start our warm-up."

They attempted to follow Jendrin's lead as he made a rowing motion, wrist-spin the quarterstaff, and switched hands. They each dropped their quarterstaffs many times before Jendrin stopped.

"These quarterstaff spinning maneuvers will form the basis of our defensive show," Jendrin said. "It will take practice to maintain control of the quarterstaff."

"I am not sure about that," Dirdin said.

"Latel can tell you I dropped this quarterstaff many times when I started," Jendrin said.

Katiana and Dirdin looked to Latel, who nodded but kept quiet. The group practiced spinning and retrieving their quarterstaffs as Jendrin encouraged them. Jendrin noticed they were tiring after a long series of practicing various spins. He called a temporary halt to the session.

"Good start, everyone," Jendrin said. "You will need to practice independently and remember to switch hands. You need to be able to use both hands equally well. Sit and rest while I go over the defensive plan."

"That is a lot more exercise than I have done in a while," Dirdin said, sitting on a rock.

"I have developed a plan that runs in phases from passive to deadly," Jendrin said. "We will follow the council's wishes and use phases one through three, which do not include the deadly phase."

Jendrin reviewed the first three phases, as he had explained to them before.

As Jendrin spoke, a group of curious villagers gathered around them. Jendrin noticed several in the group he thought would be an excellent addition to the defensive force. Looking at his teammates, he started describing his thinking on tool choice.

"I chose the quarterstaff as our tool since it will allow us the greatest defensive ability without necessarily being deadly," Jendrin said.

"You think a stick will stop hatches and knives?" A villager yelled, "It won't be able to stop anyone!" the villager laughed. Jendrin smiled back at him.

"Thank you for explaining why I chose the quarterstaff," Jendrin said. "The quarterstaff is a powerful melee tool with good defensive capabilities."

"It is just a stick," the villager chided, "prove it."

Jendrin passed Latel a hatchet and a knife.

"Latel, when I say go, do a slow overhead attack, then underneath. Switch to the knife and slice left, right, and stab." Jendrin said. Looking back at the group, he said, "We will approach each threat progressing through the three phases, stopping when the adversary redraws."

Latel took the hatchet and approached Jendrin.

"Stand with the end of the staff on the ground and watch your adversary," Jendrin said. "If they move toward us, we face them, move into our defensive stance, and twirl the staff in circles. If they attack, we will defend. Latel, start your attack."

Latel swung the axe over his head, slowly attacking Jendrin. Jendrin thrust his sideways staff up to catch the hatchet between his hands on the wood handle. Latel swung the hatchet up, and Jendrin blocked down.

"We aim for the weapon's handle to prevent their blade from cutting our quarterstaff. The ax head may break off of the hatchet. An attacker with a broken melee weapon will likely quit the fight," Jendrin said. "Let's try a knife, Latel," Jendrin said as Latel slashed left with the knife. Jendrin slid his hand down the staff and pushed the end of the staff to hit the knife, snapping the other end of the staff to stop outside his other elbow. Jendrin stopped the staff short of the knife to avoid injuring Latel. They repeated the process, going in different directions.

"We aim to knock the knife out of their hand, but they will likely be injured attacking us.

"Will it stop a strong man like Birsha if he will not stop, hurt or not?" another villager asked.

"The council has not agreed to allow us to counterattack," Jendrin said. "I will demonstrate for you but not teach it to our defense force. We could use the fourth step to counterattack when the aggressor will not stop. After we blocked their attack, we counterattacked by swinging our staff to hit a knee, ankle, chest, or shoulder. The attacker will be injured and likely turn away." Jendrin looked to Latel, saying, "Thank you, Latel."

The villager who had mocked him had grown quiet.

"I still do not believe a stick would cause an angry Birsha to stop," another villager said. "What will you do then?"

"I have agreed to avoid teaching a devastating strike," Jendrin said. "I will show the power of 'just a stick.' I placed this hard breadfruit on this stump to demonstrate. I will strike the breadfruit like it was a weapon," Jendrin said as he sliced forcefully at the breadfruit, smashing it into several pieces.

The crowd gasped as the first villager who had said it was just a stick stood quietly, holding his head.

"That breadfruit is far tougher than my head," the villager said as he left the gathering.

"It appears I need to practice," Jendrin said. "I missed my stop point and hit the breadfruit too hard." Jendrin smiled as the villager left, still holding his head.

"I have room for a few more to try out if you are interested," Jendrin said as the crowd watched silently. "Speak with one of us later if you wish to join."

Jendrin turned to face his group, emphasizing the need to be disciplined as he reviewed all phases.

"Let's begin working in a team approach," Jendrin said. "Line up on both sides of me facing the hut at the end of the clearing. Take three steps back from the person beside you. Once we learn to control the staff, we will line up within one step of each other." He looked on both sides to verify they had enough room to swing their staff without hitting someone. "Plant the butt of their staff on the ground beside you. Face away from the opponent but make no aggressive moves. On command, face your opponent and switch to a defensive stance. On command, begin spinning your staff." Jendrin said, watching the group align. "Face," he said, turning to face the crowd. "Spin," he said as he spun his quarterstaff. "Defend," he said as he stopped his spin, balanced his weight, and held his staff horizontally in front of himself.

Jendrin turned to the team, saying, "Begin again." The group slowly regrouped and stood passively. "Face," as they slowly faced the crowd and assumed a defensive stance. "Spin," he said. The group attempted to spin, but most held the staff and did circles with their wrists. "Defend," he said. They did a reasonable job of going to a balanced defensive stance. "Good," Jendrin said. "Let's practice the process and spend more time spinning. The group spent the rest of their time learning the basics of spinning and picking up the dropped staff.

Jendrin returned to the companion's hut to find Maylore sitting in a chair.

"I am pleased to see you are still here," Jendrin said, sitting on the other side.

"I wanted to see Ayare and not have Airalee think I left in the middle of the night," Maylore said. "I plan to stay and wait for Airalee to return. I hope to visit with Kelkalyn in the morning and then move to the cave. Did your new group meeting go well?"

"Yes," Jendrin replied. "I have a council member wanting to be in the group."

"Are they perhaps a spy?" Maylore asked.

"Latel and I discussed that possibility, but the council would gain little by spying on us."

"I would agree with that too," Maylore said as a knock on the door interrupted them. Marisa stuck her head in the door.

"Ayare has been born!" Marisa said. "Airalee and the baby will stay in the birthing hut tonight. She said she will be here tomorrow morning."

"She won't allow us to visit her tonight?" Jendrin asked.

"She shooed everyone out of the birthing hut and asked me to send you that message. She said she wanted to rest with the baby and to visit tomorrow."

"That seems pretty plain to me," Maylore said.

"Thank you, Marisa," Jendrin said as Marisa waved and closed the door. "Guess we eat dinner and play sticks and stones before bed." Maylore nodded and rose to collect food to add to the pot.

Chapter 38 - Preparations

The twin suns were still below the tree line when Airalee left the birthing hut. Kai had told her the night before she should rest to allow her body to start healing.

"Do not lift or do strenuous activity for ten suns," Kai had said. Airalee felt well lying on the uncomfortable bed, but now she questioned the wisdom of getting up so soon. Ayare was sleeping, but Airalee did not sleep much after the pain potion wore off. She felt stiff and sore as the cold morning air bit her face. It was a slow trip over the snowy path, but she finally found herself at her hut. She tried to open the door quietly, but it screeched like always as she entered the hut. Two men appeared from their rooms as she closed the door.

"Welcome back!" Jendrin said, hugging her but avoiding squeezing the baby. Maylore hugged her next and looked for the baby in her arms. Airalee greeted them and pulled aside the blanket covering Ayare's face. Ayare was sleeping quietly, even with the noisy adults whispering.

"Ayare, you are beautiful," Maylore said.

"Pretty as your mother," Jendrin said.

Airalee softly recovered Ayare's face, ignoring comments about her. She sat in the chair and chatted with her companions about her general experiences in childbirth.

"I learned from Kai and the birthing women what to do to help birthing women," Airalee said. "I can help Kai with Marisa, the other girls, and future mothers. She already has experienced women, but I can learn to work alongside or replace them if they are absent."

"Now the work of raising a child begins," Maylore said.

"I will be here to help," Jendrin said.

609

"I feel fortunate to have two close at hand to assist," Airalee said, smiling at them.

"I assume you are hungry," Maylore said as he retrieved a bowl from the shelf.

"Yes," Airalee said, "Ayare will be, too, when she awakens."

Maylore filled a bowl and set it before her as Airalee looked to Jendrin.

"Did you start your training group?" Airalee asked.

"Yes," Jendrin replied. "Latel, Katiana, and Dirdin were in the first session." Airalee looked askance at him when the council member's name was mentioned. "Council member Katiana seemed interested in making the defensive force succeed," Jendrin said.

He told her of the council's decision to keep the group as defensive with no intention of warring on other villages.

"The council does not want our group to counterattack even when an aggressor attacks us," Jendrin said. "That may be difficult when our people come under attack. However, I believe the four steps I outlined to them will be sufficient."

"What steps did they approve of?" Airalee asked.

Jendrin explained the approved steps and told her about his surreptitious demonstration of a killing strike.

"There was one villager who taunted me about using a stick as my tool of choice," Jendrin said. "It allowed me to demonstrate a killing strike by shattering a breadfruit with one swing of my quarterstaff. I did not tell the group about using the staff as a weapon. I claimed it was an accident, saying I did not stop the staff in time. I believe the group got the point."

"Clever, hero," Airalee said. "I also hope the council member is not there to spy. We seem established in the village enough to avoid being watched."

"I believe they will be contributors rather than spies," Jendrin said.

"I have only a passing acquaintance with them," Airalee said. "I hope you are right this time." Looking at Maylore, she asked, "What happened with you, dad?"

Maylore explained his trip to Gilriel's cave and how only Bert lived there. He told them of the warm water cave and how it would be a lovely retreat during the winter storms.

"Better keep that quiet," Airalee said. "You will have the entire village coming through the cave."

"Perhaps I should reseal the entrance," Maylore said with a smile. "I also found different fruits and berries growing in the garden." Maylore placed the round fruit and the berries he brought back on the table.

"I have not seen either of these before," Airalee said, examining the round ball. "Perhaps Mirtha will tell us if they are edible."

"Bert ate both halves after I opened the round ball," Maylore said.

"If he still lives, it is a good sign," Airalee said.

"I was going to return to the cave today," Maylore said. "If he is not well, I will return quickly to tell you. If he is well, I will stay there. I plan to move there soon."

"Yes, I know, dad," Airalee said, nodding sadly. "You do not need to hurry."

"I plan to visit Kelkalyn today to see if he can help me with my skills," Maylore said. "I believe he is in his hut."

"Unless you need help with Ayare, I will continue the defensive training class," Jendrin said.

"Ayare will be sleeping," Airalee said, smiling. "Marisa and Kai will be here soon to check on both of us. I want the defensive force to succeed almost as much as you do."

"Good," Jendrin said. "I will return to allow you to do your routine and keep Ayare safe while you are gone."

"I have no doubt she will be safe," Airalee chuckled.

A knock on the door interrupted them. Marisa and Kai entered the room smiling and greeting the group.

"Have you held your babymate's child, Jendrin?" Kai asked, looking accusingly at him.

"Not yet, Kai," Jendrin replied. "I suspect I will have my turn later in the day."

"I have been keeping her to myself," Airalee said. "I didn't want to wake her by passing her to Jendrin or Maylore."

"You don't need to worry about her," Kai said. "She will rest when she wishes." Turning to Airalee, she asked, "Do you have any bleeding or pain?"

"I do not believe so," Airalee said. "I feel aches and pains but think they are normal."

"Let me check," Kai replied. Looking at the men, she added, "You two leave."

"I will start preparing the class," Jendrin said, gathering his supplies.

"I will await Kelkalyn at his hut," Maylore said, picking up the fruit.

"You have pink ground fruit!" Marisa exclaimed. "Where did you find that this time of season? It looks to be ripe!" Marisa said, taking the fruit from Maylore.

"I found them in the garden outside Gilriel's cave," Maylore said. "Bert seemed to enjoy it, even eating the seeds."

"Oh," Marisa said. "Try to save the seeds. We will grow as much of it as possible next summer." Maylore took the fruit back.

"Shall I cut some up for you, Airalee?" Maylore asked. Airalee nodded as Maylore cut the fruit open and saved the seeds.

"Thanks, dad, it does look good," Airalee said as she ate it. "I don't need to eat all of it myself." She added, "Join me." She looked at the group, who took a piece for themselves. Airalee felt Ayare move and looked down to see her blue eyes looking up at her. "Hello, Ayare," she said softly, raising her so others could see her. Ayare's eyes paused briefly on Marisa and Kai before fixing on Maylore.

Maylore felt a tap on his throat. He looked at his communication portal and saw Ayare's dot facing him. He connected a string to the dot and listened on the portal.

"Maylore," came the whisper from Ayare's dot.

"Ayare," he replied through the portal. Ayare looked toward Jendrin, then back to Maylore.

"Jendrin, your baby-mate," he replied through the portal. Ayare looked up at Airalee and then to Maylore. "Airalee, your mom," he replied through the portal. Ayare seemed satisfied and turned to eat her breakfast.

"I guess it is breakfast time for her, too," Airalee said. Maylore decided to keep the conversation with Ayare to himself for now. He stepped back, leaving the connection to Ayare open.

"I am going to do my morning routine before going to Kelkalyn's hut," Maylore said.

"I will join you, then meet with Latel," Jendrin said. Both men waved goodbye as Kai made a shooing motion after them.

"When Ayare finishes, pass her to Marisa," Kai said. "I will check you over before looking at Ayare." Looking down, Airalee noticed Ayare had already fallen asleep.

"Here she comes, Marisa," Airalee said, passing Ayare along. Marisa seemed delighted to hold the baby as Kai checked Airalee for bleeding and infections.

"Good," Kai finally said, "I see nothing to be concerned about. I will be on my way to Gaearwen's hut. He is not doing well, and I cannot seem to help him. The passing of his lifemate Echuinis seems to have drained him of any desire to live." Kai stood and stored her things back into her satchel. "We have sung the Song of Passing for two villagers this winter. I fear he may be the third," she frowned. "I will see you both tomorrow," she added, looking at both women as she turned to leave.

"Thank you, Kai," Airalee said as Kai left. "Someday," Airalee noted, "it will probably be me to tend to the passing."

"Our village has many people approaching elder status," Marisa said. "We are just keeping even with births and deaths. We may have a few moving into the village after the snow melts. Usually, people move to a different village when summer returns."

"Well," Airalee said, "I am pleased we will raise children together. I would like to do a short wash if you don't mind staying with Ayare."

"I would be glad to," Marisa said, sitting at the table. Airalee left the hut with a clean robe to attend to herself as Marisa smiled and talked to Ayare.

Airalee arrived at the bathing area and found the fire in the pool burning brightly. "Lucky me," she said, looking around. No one was about as she slipped off her robe and used it to sit on the ground by the heater. Warm water filled the sponge as she gratefully washed off grime and sweat. Two men appeared at the edge of the pool as she washed.

"Airalee!" one said, "I understand you are our newest mom! Best wishes to you both!" he said as he came her way. Airalee was still shy around other men but wanted a bath more than covering up.

"Thank you," she said as he added more wood to the nearby fire.

"Here," he said, holding out his hand. "I will wash your back for you. I have my friend to help me, but you don't." Airalee started to protest and pull away but decided no one had tried to harm her. All the villagers went out of their way to help her.

"Thank you," she said, passing him her sponge. He washed and rinsed her back quickly with soft pressure.

"I never thanked you for helping my mate with her sickness," he said as he gave the sponge back to her. "Perhaps my thanks and this would suffice," he said, turning toward his friend.

"Your kindness is appreciated," Airalee replied, even though she did not remember him.

Airalee finished washing, turning away from the men to put on her fresh robe. She gathered the dirty robe from beneath her and turned to leave. "Thank you again," she told him as she returned to the hut.

Marisa was singing to Ayare as Airalee entered the hut.

"I didn't know you sang," Airalee said, putting the dirty robe aside.

"One of my many talents," Marisa replied with a grin. Airalee joined her at the table, noticing Ayare resting atop Marisa's baby bump. "You are not far behind me having your child," Airalee said.

"Yes," Marisa replied. "He is moving around a lot. He seemed to sense Ayare was being born," she laughed. "You think it is a boy?" Airalee asked.

"I don't know. Kai thinks it is a boy," Marisa replied. "Do you have a name picked out for him?" Airalee quizzed.

"No, I will wait to see if it is a boy or girl," Marisa said. "I will be happy to have as healthy a child as Ayare seems."

"Do you wonder who the seeder was?" Airalee asked.

"I have a preference," Marisa said, "but I do not know. I could not see the seeder's face but could see the scar on Jendrin's leg. I worked to ensure his seed was firmly planted. For the others, I tried to leave their seed at the gate but did not always succeed."

"Do the seeders try to guess if their seed made the child?" Airalee asked.

"I suspect they do," Marisa said. "It is of no concern."

"Your baby-mate Gobelben did not try to seed you?" Airalee asked.

"Oh, my yes," Marisa said. "We had many encounters, but I used Kai's portions to close the baby chamber to his seed. Kai said I had to stop using the potions for several months before I could join the baby seeding group. I devised other ways to entertain Gobelben to avoid full encounters," Marisa said, smiling slyly. "Gobelben does not have what I wanted in a child. He is a small man who avoids heavy work. He is willing to help me and is a person who is easy to live with. I did allow him a separate seeding after the seeding group but ensured his seed would remain outside."

"How did you decide on a seeding group?" Airalee asked, checking Ayare.

"I wanted to use the traditional seeding group our village women used for their children," Marisa replied. "I considered following the old tradition of seeders traveling from village to village, but the snow prevented them from arriving when I was ready. Since Jendrin could be in the seeding group, I would not need to wait for outsiders. I know all of the men in the village, as I picked four, ensuring Jendrin was in the group. The other girls picked four and wanted Jendrin in their group. We quickly settled on a group since we all wanted similar characteristics for our children. I hoped Jendrin would be the final seed, but I won't know. Melronna told me I had many seeds and had not chosen one when I visited her. She did not say anything about my baby after that. She always seemed surprised I was with child each time I visited her. She forgets some things now. Meliniel has asked Kai if we can help her remember things. Kai did not know of anything to help her."

"You certainly thoroughly planned it," Airalee said.

"I also may be able to have another Lemidge experience since they will arrive in the summer," Marisa said. "They never produce children, but they create very happy women!" Marisa laughed.

"I remember," Airalee said, looking wistful. "I remember floating the warm air to a far-away meadow of many colors," Airalee said, wiggling her fingers above her head.

"I felt wrapped up in soft, warm cushions," Marisa recalled. "When he pressed into me, I saw a huge explosion of small lights flying through the air. I remember being sad when the colored lights finally faded."

The two women were quiet, remembering their experiences when Ayare awoke with soft moans.

"All right, back to mom, you go," Marisa said, passing Ayare back to Airalee.

"Speaking of seeding and Kai," Airalee said, "I forgot to ask Maylore if our potion was working. I will ask him tonight."

"I could help test him for you," Marisa said slyly. "I may be with the child, but I know ways to find out if he is interested."

Airalee looked at her in surprise.

"I will just ask him," Airalee said. "He will be truthful."

"My offer stands if you need help," Marisa said.

"Yes," Airalee replied, "what would you do if he accepted your offer?" Airalee countered.

"I would not be more with a child than I am now!" Marisa smiled.

Jendrin

Jendrin was not surprised to be the first to arrive at the practice area. It was early morning, and many were doing morning routines.

"I need to set up practice targets for knife and hatchet attacks," Jendrin said. "Perhaps I can make them move for high and low attacks."

Latel heard what Jendrin said as he arrived.

"If we move the defense training to the trees by the creek, we can use old ropes to suspend knives and hatchets from them," Latel said. Jendrin looked at the short distance to the trees and their branches.

"It would be far better to have the knife knocked off the rope than from my hand," Jendrin said. "I suspect I would quickly be injured holding a knife!"

"I would not volunteer to have someone swing a quarterstaff at me," Latel said. "I would not expect our untrained group only to hit the knife or hatchet!"

"It is why I wanted to set up a practice area where no one has to be injured to help train," Jendrin said. "I will do the initial slow attack with my quarterstaff to have everyone defend themselves. We need to find some rope to hold our target weapons."

"The old ropes from fishing are taken to our cloth-making area," Latel said. "They are unwound and turned into cloth for our clothes. Many are very worn but good enough to create cloth. I can get several ropes and throw them over the branches. We can tie test weapons on the other end, then raise and lower them by pulling on the other end."

"Good, Latel," Jendrin said. "I will find something to pose as a hatchet. We will use Oleg's knife for the practice knife."

"That's a fitting use for the attacker's knife that tried to kill you," Latel said.

"Indeed," Jendrin said. "If you gather the ropes, I will fashion a stick with a rock tied to it as a hatchet." Jendrin pulled out the white knife Oleg had carried. "We can tie this to a branch and loop the rope through it on another rope to allow it to move. If you see our trainees, have them join us."

Latel turned to complete his tasks when Jendrin spoke again.

"We need to develop a signal to have the team gather in the training area," Jendrin said. "We also need it when trouble comes calling. We should have a danger signal to gather at the visitor's huts."

"Good idea. For now, I will tell the ones I find we are starting to train," Latel said as he strode away.

Jendrin found two trees close together but far enough apart to allow training without hitting each other. He located three sticks to hold the knife, a high hatchet, and a low hatchet. He found two rocks he could lash onto the ends of the sticks to serve as hatchets. He laid the training knife and hatchets on the ground where he anticipated the ropes would hang. Returning to the area between the huts, Jendrin planned the day's training course.

"I will start each session reviewing the charter the council gave us," Jendrin said, thinking aloud. "I will review each phase of our system while the team practices their warm-up quarterstaff spins. I will have the team line up and practice phases one and two. I must ensure they are far apart to avoid hitting each other." Jendrin said, looking around the area to verify there was enough space. "Next, practice phase three using imaginary attacks and aggressive blocks in all directions." Jendrin looked at the new area where they would practice defending against knives and hatchets.

He realized his plan was optimistic for now and the near future. "If I can get them to line up and spin without hurting each other, we will be doing well," he said aloud. "We won't be ready for test hatchets and knives for many days. If we have a confrontation before we finish training, we will put on a show and stand aside," Jendrin decided. "I will need to inform the council of that."

The crunch of the slowly melting snow announced Latel's return with others.

"I found everyone on the way back," Latel said as they stopped before Jendrin.

"Good," Jendrin said, noting a new addition. "Are you joining our group, Callon?"

"I would like to try out," Callon replied, moving to the front. "Dirdin seemed proud that I wanted to join the group. He assured me there would be work when I return each day."

"It will do one even better. I will give us some of the brews at the end of each day." Dirdin chuckled.

"That is another good reason to join up!" Katiana said. The men nodded at her as Jendrin spoke.

"Welcome, Callon," Jendrin said. "I will let you borrow one of the clear quarterstaffs until you decide to join or leave. We are at the beginning of training. You will catch up with practice."

"Thank you, Jendrin," Callon said.

"First," Jendrin said, "I would like to agree on a meeting time for our training. As you know, I am Airalee's baby-mate. Now that Ayare has been born, I will dedicate time to helping her in the mornings and evenings."

"Airalee had her child?" Katiana said.

"Yes," Jendrin replied, "last night. She has named her Ayare."

"I am happy for her and will visit them when she is ready," Katiana said. The rest of the group added their well wishes as Jendrin assured them he would tell her.

"I assume Airalee will be presenting her to the village soon," Jendrin said. "Shall we continue our discussion?"

The group nodded as he started his teaching.

"I suggest we meet at quarter twin suns and finish by half twin suns each day," Jendrin said. "Do you have any comments or suggestions?"

The gathered group looked at each other, saying it would be good for them.

"Well, that was easy," Jendrin said with a smile. "I would like a way for us to gather quickly if the village is threatened. Does anyone have an idea?"

The group suggested yells, drums, animal noises, and whistles. They decided on a whistle because it would be distinct and loud enough for many to hear.

"Who suggested a whistle?" Jendrin asked.

Katiana stepped forward.

"My life-mate Aylendel made one for each of us if we need the other. It is loud and unique."

"Can you demonstrate?" Jendrin asked.

"I can," Katiana said. "I will signal her to tell me her location." Katiana blew a short whistle, then paused before sounding two more short whistles. A few seconds later, a similar signal came from across the village.

"I have heard that before," Dirdin said. "I didn't know what it meant, and it was some time ago."

"Yes," Katiana said. "We don't whistle often. She may come here looking for me even though I didn't whistle for her to come."

"I think that may be a good solution," Jendrin said. "What do the rest of you think?" he asked. The others nodded and voiced their agreement with the idea.

"I can ask Aylendel to make each of us a whistle if you wish," Katiana said.

"Katiana?" a voice called a short distance away.

"Here Aylendel!" Katiana called back. Aylendel appeared in the area and stopped seeing the gathered group.

"Are you all right?" she asked.

"Yes," Katiana said. "This is the defense group I was talking about. We were looking for a way to communicate when I suggested trying a whistle like yours. Would you make six whistles with a pitch different from ours for us?"

"I would be glad to," Aylendel said.

"If you were not busy, why don't you watch?" Katiana suggested.

"Oh," Aylendel replied, "I was not busy and will be glad to watch." Jendrin noticed that Aylendel was a strong woman and slightly younger than Katiana. He also saw several villagers had gathered along with Rendal and Throc to watch. Jendrin decided it was a good time to start the session.

"If everyone would form a staggered line along here," Jendrin said. "We can begin." The group lined up in front of Jendrin with their quarterstaff in hand. "Every other person takes two steps back and spreads two paces from the person on either side. Make sure you don't hit your neighbor with your staff. Face away from the gathering, feet apart, with the butt of staff on the ground. Your quarterstaff is outside your foot. This is the start of the phase one stance." Jendrin instructed, moving around the group. He spoke loud enough for the observers to listen, especially Rendal.

"This beginning passive stance may make the mildest of aggressors see they face some resistance and leave," Jendrin said, moving to the front of the group. "The next phase is to face the aggressor and wait for their response. If they approach, take your defensive stance and start spinning your quarterstaff. Start with the rowing motion, then switch to rotating the staff in your hand. Change to the opposite hand and repeat. Callon, watch another member to learn the process. While you do that, I will recount our agreement with the council and the phases we will use in defending Olona." Jendrin said, moving and correcting each member's stance.

"Your council has set a fair policy for us to use," Jendrin continued. "We do not attack other villages. We do not use more aggression than is needed. We do not attack an aggressor first. We strive to disarm the aggressor if they continue their attack. We do not kill. I will add one more. Do not practice attacking each other!" Jendrin almost yelled at them. "I do not want someone injured or worse due to practice." Jendrin continued to walk around the group as he repeated the steps they would use to meet that agreement. There were fewer drops today as Jendrin watched.

"Stop," Jendrin told the class. "Today, I want you to add a rollover of the staff instead of twisting your wrist. We will add an overhead spin, which needs the rollover to switch hands." Jendrin demonstrated rolling his wrist and overhead transfer spin. Anticipating the question of why they were doing this from the crowd, he spoke to his group. "I hope to discourage the less aggressive attacker by showing staff action while they think about attacking us."

Jendrin noticed many staff drops were occurring, trying the rollover.

"Expect to drop the staff many times before you learn to spin and transfer successfully."

Jendrin noticed the villagers were still watching along with Beacon Rendal. Jendrin decided a demonstration of the first two phases for Rendal would help.

"Throc, would you approach me so I may demonstrate?" Jendrin asked, "Stop when you feel you are too close."

Jendrin stood facing Throc in the first phase stance. As Throc approached, Jendrin turned and faced him. Throc took another tentative step. Jendrin took a defensive step and started spinning the staff slowly. Throc stopped and watched as Jendrin spun the staff and rolled it over to the other hand to turn on the other side.

"Move a little closer, Throc," Rendal said. Throc looked unsure at the Beacon before slowly moving a little closer. Jendrin increased the spin speed as Throc raised his hands before him.

"I would not approach anyone who looks that dangerous," Throc said, moving backward. Rendal patted Throc on the back.

"Good man, Throc," Rendal said. "We have our work to do." Rendal smiled at the group as they walked away.

Jendrin returned to the front of the group.

"That would be the reaction we hope to achieve," Jendrin said. "I will work with each of you on the spin. Expect it to hit the ground many times before you achieve any real success." Jendrin showed each person how to spin the staff and roll it over their hand to the next hand. "Stay apart from each other! Let's see how you are doing." Jendrin said, standing at the front. Most could do a one-handed spin without losing control. None managed to transfer to another hand successfully.

"We will practice the spin each day. We will also set up safe training dummies for you to practice with when our training gets that far." Jendrin walked around the group, demonstrating and encouraging the group as he went. Moving back to the front, he spoke to the group.

"Let me demonstrate what the third phase of defense will be," Jendrin said, pointing to Latel. Jendrin restarted in phase one, and as Latel approached, he went to phase two.

"When the aggressor continues to advance, we go to phase three." Jendrin caught the quarterstaff in both hands and centered his weight over his stance. "High hatchet or club," he said as he thrust the staff up with both hands spread so he could see the weapon. "Low hatchet or club," as he thrust the staff down to block the imaginary attack. "Reset to the middle for the next attack. We will discuss a knife attack at a future meeting. I realize it is much to think about as you learn." Jendrin stood straight with the staff in one hand. "You will learn the process, I am sure. Practice your spins when you can, and we will do them daily." Jendrin noticed several members looked tired and decided to suggest an adjournment.

"Good work today, everyone," Jendrin said. "We will meet again tomorrow, but if you have extra time, I will help you train."

No one left the training area, and the group practiced together until Jendrin needed to go to help Airalee.

Maylore opened the door to find Airalee and Marisa sitting at the table, looking at Ayare. Both looked up at him with a similar grin he felt he did not trust.

'Now what?' he thought as he entered.

"Welcome back, Dad," Airalee said.

"Greetings, Maylore," Marisa said, pointing at a chair near her. Maylore first looked at Ayare, who was awake and looking at him.

"She recognizes you," Marisa said.

"Yes, we have met before," Maylore said. "She will be an interesting young woman as she grows," Maylore said, sitting in the chair Marisa had indicated.

"Another prophet amongst us?" Marisa said. Maylore smiled and set his satchel on the floor.

"Did you meet with Kelkalyn?" Airalee asked.

"I did," Maylore said, "He was a little more open than he has been." Maylore could sense they were up to something.

"I suspect you two have been conspiring," Maylore said.

"Us?" Marisa said, sitting back in mock surprise. "We wouldn't do anything like that unless given a chance to!" Marisa laughed.

"Actually," Airalee started, "we have been discussing how to get the potion over to Gilda to slow down the bandits' libido if it works. Do you feel like your libido has gone down after using the potion?"

"Yes," Maylore said. "In fact, Kelkalyn noticed some kind of chemical blocked my belly portal."

"We can test it," Marisa said, moving quickly onto Maylore's lap.

"Kelkalyn can see the portals?" Airalee said, ignoring Marisa as she wiggled. Maylore was only mildly surprised at Marisa's actions.

"He does not want others to know about it," Maylore replied.

He had no appetite for using Marisa but decided to play along. He winked at Airalee as she looked askance at him. He wrapped his arms around Marisa and hugged her fiercely to his body.

"I would gladly join your next baby seeding group," he said, looking at her. He saw a wry smile come to her lips as he released her.

"I may consider it," Marisa said, putting her arm around his shoulders. Maylore smiled and patted her on the back.

"You are my second favorite woman," Maylore said. "I desire you only for your friendship." Marisa looked slightly disappointed but wiggled a few more times.

"I am pleased to hear that," Marisa said as she returned to her chair. Looking at Airalee, she said, "I didn't get any reaction from him. He must be drugged."

Maylore

Maylore trudged through the snow to Kelkalyn's hut. He met Kai on the trail coming from his hut.

"That is one difficult man," she said as she approached. "I wish you luck visiting him," she said as she passed.

"Thank you," Maylore said, thinking, 'Two peas in a pod' as he smiled at her.

Knocking on his door, he heard no reply, and no one came to the door. He checked his portal and saw Kelkalyn was inside, so he opened the door.

"Kelkalyn?" he called. He got no response but entered anyway. No one was in the room as he stood perplexed, looking around. He turned back to the rear of the hut as Kelkalyn suddenly appeared. Maylore jumped back in surprise but remembered the portal showed he was there.

"I was doubting the portal showing you were here!" Maylore said.

"I have not used that trick in a long time," Kelkalyn laughed. "I should have tried it when Kai came knocking. She is a good person, but she is difficult sometimes."

"She said the same about you when I passed her outside!" Maylore said.

"We are alike in a few ways," Kelkalyn nodded. "Come, sit by the fire, and I will show you how to do the cloaking trick," he said.

"That would be far better than I had hoped to talk about," Maylore said, moving to a chair near the fire.

"What did you want to talk about?" Kelkalyn asked.

"I used a mushroom to check on Airalee and saw pearl energy threads. Do you know what they are?" Maylore asked.

627

"You saw it," Kelkalyn said. "Well, you continue to surprise me. It is surplus energy from another person. It transforms into pearl energy when it leaves one person and is accepted by another. Some can unknowingly send it, while others can use it. I know little about it and cannot use it. Can you use it?" Kelkalyn asked.

"No," Maylore replied. "I am unsure if I could use it. Will it harm someone if I try?"

"I have heard that if all surplus energy is used, the person will stop creating it before it harms them," Kelkalyn replied.

"I brought a blue spot mushroom with me if you need to use it," Maylore said, offering it to Kelkalyn.

Kelkalyn sat back as if he were being offered poison.

"Using the blue spot to enter another is a very invasive, personal thing," Kelkalyn said. "I do not use them since I do not want to enter another person, nor do I want someone rummaging around inside of me."

"I apologize," Maylore said. "It is invasive, I agree," Maylore said, putting the mushroom back into his pocket. Kelkalyn leaned forward again.

"I truly trust no one," Kelkalyn said. "If you prove trustworthy, I will consider working with you."

"Thank you," Maylore replied. "Would you check to see what portals I can use?"

"It is one of the few skills I have without using a mushroom," Kelkalyn said, looking slightly down. "Your head portal has no outside dome on it. Your eye portal has no outside dome on it. Your communication portal is fairly large and has an outside dome. You have extra threads connecting it to your body, which most people don't have. Your heart portal has no dome and inactive threads attached to it. The spine portal has no dome on it, either. Something seems to block the belly portal. It has no dome on it but should not be blocked. The belly portal gives people sexual desire. Did someone block it?"

"Airalee and Kai are trying to develop a potion to stop the bandits' libido," Maylore said. I tried it for her, and it appears to be working."

"Indeed," Kelkalyn said. "Some lady here will not be happy."

"No one fits that description," Maylore laughed.

"What skills did Gilriel work with you on while he was here?" Kelkalyn asked.

Maylore told him of the skills he had been working to learn and his success rate.

"If you can twist energy left and right, did he tell you how to cancel a cast if you wish?" Kelkalyn asked. Maylore considered why he would want to cancel a cast before answering.

"I do not know how to do that," Maylore said. "Why would I want to do that?"

"You may cast energy toward an enemy only to realize it is an ally," Kelkalyn said. "You would want to stop the energy from hitting them. I will show you by throwing a small amount of heat energy at the wall and then canceling it. Watch what happens," he said. A small amount of right-spin fire erupted from in front of Kelkalyn, followed by a faster-moving left-spinning fire. A large shower of sparks erupted as the spins cancel each other out. "It is a practical skill but can also entertain others you trust." Maylore realized what could happen and the practicality of the skill.

"Thank you," Maylore said. "I am not sure I need the sparkling trick, but I might need to cancel a mistake."

"Sometimes, you need to have fun," Kelkalyn said, smiling. "My bag of tricks is nearly empty. Can I answer another question?". Maylore considered for a moment.

"Could I develop domes for the other portals?" Maylore asked.

"I have heard it happens," Kelkalyn replied. "If you practice, you may develop a dome for a portal that will pop open when you use the right skill. Consistent training and help from a master sorcerer could make that happen. I do not believe any master-training sorcerers remain alive on Almora. There are a few partially trained ones like me who are still alive. Most stay hidden from the master's wrath, meeting only in secret. With Gilriel now gone, it will be hard to find others to meet with, even in secret".

"I understand," Maylore replied.

"You must understand you are not to allow others to see what we have done here," Kelkalyn said sternly. "Especially that you learned it from me! If the wrong ears hear it, I would be the next one missing from Almora, and they would not be subtle this time."

"I understand. I appreciate you are teaching me some valuable skills," Maylore said, nodding.

"You are welcome," Kelkalyn said, smiling. "Those small things may become useful someday."

"Do you want to discuss the cloaking trick?" Maylore asked.

"I shall keep that for another day," Kelkalyn said. "It would be an incentive for you to return."

Maylore stood and walked to the door.

"I would like to visit again," Maylore said.

"Anytime," Kelkalyn said.

Maylore nodded as he closed the door and returned to the companion's hut.

CHAPTER 39 - MARISA'S TURN

Marisa was near the bathing pool when she felt her baby moving around.

"On the move," Marisa said aloud as more small contractions began. "Is today the day?" she asked, looking down and rubbing her baby bump. Marisa washed and dressed before adding more wood to the pool firepit. She headed toward Kai's hut for her weekly visit.

Kai was talking with Jasal as she entered the hut.

"Marisa," Kai said. "Are you having baby pains?"

"Perhaps," Marisa replied. "The baby is moving, and the baby chamber is sometimes contracting."

"Good," Kai said. "Jasal and the other girls will be due soon. If yours starts soon, it would be good timing for the birthing women and myself."

"Is Airalee going to help with the birthing?" Marisa asked, sitting in a chair.

"She will attend to you when it is your time," Kai said. "She will help me with wellness checks this morning. We will check with you later to see how you are coming. Did you tell your baby-mate Gobelben to stay away when you go to the birthing hut?"

"We discussed it before, and he seemed happy to stay away," Marisa replied. "I will return to the hut to remind him and get ready for the baby's arrival."

"Baby may not be ready," Kai said. "The baby chamber may be getting ready for the birth."

"I understand," Marisa said. "I will ensure our hut is ready when it decides it is time."

A knock on the door announced another arrival.

"Good morning, all," Airalee said as she entered carrying Ayare. Ayare was 60 sunrises in age and was held in a sling in front of Airalee. Airalee still wore the amulet, hoping Ayare would try to speak to her.

"Jendrin is not with the baby?" Kai asked.

"He has done his morning duties with Ayare and is getting ready to train the defense group," Airalee said. "We worked out a good system where he takes Ayare in the morning and evening until Ayare decides she needs Mom. It gives me a good amount of time to myself. I usually miss her before she calls for me," she chuckled.

"The villagers will welcome her as we visit this morning," Kai replied. "Are you ready to start our rounds?"

"I am," Airalee said.

"Marisa believes she is approaching her baby's birth," Kai said, looking at Marisa.

"Wonderful, Marisa!" Airalee replied. "I will be there to help you through it."

"Thank you," Marisa replied. "I hope I am near the end of carrying this one around."

"Not so fast," Airalee said. "After he is born, you still carry him around like this," she said, pointing at Ayare in her sling.

"Yes, but Gobelben will get to carry him, too," Marisa said.

"It was nice when Jendrin could help carry the load," Airalee smiled.

"Let's be on our way," Kai said, opening the door.

As they left the hut, the loud caw of a bird sounded outside. An IB sat in a nearby tree, cawing at them.

"It is Gilda's bird," Kai said, moving toward the bird.

"How did she know that?" Jasal asked, moving outside with the others.

"This bird has a red feather extending out from each eye," Airalee said.

"It may be carrying a message from Gilda," Marisa said.

The bird extended its leg to Kai as she approached.

"Thank you, bird," Kai said as she removed the note from its leg. The bird cocked its head at her but did not fly. Kai opened the short notice and moved back toward her hut.

"It says the bandits plan a gathering trip when the snows melt from the passes," Kai said. "It means they plan to steal more of our supplies. It is a nice warning, but it is how the bandits normally work." The bird suddenly straightened as another IB cawed its arrival and landed just above the other bird. The two birds cawed at each other and bobbed their heads at each other.

"It looks like they know each other," Jasal said.

"That is Maylore's bird, Bert," Airalee said. "It has two feathers going up from its beak to its head."

"It has a name?" Jasal said in amazement.

"Maylore named the bird since he can recognize him," Airalee said, not wanting to reveal the truth.

"I am here, Bert," Maylore said as he approached Kai's hut. Bert softly cawed as Maylore stood before him. "Greetings, everyone," Maylore said, smiling toward the women and facing Bert. "You want me to meet your friend?" he asked Bert. Maylore looked at his portal and tied a string to Bert. Maylore received a picture from Bert asking him to identify his friend so he could talk with Maylore. Maylore looked at his portal, noting there was a dot near Bert. He tied another string to that dot and sent a picture of the bird with a questioning look on his face. The bird vocalized a sound that, to Maylore, sounded like Muninn. "Muninn?" Maylore said, looking toward Gilda's crow.

Both crows seemed to laugh at him but quickly settled on their branches. Maylore added the bird's name to the new dot. "The bird's name is Muninn. At least that's what I think it is," Maylore said, realizing he should have kept quiet. Kai cocked her head at him.

"That is a good name for an IB," Kai said. "Could you ask him if he needs something from us?"

"Marisa and I discussed having the bird, Muninn, carry the libido potion to the bandit camp," Airalee said.

"That would be much safer than Jendrin trying to sneak into their camp and add the potion to their reeb," Kai said. Looking toward Maylore, she asked, "Can you ask Muninn if he could carry a small vial?"

Maylore decided Kai knew his secret and sent both birds a picture of a claw carrying a vial through the air. Both birds returned a picture of them flying with a vial.

"I believe they said they could each carry one," Maylore said, looking at Kai.

"It can't be too heavy," Airalee said. "We can send just the powder and have Gilda add it to their drink."

"She can do that," Kai said. "We have much of the powder ground up in the storage hut. We can fashion a light container from small pieces of thin leather for them to carry." Airalee and Marisa nodded and headed toward the storage hut.

Jasal looked in wonderment at the activity around her. She shook her head and started walking back to her hut. Kai faced Maylore as the others left the area.

"When did you learn this skill?" Kai asked.

Maylore explained that he was still learning the skill as Airalee and Marisa returned with two small tubes.

"I know very few who could communicate like that," Kai said. "It is a valuable skill. You must avoid showing or discussing it with anyone outside the village," she said, pointing her finger at him for emphasis. Kai returned to her hut to create a new message for Gilda as he determined the best way to attach it to the birds. Kai returned and joined the group near the birds.

"I wrote that Gilda should add this powder to Birsha's drink to slow or stop libido," Kai said. Muninn waited as Kai attached the paper and a tube to its leg. Maylore attached a tube to Bert's leg and stood back. The birds squawked and flew off in the direction of the bandit camp. They watched the birds disappear as another pregnant girl walked up the path to Kai's hut.

"Would you do the rounds on your own today, Airalee?" Kai asked.

"Yes. I can start now," Airalee answered.

"All right, I will take care of the girls this morning," Kai said, motioning for the girl to enter the hut.

"I will go clean my hut," Marisa said, rubbing her baby bump. "The pains are getting stronger and lasting longer," she said, wincing slightly.

"Perhaps we will soon meet in the birthing hut," Airalee said.

"Perhaps," Marisa said, waving as she turned toward her hut. Maylore waved to her before turning to Airalee.

"I will return to our hut, then visit Kelkalyn," Maylore said.

"See you tonight, Dad," Airalee said as she headed toward the first hut to be visited.

The villagers Airalee visited were all in good spirits and did not require anything. Gaearwen did not look well during her visit and had little to say outside of watching Ayare. He fell asleep in his chair, so Airalee quietly closed the door and continued her rounds. She moved on to the elder's huts. Climbing the short incline, she knocked on Melronna's door.

"Come in!" came two voices as she opened the door.

"Greetings, ladies," Airalee said as she moved to where Melronna and Lalien sat by the fire.

"Nice to see you, Airalee," they both said.

"I see you have had your baby," Melronna said.

"Yes, I did, Melronna," Airalee replied as Lalien looked at Melronna.

"She brought the baby with her the last several times, Melronna," Lalien said.

"Oh, I lose track too often," Melronna replied.

Airalee smiled as the two women fussed at each other.

"Do you ladies need anything I can bring you?" Airalee asked. Both women shook their heads as Melronna spoke.

"Summer season begins in 15 sunrises," Melronna said, staring past the door. "Be ready to plant your crops."

Airalee had seen the look on Melronna's face enough to know she would be correct.

"I will pass it on to Mirtha," Airalee said.

"May we see Ayare?" Lalien asked. Airalee moved closer to them so they could see Ayare in her sling. Ayare was sleeping when she pulled back her covering.

"Pretty girl!" Melronna exclaimed as she peered into the sling. Lalien smiled and waved to Ayare. "Where is Marisa?" Melronna asked, looking at Airalee.

"She may be having labor pains and went to her hut," Airalee replied.

"Marisa is with child?" Melronna asked in surprise.

Lalien looked at her and then let out a sigh.

"Marisa has been that way most of the winter," Lalien said.

Airalee smiled again, covering Ayare with the blanket.

"I will be on my way then if you are both doing well," Airalee said as she stood.

"We are well," Lalien said.

"Goodbye, ladies," she said as she approached the door. They both bid her farewell as she walked out the door to the next hut.

Selakiir met her at the door to his hut.

"Greetings, Airalee and Ayare," he said, standing in the doorway. "My children are here, and I have everything I can use. You are welcome to come in, but my hut is already crowded." Airalee waved to the group inside his hut.

"Since you are well, I will continue on my path," Airalee said. "I am sure one of us will check on you tomorrow." Selakiir thanked her and closed the door.

Airalee walked to Phaerl's hut and knocked on its door. Phaerl opened the door wide, bidding her to enter. Phaerl was lonely after Adandir's passing, but her daughter spent time with her. Phaerl had made baskets again since a half-completed one was near her chair.

"Is Ayare asleep?" Phaerl asked. Airalee pulled aside the cloth covering her face so Phaerl could see. "Asleep or awake, children can be pure joy," she said, indicating a chair for Airalee. Airalee sat in the chair, realizing her legs could use some rest from carrying Ayare.

"My daughter says Jendrin has started building a defensive force for the village," she said as she sat in another chair. Airalee told her it was true and explained why the force was being created. Phaerl looked down as she said, "One of the girls I worked with in the baby center was taken when she turned 15 seasons. It was tough for me,

637

almost as much as when my daughter was taken. She returned two seasons later to have her baby but moved to another village with the child. It still makes me sad we allowed it to happen to her and the others before her."

"We agree," Airalee said. "We hope to stop our children from being taken by diverting the bandits from our village. The bandits are planning a trip to the village to collect food, but we plan a passive show of force when they arrive, hoping they will not attempt to raid our village of our young in the future."

"I hope we are successful," Phaerl said. The two women discussed the council's approved charter and who Jendrin had been training. Phaerl nodded as Airalee related the tale and seemed satisfied with the conversion. "Thank you for taking the time to explain it to me, Airalee," she said.

"My pleasure," Airalee said as she rose from her chair. "I have two more huts to visit, and then it is my rest time. Ayare may yet change my plan," she chuckled. Phaerl opened the door for her and bid her goodbye.

Werloth had not been seen since his mother's funeral. Airalee opened the door to his hut, but it smelled empty like no one had lived there for a long time. Airalee securely closed the door and walked toward Kelkalyn's hut.

She had not seen Kelkalyn for many days but checked his hut anyway. Smoke was coming from his fireplace as she knocked on the door. There was no answer, so she opened the door. The fire burned merrily, but no one was in the hut. Ayare was stirring, so she pulled the cloth from over her face. Ayare turned her head to look at an empty spot near the fire.

"I don't see anyone either, Ayare," Airalee said, looking around. "There is a good supply of wood and food in the cabinet. "He could not have gone far. I guess that is all I needed to know anyway," she said aloud as she turned to leave. Ayare made a noise, still looking at the corner. "All right, we are leaving Ayare," she said, opening the door. She returned to the village and descended the rocks leading up to the elder's huts. Maylore was approaching the path as she reached the bottom. "Dad," she said.

"Kelkalyn was not in his hut. He probably ran off when he heard me coming," Airalee chuckled as they met on the trail.

"I guess I will wait for him anyway," Maylore said, smiling at her.

"Ayare and I are going to the child center," Airalee said. "I would rather be with them than Kelkalyn anyway."

"He can be a challenge," Maylore said. He gave them both a hug and started toward Kelkalyn's hut.

"Good luck, Dad!" Airalee said as they walked away.

Maylore reached Kelkalyn's hut and decided to knock in case he had returned. Knocking on the door, he got no reply. Maylore opened the door and walked inside. He looked around but didn't see anyone.

"I think I will wait," he said as he walked to a chair and sat down.

"Hope I didn't keep you," Kelkalyn said as he appeared beside the fire. Maylore looked up in surprise.

"I didn't see you, sorry," Maylore said.

"Good," Kelkalyn said, laughing. "It is one of the few tricks I have to avoid people. Your companion and her daughter were just here. She didn't see me as I intended, but I suspect her child did."

"Ayare is indeed a special child," Maylore said. "She already has some communication ability with me."

Kelkalyn's smile disappeared.

"That is extraordinary," Kelkalyn said. "You are the only one I know who has that ability." Kelkalyn cocked his head, asking, "Are you the one who seeded her?"

Maylore was taken aback but answered quickly.

639

"No," Maylore said. "Ayare comes from Jendrin's seed. I view Airalee as a daughter."

"Did Airalee use a seeding party?" Kelkalyn asked.

"No, just Jendrin," Maylore replied.

"Interesting," Kelkalyn said. "Does Ayare initiate the conversation, or must you select her first?"

"I have to start the communication," Maylore said. "Ayare can already request a conversation."

"The baby can speak?" Kelkalyn said in surprise.

"No," Maylore replied, "She can use thoughts through the portal, but nothing else yet."

"Even so," Kelkalyn said, "we must watch her as she grows. She could be an important addition to our world. Be sure not to mention anything about her to the master. I would fear for her safety if he finds out."

Maylore became very sober as Kelkalyn spoke.

"I have never seen the master," Maylore said. "I intend to stay away from him. I will also inform my companions of your warning," Maylore replied.

"Does her mother use her communication portal?" Kelkalyn asked.

"I feel a knock on my portal like I do for Ayare, Bert, and yourself," Maylore said. "She can speak to me through her amulet after I open the connection."

"Good," Kelkalyn said. "You are indeed becoming a central communication point."

"It seems so," Maylore said.

"Are you ready to learn another skill?" Kelkalyn asked.

"I am," Maylore replied.

"It is the right time to teach you my hiding skill," Kelkalyn said. "It may become a valuable skill for you in the future."

"I am ready to learn," Maylore said.

"To make this trick work," Kelkalyn said, "an object must remain stationary. Any movement changes the energy flow, and part of the object will show through until the energy flow can adjust. I start by asking an energy source, such as the planet's energy, to copy light from behind an object. I ask the energy to flow around the object and stop at the same height in front of the object. It creates a circle of light from behind the object and displays it in front of it." Kelkalyn demonstrated by setting up a log and then sitting quietly as the log faded from view.

"Amazing," Maylore said in awe.

"Try and see if you can do it," Kelkalyn said. Maylore tried asking the blue energy to copy the light from behind the log and move it to the front of the log. Maylore worked at this for some time before Kelkalyn interrupted.

"I saw a few holes appear in the image," Kelkalyn said. "It will take practice to get this to work." Kelkalyn coached him on copying and projecting the image until the sun reached its halfway point. "I believe you will be able to do it. It just takes patience and practice," Kelkalyn said. "Have you practiced the reverse or sparks skill?"

"I have," Maylore replied. "I can stop the skill sooner, but more sparks erupt. It would make a good trick for others to view."

"Let's go outside," Kelkalyn said, opening the door. "Throw the skill about fifty feet, then reverse it to sparks."

Maylore gathered earth energy and pushed it out to about fifty feet. He reversed the spin, and the energy turned to sparks and fell to the earth.

"Use a right spin to start," Kelkalyn said. "If you fail to stop the spin, it won't put a hole in something," Kelkalyn instructed.

Maylore tried different spins and distances as Kelkalyn coached him through the process.

"Good. You are getting better at it already," Kelkalyn said, nodding.

"Thank you, Kelkalyn," Maylore said. "Your training has saved me many hours of experimenting to get results."

Kelkalyn smiled and nodded to him.

"I believe that is enough for one day," Kelkalyn said.

"It is nap time for me anyway," Maylore agreed.

"I will visit with Airalee and then return to the cave," Maylore said. "Thank you again," he said as he walked away.

Jendrin

Jendrin cleaned up the hut after Airalee left with the baby. He set up more firewood, added food to the cookpot, and cleaned necessities for the baby. He arrived at the training ground while all the members practiced independently. He checked the recently completed training dummies he and Latel had made. The dummies had ropes attached from their arms to the tree limbs above. The ropes allowed a trainer to lift or drop a weapon from the dummy to the trainee. Satisfied they would work for the training session, he moved to the front of the group.

"Greetings, everyone!" he said as he looked to see who was present. The group had grown to nine members before four dropped out to settle at five plus Jendrin. Jendrin was pleased with the group that remained. Latel had proven his ability to take on a secondary training role by working hard to learn skills. Katiana was very quick with her quarterstaff and would be a challenge for anyone. Aylendel had joined the group to be with her mate Katiana. She was more of a warrior than Katiana and aggressive in her defense. Dirdin and

Callon were slower but much more potent. Jendrin was sure any of them was a good match for any intruder.

"It appears this is our final group, which is a good group!" Jendrin said, smiling.

Aylendel came forward and presented him with a whistle for each member.

"I created these for the group to use," Aylendel said. "They have the same note so that we can call the group. Katiana and I will have our own to call each other," she said, smiling.

"Thank you, Aylendel!" Jendrin said, putting one around his neck. "Please pass the others to your teammates. Shall we try out our whistles to know what they sound like?" Jendrin said, blowing his whistle. All the team members blew their whistles, putting a big smile on Aylendel's face.

"Let's start today's practice," Jendrin said.

He reviewed the council's mandate and emphasized not attacking another or killing. The group had heard these same statements many times and simply rested while he talked. After completing his rehash of the charter and reviewing the process phases, he moved on to a new business.

"Today, I want to complete our training by discussing phase four," Jendrin said. "This is the counterattack phase we will only use if the attacker refuses to stop their attack." Jendrin moved away from everyone before continuing his demonstration. "We will begin this after we block their attack, then immediately force the other end of your quarterstaff out to strike a joint of your attacker. We want to strike an ankle, knee, hip, or shoulder. The other end of the staff must stop on the outside of our elbow. If the attacker is injured enough, they will stop their attack. Remember, we do not continue our attack." Jendrin moved to the training dummies to illustrate each block and joint's counterattack.

"If they rush forward at us," Jendrin said, "use the end of the staff to poke them in the body forcefully. Reset to the ready position after each counterattack to see if they attack again." Jendrin looked over his group and saw they were ready to work on their counterattacks. "Latel and I have set up training dummies where we will practice," he said. "You may want to set up your own practice area or use this one when you want to practice. Any questions before we practice?" The group looked at each other but remained quiet.

"Line up behind each dummy, and we will practice together," Jendrin said, standing beside one dummy. Jendrin spent the rest of their practice time working on the fourth phase with each person.

Airalee

Airalee was in the children's area when she saw Marisa approaching the birthing hut with Kai and one of the birthing women. The three other girls in her seeding group followed behind them. Airalee picked up Ayare and walked to join them.

"My turn!" Marisa said when she saw Airalee approaching.

"I'm afraid the smile may not last long," Airalee said as they entered the birthing hut.

"I fear not," Marisa replied.

"It may happen sooner than I thought," Kai said, pointing at the bed for Marisa.

"If she is lucky," Airalee said, looking at Marisa. "Ayare and I plan to stay to help if we can."

"I suspect Ayare will be no help," Kai said, "but you can help support Marisa as she did for you."

Airalee sat in a chair next to Marisa and changed Ayare's sling so she could face forward. Ayare seemed content to watch the activity as her mom chatted with Marisa. Time passed as activity in the room began to pick up. Ayare had fallen asleep, and Airalee had laid her on a nearby bed.

"Would one of you watch Ayare for me?" Airalee said, looking toward the girls in the back.

"I will," Jasal said, moving her chair near Ayare's bed.

Marisa felt confident as long as Airalee held her hand. When Airalee pulled her hand out with more extensive contractions she looked concerned.

"You are doing well," Airalee would tell Marisa. The birthing room women reassured Marisa, trying to calm her down.

"I don't know what I am doing," Marisa said with a slightly wild look in her eyes. "My body has its own idea of what to do!" Airalee chuckled with her as she rubbed her when Marisa sat up.

Night came as the birth process continued. The three girls took the task of using torches to light the room. Airalee would feed Ayare as one of the girls held Marisa's hand. Marisa was talking less and concentrating on getting it over with. Kai kept rubbing her along with Airalee, who spoke quietly to her.

"I believe she is ready," Kai said, preparing for the baby. Marisa could not contain the pain in her throat, and it often escaped in loud wails. Ayare awoke but didn't cry at the sudden noise. Airalee noticed Ayare was awake between contractions and put her back into the harness. A sudden crescendo erupted from Marisa's throat as Kai announced, "You have a boy!"

Marisa slumped back on the bed, laughing and crying simultaneously. Airalee hugged her the best she could and cooed congratulations in her ear. The three girls took the baby and cleaned him up before presenting him to Marisa. She hugged and rocked her new son while he protested being in the cold world. He quieted as she bound him up in the cloth and cradled him to her shoulder.

"Look Ayare!" Marisa said, "You'll have someone your age to play with." Ayare hung in her sling and continued to watch.

"Would you like to see him?" Airalee asked, moving to where Ayare could see him closely. Airalee took one of Ayare's hands and touched her fingers to his head. He went silent and looked at Ayare briefly before resuming his protests. "It may be dinner time," Airalee said, pulling Ayare away as she stood up.

"Let's find out," Marisa said. He immediately quieted as she fed him. Kai returned with pain medication, telling her to drink it all.

"You will sleep here tonight with the baby," Kai said. The birthing women watch over you. You may leave tomorrow. I will visit you tomorrow and recheck you both for potential problems. Allow the birthing woman to clean you up. You will probably sleep when he does. Congratulations," Kai said as she moved away.

Maylore had settled in for another night in the cave when he received a knock on his dot. He looked at the dots on the dome and saw that Ayare was trying to send him something. He opened her dot and received a single word, 'Torbin.' Maylore sent it back, asking if it was a name. He didn't receive a reply, which didn't surprise him. Maylore attached a string to Airalee's dot, asking, 'Does Torbin mean something?'

Airalee had just sat back in the chair near Marisa's bed when Maylore contacted her. She decided to move away from everyone before she replied to Maylore.

"No," Airalee replied. "Marisa has given birth to a son."

"I heard what I think is the name Torbin from Ayare," Maylore said.

"I wish she could talk to me!" Airalee said.

"I guess I will be the communications hub for now," Maylore said, chuckling.

"I will ask Marisa if it is a name," Airalee said. "I don't want her to think I am pushing a name on her."

"Understood," Maylore replied.

"Thanks, dad," Airalee said.

Maylore decided to leave the strings attached for her and Ayare.

"I am not sure why I disconnect those strings anyway," he said aloud.

Airalee moved back to Marisa's bed and shifted Ayare to the front. Not wanting Marisa to think she was pushing a name on her, she considered how to question her.

"Have you thought of a name for him?" Airalee asked.

"No," Marisa replied. "Let's try to come up with a few names," she said as she cradled him. Marisa tried several names, not liking any of them. Airalee tried several, and Marisa shook her head until Airalee included Torbin.

"Torbin?" Marisa replied, looking at her. "I don't know why, but I like that one. How does Torbin sound to you, little one?" she asked as she rocked him slightly. "Welcome, Torbin."

CHAPTER 40 - WARNING

Thirty sunrises proved Melronna's prediction of summer's return correct. The warm twin suns quickly melted the snow farther and farther into the hills. Two villagers had succumbed to winter's death grip as the village mourned the loss of two more lives between winter storms.

The three pregnant girls became mothers as their children were born shortly after Torbin's birth. Two girls and one boy joined Torbin and Ayare daily in the children's area as mothers traded tips, and the older children marveled at the newborns. Marisa did not have enough milk for Torbin soon after his birth. Airalee quickly offered to feed him and Ayare until Marisa's milk was ready. The babies seemed happy to eat together, and Marisa was delighted she had Airalee to depend on.

The village was waking up and starting repairs to winter's damage. Jendrin repaired broken water pipes and helped others repair the damage caused by winter. A large group began preparing the garden for the new season. Marisa and Airalee carried their babies on their backs as they helped clean up the garden.

"Jendrin said Fenhild will soon call for the first fishing of the season," Airalee said as she picked up the area of the row they would be planting.

"Gobelben told me he was going to help pull up the fish they caught," Marisa said, cleaning the next row.

"We need to plan a gathering of herbs and fresh vegetables," Airalee said, standing.

"We can take a quick trip through the meadow area today after the little ones eat," Marisa replied, nodding.

"I hope they will sleep while we gather," Airalee said before her smile disappeared. "Jendrin worries that Oleg may soon return and does not want me to gather alone."

"We would meet Oleg with knives and screaming if he appeared!" Marisa said, standing tall with a fierce tone.

"I have no doubt you would," Airalee smiled. "I just hope we don't need to."

The large group that gathered to clean the garden soon finished. Planting had begun with a much smaller group directed by Levyna on what to plant where. Airalee had given her pink fruit seed to Levyna for planting.

"I will plant them at the top of the row near the water source so they will get the water they need to grow," Latel's mother said. "This time, I will gather some of the fruit for seeds before they disappear!"

Airalee volunteered to stay and help but was told she would be busy enough with the baby.

"My group can plant seeds but not care for a baby," Levyna told her. Airalee smiled and bid them goodbye as she returned to Marisa.

"Let's feed our children and look for fresh food in the meadow," Airalee said as Marisa led the way.

Jendrin

Jendrin decided that the defense group could practice more regularly. The team members' skills varied greatly, with Katiana and him having the most vital skills. Baruo was the least skilled but would be a formidable opponent to anyone.

Ayare had taken up morning and evening hours with Jendrin as he enjoyed being a parent. Feeding, bathing, dressing, and playtime had become normal daily activities.

"Fishing day," Fenhild told him as he walked by.

Jendrin fell in behind him as they walked to the cliff. Jendrin checked the ropes they used for fishing as they dropped them down the ocean slope. Fenhild again led the group and prepared them for the descent to the shore.

"The sea is calm today," Fenhild said. "We have an experienced group, so we should be able to gather our fish quickly. If you find shellfish, gather them and save some for Mirtha to cook for the community lunch. I hope to gather crabs as we clean the fish." Looking over his shoulder, he saw a group of men and women ready to haul the baskets up and down the cliff.

Fenhild led the group down the cliff, with the other men and women following him down the rope. The fishermen spread along the rocks, looking for fish amongst the seaweed. The group found fish to spear almost immediately. Jendrin found it much easier to spear and retrieve the fish this time. He had speared several fish and laid them on the bank for others to take to the baskets. He spotted another fish just as it saw him and started to submerge into the depths. The rope attached to his spear was near the end of its reach when he managed to spear the fish. The rope suddenly jerked, almost pulling the spear from his grasp. Thanks to his quarterstaff strengthening his arms, he twisted the rope back in his direction. Latel noticed Jendrin struggling with the rope and came to help him.

"You may have an anut! It looks heavy," Latel said. "Pull back!" he said as they both pulled to regain the rope. A large fish splashed the water as they pulled it onto the shore.

"It is an anut and a big one!" Latel said as the fish tried to get back to the water. Fenhild appeared with a large club and smashed the anut on the head to quiet it. Latel examined the spear in the now quiet anut's mouth. "You speared an anut in the mouth?" Latel asked in amazement. Jendrin did not know what to say.

"Dinner for a whole village on its own!" Fenhild said. "We usually get one each season, so we are off to a good start!" He said, examining the fish. Pulling up on the spear, he saw the speared sabb fish in the anut's closed jaws. "It refused to give up your speared dinner, and now it is our feast," he laughed. Fenhild whistled to stop the fishing and shouted, "Shellfish!" as he returned to the anut. "Get your knives out, men. We have a lot of cutting to do to get this up to the village." Latel and Jendrin helped the fishmonger clean, cut up, and haul the large pieces to the waiting baskets. The crab came to claim the anut's cleanings and, in turn, were caught themselves. The fishmonger called the fishing outing a success and told the fishermen to return to the village.

Maylore

Maylore had become quite comfortable in the cave, finding he could practice his skills anytime. He found an abundance of food in the garden outside his door.

"No wonder the village thought Gilriel antisocial," Maylore said aloud. "He never had to leave here to have a comfortable living!" He had spent much of the winter trying to decipher what was in the spell book Gilriel had left him. He was very disappointed he could not determine anything from the hefty tome. The months he spent looking at the book convinced him they were notes written by different authors about spells that worked for them.

"I suspect the same results are written here using different methods," he muttered. "Someone could have collected the notes from different people and translated them into a guild language few knew. I wonder if they destroyed the original notes."

Long ago, he decided to create notes on his scroll of the skills he had learned and how he did them. "I don't know who I am making this for. I will likely remember all of this," he said, setting his pen down. Unlike the large tome, he wrote all his notes in plain language.

"Caw." A soft sound came from the back of a chair. Maylore looked up to see Bert staring at him. Bert apparently decided to become a constant companion to him. Bert only left his chair back to eat and fly with the other birds. Sometimes, Bert would send him a picture of the birds as they flew to find food or just to fly.

"Let's go for a warm water bath," Maylore said as he stood. He told his companions about the pool, and they joined him swimming in light clothes in the warm waters. Maylore had washed Ayare as her mother and Jendrin swam behind him. Marisa occasionally

651

joined them but would not leave Torbin with Maylore while he washed Ayare. Marisa would leave her clothes on the side and sit beside him as she washed Torbin. She would swim after Airalee returned to claim Ayare, and Maylore could watch Torbin.

Maylore let that memory fade as he reached the entrance to the swimming cave. He picked some soapweed he had planted there and stepped into the cave. Leaving his robe on the side of the cave, he slipped into the water to enjoy the warming sensation as it seeped through him. He floated for what seemed to be a single minute when a caw came from Bert outside the cave.

"Time already?" Maylore sent him. Bert sent him a picture of birds flying. "Messenger," Maylore translated, getting out of the water and slipping on his robe. "Well, Bert," Maylore said, "Perhaps we should go to the village." Bert cocked his head, listening as he spoke. Maylore sent him a picture of Kai's hut. The bird nodded and flew off in the direction of the village. Maylore opened the connection to Ayare as he walked back to the cave. Ayare was probably asleep since he did not receive anything from her. Maylore had taken the time to leave the connection to Ayare closed. Ayare could not yet control what she sent, and he would receive pictures of feeding, which Maylore did not need to see. He closed the connection again and left the cave to return to the village.

Kai had finally cast off all of the stiffness in her knee during the winter. She strode confidently between the huts of her patients as she did her daily rounds without the snow impeding her. Village patients seemed to be doing well, and now she traveled to the elders' huts.

"I suspect one of these will be my home someday," Kai said. "I already crave the privacy these huts will afford," she muttered as she walked the coastal huts. Kelkalyn was not in his hut. Werloth had not returned. Phaerl was visiting children, leaving only two others to check on. Kai enjoyed visits with Melronna and Lalien most of the time. People, in general, seemed to grow more tiresome as she got older.

Knocking on their door, she heard two voices inviting her in.

"Greetings, ladies," Kai said as she closed the door.

"Sit, Kai," Melronna said, indicating a nearby chair.

"Have you news for us?" Lalien asked, smiling up at her.

"The village awakens, fishing starts today, and new vegetables are being planted," Kai said. "It is a newsworthy day," Kai said with a hint of mockery in her voice.

"The weather smiles on us and should be fair for some time," Melronna said. Melronna's smile disappeared as she turned her head toward the sunset.

"Heed the warning that flies your way. It will foretell death before the rebirth of an entire village." Melronna's smile returned. "There won't be any rain for several weeks." Her voice trailed off, seeing the other two women staring at her. "Did I say something interesting?" she asked.

"You said we should heed a warning flying our way. It will be the entire village's death and rebirth," Lalien replied.

"That is one possible summary," Kai said. "I will be watchful for any unusual message. Do either of you need help while I am here?" Both shook their heads.

"We were getting ready to walk to the edge of the rocks as you arrived," Lalien said. "Would you join us?" Kai agreed and opened the door for them to go together. The three women sat at the cliff's edge, discussing topics interesting to older women.

Marisa and Airalee finished feeding Torbin and Ayare as the sound of the fishing group hauling food to the kitchen increased.

"Let's check in with Mirtha to see if she needs our help," Marisa said, putting Torbin into the baby carrier. Ayare was already asleep as she settled into her carrier. The two women arrived to find the kitchen full of people preparing the fish for drying and dinner.

"Do you need more help, Mirtha?" Marisa asked as they approached the kitchen fire. Mirtha held up her hands before she spoke.

"We are well stocked for help now," Mirtha said. "If you could find some fresh herbs for our fish, especially tarragon, that would be helpful," Mirtha said as she sailed by to direct another group arriving with fish.

"I know where to find that," Marisa said. Mirtha had left several gathering bags sitting on the table. "Grab a bag, and let's head to the meadow," Marisa said as she walked toward the meadow.

"I will see if I can find some green plants," Airalee said, following her. "The first pickings of the season should easily feed many villagers." She had little trouble filling her satchel as they walked through the outer meadow. Marisa was a few feet away gathering tarragon when two short IB whistles echoed from the trees. Both women stood straight as they looked at each other before running back toward the village.

"I don't know if the sentinel saw a beast or a bandit, but let's hope he doesn't whistle again," Marisa shouted as she ran.

"Another would mean we are being pursued?" Airalee said, running beside her.

"Yes," Marisa answered simply. The two women were already close to the village when the warning sounded. They didn't stop running until they reached the huts near the garden area. The two babies were quiet, perhaps sensing their mothers' anxiety. Looking over their shoulders, they saw no pursuit. There were no further warning whistles from the trees.

"I will speak with Rendal to ask Olach about what they saw," Marisa said. Both babies seemed to have enjoyed the run in the forest and now smiled up at their mothers. "Glad you had a good time, Torbin," Marisa said, leaving his head uncovered.

"Let's deliver our collection to Mirtha," Airalee said, starting toward the kitchen.

Jendrin heard the distant IB whistle as he helped carry the fish to the kitchen. He wasn't sure what to think of the whistle since it was not the whistle of the defense group but a sentinel warning.

"A warning from the meadow," Latel said, picking up his pace.

"Airalee may have gone to the meadow for greens," Jendrin said as the thought moved his anxiety level up several degrees. He started running with his load, arriving quickly at the kitchen. He placed his load near the fire and started toward the meadow.

Maylore was approaching the edge of the kitchen when he heard the IB warning.

"Warning about what, I wonder?" he said as he looked around. He didn't see anything but decided to continue toward the kitchen. Entering the kitchen area, he saw Jendrin drop his load and run toward the forest. Maylore quickened his pace until he saw Airalee coming from the other direction. She and Marisa were walking fast but did not seem concerned, so he slowed to a walk again. Jendrin spotted the two women and slowed until he met up with them on the path.

"Are you alright?" he asked Airalee. Airalee looked slightly surprised.

"Was that warning for me?" Airalee asked.

"I am not sure," he replied. "I probably assumed the worst." As they looked toward the meadow, a single sharp whistle echoed from the trees.

"All clear," Marisa translated. "Whatever they saw has left."

"Let's deliver our collection," Airalee said, moving toward the kitchen. Mirtha looked pleased to see the greens and tarragon the women had shared with her. The two women had finished when Maylore arrived.

"I am meeting Bert at Kai's to see if Muninn has brought us any news from Gilda. Would you like to join us?" Maylore said.

"I would, dad," Airalee said. "I will take care of Ayare, then join you."

"I will join you, too," Marisa said as she walked toward her hut. Maylore noted the large number of fish in the baskets.

"It looks like the village had a good fishing trip," Maylore said as Jendrin picked up his basket.

"Yes, I somehow captured a hungry anut," Jendrin said. "It is a big fish and ended our trip for this day. Will you join us for a fish dinner, Maylore?"

"I was hoping you would ask," Maylore said. "I would like to visit with Ayare anyway. It would be two treats at once that way. How did you capture such a large anut?" Jendrin recounted his story of the fishing trip and the lucky snagging of the anut. Maylore felt a bump in his throat as he listened to Jendrin. Maylore checked his communication dome to find Bert had sent him a picture of a message attached to Muninn's leg. Maylore waited until Jendrin finished his story before speaking.

"Bert is on his way here with Muninn and a message for Kai," Maylore said. "I will join you tonight for dinner."

"Good. See you at dinner," Jendrin said as he carried his fish to be stored.

A chorus of IB caws greeted Maylore as he walked to Kai's hut. Kai was outside her door looking at the two birds sitting in the tree above her.

"Come down, silly bird!" she called at Muninn as the bird continued to caw. Bert saw Maylore approach and flew down to his shoulder.

"Ah, you have made friends with the bird," Kai said with approval in her voice.

"I feed him treats," Maylore replied, standing near Kai. Muninn had stopped crowing and watched Bert on his new perch.

"I should try that," Kai said. "Can you get the other bird to drop its message?" Maylore looked up at Muninn as he sent a picture to untie the message. Muninn flew to Maylore's shoulder next to Bert. Maylore pulled the message loose and handed it to Kai.

"Two birds, huh?" Kai said as she read the message. Kai studied the shorthand before saying, "It says the potion works, and she wants more. She used it on the worst offenders, too many to treat all bandits. Birsha is planning a trip here to collect his tithe. The passes are nearly clear."

"I don't think we can shuttle enough powder to treat that many," Maylore said. "I believe she understands that. I hope we can keep a few of them under control."

"I will gather some more powder and write her a return message," Kai said as she returned to her hut. When Kai opened the door to her hut, both birds flew into the tree.

"How can I get you two to help scout for us?" Maylore thought, watching the two birds chatter to each other. He sent Bert a picture of a scout in a tree. Bert returned several pictures of bandit scouts in positions challenging to see from the ground. "Oh my," he said, realizing they were unlikely to be able to sneak anyone by them. Maylore considered his options as the two birds continued chatting in the tree.

Beacon Rendal arrived as they awaited Kai's return.

"Greetings, Maylore," Rendal said, stopping near Maylore. "Is Kai inside?" he asked.

"Yes," Maylore replied, nodding to him. "She is gathering more powder after Gilda's message arrives."

"A new message?" Rendal asked.

"Yes, Kai has it with her," Maylore replied as Kai opened her door again.

"Kai," Rendal said as she approached. "What does the message say?" Rendal asked her. She passed him the note and handed the full-power vial to Maylore.

"Gilda believes our potion works," Kai said, "but she needs much more of it."

Rendal read the note and passed it back to Kai.

"I talked with Calel about trying to enhance their reeb supply with the powder," Rendal said. "She told me they have guards watching the camp at all times. They are watching for women trying to escape but would notice any stranger in their village. I am afraid we are unlikely to bring in a large amount that way."

"Bert tells me there are guards in the trees who would see us before we reach their village," Maylore said.

"The good news is Gilda is still alive," Rendal said. As Rendal finished speaking, Airalee and Marisa arrived at the hut with their babies.

"May I see your little ones?" he asked as the women turned sideways so he could see their faces. "Wonderful," he said, "I am pleased for both of you."

Maylore looked up at the birds and sent a message to fly to his shoulder. Bert and Muninn flew to Maylore's shoulder as Rendal gasped in surprise.

"I have not heard of IBs being near humans, let alone two landing on one's shoulder!" Rendal said. "How did you do that, Maylore?"

"One of the birds lives in Gilriel's cave," Maylore said. "He has grown accustomed to me being around and trusts that I won't hurt him. The other bird is his friend, whom I call Muninn. Muninn has agreed to carry powder vials to the bandit's camp for us. Bert will carry a vial, too." Kai disappeared into her hut as Maylore tied the first vial to Muninn's leg. Kai quickly returned with another vial, which Maylore tied to Bert's leg. "Off you go," Maylore said, sending both of them a picture of him bowing to say thank you. Both birds seemed nervous with the crowd of humans around them and were glad to be away.

"Goodbye, Bert," Airalee said as the birds flew out of sight.

"Did they bring any message with them?" Marisa asked.

Rendal recounted the message and their discussion about trying to sneak someone into the bandit's camp.

"The message also said Birsha will be coming to steal from us again," Kai said.

"We are fortunate we have supplies left over from last season," Rendal said, ignoring her commentary. "The fishing went well today. We have plenty to share with them, too."

"Thieves," Kai grumbled.

"Agreed," Marisa said.

"Perhaps that will change too," Airalee said. "Do you know what caused the sentinel's warning, Beacon?"

"I understand the new meadow guard saw an intruder in the forest and sounded an alarm," Rendal said. "We don't speak each other's language, so the hand signals the Tocor used told me: 'New,' 'sentinel,' 'forest,' 'intruder.' I didn't understand if it was an animal or a human. It appears the warning frightened the intruder away."

"I wonder if Oleg was scouting the area," Airalee said.

"I hope not," Marisa said. "Let's not assume evil will be behind every bush when we collect."

"You're right," Airalee sighed. "I would become frightened of my own shadow very quickly."

"I will help Mirtha with the catch if you join me, Airalee," Marisa said, looking at Airalee.

"That's a good idea," Airalee said. "It is almost time for Jendrin to take care of Ayare anyway."

"Airalee?" Kai said, "We will need more of the monk's berry soon."

"I will get Jendrin to go with Ayare and me to collect more," Airalee said. "Would you like me to do rounds tomorrow, Kai?"

"Yes," Kai replied, "I will inventory what we will soon need to collect."

"Thank you," Airalee said. "Are we ready, Marisa?"

"Yes," Marisa replied. "Goodbye, everyone," she said as they walked away.

"Is Kelkalyn in your hut?" Maylore asked, turning to Rendal.

"He is," Rendal replied. "Would you like to speak with him?"

"I would like to ask both of you a favor," Maylore said.

"Of course," Rendal said. "This way," Rendal said, starting toward his hut.

Kelkalyn gave Maylore a small smile as they entered Rendal's hut.

"I assume you knew I was here," Kelkalyn said.

"Yes," Maylore replied. "I saw you on the communication dome while communicating with Bert. I was hoping you would help me identify villagers who may have abilities they do not know about."

"I don't want anyone to know I can do that," Kelkalyn said, shaking his head.

"I suggest Rendal, and I will talk with the villagers while you sit behind this wall looking for their portals," Maylore said. "After you have examined them, tap my chair, and we will show them out."

Kelkalyn considered the idea instead of rejecting it.

"We tested some of the villagers with Gilriel," Rendal said. "That was before you and your companions arrived. We found no one with abilities, but we tested very few."

"I will help if no one knows I am there," Kelkalyn said. "You must promise to bring me ground fruit," Kelkalyn said, grinning.

"I did plant more ground fruit in my garden," Maylore said, chuckling. "I didn't think they would serve as payment, but it is a good trade for all of us."

"You should not let the word of them in your garden get around," Kelkalyn said, smiling. "They are everyone's favorite treat on Almora, and you would be overrun!"

"I have been forewarned," Maylore replied. "Shall we start tomorrow?"

"I will create a list of those we haven't tested," Rendal said as Kelkalyn nodded. "Throc can help bring them to my hut. Today, the council wants to see what the defensive force is about. A council member is on the team, but the rest want to see what Jendrin has built to approve or reject their existence. I leave you two to your ways as I find Jendrin," Rendal said, bowing and leaving the hut.

Rendal found Jendrin helping cut and store the catch.

"Jendrin," Rendal said as he approached.

"Beacon Rendal," Jendrin said, finishing his cuts.

"The council would like you to review your defensive force in person," Rendal said as Jendrin wiped his hands.

"I was wondering when they would get around to us," Jendrin said with a smile. "We are ready even though we have not defended or attacked anyone except practice dummies."

"It is a formality," Rendal said. "I expect the vote will be the same as when we started the force. Can we do the demonstration today?"

Jendrin considered for a moment.

"I believe so," Jendrin replied. "Can we meet at ¾ sun?"

"Perfect," Rendal replied. "We will see you all at the council hut later today," he said as he turned to leave.

Jendrin finished his duties and visited each defensive force member individually.

"The council wants to see what we are made of," Jendrin told each one. "Come to the council hut when I blow the whistle. Be sure to sound your whistle to alert those out of range of my whistle. We will demonstrate our range of passive to defensive moves for them. Katiana will attend the meeting but will join the group for the demonstration."

Time passed quickly, but there was enough time for Jendrin to talk to Airalee and Ayare and arrange baby duties with Airalee. Airalee decided to bring Ayare to watch the demonstration and followed Jendrin to the council hut. Jendrin opened the door enough to nod to Rendal and then closed it.

A short time later, the door opened, and all the council members stood outside in a semicircle.

"I will summon the team members," Jendrin said as he blew a lengthy note on the whistle. Two other whistles answered him as Katiana grabbed her quarterstaff and stood behind Jendrin. Aylendel, Latel, Baruo, and Callon arrived quickly and stood behind Jendrin.

"I will reiterate what I tell this group each time we meet," Jendrin said, looking at the council. "We do not attack, we do not kill, we do not wage war on other villages. We are here to defend our village."

Caudra made a sour face at the group but kept quiet.

"For this demonstration, we will pretend Rendal represents the group we want to dissuade from approaching us. We start with a passive stance by facing away from the aggressor group." The defensive force faced away from Rendal with their quarterstaffs anchored near their feet.

"If the potential aggressor begins to advance," Jendrin continued, "the force turns to face the aggressor in the same stance."

The group turned to face Rendal and remained in a resting stance.

"If they continue to advance, the group starts spinning their quarterstaffs."

The group started spinning their quarterstaffs, changing hands, and spinning overhead. No one lost control of their quarterstaff, and all turned quickly. Katiana spun the fastest, followed by Aylendel, Latel, and then the less dexterous men.

"If they continue to advance," Jendrin continued, "we stop our spin, set a rear foot at an angle, and balance our weight between our feet. We will not attack. If they attack us, we will defend ourselves by blocking their attacks. If they continue to attack, we will knock the weapons from their hands. Let me simulate an attack on one of the defensive forces so you may see what we would do."

Jendrin moved to the front of the force. He turned to find himself facing Katiana, causing him to hesitate. He turned back to the council.

"A word of advice: do not attempt to attack Katiana," Jendrin said. "She is swift and will leave any opponent gasping. Our defensive force can all take care of themselves, but her speed is amazing."

Jendrin turned back to smile at Katiana, then slowly swung his staff like an overhead axe. Katiana used both hands to raise her staff over her head to stop his attack. Jendrin swung up and was blocked. He swung from the left, then the right, and was blocked each time.

"If I persist in attacking her, she will knock the weapon from my hand," Jendrin said. "I will pretend my staff is a knife." He stabbed at her with his quarterstaff. Katiana blocked the attack with enough force to knock a knife from his hand. Jendrin bowed slightly to her as Katiana grinned and stood with her staff at her foot. Jendrin turned to the council.

"You will note I did not say we kill the opponent. We have taken to heart your directive and did not teach killing anyone. I hope I have shown our group can be the basis for a defensive force and approve our continuation." Jendrin nodded to the council members as they all reentered the meeting hut.

"Impressive, hero!" Airalee said as he walked toward her.

"I hope they believe we should continue," Jendrin said, reaching for Ayare. Aylendel and Latel joined them as they discussed the demonstration and waited for the council's decision. A short time later, the council door opened as Rendal left the hut to talk with them.

"The vote is four to one to continue. Caudra was the only one who voted no, and Nenaias abstained. I did not think she would change, but she saw the value in the group's existence. Thanks for getting our group set up, Jendrin."

"It was my pleasure," Jendrin said, smiling. Rendal returned to the meeting as Jendrin and the others conversed.

"You did not mention a counterattack," Latel said.

"I did not," Jendrin said. "Rendal and I decided to add this to the council discussion after time proved we were not a warring group."

"I hope we never face the need to use the group at all," Airalee said.

Chapter 41 - Collect His Due

Maylore arrived at the companions' hut the following day as Airalee passed Ayare to Jendrin for their morning routine.

"Greetings, everyone, especially Ayare," Maylore said, entering the hut.

"Dad, how nice you could visit this morning!" Airalee said, picking up the breakfast foods. "Have you eaten today?" she asked.

"Yes, thank you," Maylore replied, tickling Ayare. "I hoped to catch you three before you searched for more monk berries."

"We plan to leave soon since it is a half-day trip there and back," Jendrin said, cradling Ayare.

"Good," Maylore said. "The reasoning is I asked Beacon Rendal to have some villagers visit his hut today. He will tell them he wants to find out how well they are doing in the village. The real reason will be for Kelkalyn to determine if they have hidden abilities. I would like you to keep the last part to yourselves. We plan to talk to those who have some ability to see if they want to develop it. It could be they have one we know nothing about. We plan to inform them so they are aware of it but continue to live their lives as before."

"You believe we have hidden abilities?" Jendrin asked.

"I know Airalee does," Maylore said. "I suspect Ayare does, too. Perhaps you do, also, Jendrin."

"My only skill is hard-headedness," Jendrin said, smiling at him.

"I think he is right, dad," Airalee grinned. "He is only special at creating babies."

"I did that," Jendrin said, puffing out his chest.

Maylore saw this was going downhill fast.

"Please drop in at Rendal's hut before you leave," Maylore said. "We will do a quick check."

"We will be there soon, dad," Airalee said as Maylore left the hut.

The village was busy this morning as Maylore went to Rendal's hut. Word of Birsha's upcoming visit had creative villagers gathering clothes, tools, and food for the bribe payment. All the faces he saw were now familiar, and a few stopped to exchange words with him briefly. He reached Rendal's hut as Rendal stood out front with Throc. He was chatting with a few villagers.

"Maylore!" Rendal said as he arrived. "Are we ready to begin?" he asked. Maylore nodded to him and entered the hut when Rendal opened it. "You three may as well start us off. Please enter," he said, indicating the chairs around the table inside. "Throc, please gather the next group on our list," he said as Throc walked back into the village.

The three villagers sat at the table, and Maylore sat in a chair in front of the door to the back room. Kelkalyn sat behind the wall, out of sight. He would tap Maylore's chair when he finished examining the villagers.

Rendal began reciting from a short list of topics while Kelkalyn quickly examined each person. Rendal had just finished reviewing the council's decision about the defensive force when Maylore felt a tap on his chair.

"Beacon," Maylore interrupted him. "I believe we have kept our guests long enough."

"Excellent," Rendal said, looking at three visitors. "Unless you have questions, you are free to enjoy the day, and thanks for stopping by," he said as he arose. The villagers were all aware of the subject he covered and were happy to leave the hut.

"Did you sense anything?" Rendal quietly asked after they left.

667

"They are three normal villagers with no special ability," Kelkalyn quietly said.

"I will see if Throc has our next guests," Rendal said, opening the door. Throc was coming to the hut with four villagers. Rendal knew they were unrelated but asked them to sit around the table as Throc started his search anew.

Rendal began his list of subjects again, waiting for Maylore to interrupt him. Rendal had just finished discussing the defensive force when Maylore signaled him. "I believe that is all we need for today. Thank you all for stopping by," Rendal said as he arose.

"Do you plan to add more members to the defensive group?" a young man asked as they all rose.

"Yes, would you like to join?" Rendal asked him.

"Yes," he replied, a smile growing on his face.

"I will tell Jendrin of your interest. He will contact you," Rendal told him. The villagers said nothing else and left the hut.

"Anything?" Rendal asked, looking toward the back of the room.

"No," came a quiet answer from Kelkalyn.

"Do you need more water or food?" Rendal asked, moving toward his cabinet.

"That would be good," Kelkalyn replied. Maylore stood to move his chair, allowing Rendal to set food and water inside the back room. As Maylore set his chair back in place, a knock came at the door, and Rendal opened it.

"Did we pick a good time?" Jendrin said, carrying Ayare with Airalee nearby.

"Yes," Rendal replied, stepping aside. "Sit in any chair," Rendal said. They sat in chairs nearest the door as Maylore smiled and waved to Ayare. Rendal sat and started his practice speech. He discussed additional details about the council and possible openings. He told

Jendrin of a potential recruit he should talk to. Jendrin and Airalee were listening to his speech when Ayare squirmed and looked toward the back room. She pointed in the direction of where Kelkalyn was seated and watched intently. Maylore received a blank message from her that he interpreted as a question. Maylore smiled and returned a picture he had used with her to denote quietness. Ayare dropped her pointing hand but continued to watch where Kelkalyn was hiding. Rendal was running out of things to speak on when Maylore finally interrupted him.

"Yes," Rendal said, "we have taken enough of your time for this. Do you have questions for me?"

"No, thank you, Beacon," Jendrin said as he stood.

"We will travel to gather more monk berries today," Airalee said, smiling. "We know the route and will return late afternoon."

"Excellent," Rendal said, opening the door for them as the three exited.

"That was an odd meeting," Airalee said after they left the hut. "I hope Kelkalyn got the information he wanted.

"He did say a few council positions would be open soon. Perhaps we should add our names to the list of candidates."

Airalee looked surprised at him.

"You surprise me, hero," Airalee said. "I had not considered either of us wanting such a position, especially you, since you wanted to tour the world rather than live in a village."

"Perhaps," Jendrin replied, "I suspect it will be some time before a spot opens, but we should consider running."

Airalee stopped and gave him a crooked smile.

"I would like the opportunity to best you in that race, hero," Airalee said.

"Bah," Jendrin replied, smiling back at her. "You would stand little chance against me!"

Airalee's smile grew larger before she started walking again.

"We shall see, hero," she said.

"What did you find, Kelkalyn?" Rendal asked as he closed the door. Kelkalyn was silent for a few moments.

"Jendrin has no ability he can use," Kelkalyn said. "His heart portal does have one section that creates pearl energy, which others may be able to draw from him. I watched it flow from his heart portal to his skin, then return." Maylore perked up hearing Kelkalyn's description of Jendrin.

"Airalee can use it," Maylore said. "I used a mushroom once to see her pull pearl energy from her skin to her heart. It turned into healing green energy which flowed to her skin."

"Jendrin would have to be very close for her to do that," Kelkalyn said.

"She was," Maylore said. "She was touching his infected wounds when I saw it. If she had not used her healing energy, Jendrin would not have survived his wounds. Kai told me she was surprised he survived after the infections set in. Did you see anything else about Airalee?"

"She has a small ability to use her communication portal," Kelkalyn said. "I see she wears a blue amulet around her neck. I believe it may help her communicate."

"I can contact her through my communication portal when she wears it," Maylore said.

"She also has strings that run to her head portal," Kelkalyn said. "They were empty when I watched, and I don't know the portal's purpose. She has a large heart portal filled with dead energy. I don't know how it got there, and it seems locked and difficult to remove. I have heard that people who use the portal can create strong energies.

670

I don't know anyone on Almora who has that ability." Kelkalyn was silent for a short time before continuing. "The child is a different story. She has a clear heart, communication, and head portal. She will be a good study of what the portals can do if she allows it. She sensed I was probing her and tried to force me away. Fortunately, she is a child and cannot yet focus her energy."

"Unlike her mother," Maylore said, "Ayare can start a conversation from her communication portal. She sent me a message questioning what was happening to her. I replied for her to be calm."

"That may be why it suddenly became easier to examine her," Kelkalyn said. "She slowed her pushing and seemed to follow me around. I saw her drawing pearl energy from Jendrin, which circled through her heart and head. She didn't seem to use it. Perhaps that was the source of her energy to push me around. Yes, I believe her heart portal created a wave of energy that pushed at me. It was a golden-colored wave that bounced around but pushed at me, nonetheless. When she learns to control it, she would be nearly impossible to examine without her consent."

"Thank you, Kelkalyn," Maylore said. "It explains many things I have wondered about. I will discuss this with Jendrin and Airalee in the future."

"I suspect there is more to each one that my meager abilities cannot see," Kelkalyn said. "I will learn with you what these portals can do as they reveal themselves in the future."

Rendal opened the door to see another family of four villagers approaching the hut.

"Come in!" he said as they reached the hut. "Sit around the table, and we will begin." Maylore nodded to the group as they sat, and Rendal began his talk. Rendal had just finished reviewing the village charter when Maylore signaled him. "I believe I have covered what I needed to discuss. Do you have any questions?" Rendal asked. The villagers asked a few questions about the defensive force before leaving.

"Anything?" Rendal asked after they left.

"No," Kelkalyn said. "Normal people."

Several more groups came to the hut, with Kelkalyn reporting no special abilities. Rendal was bidding the latest group farewell as Marisa approached carrying Torbin.

"Marisa, glad you came," Rendal said, extending his hand toward the chairs in his hut.

"Thank you, Beacon," Marisa said, sitting in a chair. Torbin was nestled in her arms, watching the action around him. Rendal skipped several parts of his planned discussion and discussed the bandit's situation. Marisa was well-versed in the plan to curb the bandit's libido, and Rendal used the time to bring himself up to date.

"I expect Birsha to arrive today to collect his tithes," Rendal said.

"Steal from us, you mean," Marisa replied.

"As you will, Marisa," Rendal said.

Maylore signaled that Kelkalyn finished his examination.

"I believe I have said my piece for today," Rendal said. "I wish you and Torbin a good day," he said, rising. Marisa was happy to be done and bid the men goodbye. Rendal watched Marisa walk away before closing the door. "Kelkalyn?"

"Marisa has no special ability other than being a lovely woman," Kelkalyn said, causing Maylore and Rendal to look in his direction. "Torbin, however, generates pearl energy within himself as Jendrin does. Torbin does not seem to have any other ability."

"It is possible Jendrin's seed created Marisa's child." Rendal started, "He was one of the group seeding the latest group."

"Likely," Kelkalyn said.

"It would not surprise me if Marisa made sure it was his seed that created Torbin," Maylore said with a smile.

"Be that as it may, do we inform Marisa of Torbin's ability?" Rendal asked.

"Yes," both men said at once. "It is a minor ability that does not impact anyone except Airalee and Ayare," Kelkalyn said.

"Agreed." Rendal said, "I will inform her shortly."

Throc gathered other villagers who arrived in small groups or one at a time. None of them had any ability Kelkalyn could detect. Throc appeared at the door with the new mothers and their children. Rendal bid them to enter.

"I will see if I can persuade the elders to come next," Throc said. Rendal started to say they need not come but decided to have Throc invite them.

"Good, thank you, Throc," Rendal said as he indicated chairs for the three women. Rendal started his speech as the three women cuddled their children. It didn't take long for Maylore to feel Kelkalyn's tap on his chair. Maylore waited until Rendal finished his thought before he interrupted.

"The little ones seemed to have heard enough from us already, Rendal," Maylore said, looking at the babies.

"Indeed," Rendal replied. "I appreciate you three coming to visit. Is there a question I could answer for you?" All three shook their heads no and started to rise. Rendal opened the door for them and smiled at each child as they left.

"Anything Kelkalyn?" Rendal asked.

"The female child in the middle has pearl energy streaming from her heart. I didn't see any other ability in her or the rest of the group."

"You could tell her child was female?" Rendal asked.

"Yes," Kelkalyn replied. "Portals have distinctive features that tell me something about the body they are in. Her reproductive portal also indicates she is female."

"My," Maylore said. "There is little hidden from you."

"There is a lot hidden from me," Kelkalyn said, laughing. "Experience doing surreptitious examinations has taught me a few things over the seasons."

A knock on the door interrupted their discussion as Rendal opened it.

"Melronna and Meliniel were willing to come," Throc said. The others asked to be excused. I could not find Kelkalyn."

"Excellent work, Throc," Rendal said. "I thank you for completing this task for me." Throc gave him a slight bow as he left. Rendal indicated chairs for the two women to sit in as he sat. Rendal did not need to start his usual talk as both women asked him questions on their minds. A short time passed before Maylore felt the tap on his chair. Maylore found it challenging to find a point to interrupt them as the two peppered Rendal with questions. Maylore felt a firm whack on his chair, causing him to speak.

"Beacon," Maylore said, "we should allow these ladies to leave so we may move on to the next group." Both women stopped talking and expressed thanks for meeting with them as they stood to leave.

"Thank you both for joining us," Rendal said, opening the door for them. Rendal then locked the door.

"You can join us now, Kelkalyn," Rendal said as he returned to his seat. Maylore moved his chair to the table as Kelkalyn emerged to join them.

"Their prattle was becoming more than my ears could stand," Kelkalyn grumped.

"They had good questions for me, Kelkalyn," Rendal replied, "Did you see anything in either one?" The irritability in his voice disappeared as he spoke.

"Meliniel still has no ability," Kelkalyn said. "Melronna has developed a new connection to her head portal. I know from

674

examining her before she could read weather patterns. The new connection is to an area I don't know about. I did not see that connection in anyone except perhaps Airalee and Ayare." Kelkalyn was silent, as if deep in thought. "I ignored the connection in Airalee since it did not seem to have any activity. I have examined Melronna in the past; she did not have that connection. She had no portal activity today, but the connection is there. Has she shown any new ability that you have seen?"

Rendal considered for a moment.

"I have heard Meliniel say Melronna occasionally speaks in an odd voice of future things," Rendal said. "Meliniel says Melronna does not remember speaking. I have heard from Marisa and others that Melronna stares into the distance when she prophesizes."

"Jendrin told me Airalee does similar things," Maylore said. "He told me she pointed to different locations on the tree to cut his quarterstaffs. She then denies speaking to him."

Kelkalyn leaned on the table and listened to them.

"Interesting," Kelkalyn said. "Does the mind portal allow them to prophesize? It may be unrelated, but we know more than before."

The three men discussed their findings from their morning's activity when a sudden squawk and flutter of wings sounded outside the door.

"What is this?" Kelkalyn said, looking toward the door.

"Bert is here," Maylore said, moving to the door. He opened the door to see Bert perched on the hut, screeching at him. "All right, Bert," Maylore said. Bert flew in the direction of Kai's hut. "It appears Bert wants me to follow him," Maylore said to Rendal and Kelkalyn as he left the hut.

Muninn and Bert were on a high branch near Kai's hut as Maylore followed them. Kai was staring up at them as Maylore arrived.

"Can you ask your birds to be quiet and give me their messages?" Kai asked.

"They answer only to themselves, I am afraid," Maylore said as he sent messages to both birds, asking them to allow him to untie the messages on their legs. Bert flew to his shoulder and held out his leg. Maylore untied the vial, and then Bert flew back to the tree. Muninn repeated the procedure. Maylore passed both vials to Kai. Kai read the message from the vial before passing it to Maylore.

"Birsha wants two girls and his due," Maylore read from the message. "He left before I realized he was gone."

Kai pulled the message from the second vial, but it repeated the first message.

"It appears she wanted to be sure we got a message," Kai said as she walked toward Rendal's hut.

Rendal was alone in his hut when they arrived. Kai gave him the note Gilda had written as Rendal's expression fell.

"Spread the word for our young girls, go to the cave," Rendal said. "Have villagers start collecting food, clothing, and spare tools and bring them to the visitor's hut. Kai, go to the child-card area to warn them to go to the cave. Maylore, you warn the clothing and pottery people. I will warn those in the kitchen and homes in between."

Word spread quickly about the bandit group's pending arrival. Young girls gathered in the council hut before entering the cave. Crafters gathered clothing and took it to the visitor's hut. A collection of pots, food, fur, and a few tools was placed alongside the clothing.

Rendal stood at the entrance to the visitor's hut and nodded as the last villager delivered their contribution.

"Now, we wait," Rendal said.

Airalee

Jendrin, Airalee, and Ayare successfully completed their quest to gather monk berries from the desert oasis. They approached the village entrance when they saw villagers putting their burden down by the visitor's hut.

"I wonder if Birsha is here," Airalee said, looking at the collection.

"Rendal is standing alone near the visitor's hut," Jendrin said. "I suspect Birsha has not yet arrived. Let's check with Rendal before we go to our hut," Jendrin said as they approached the hut.

"I am glad to see you both," Rendal said as they stopped before him.

"I assume you are expecting Birsha?" Jendrin asked.

"We received a message he was on his way," Rendal said. "Gilda warned us he is coming for his share and replacement girls."

"We cannot allow the slavery of girls to him," Airalee said.

"We will try to dissuade him from our girls," Jendrin said. "I am hopeful the gathering of the defensive force will convince him to look elsewhere."

"That isn't much better," Airalee said. "It enslaves the children of another village."

"If Oleg is with him, it puts Airalee in danger, too," Jendrin said.

"Birsha demoted him when he attacked you," Rendal said. "He will not be with Birsha."

"We should go to our hut and then hide you and Ayare until this is over," Jendrin said, starting toward their hut.

"I won't run from Oleg," Airalee said.

"You hide for Ayare's sake," Jendrin said, turning toward the hut.

Airalee looked at Ayare as she took Jendrin's hand and followed.

Maylore stood outside their hut as they hurried to the door.

"Birsha comes," Maylore said as they arrived.

"Yes," Jendrin said. "I will gather my quarterstaff while you take Airalee and Ayare to the caves," Jendrin said, opening the door. They dropped their load of monk berries as Jendrin helped Airalee with Ayare.

"Birsha is not interested in us," Airalee said. "I am sure we have time for me to care for Ayare," Airalee said, sitting at the back of the hut.

"Be ready," Jendrin said, grabbing his quarterstaff and whistle as he left the hut. Jendrin sounded his whistle as he ran toward the visitor's hut. Several other whistles soon followed.

Maylore sat at the table near Airalee and started recounting the messages they received from Gilda.

"Birsha could be here soon," Airalee said, looking at the nursing Ayare. "Sorry, Ayare, we should move you to the cave. Even if it is unnecessary." They gathered a few items in a pouch and prepared to leave the hut. A sentinel's warning suddenly sounded from the trees.

"Birsha must be here," Maylore said. "We should hurry to the cave."

"Ayare and I are ready," Airalee said, turning toward the door.

Another sentinel warning sounded farther from the original signal.

"Oh my, now what," Maylore said, peaking out the door.

Oleg was running into the middle of the empty village, looking at the huts. Oleg spotted him at the door and started in his direction.

"Oleg is coming this way," Maylore said, closing the door.

"He is likely to kill all three of us," Airalee said with alarm on her face. "We have no place to hide here. We can't lead him to the hiding cave even if we could escape."

"I know of a possible way to hide you and Ayare," Maylore said. "Sit on the edge of the fireplace while I sit in a chair near you."

Airalee gathered Ayare close to her and wrapped them in a nearby blanket.

Maylore returned to the chair nearest Airalee, saying, "Do not move. I can hide you both if you remain silent and motionless." Maylore concentrated on creating an image from behind them to appear in front of them. He completed his spell as Oleg tore open the door. Oleg had a bone knife in his hand and looked around inside the hut.

"Where is she, old man," Oleg demanded, not seeing anyone else in the hut.

"Old man indeed," Maylore said. "My companions are waiting for you thieves at the visitor's hut," he said with disdain. Oleg checked both bedrooms before turning to Maylore again.

"You aren't worth killing," Oleg said. "I want the woman who disrespected me dead," he said, bursting out the door.

Maylore waited a few seconds before checking outside to see which way he went. Oleg was searching in the direction of the council hut.

"He is moving toward the council hut entrance. We must go a different way to avoid him," Maylore said, watching Oleg.

"Let's take Ayare to your cave, Dad," Airalee said as he watched.

"We would have to pick a path through the village to avoid him,'" Maylore said. "Perhaps it is safer here since he has already checked here."

"Let's go," Airalee said, passing behind him into the village.

"Perhaps not," Maylore said as he followed after her. "Don't go toward the visitor's hut Airalee!" Maylore said. "We go sunrise and avoid it."

"I will not let Jendrin face them without me," Airalee replied.

"Oh my," Maylore said, "What happened to hide in my cave?" as Airalee continued behind the huts.

Jendrin arrived at the visitor's hut, quickly followed by the other team members. None of the bandits were present, but Rendal seemed relieved to see the team.

"Remember, do not attack them," Rendal shouted. "Let me convince them to look elsewhere for their requirements."

"Requirements indeed," Katiana said in a low voice.

"Set up our wing formation on this flat," Jendrin told as he scanned the area. He moved to the edge of the slight rise. The team members created their V-formation facing, facing toward Rendal. "Warm-up drill," Jendrin said as he spun his staff to the side and over his head.

A sharp warning whistle sounded, causing the team to stop spinning and turn away, assuming the first-phase position.

Birsha appeared with six other bandits carrying a litter and leading two women. Oleg was not in the group. They walked to where Rendal was standing and stopped before him.

Another sharp warning whistle sounded from farther in the camp.

"Rendal, you created a welcoming committee for me?" Birsha said, towering over Rendal. "How nice. Why do they carry sticks?"

Rendal simply pointed to the supplies.

"We have collected food, clothing, and decorations for you," Rendal said. "I wish you to take them and return to your village."

Birsha laughed a low rubble.

"This is only part of my requirements," Birsha said. "I have a broken woman and one old-age female to exchange. Bring me two appropriate females, and we will leave."

Rendal looked at the two women. One was a Tocor, and the other was a human he did not recognize.

"We will accept the two women," Rendal said. "but ask you to look elsewhere for female replacements. We have been very generous with our gifts and believe it will suffice," he said, pointing again at the pile of supplies.

Birsha stood silent for a moment, looking from Rendal to the pile. Jendrin and his team watched the confrontation with sidelong looks. Jendrin noticed movement behind Birsha's group as Oleg emerged from the village and joined the bandit lineup. Jendrin was concerned at first but knew Airalee and Maylore were resourceful and would have evaded Oleg, he hoped. Birsha pointed his hatchet at the village, Rendal, and then the defensive force.

"I have been very patient with you today, Rendal," Birsha said, his voice grew louder. "Give me what I require, or face my wrath!"

Rendal knew Birsha had never led any kind of attack. His size, weapons, and henchmen were enough to convince every village to bend to his will in the past. Rendal was considering his option as Birsha took a step toward him.

Jendrin chose to turn to face Birsha when Birsha stepped toward Rendal. The team moved to face Birsha when Jendrin turned.

Birsha noticed they all faced him now.

"Ah, children with sticks," Birsha said. "Fearsome? No. Perhaps they will gather the two females I require." Birsha looked at Jendrin, saying, "You, go gather what I need." Jendrin was silent and merely stared at Birsha. "You will get what I need or be the first to die!" Birsha shouted as he started toward the defensive force.

Jendrin started spinning his staff as the group followed suit. Birsha stopped and looked at the spinning quarterstaffs.

"Tricks?" Birsha said. "Do tricks later. Bring me the women I need."

A sound came from behind the defensive force as Airalee, Ayare, and Maylore appeared.

"NO!" Birsha thundered, waving his hatchet at Airalee. "She is too old and already broken. Send me two unbroken females!" he shouted. Jendrin stopped spinning his quarterstaff and assumed the ready phase position. The team followed his lead. Noise erupted from the back of Birsha's group as Oleg moved to the front of the group.

"They are cowards hiding what is ours!" Oleg shouted, looking at the bandit group.

"Quiet, Oleg!" Birsha said. "You are no longer a lieutenant. Why are you here? I didn't invite you!"

Oleg continued raising his fists and encouraging his companions to attack as he complained about Airalee's disrespect toward him.

"She has shown nothing but contempt for me and all of you!" Oleg yelled at the bandits, pointing toward Airalee. "She tells others you are less than woca dung!"

"That girl has blinded you beyond all reason, Oleg," Birsha yelled at Oleg. "Remain quiet or leave!" Birsha turned again to rage at Jendrin. "Leave now, boy, before you are injured again," Birsha said threateningly.

Jendrin merely stared and shifted his stance, ready for an attack.

"Oh, more tricks," Birsha said, waving a dismissive hand at Jendrin. Turning back to Rendal, he said, "Tell your children to put down their sticks, Rendal."

A battle cry echoed from behind Birsha.

"Kill them!" Oleg yelled as he led a few others past Birsha to confront the defensive force. Battle cries filled the air as the group attacked the defensive force. The bandits picked one target, and the mele began in earnest.

Birsha was shocked and speechless to see his men attack. Rendal stepped back as the cries grew louder. A small group of villagers had arrived, standing beyond Rendal. A few of them started yelling at the bandits.

One bandit attacked Katiana, who blocked his overhead hatchet, then blocked one from the side before he tried another overhead attack. Katiana's staff sang as she blocked each attack. She stopped his last attack by blocking his hatchet on its handle. The head of the hatchet snapped off and fell to the ground. The amazed bandit ran away from her as she prepared for another bandit. The second bandit attacked Latel, but each attack was blocked several times before Latel used the end of his staff to punch the bandit in the gut. The bandit fell to the ground, gasping for breath before he moved bent over behind Birsha. The defensive force's staffs sang louder as the battle continued.

Oleg attacked Jendrin as two others started their attack. Jendrin's singing staff quickly blocked his hatchet attacks as Oleg grew visibly angrier. "I will finish killing you this time before I kill her!" he shouted, attacking again.

"No!" Airalee shouted, moving toward Jendrin before realizing she held Ayare and stopped.

Maylore reached to grab her arm, but she had already stopped. He focused on gathering the wind's energy and pushed it toward Oleg. The energy he gathered struck Dirdin and Callon instead of the bandits and knocked them to the ground. The two bandits attacking them turned to rush Jendrin as Dirdin, and Callon rolled up to their feet.

"Basrah!" Maylore shouted as he attempted to redo his spell.

The melee in front of him moved too fast for him to try again.

Jendrin blocked Oleg's attack each time before knocking the weapon from his hand. A bandit rushed in to take Oleg's place as Oleg stepped to the side.

Oleg turned to glare at Airalee. Seeing she was unprotected, he pulled a white bone knife from his belt and started toward her.

"Time to die, vicious woman!" Oleg said as he crouched down and quickened his pace.

Airalee pushed Ayare into Maylore's arms, stopping his next wind force. She flung away Ayare's blanket, pulled her knife, and stepped in front of Ayare.

"You want to make a sport of it?" Oleg said, "Wonderful!" as he continued his stalk.

Airalee had no idea of how to defend herself. She raised her knife in front of her, raised her other hand before her, and crouched, awaiting his attack.

"Be gone, vindictive evil," Airalee snarled at him.

"NO!" Jendrin yelled as he punched his opponent to the ground.

He spun to follow Oleg as Dirdin filled his spot on the line.

Oleg shifted his knife to stab and rushed at her, yelling.

A silent blinding bolt of light blasted from Airalee's amulet, hitting Oleg in the chest and pushing him back three sticks. He landed beyond Jendrin's charge and sat staring at Airalee.

"A sorcerer," Oleg spat. "I knew you should die," he growled, scrambling to his feet.

Jendrin stepped between them as Oleg pulled another hatchet from his belt.

"You still live?" Oleg snarled, "Not for long!" as he rushed at Jendrin.

Jendrin blocked his hatchet and knife attacks several times. He finally gut-punched Oleg with the end of his quarterstaff.

Oleg stumbled back behind Birsha and collapsed, fighting for breath.

Birsha was not only surprised to see his bandits attack; he was shocked to see that his forces would surely lose this battle. Many of his bandits had already lost their weapons.

"Stop!" Birsha roared. "I did not order an attack!"

The rest of the fighting bandits stopped their half-hearted attacks and turned to watch their leaders. Olona's defenders' singing staffs quieted as they stood ready, watching their former attackers retreat.

"You are not in charge, Oleg," Birsha snarled, pointing at Oleg. "I will see you do women's work from now on. Perhaps I should have you killed or ejected from the village. I will deal with you later!" he growled. Birsha turned to Rendal.

"I will accept your offer, Rendal. We will find unbroken women in another village." Birsha said, sounding almost conciliatory.

Oleg regained his breath and stood looking incredulously at Birsha.

"You are weak," Oleg yelled, twisting his lips as he buried his spare hatchet in Birsha's chest.

"You attack me?" Birsha yelled, ignoring the hatchet. Birsha proved fast for a big man and buried two hatchets in Oleg, nearly cutting him in half. Oleg fell onto his back from the force of Birsha's blows. Birsha turned to the rest of his bandits, who had moved farther behind him. "Does anyone else object to my decisions?" He said with a sarcastic voice. He glared at his team when he realized something was buried in his chest. "A bee stung me," he said as he yanked on the buried hatchet. Blood poured from his chest as he tossed the weapon to the ground. Birsha stared at the blood running down his chest before collapsing to his knees and toppling over to his side.

The gathering stared silently at the carnage before one of the bandits stepped forward.

"Are they dead?" the bandit asked, looking at the two bodies.

A muscular bandit, who had not participated in the attack, stepped forward and bent to examine both bodies.

"I am sure they are both dead," he said, rising.

The first bandit sunk to one knee, appearing to morn. Laughter betrayed him as he arose and tossed his remaining weapon over his head into the bush.

"My pleas have been heard!" he said as he started dancing in place. "I'm overjoyed!" The other bandits stared at him before they began to smile and join him in celebration.

The second bandit stood before Rendal.

"I am Dorongwe," he said. "Birsha left no one to assume his command after Oleg attacked one of your people before the last snow. I am the village deputy. I would be next in line without his appointment until a new leader can be chosen."

A third bandit pushed Birsha over to reveal a large gash in his chest, draining blood to the ground. He then pushed Oleg over, who showed bones and internal organs outside his chest. He arose with a giant smile on his face to continue a celebration.

Cheers continued from bandits as they threw their weapons into the air behind them and continued dancing. Dorongwe smiled at them as he turned to Rendal.

"Most village men hated and feared Oleg and Birsha," Dorongwe said. "Many came to the same conclusion as me. The life of a bandit is not good. Fear forced us to follow them since they would execute us if we disobeyed. Most of us want to live a peaceful life of self-sufficiency like this village. I, too, am glad that these two collected their due."

The remaining bandits surrounded Dorongwe, all talking at once.

Airalee ran to Jendrin with Ayare as Dorongwe spoke with the other bandits.

"Jendrin," she said, putting her arms around him. He hugged her tightly as he considered whether to chastise her or just be relieved she was well.

"I was not sure you were brave to face Oleg untrained with a knife or believed you could defeat him," Jendrin said.

"It was a reaction of Oleg coming to get our daughter," Airalee said. "I could slow him enough for you to stop him even if I were to die."

"I did not know you could blast him away from you," Jendrin said.

"I didn't either," Airalee said. "It seemed to come unbidden from the amulet," she stopped his comments with a kiss.

Dorongwe raised his hand.

"Thank you, I agree to it," Dorongwe said. He turned to Rendal to say, "These men remind men the village has been asking me for many seasons to assume leadership of our village. I could not accept knowing Birsha and Oleg had spies who would see us dead for considering such a thing. I will assume my prescribed temporary leadership until the village elects a new leader."

The small group of villagers who had heard the commotion had gathered behind the visitor's hut. Most villagers had hidden in their homes.

"Where may we dispose of the two bodies, Rendal?" Dorongwe asked, looking down at the two bodies.

Rendal was still in shock but pointed to the cliffs behind him.

"Give them to the sea," Rendal said. "They were not honorable men, but the sea will know what to do with them."

Dorongwe motioned for the bandits to pick up the bodies.

"I will bear Oleg, the death bringer," Jendrin said as he moved forward.

"I will gladly join you," Airalee said as Maylore held Ayare. A bandit and another villager joined them to carry him away. The other bandits lifted Birsha, but he was too heavy to carry. Latel and two other villagers joined them as the group carried him toward the cliffs. Rendal led the way to the burial cliff.

"The flash from your amulet was well-timed to stop Oleg," Jendrin said as they carried Oleg. "Did you summon it in some way?"

Airalee turned her head toward him with a faraway look in her eyes.

"I assisted you. She is to be protected," she said before again looking ahead.

"Your assistance was appreciated," Jendrin said.

"My assistance?" Airalee asked. "I was prepared for Oleg to kill me."

"You just said you assisted me," Jendrin said.

"I said no such thing," Airalee said. "I was just wondering if Maylore could have powered the amulet,"

"Well, we were fortunate," Jendrin said. "The flash was brief, and I do not think others saw it anyway."

"I will ask Maylore if he created it," Airalee said.

Maylore followed the group, and Ayare silently watched.

The group climbed the hill past the elder's huts and arrived at the cliffs.

"They do not deserve an Olona burial," Rendal said. "Throw them off here," Rendal said, pointing at the cliff. They carelessly tossed Oleg over the cliff. Birsha was too heavy to toss. The villagers helped the bandit crew roll him over the edge to the rocks far below. Many bandits fell to their hands and knees, muttering happily under their breath.

"My apologies for our actions against you and my thanks for not killing us too, Rendal," Dorongwe said.

"Accepted," Rendal said. "We are a peaceful people and opposed to killing. Please walk with me to the visitor's hut," Rendal said. "I would like a short discussion of our future."

"I have no authority to speak on behalf of our village," Dorongwe said.

"It is only a beginning I seek," Rendal said.

"I will take your message to our village," Dorongwe said. "Come, my fellows, we depart."

The bandits arose with smiles on their faces and followed him.

The Olona villagers who witnessed the burial sang no songs of departure or words of leaving that day.

CHAPTER 42 - NOUVEL

Rendal led Dorongwe and the remaining bandits from the cliffs back to the village entrance. He stopped at the visitor's hut.

"I am sorry for the death of your companions," Rendal said.

"No one will miss them," Dorongwe stated. "The few that followed them will perhaps mourn. I suspect not."

"As the Beacon of Olona," Rendal said, "I hope our two villages can now begin a mutually advantageous future."

"There is a chance if I gain leadership of our village," Dorongwe replied. "Few left believe in Birsha's and his father's vision. Many want change. On my visits to Olona with Birsha, I admired how your village and its people lived peacefully. I often wished my village would become industrious like Olona."

"We would welcome those changes in your village," Rendal said.

"I consider your village an example of what we could be," Dorongwe said.

"Olona would be glad to assist if we may," Rendal said, surprise showing on his face.

"Do you have an ambassador who could accompany me to start the process?" Dorongwe asked.

Rendal was surprised by his request. It took time for him to respond.

"I will consider who could accomplish the task," Rendal said. "I will ask if they would be interested."

Dorongwe nodded and gave a slight bow.

"Would you gift us some of this fish?" Dorongwe asked. "We will return some of our hides in trade."

"Yes, yes, of course," Rendal said with happiness in his voice. "A trade like that is valuable to us."

Dorongwe motioned to his team to gather fish into their carriers.

"If you wait here," Rendal said, "I will see if I can send a diplomat with you now." Rendal started to walk to the village when he noticed Throc observing the proceedings.

"My apologies for eavesdropping, Beacon," Throc said as Rendal stopped before him.

"No," Rendal said, "The way to learn is by observing situations unfolding. I want to ask you for a favor. Would you be interested in being our ambassador to Dorongwe's village? I realize it is dangerous, so I understand if you would reject the offer."

Throc showed the biggest smile Rendal had ever seen from the man.

"I accept!" Throc exclaimed. "Allow me to gather my pack and go with them!" He turned and ran to his hut.

"I wish all my requests were met so enthusiastically," Rendal said to no one. "I expected to twist his arm a little," as Throc disappeared. Rendal returned to Dorongwe, saying, "My assistant Throc will serve as ambassador to you."

"He is welcome," Dorongwe said.

"If he fails you in some manner, let me retrieve him before he is killed," Rendal almost pleaded.

"Oleg is dead," Dorongwe said, looking at him. "He is the only one in our camp who would kill for a small reason. Birsha ignored his killing, but the rest of us rejected his killings. Your ambassador is free to come and go as he wishes. He is not a prisoner."

Rendal felt himself relax as he nodded. He decided to take a chance and request another boon from this new relationship.

691

"May I ask for the return of our villagers?" Rendal asked in a steady voice.

Dorongwe considered for a moment before replying.

"If I am selected chief," Dorongwe started, "we will ask everyone if they wish to stay. Those who wish to leave may do so."

Rendal could feel heavy weights lifting from his shoulders and felt himself standing straighter. Throc returned to the clearing on the run.

"He is such a young man," Dorongwe said as Throc approached.

"He is in his 27th summer," Rendal replied. "He is perhaps young but wise in running a village and its laws. He has assisted me in many negotiations for our village. I believe he will work well with you."

"He will return unharmed to you if he does not," Dorongwe said with a smile. Dorongwe motioned for the group to start moving.

Rendal stopped Throc.

"Do not force things on them," Rendal said. "Suggest ideas but do not demand. Speak honestly and politely when asked your opinion."

"Yes, Beacon," Throc replied. "You have shown me many times the correct ways of diplomacy. I will be careful," he said, turning with a smile to run after the group. Rendal watched him go as if he were his child rather than his apprentice. "I wonder if he told his mother he was leaving? I will visit her to be sure he did."

Rendal returned to the community kitchen to find a large crowd of villagers talking excitedly. The group buzzed with the news of Birsha and Oleg's deaths. Jendrin, Katiana, and Baruo were repeatedly telling individuals they had not killed anyone. Nenaias and Cauladra saw Rendal return and hurried to meet him. They both stood staring at him with angry looks on their faces.

"You told us the defensive force would not kill anyone," Cauladra nearly yelled.

"They did not kill anyone," Rendal said, holding up his hands.

"The story we hear is Jendrin killed two men with his stick," Cauladra said.

Rendal stood staring at Cauladra.

"I was there, Cauladra," Rendal said. "Our group defended from attacks by Oleg and his henchmen. Our force seriously hurt none of the bandits. Their pride was hurt when their weapons were swatted away."

"If he did not kill them, who did?" Cauladra spit the words in Rendal's face.

"I will explain it to everyone at once," Rendal said calmly, standing atop a nearby table.

Katiana, Baruo, and Airalee had joined Rendal as he raised his hands. Staring at Katiana, Nenaias started raging at her.

"You will bring down more killing upon us by defending our villagers," Nenaias yelled. It matters not who killed who. It will bring trouble!"

Katiana remained calm as Aylendel moved to step between them. Katiana placed her hand on her shoulder, saying, "Hold my mate, wait for Rendal to speak.

Nenaias turned toward Rendal as she began to rage at him.

"They came to kill," Nenaias said, pointing a finger at Rendal. "If you had allowed them to finish their destiny, they would have left the rest of us alone!"

Rendal had heard these arguments many times before. He calmly looked at her before asking for quiet.

"They did indeed come to kill," Rendal replied. "Their destiny, however, was to kill each other, not us."

Nenaias and Cauladra cocked their heads at him before a relenting smile came to Cauladra's lips. Nenaias relaxed, realizing Rendal could be right.

"I hope you are correct, Beacon," Nenaias said, turning away.

"Was Birsha here just to confiscate our work?" a voice called from the crowd.

"Did they take any more of our girls?" another asked.

"Did they want more of our goods than we offered?" another villager asked.

"I will tell you the events as they transpired in my presence," Rendal said as the crowd quieted. "Birsha arrived with his henchmen and captive women. He demanded his share of our work, plus two of our girls. I did offer the food and goods we had made, but I did not offer any of our village girls."

"We have been offering the same offerings for many seasons? It prevents us from being attacked," another villager yelled.

Nenaias and Cauladra smiled as they moved to the back of the crowd.

"No!" Airalee shouted above the noise. "We have sacrificed our young to satisfy evil men's desires for too long. It must stop!"

The crowd seemed split between cheers and jeers. Rendal calmly placed his hand on Airalee's shoulder.

"Please," Rendal said to Airalee, "Let me lead them to our conclusion. Many will only be angry with your approach. It may take several peaceful conversations to convince all of them. If Dorongwe succeeds, it will be easy to convince all of our doubters."

Airalee nodded, deciding to step back to stand with Jendrin. Rendal calmly raised his hand and asked for calm.

694

"Let me continue," Rendal said as the crowd quieted. "Birsha approached me with hostility, demanding we agree to his terms. My refusal surprised him since Birsha expects obedience from everyone. That is especially true of us since he considers us his servants."

"Why did he kill Oleg?" someone asked.

"Birsha demoted Oleg for hurting one of his little people when Oleg attacked Jendrin last winter," Rendal said. "Oleg was not invited to Olona this time but followed the group anyway. Oleg surprised Birsha with his sudden appearance. He surprised him again when he attacked our defensive force and tried to kill Airalee. Our team repelled them by knocking them to the ground. Birsha ordered Oleg to stop, but Oleg called Birsha weak and attacked him with a killing strike. Birsha ignored Oleg's attack and quickly struck Oleg with two killing hatchets. Birsha appeared more disturbed by the disobedience than the hatchet in his chest. He finally noticed Oleg's hatchet, saying it was a bee sting as he pulled it out. He bled from the wound and soon dropped to the ground. Birsha and Oleg both died from their violence. You all saw them as we gave their bodies to the sea." Rendal stopped, hoping that would satisfy most of them.

The crowd quieted as they absorbed what they had just heard.

"I do have some good news for everyone," Rendal said, looking at the crowd. "Dorongwe is the man assuming temporary leadership of the bandit village. He asked me for an ambassador to help him rebuild in the mold of our village. I asked Throc to assist Dorongwe as our ambassador, and he accepted.

"Will he send my daughter back?" Gilda's mother asked.

"If Dorongwe successfully becomes their chief," Rendal said, "he will stop the practice of enslaving girls from other villages and allow those already there to leave if they wish. Our girls may be coming home soon."

This pronouncement drew hearty cheers from the gathering and many tears at the hope that their own would soon return. Nenaias and

Cauladra had moved to the crowd's edge but turned around after hearing Rendal's last statement. Both women smiled and hugged each other as they joined the impromptu celebration.

The villagers began exchanging stories of hiding. Maylore, Jendrin, and Airalee stood together, laughing and joining the celebration. Ayare bounced in her carrier and didn't seem to mind.

"Airalee!" came a call from behind them. Marisa was coming to them with Torbin on her chest and two young girls holding each of her hands. "I am glad to see you are well!" she said as she hugged Airalee. "I was worried when you did not come to the cave."

"I was preparing to leave when Maylore saw Oleg alone in the village," Airalee said. "Oleg saw Maylore looking out our door and charged in our direction. We were trapped in our hut. Fortunately, Dad had learned the hiding skill and could hide Ayare and me when Oleg burst into the hut. Oleg was intent on killing me, but Dad managed to direct his attention elsewhere."

"I tried to convince her to go to the cave after Oleg left," Maylore said.

"I wanted to warn Jendrin that Oleg was in the village and to be sure he was all right," Airalee said.

Jendrin was still unsure if he should chastise her or just be pleased they were all right. "I am pleased you and Ayare are well," he said.

"Me too," Airalee said, looking at him.

"Did you know of the power inside your amulet?" Maylore asked in a low voice.

"No," Airalee answered. "I thought you created the energy."

"I have no such ability," Maylore said.

"I am not sure where it came from," Airalee replied.

"I don't think anyone besides Jendrin, and I saw it," Maylore said in a low voice. "It was short and silent. The rest of the group was watching the other bandits."

"Something stopped, Oleg," Airalee said quietly. "I am willing to leave it at that. Shall we join the celebration?"

"Yes," Maylore said. "I will leave it at that."

The four of them began dancing with the babies in between.

Two sunrises passed as villagers became more hopeful for a peaceful future for all of Molia. Rendal had asked the sentinels to post more Tocor around the area to watch for possible bandit attacks if Throc and Dorongwe were unsuccessful. The sentinels' warning calls had remained silent. Daily activity returned to normal as villagers planted crops, made necessary repairs, and harvested forest gifts. The lone whistle from a sentinel caught the village's attention.

"Another attack?" Airalee said.

"No," Marisa said. "It is a signal that someone is approaching."

"I will see who is approaching," Jendrin said, gathering his quarterstaff and leaving the hut. Jendrin arrived at the visitor's hut as Rendal and Latel watched the road. The three stood in silence as seven figures appeared coming down the hill. Throc appeared walking with Gilda and two other girls who had been taken in the seasons before her. Two Tocor girls followed them with a bandit trailing behind. The group split and waved to each other as the Tocor and the bandit waited on the road.

"Welcome, Ladies!" Rendal shouted as they drew closer. The girls started running toward the village, laughing and crying with relief. They hugged Rendal as a physical verification they were home before running into the village to find their own families.

"I will escort my women home," sentinel Olach said, walking past Rendal to the road.

"Thank you, Olach," Rendal called after him. Olach signaled the women to follow him as their bandit escort waited on the road.

"You worked fast, Throc!" Rendal said as Throc stopped in front of them.

"Tense negotiations went well, Beacon," Throc said. "May we sit in the visitor's hut with a drink?" he asked.

"Yes, come all, let's sit and hear of Throc's adventures," Rendal said, opening the door. Rendal poured drinks as Throc cleared his throat and started his tale.

"Dorongwe called all the bandits to a meeting in the large hut," Throc said. "They asked why Dorongwe was conducting this meeting, and he told them he would explain when all were seated. The news he told of Birsha and Oleg's death shocked all the bandits," Throc said. "Dorongwe explained how they killed each other. A very few seemed saddened by the news and started demanding retribution. Dorongwe allowed them to vent their anger as even fewer agreed with them. He eventually asked for calm and allowed the others at Olona to describe the attack. Their common story quieted the group of angry men. I noted who complained, but Dorongwe already knew they were ardent followers of Oleg."

"Dorongwe reminded them Birsha had left no second. The bandit's code read that the eldest member would become the default second or sheriff. The group was quiet when they realized he was correct. They then questioned why I was there. Dorongwe told them he would explain later. I was allowed to stay as long as I sat behind Dorongwe.

Dorongwe explained they would need a new leader and asked for those who would like to lead the village to stand. Two of Oleg and Birsha's followers stood. One other stood but sat down again when the other two stared at him. Dorongwe announced he was in the running, and a few bandits smiled at him. The room was very tense as arguing amongst the gathering continued for some time. Dorongwe finally raised his hands, asking for quiet.

"Tell us how you would lead our village," Dorongwe asked each of the two other candidates. Both said they would hold to the old ways of Birsha and Oleg. They would demand a larger share of their due from all of the villages in Molia. They promised to do away with the constraints Birsha had placed on them. They would collect anytime, replacing girls of any age and quickly removing broken ones. They especially wanted to expand their empire to include all villages throughout Molia. They insisted on forcing all others to bow down to them. The gathering applauded softly in a fearful way when they finished speaking. Few would look at the two men as they spoke.

Dorongwe gave a more subdued presentation, telling them he wanted a village of peace, self-reliance, trade, and cooperation with other villages. His voice strengthened as he said he wanted no warring with other villages. He wanted a village council elected by the villagers to run the village."

"No more chiefs to bend you to their rules!' Dorongwe shouted. The group looked at him in astonishment but stayed quiet. "I will lead the start of our council selection, then step down as leader, asking you to allow me to serve as one of your council members. The elected council will establish our village's rules, and you will help select a lead council member to help when old council members leave and new ones join."

Dorongwe looked at me and pulled me to my feet.

"The man with me today is named Throc from the village of Olona. He is here to suggest how we can get started on that path. He will teach us how Olona runs their village. We will then choose our own course."

Dorongwe talked more about the future he saw for their village, but that is the most essential part of it," Throc said.

699

"It may be obvious Dorongwe won, but how did they vote?" Rendal asked.

"Dorongwe used a hut with a divider in it so no one could see how anyone voted," Throc said. "The three candidates stood facing a cup and the wall on one side. Each villager was given a small rock and passed through the wall into a cup with the name of the person they voted for. No one could see who voted or who they voted for. The village guards watched to verify that the villagers only voted once and that no one harassed them. Oleg's followers got two votes each, and Dorongwe got the rest."

"Excellent!" Rendal said, "The defeated ones and their followers left?"

"Yes," Throc replied. "They left with a few diehard bandits to form a new village. Dorongwe asked them to go into the northern mountains along its lakes."

"That is a long distance," Rendal said. "Did the rest of the village accept Dorongwe's vision?"

"They were enthusiastic Dorongwe won," Throc said. "The village of bandits are mostly good people only performing what Birsha, Oleg, and his henchmen wanted. Those who remained were relieved to see both were dead and their followers banished. Dorongwe asked the scouts to leave their trees and to discreetly follow the departing bandits to verify they left the valley."

"Your tale brings happiness to my ears!" Rendal exclaimed. "I am also pleased they allowed the girls to leave."

"Dorongwe asked every villager if they wished to stay or leave," Throc said. "The captive girls wanted to leave. A few women had become attached to a certain man and stayed. Dorongwe told them they could visit their homes if they wished."

"Are you staying or going back?" Rendal asked.

"I will return to help them get started," Throc said. "I walked back with these girls to inform you of their decision. I believe the former bandits will become good neighbors."

"Excellent!" Rendal said. "My thanks to you. You accomplished a great deed," Rendal said.

Throc smiled and waved as he turned to leave. He suddenly turned back to face Rendal.

"They named their village Nouvel," Throc shouted. "I will remain there until winter returns," he said, waving again and walking back with the Nouvel escort.

Rendal, Latel, and Jendrin walked back to the village. Rendal's steps felt so light that he was scarcely touching the ground. Villagers chattered excitedly in the kitchen area as Gilda and the other girl passed among them on their way to their families. Rendal climbed atop one of the tables.

"I have news from Throc!" Rendal shouted. "Gather around!" The villagers gathered and quietly waited for Rendal to start. The crowd grew louder as Rendal related the tale Throc had told him.

"We welcome our new neighbors from the village named Nouvel!" he said, pumping his fists. Villagers started celebrating again, even more so than two days ago. Dirdin brought out the last of his strong drink, and it quickly vanished into happy throats. Rendal downed his small cup when he noticed a small group of men standing outside the gathering. They were dressed in traveling clothes and did not seem familiar to him.

"Jendrin," he said, "come with me," as he started in their direction. The one-bearded face he could see looked slightly familiar, but the others huddled together, so he could not tell who was who. "Greetings," Rendal said as he approached.

Kelkalyn turned around.

"Beacon, may we help you?" Kelkalyn asked as Gilriel and Neldor turned to face him.

"You are well, Gilriel!" Rendal said.

"Yes," Gilriel replied. "I have been hiding in Neldor's dome. I feared the master would find me."

"Fearing him?" Rendal said. "I mistrust him but do not fear him."

Gilriel looked to the others before speaking.

"We will discuss it another time," Gilriel said. "We have come to see Maylore. Kelkalyn and I have discussed Maylore with Neldor, and he wishes to measure Maylore for himself."

Rendal looked to where Maylore had been standing.

"Maylore stands there with his companions and the baby," Rendal said.

"Maylore has a child?" Gilriel asked.

"No," Rendal replied. "The child is Airalee's by Jendrin."

"I see," Gilriel said.

"What is the celebration about, Beacon?" Kelkalyn asked.

"Good news!" Rendal replied. "Birsha and Oleg have killed each other. Dorongwe was elected to lead the bandit village, renamed Nouvel. He promised to turn it into a peaceful village. Our captive girls have returned to us. Throc is working with Dorongwe to create a village similar to ours."

All three men smiled before Neldor spoke.

"That is good news," Neldor said. "Now that his henchmen are gone, the master will likely disappear into his caves again. He will return, I am sure of it."

The rest of the men nodded at his assessment.

"The news removes the immediate need to see Maylore," Neldor said. "We will discuss our business another day. We should join the celebration since there has been little to celebrate recently. I would like to meet Maylore."

Rendal understood little of what they said but turned toward the companions. He signaled for Maylore to join them. Maylore looked surprised when he saw Gilriel.

"I thought you were lost!" Maylore said. "I am pleased to see you!"

"And I am glad to see you," Gilriel said.

Maylore turned to Kelkalyn.

"Greetings, Kelkalyn," Maylore said. "I am glad you have remained."

"Thank you, Maylore," Kelkalyn said.

"You are the red sorcerer," Maylore said, looking at Neldor.

"The red sorcerer?" Neldor said. "Indeed, my travel clothes are red, but my name is Neldor," he said, ending with a bow.

"I am pleased to meet you, Neldor," Maylore replied.

"We have some business to discuss, but not today," Neldor said. "We should all join the celebration. Where can we go so we are hidden?"

Maylore pointed toward the lava rock hill behind them.

"Yes, we will climb up the rock, lead the way, Maylore," Neldor said. Neldor whispered to Rendal before the four men left the kitchen and moved toward the hill.

Rendal nodded as he walked toward Airalee. Melronna and Lalien approached as he arrived. The women both smiled at Ayare and exchanged greetings with Airalee and Jendrin. Melronna smiled at Rendal.

"A reason to celebrate is what this village needed, Beacon," Melronna said. She started to turn when her face went blank, and she stared at Rendal. "Peace has forced its way to your homes." Melronna's smile returned, and she started walking away when Meliniel stopped.

"Peace, Melronna?" Meliniel asked.

"Did I again say something interesting?" Melronna asked. "What did I say?"

"You said, 'Peace has forced its way to your homes,'" Rendal replied. "I hope that is correct."

"Yes," Melronna replied. "I hope it is true. I do wish I knew where it comes from." She wandered off into the crowd.

A low buzz filled the air as Jendrin saw an empty firebird flying overhead.

"The woca have returned," a voice said behind him. Jendrin turned to see Werloth looking up. Airalee moved out of his reach as he noticed Ayare.

"You have a child?" Werloth asked. "I regret I was not here to join your baby seeding group," he finished with a grin. Airalee stared at him with an icy look.

"My baby-mate Jendrin was all the help I needed," Airalee said.

Werloth nodded to Jendrin.

"Indeed," Werloth said. "He is more than sufficient." Looking up as the firebird made its way back toward the mountain, "The woca herd has moved to different valleys. The firebird flies the same route regardless of where the herds are feeding. Do you wish to join me in locating the herds?"

"Airalee and I will discuss it," Jendrin replied.

"Good," Werloth replied. "I will remain in Olona for a while and await your decision." He nodded to Airalee and walked into the crowd.

"Dirty old man," Airalee said in a low voice.

A sudden show of sparkling light appeared above the village as it spread to the width of the village. Villagers looked up, wondering if they should run or watch.

"Fear not!" Rendal said. "We have some travelers who brought sparkling lights for our entertainment. Enjoy it and celebrate our new peace!"

ABOUT THE AUTHOR

From the structured world of computer programming to the boundless realms of fantasy fiction, Curt Sylvester embarks on a literary journey that mirrors the epic quests of his characters. Born in Keizer, Oregon, Curt's early fascination with storytelling blossomed alongside a successful career in technology, where he harnessed the logic of code before turning his attention to the magic of words upon his retirement.

Curt's debut novel emerges from a vibrant imagination honed by decades of technical precision and a lifelong passion for fantasy's greats like Robert Jordan and George R.R. Martin. His narrative weaves together themes of freedom from oppression, the power of community, and the nuanced balance between magic and might. These themes unfold through a group of characters who, much like Curt in his second act as a novelist, are on a quest to redefine their destinies.

Currently in the planning stages of Sorcerer Scroll, the next chapter in his burgeoning series, Curt delves further into the intricate dynamics of his created world, where dialogue can resolve conflict and where old traditions give way to new hopes. As he envisions this evolving saga, Curt invites readers to lose themselves in the layers of his imaginative universe, drawing parallels to our own through the universal language of myth and lore.

Explore Curt Sylvester's work, available wherever books are sold, and let his stories transport you to worlds unknown.

www.ingramcontent.com/pod-product-compliance
Lightning Source LLC
Chambersburg PA
CBHW031017030726
47497CB00004B/897